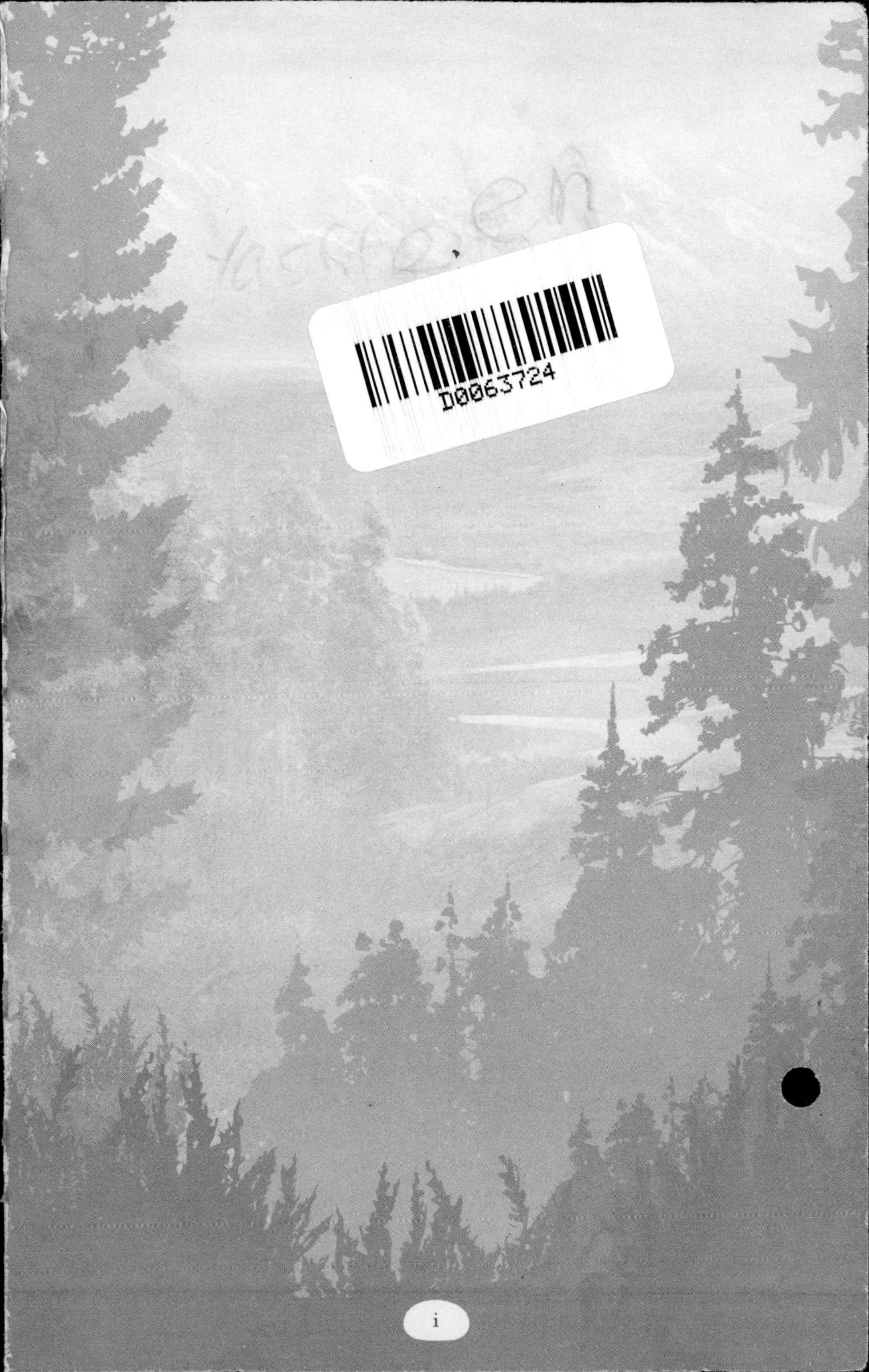

ALSO FROM JOE BOOKS

Disney Frozen Cinestory Comic

Disney Cinderella Cinestory Comic

Disney 101 Dalmatians Cinestory Comic

Disney•Pixar Inside Out Cinestory Comic

Disney Big Hero 6 Cinestory Comic

Disney Princess Comics Treasury

Disney•Pixar Comics Treasury

Disney's Darkwing Duck:
The Definitively Dangerous Edition

Disney · PIXAR

THE GOOD DINOSAUR

CINESTORY

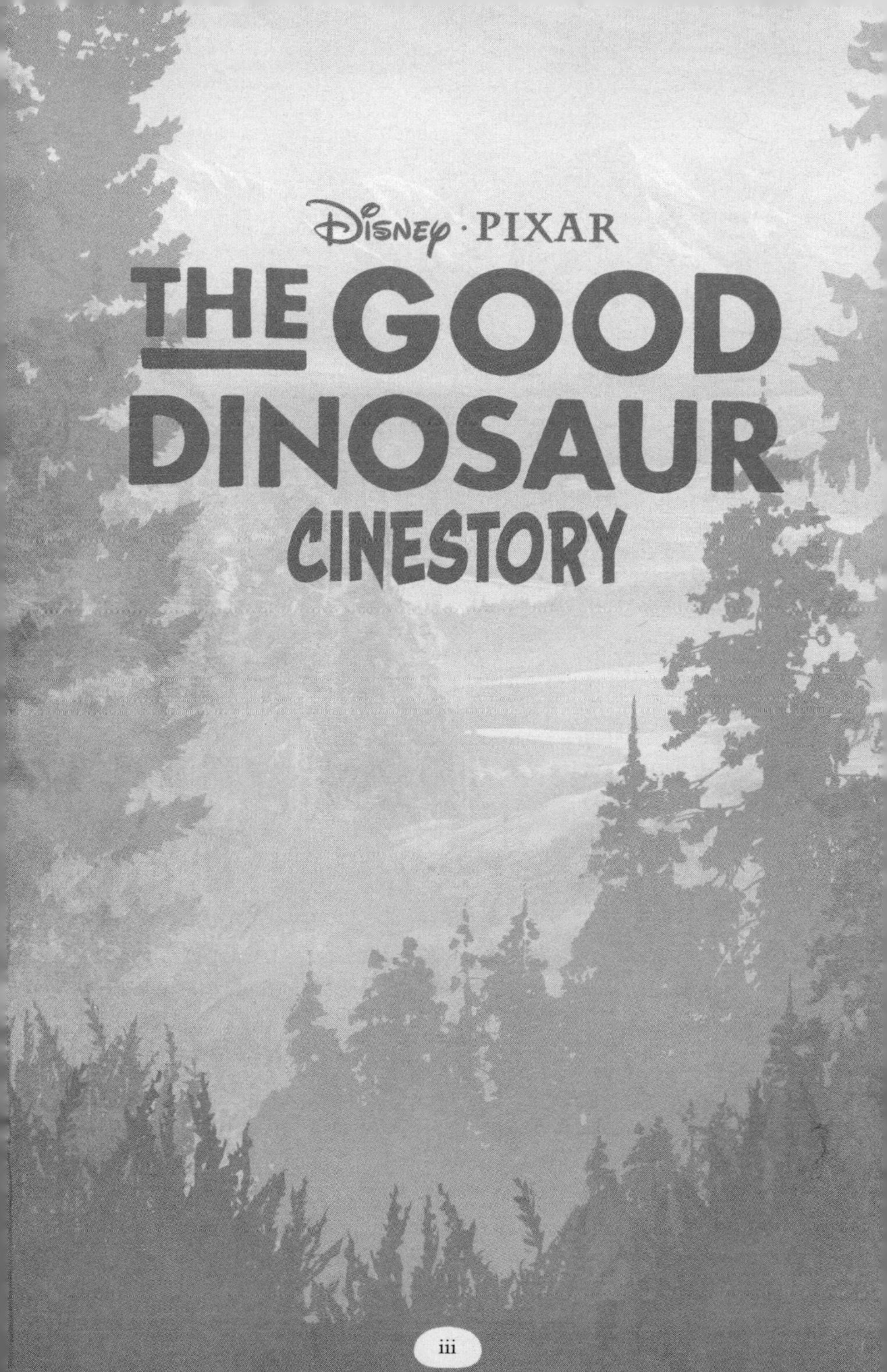

JOE BOOKS INC

Published in the United States and Canada by Joe Books, Inc.
567 Queen St W, Toronto, ON M5V 2B6
www.joebooks.com

Library and Archives Canada Cataloguing in Publication information is available
upon request.
ISBN 978-1-92651-628-8
ISBN 978-1-77275-238-0 (Ebook edition)

First Joe Books, Inc edition: January 2016

Printed in the USA through Avenue4 Communications at Cenveo/Richmond, Virginia

Disney · PIXAR
THE GOOD DINOSAUR
CINESTORY

ADAPTATION, DESIGN, LETTERING, LAYOUT AND EDITING:
For Readhead Books: Aaron Sparrow, Heidi Roux, Salvador Navarro, Ester Salguero, Puste, Ernesto Lovera, Eduardo Alpuente, Alberto Garrido, and Carolynn Prior.

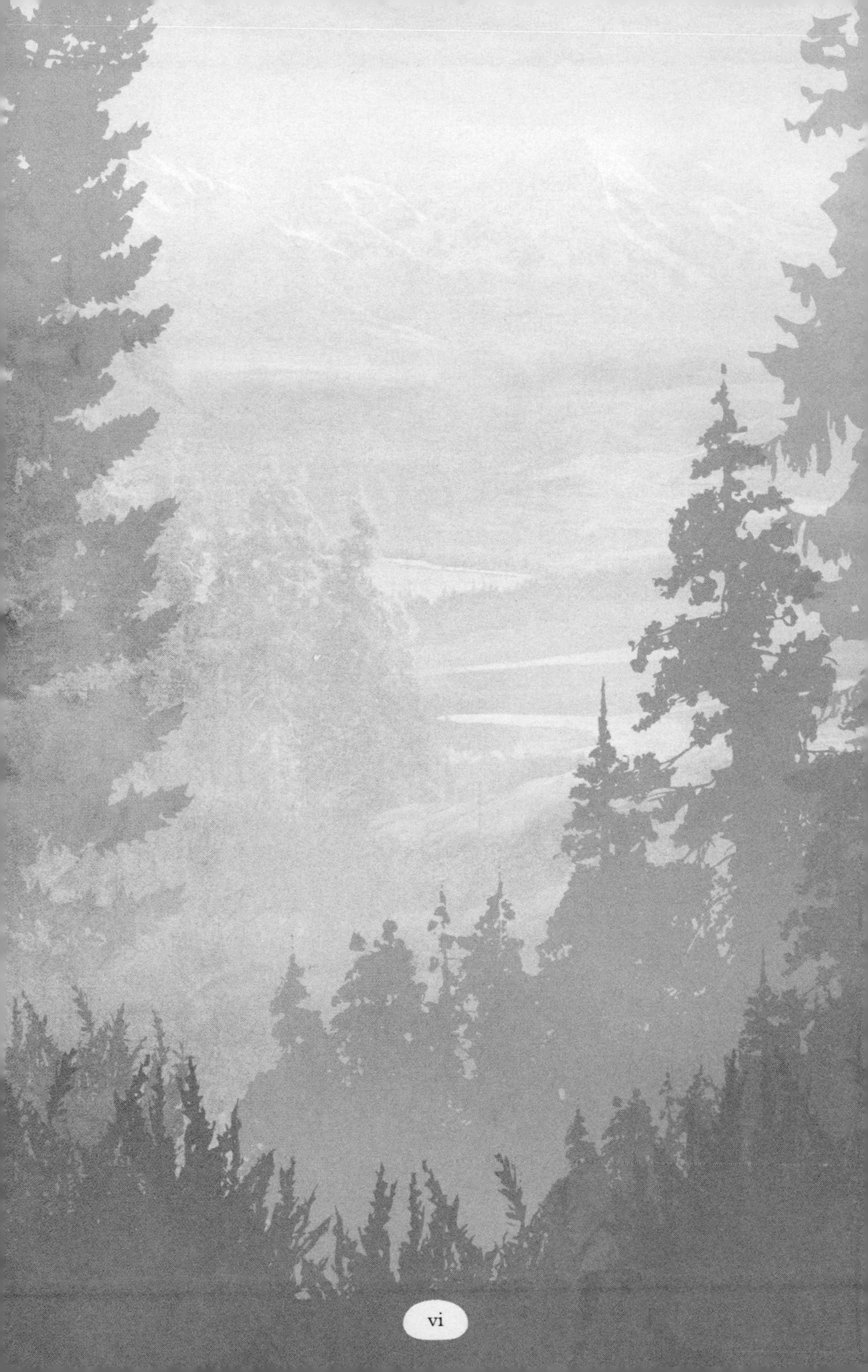

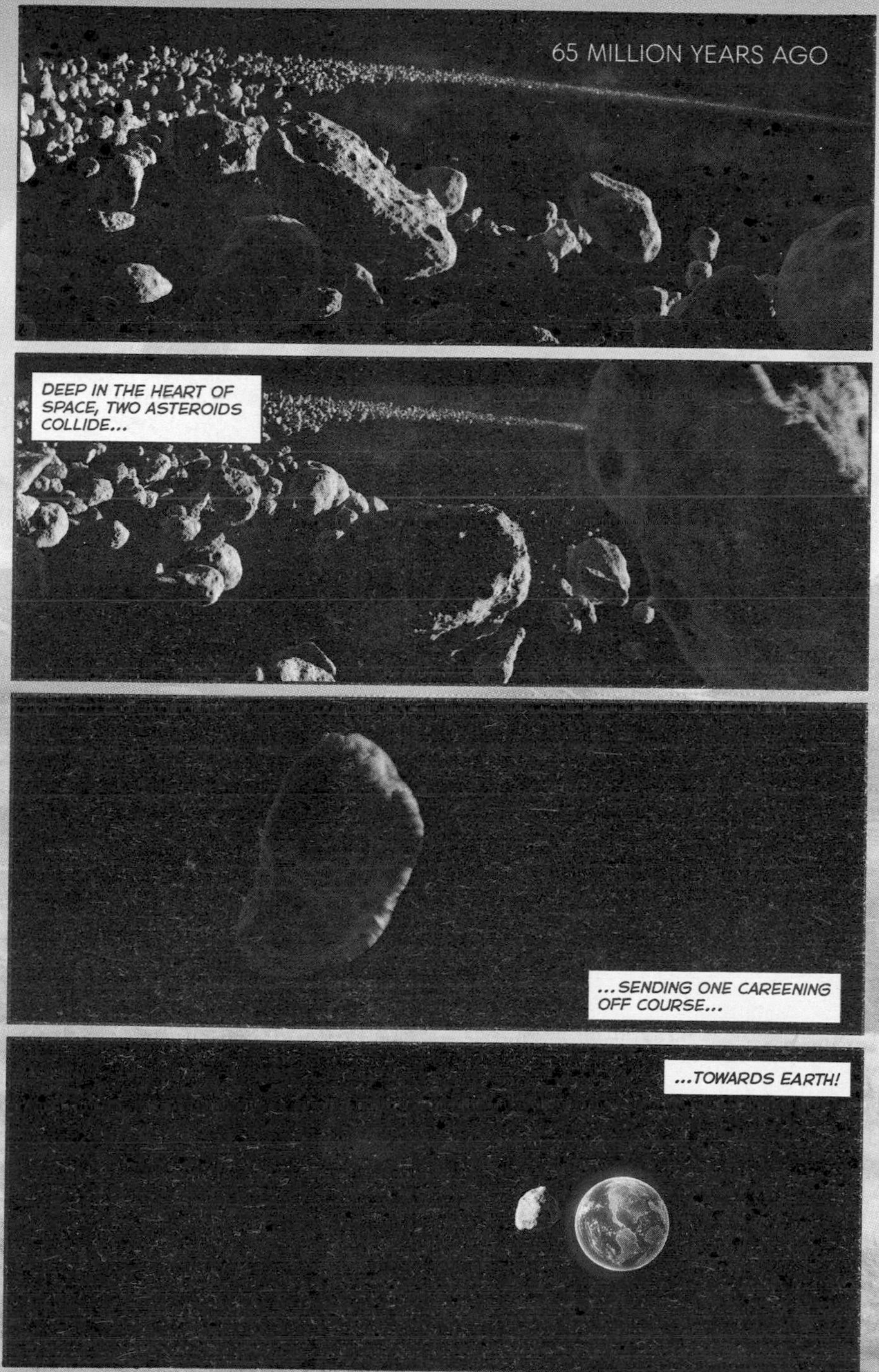
65 MILLION YEARS AGO
DEEP IN THE HEART OF SPACE, TWO ASTEROIDS COLLIDE...
...SENDING ONE CAREENING OFF COURSE...
...TOWARDS EARTH!

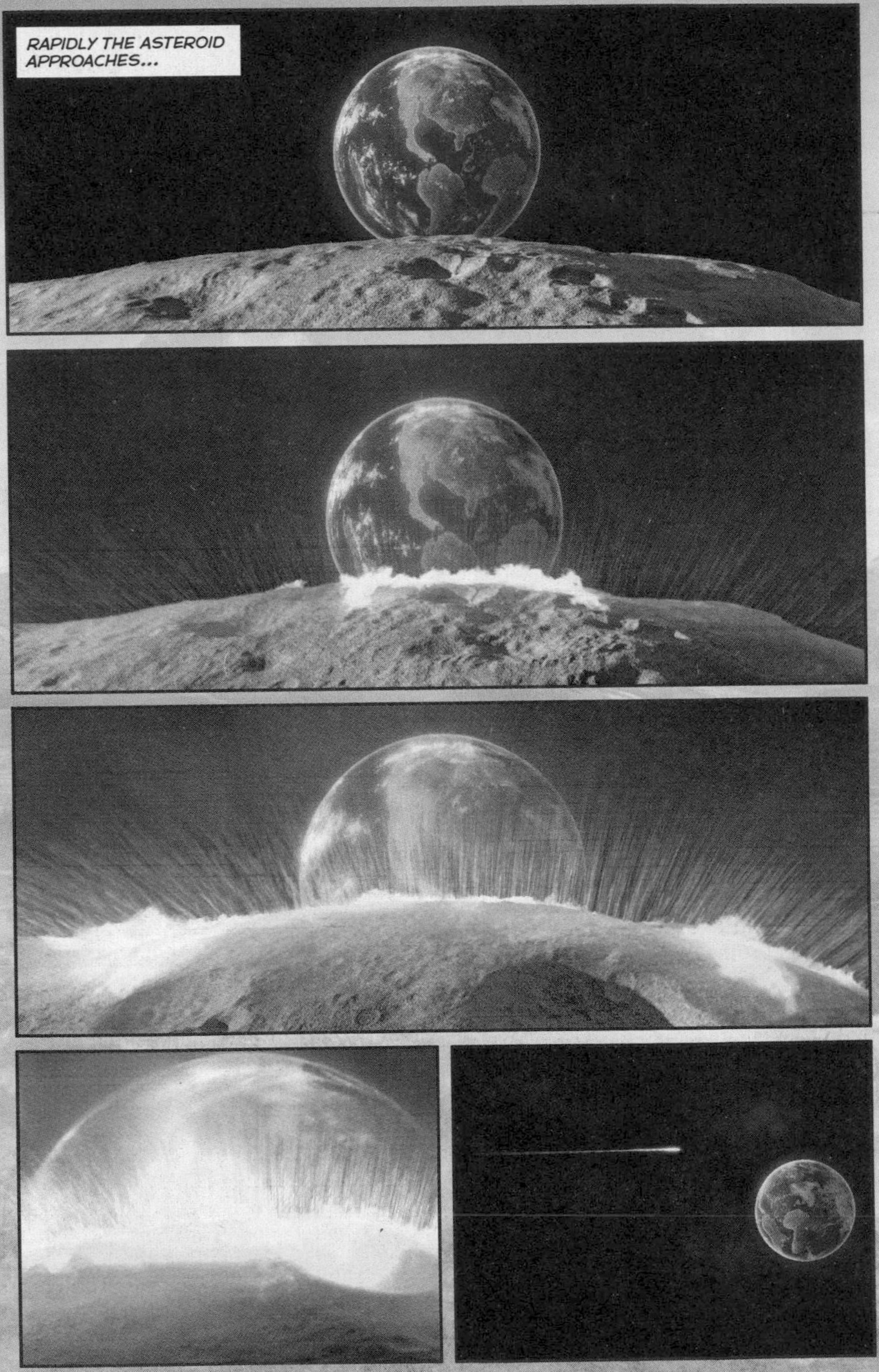
RAPIDLY THE ASTEROID APPROACHES...

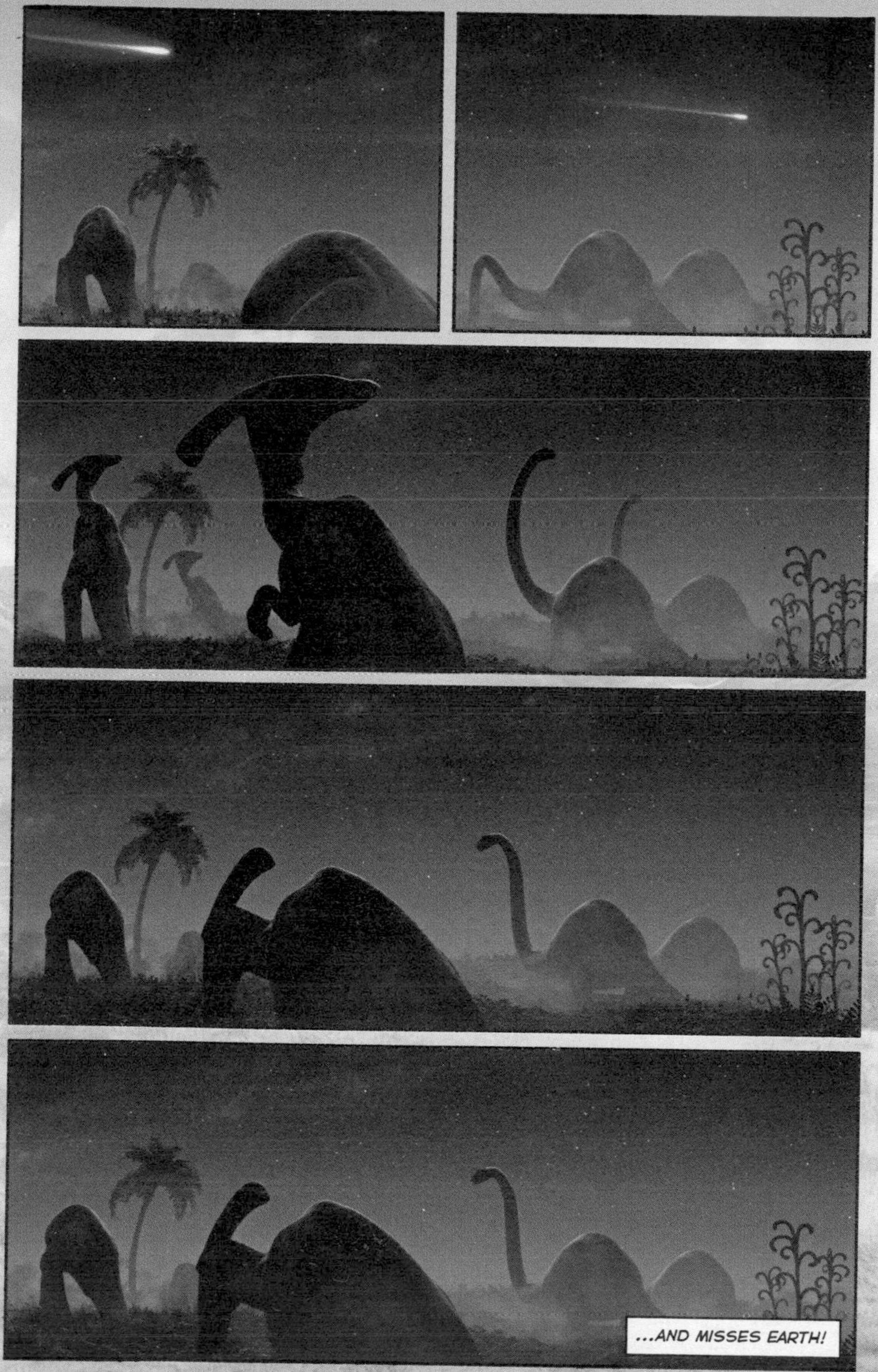
...AND MISSES EARTH!

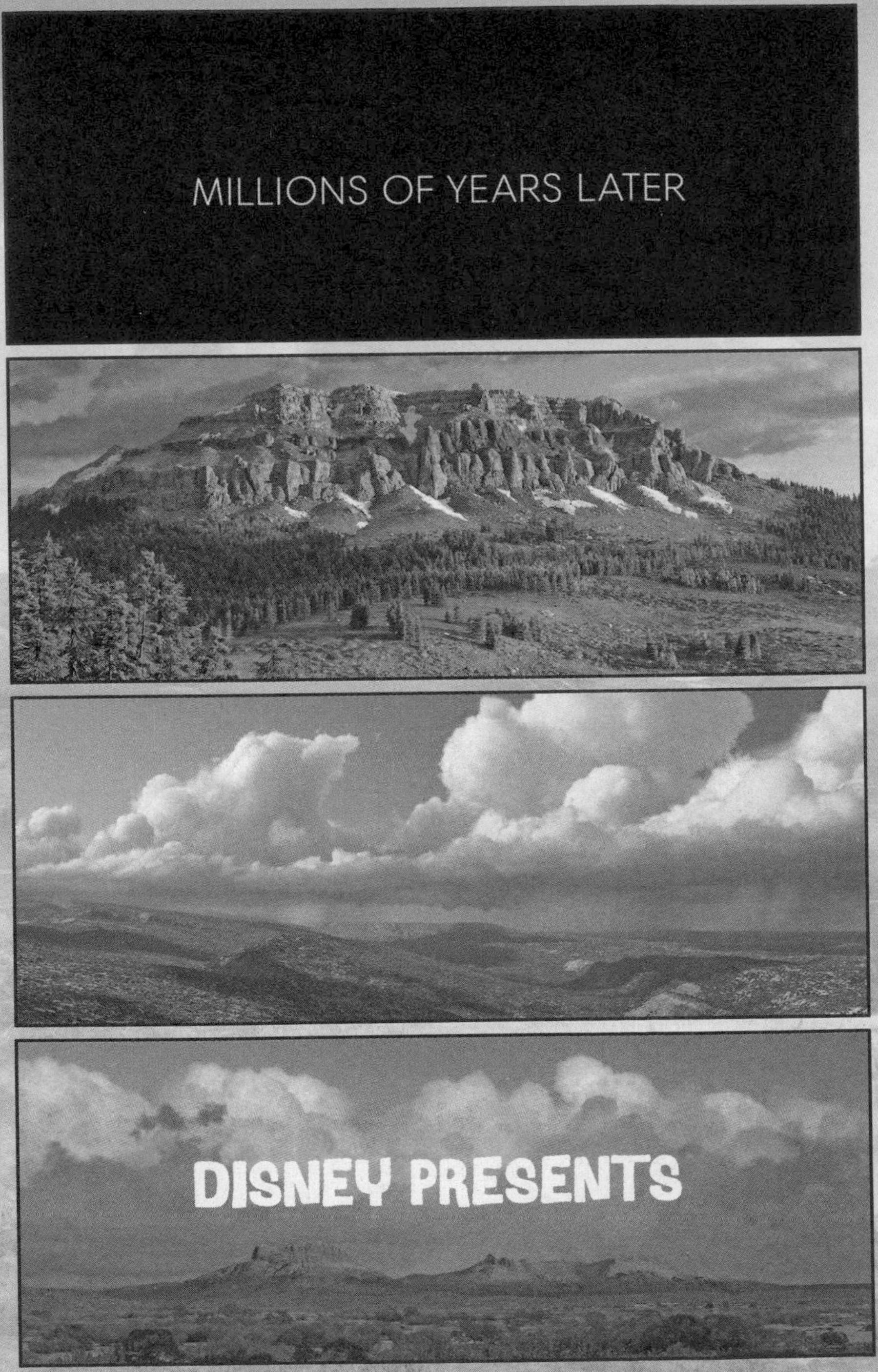
MILLIONS OF YEARS LATER
DISNEY PRESENTS

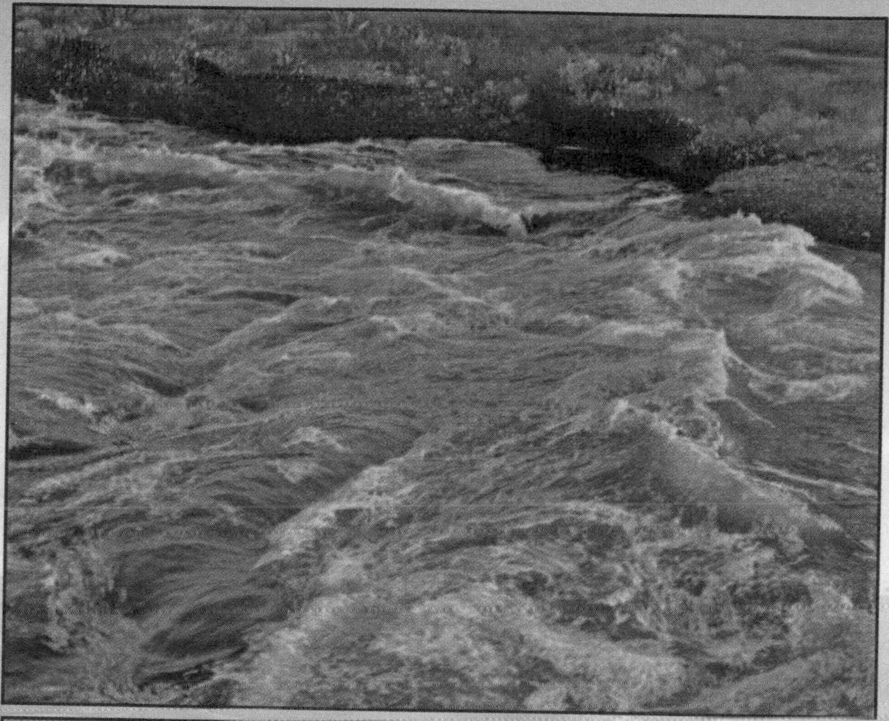

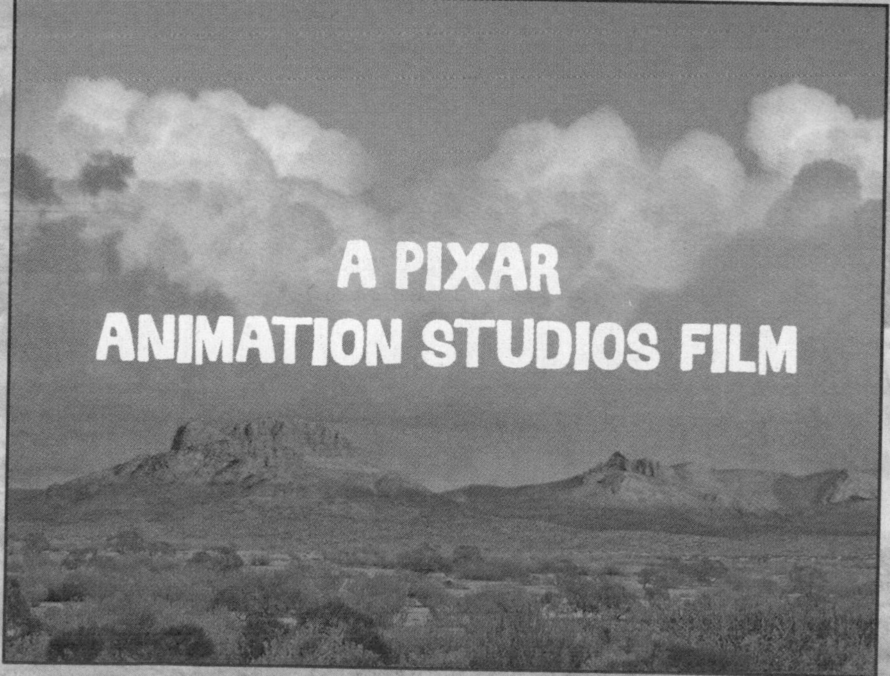
A PIXAR
ANIMATION STUDIOS FILM

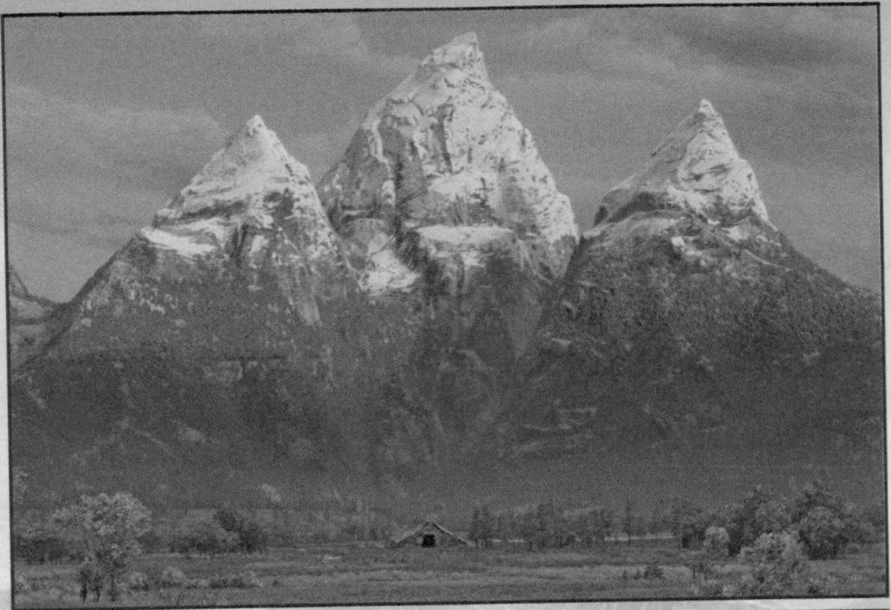

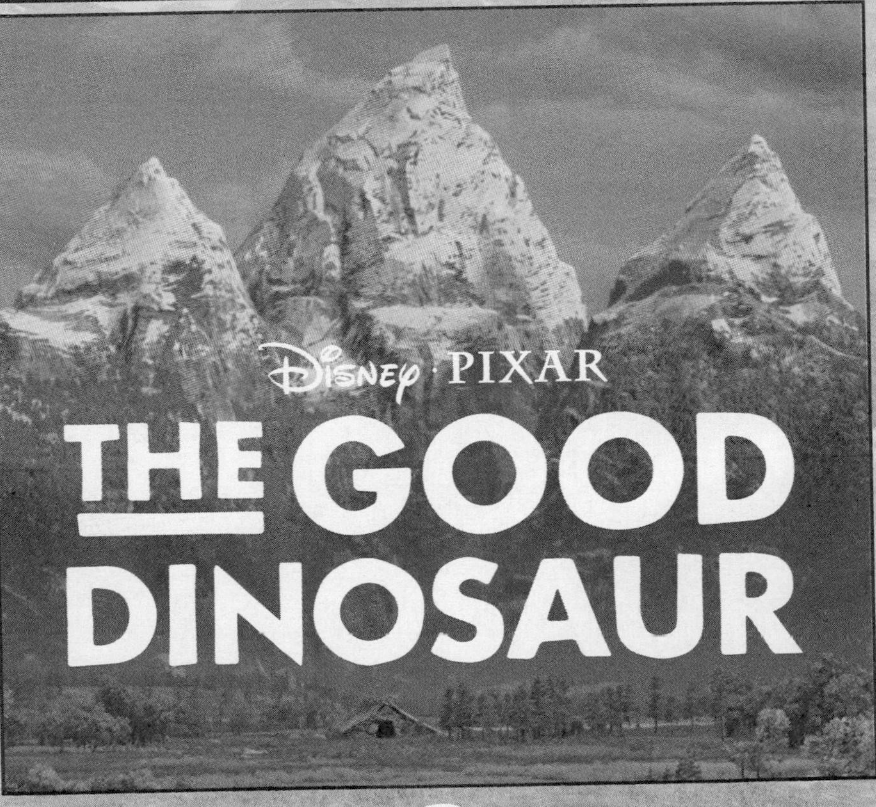
Disney · PIXAR
THE GOOD
DINOSAUR

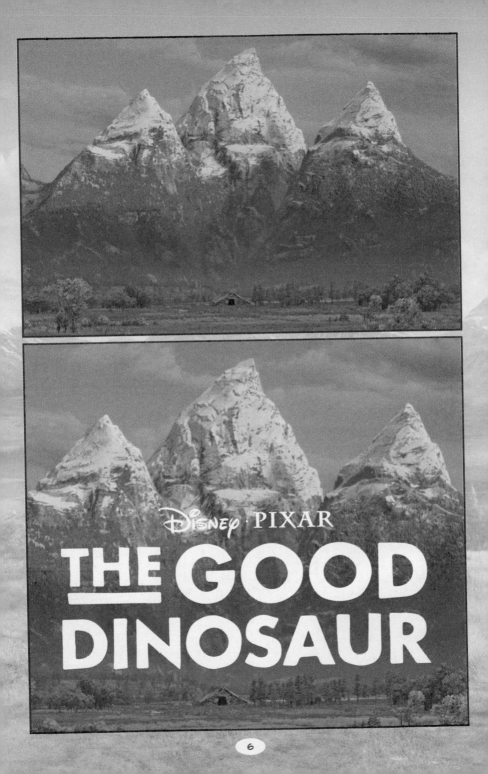

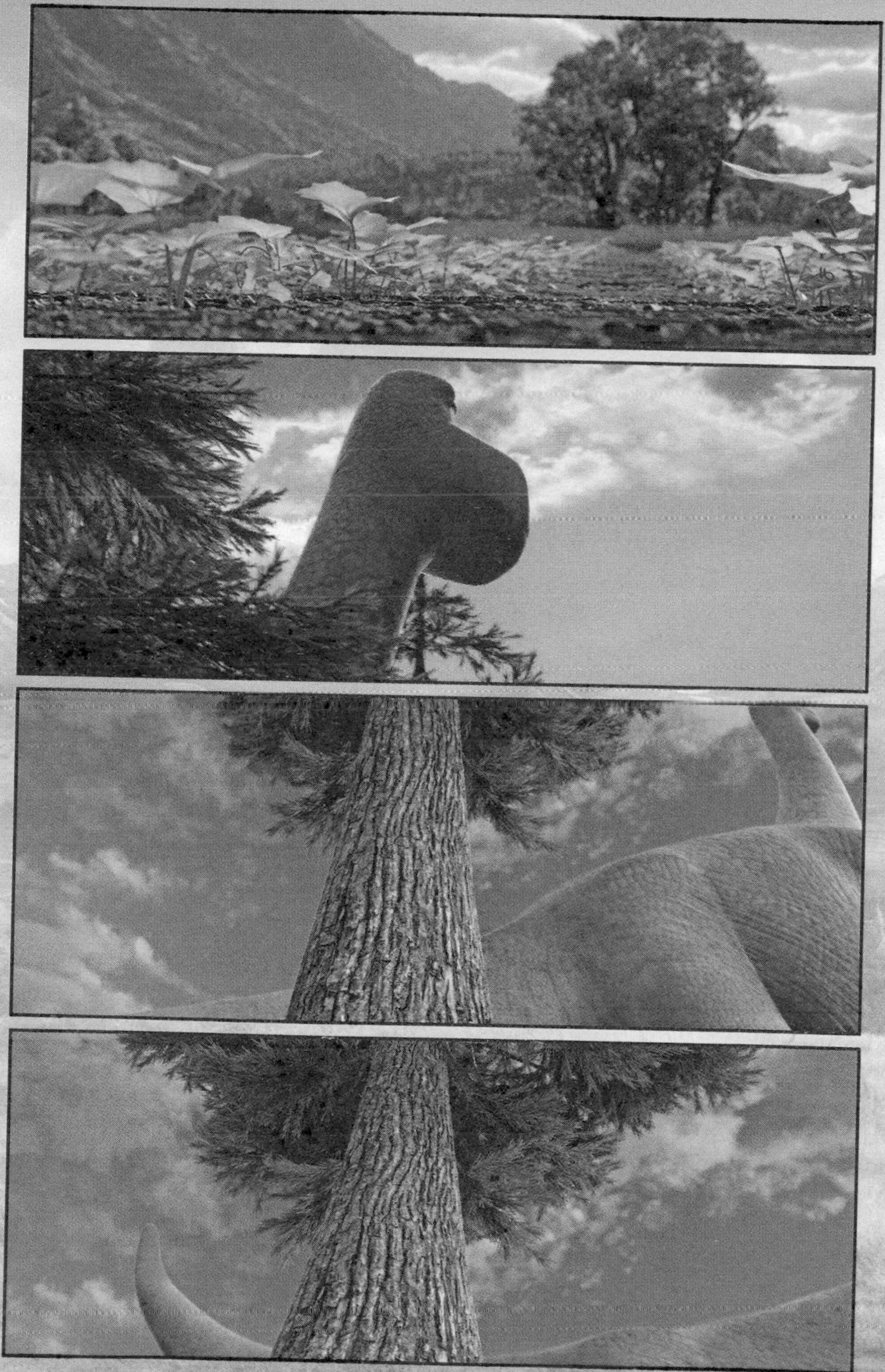

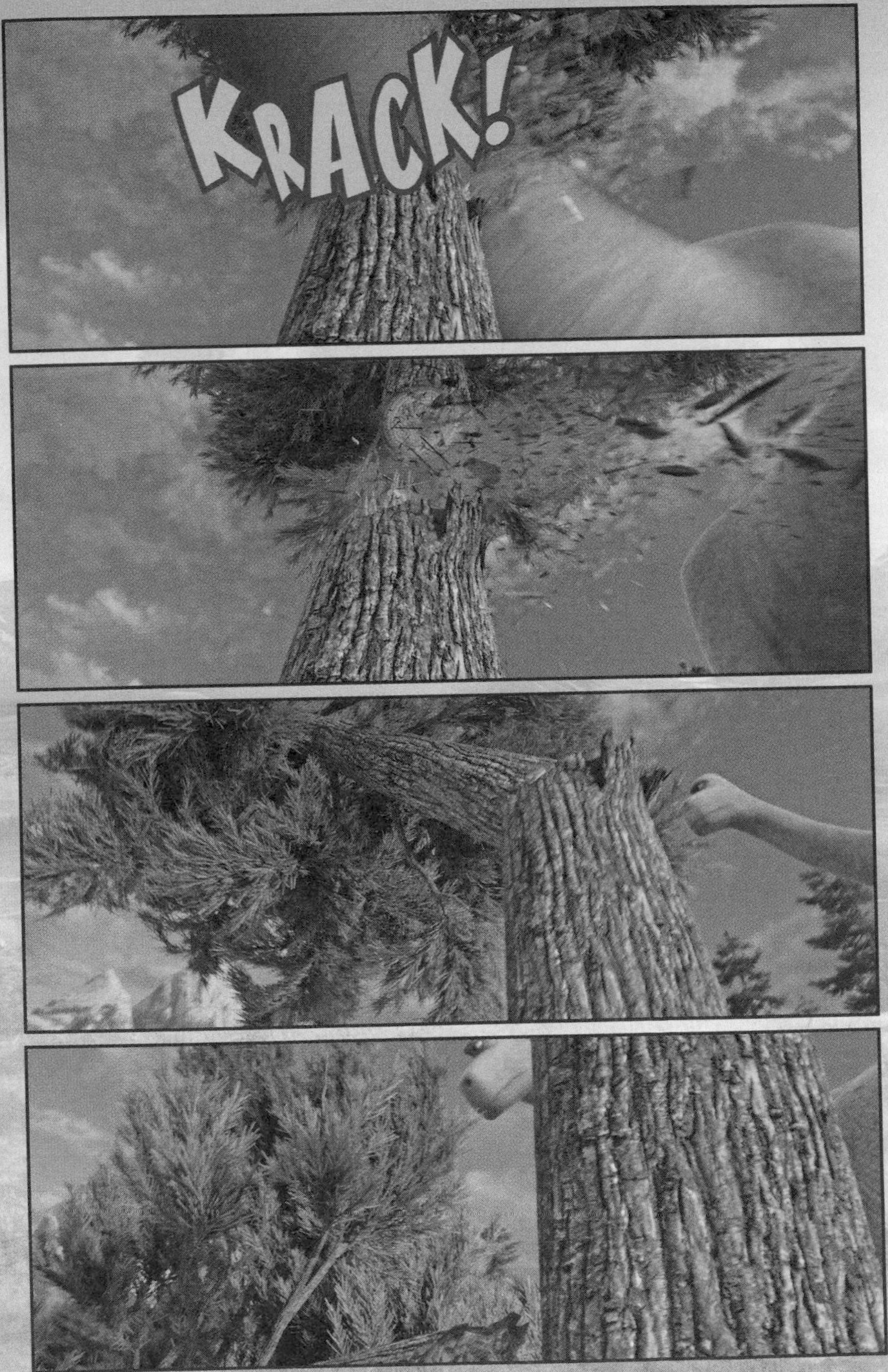
KRACK!

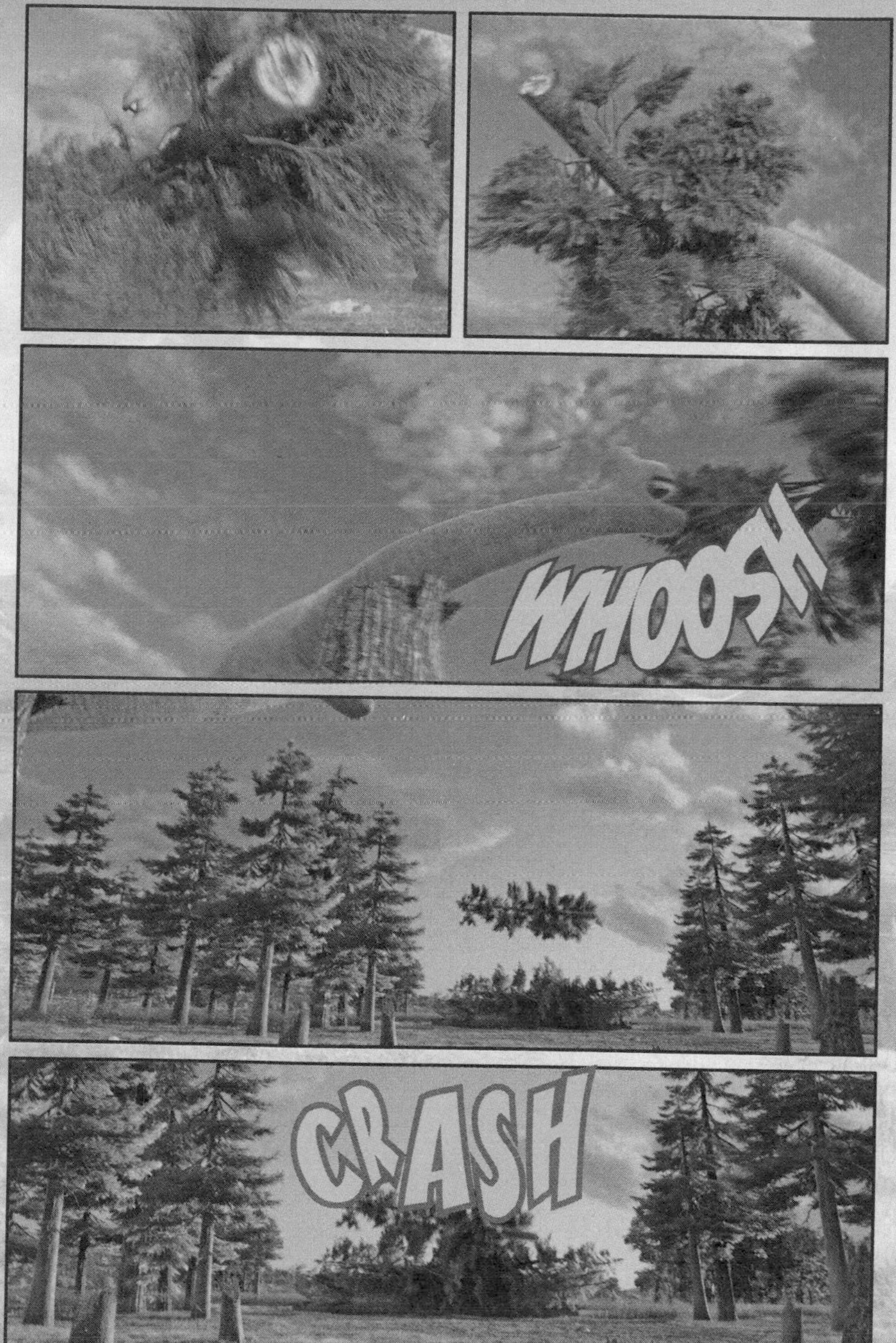
WHOOSH
CRASH

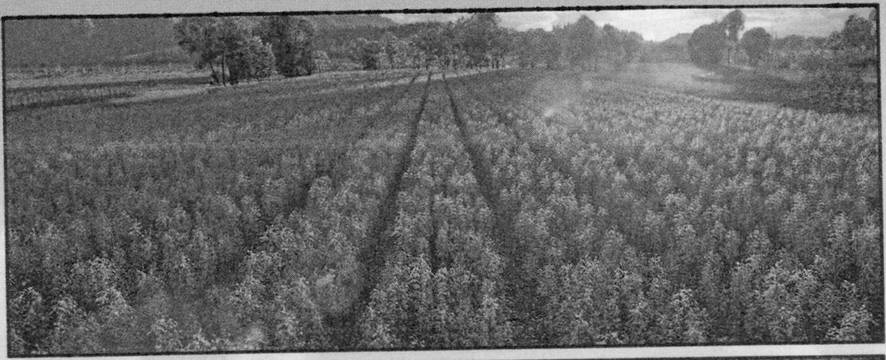

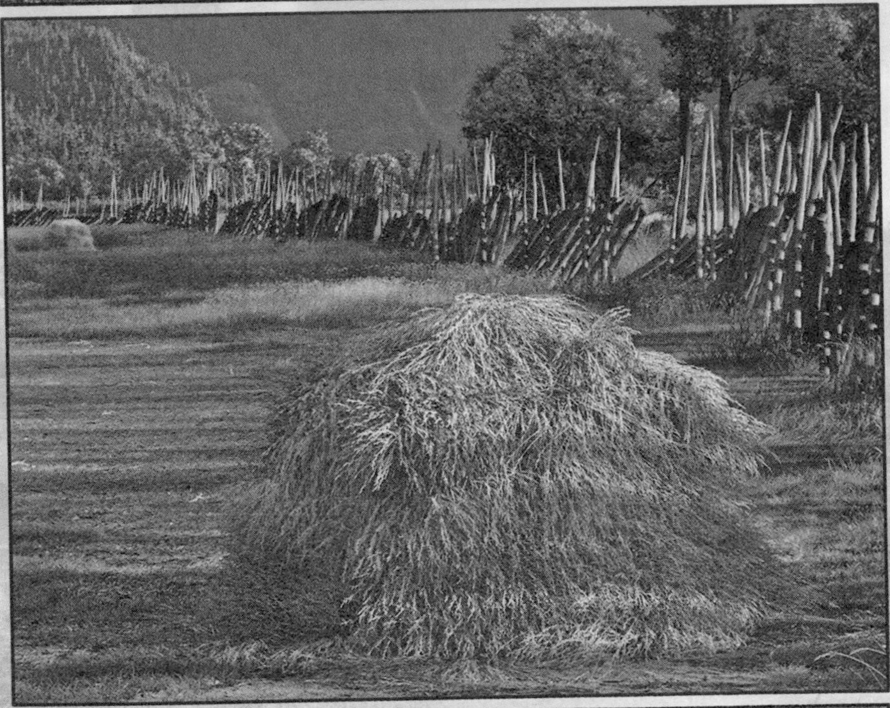

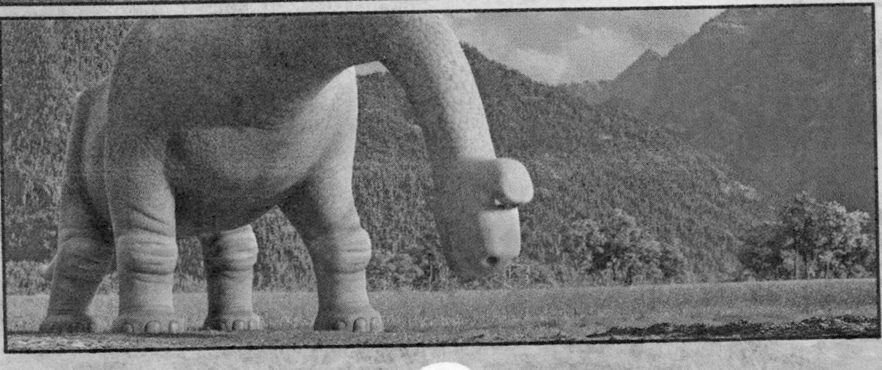

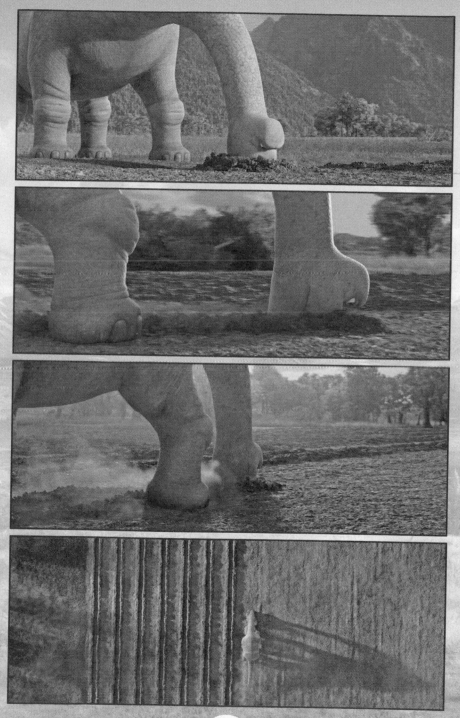

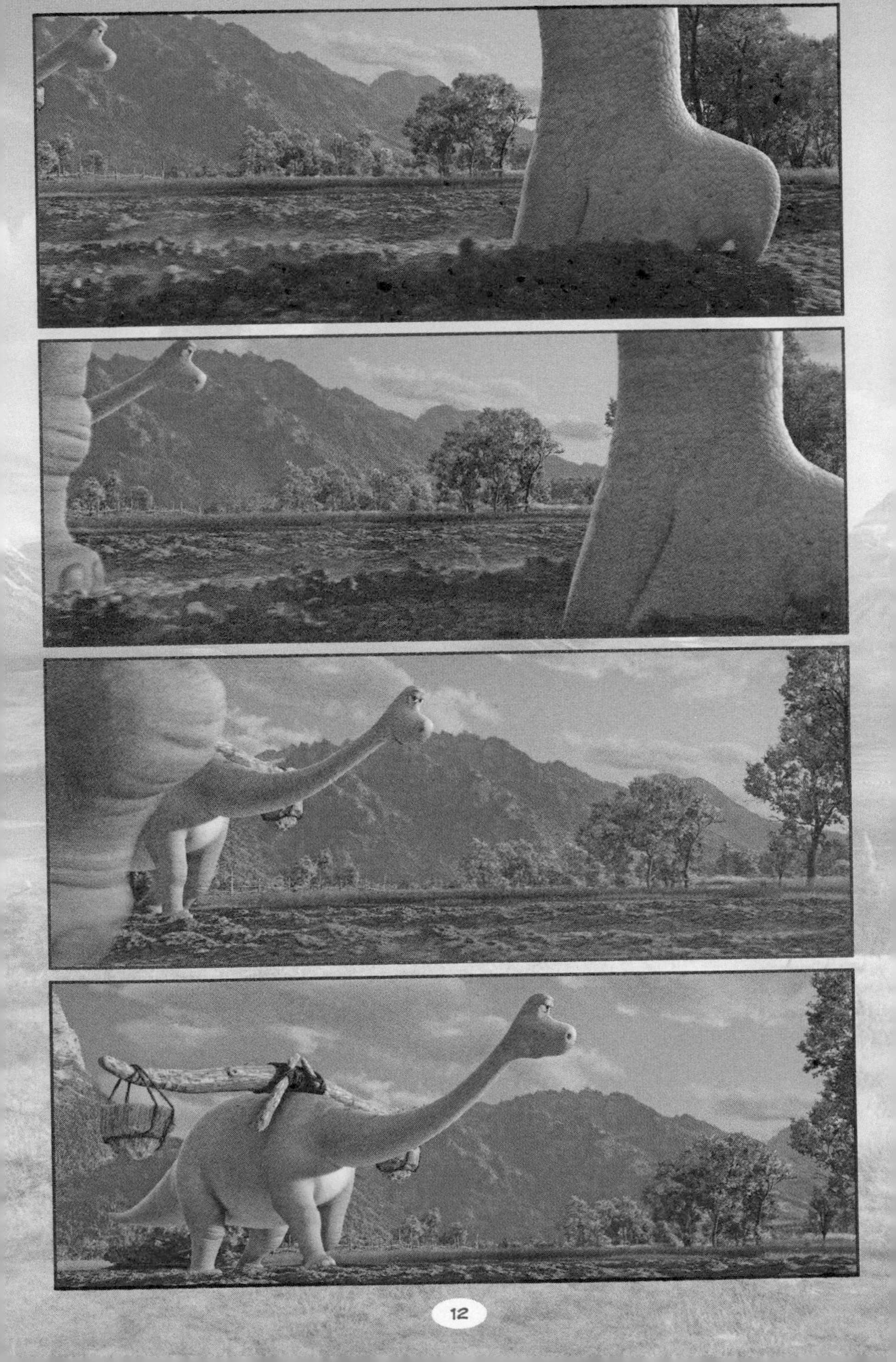

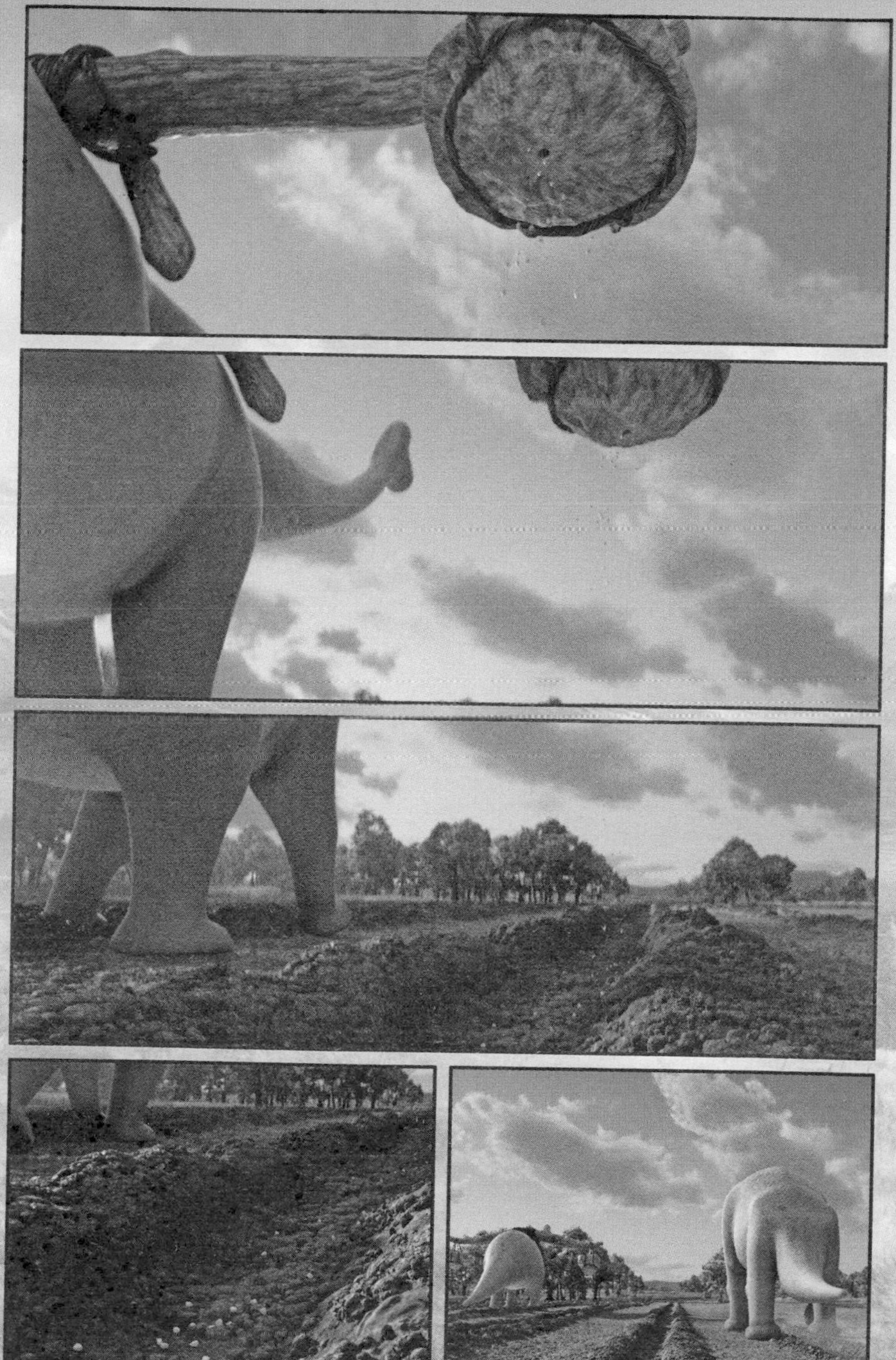

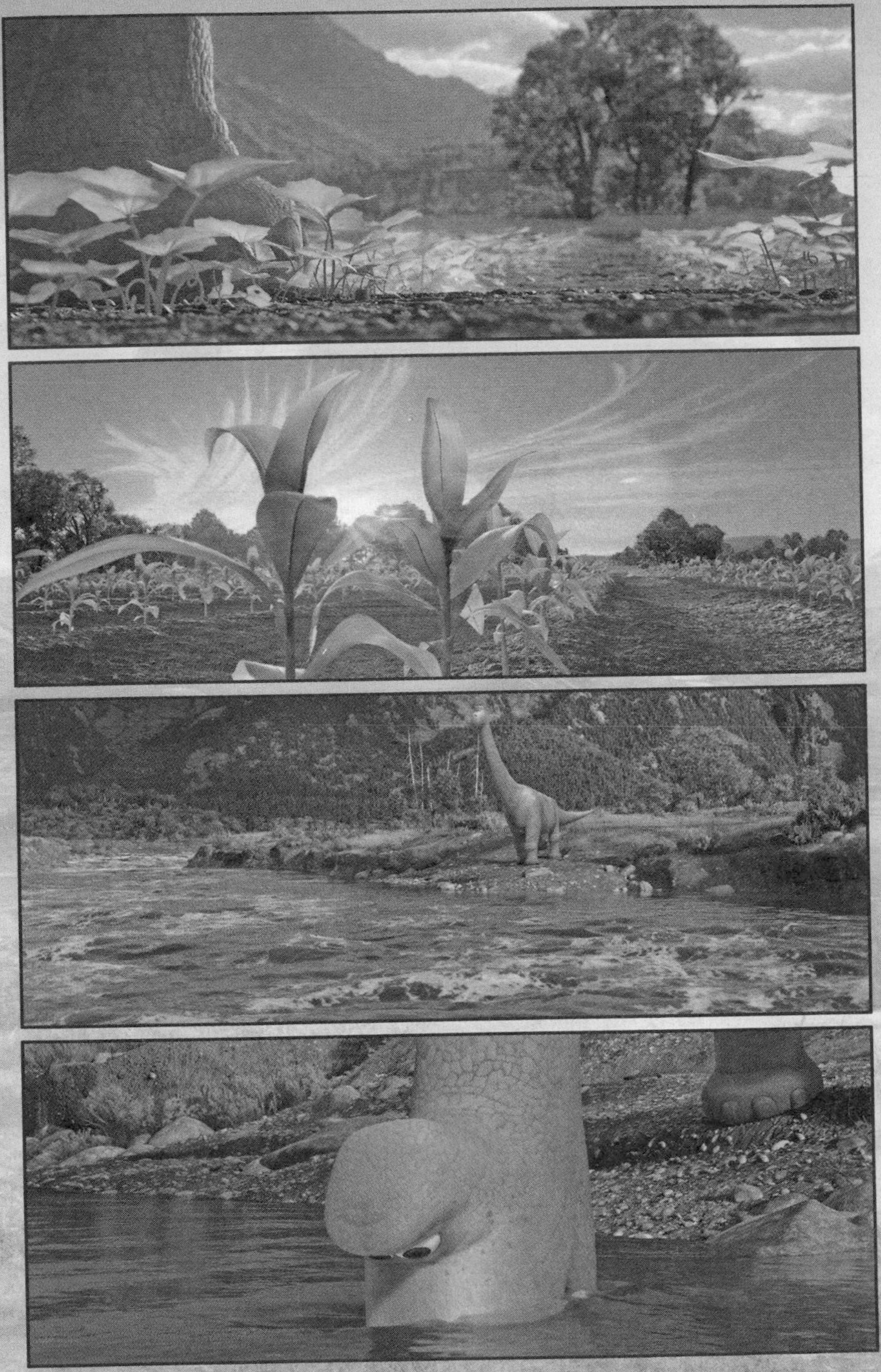

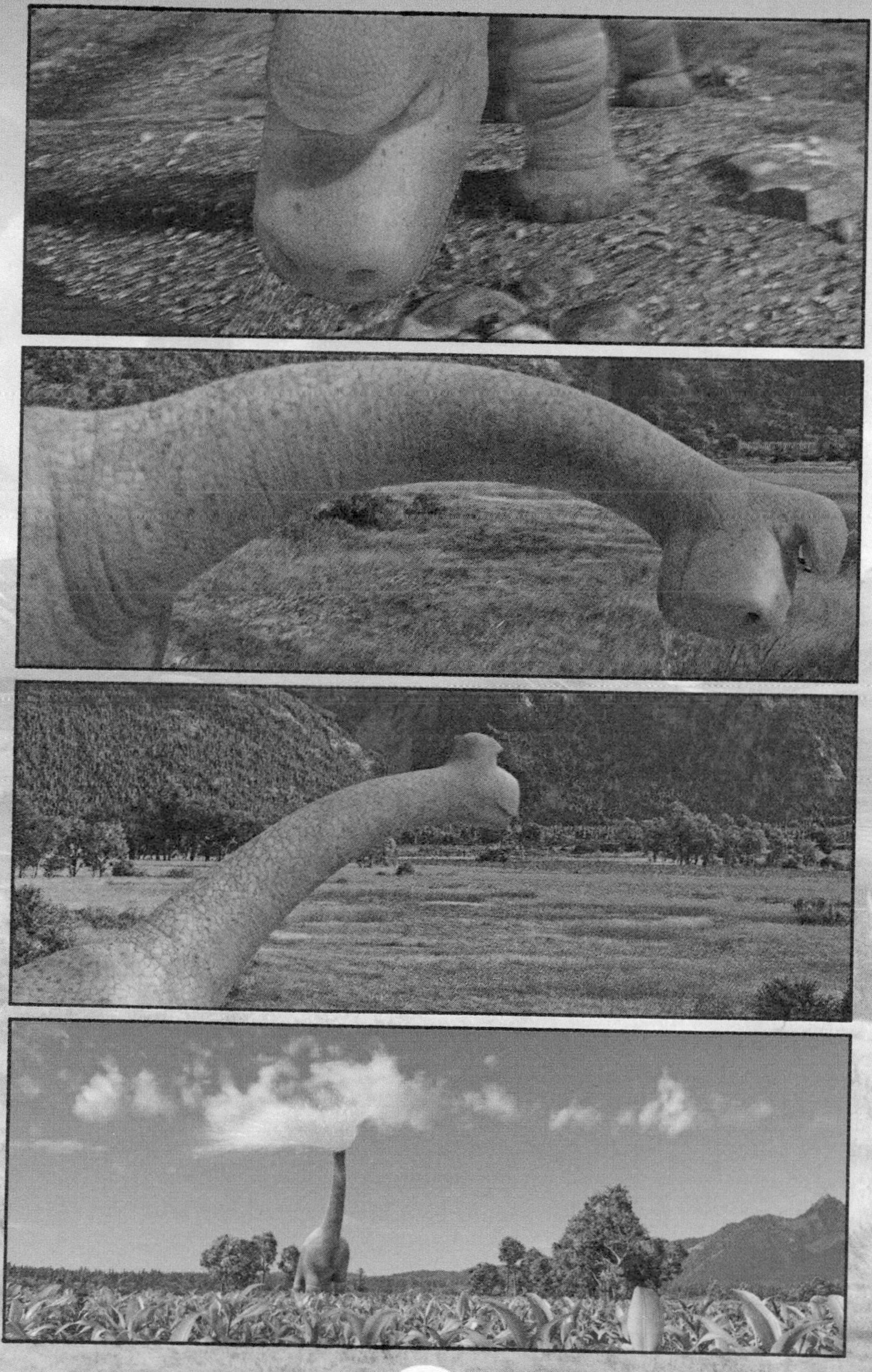

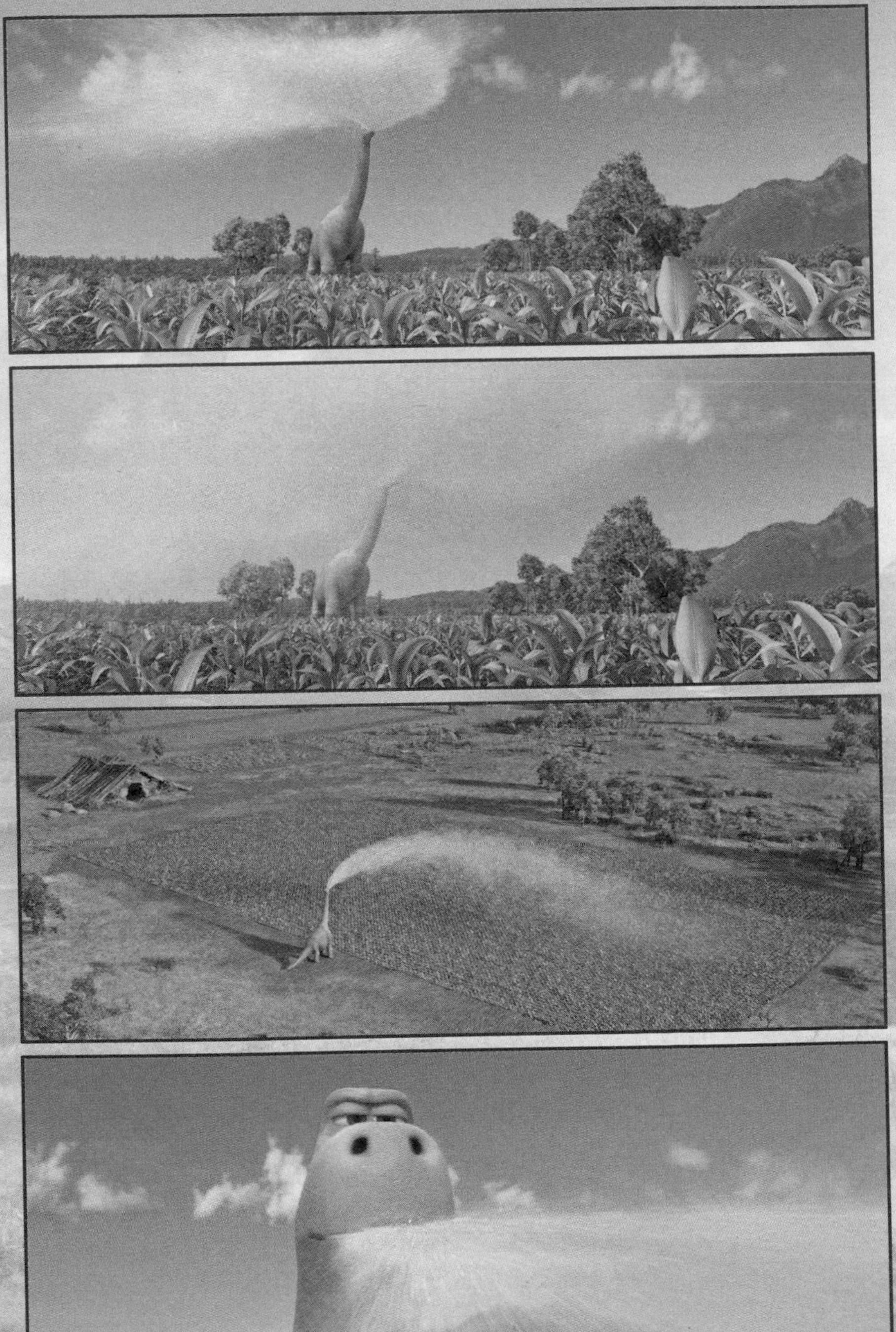

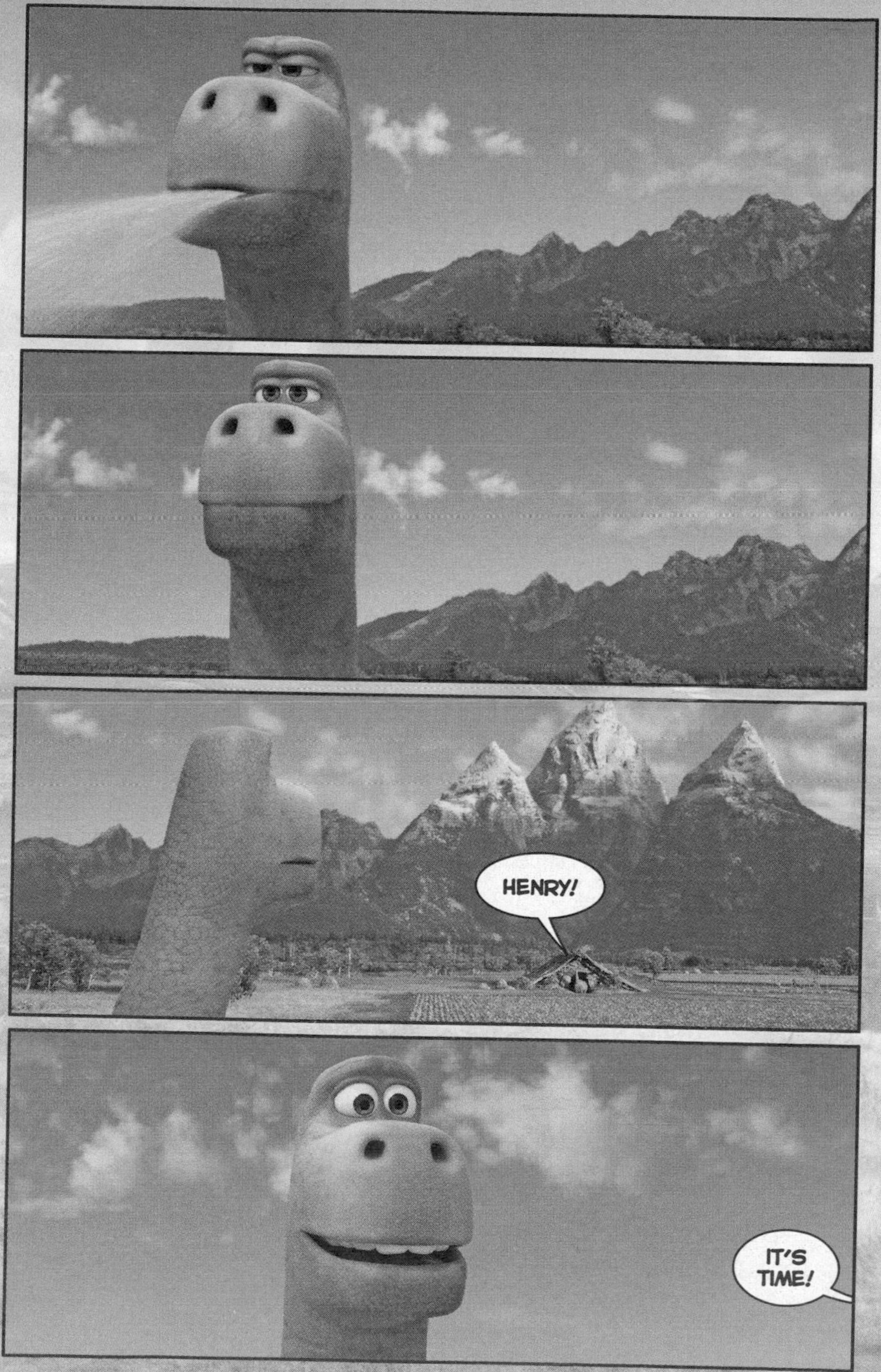
HENRY!
IT'S TIME!

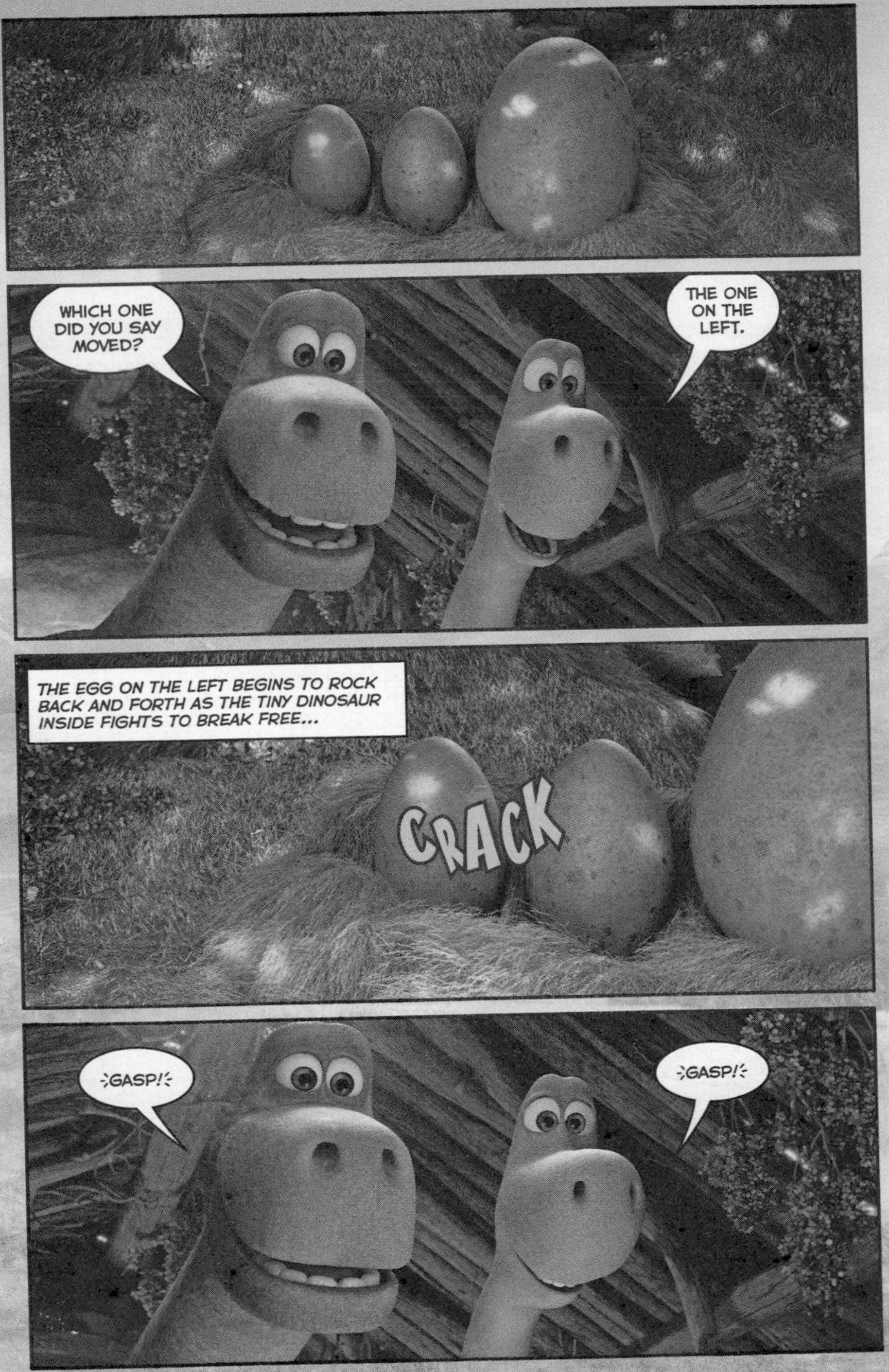
WHICH ONE DID YOU SAY MOVED?
THE ONE ON THE LEFT.
THE EGG ON THE LEFT BEGINS TO ROCK BACK AND FORTH AS THE TINY DINOSAUR INSIDE FIGHTS TO BREAK FREE...
CRACK
GASP!
GASP!

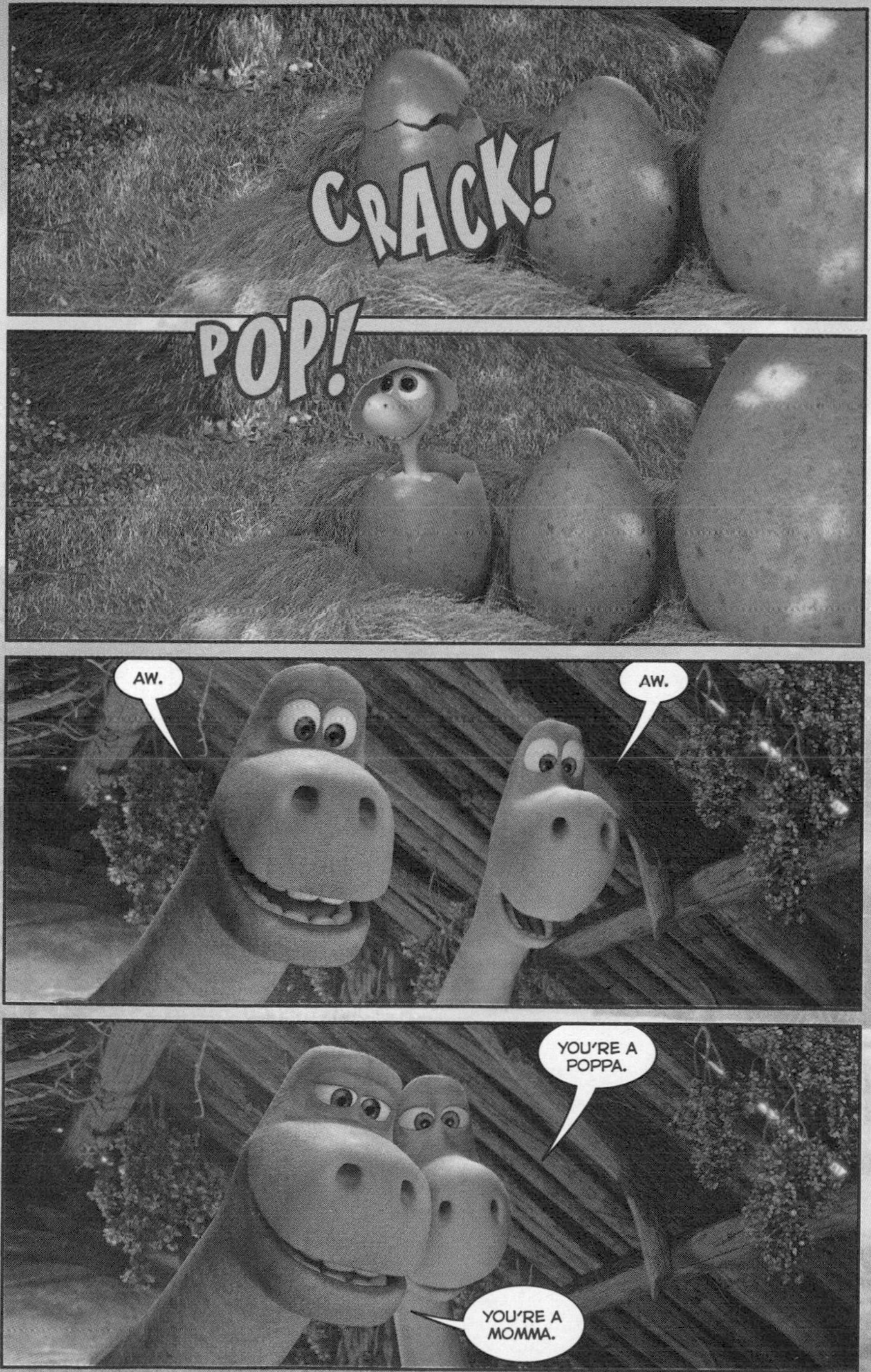
CRACK!
POP!
AW.
AW.
YOU'RE A POPPA.
YOU'RE A MOMMA.

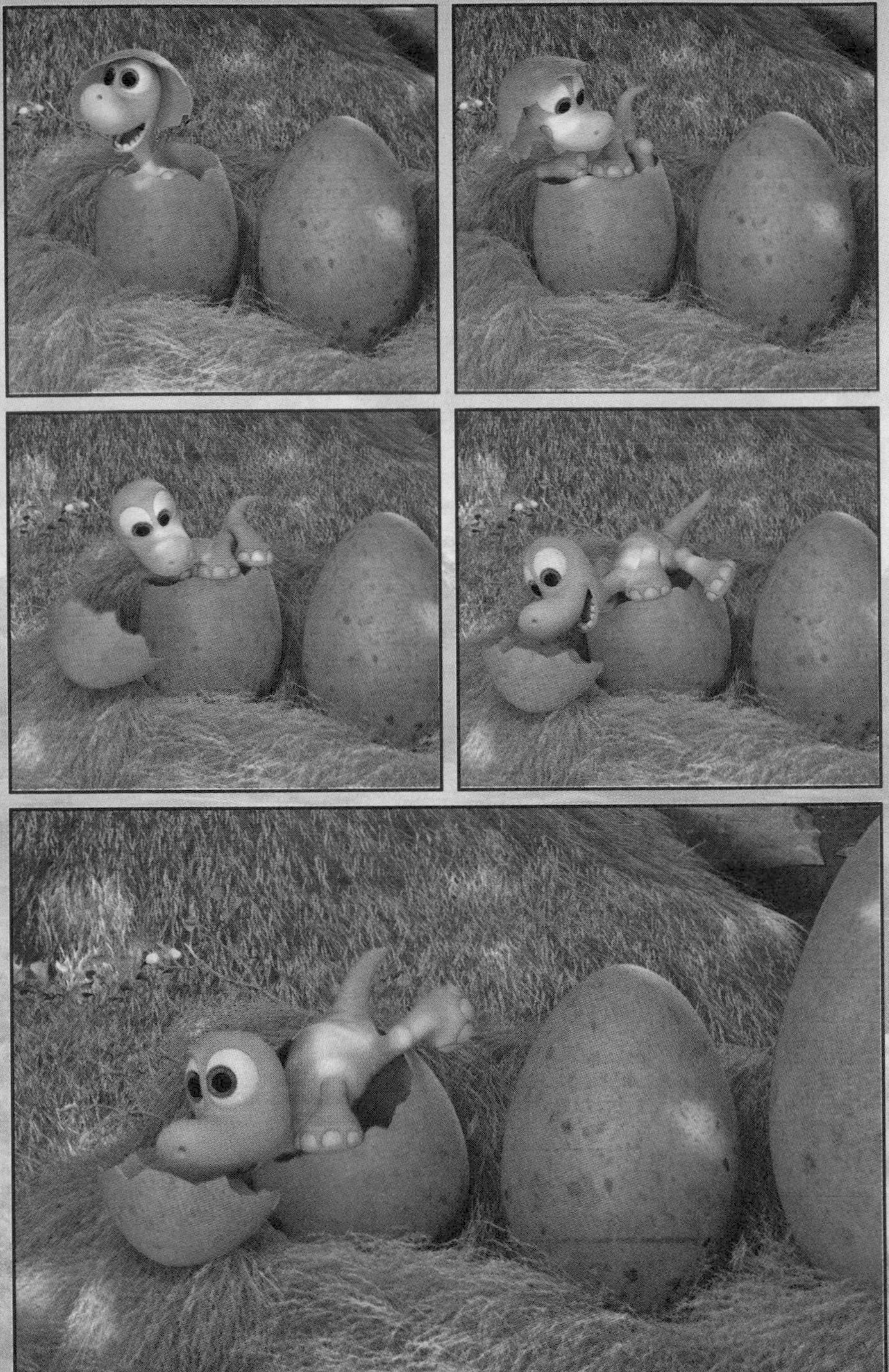

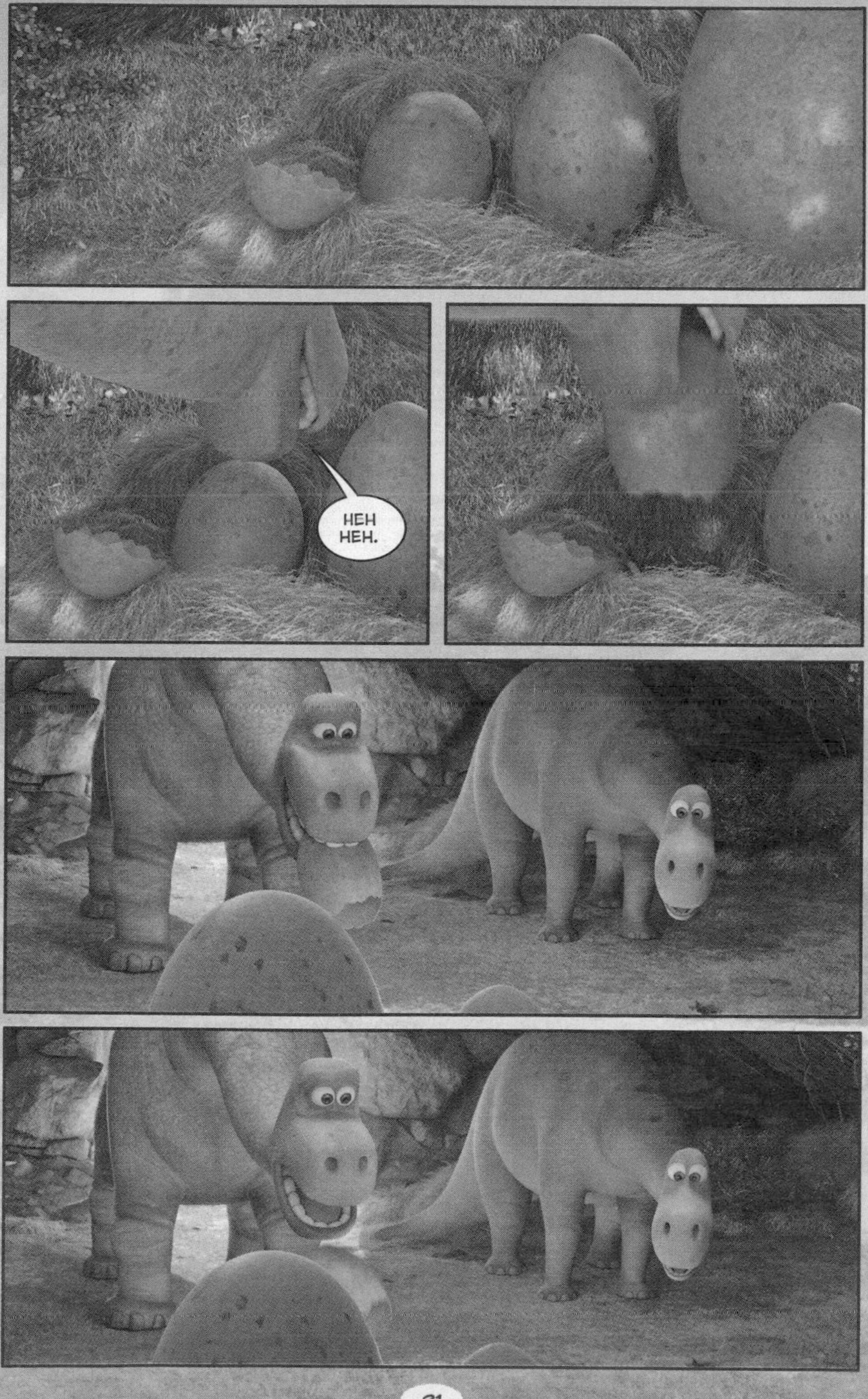
HEH HEH.

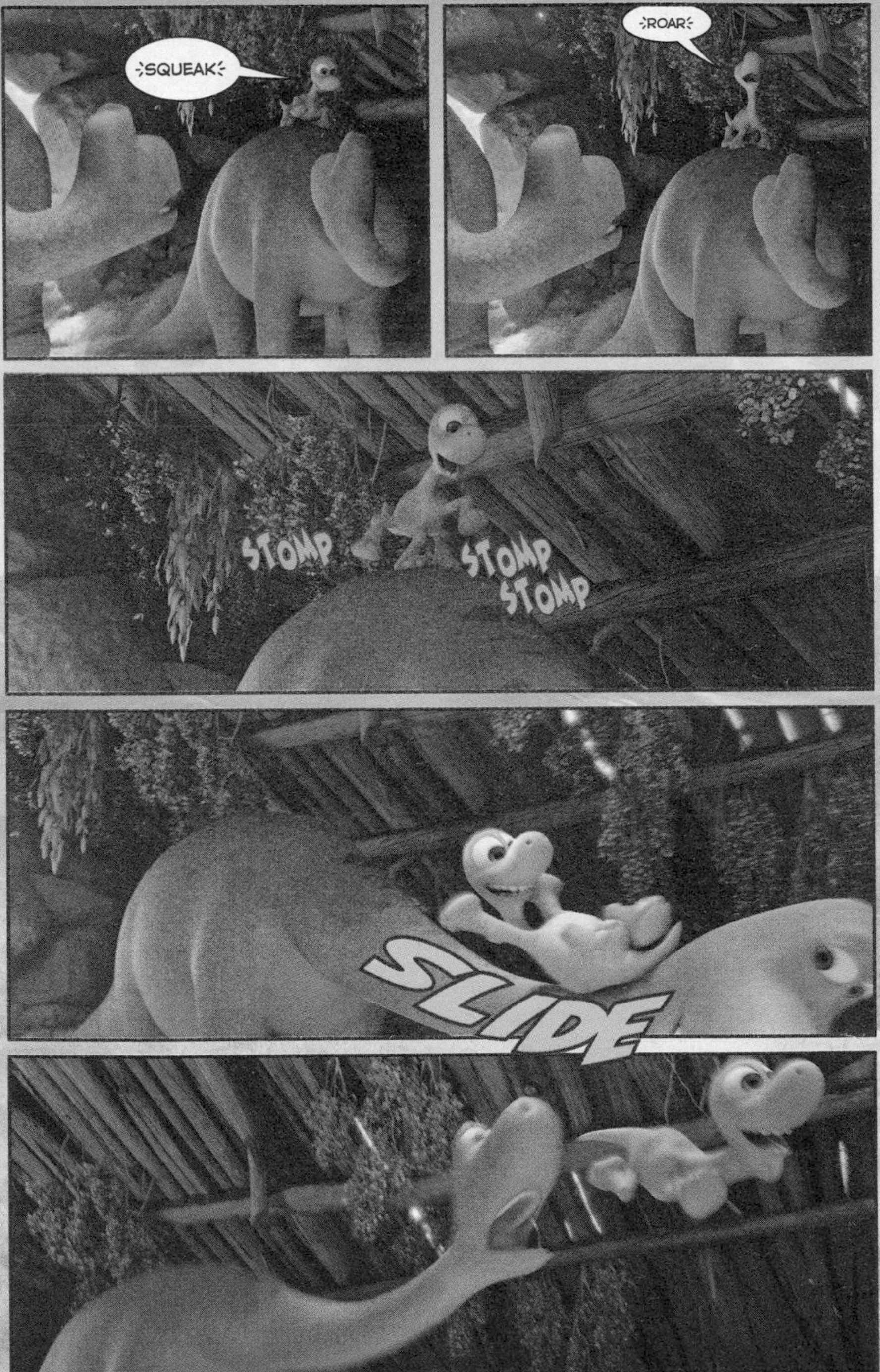
SQUEAK
ROAR
STOMP
STOMP
STOMP
SLIDE

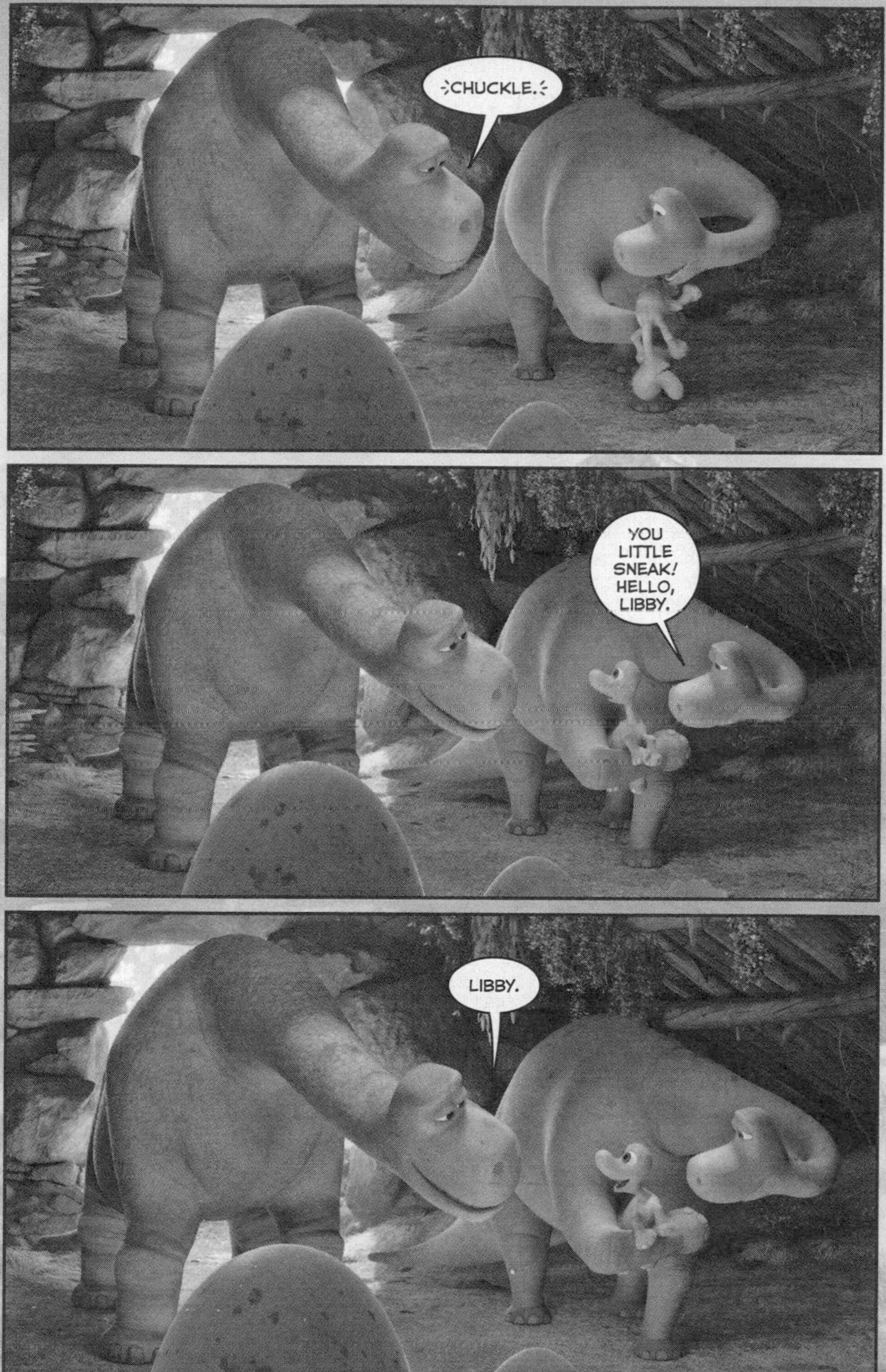
CHUCKLE.
YOU LITTLE SNEAK! HELLO, LIBBY.
LIBBY.

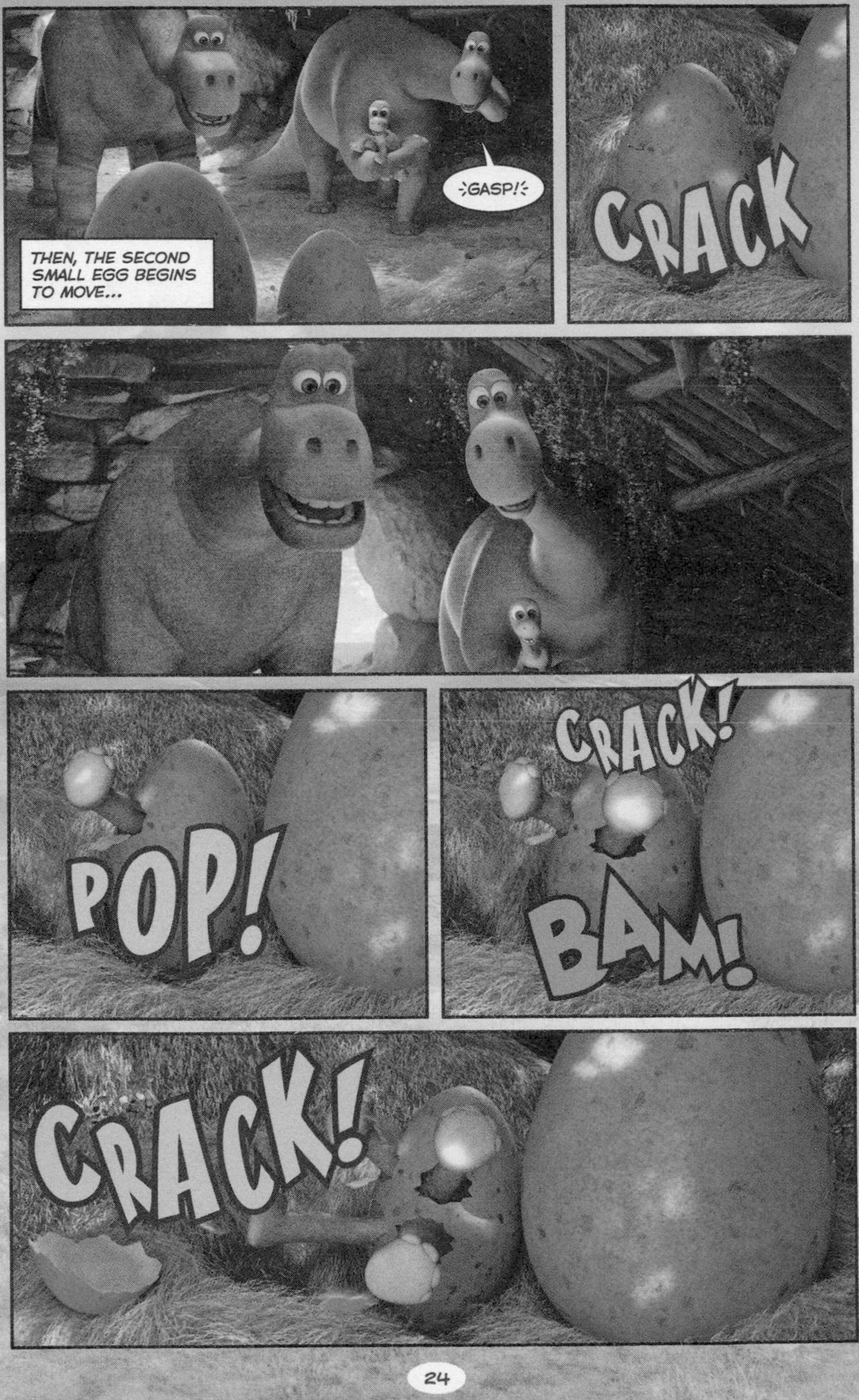
THEN, THE SECOND SMALL EGG BEGINS TO MOVE...
GASP!
CRACK
POP!
CRACK!
BAM!
CRACK!

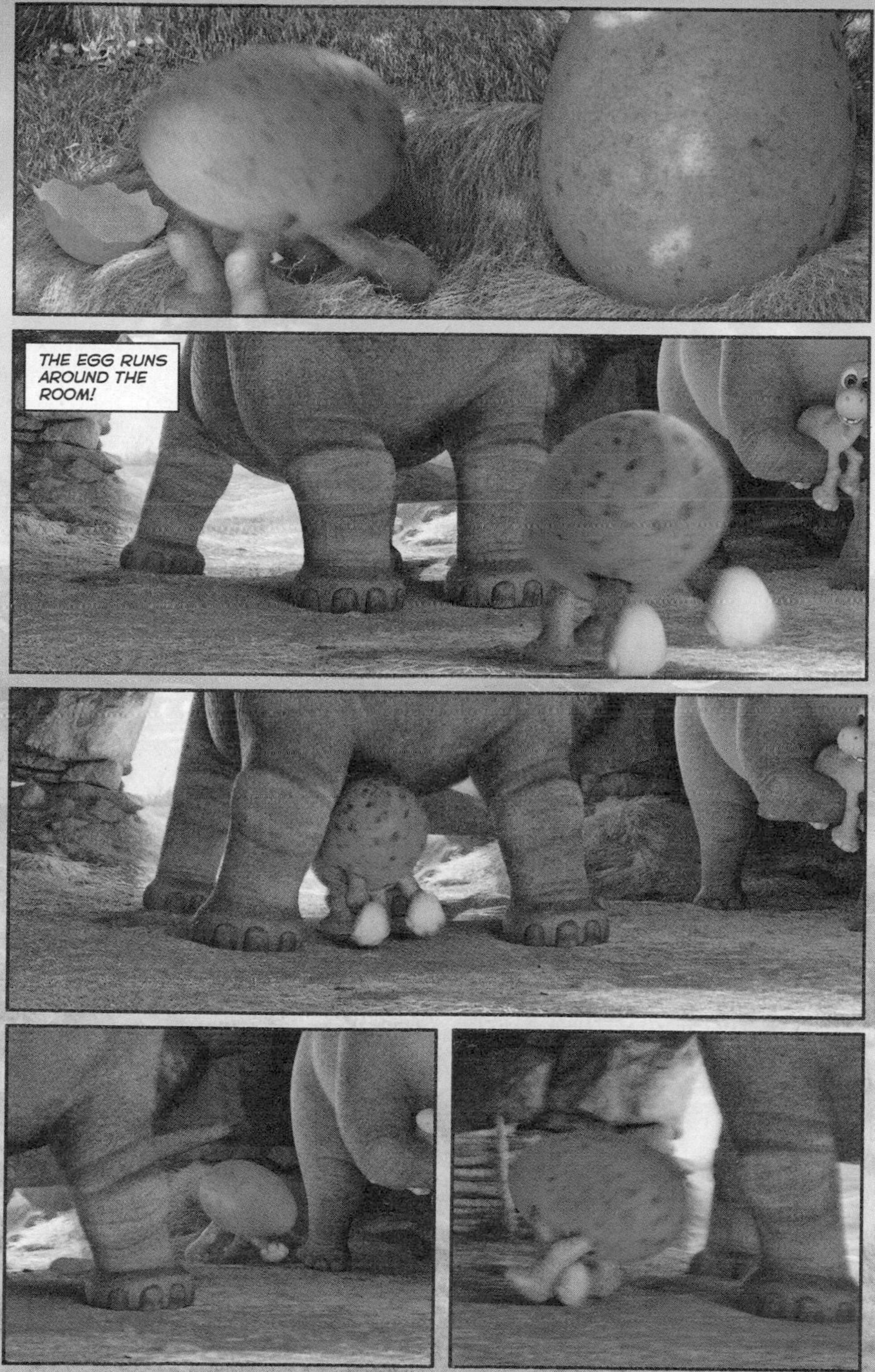
THE EGG RUNS AROUND THE ROOM!

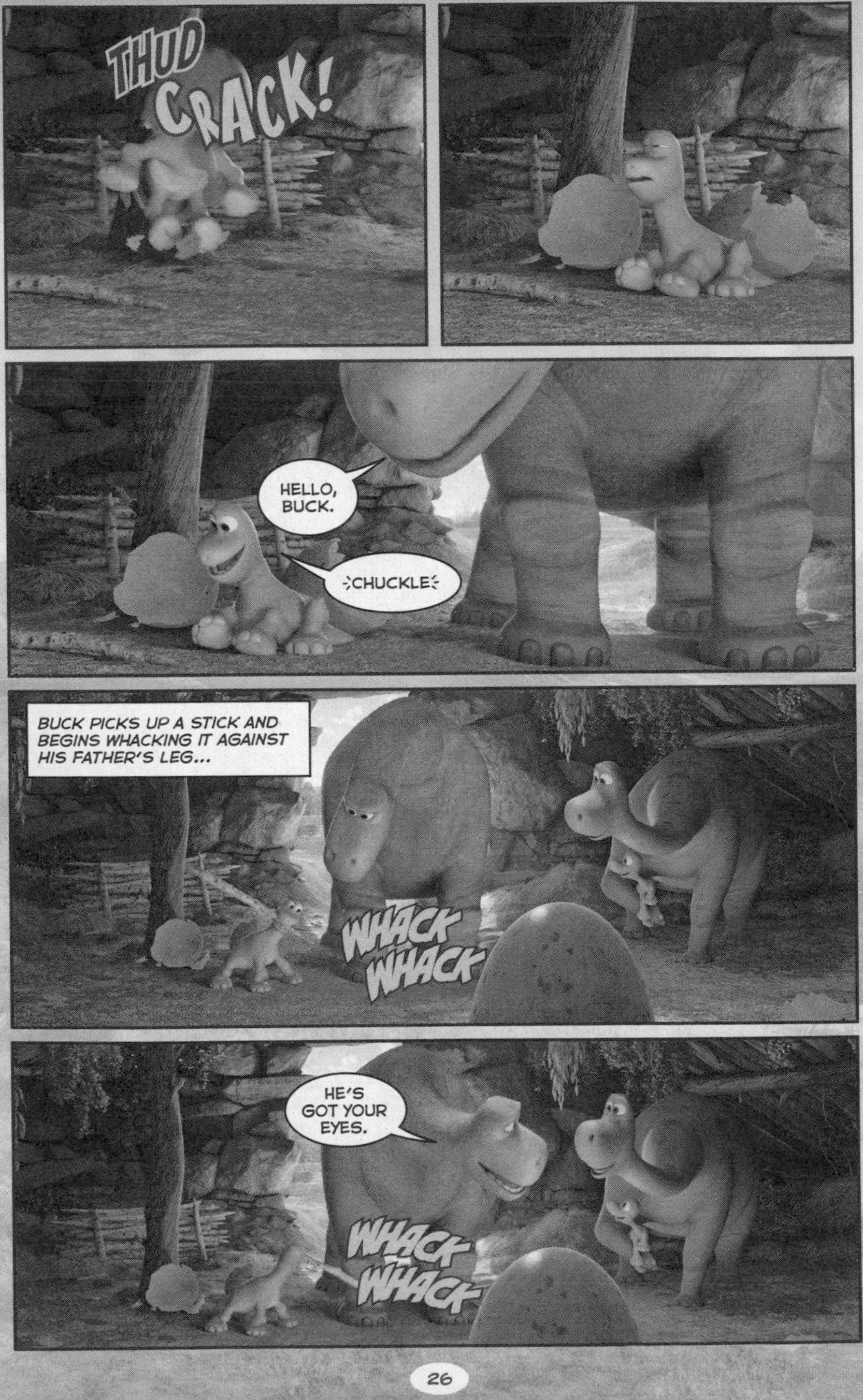
THUD
CRACK!
HELLO, BUCK.
CHUCKLE
BUCK PICKS UP A STICK AND BEGINS WHACKING IT AGAINST HIS FATHER'S LEG...
WHACK
WHACK
HE'S GOT YOUR EYES.
WHACK
WHACK

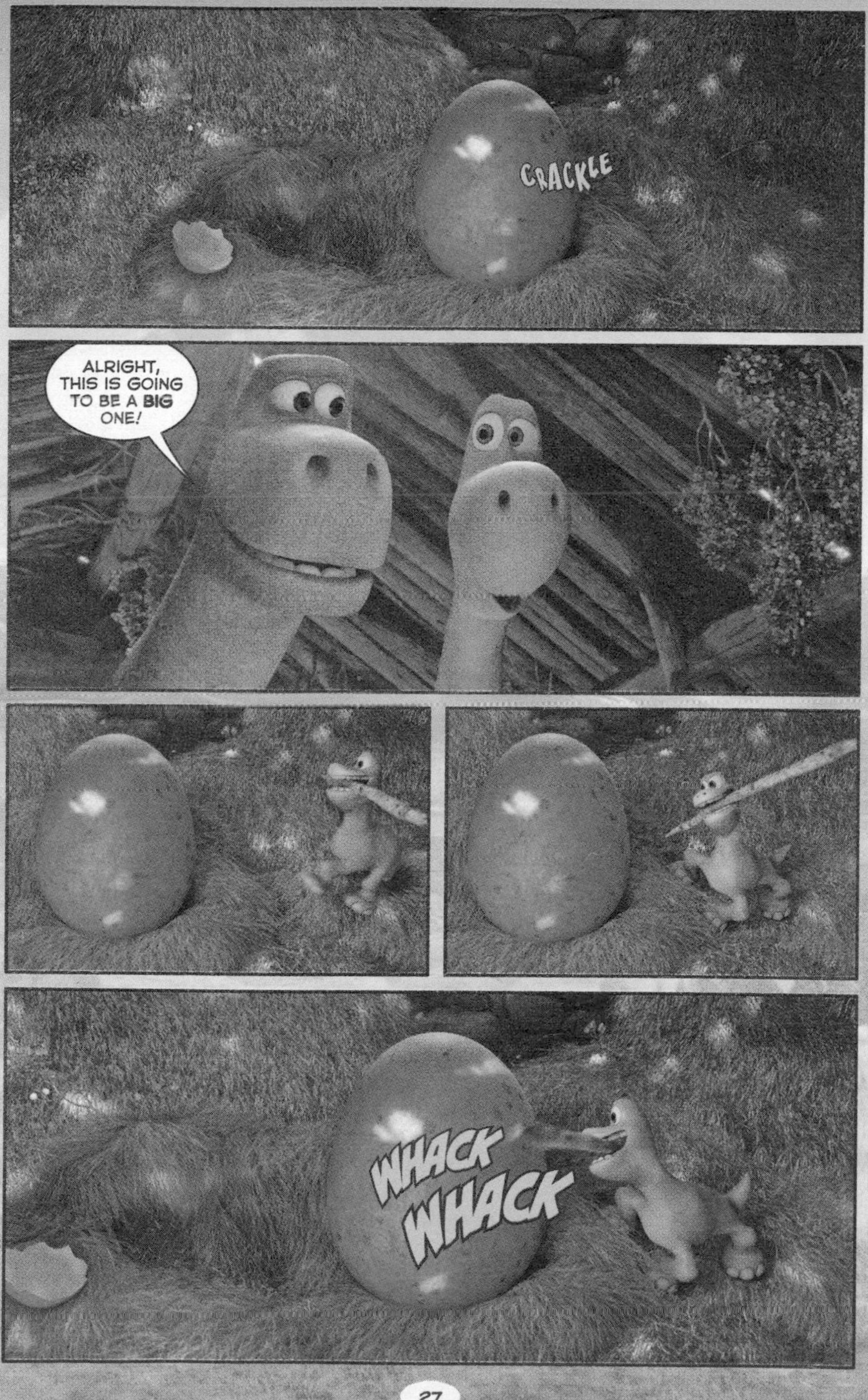
CRACKLE
ALRIGHT, THIS IS GOING TO BE A BIG ONE!
WHACK
WHACK

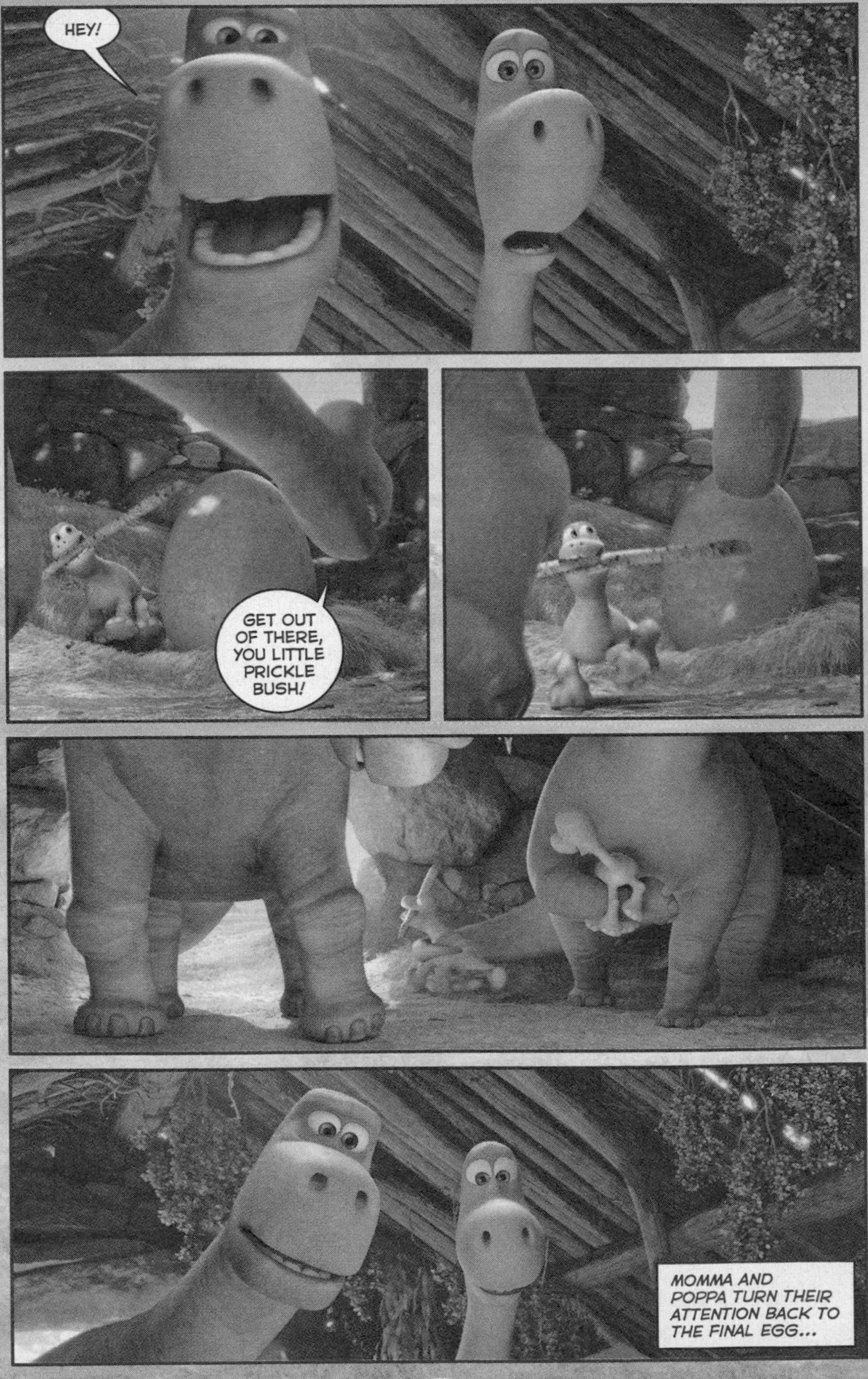
HEY!
GET OUT OF THERE, YOU LITTLE PRICKLE BUSH!
MOMMA AND POPPA TURN THEIR ATTENTION BACK TO THE FINAL EGG...

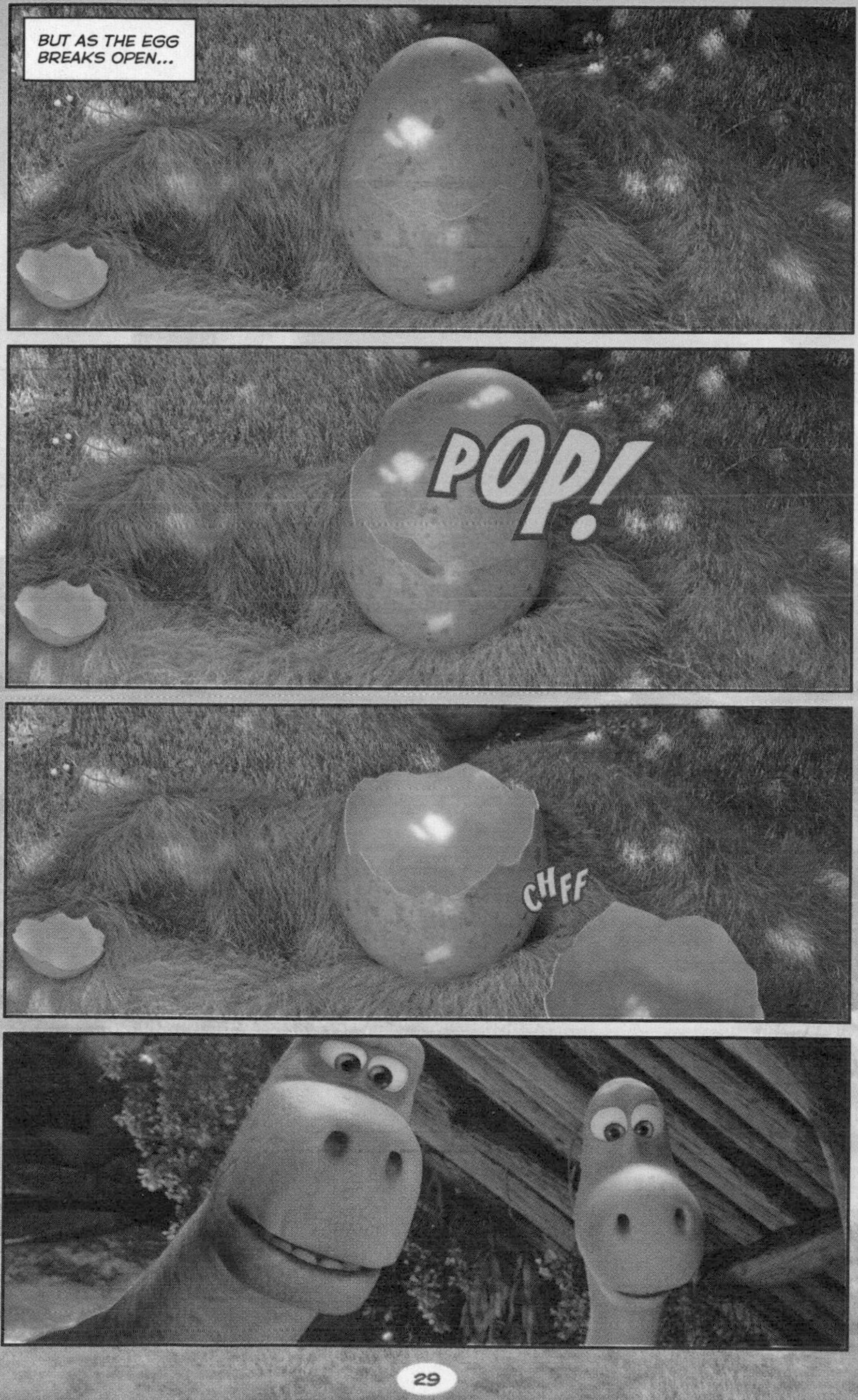
BUT AS THE EGG BREAKS OPEN...
POP!
CHFF

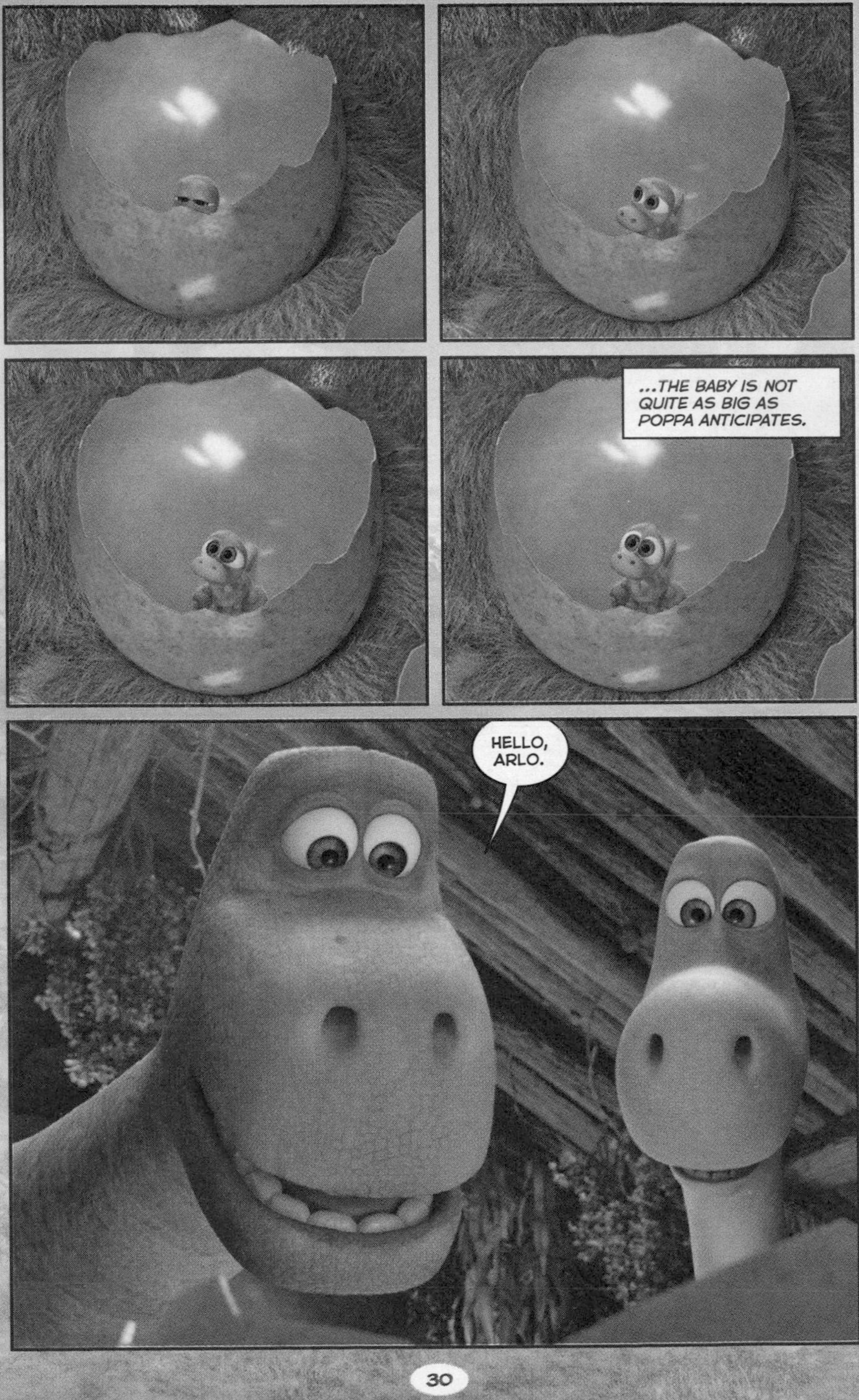
...THE BABY IS NOT QUITE AS BIG AS POPPA ANTICIPATES.
HELLO, ARLO.

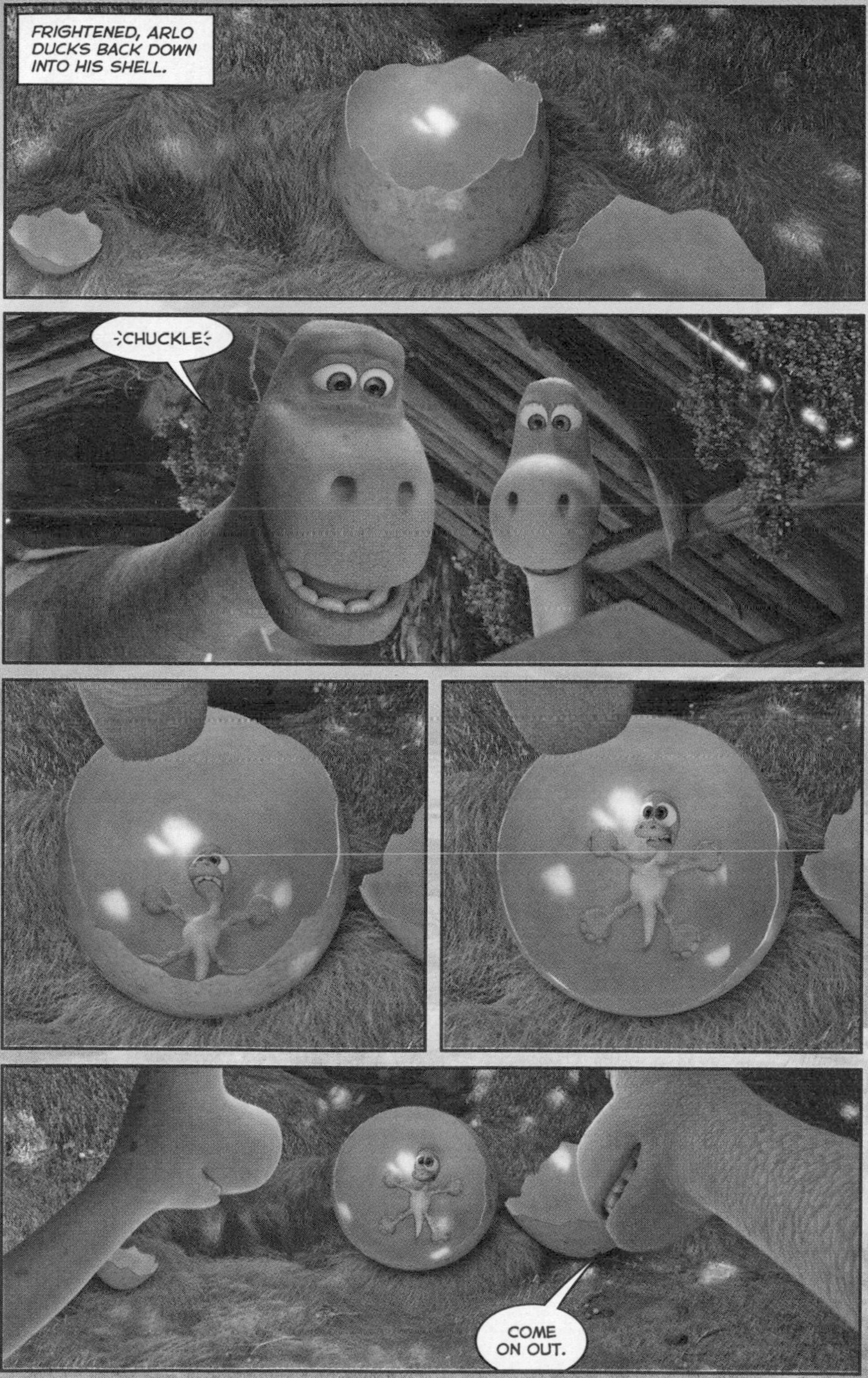
FRIGHTENED, ARLO DUCKS BACK DOWN INTO HIS SHELL.
CHUCKLE
COME ON OUT.

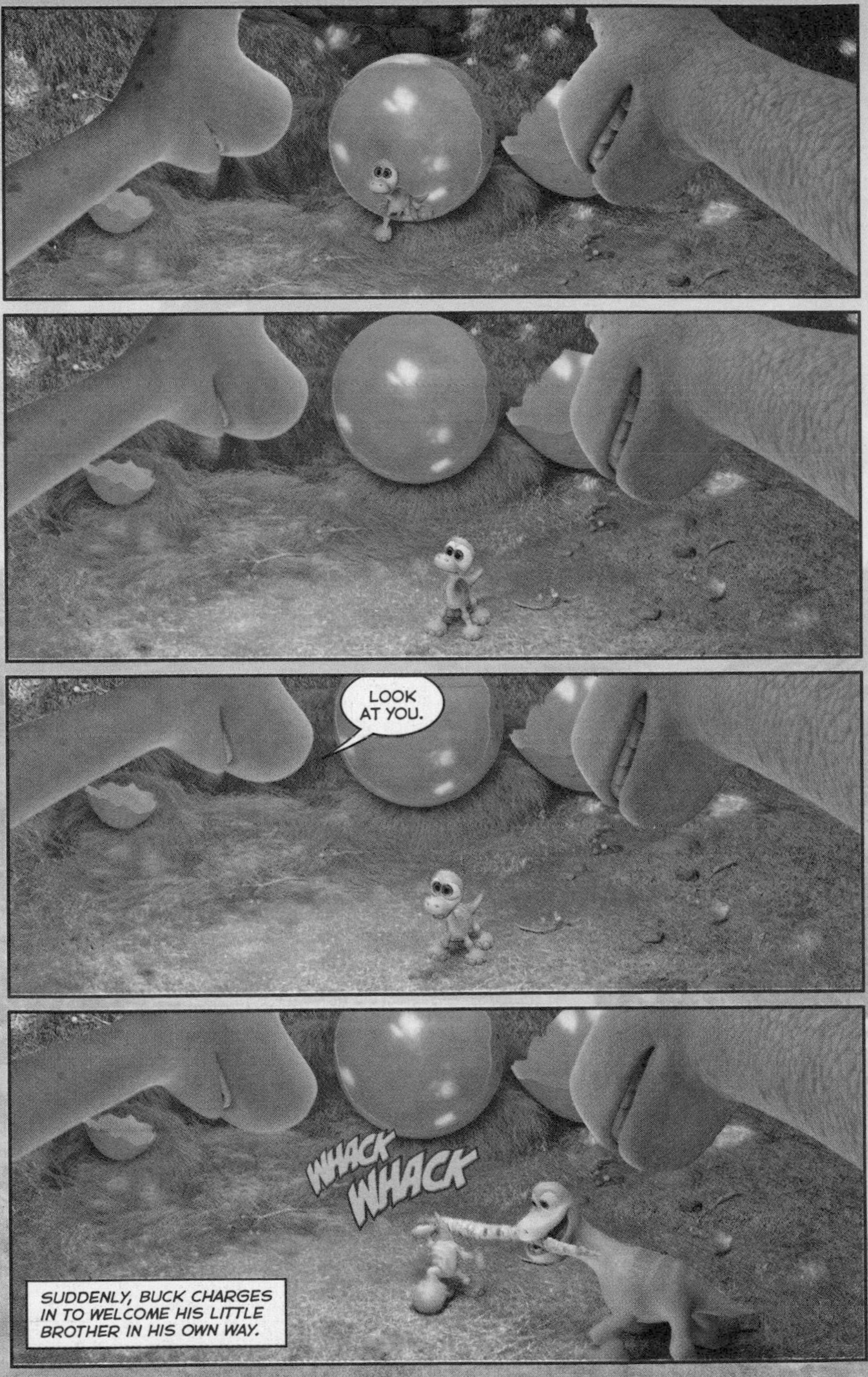
LOOK AT YOU.
WHACK
WHACK
SUDDENLY, BUCK CHARGES IN TO WELCOME HIS LITTLE BROTHER IN HIS OWN WAY.

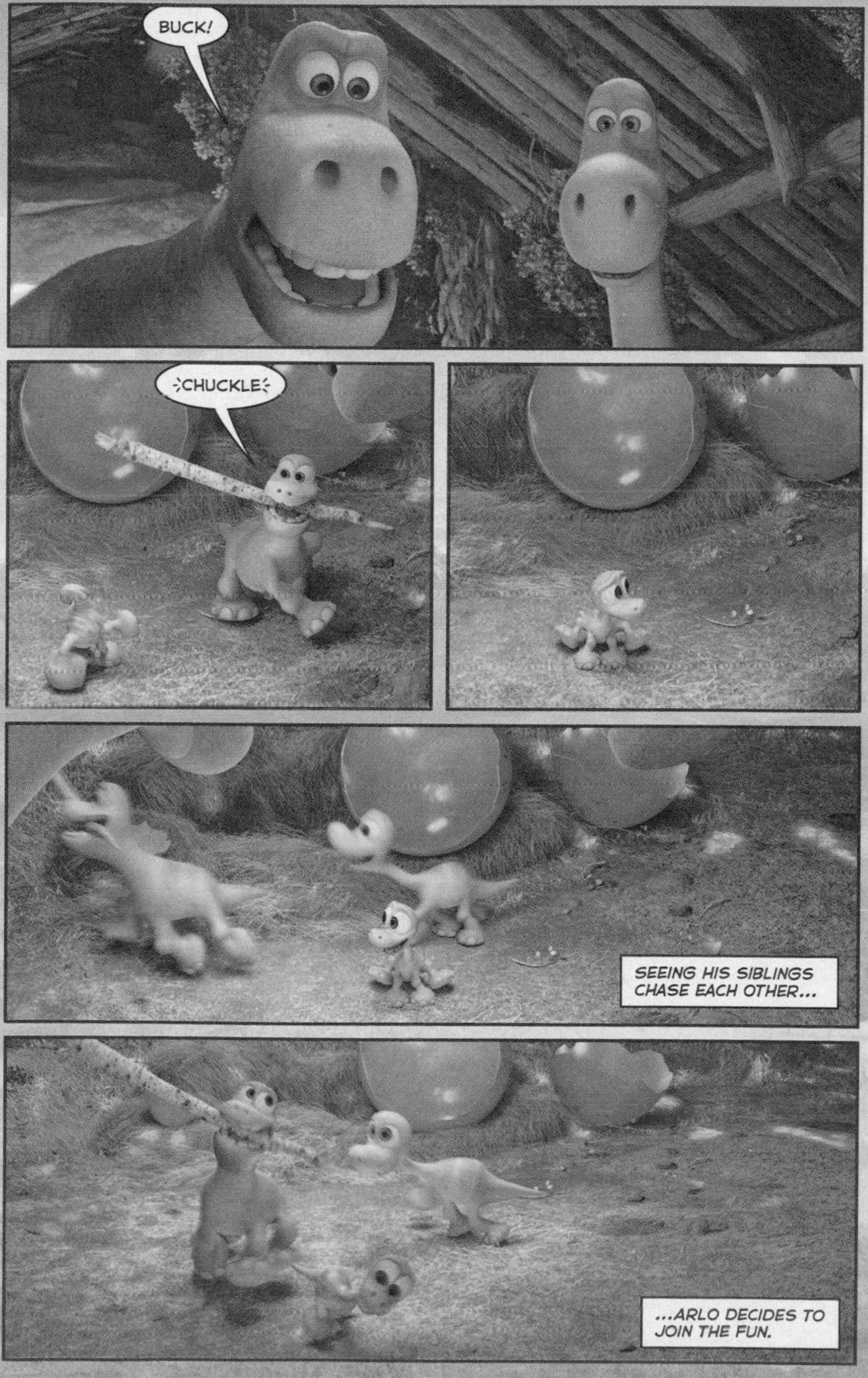
BUCK!
CHUCKLE
SEEING HIS SIBLINGS CHASE EACH OTHER...
...ARLO DECIDES TO JOIN THE FUN.

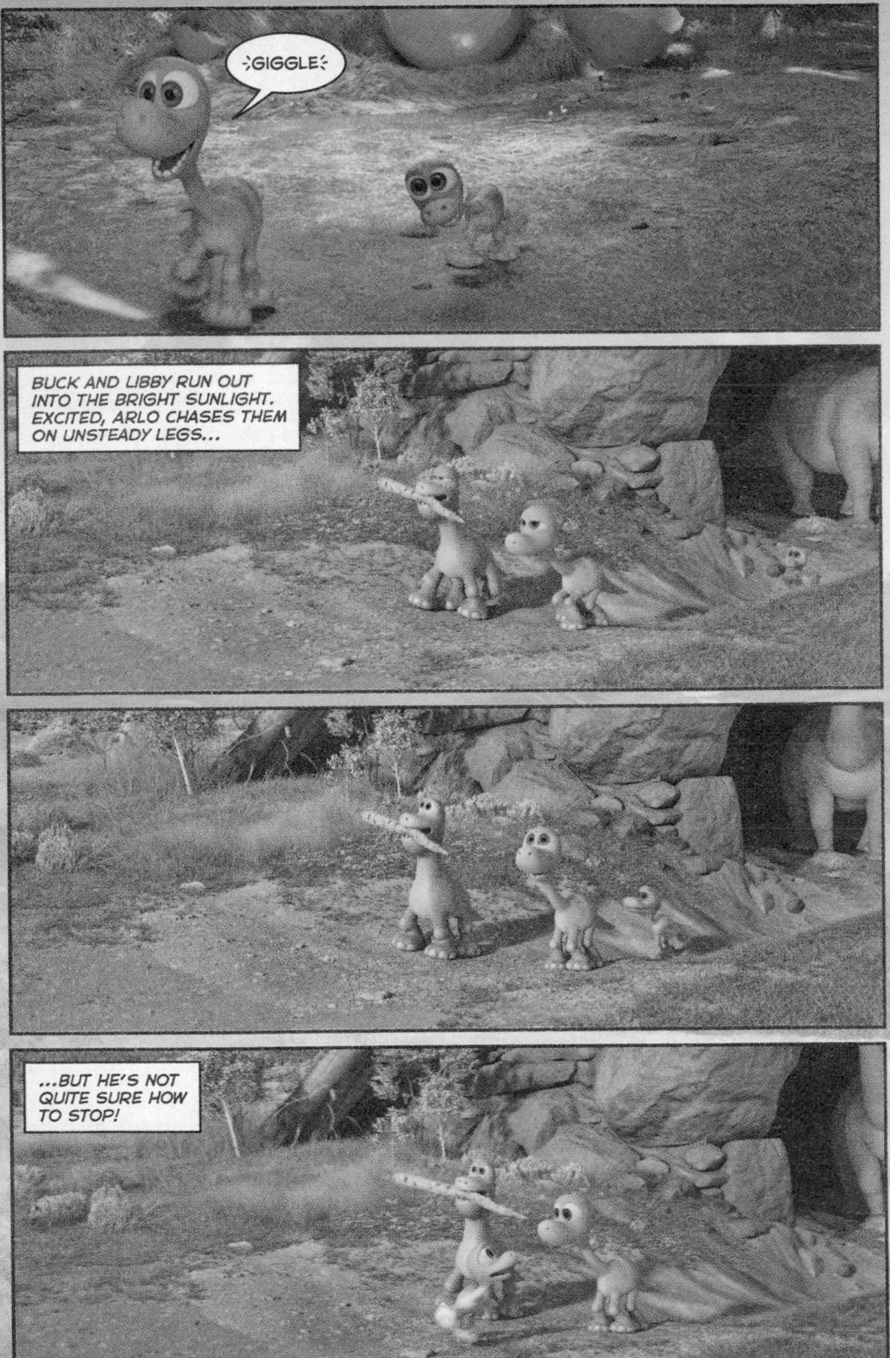
GIGGLE
BUCK AND LIBBY RUN OUT INTO THE BRIGHT SUNLIGHT. EXCITED, ARLO CHASES THEM ON UNSTEADY LEGS...
...BUT HE'S NOT QUITE SURE HOW TO STOP!

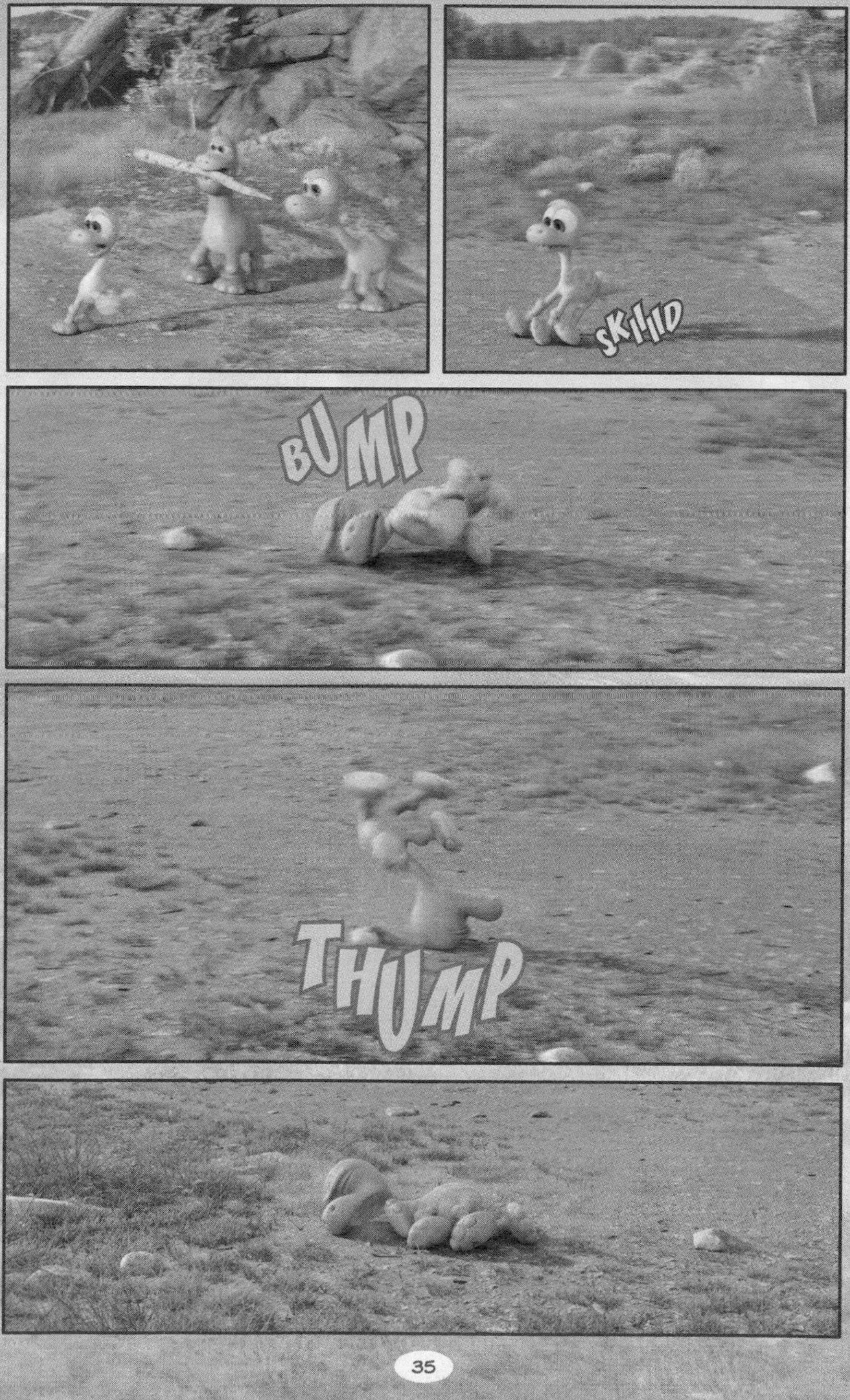
SKIIID
BUMP
THUMP

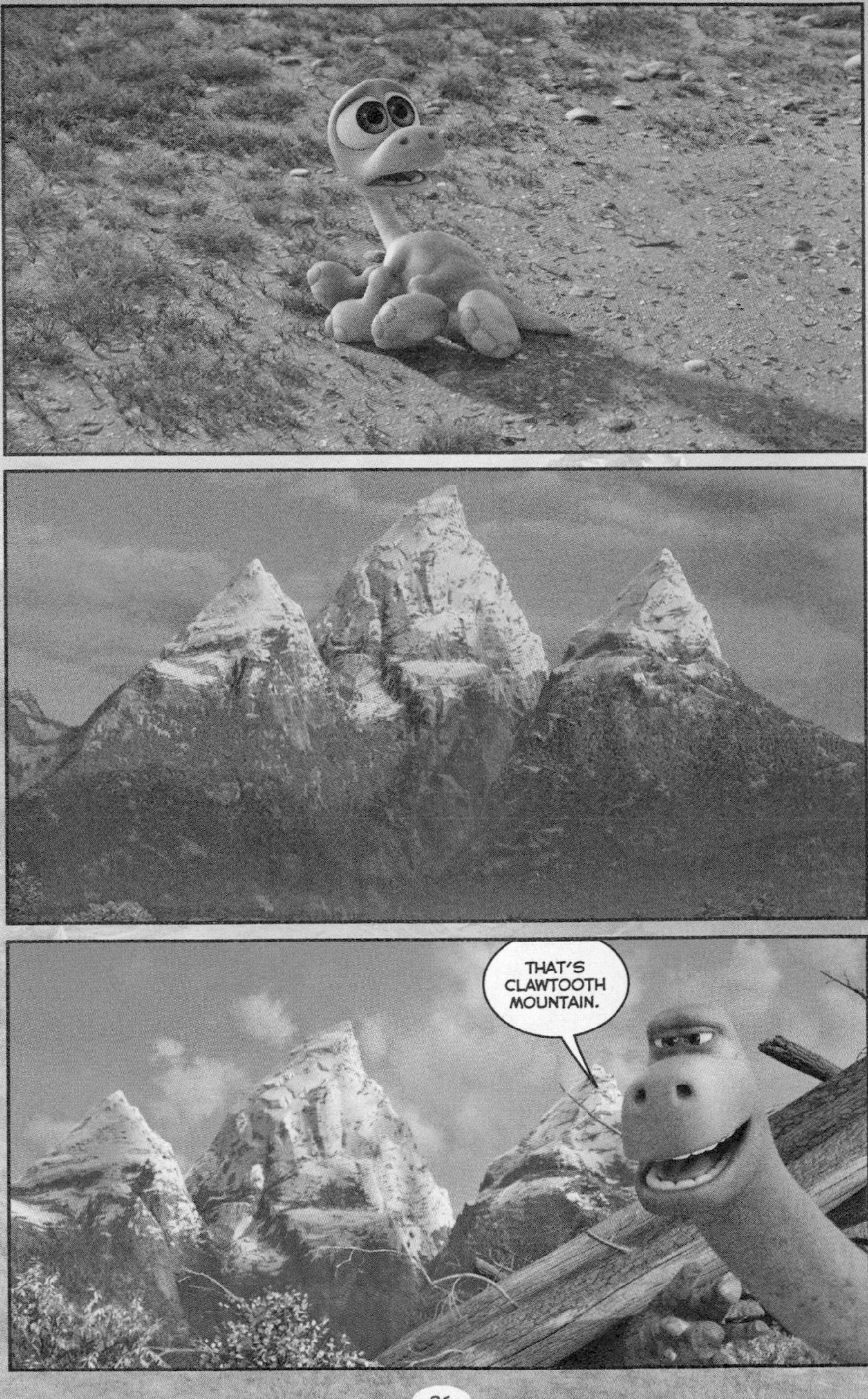
THAT'S CLAWTOOTH MOUNTAIN.

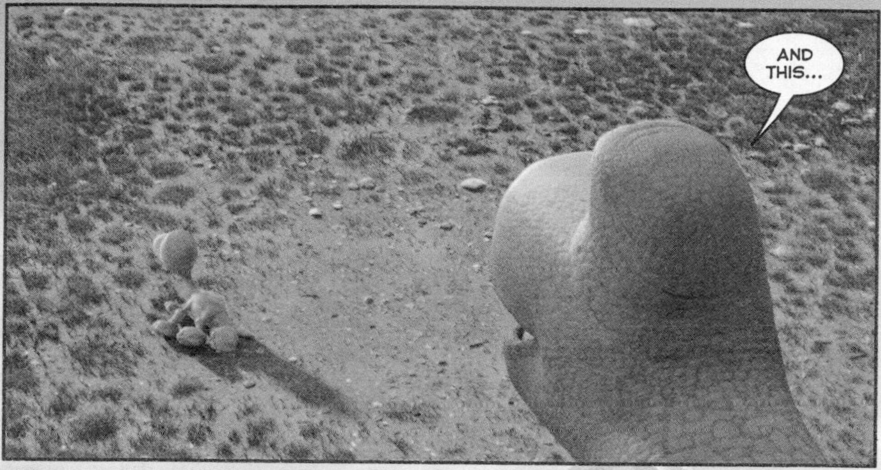
AND THIS...

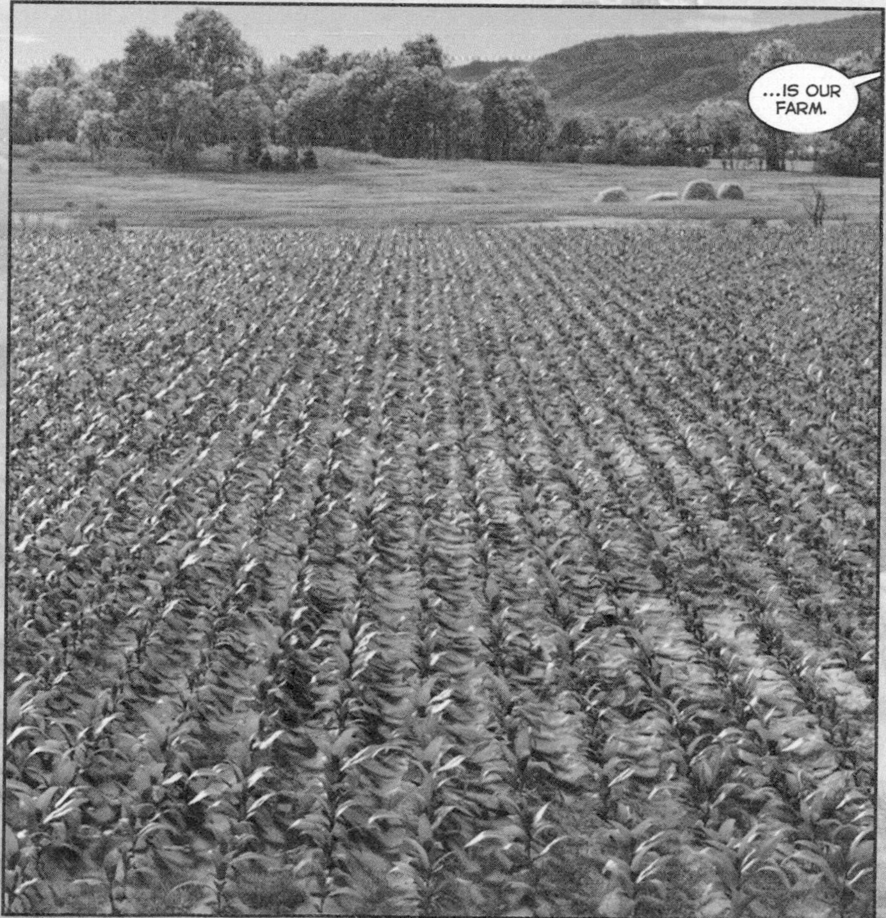
...IS OUR FARM.

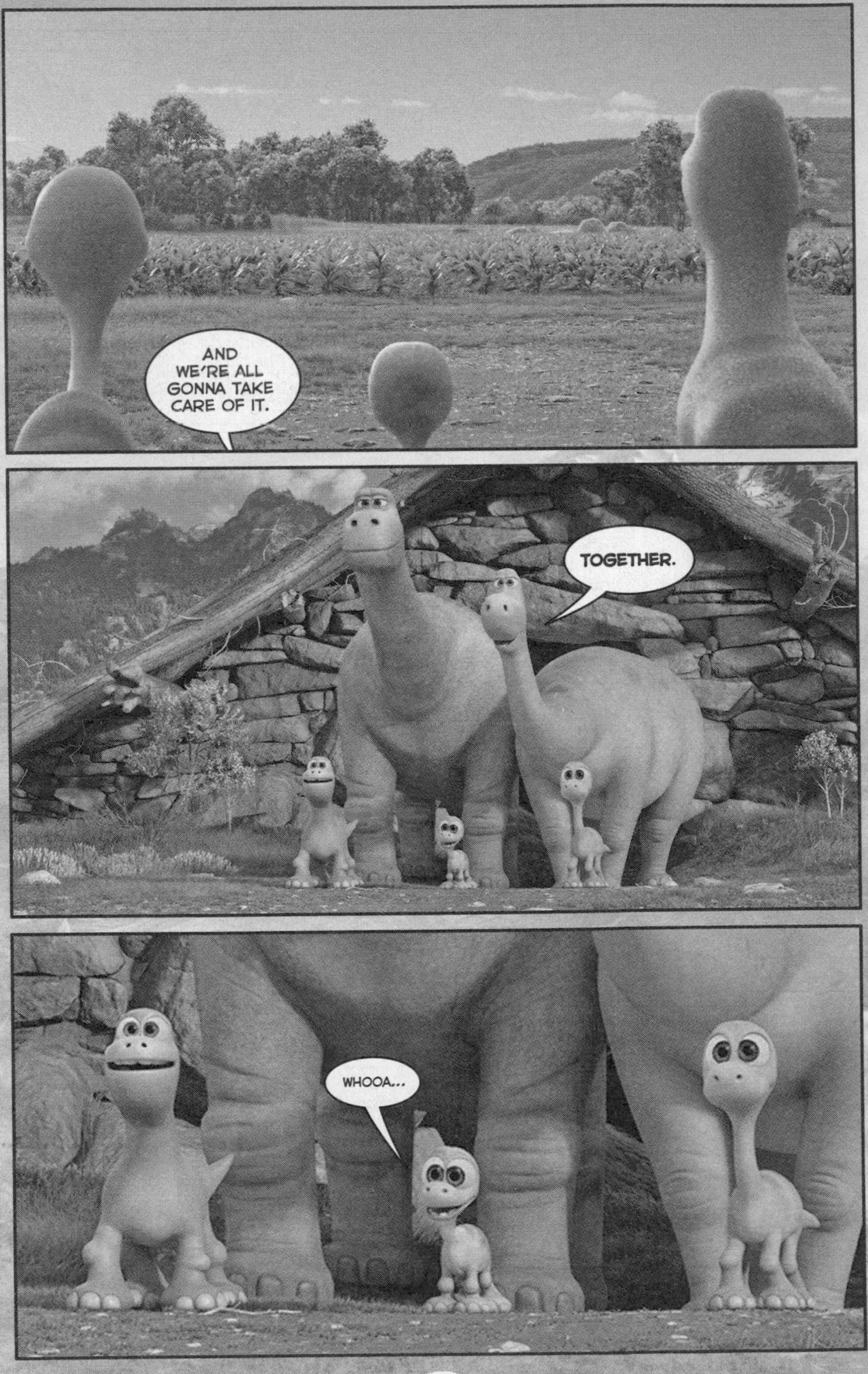
AND WE'RE ALL GONNA TAKE CARE OF IT.
TOGETHER.
WHOOA...

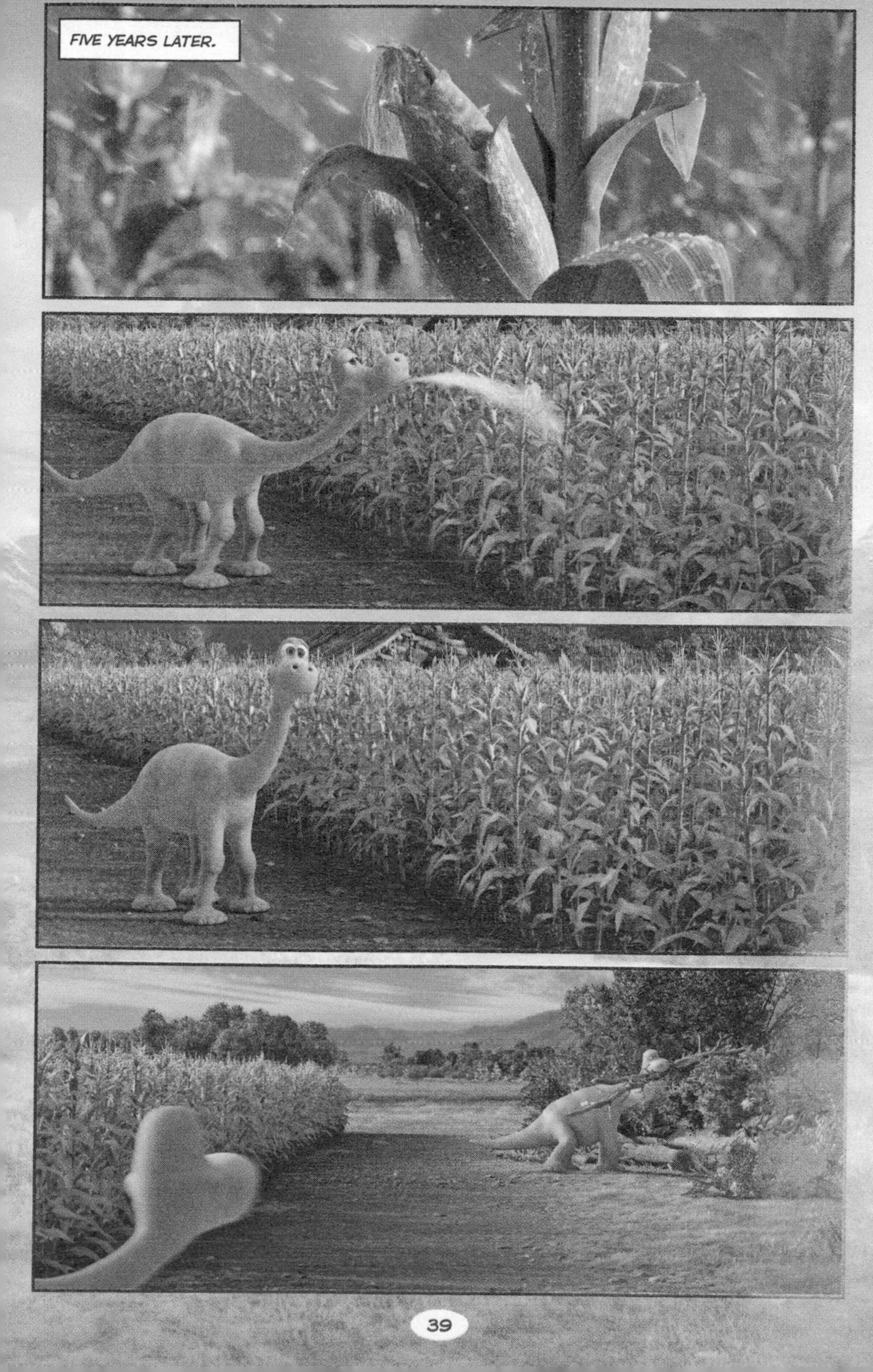
FIVE YEARS LATER.

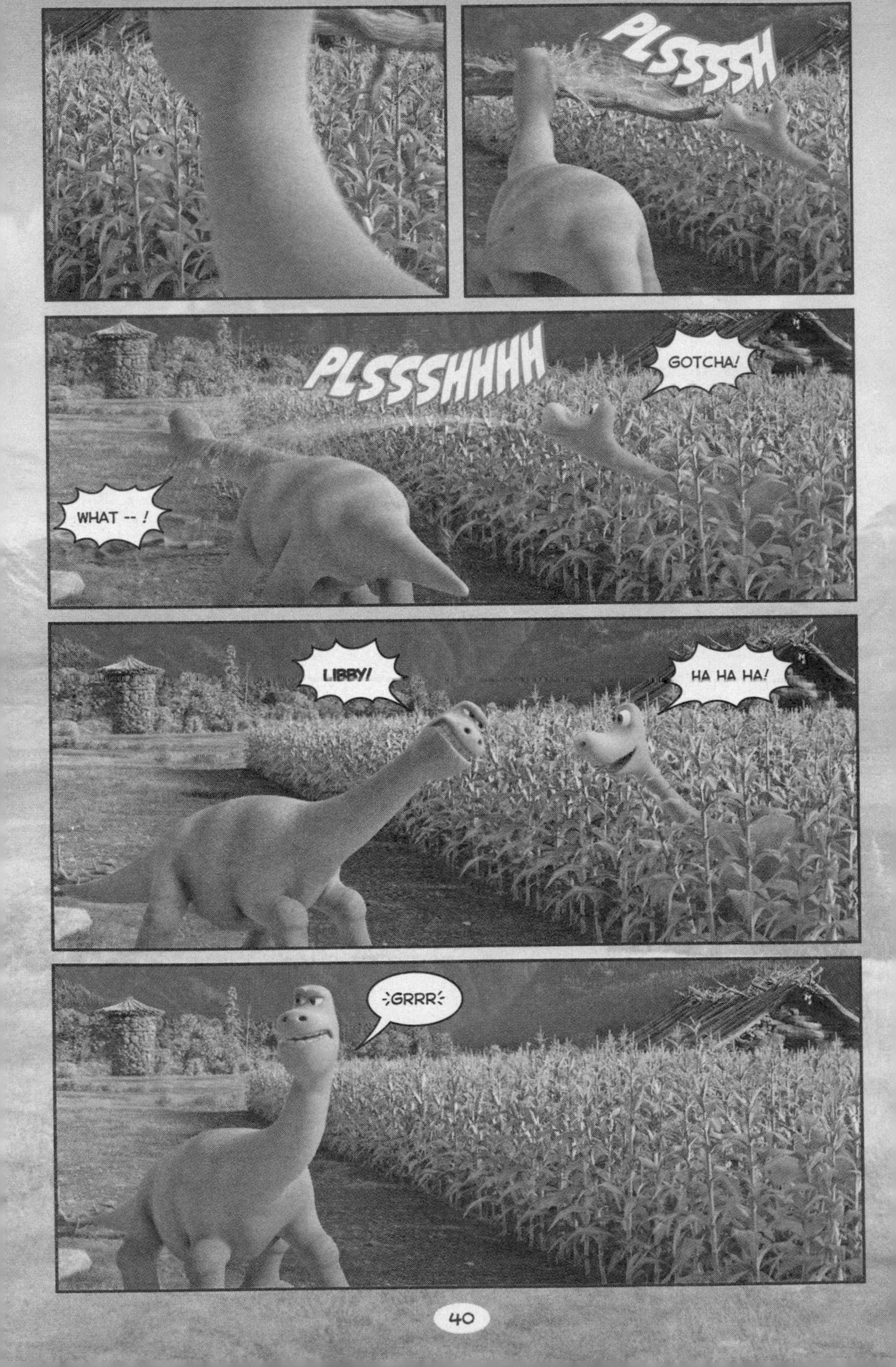
PLSSSSH
PLSSSHHHH
GOTCHA!
WHAT -- !
LIBBY!
HA HA HA!
GRRR

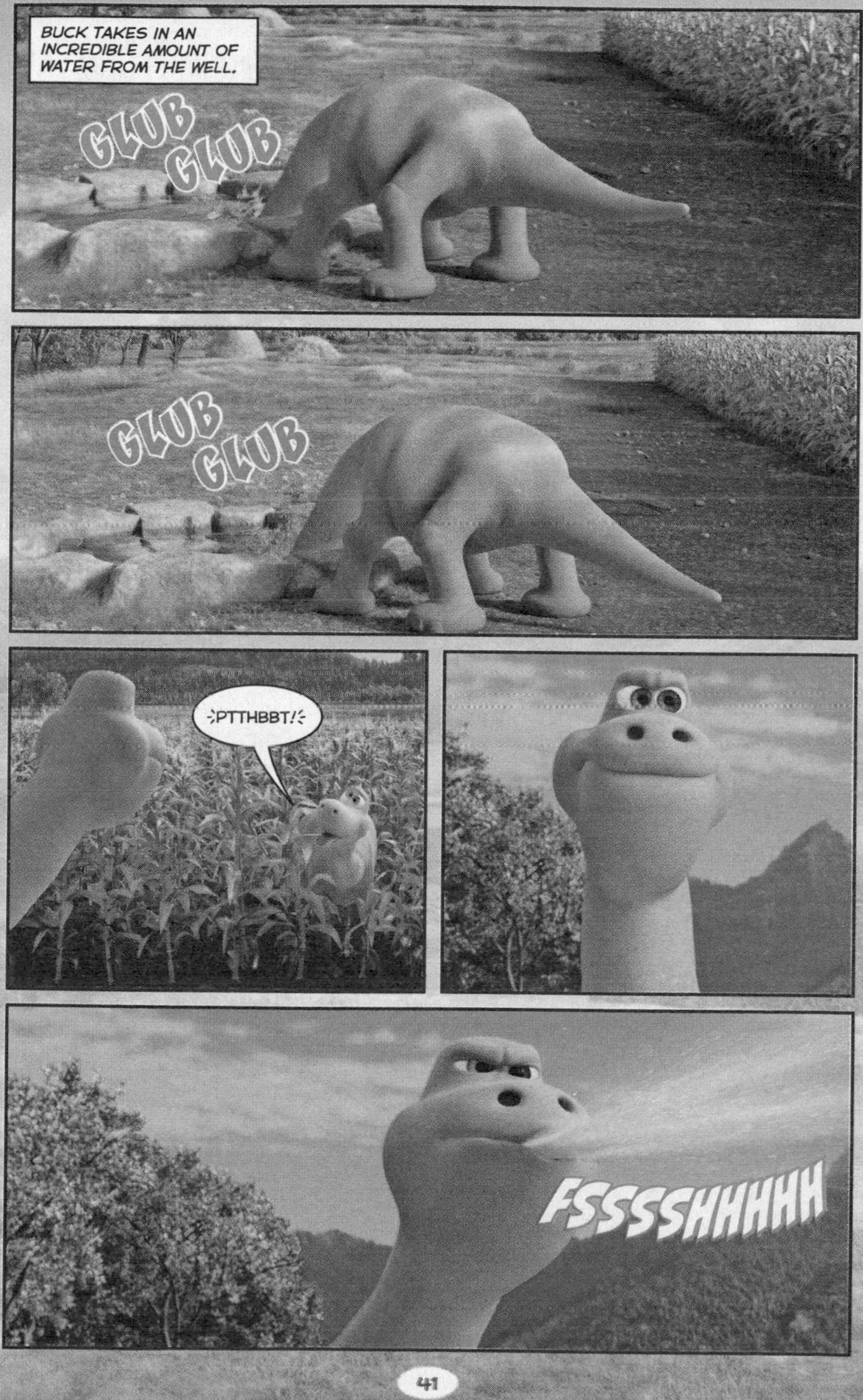
BUCK TAKES IN AN INCREDIBLE AMOUNT OF WATER FROM THE WELL.
GLUB GLUB
GLUB GLUB
PTTHBBT!
FSSSSHHHHH

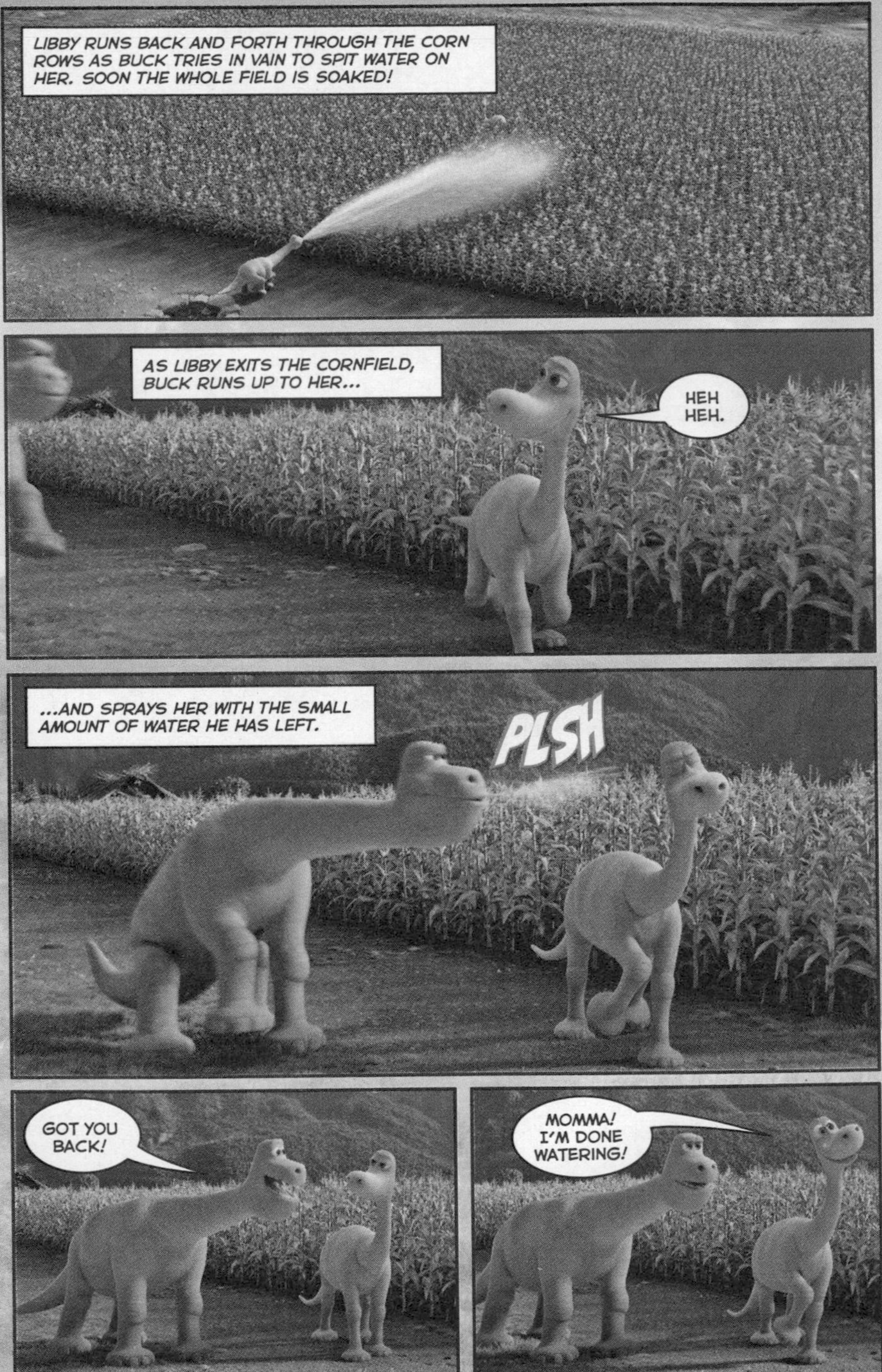
LIBBY RUNS BACK AND FORTH THROUGH THE CORN ROWS AS BUCK TRIES IN VAIN TO SPIT WATER ON HER. SOON THE WHOLE FIELD IS SOAKED!
AS LIBBY EXITS THE CORNFIELD, BUCK RUNS UP TO HER...
HEH HEH.
...AND SPRAYS HER WITH THE SMALL AMOUNT OF WATER HE HAS LEFT.
PLSH
GOT YOU BACK!
MOMMA! I'M DONE WATERING!

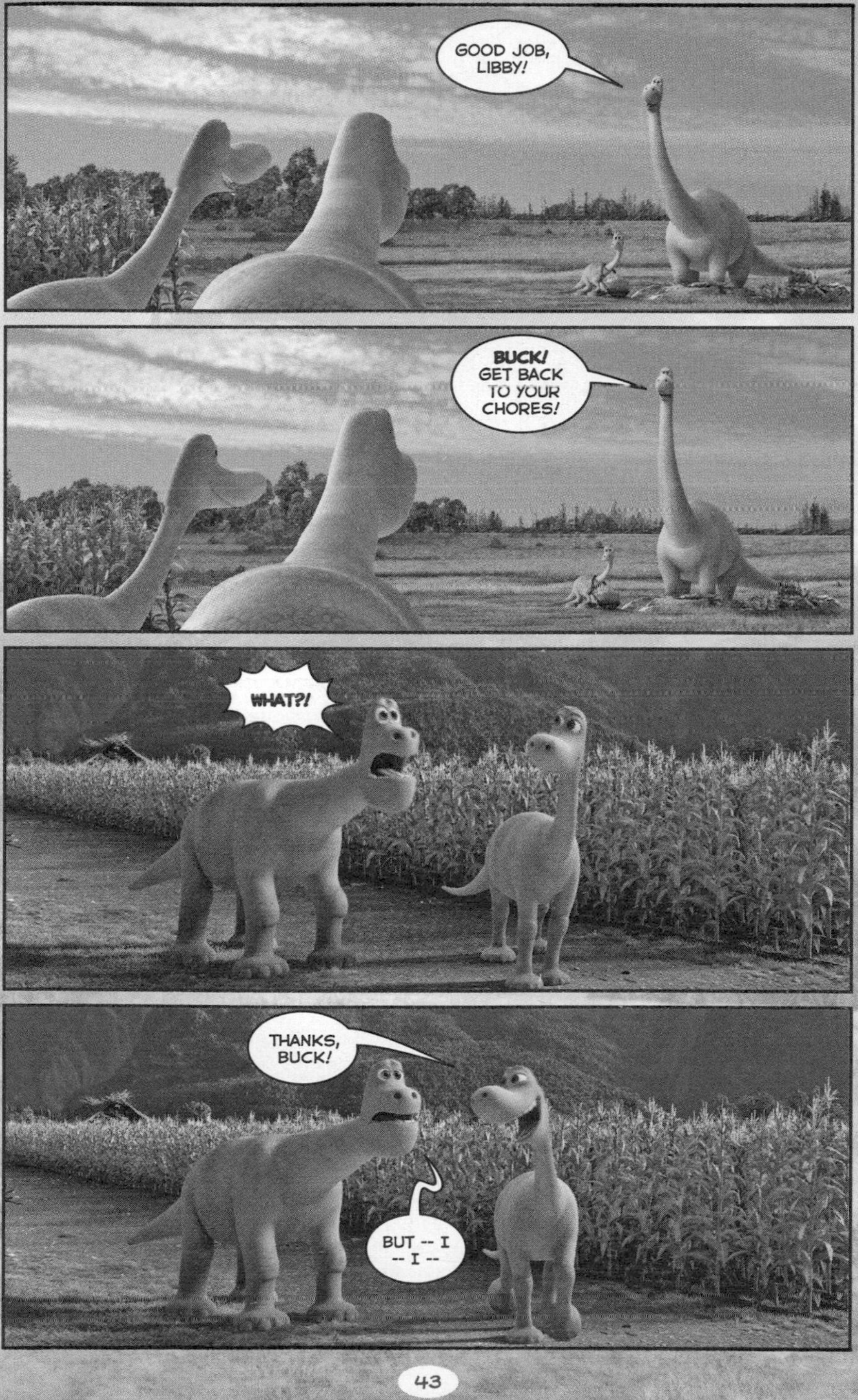
GOOD JOB, LIBBY!
BUCK! GET BACK TO YOUR CHORES!
WHAT?!
THANKS, BUCK!
BUT -- I -- I --

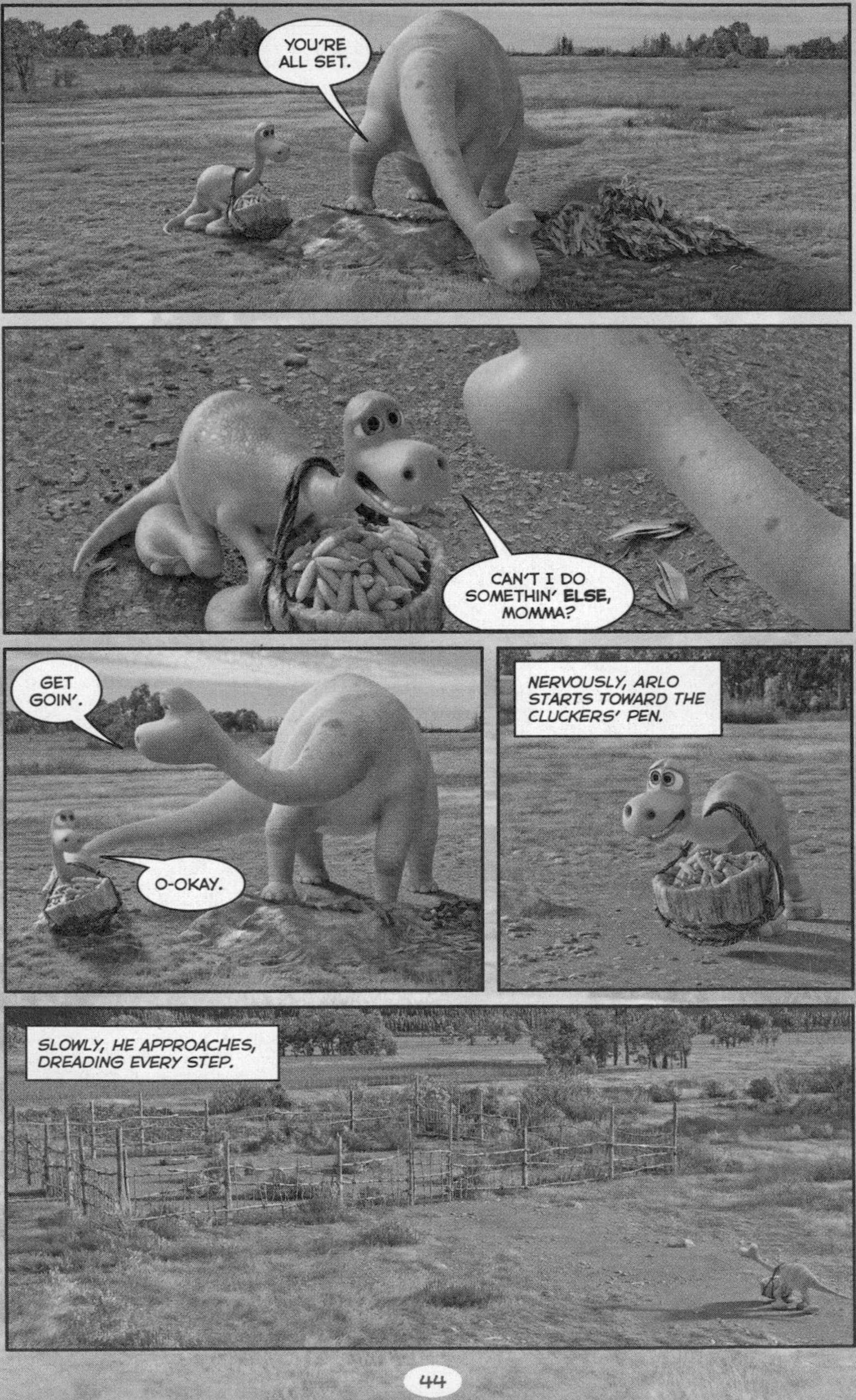

YOU'RE ALL SET.
CAN'T I DO SOMETHIN' **ELSE**, MOMMA?
GET GOIN'.
O-OKAY.
NERVOUSLY, ARLO STARTS TOWARD THE CLUCKERS' PEN.
SLOWLY, HE APPROACHES, DREADING EVERY STEP.

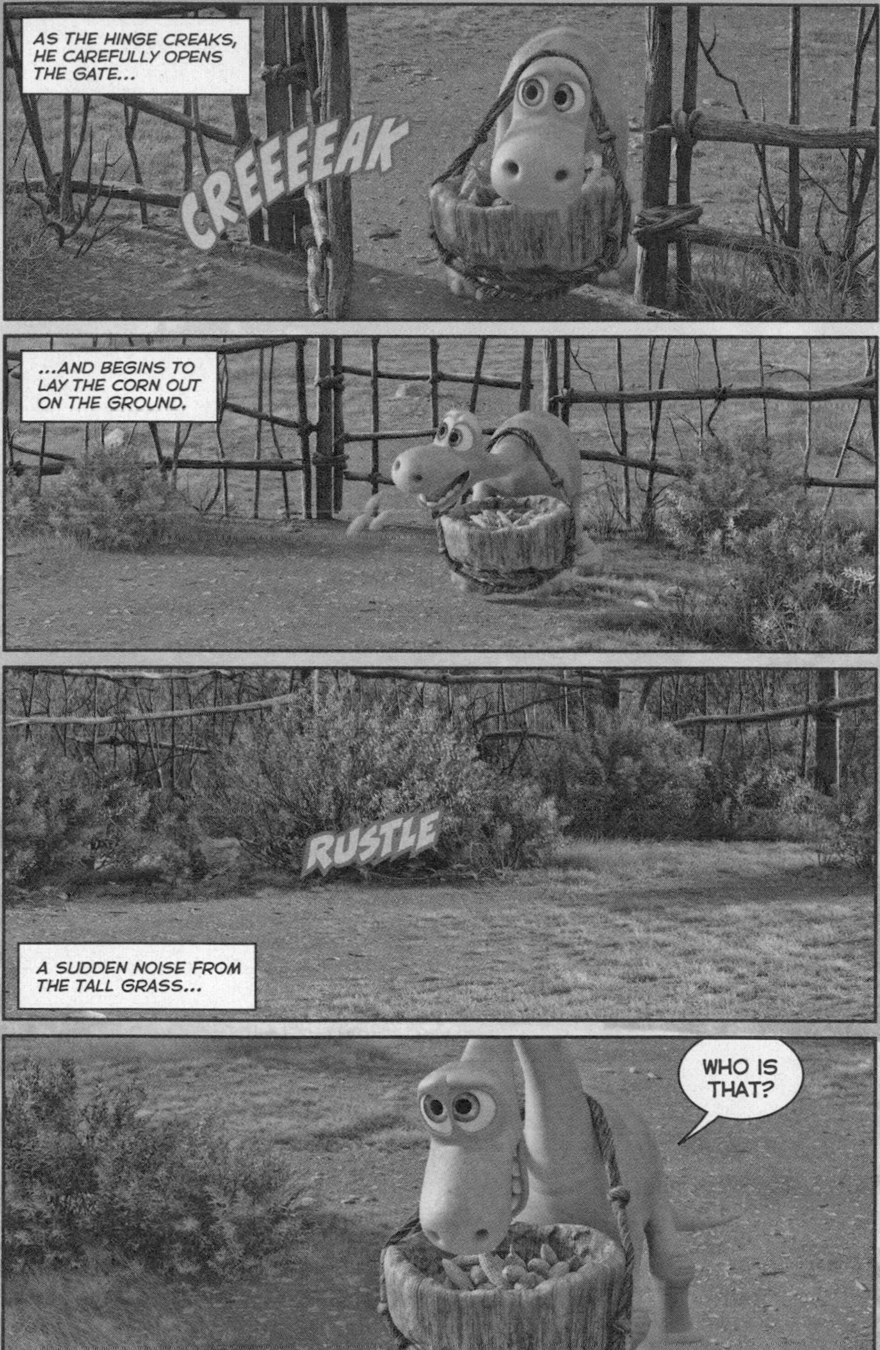
AS THE HINGE CREAKS, HE CAREFULLY OPENS THE GATE...
CREEEEAK
...AND BEGINS TO LAY THE CORN OUT ON THE GROUND.
RUSTLE
A SUDDEN NOISE FROM THE TALL GRASS...
WHO IS THAT?

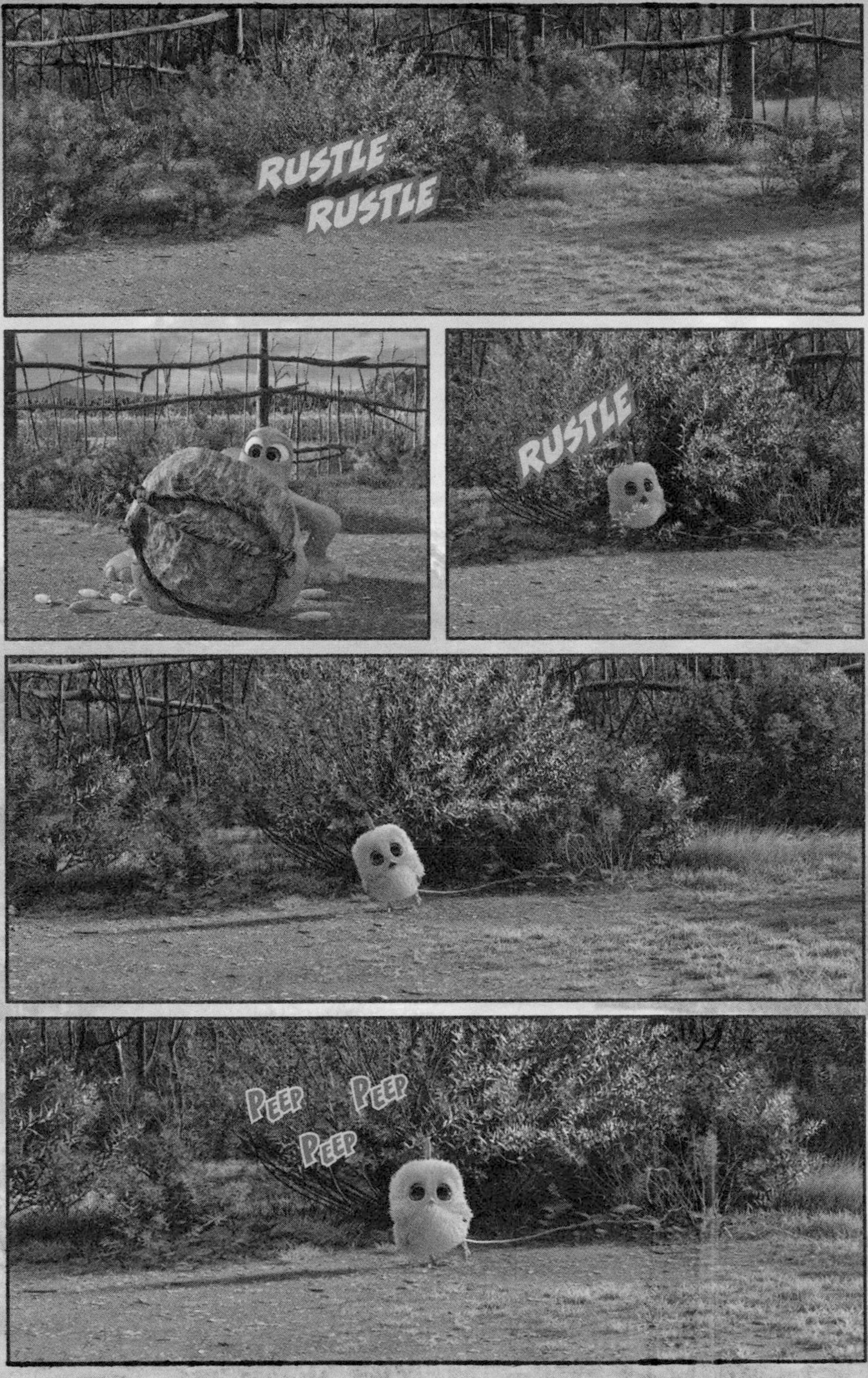
RUSTLE
RUSTLE
RUSTLE
PEEP
PEEP
PEEP

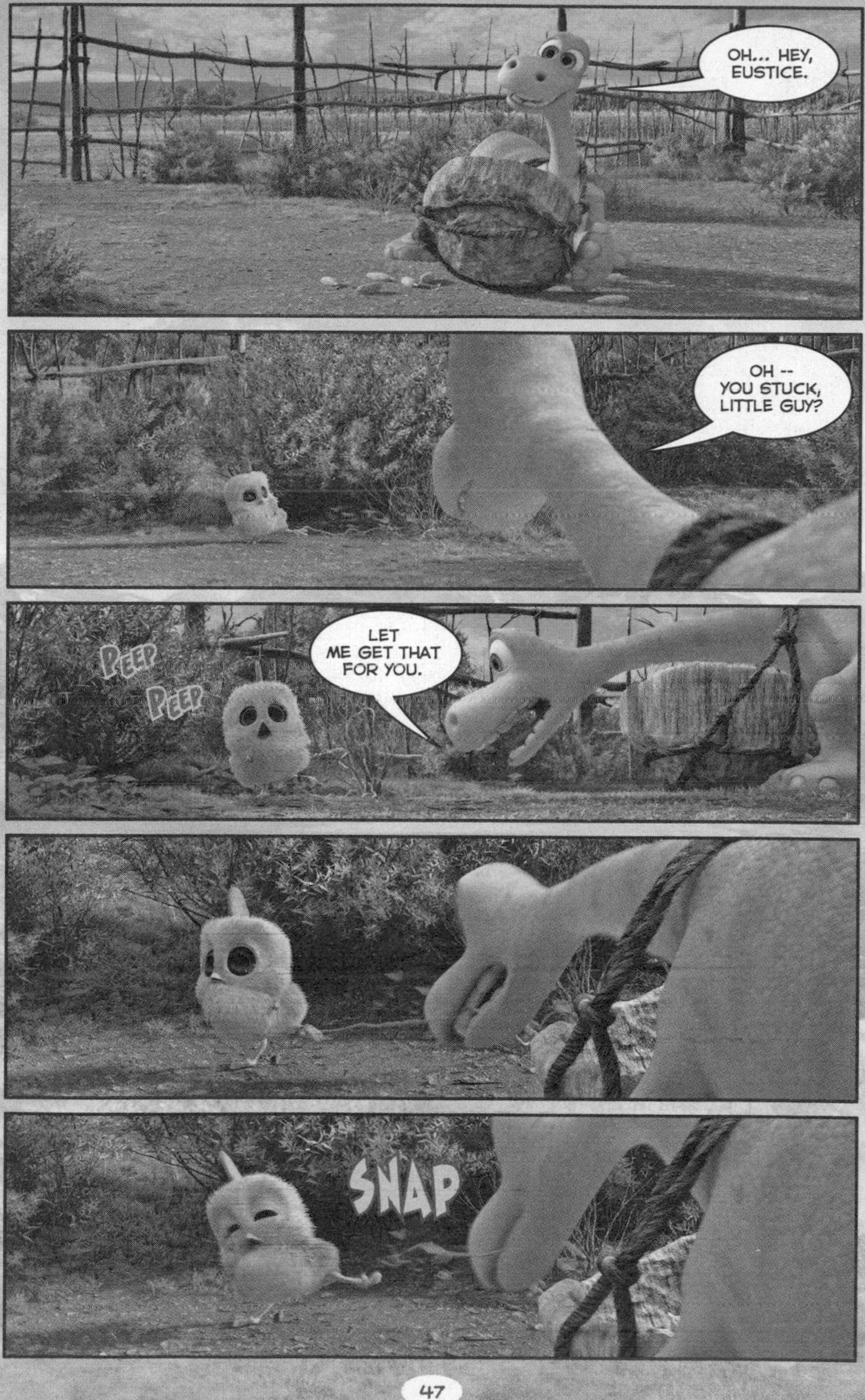
OH... HEY, EUSTICE.
OH -- YOU STUCK, LITTLE GUY?
PEEP
PEEP
LET ME GET THAT FOR YOU.
SNAP

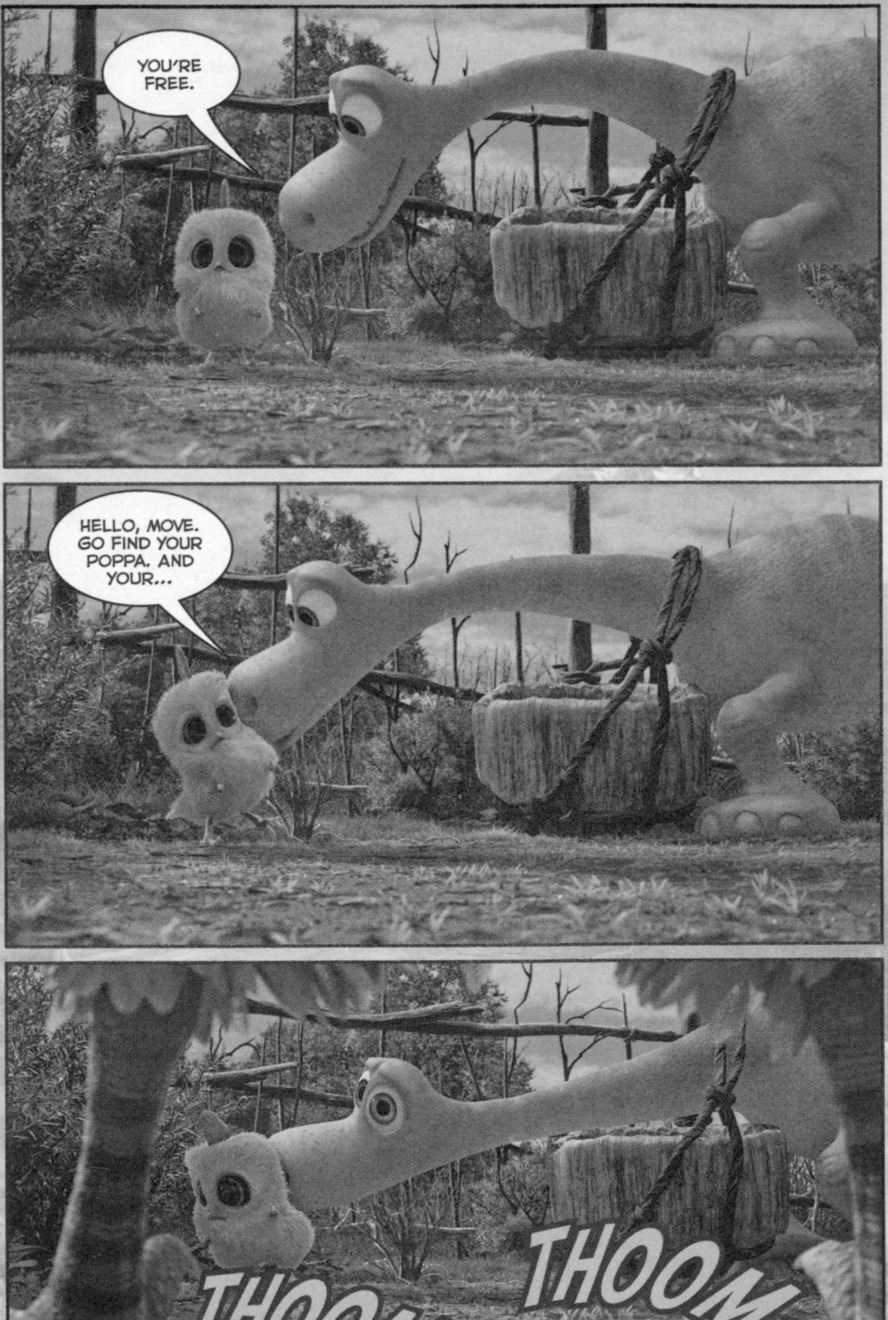
YOU'RE FREE.
HELLO, MOVE. GO FIND YOUR POPPA. AND YOUR...
THOOM
THOOM

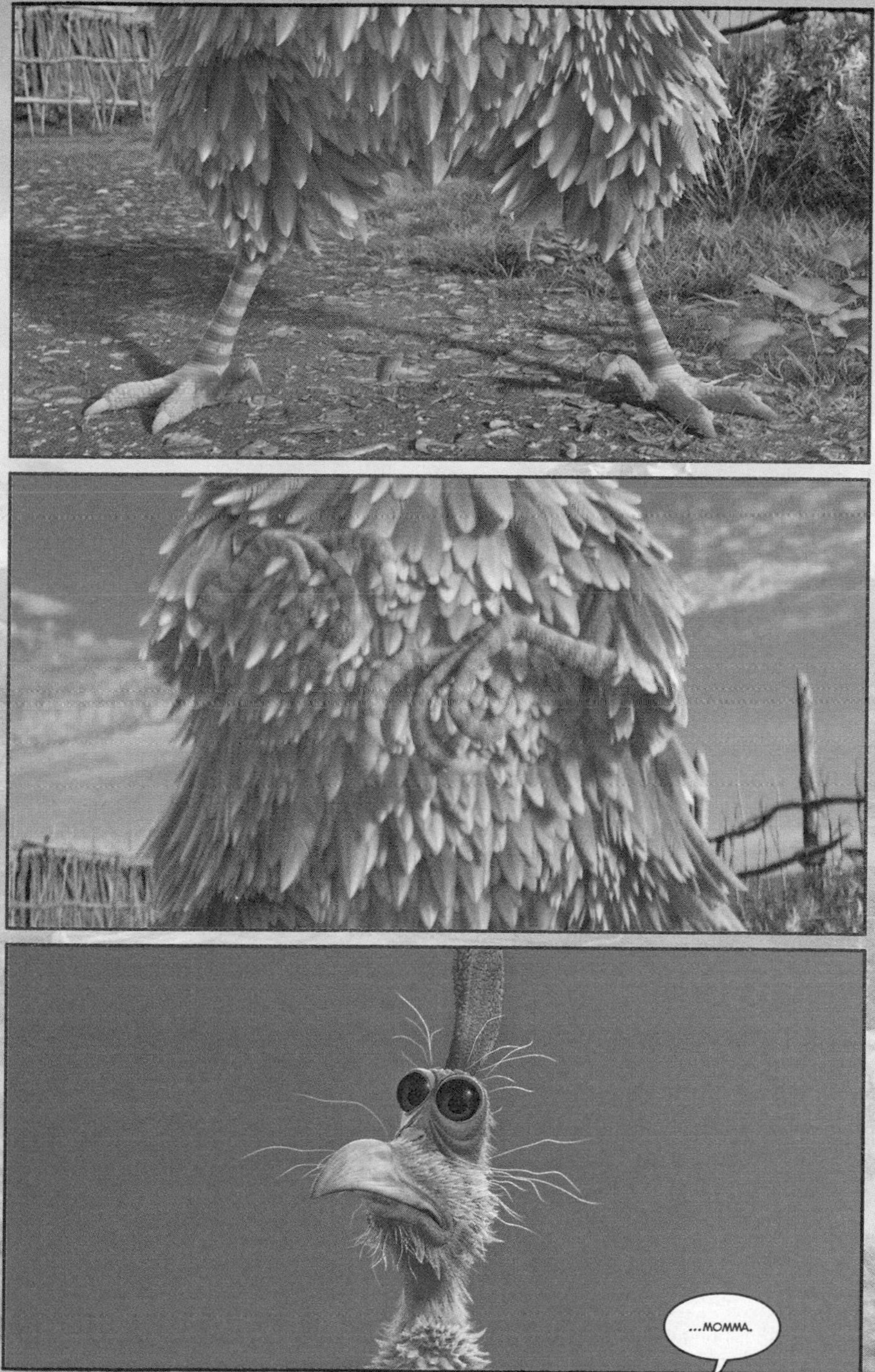
...MOMMA.

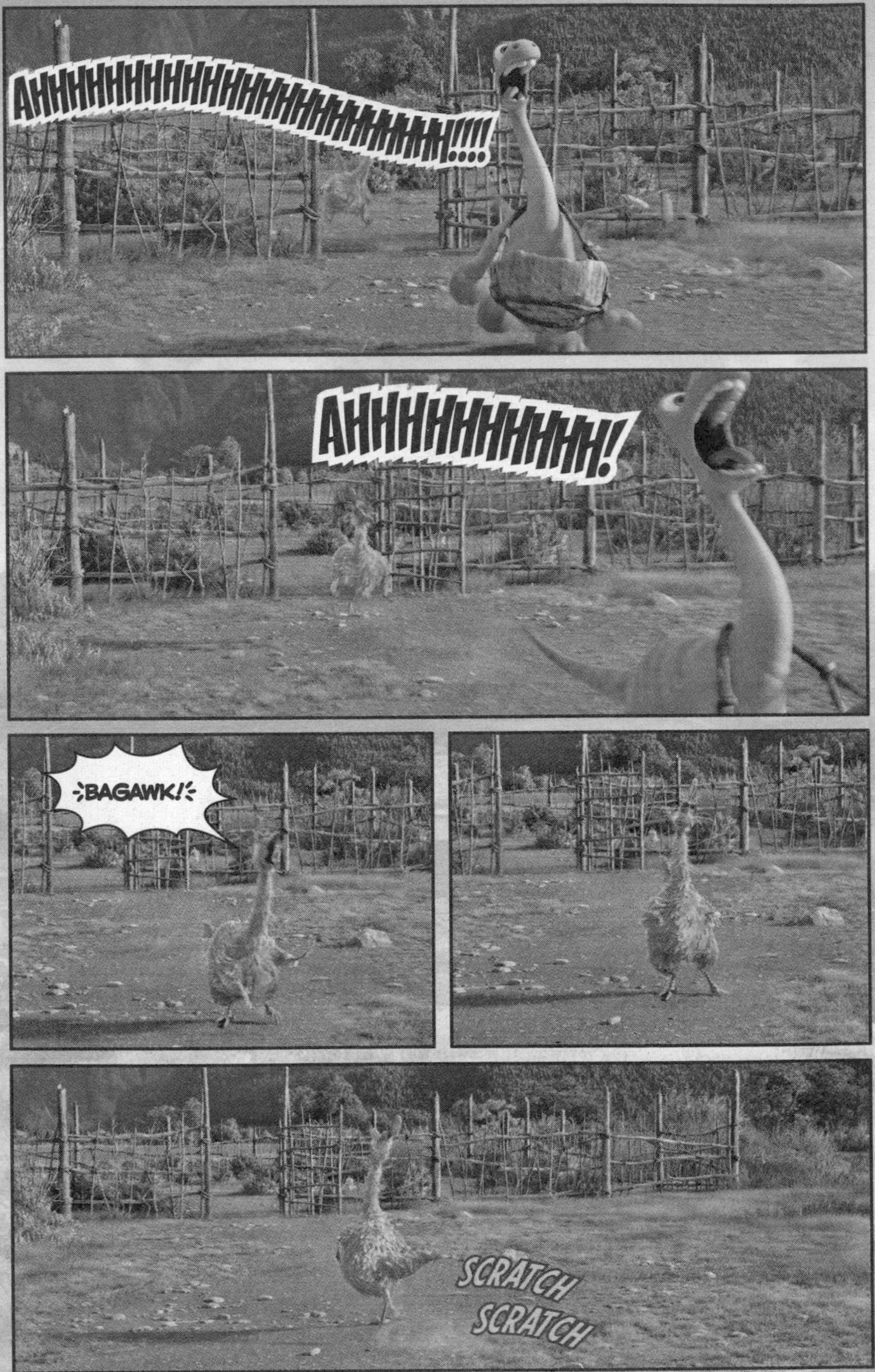
AHHHHHHHHHHHHHHHHHHHHHHHHHH!!!!
AHHHHHHHHHHH!
BAGAWK!
SCRATCH
SCRATCH

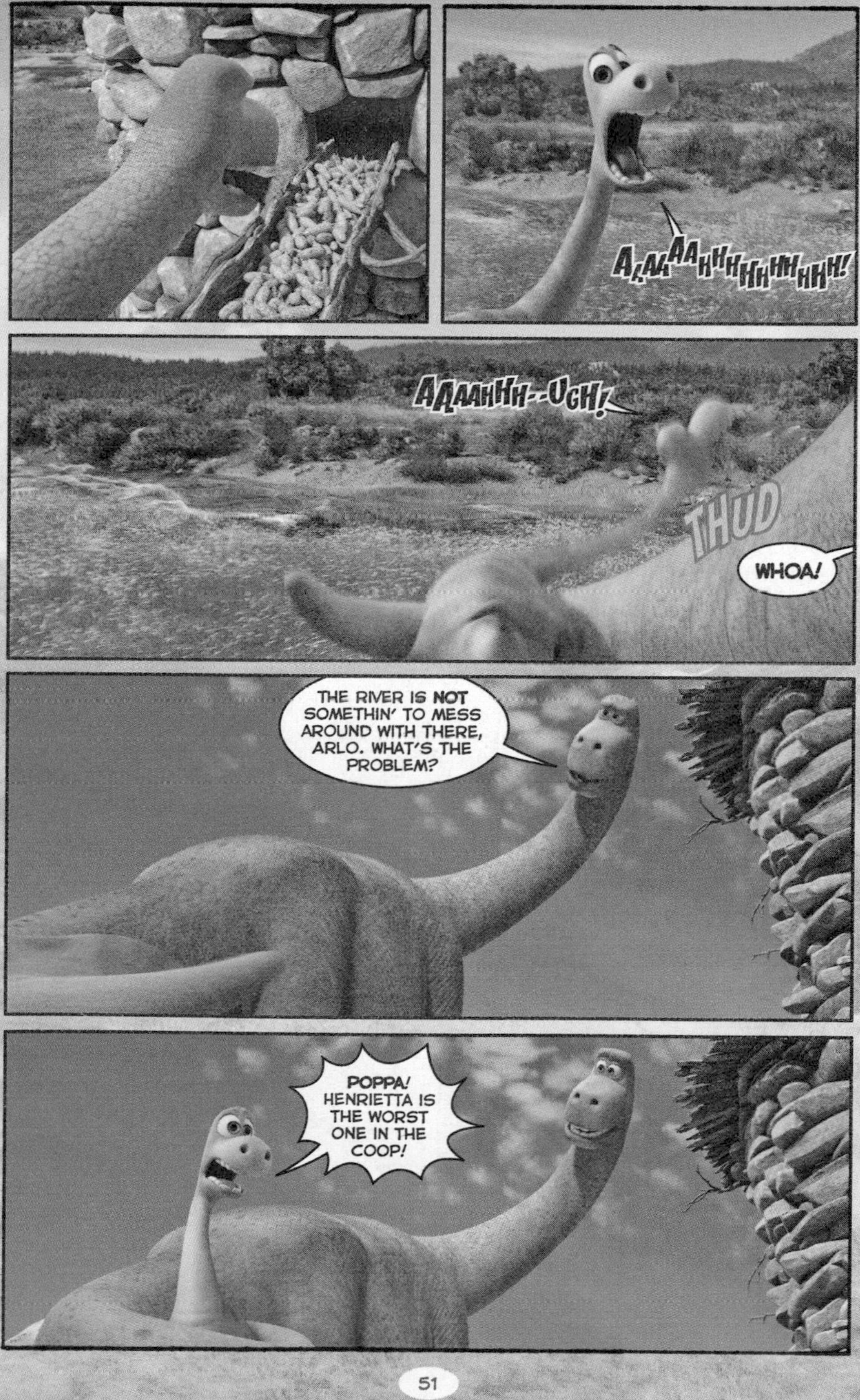
AAAAAAHHHHHHHHHHH!
AAAAHHH--UGH!
THUD
WHOA!
THE RIVER IS NOT SOMETHIN' TO MESS AROUND WITH THERE, ARLO. WHAT'S THE PROBLEM?
POPPA! HENRIETTA IS THE WORST ONE IN THE COOP!

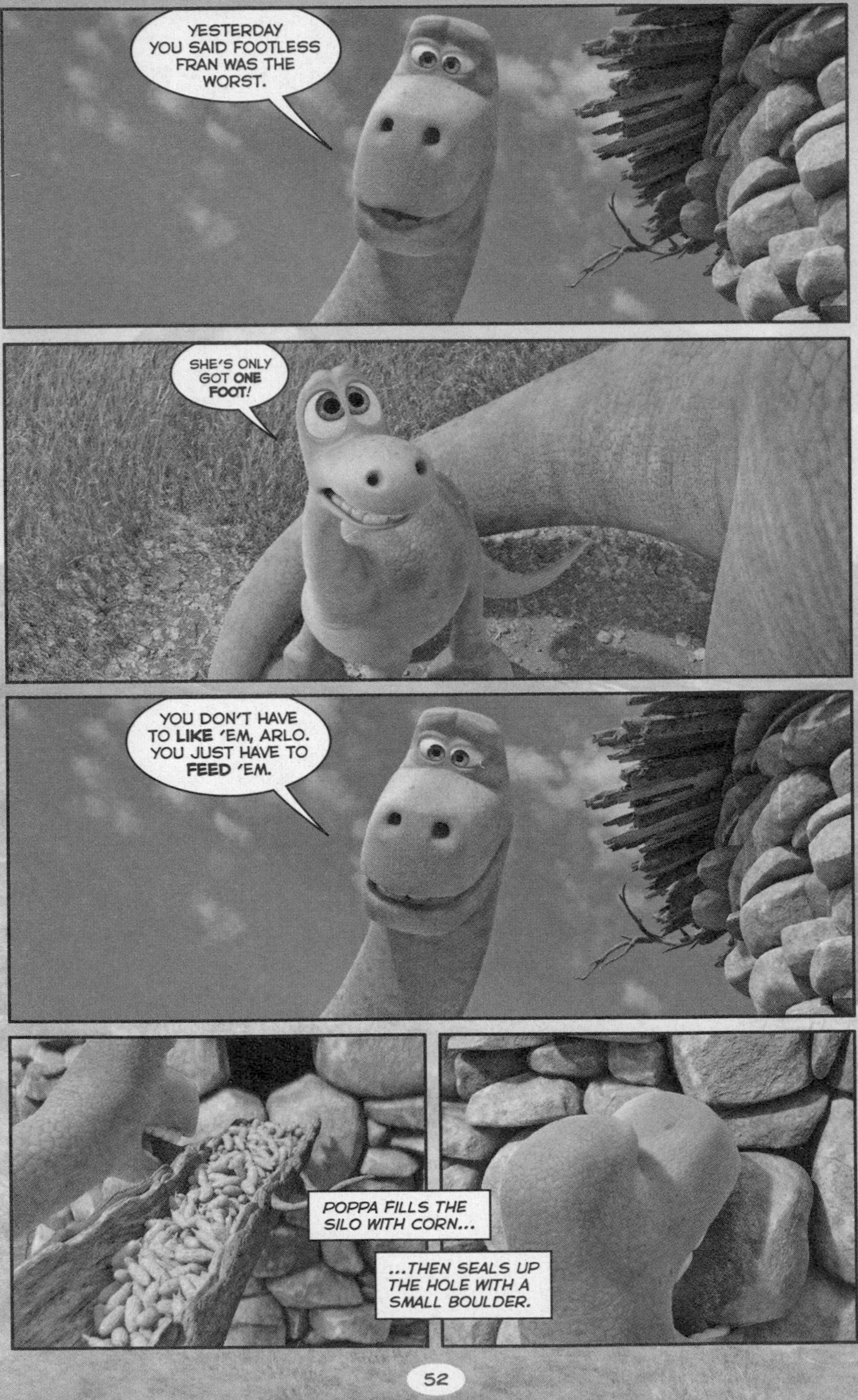
YESTERDAY YOU SAID FOOTLESS FRAN WAS THE WORST.
SHE'S ONLY GOT ONE FOOT!
YOU DON'T HAVE TO LIKE 'EM, ARLO. YOU JUST HAVE TO FEED 'EM.
POPPA FILLS THE SILO WITH CORN...
...THEN SEALS UP THE HOLE WITH A SMALL BOULDER.

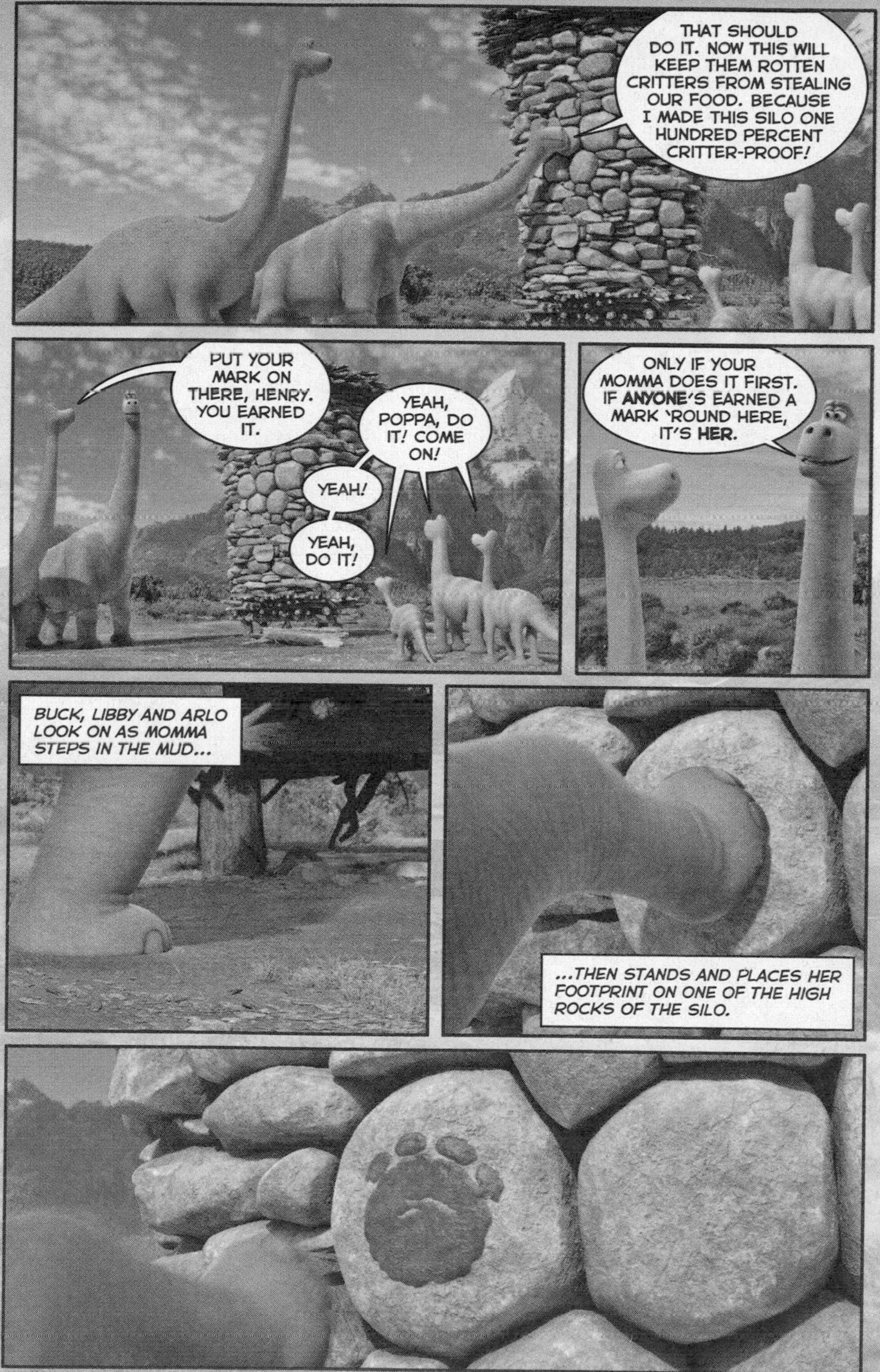

THAT SHOULD DO IT. NOW THIS WILL KEEP THEM ROTTEN CRITTERS FROM STEALING OUR FOOD. BECAUSE I MADE THIS SILO ONE HUNDRED PERCENT CRITTER-PROOF!
PUT YOUR MARK ON THERE, HENRY. YOU EARNED IT.
YEAH, POPPA, DO IT! COME ON!
YEAH!
YEAH, DO IT!
ONLY IF YOUR MOMMA DOES IT FIRST. IF ANYONE'S EARNED A MARK 'ROUND HERE, IT'S HER.
BUCK, LIBBY AND ARLO LOOK ON AS MOMMA STEPS IN THE MUD...
...THEN STANDS AND PLACES HER FOOTPRINT ON ONE OF THE HIGH ROCKS OF THE SILO.

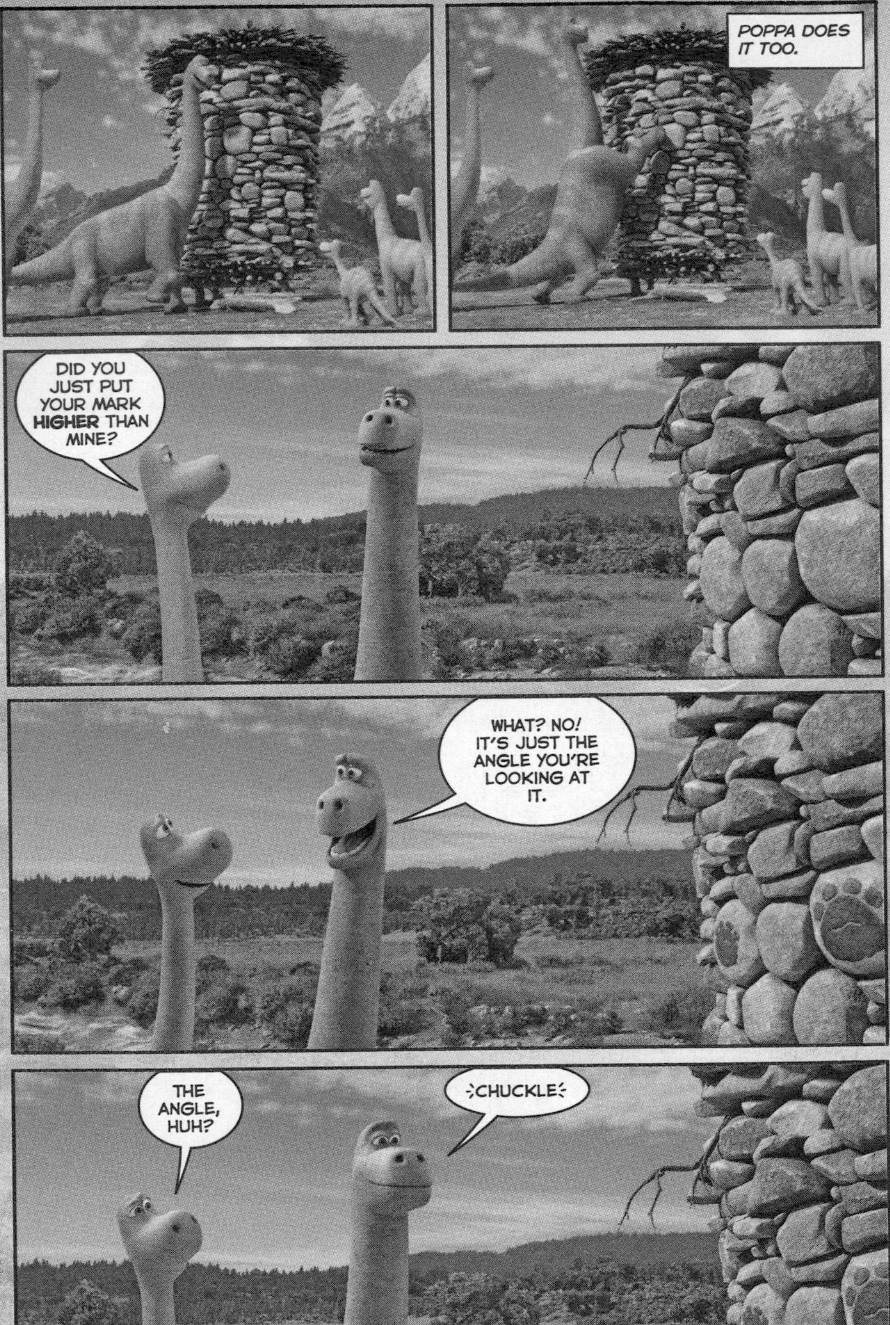
POPPA DOES IT TOO.
DID YOU JUST PUT YOUR MARK HIGHER THAN MINE?
WHAT? NO! IT'S JUST THE ANGLE YOU'RE LOOKING AT IT.
THE ANGLE, HUH?
CHUCKLE

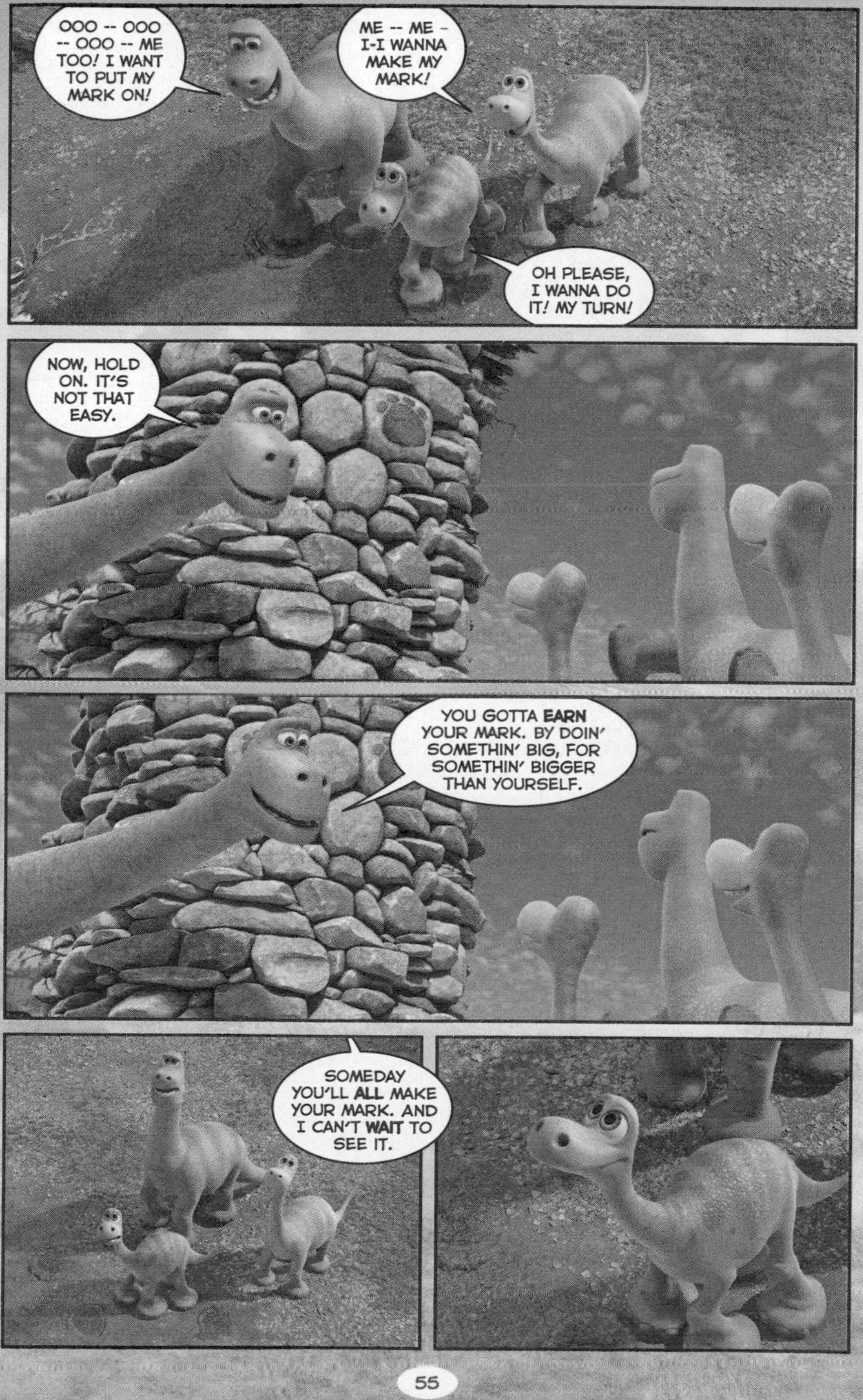
OOO -- OOO -- OOO -- ME TOO! I WANT TO PUT MY MARK ON!
ME -- ME -- I-I WANNA MAKE MY MARK!
OH PLEASE, I WANNA DO IT! MY TURN!
NOW, HOLD ON. IT'S NOT THAT EASY.
YOU GOTTA EARN YOUR MARK. BY DOIN' SOMETHIN' BIG, FOR SOMETHIN' BIGGER THAN YOURSELF.
SOMEDAY YOU'LL ALL MAKE YOUR MARK. AND I CAN'T WAIT TO SEE IT.

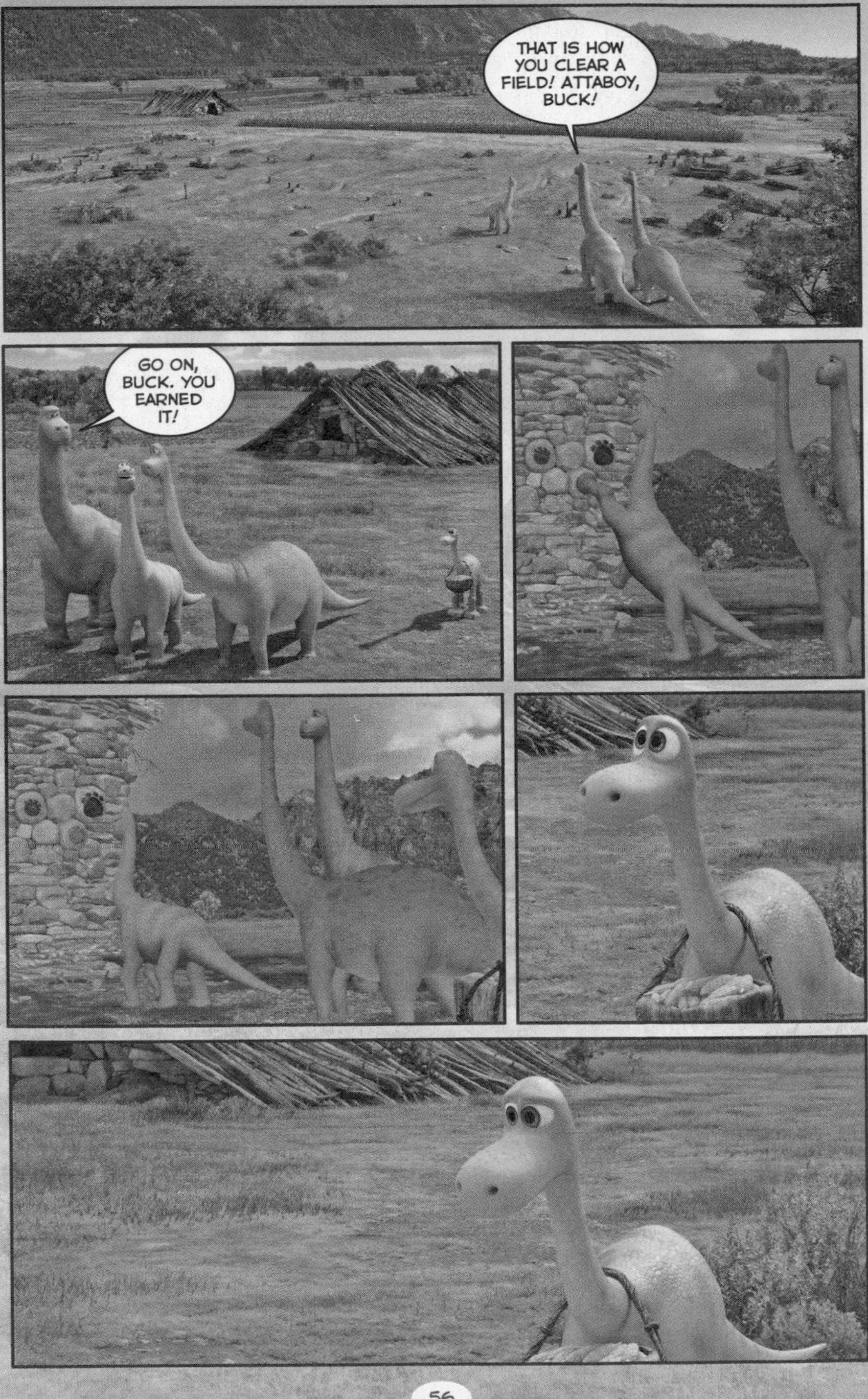
THAT IS HOW YOU CLEAR A FIELD! ATTABOY, BUCK!
GO ON, BUCK. YOU EARNED IT!

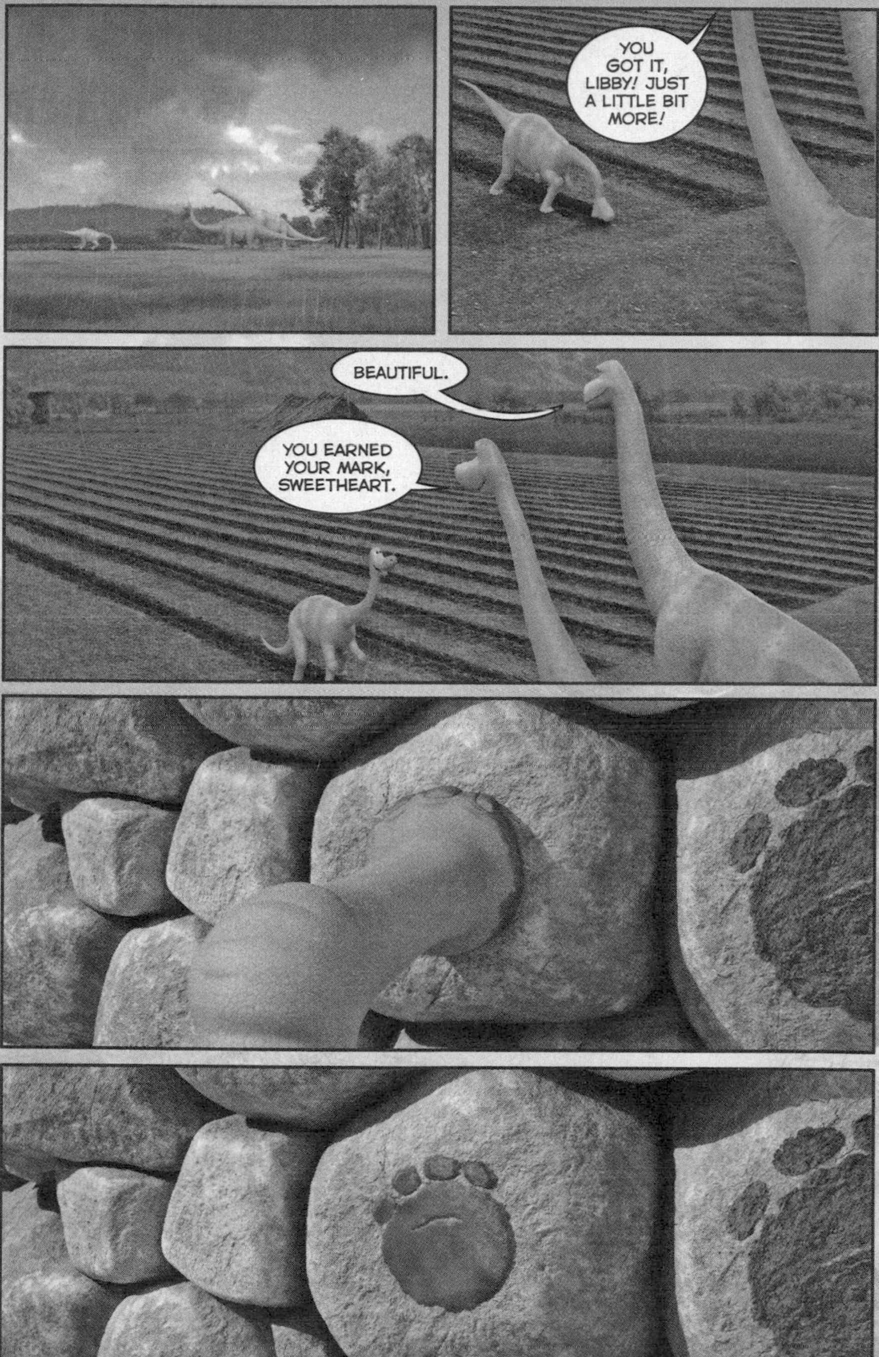
YOU GOT IT, LIBBY! JUST A LITTLE BIT MORE!
BEAUTIFUL.
YOU EARNED YOUR MARK, SWEETHEART.

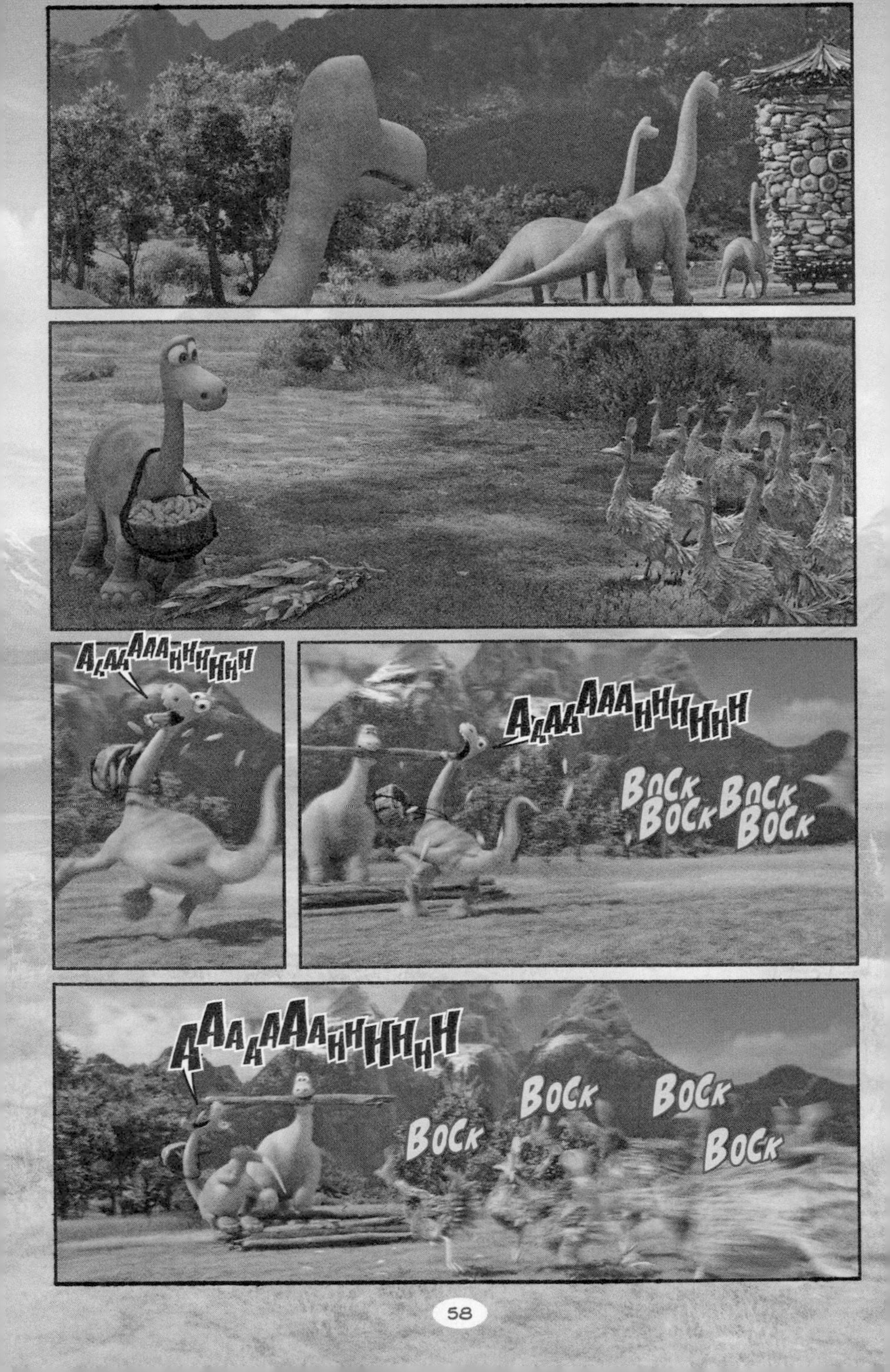
AAAAAAAHHHHHH
AAAAAAAHHHHHHH
BOCK BOCK BOCK BOCK
AAAAAAAAHHHHHH
BOCK
BOCK
BOCK
BOCK

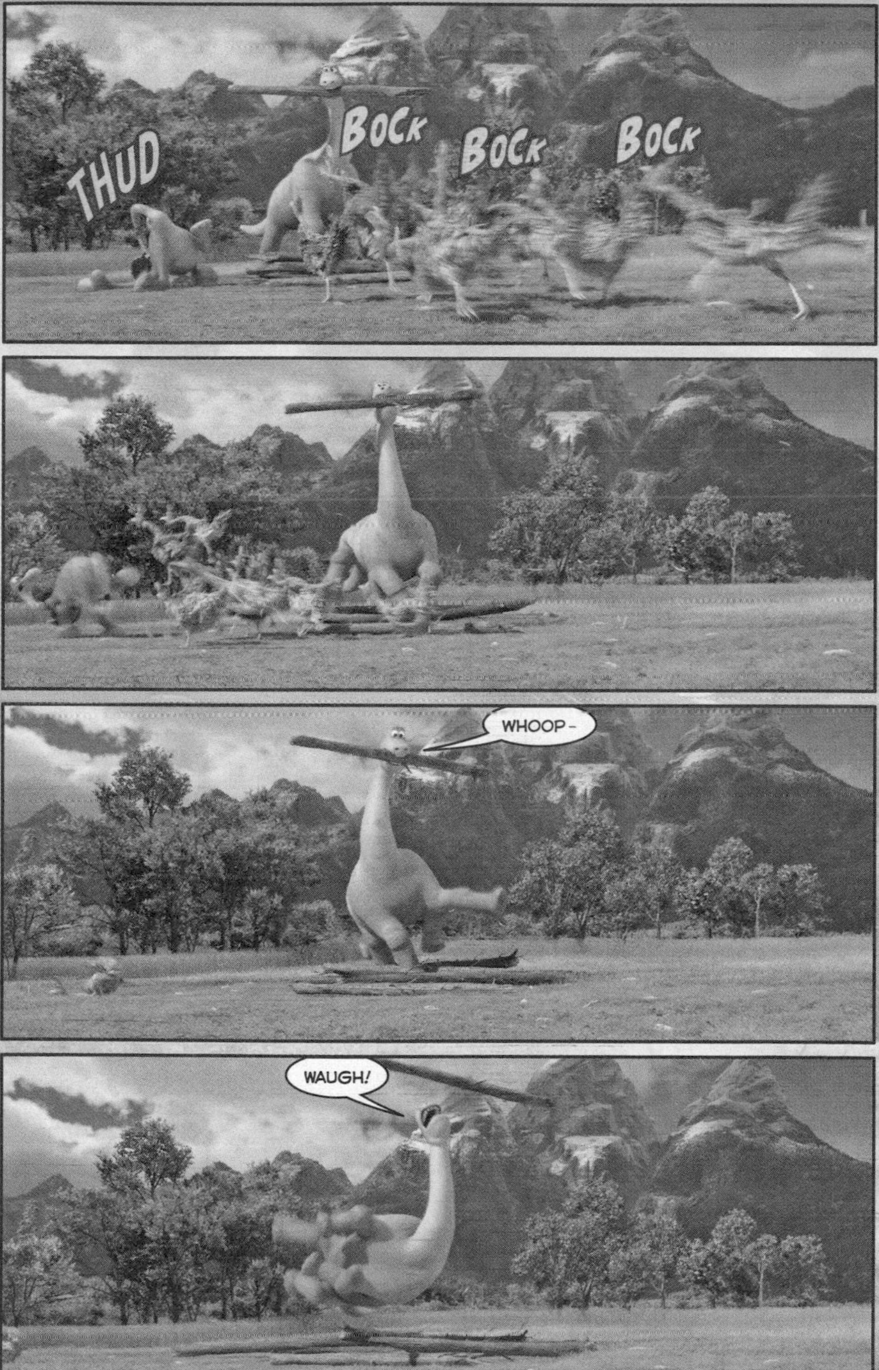
THUD
BOCK
BOCK
BOCK
WHOOP-
WAUGH!

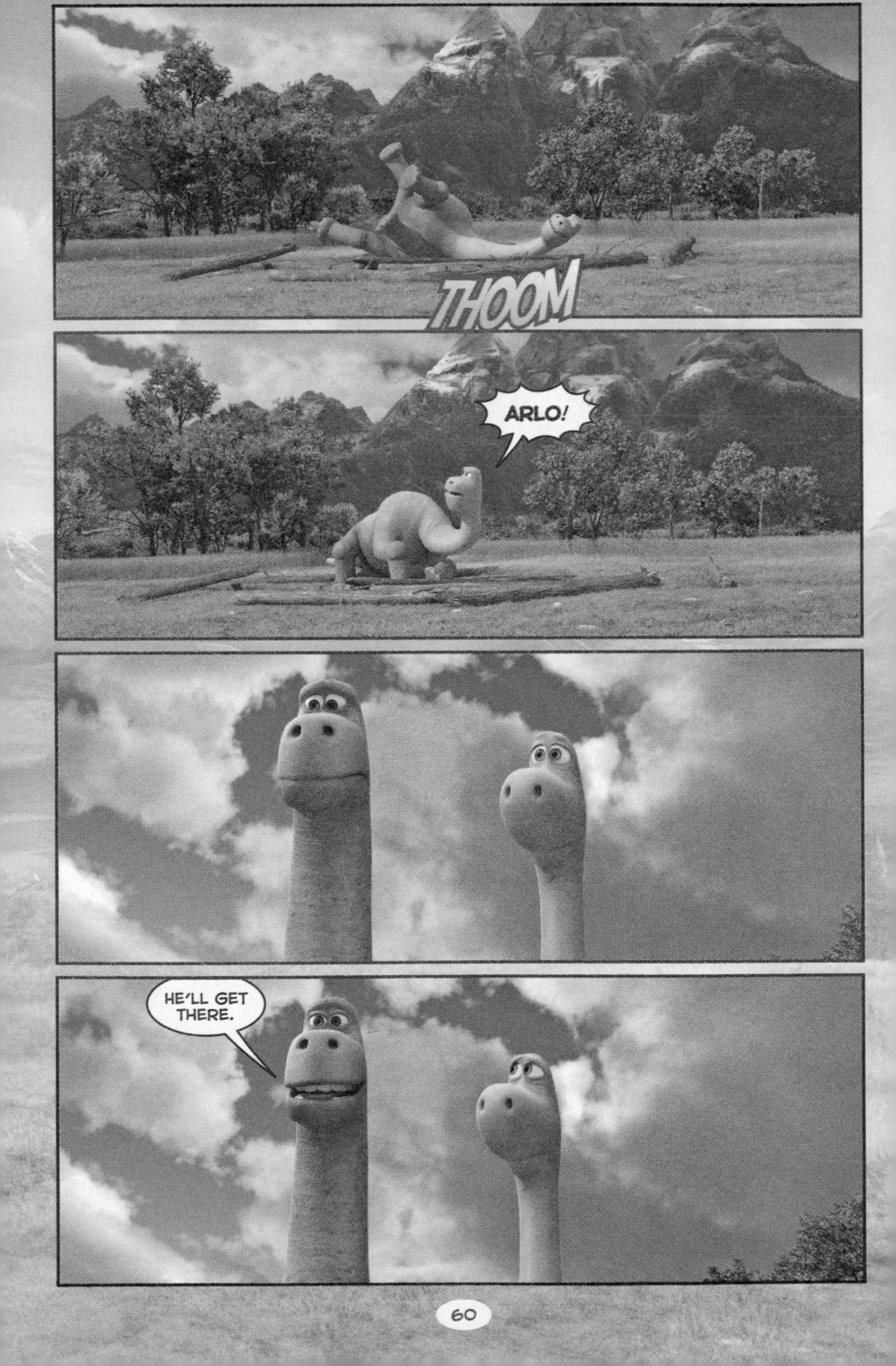
THOOM
ARLO!
HE'LL GET THERE.

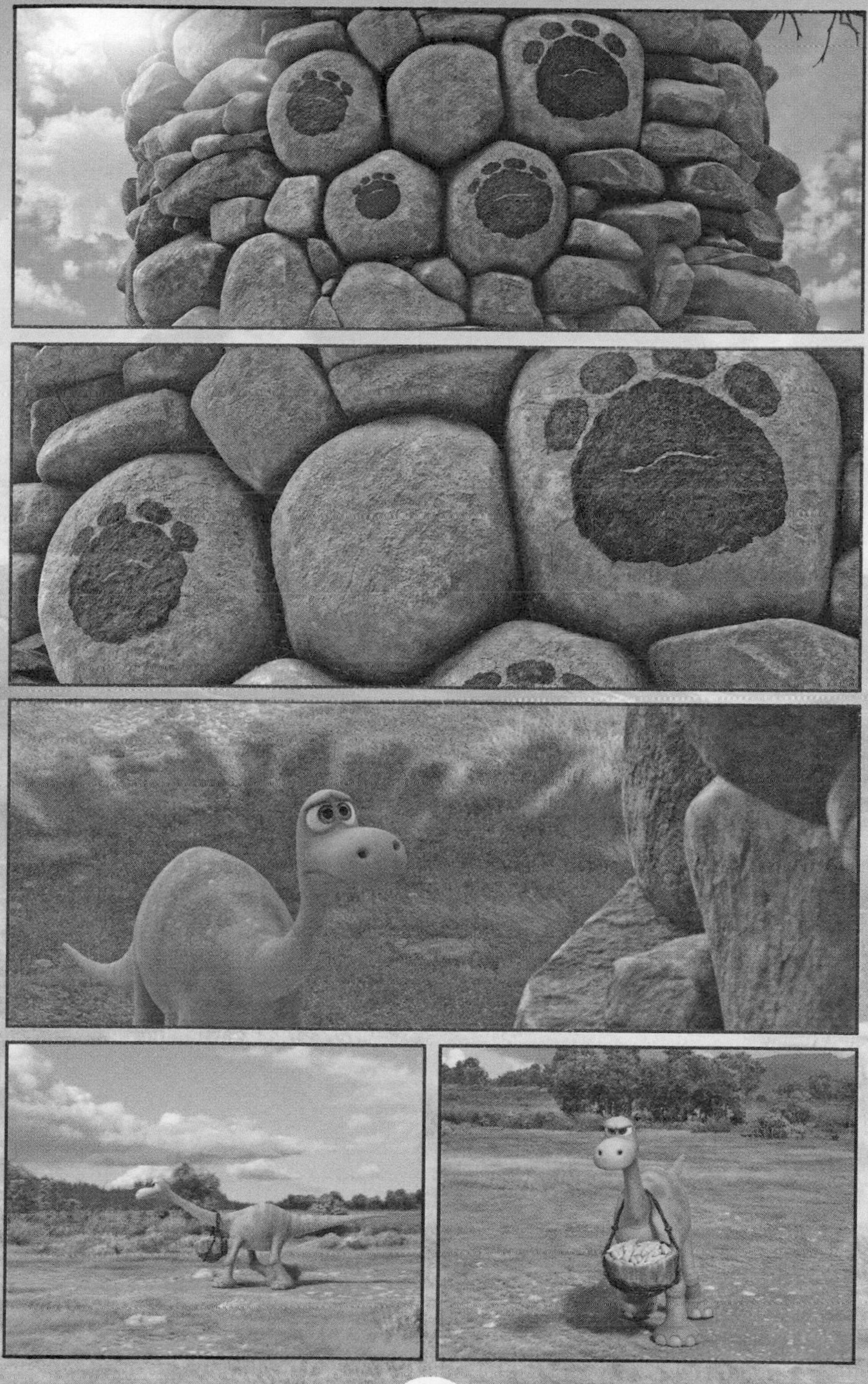

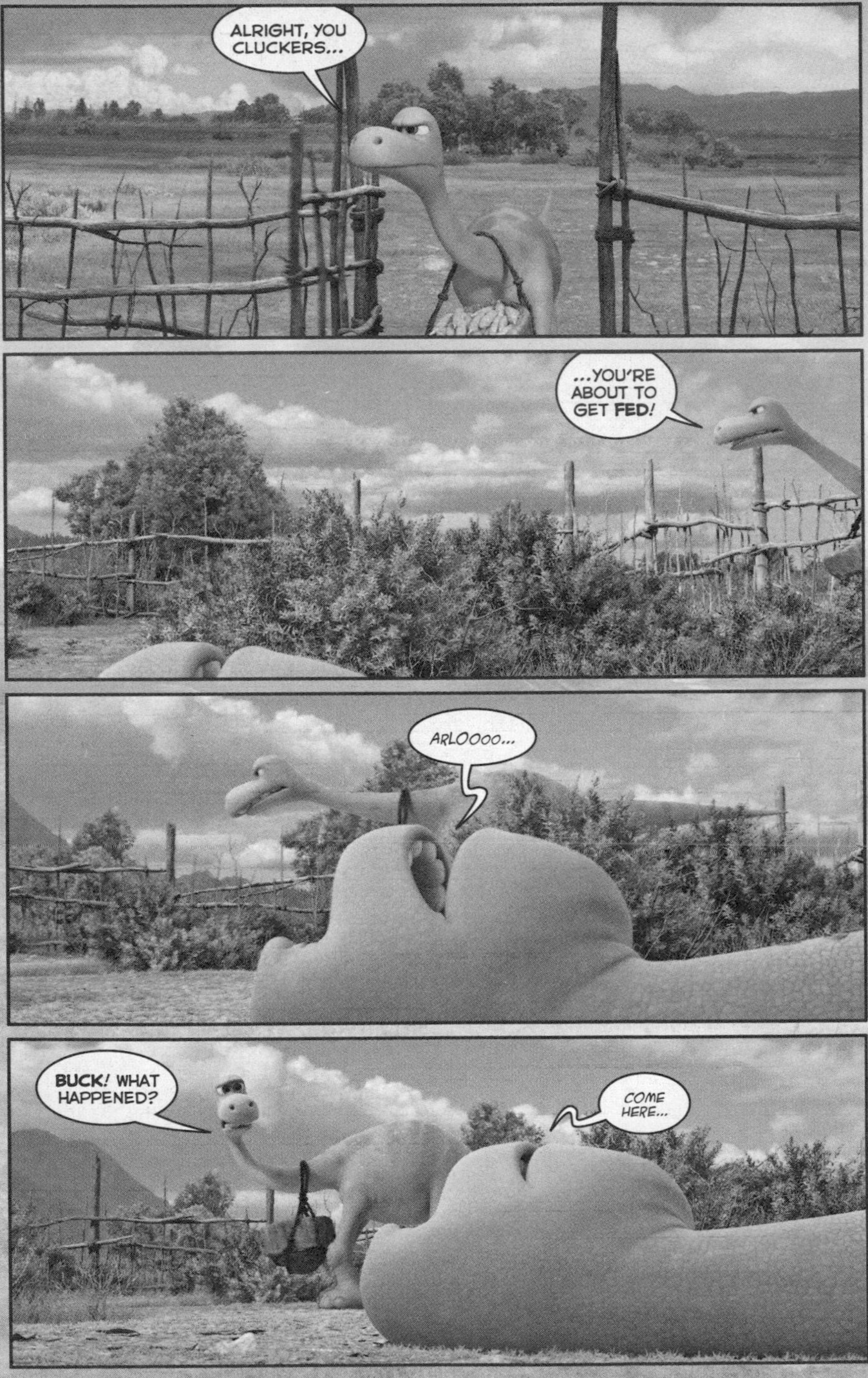
ALRIGHT, YOU CLUCKERS...
...YOU'RE ABOUT TO GET **FED**!
ARLOOOO...
BUCK! WHAT HAPPENED?
COME HERE...

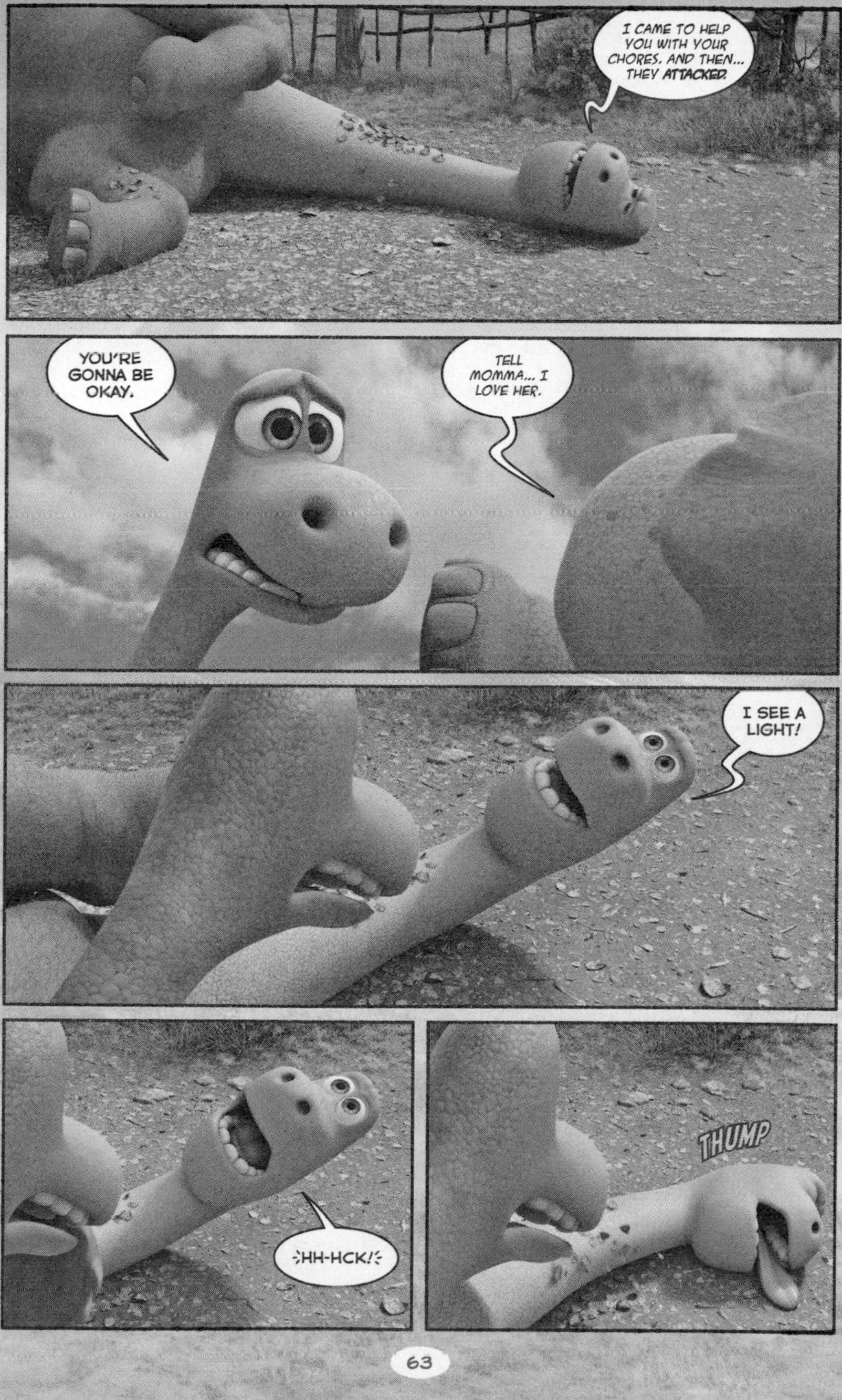
I CAME TO HELP YOU WITH YOUR CHORES. AND THEN... THEY **ATTACKED**.
YOU'RE GONNA BE OKAY.
TELL MOMMA... I LOVE HER.
I SEE A LIGHT!
HH-HCK!
THUMP

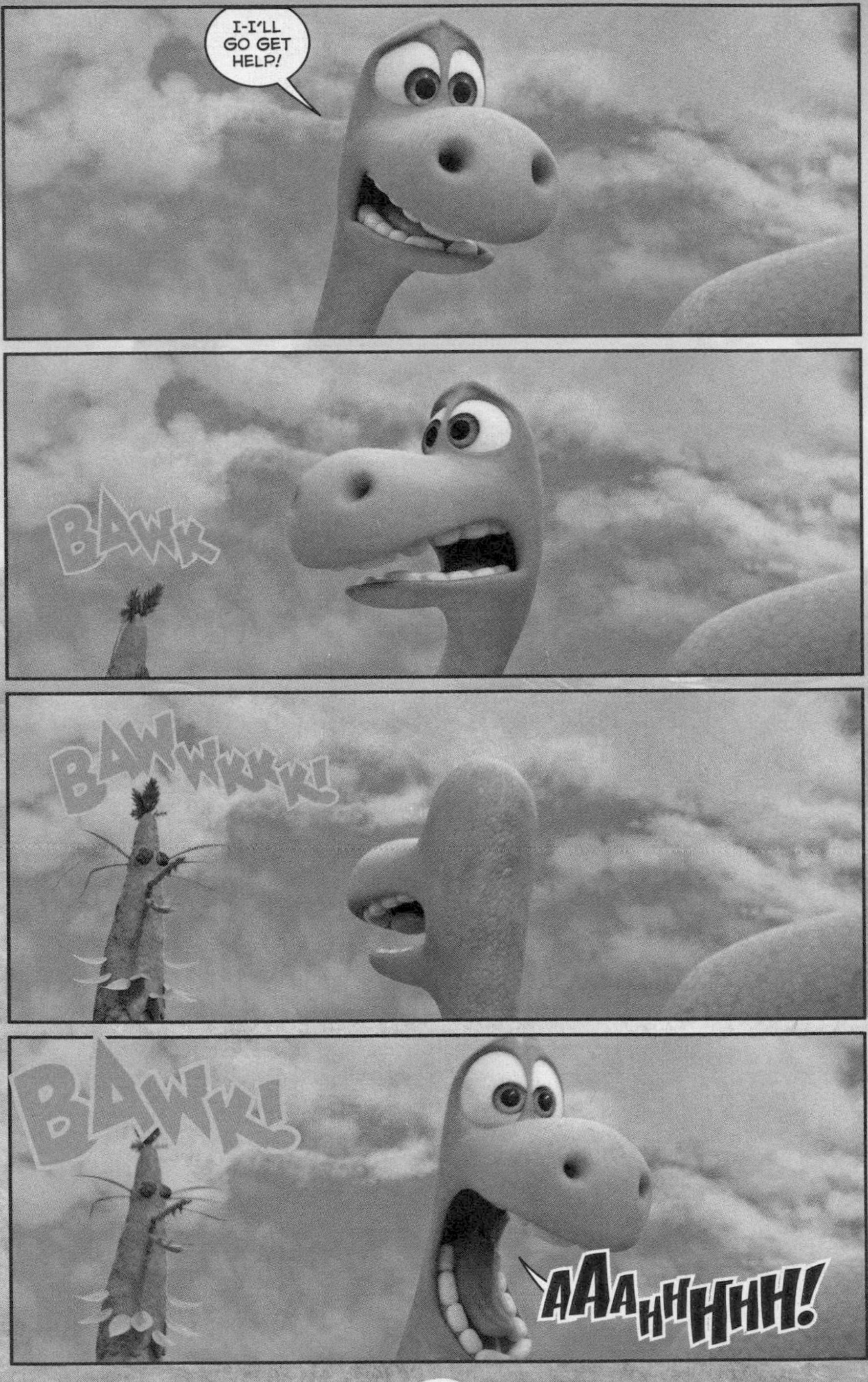
I-I'LL GO GET HELP!
BAWK
BAWWKKK!
BAWK!
AAAHHHHH!

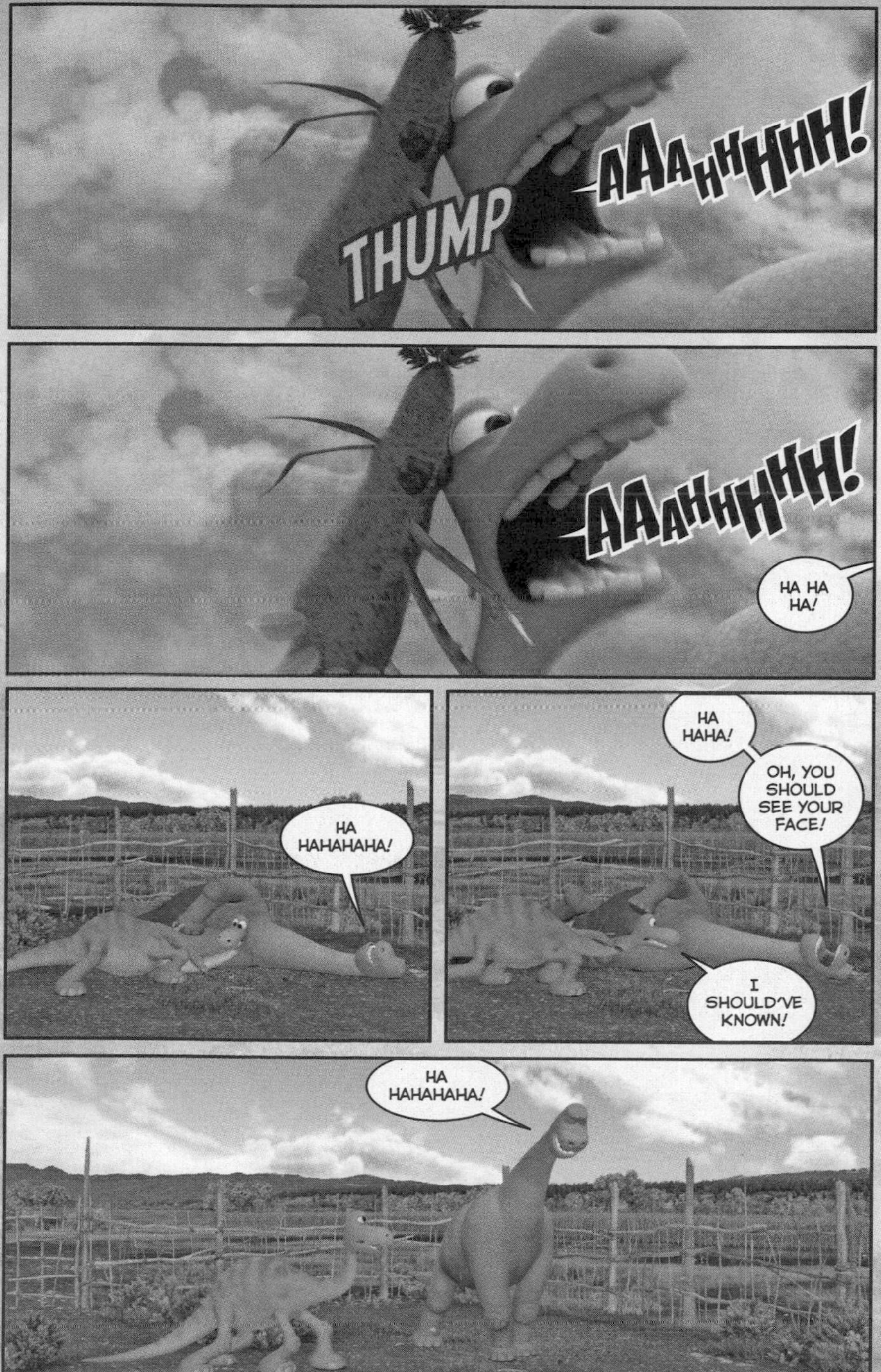
THUMP
AAAHHHHH!
AAAHHHHH!
HA HA HA!
HA HAHAHAHA!
HA HAHA!
OH, YOU SHOULD SEE YOUR FACE!
I SHOULD'VE KNOWN!
HA HAHAHAHA!

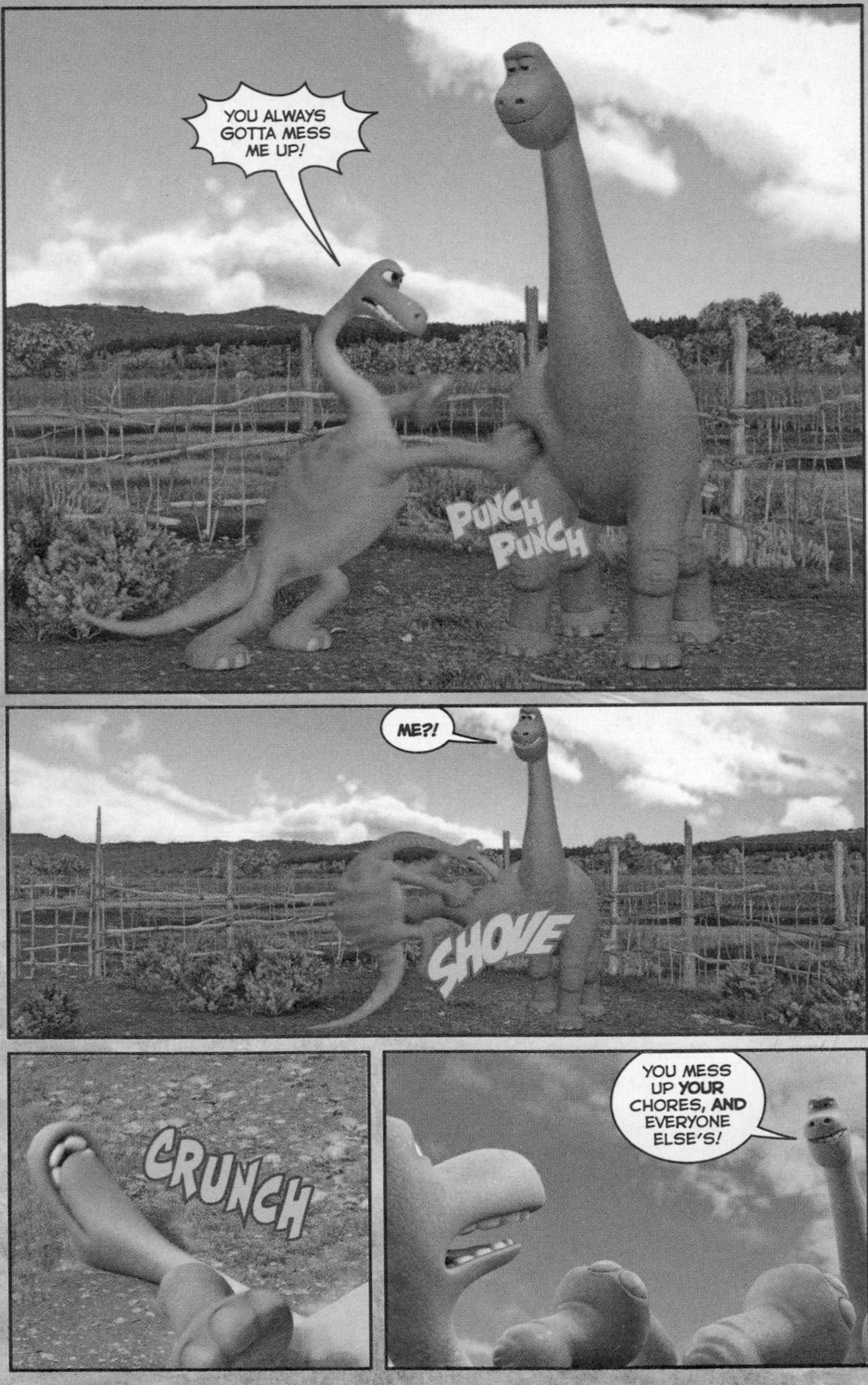
YOU ALWAYS GOTTA MESS ME UP!
PUNCH PUNCH
ME?!
SHOVE
CRUNCH
YOU MESS UP **YOUR** CHORES, **AND** EVERYONE ELSE'S!

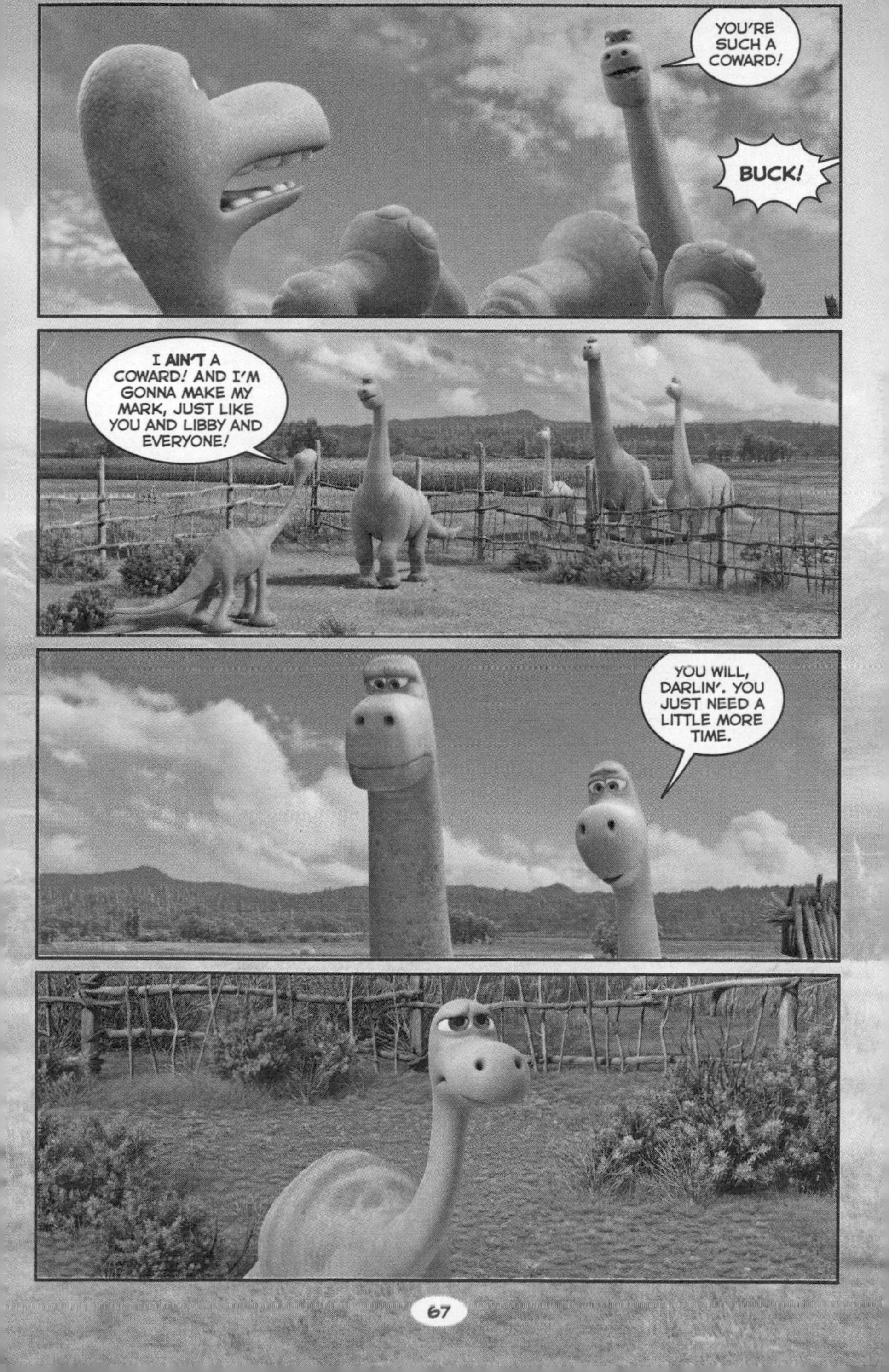
YOU'RE SUCH A COWARD!
BUCK!
I AIN'T A COWARD! AND I'M GONNA MAKE MY MARK, JUST LIKE YOU AND LIBBY AND EVERYONE!
YOU WILL, DARLIN'. YOU JUST NEED A LITTLE MORE TIME.

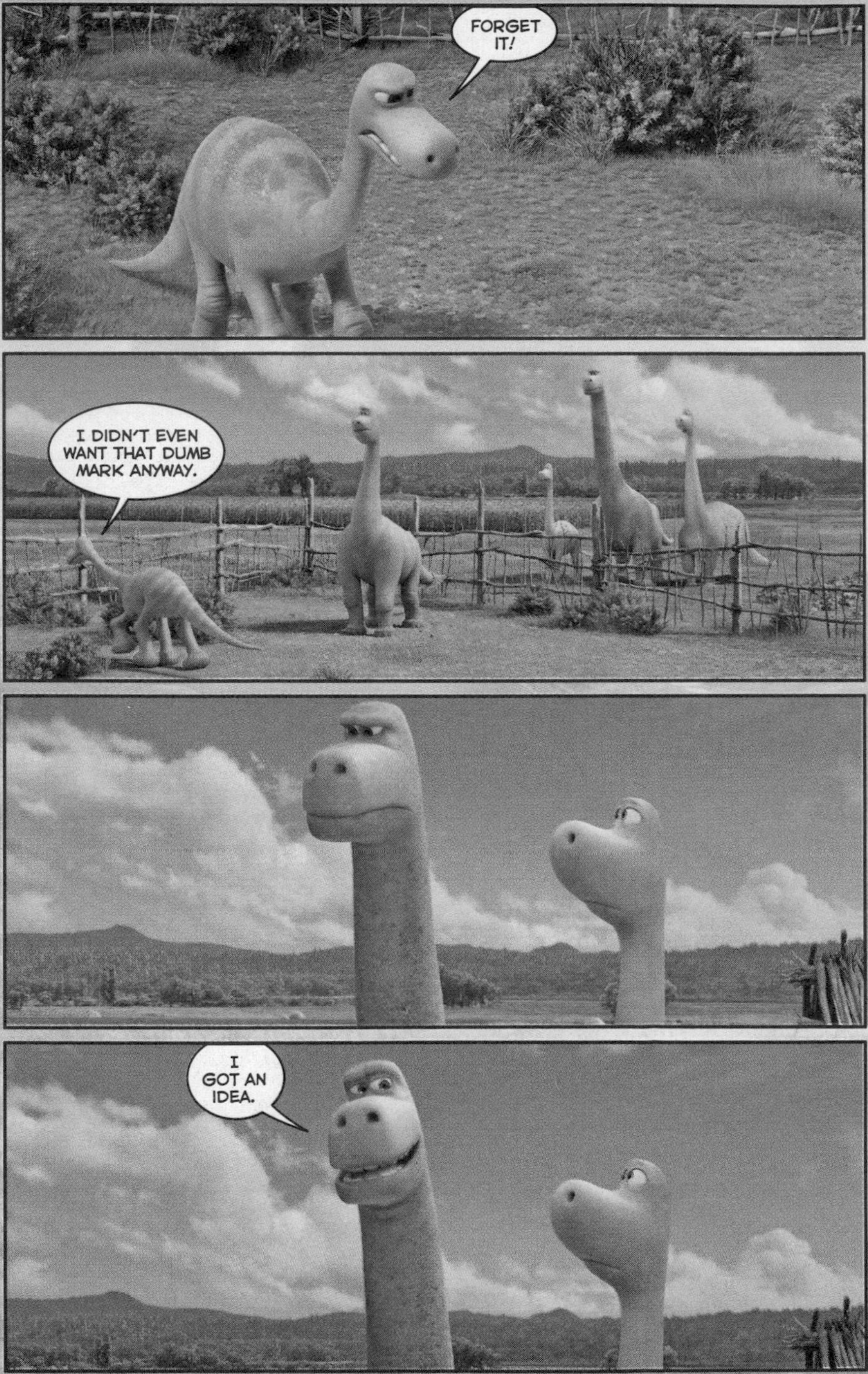
FORGET IT!
I DIDN'T EVEN WANT THAT DUMB MARK ANYWAY.
I GOT AN IDEA.

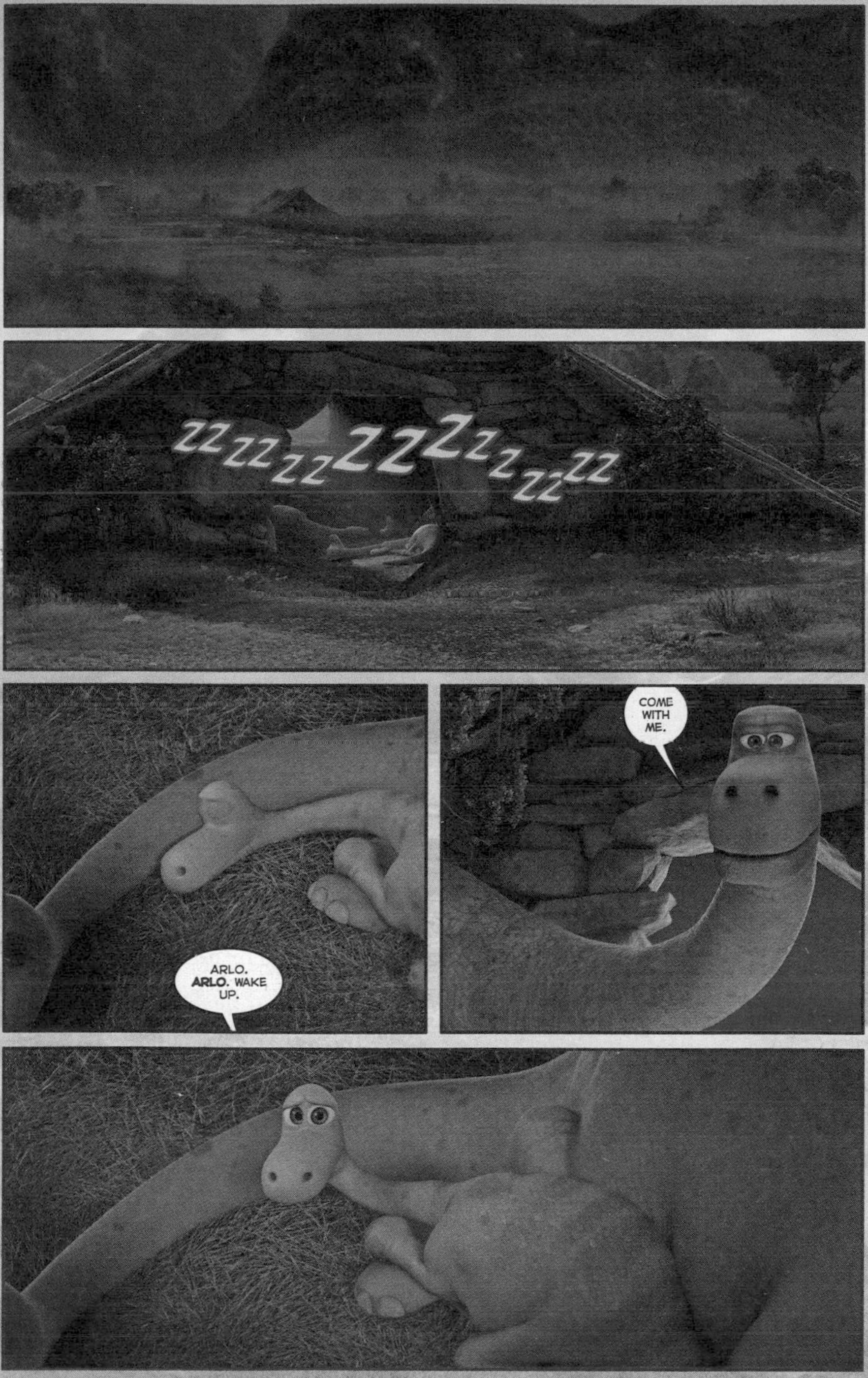
ZZZZZZZZZZZZZZZZZ
ARLO. **ARLO.** WAKE UP.
COME WITH ME.

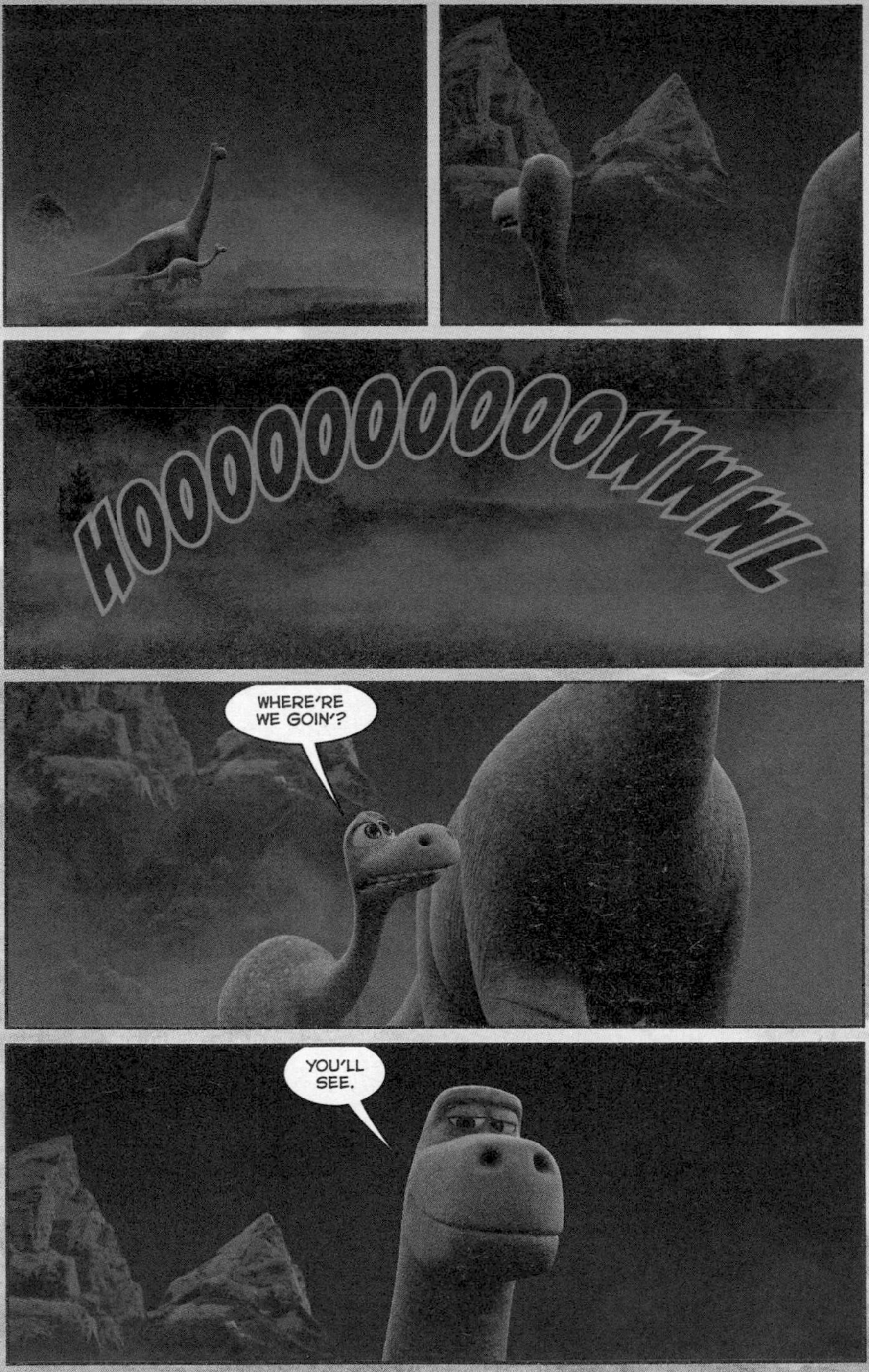
HOOOOOOOOOOWWWL
WHERE'RE WE GOIN'?
YOU'LL SEE.

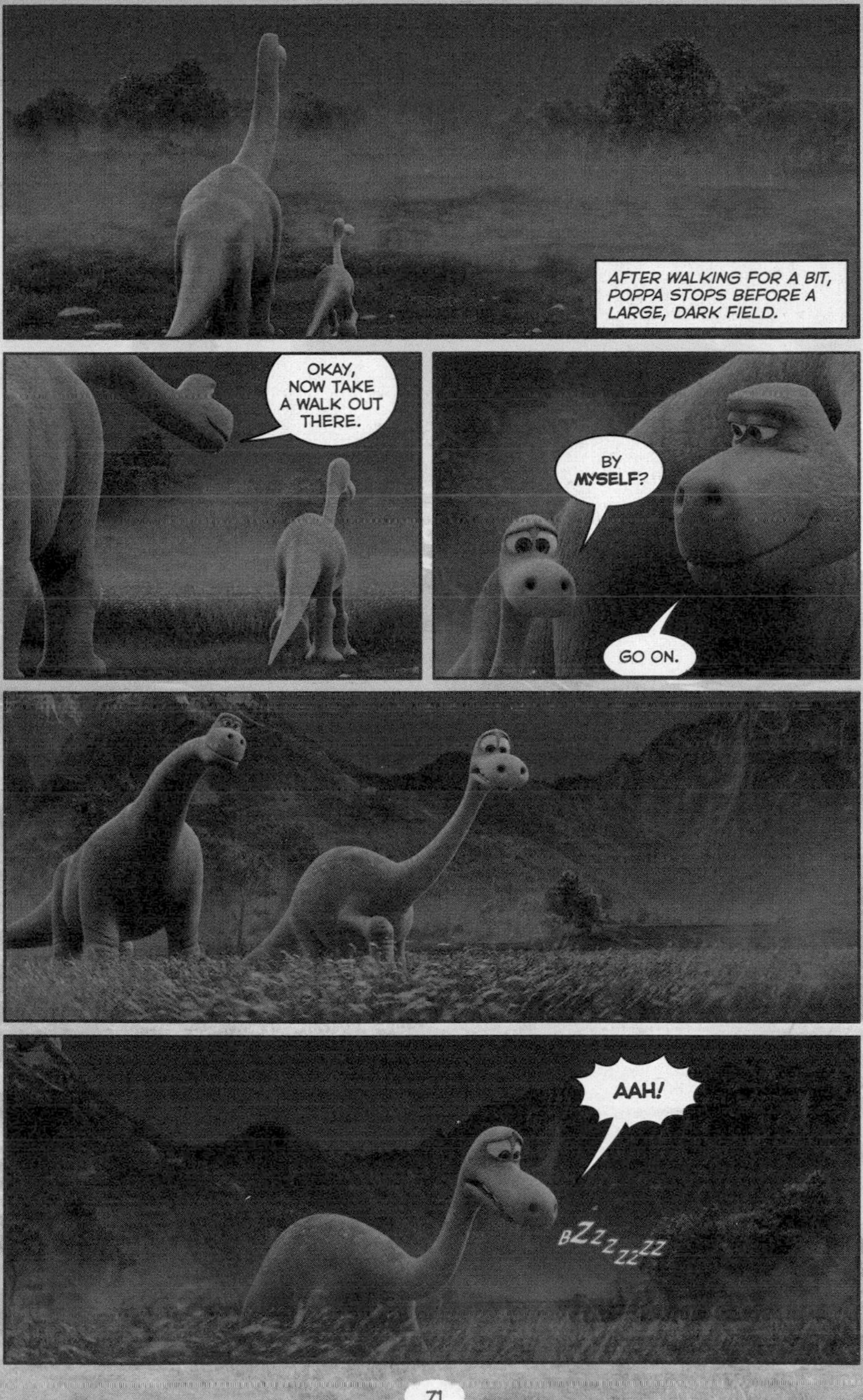
AFTER WALKING FOR A BIT, POPPA STOPS BEFORE A LARGE, DARK FIELD.
OKAY, NOW TAKE A WALK OUT THERE.
BY MYSELF?
GO ON.
AAH!
BZZZZZZZ

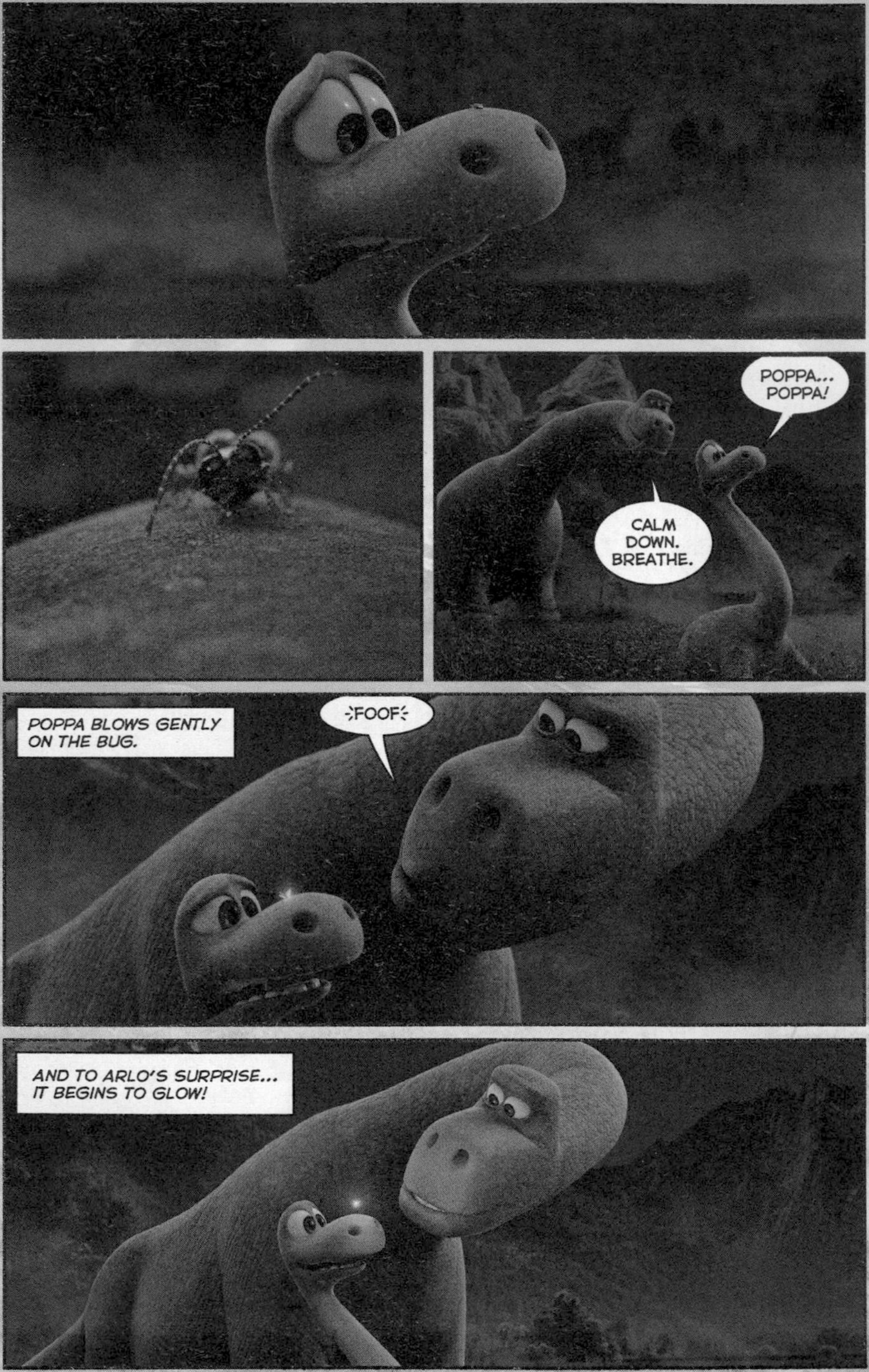
POPPA... POPPA!
CALM DOWN. BREATHE.
POPPA BLOWS GENTLY ON THE BUG.
FOOF
AND TO ARLO'S SURPRISE... IT BEGINS TO GLOW!

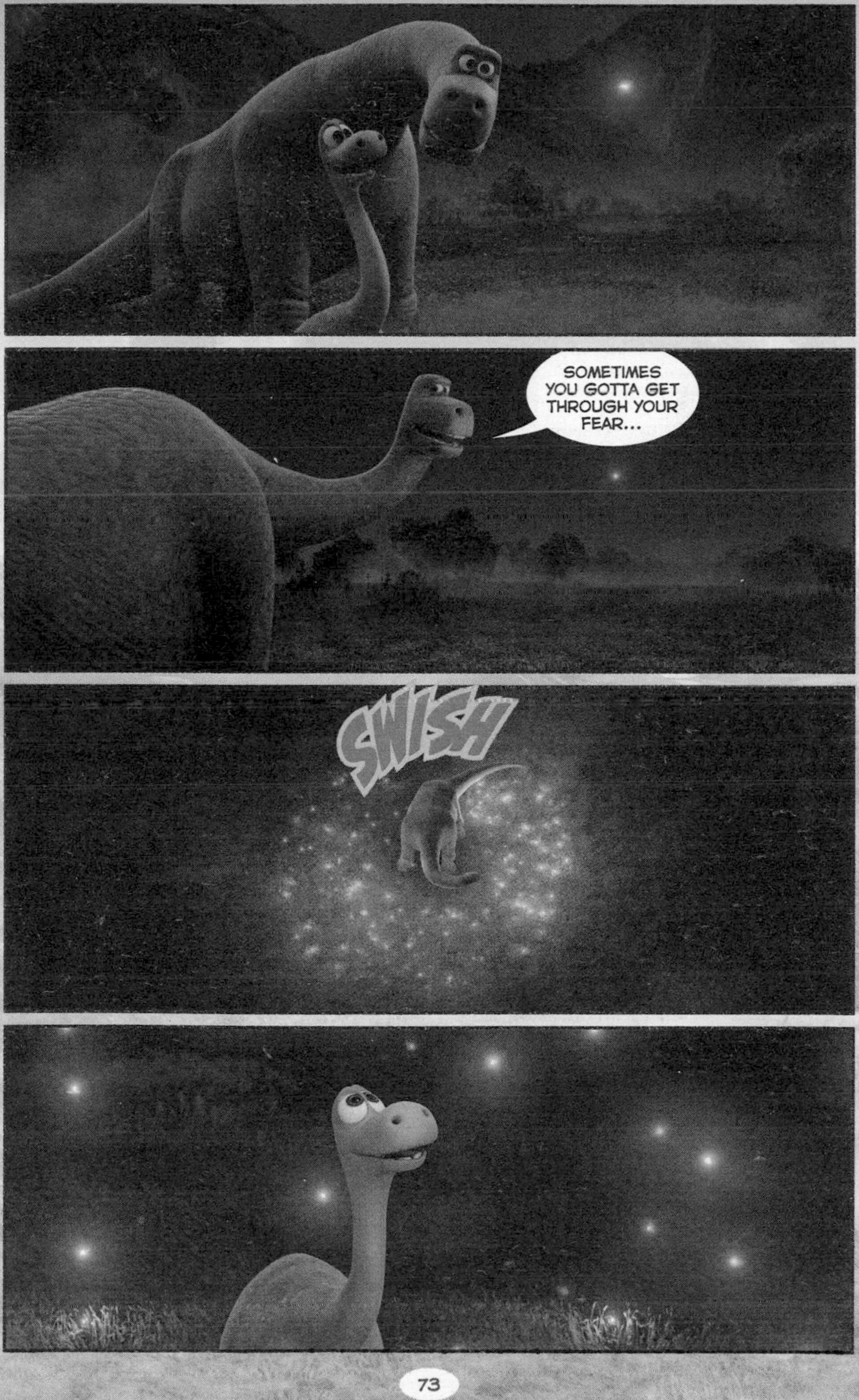
SOMETIMES YOU GOTTA GET THROUGH YOUR FEAR...
SWISH

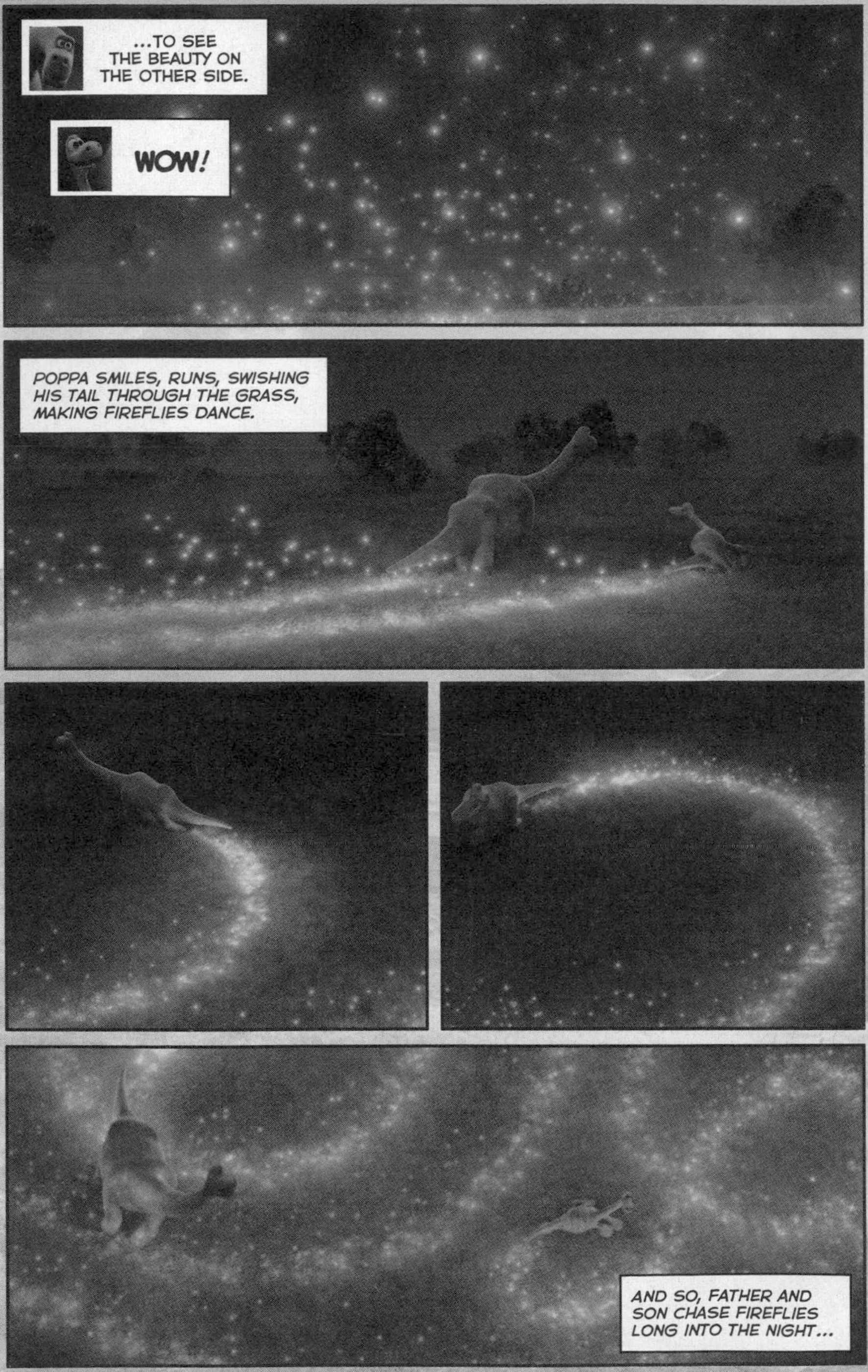
...TO SEE THE BEAUTY ON THE OTHER SIDE.
WOW!
POPPA SMILES, RUNS, SWISHING HIS TAIL THROUGH THE GRASS, MAKING FIREFLIES DANCE.
AND SO, FATHER AND SON CHASE FIREFLIES LONG INTO THE NIGHT...

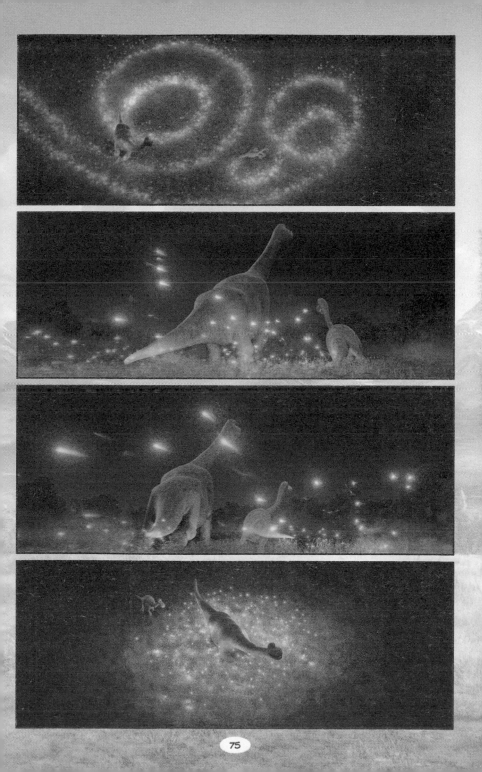

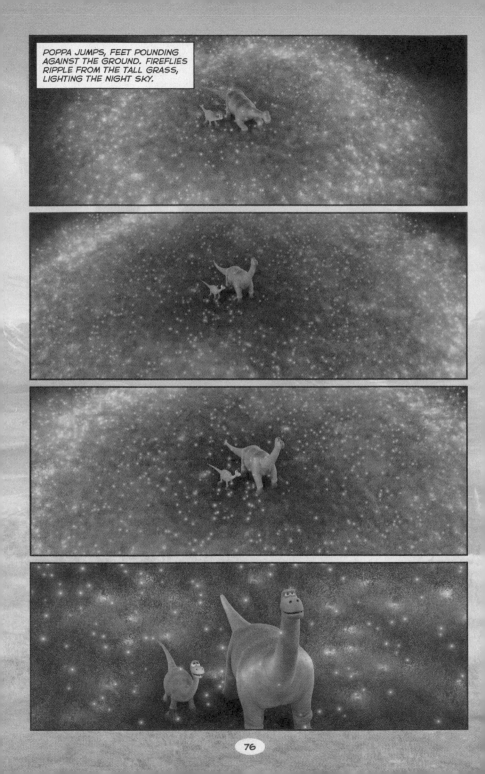

POPPA JUMPS, FEET POUNDING AGAINST THE GROUND. FIREFLIES RIPPLE FROM THE TALL GRASS, LIGHTING THE NIGHT SKY.

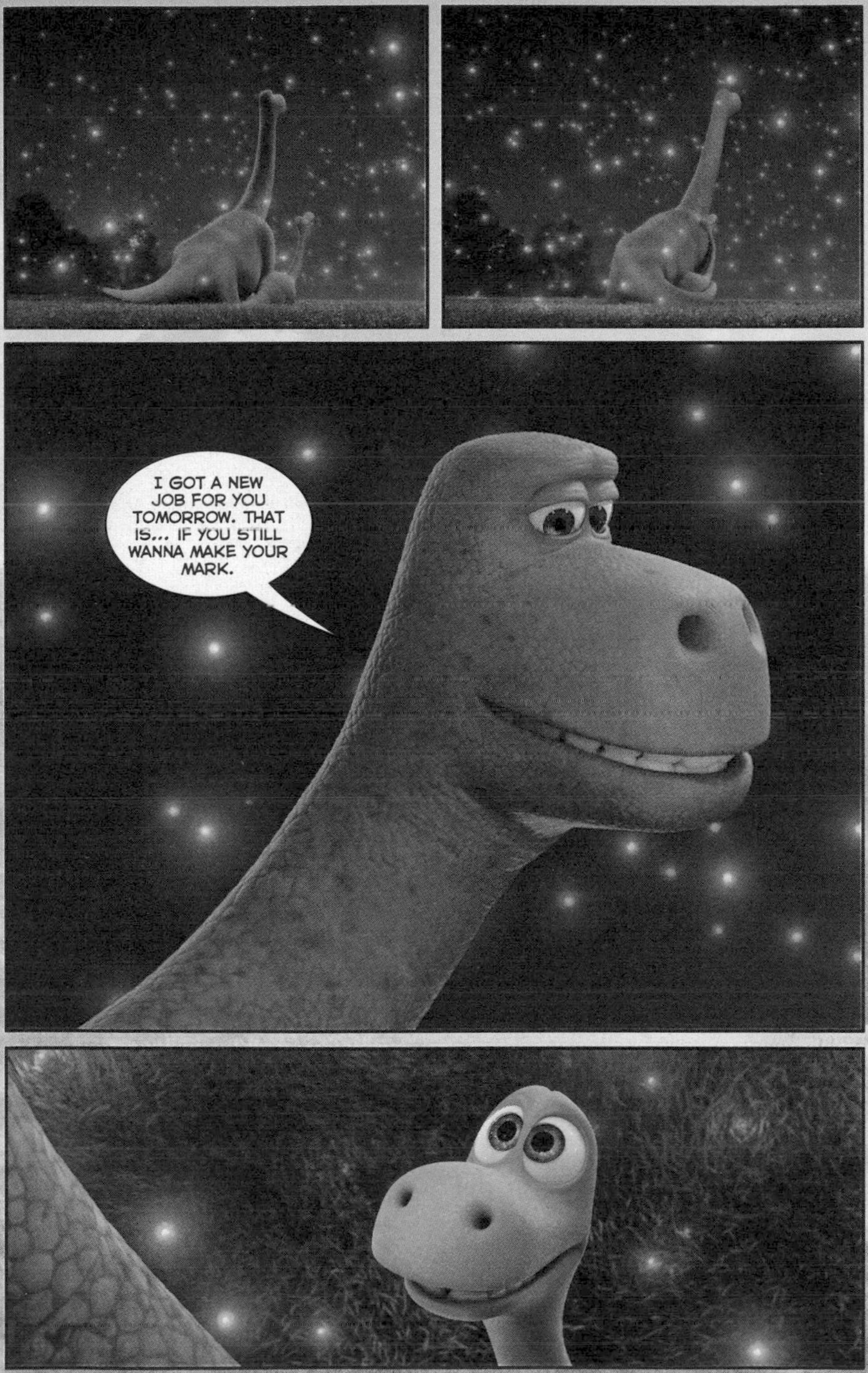
I GOT A NEW JOB FOR YOU TOMORROW. THAT IS... IF YOU STILL WANNA MAKE YOUR MARK.

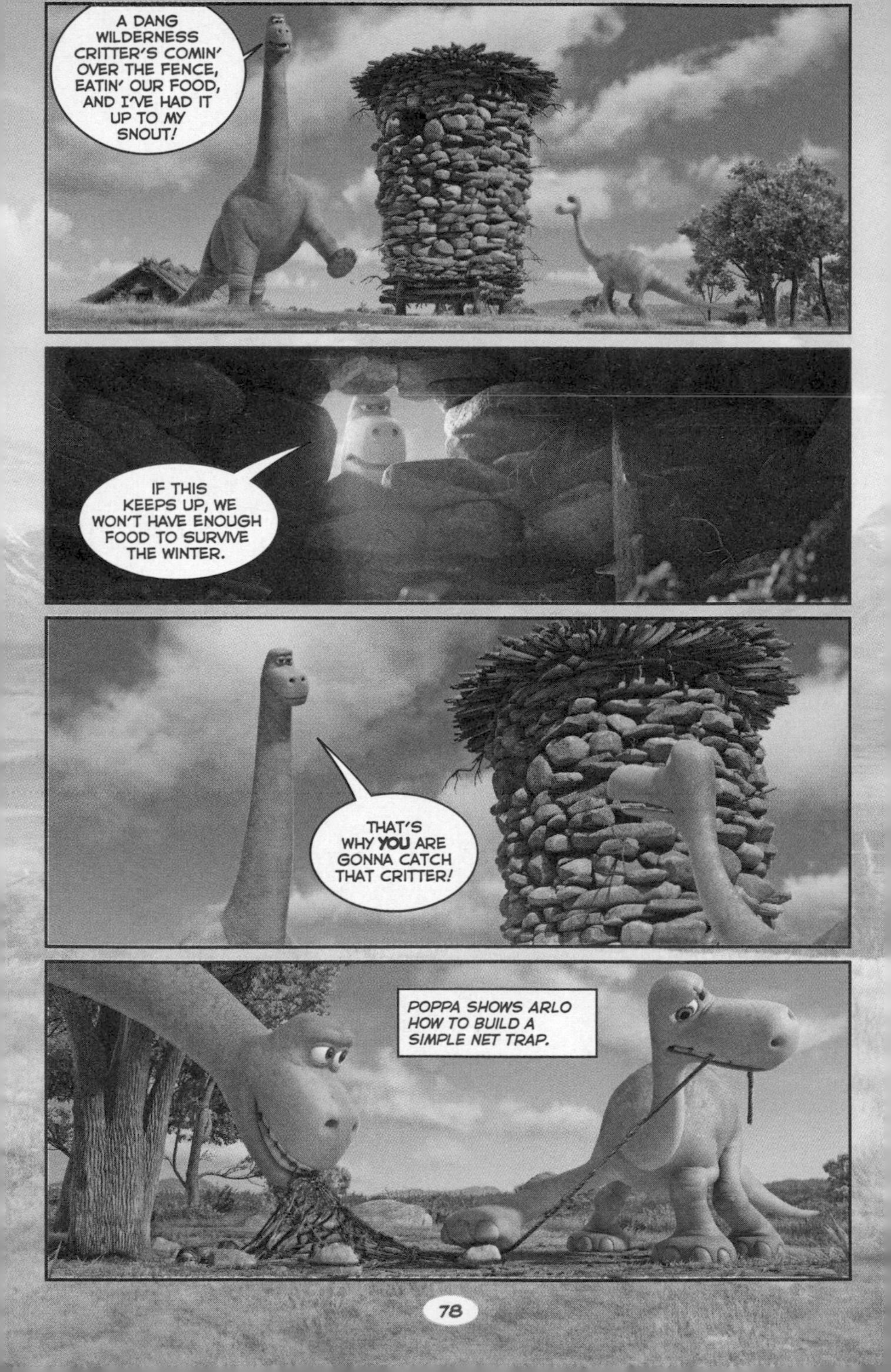
A DANG WILDERNESS CRITTER'S COMIN' OVER THE FENCE, EATIN' OUR FOOD, AND I'VE HAD IT UP TO MY SNOUT!
IF THIS KEEPS UP, WE WON'T HAVE ENOUGH FOOD TO SURVIVE THE WINTER.
THAT'S WHY **YOU** ARE GONNA CATCH THAT CRITTER!
POPPA SHOWS ARLO HOW TO BUILD A SIMPLE NET TRAP.

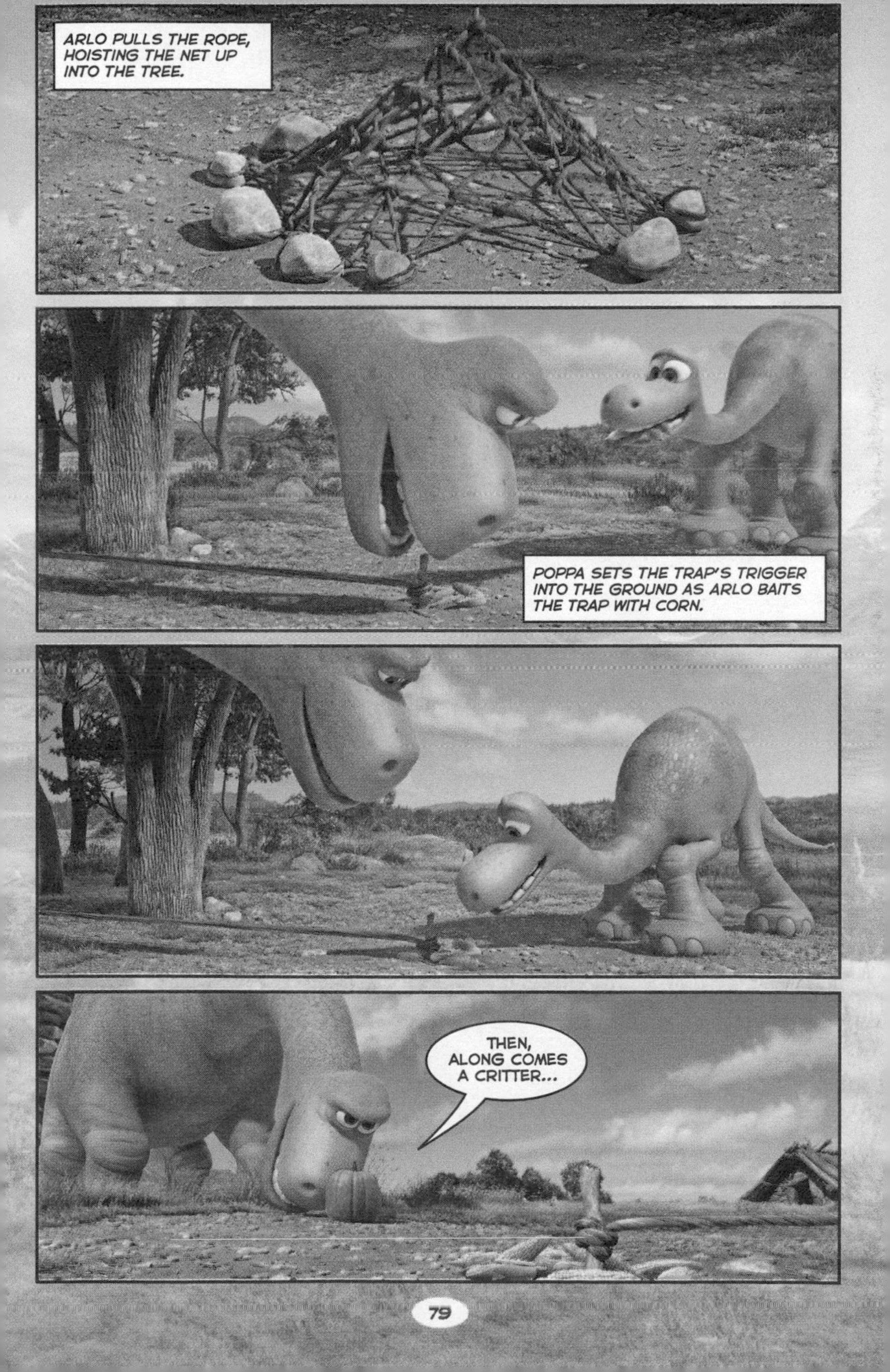
ARLO PULLS THE ROPE, HOISTING THE NET UP INTO THE TREE.
POPPA SETS THE TRAP'S TRIGGER INTO THE GROUND AS ARLO BAITS THE TRAP WITH CORN.
THEN, ALONG COMES A CRITTER...

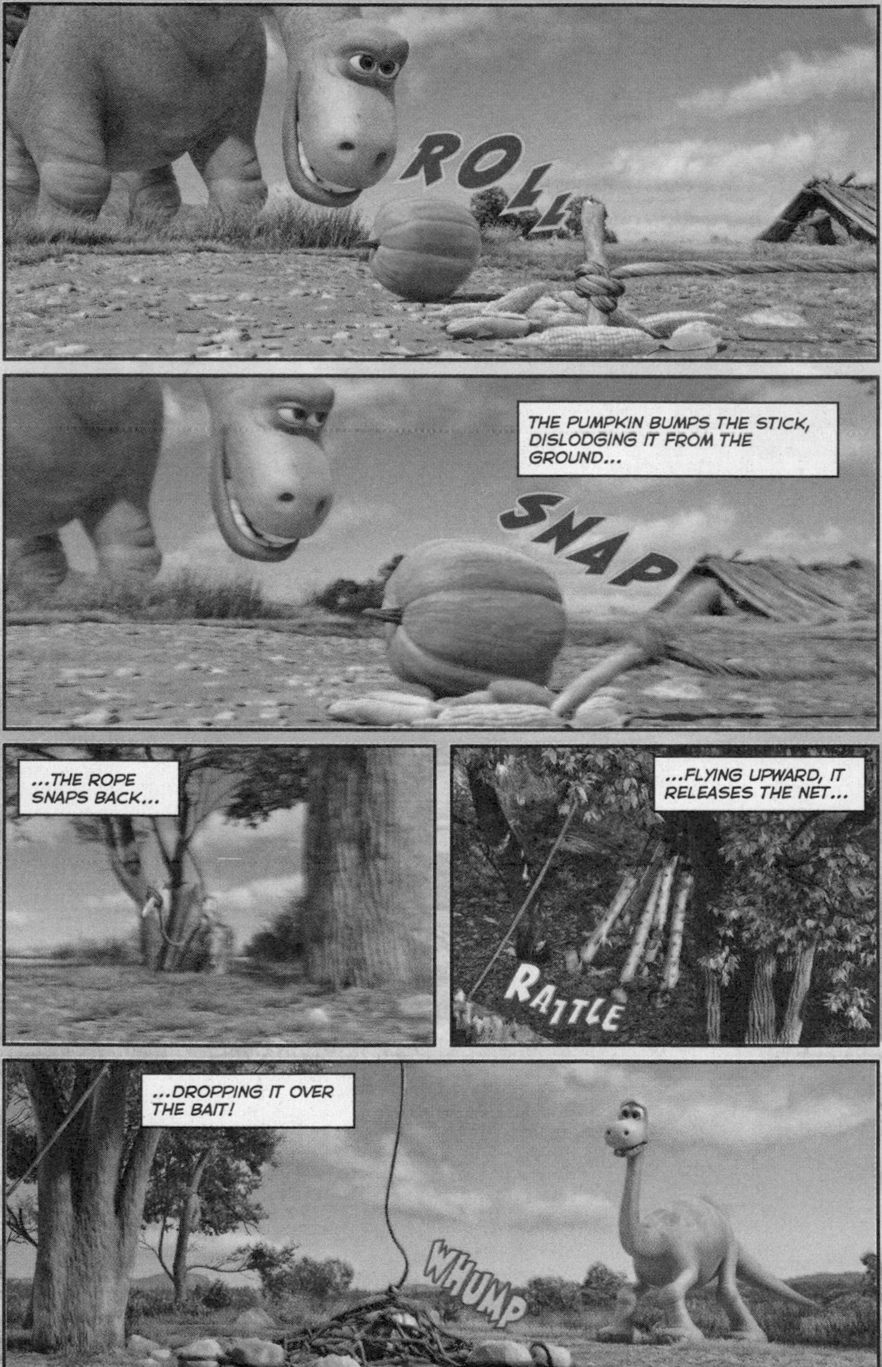
ROLL
THE PUMPKIN BUMPS THE STICK, DISLODGING IT FROM THE GROUND...
SNAP
...THE ROPE SNAPS BACK...
...FLYING UPWARD, IT RELEASES THE NET...
RATTLE
...DROPPING IT OVER THE BAIT!
WHUMP

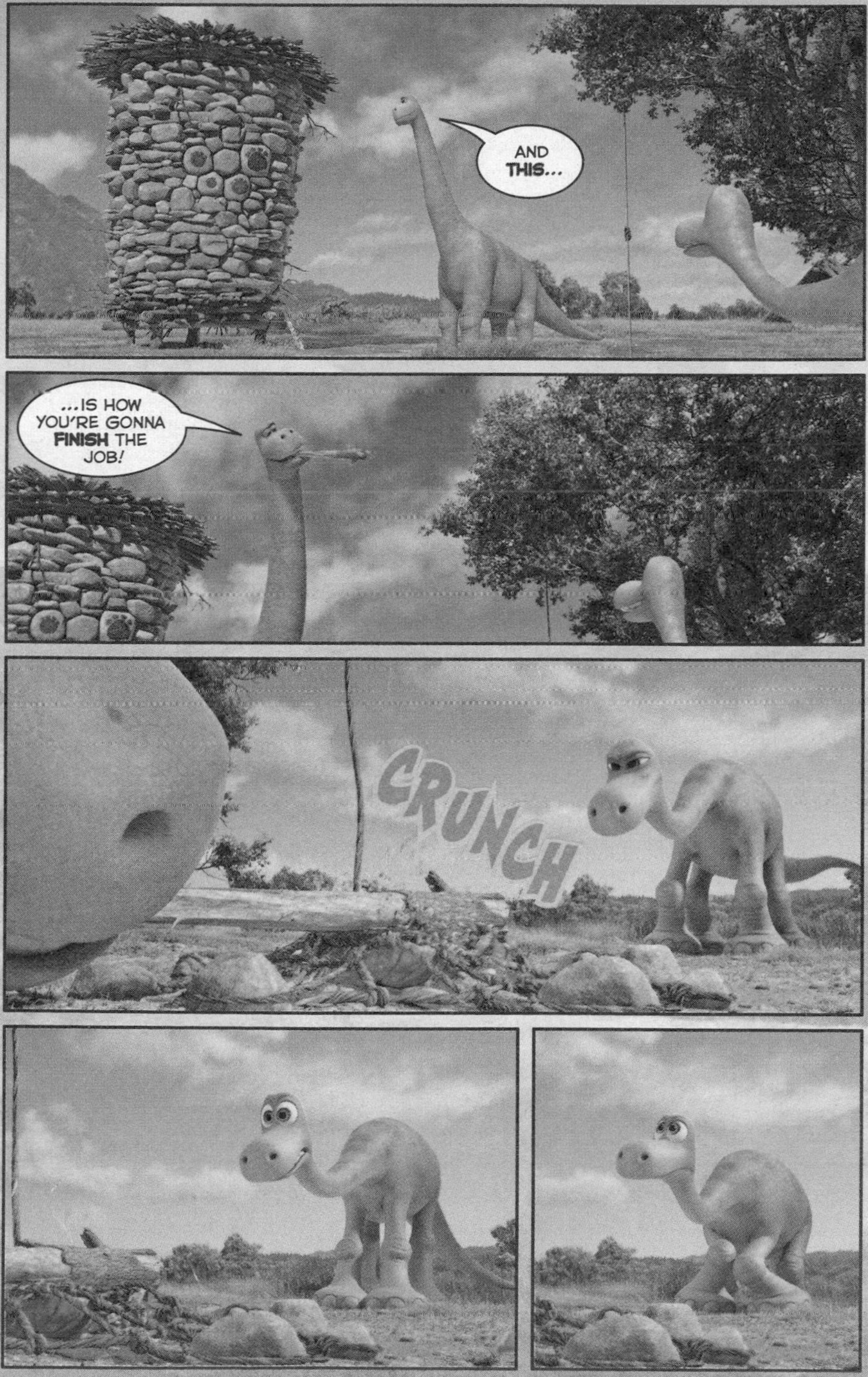
AND THIS...
...IS HOW YOU'RE GONNA FINISH THE JOB!
CRUNCH

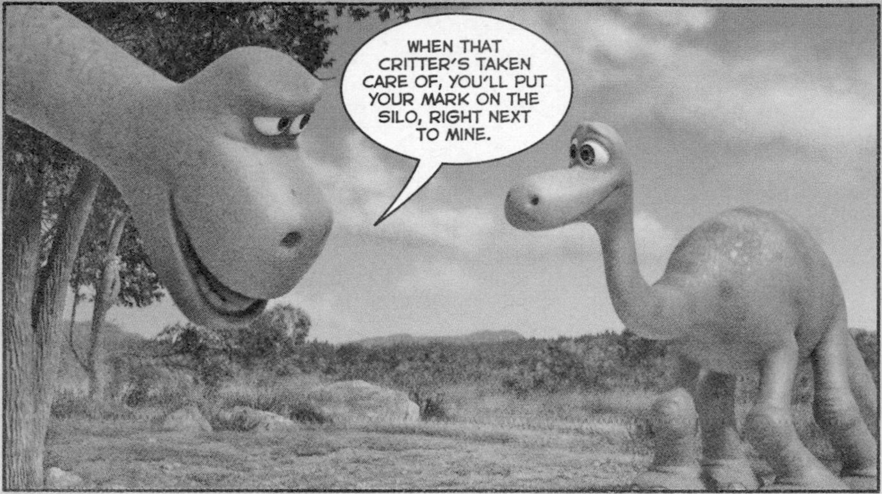
WHEN THAT CRITTER'S TAKEN CARE OF, YOU'LL PUT YOUR MARK ON THE SILO, RIGHT NEXT TO MINE.

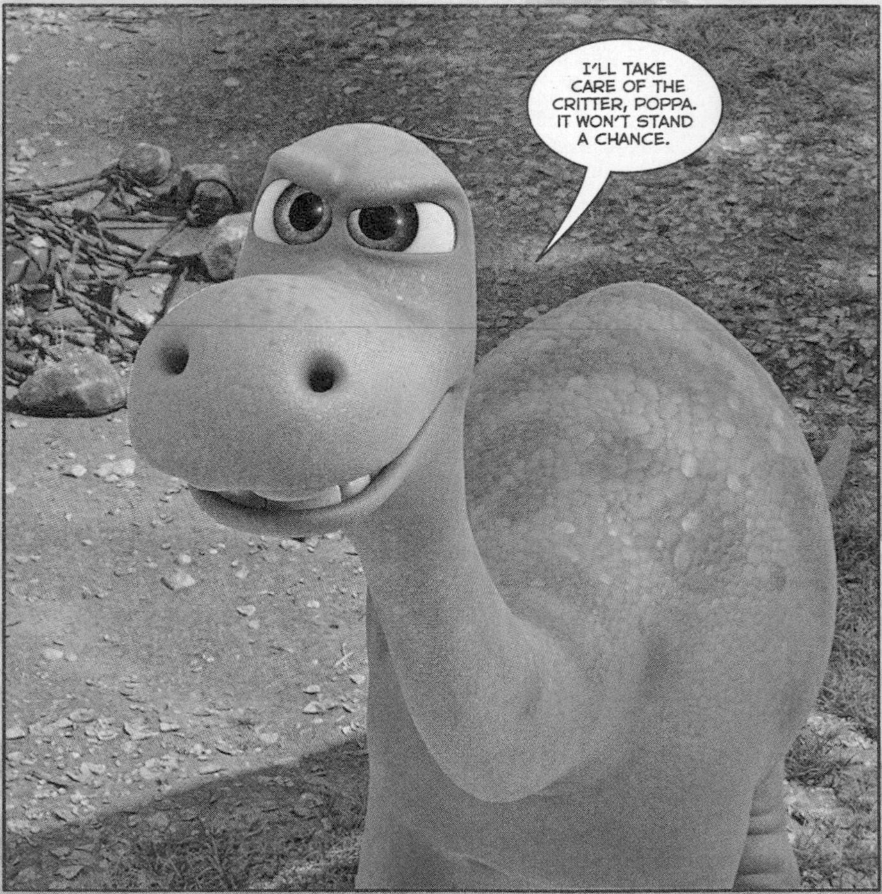
I'LL TAKE CARE OF THE CRITTER, POPPA. IT WON'T STAND A CHANCE.

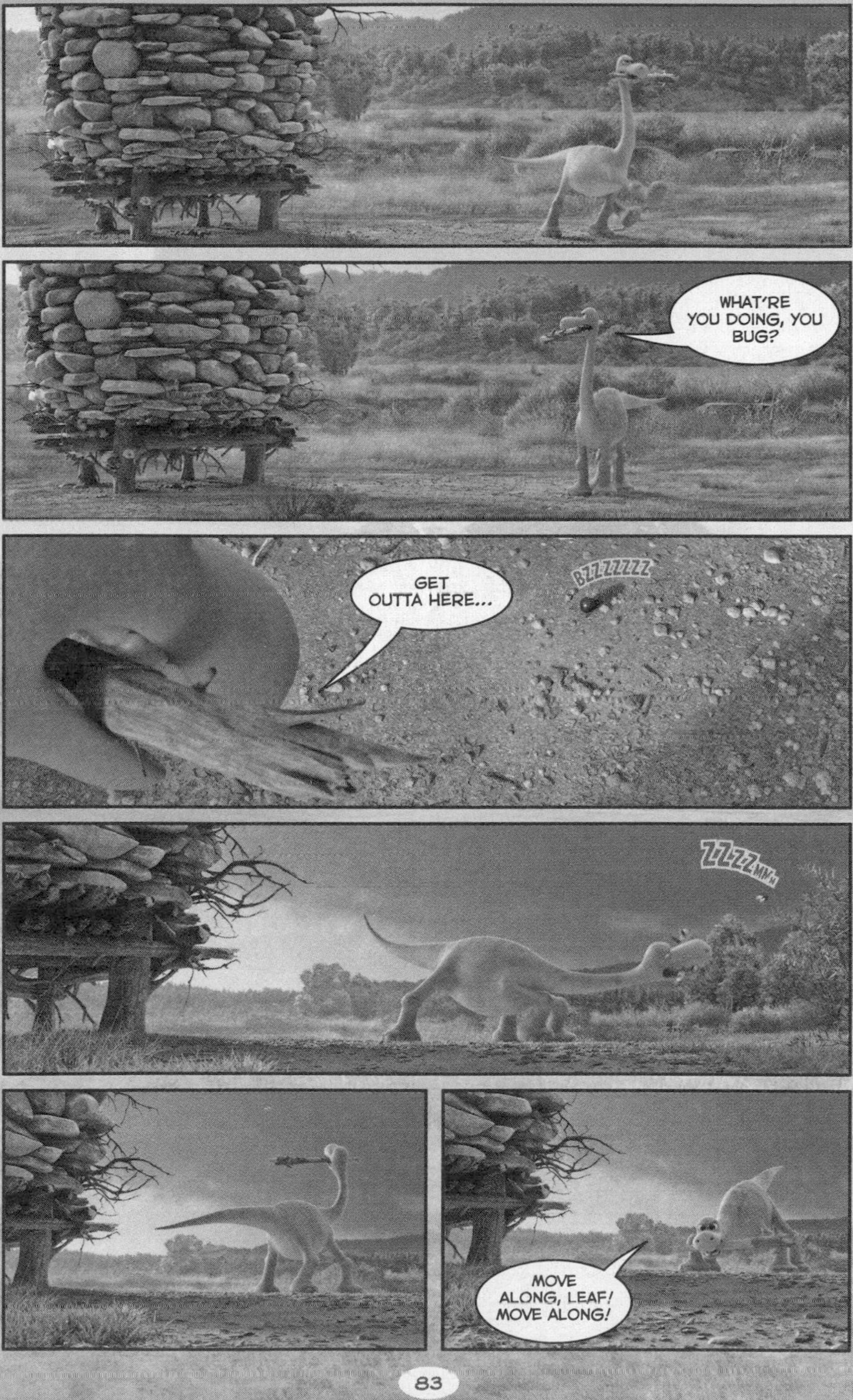
WHAT'RE YOU DOING, YOU BUG?
GET OUTTA HERE...
BZZZZZZZ
ZZZZMMM
MOVE ALONG, LEAF! MOVE ALONG!

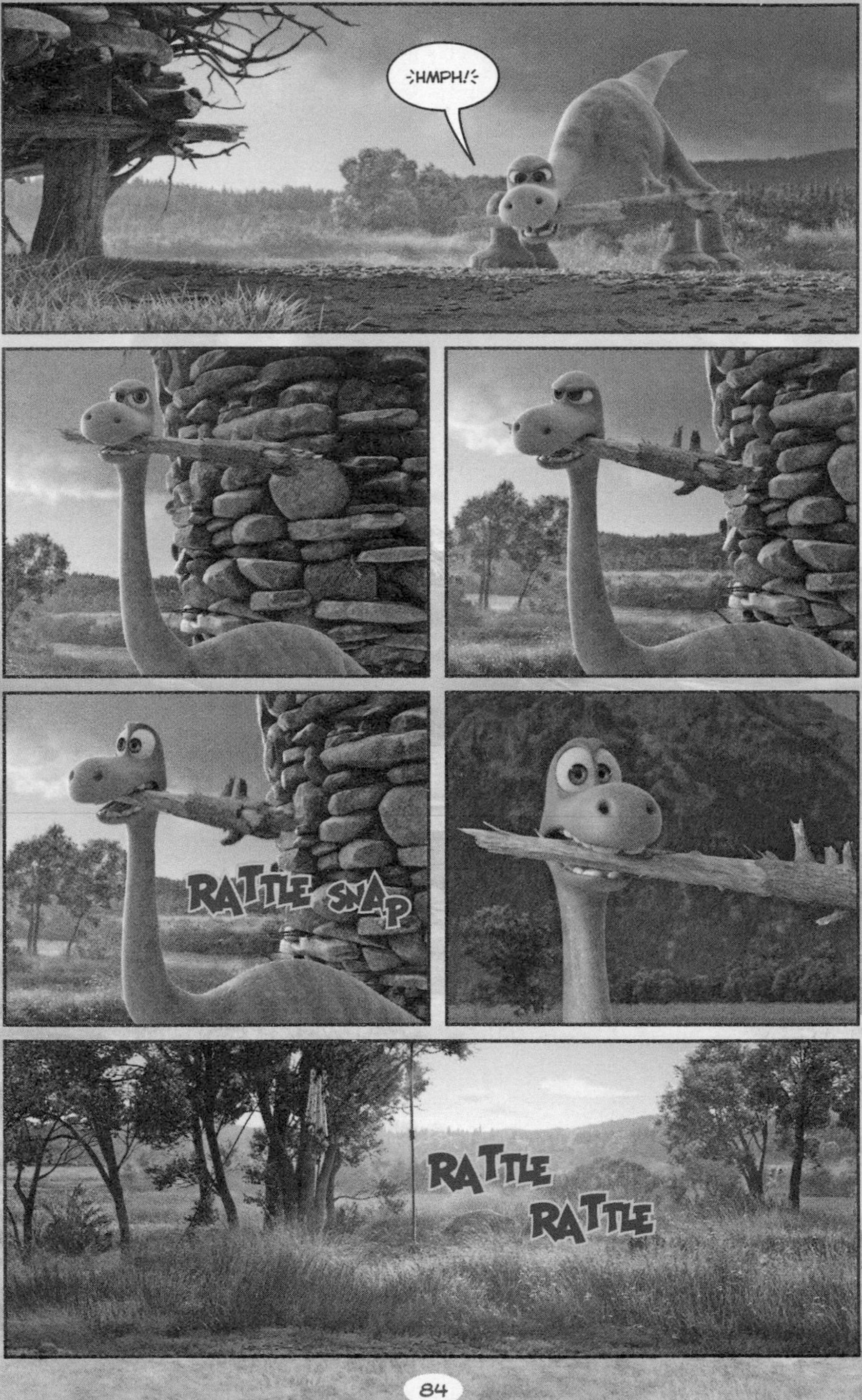
HMPH!
RATTLE SNAP
RATTLE
RATTLE

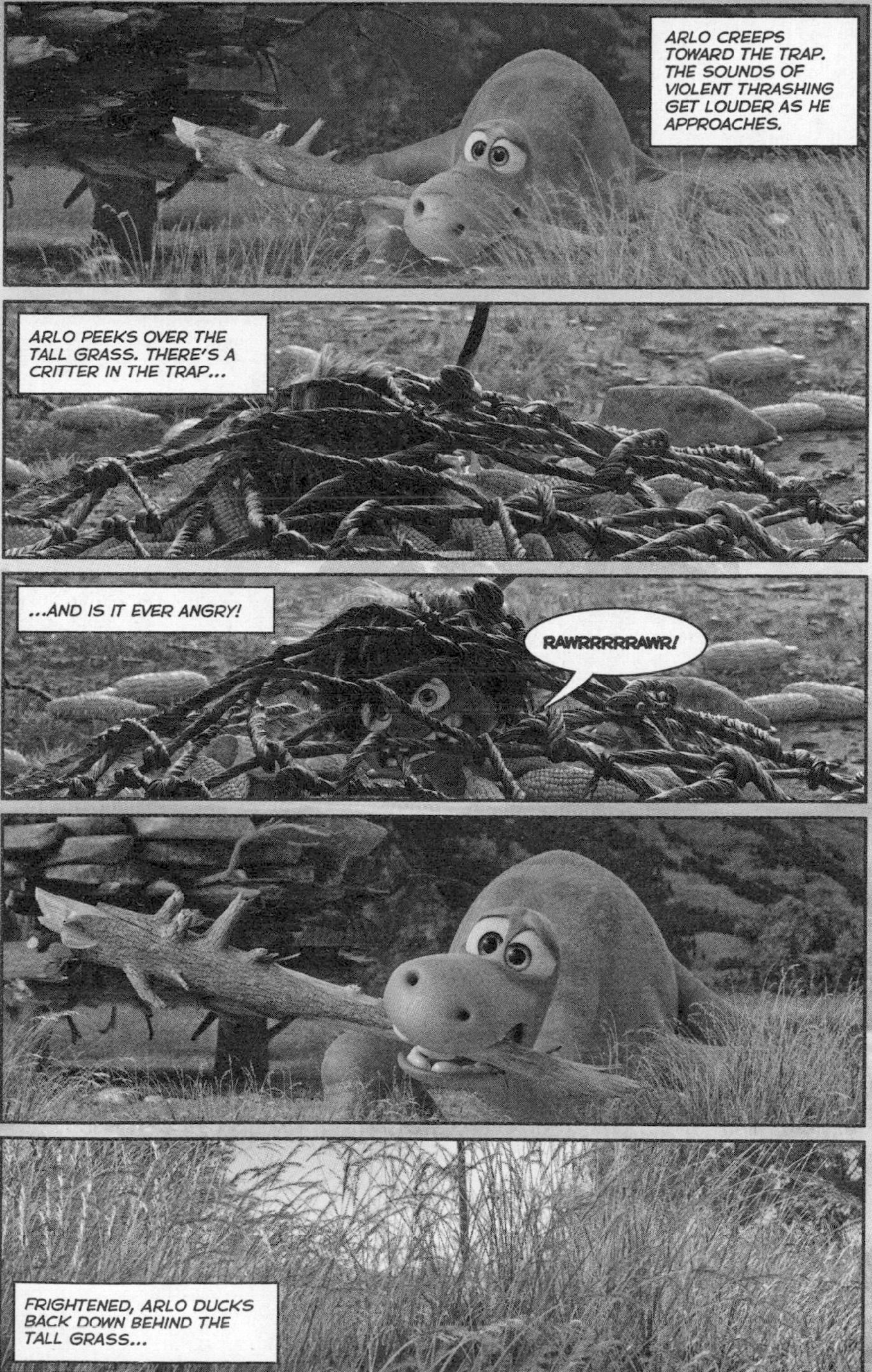
ARLO CREEPS TOWARD THE TRAP. THE SOUNDS OF VIOLENT THRASHING GET LOUDER AS HE APPROACHES.
ARLO PEEKS OVER THE TALL GRASS. THERE'S A CRITTER IN THE TRAP...
...AND IS IT EVER ANGRY!
RAWRRRRRAWR!
FRIGHTENED, ARLO DUCKS BACK DOWN BEHIND THE TALL GRASS...

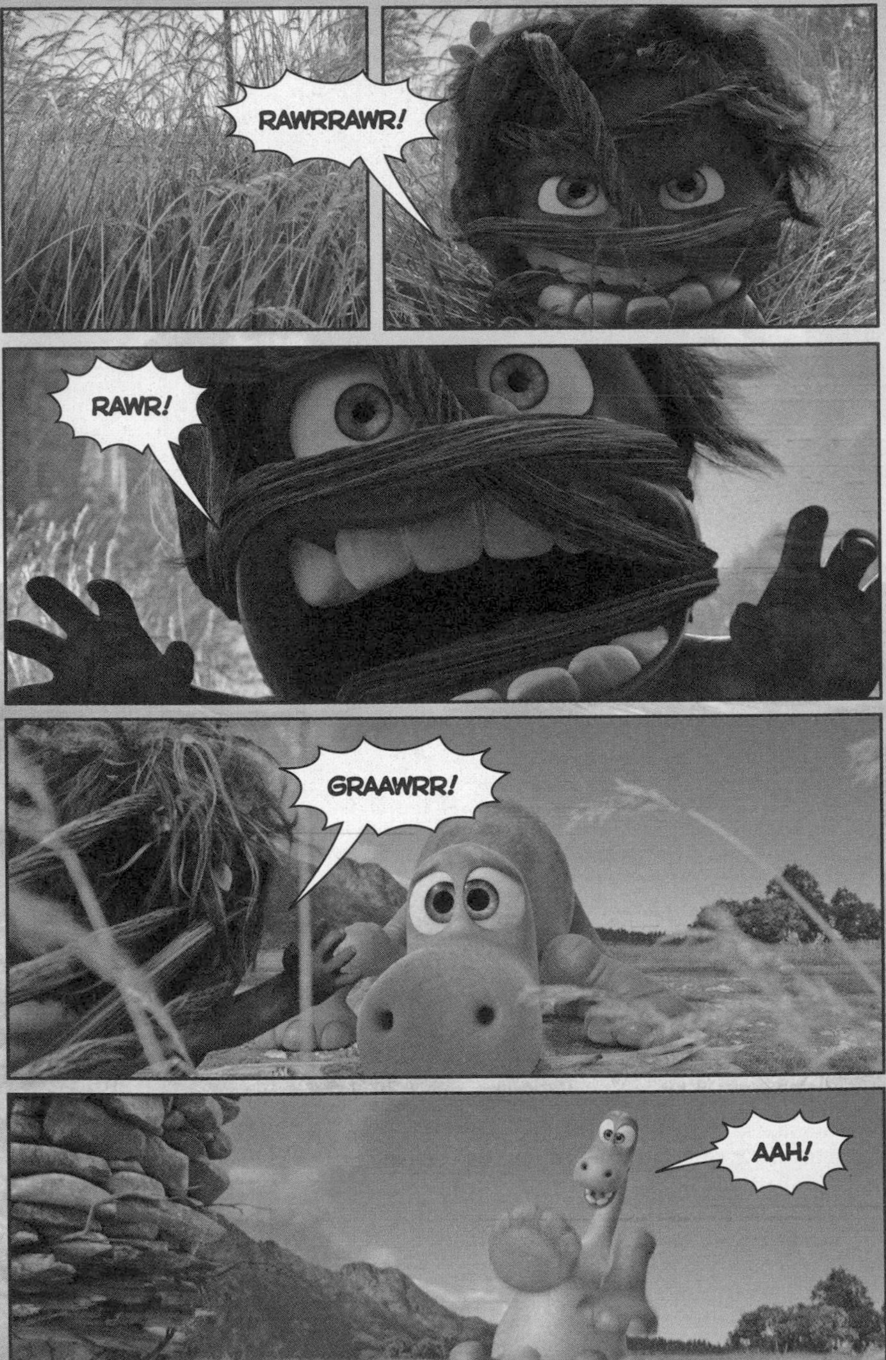
RAWRRAWR!
RAWR!
GRAAWRR!
AAH!

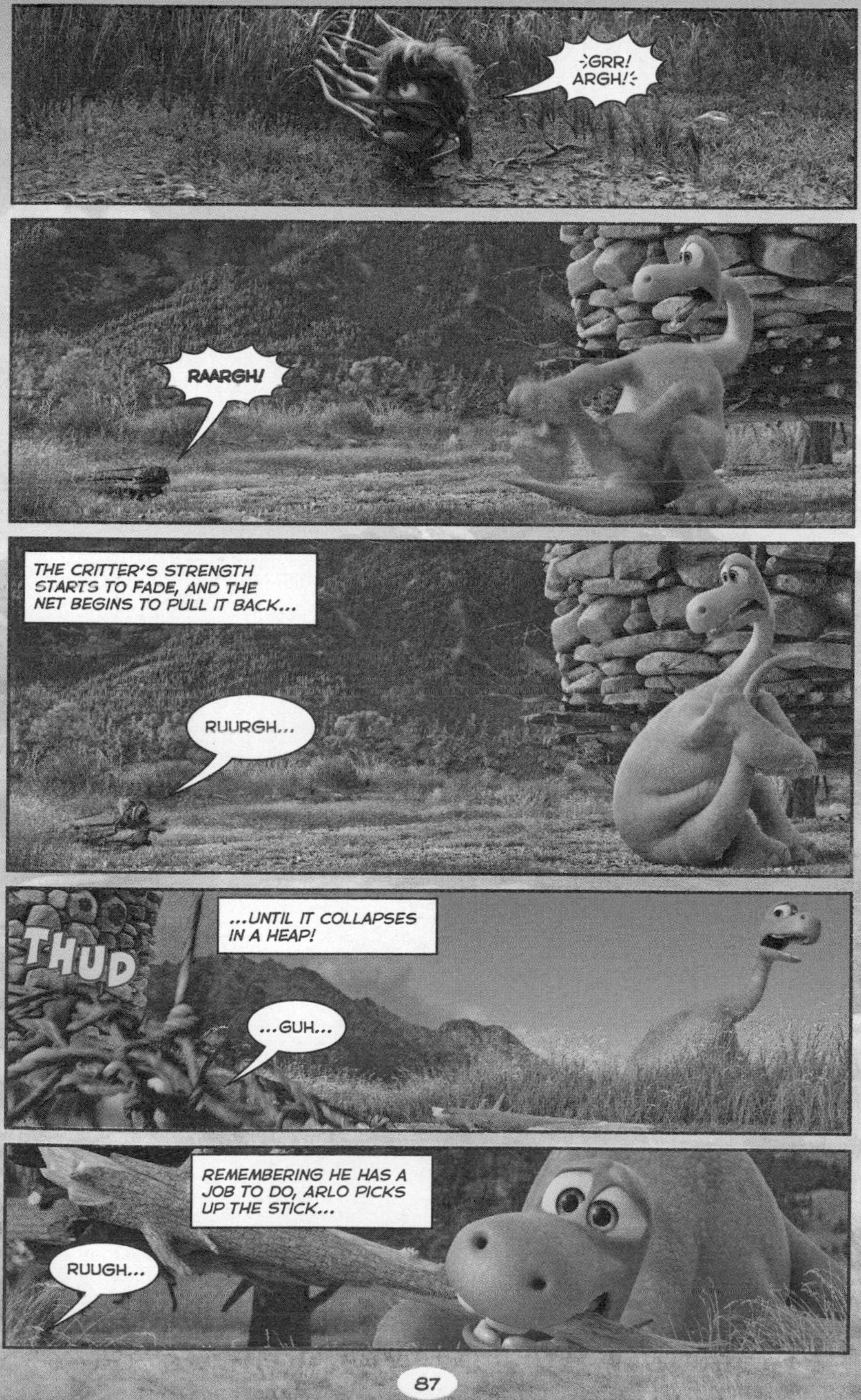

GRR! ARGH!
RAARGH!
THE CRITTER'S STRENGTH STARTS TO FADE, AND THE NET BEGINS TO PULL IT BACK...
RUURGH...
...UNTIL IT COLLAPSES IN A HEAP!
THUD
...GUH...
REMEMBERING HE HAS A JOB TO DO, ARLO PICKS UP THE STICK...
RUUGH...

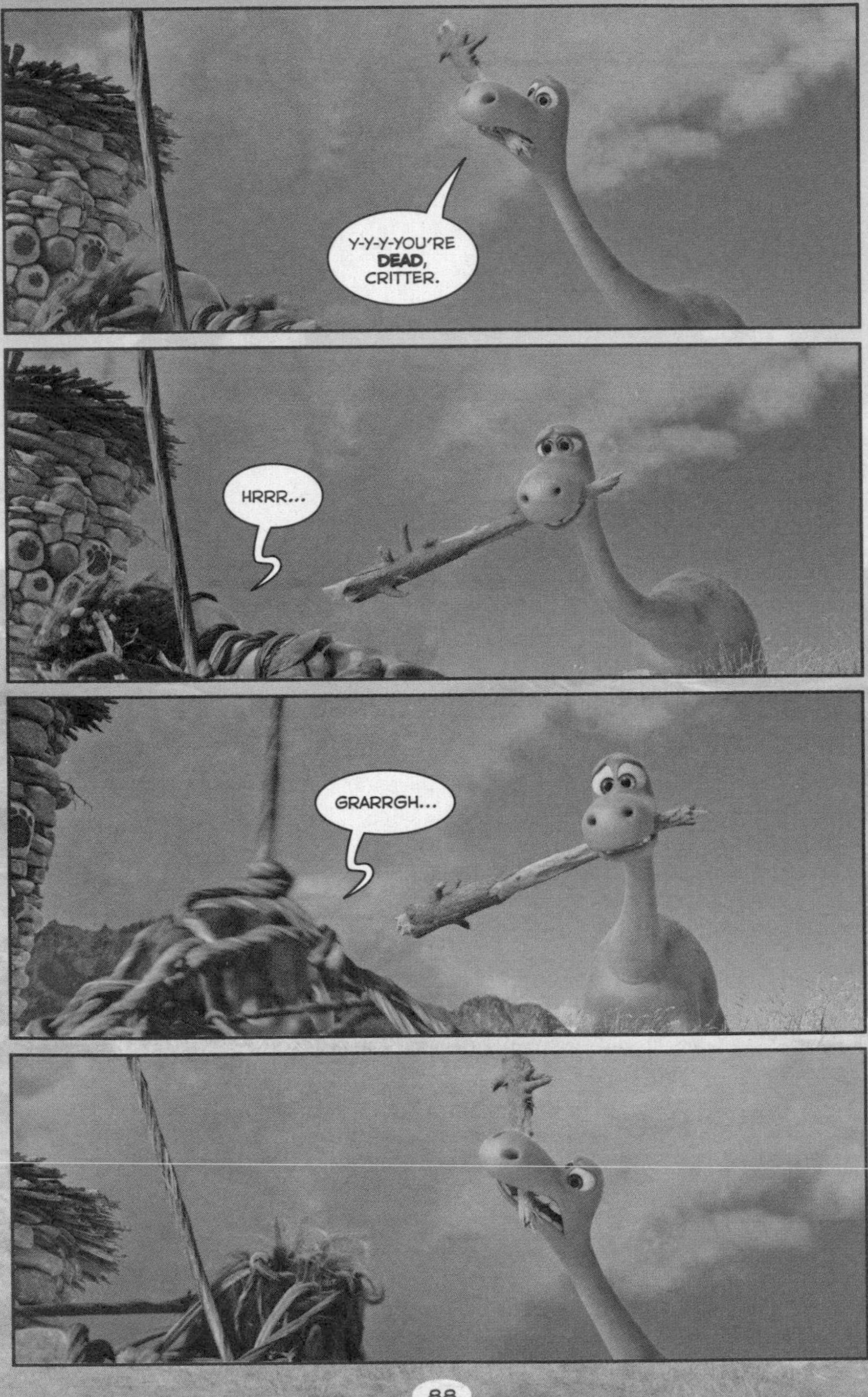
Y-Y-Y-YOU'RE **DEAD**, CRITTER.
HRRR...
GRARRGH...

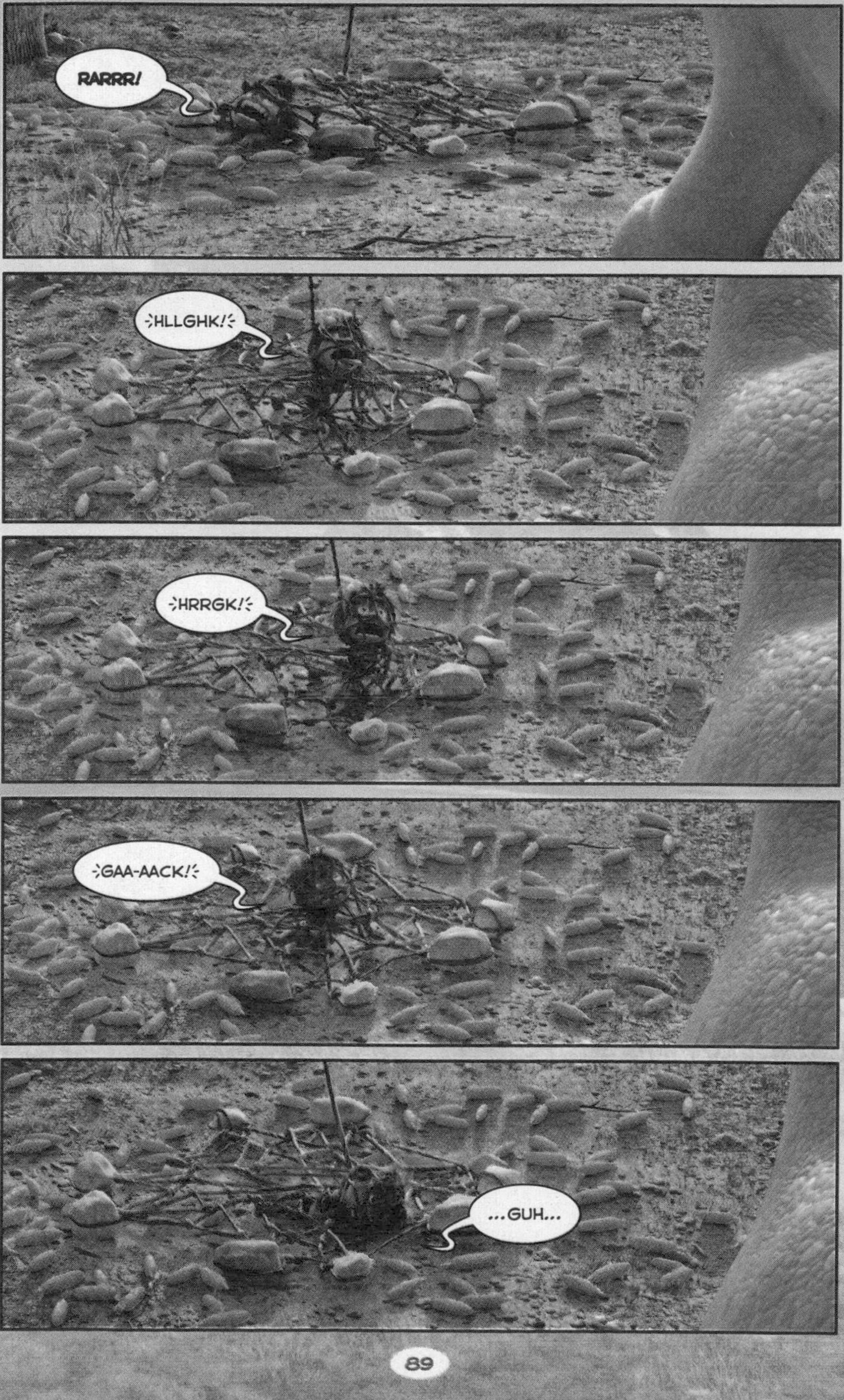
RARRR!
HLLGHK!
HRRGK!
GAA-AACK!
...GUH...

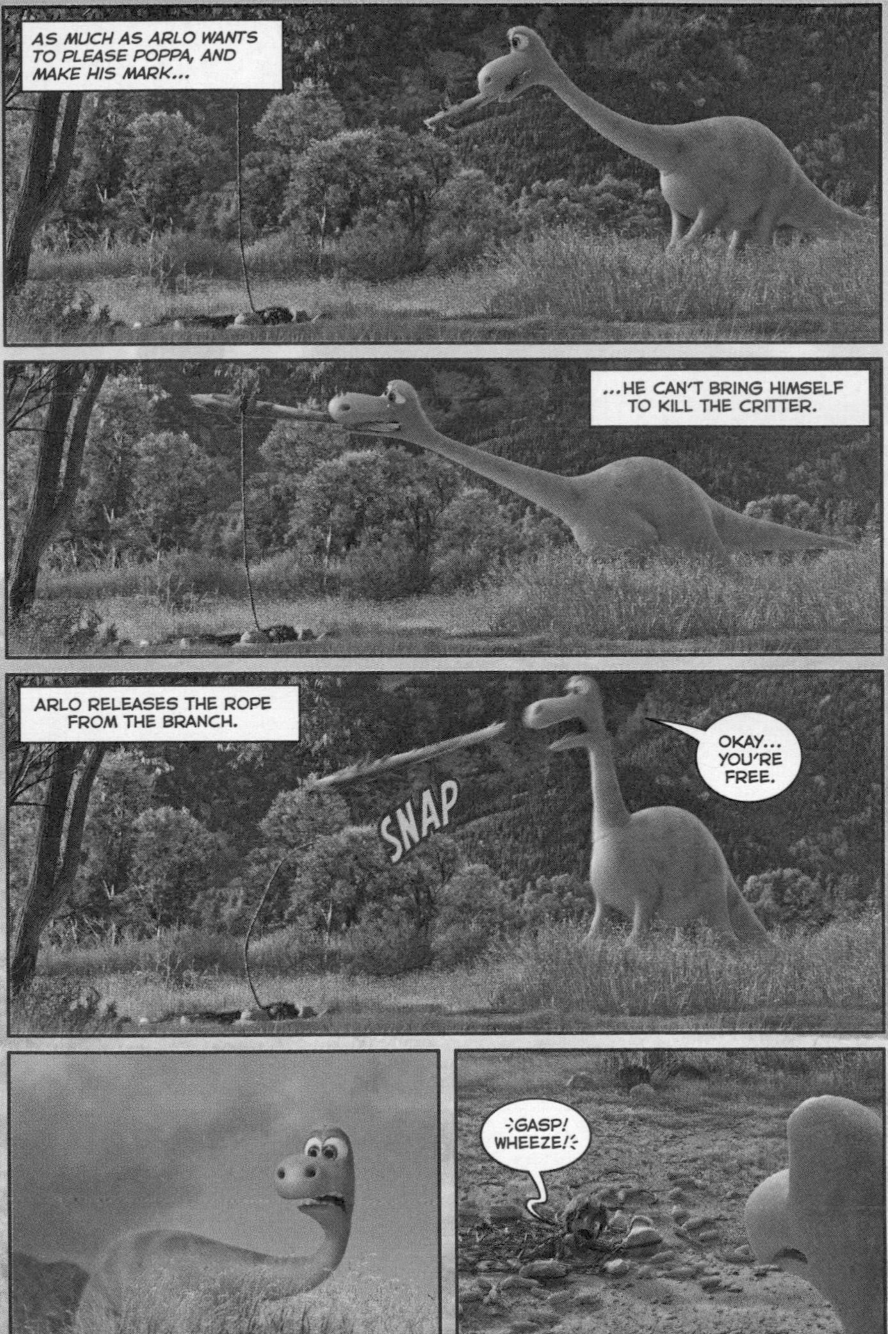
AS MUCH AS ARLO WANTS TO PLEASE POPPA, AND MAKE HIS MARK...
...HE CAN'T BRING HIMSELF TO KILL THE CRITTER.
ARLO RELEASES THE ROPE FROM THE BRANCH.
OKAY... YOU'RE FREE.
SNAP
GASP! WHEEZE!

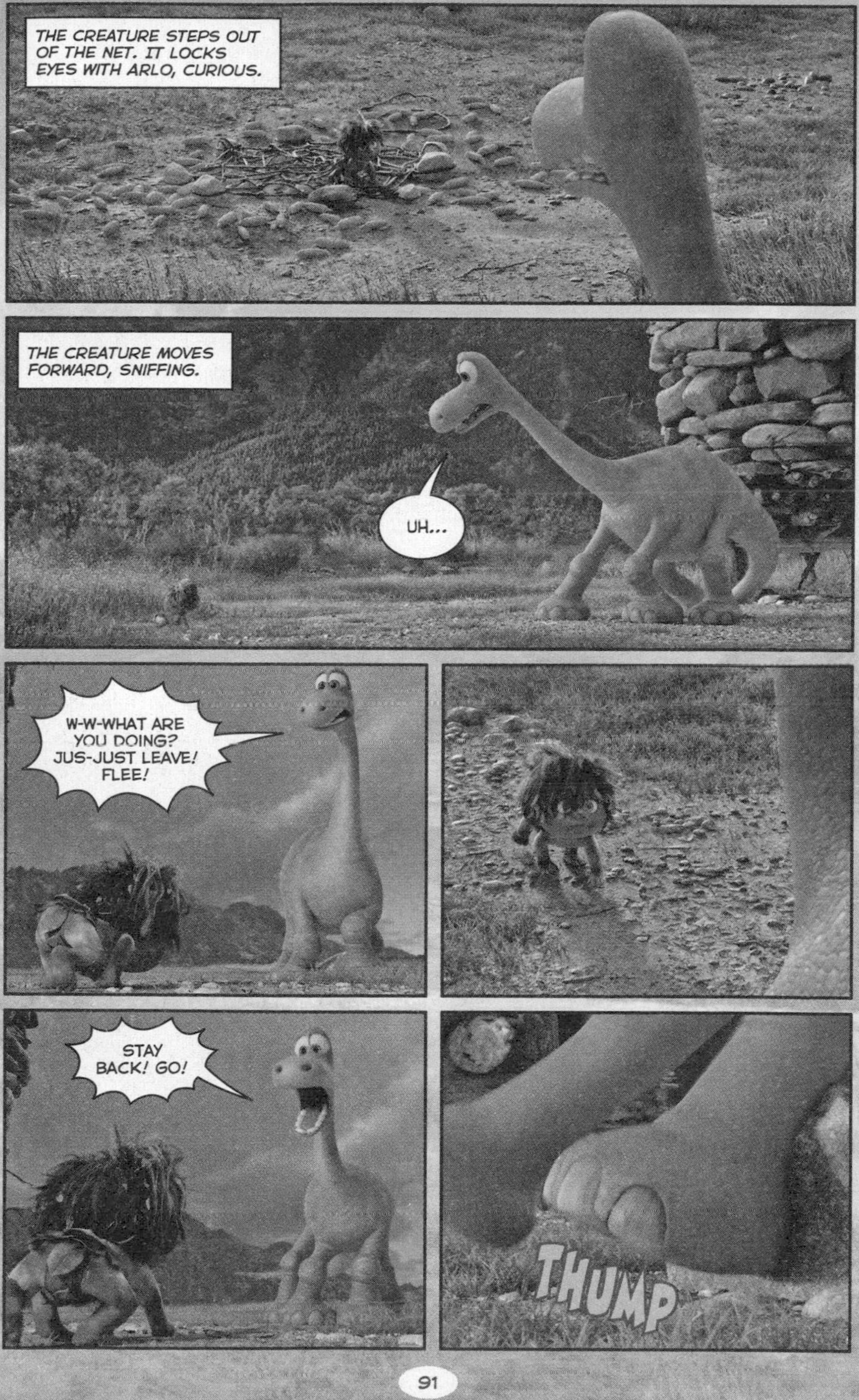
THE CREATURE STEPS OUT OF THE NET. IT LOCKS EYES WITH ARLO, CURIOUS.
THE CREATURE MOVES FORWARD, SNIFFING.
UH...
W-W-WHAT ARE YOU DOING? JUS-JUST LEAVE! FLEE!
STAY BACK! GO!
THUMP

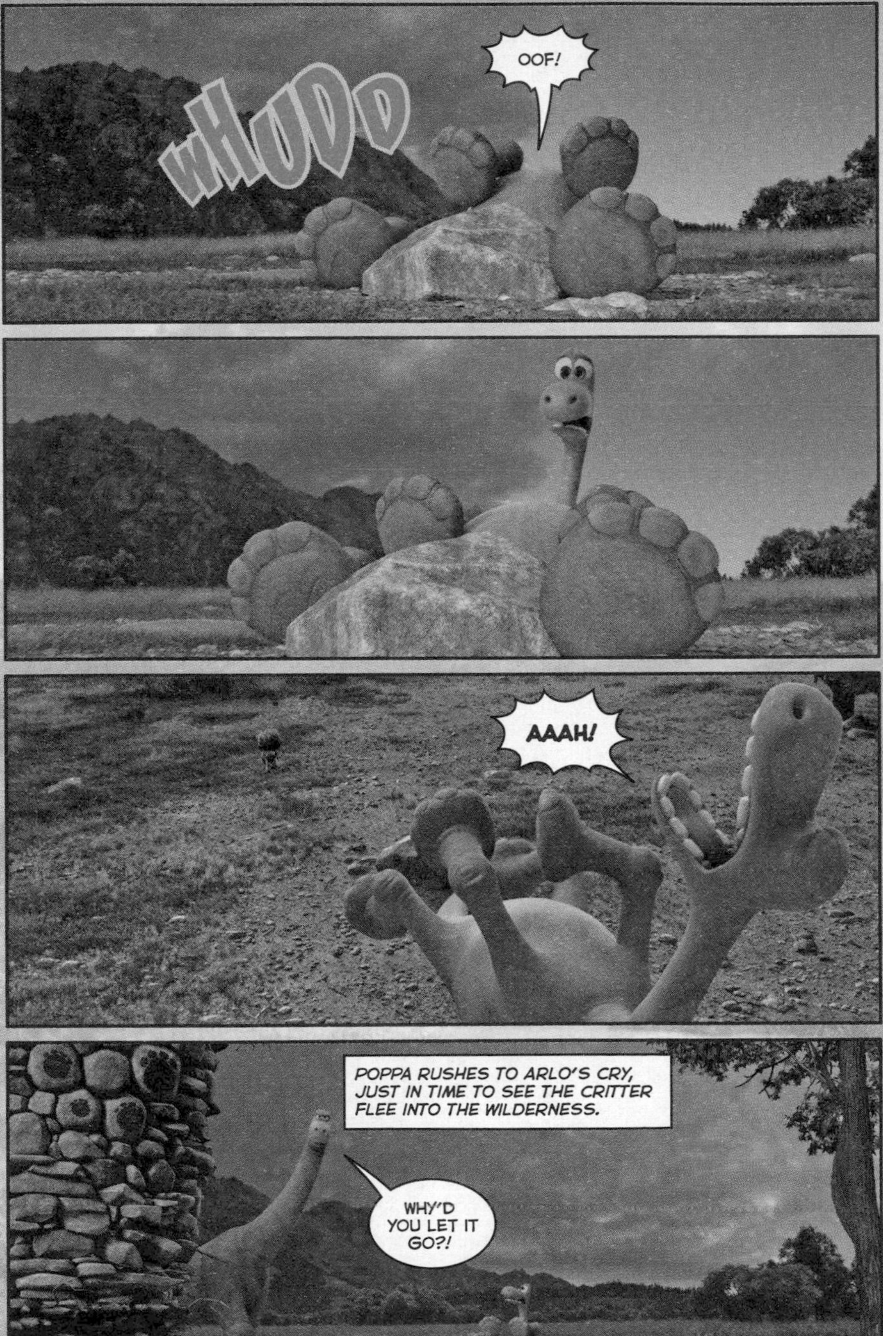
WHUDD
OOF!
AAAH!
POPPA RUSHES TO ARLO'S CRY, JUST IN TIME TO SEE THE CRITTER FLEE INTO THE WILDERNESS.
WHY'D YOU LET IT GO?!

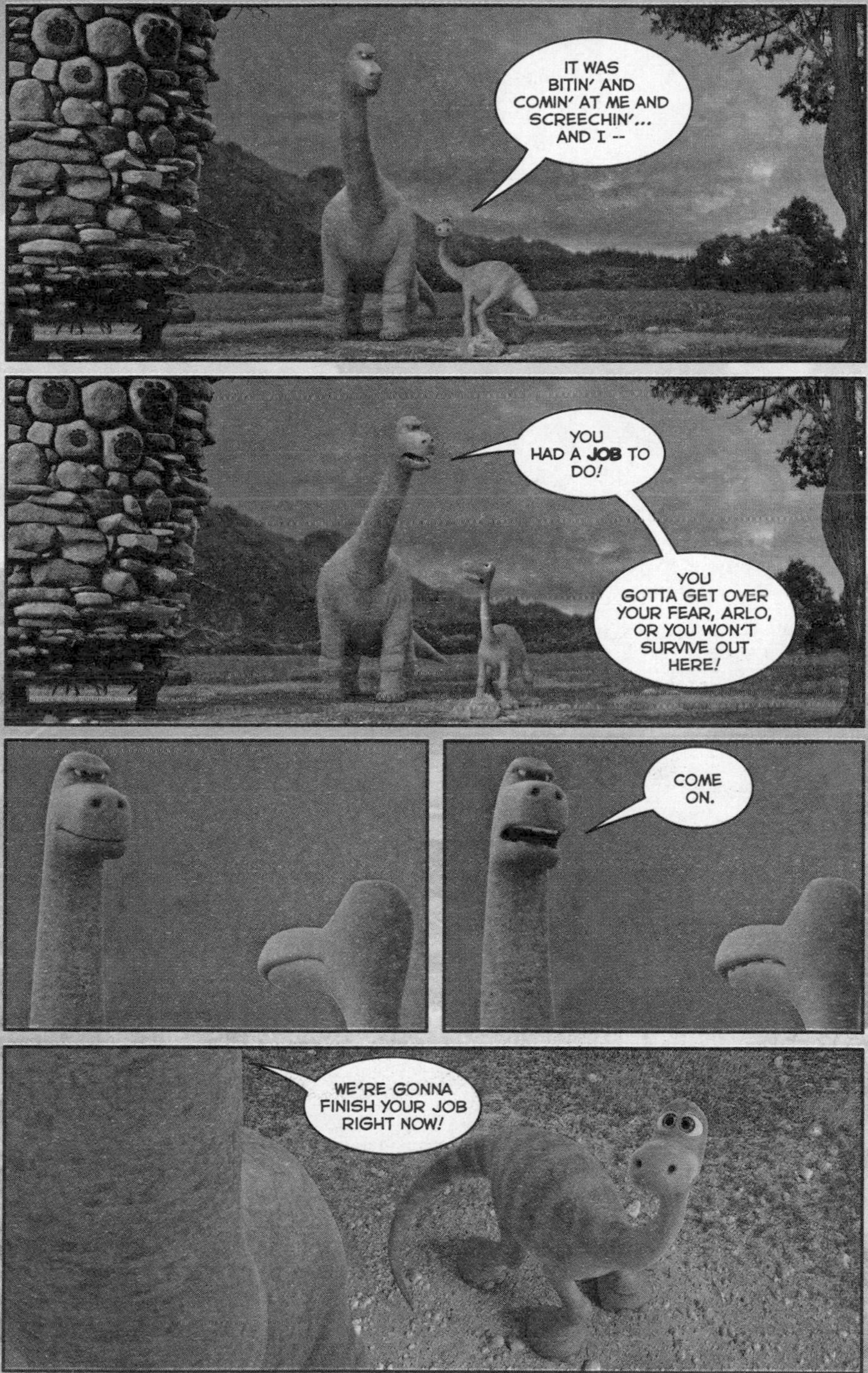
IT WAS BITIN' AND COMIN' AT ME AND SCREECHIN'... AND I --
YOU HAD A JOB TO DO!
YOU GOTTA GET OVER YOUR FEAR, ARLO, OR YOU WON'T SURVIVE OUT HERE!
COME ON.
WE'RE GONNA FINISH YOUR JOB RIGHT NOW!

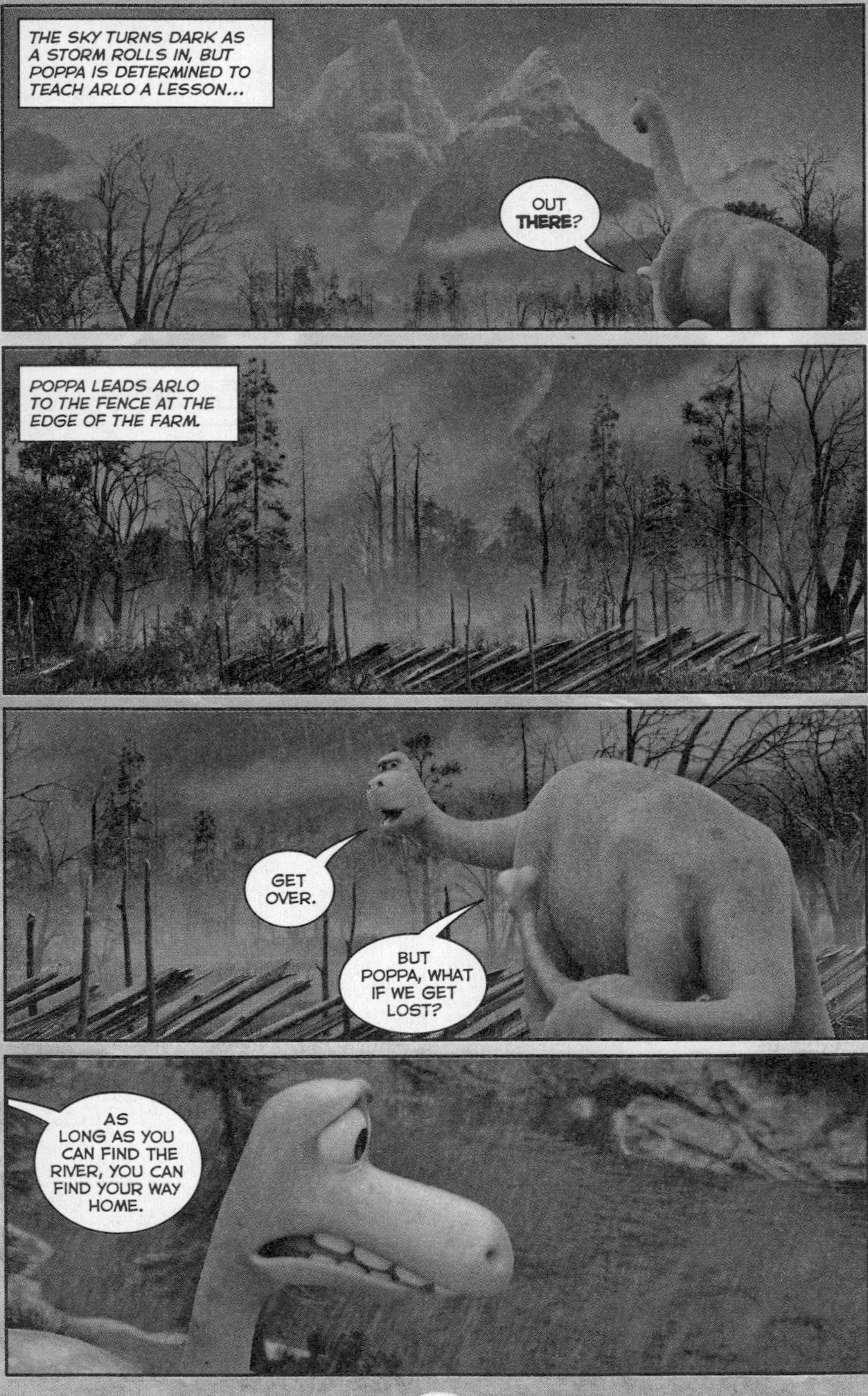
THE SKY TURNS DARK AS A STORM ROLLS IN, BUT POPPA IS DETERMINED TO TEACH ARLO A LESSON...
OUT THERE?
POPPA LEADS ARLO TO THE FENCE AT THE EDGE OF THE FARM.
GET OVER.
BUT POPPA, WHAT IF WE GET LOST?
AS LONG AS YOU CAN FIND THE RIVER, YOU CAN FIND YOUR WAY HOME.

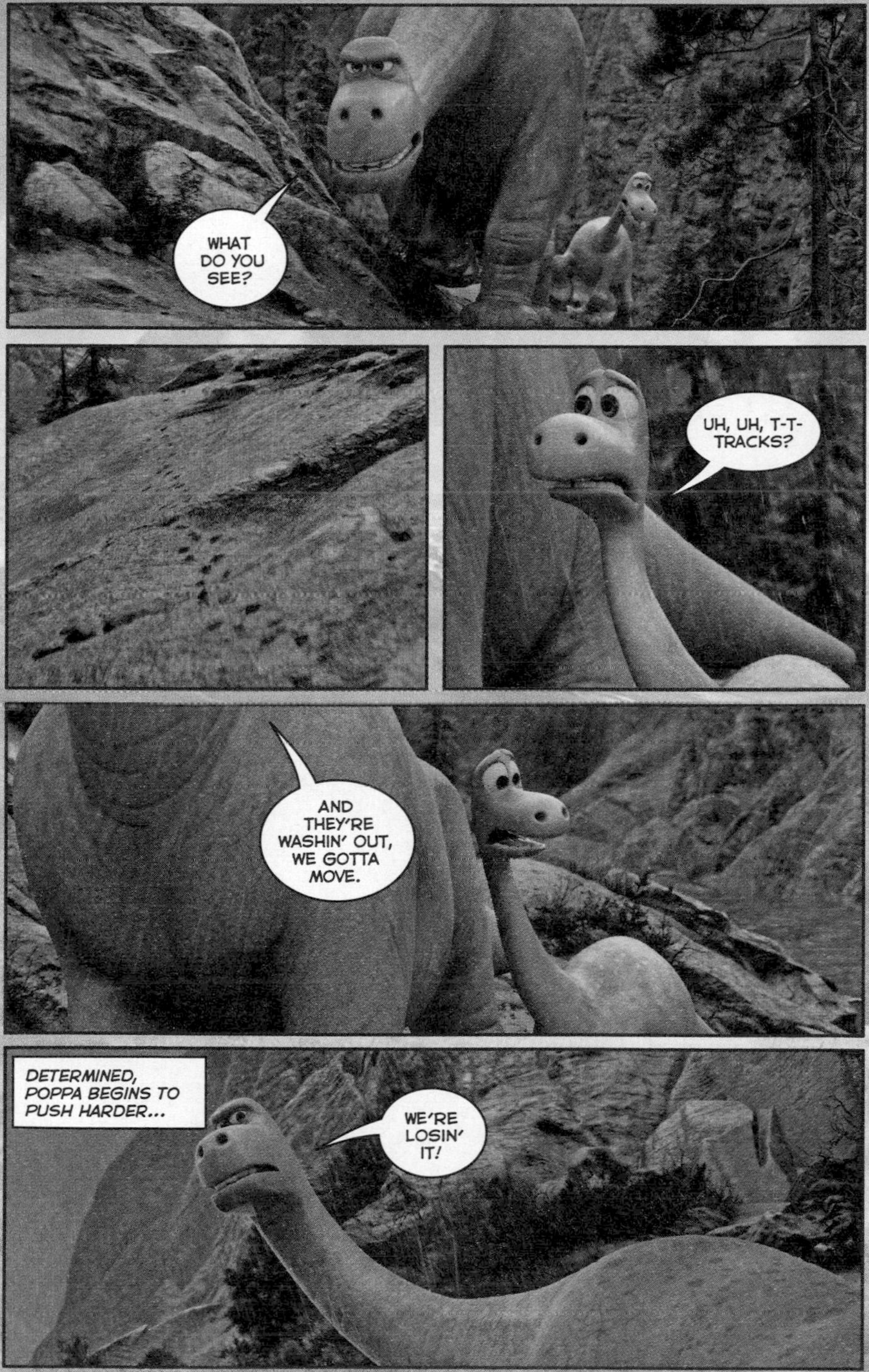
WHAT DO YOU SEE?
UH, UH, T-T-TRACKS?
AND THEY'RE WASHIN' OUT, WE GOTTA MOVE.
DETERMINED, POPPA BEGINS TO PUSH HARDER...
WE'RE LOSIN' IT!

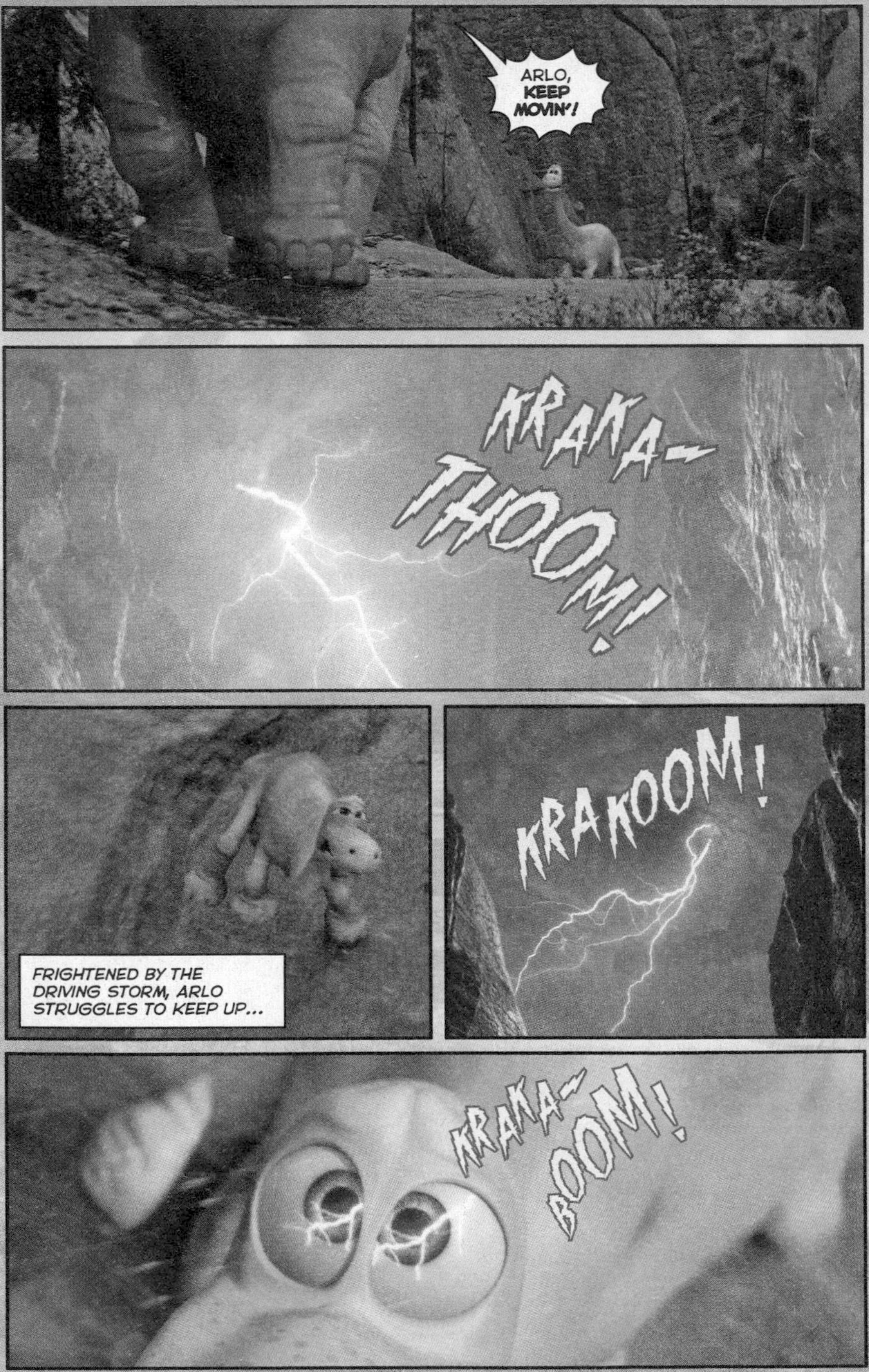
ARLO, KEEP MOVIN'!
KRAKA-THOOM!
FRIGHTENED BY THE DRIVING STORM, ARLO STRUGGLES TO KEEP UP...
KRAKOOM!
KRAKA-BOOM!

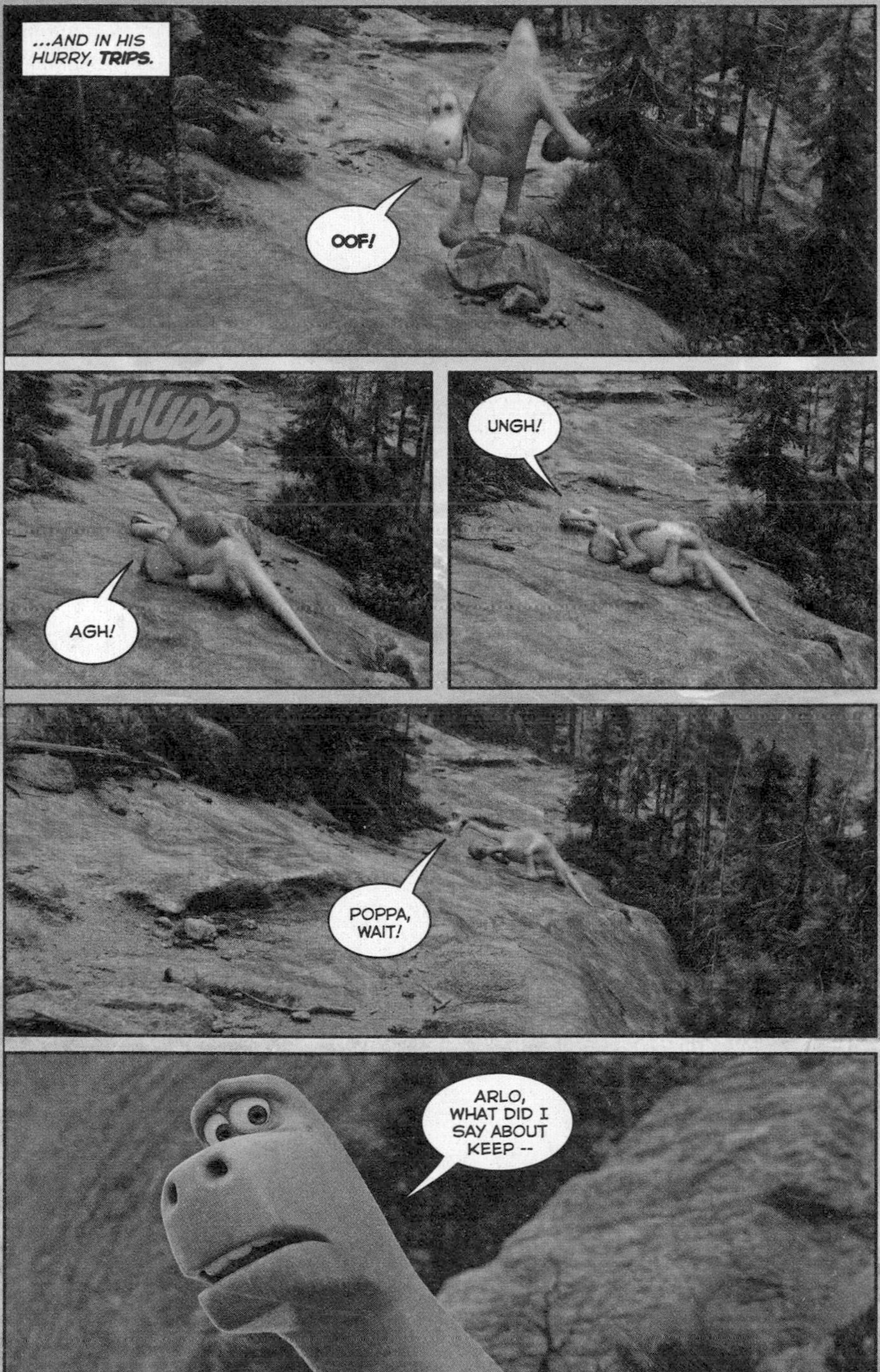
...AND IN HIS HURRY, **TRIPS**.
OOF!
THUDD
AGH!
UNGH!
POPPA, WAIT!
ARLO, WHAT DID I SAY ABOUT KEEP --

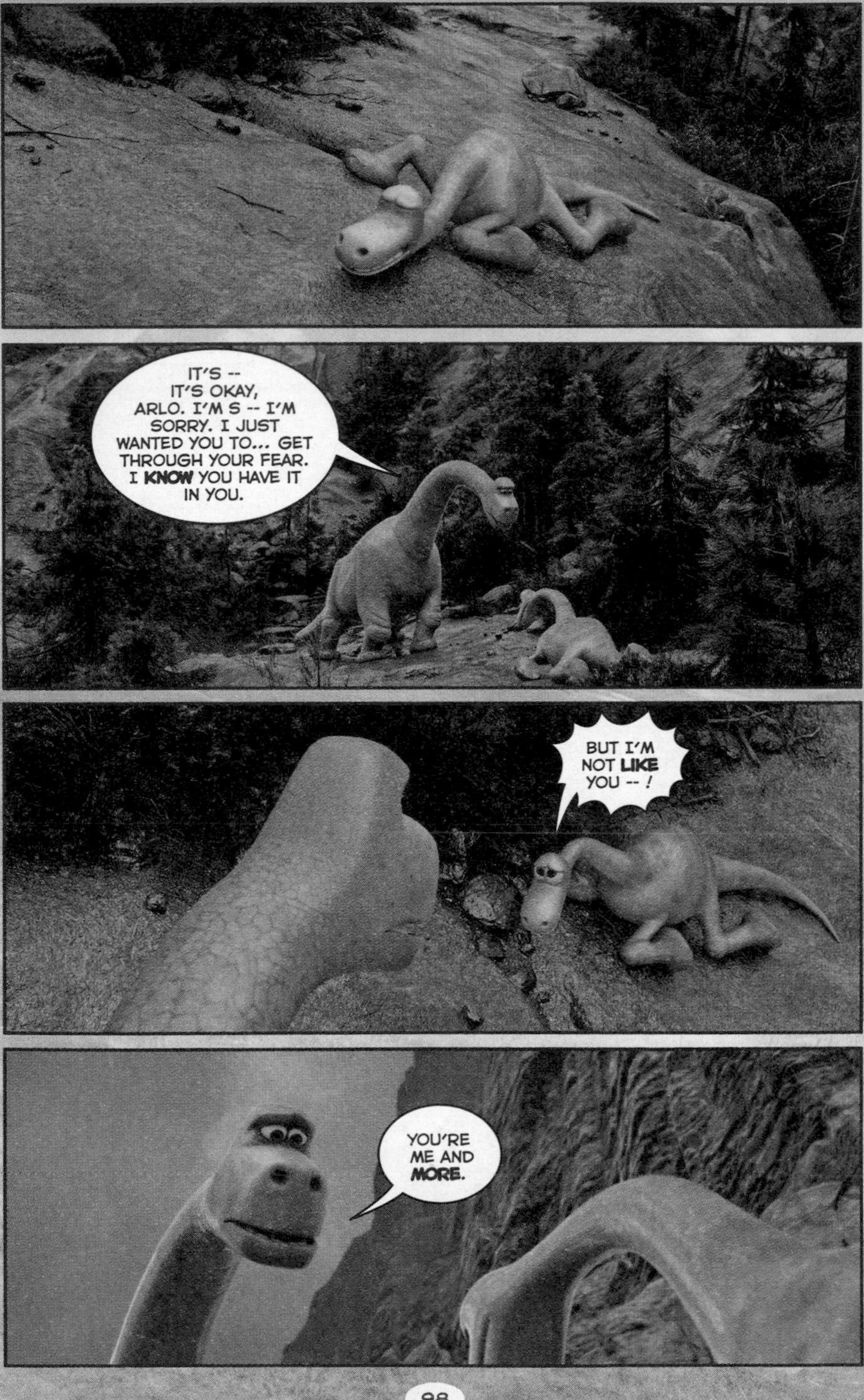
IT'S -- IT'S OKAY, ARLO. I'M S -- I'M SORRY. I JUST WANTED YOU TO... GET THROUGH YOUR FEAR. I **KNOW** YOU HAVE IT IN YOU.
BUT I'M NOT **LIKE** YOU -- !
YOU'RE ME AND **MORE**.

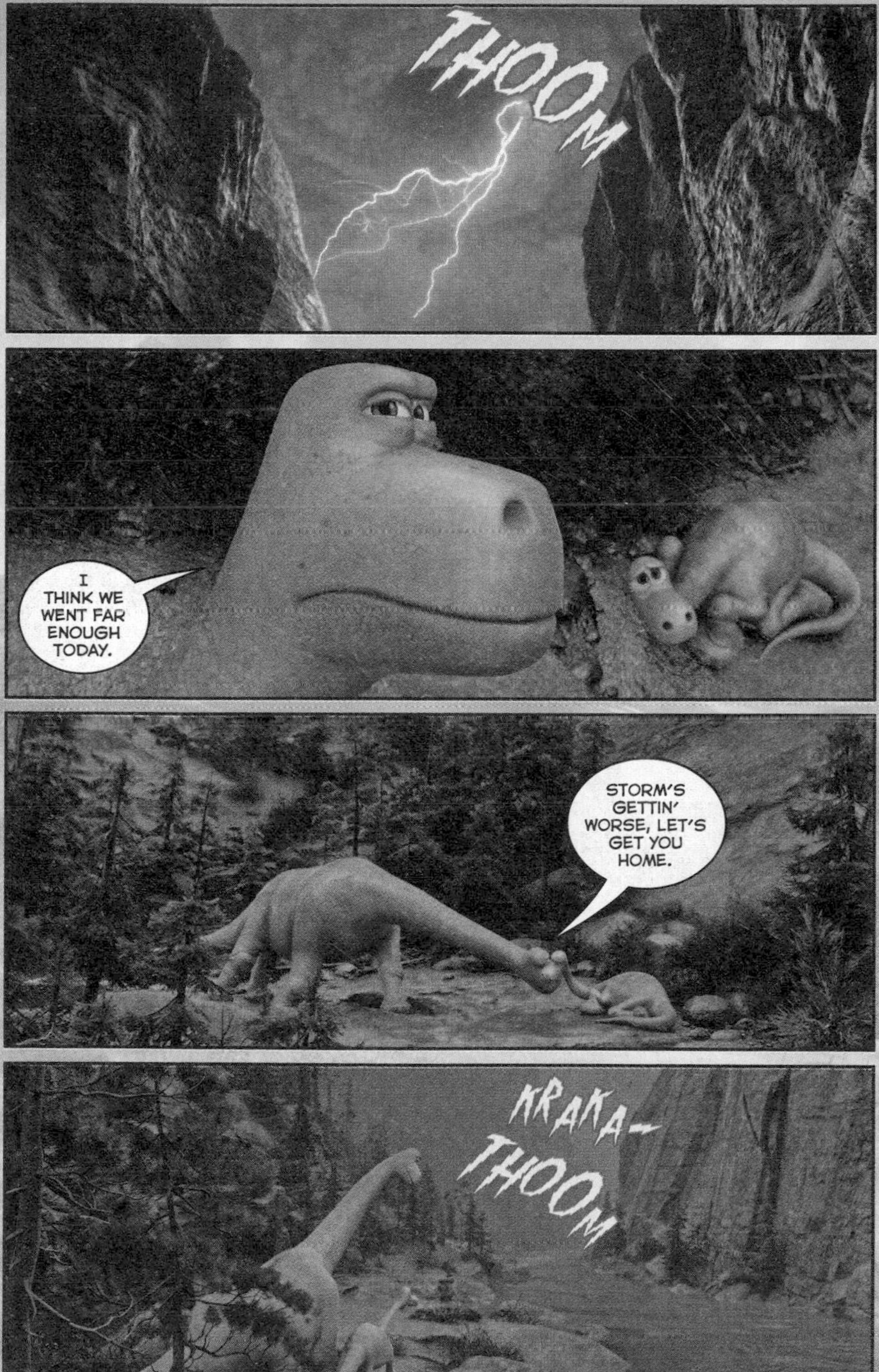
THOOM
I THINK WE WENT FAR ENOUGH TODAY.
STORM'S GETTIN' WORSE, LET'S GET YOU HOME.
KRAKA-THOOM

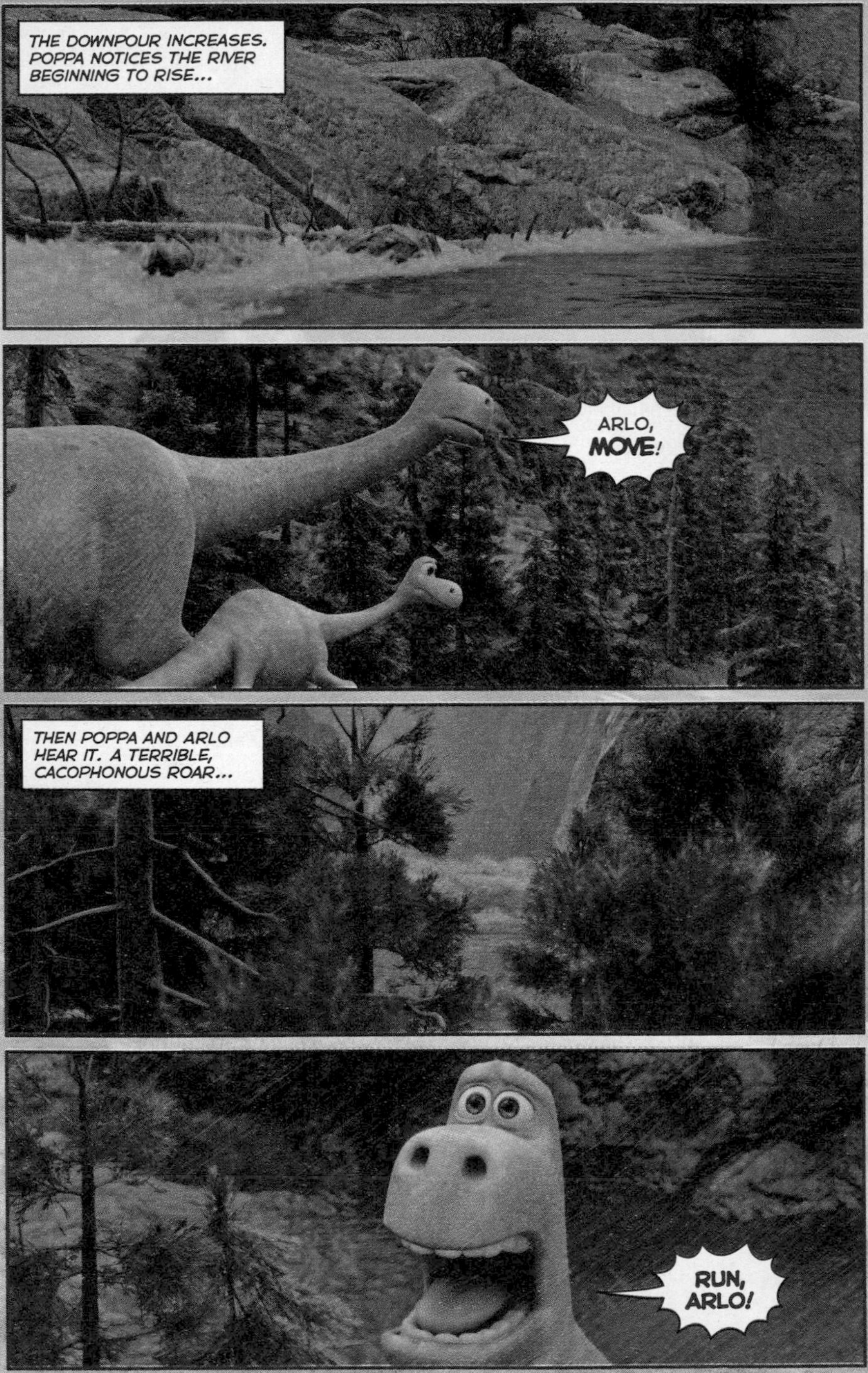
THE DOWNPOUR INCREASES. POPPA NOTICES THE RIVER BEGINNING TO RISE...
ARLO, MOVE!
THEN POPPA AND ARLO HEAR IT. A TERRIBLE, CACOPHONOUS ROAR...
RUN, ARLO!

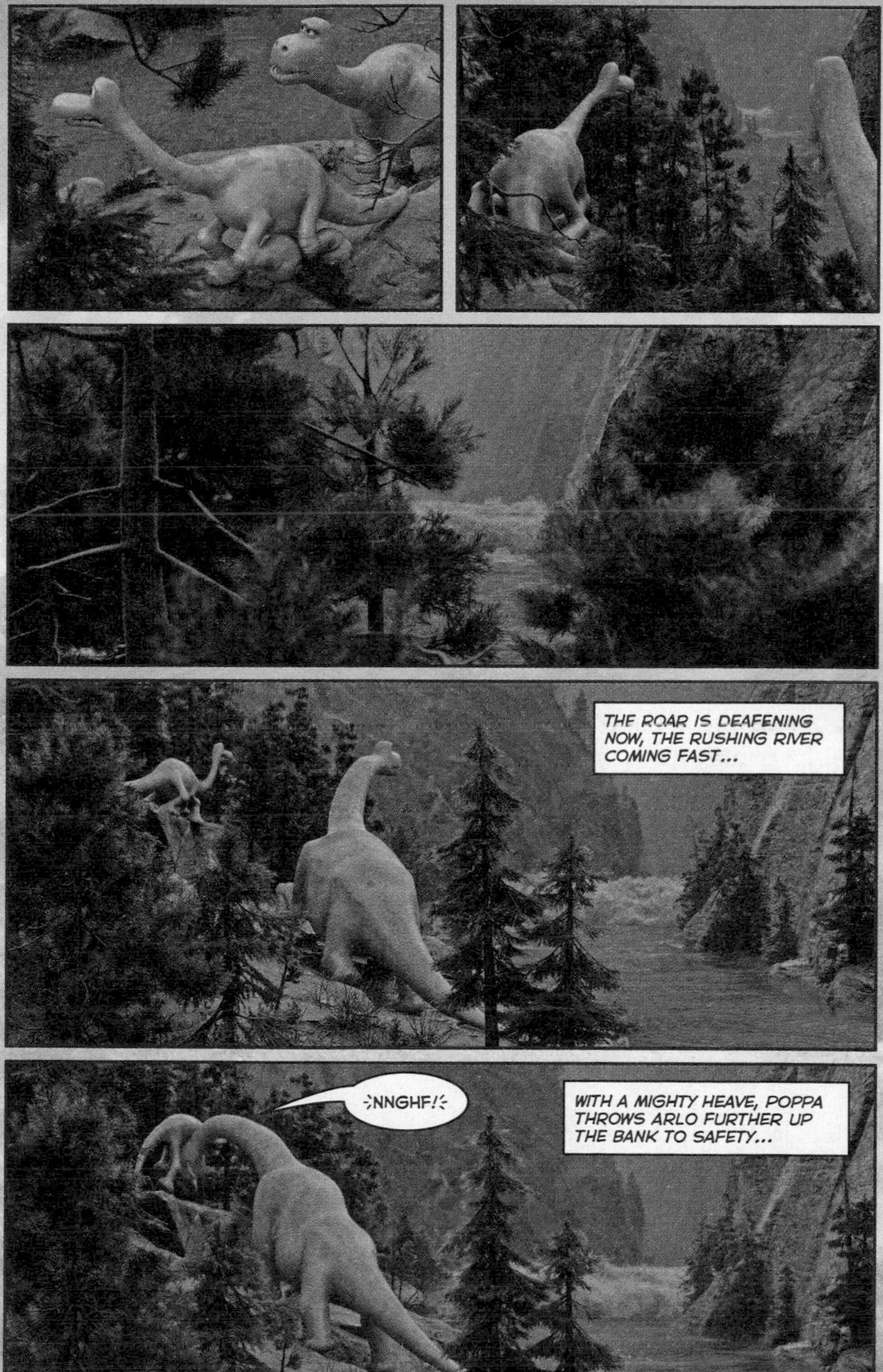
THE ROAR IS DEAFENING NOW, THE RUSHING RIVER COMING FAST...
NNGHF!
WITH A MIGHTY HEAVE, POPPA THROWS ARLO FURTHER UP THE BANK TO SAFETY...

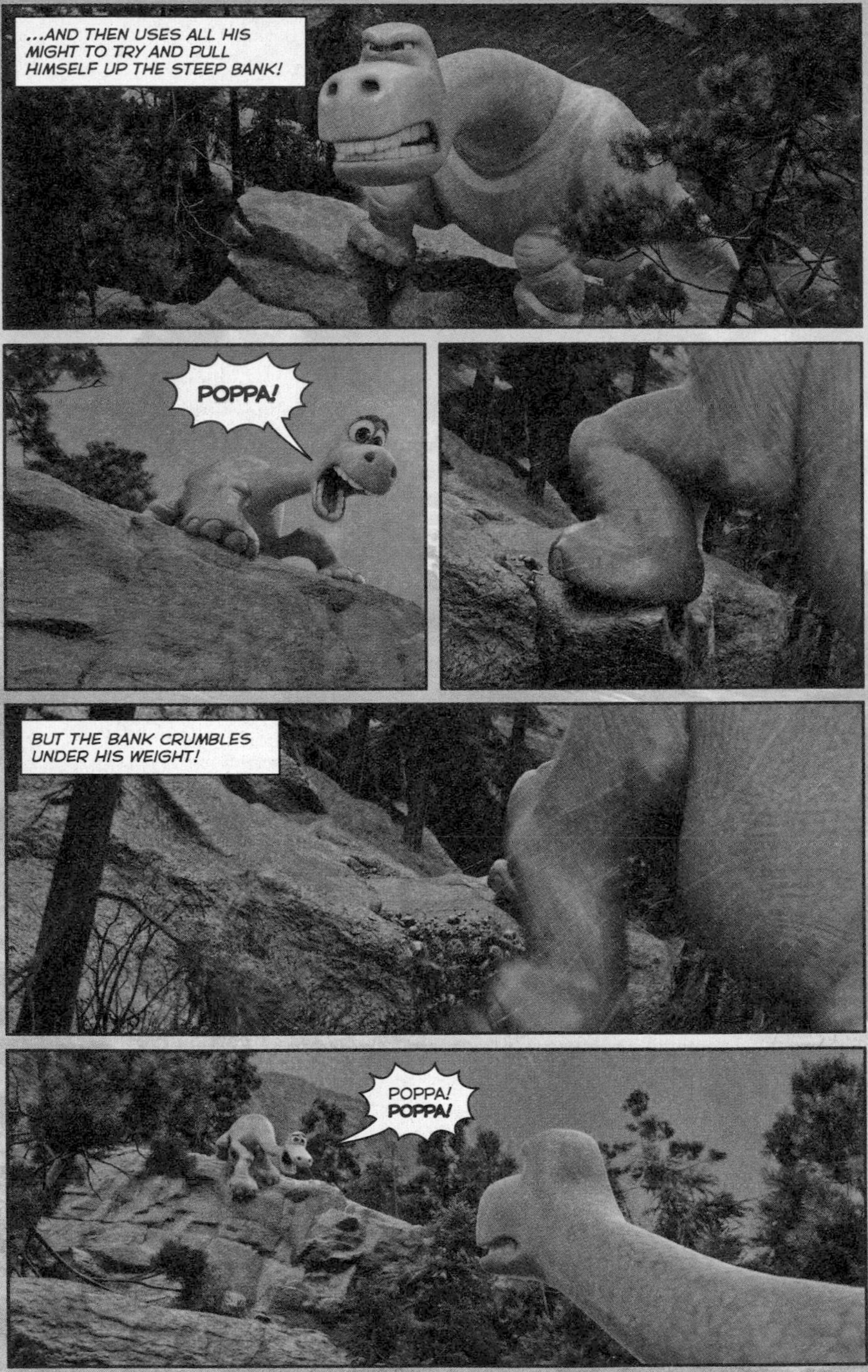
...AND THEN USES ALL HIS MIGHT TO TRY AND PULL HIMSELF UP THE STEEP BANK!
POPPA!
BUT THE BANK CRUMBLES UNDER HIS WEIGHT!
POPPA! POPPA!

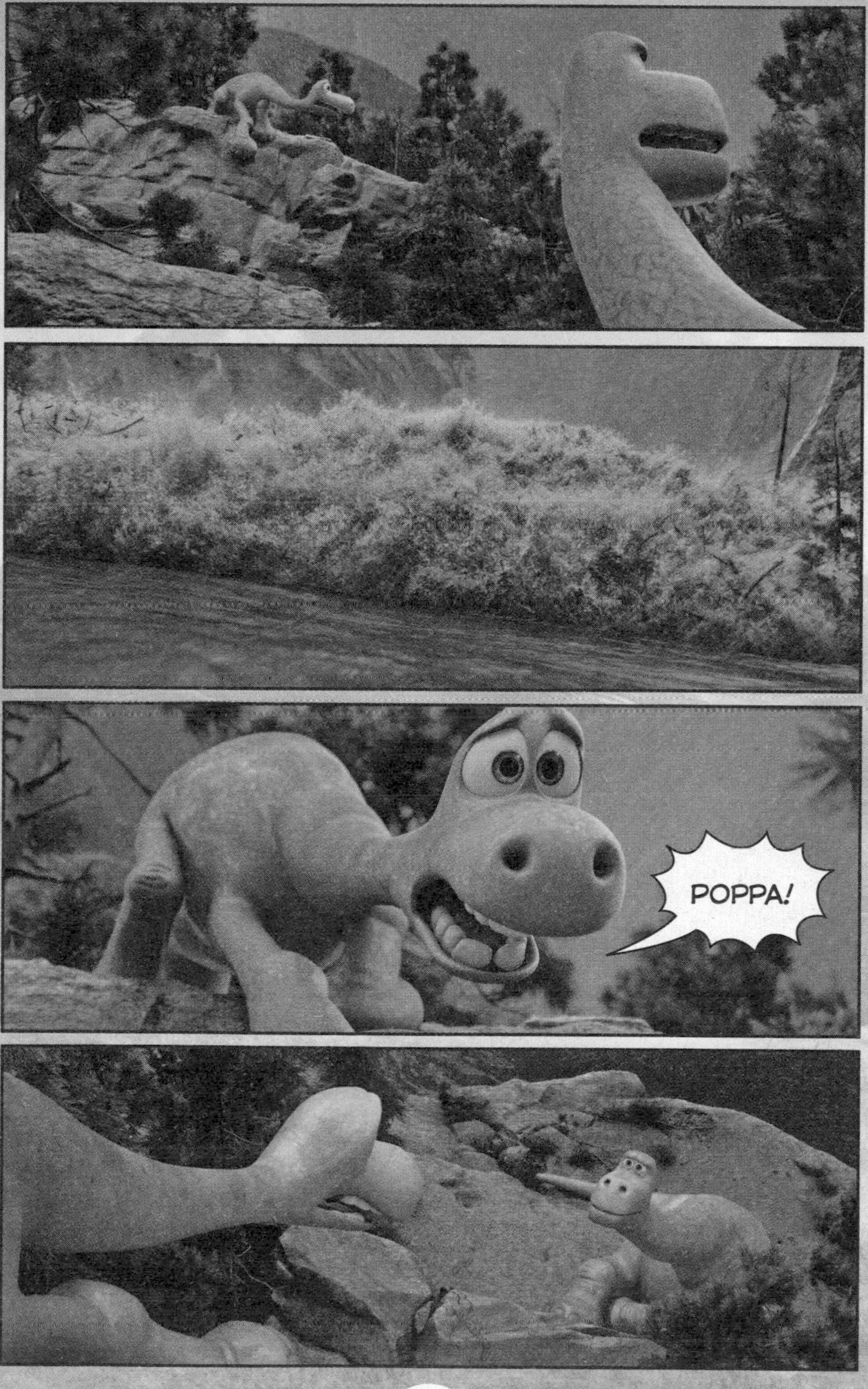
POPPA!

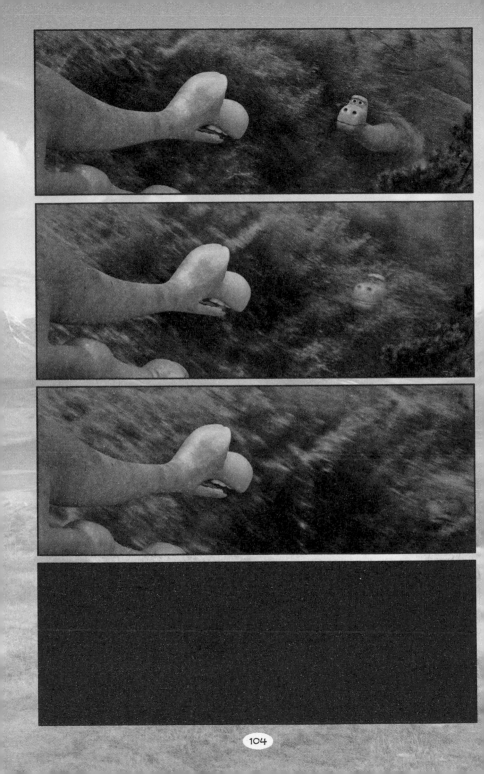

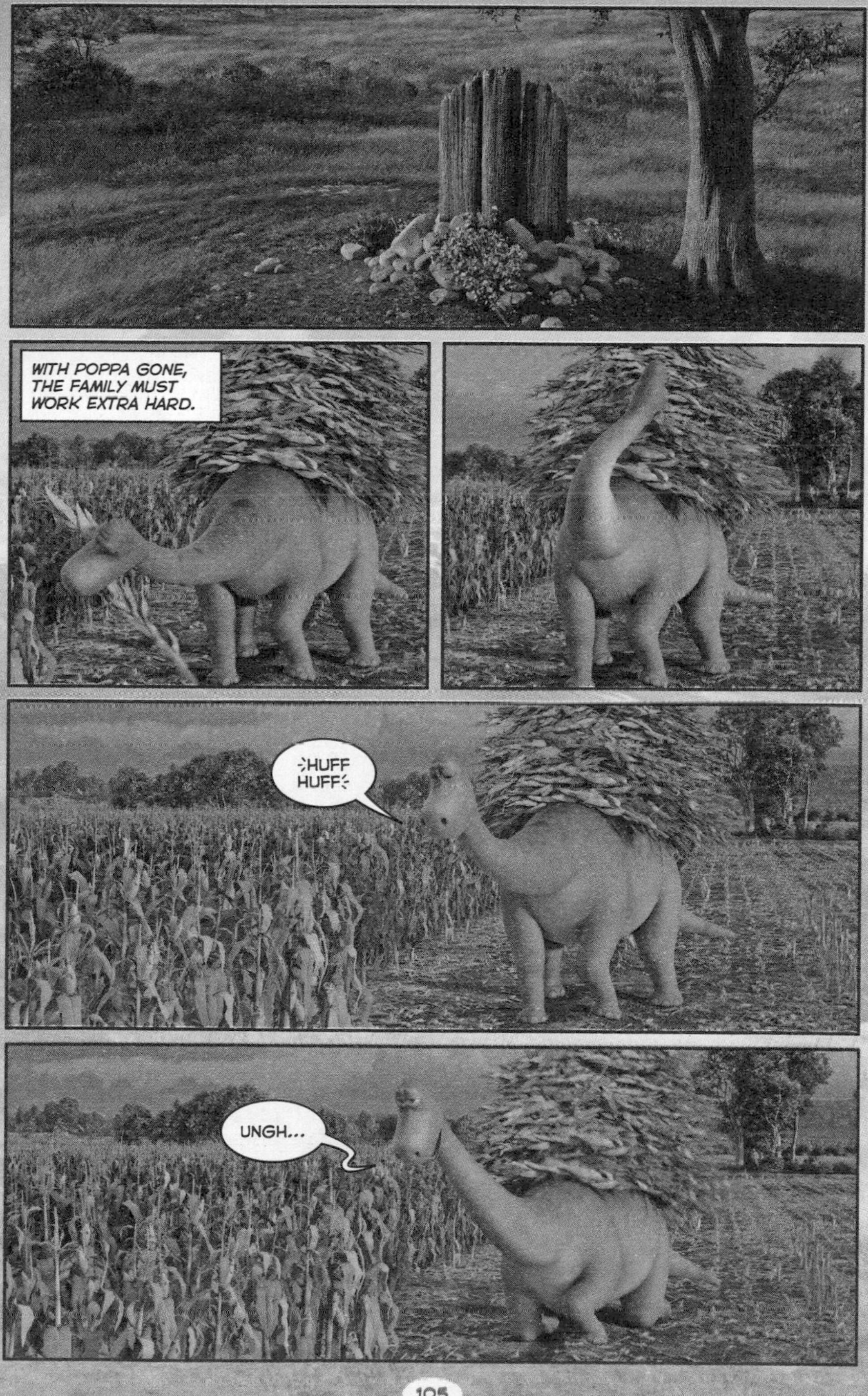
WITH POPPA GONE, THE FAMILY MUST WORK EXTRA HARD.
HUFF HUFF
UNGH...

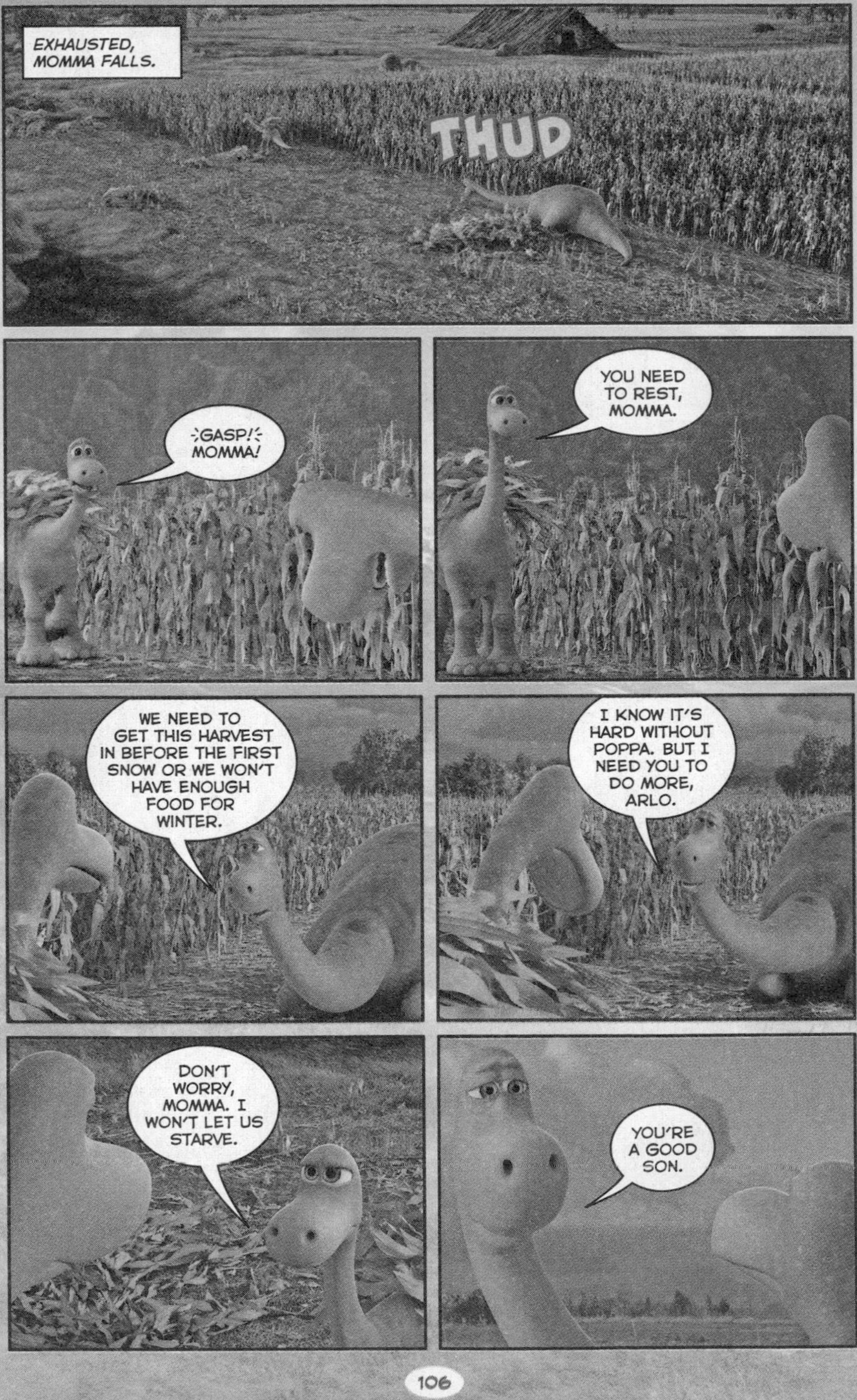
EXHAUSTED, MOMMA FALLS.
THUD
¡GASP!¡ MOMMA!
YOU NEED TO REST, MOMMA.
WE NEED TO GET THIS HARVEST IN BEFORE THE FIRST SNOW OR WE WON'T HAVE ENOUGH FOOD FOR WINTER.
I KNOW IT'S HARD WITHOUT POPPA. BUT I NEED YOU TO DO MORE, ARLO.
DON'T WORRY, MOMMA. I WON'T LET US STARVE.
YOU'RE A GOOD SON.

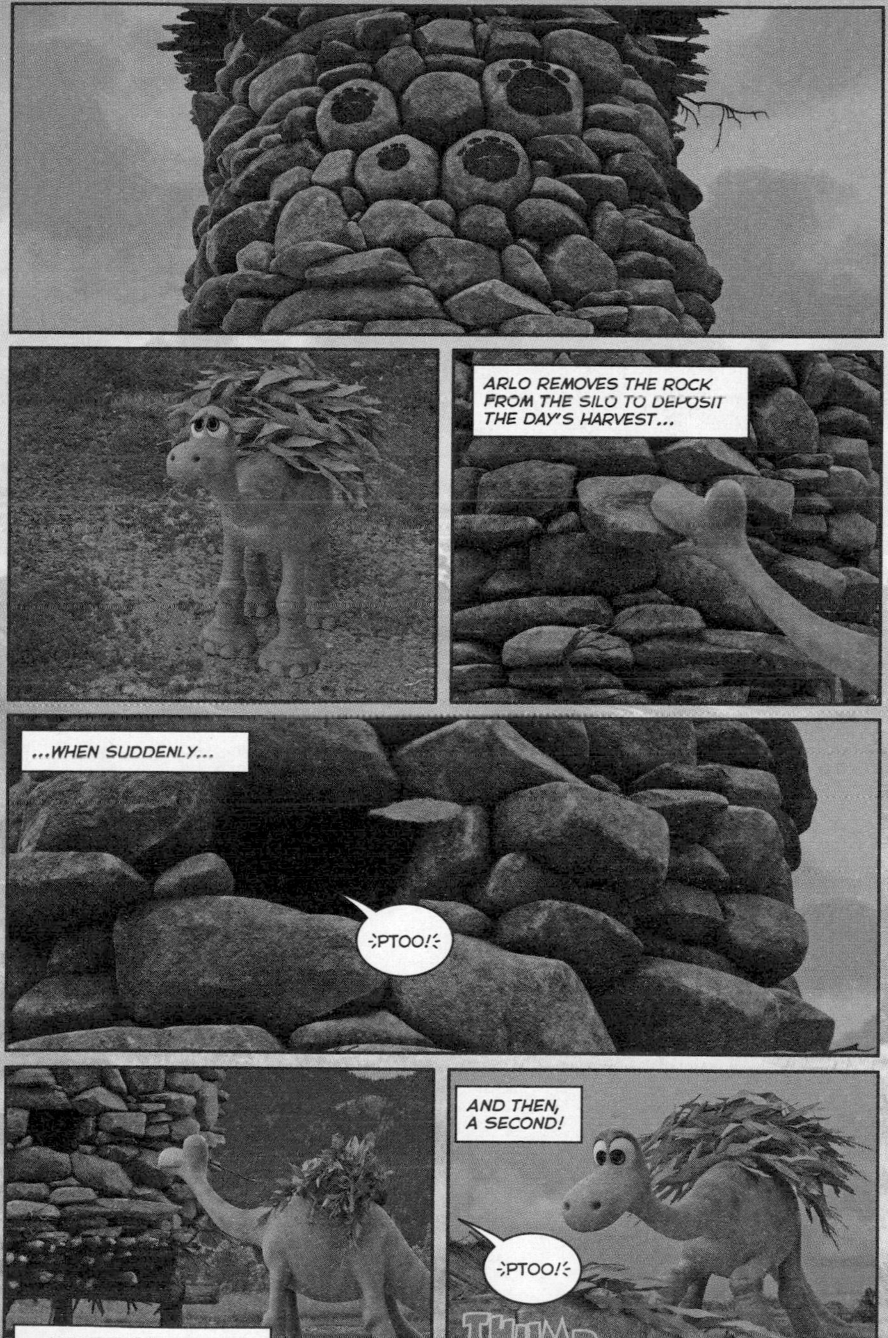
ARLO REMOVES THE ROCK FROM THE SILO TO DEPOSIT THE DAY'S HARVEST...
...WHEN SUDDENLY...
PTOO!
...A HALF-EATEN PIECE OF CORN FLIES OUT!
AND THEN, A SECOND!
PTOO!
THUMP

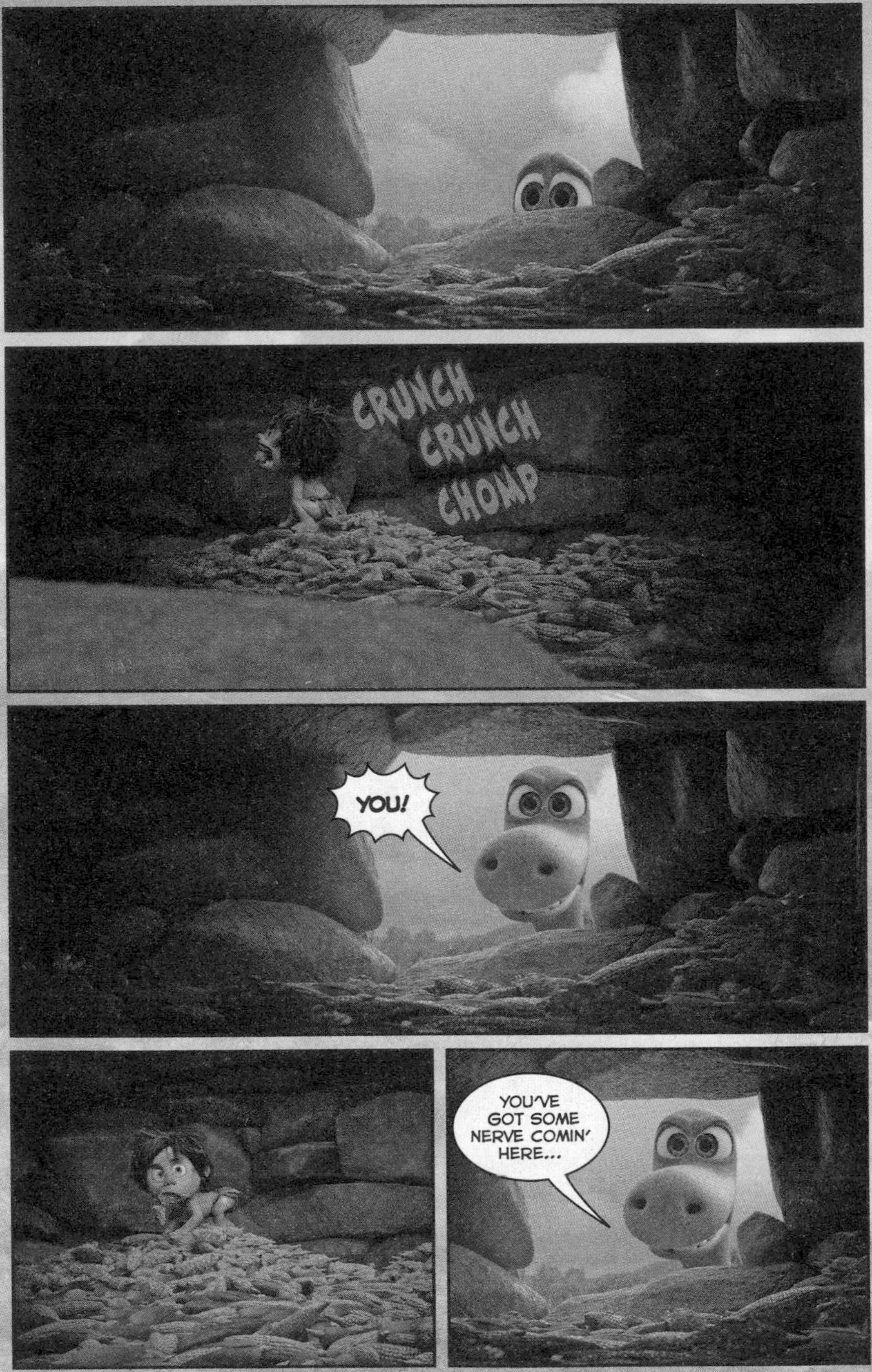
CRUNCH
CRUNCH
CHOMP
YOU!
YOU'VE GOT SOME NERVE COMIN' HERE...

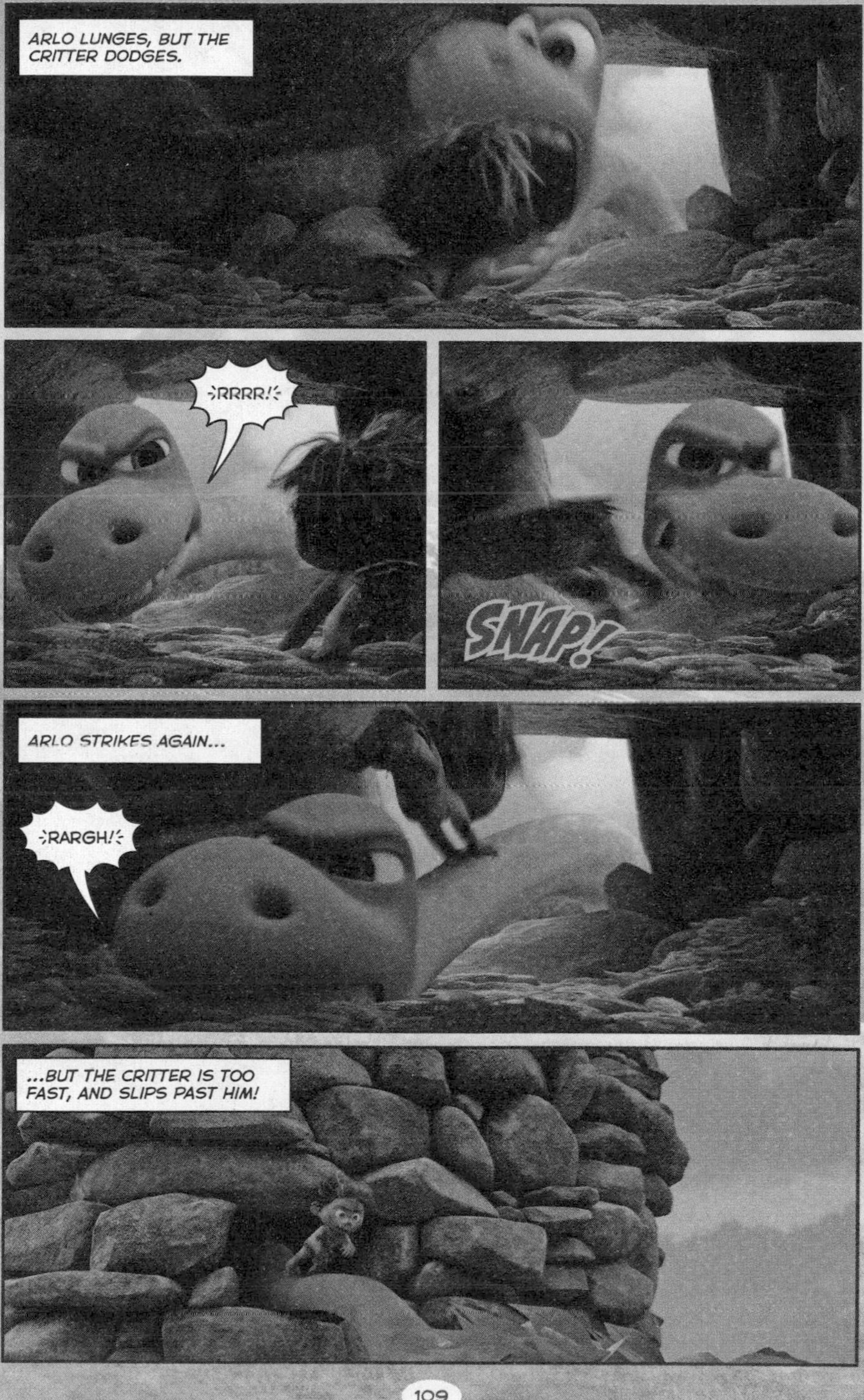
ARLO LUNGES, BUT THE CRITTER DODGES.
RRRR!
SNAP!
ARLO STRIKES AGAIN...
RARGH!
...BUT THE CRITTER IS TOO FAST, AND SLIPS PAST HIM!

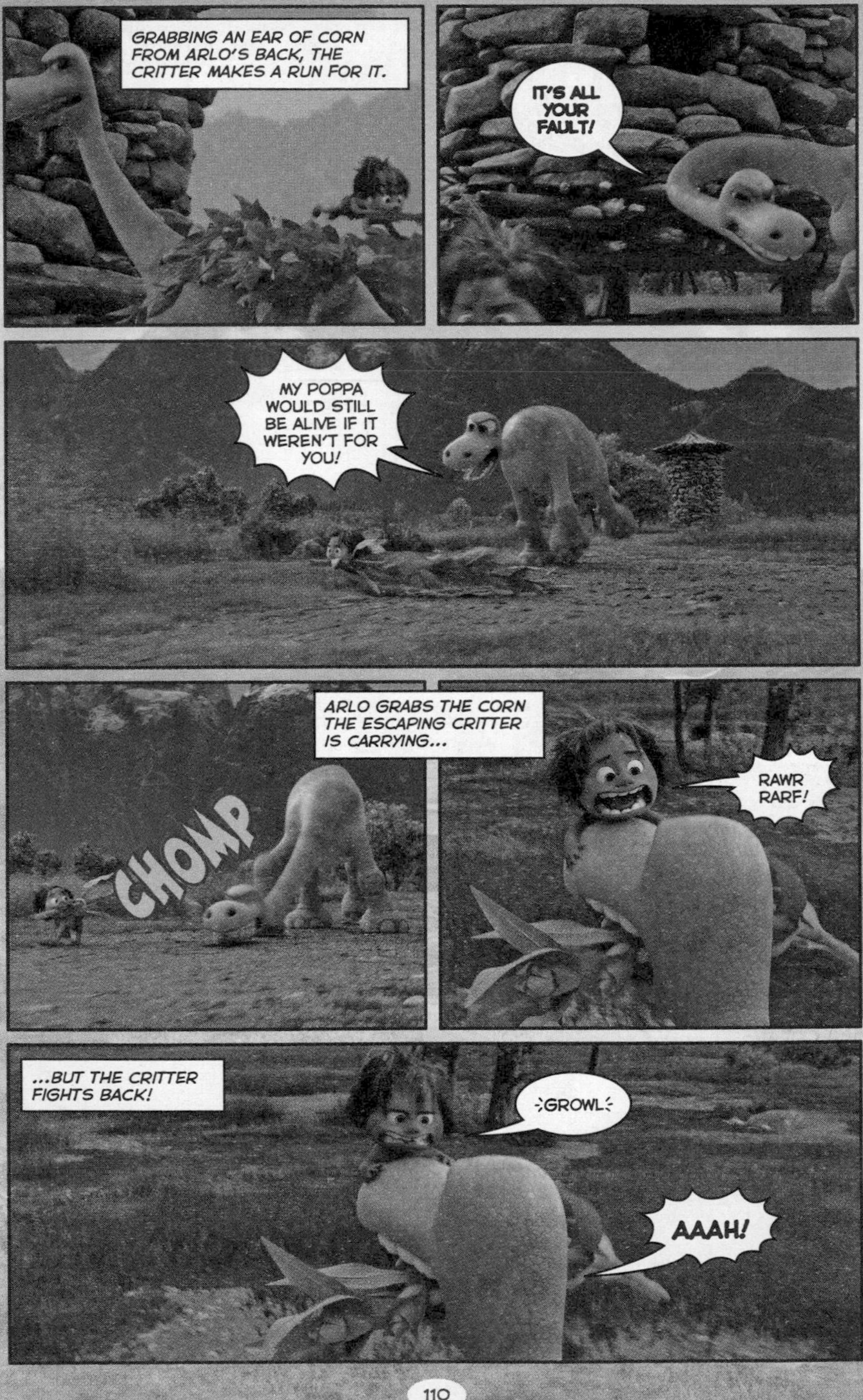
GRABBING AN EAR OF CORN FROM ARLO'S BACK, THE CRITTER MAKES A RUN FOR IT.
IT'S ALL YOUR FAULT!
MY POPPA WOULD STILL BE ALIVE IF IT WEREN'T FOR YOU!
ARLO GRABS THE CORN THE ESCAPING CRITTER IS CARRYING...
CHOMP
RAWR RARF!
...BUT THE CRITTER FIGHTS BACK!
GROWL
AAAH!

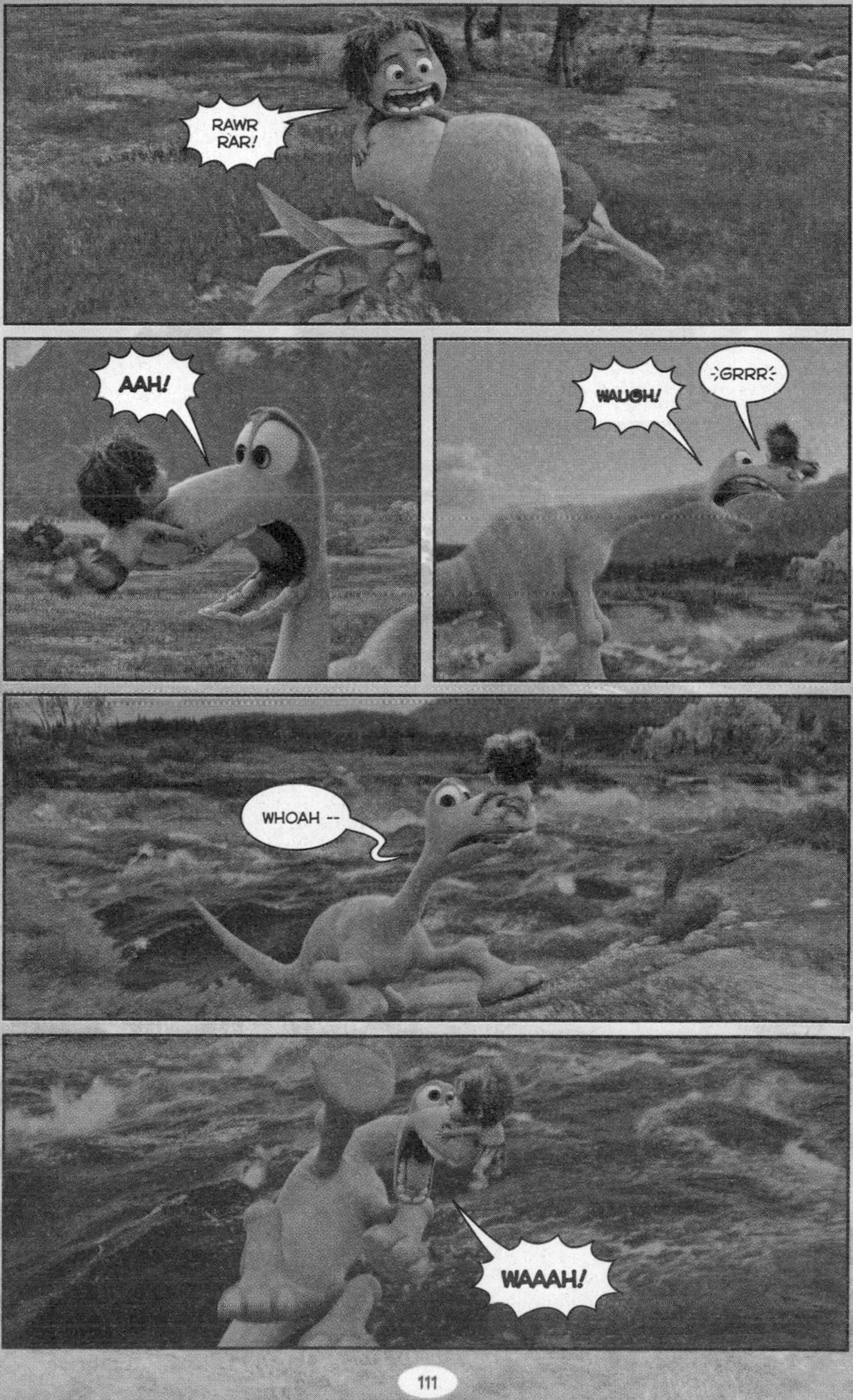
RAWR RAR!
AAH!
WAUGH!
GRRR
WHOAH --
WAAAH!

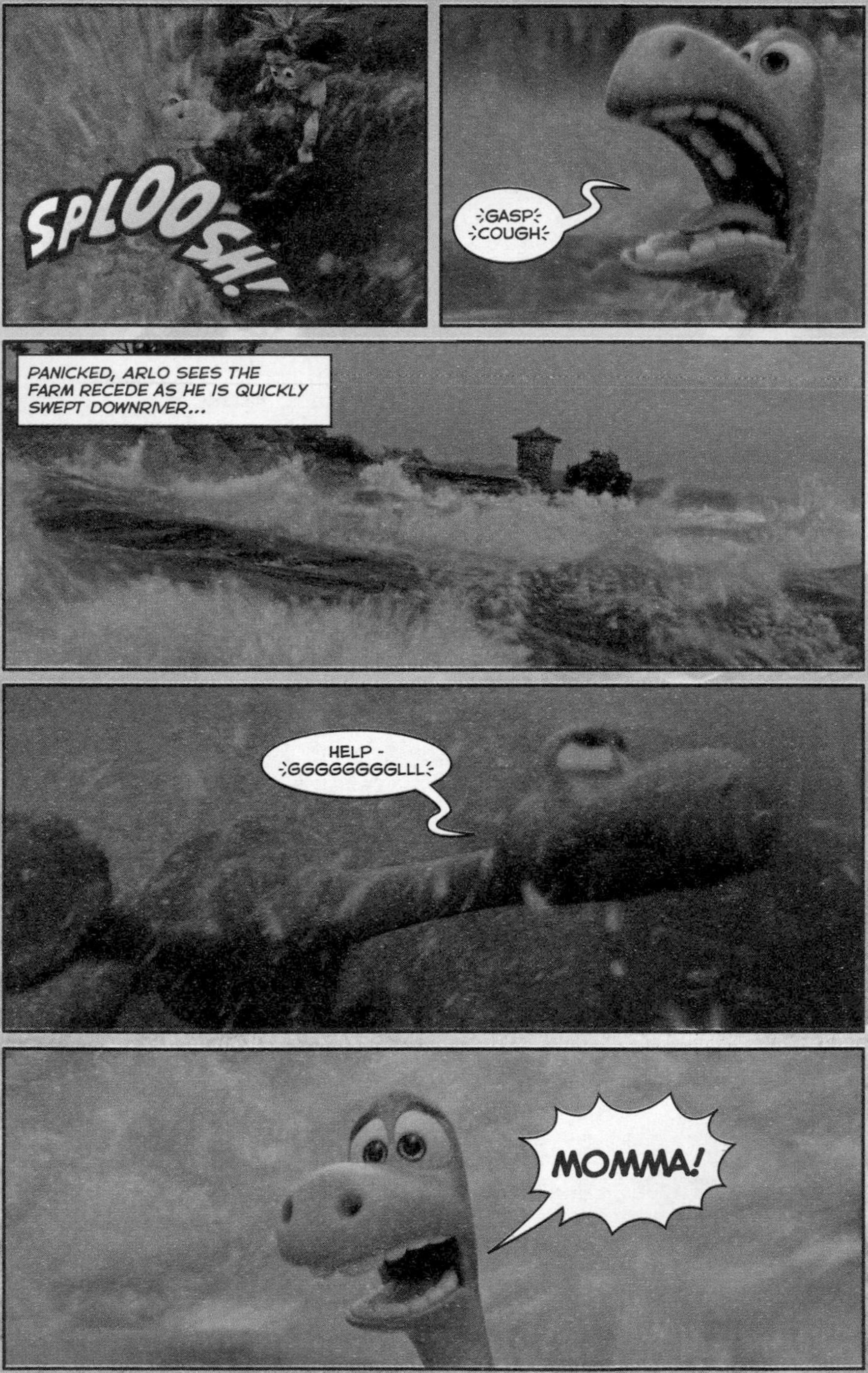
SPLOOSH!
GASP
COUGH
PANICKED, ARLO SEES THE FARM RECEDE AS HE IS QUICKLY SWEPT DOWNRIVER...
HELP -
GGGGGGGGLLL
MOMMA!

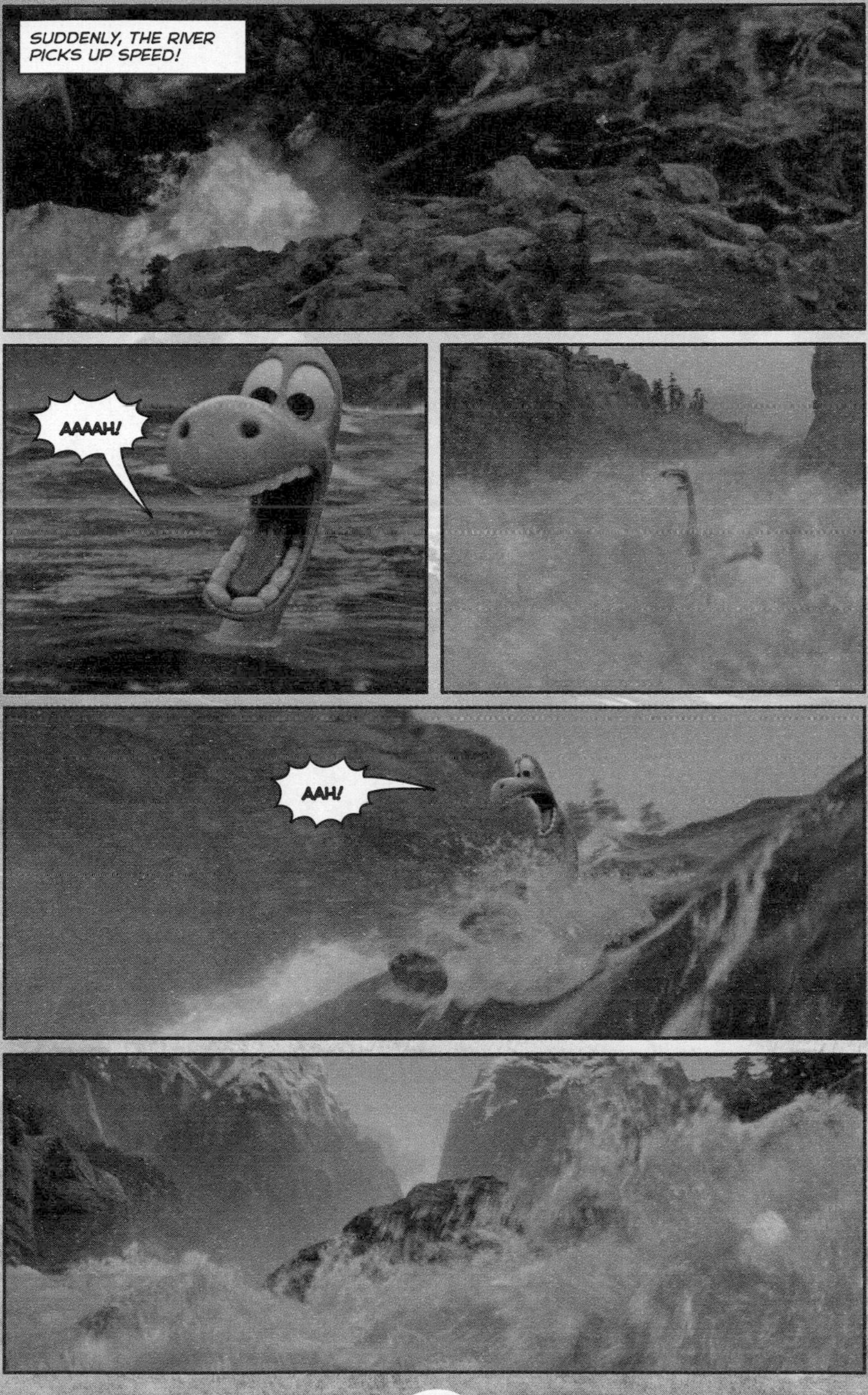
SUDDENLY, THE RIVER PICKS UP SPEED!
AAAAH!
AAH!

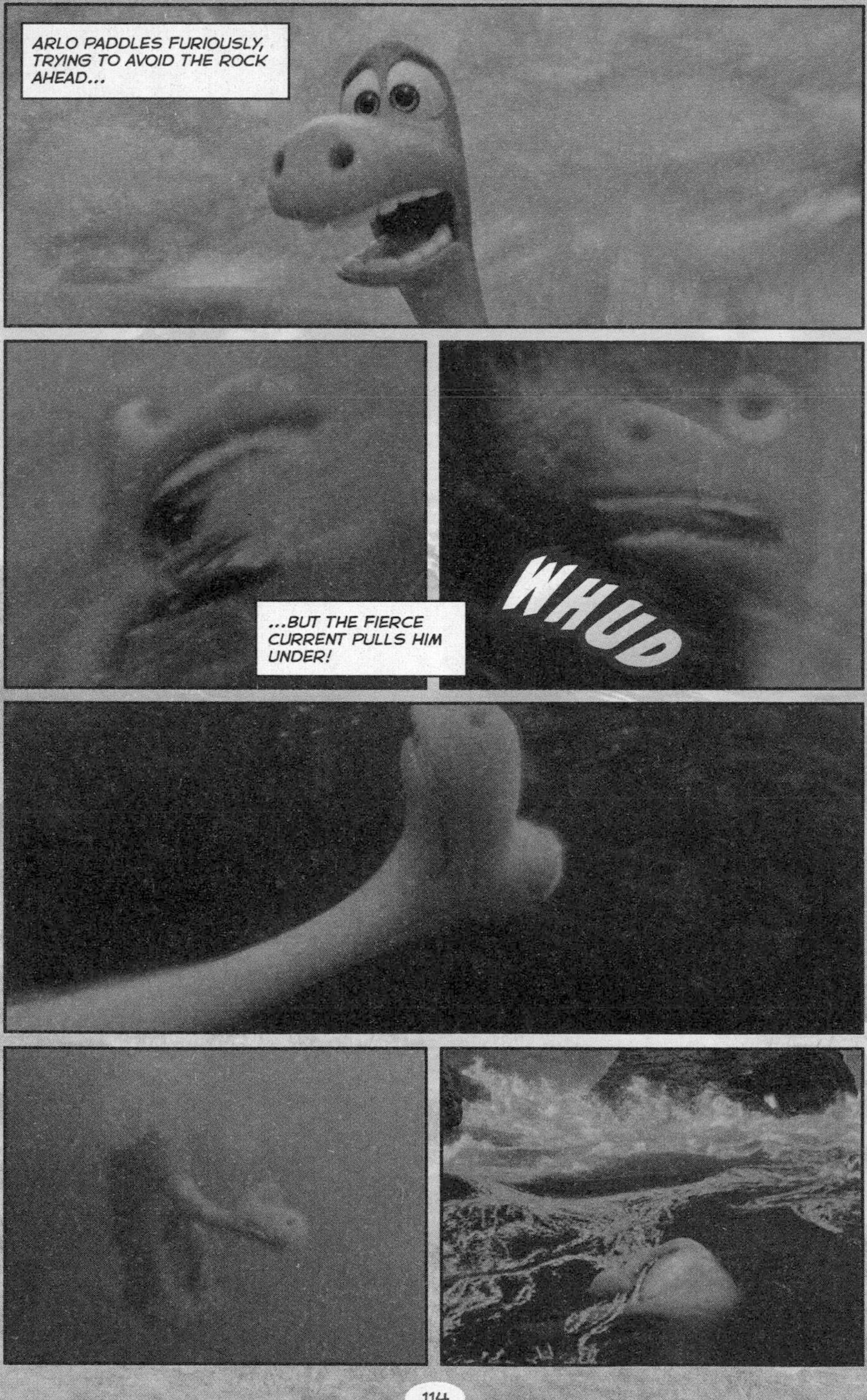
ARLO PADDLES FURIOUSLY, TRYING TO AVOID THE ROCK AHEAD...
...BUT THE FIERCE CURRENT PULLS HIM UNDER!
WHUD

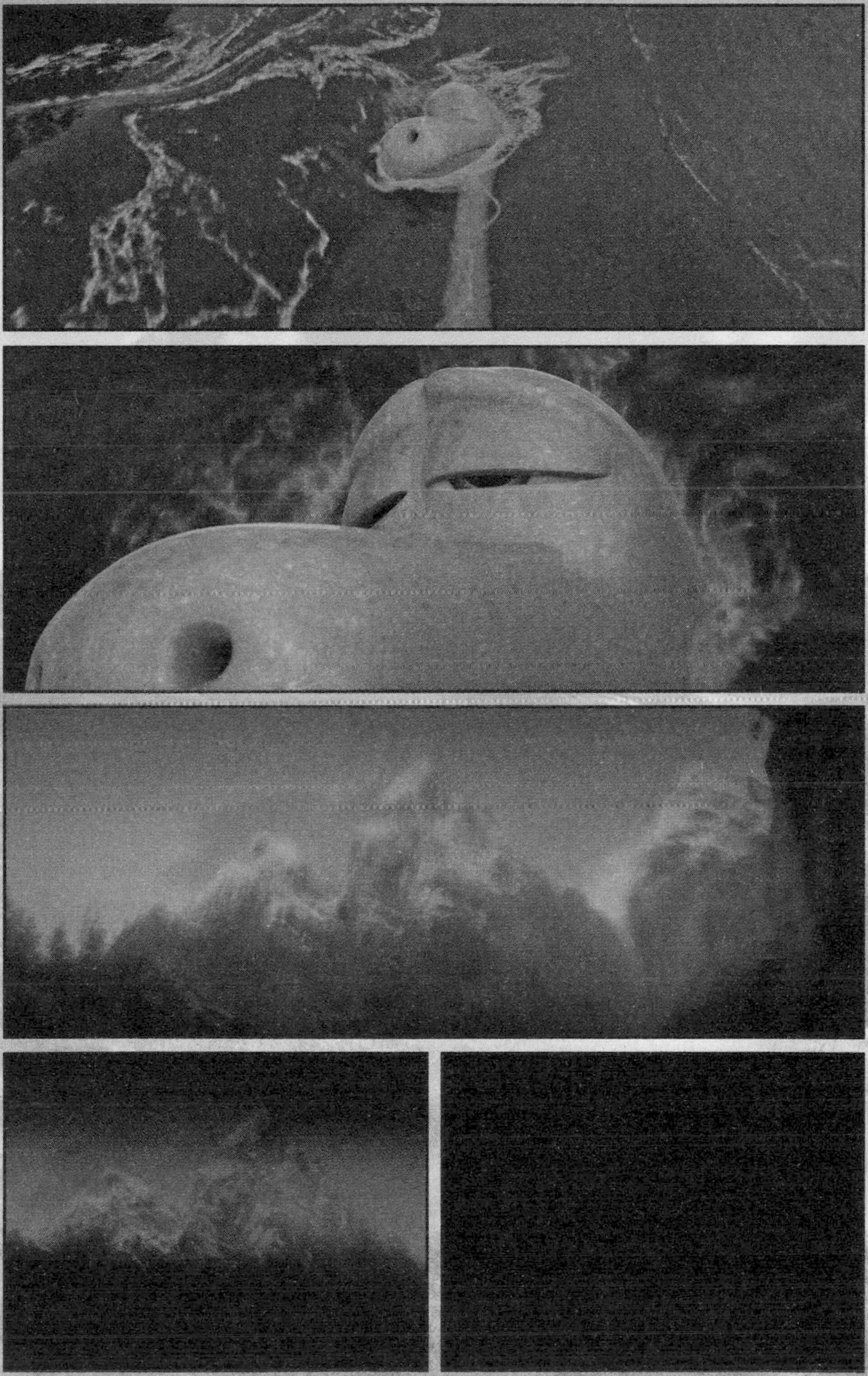

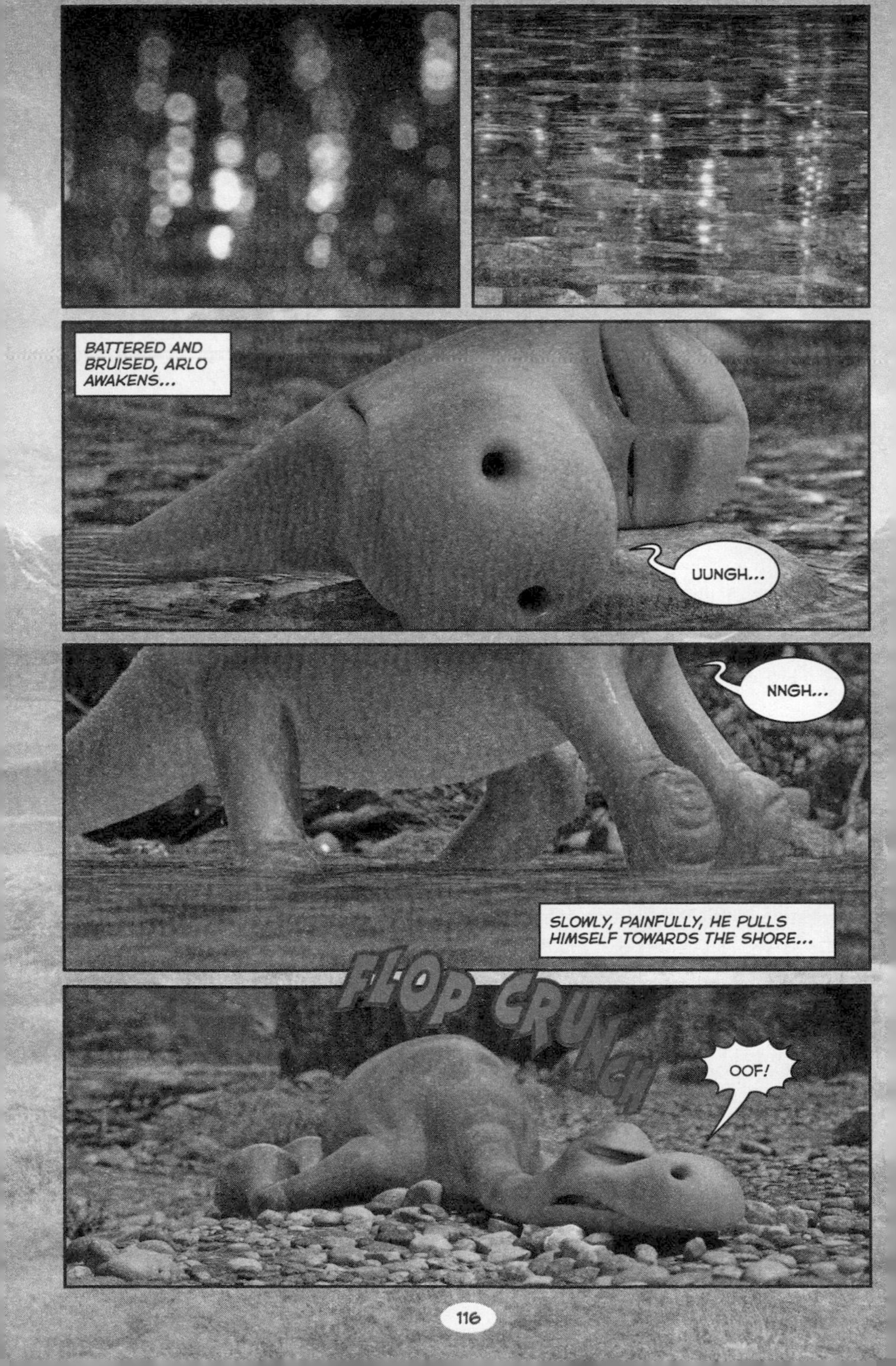
BATTERED AND BRUISED, ARLO AWAKENS...
UUNGH...
NNGH...
SLOWLY, PAINFULLY, HE PULLS HIMSELF TOWARDS THE SHORE...
FLOP CRUNCH
OOF!

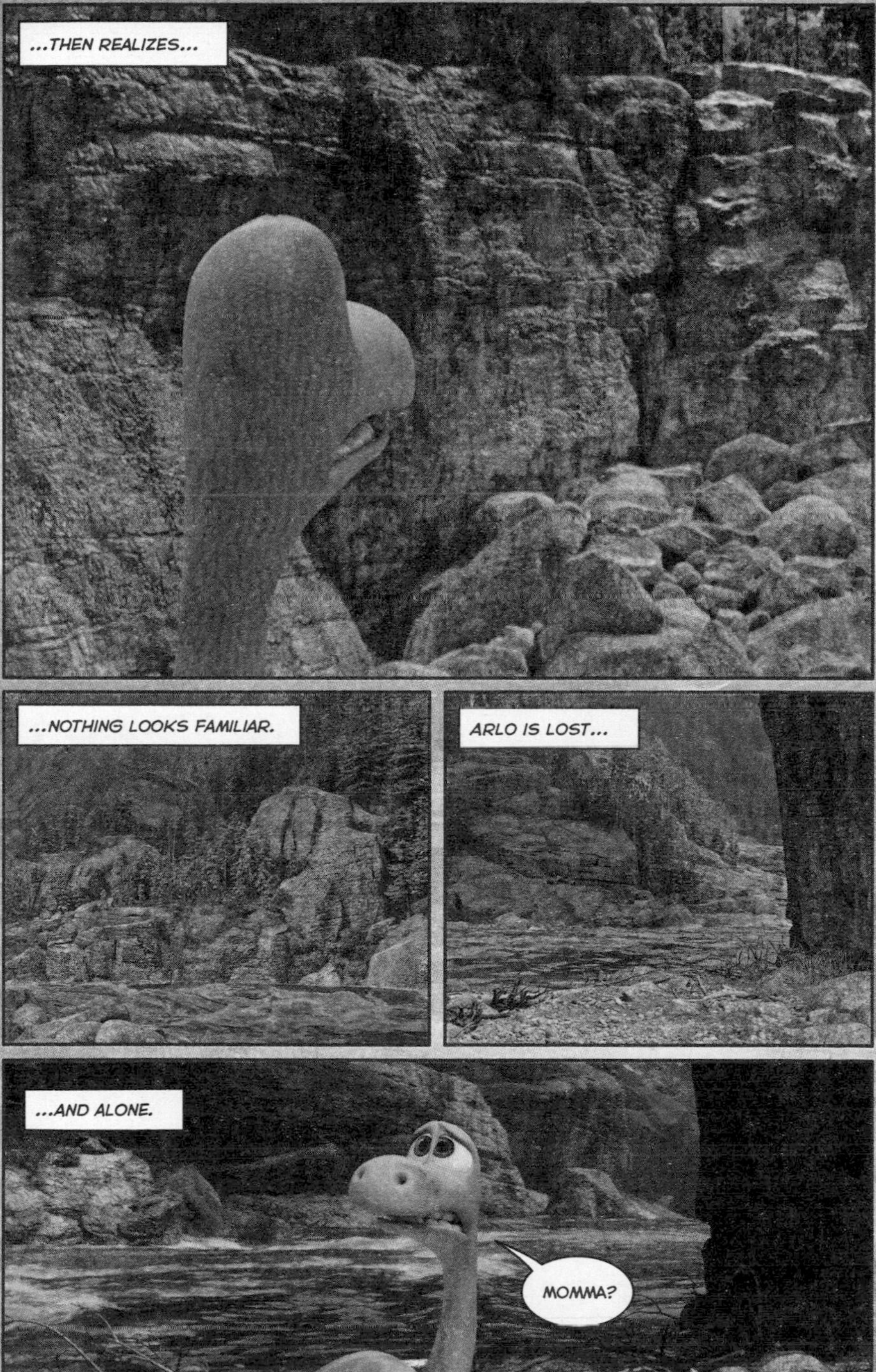
...THEN REALIZES...
...NOTHING LOOKS FAMILIAR.
ARLO IS LOST...
...AND ALONE.
MOMMA?

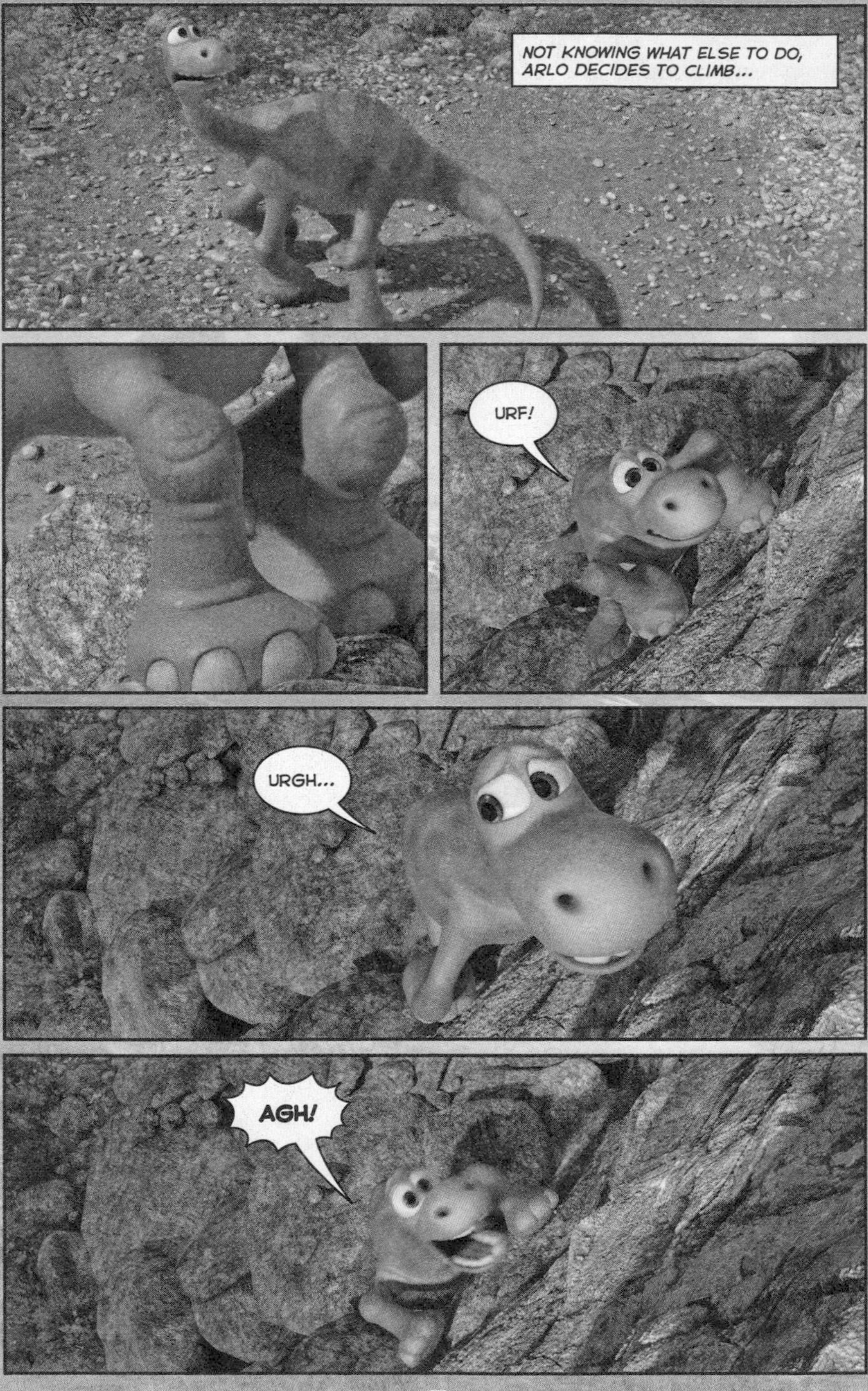
NOT KNOWING WHAT ELSE TO DO, ARLO DECIDES TO CLIMB...
URF!
URGH...
AGH!

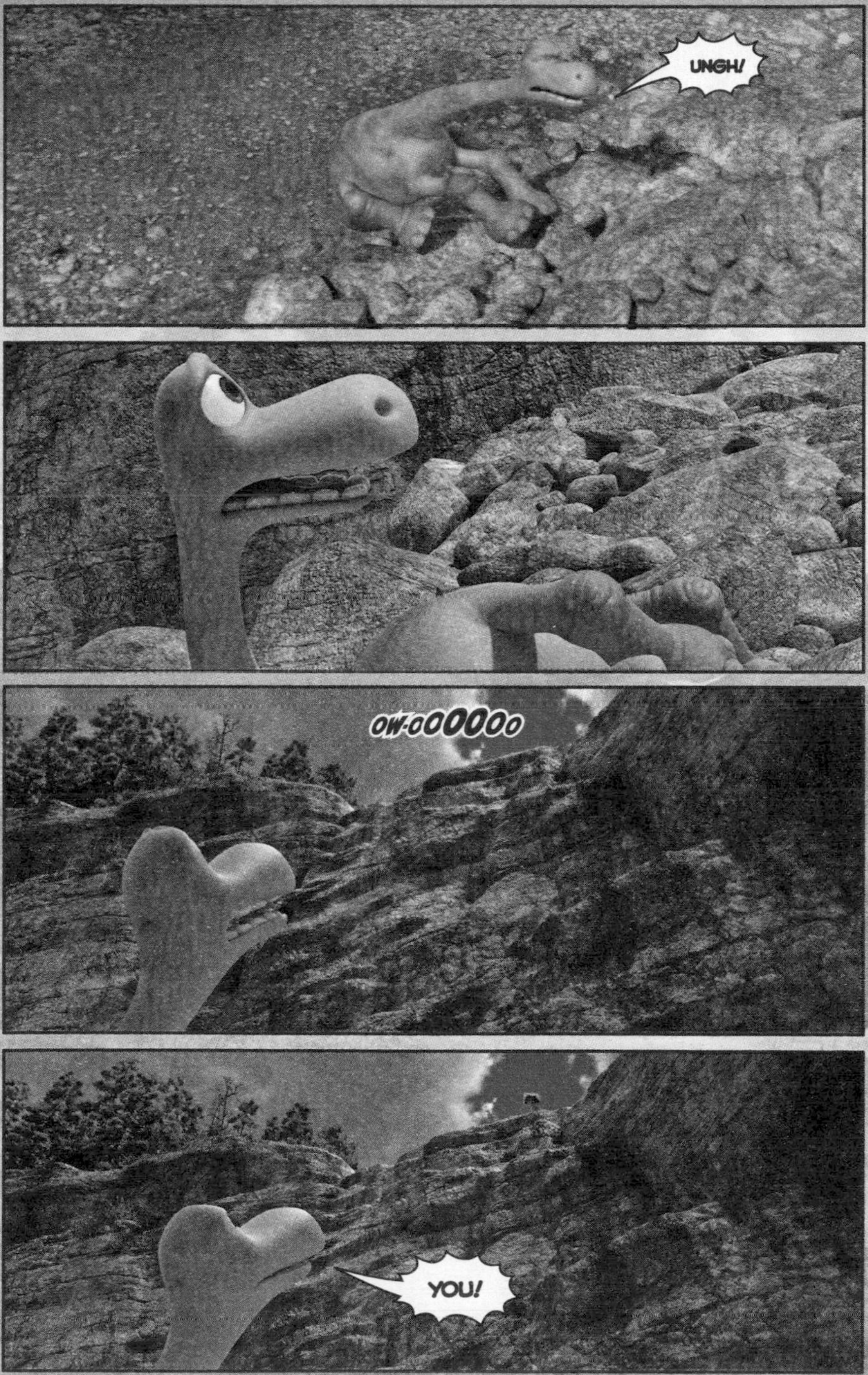
UNGH!
OW-oOOOOo
YOU!

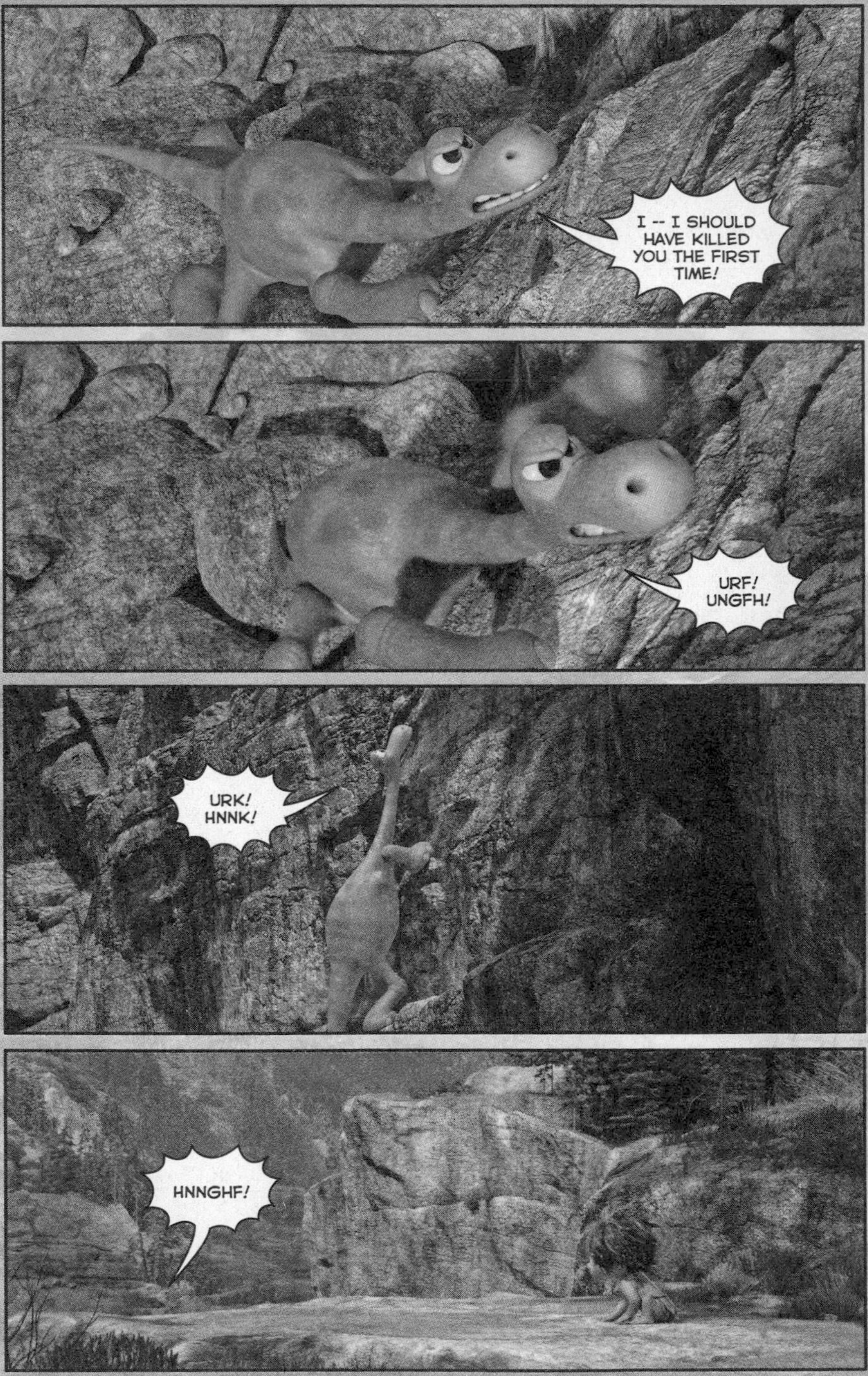
I -- I SHOULD HAVE KILLED YOU THE FIRST TIME!
URF! UNGFH!
URK! HNNK!
HNNGHF!

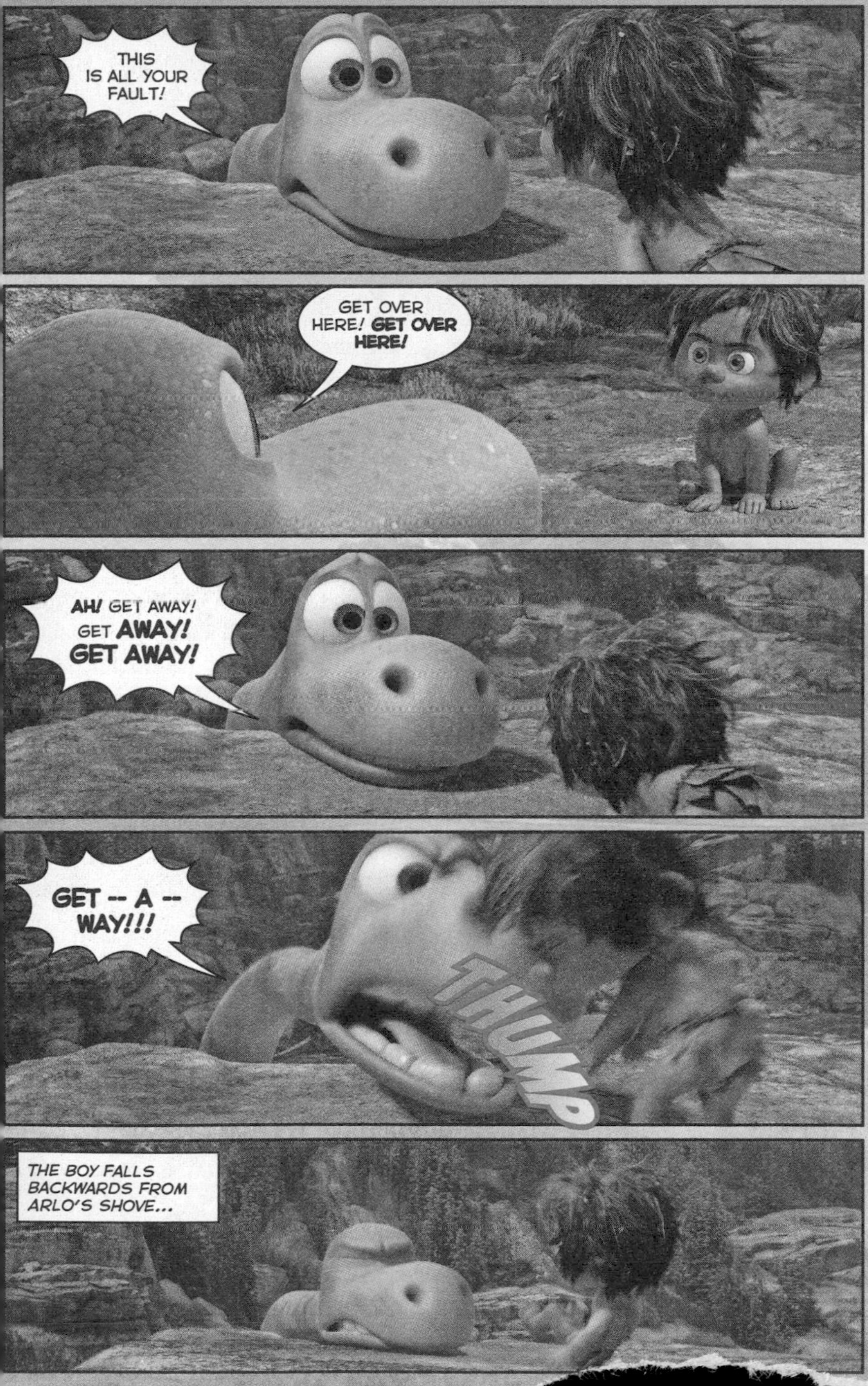
THIS IS ALL YOUR FAULT!
GET OVER HERE! GET OVER HERE!
AH! GET AWAY! GET AWAY! GET AWAY!
GET -- A -- WAY!!!
THUMP
THE BOY FALLS BACKWARDS FROM ARLO'S SHOVE...

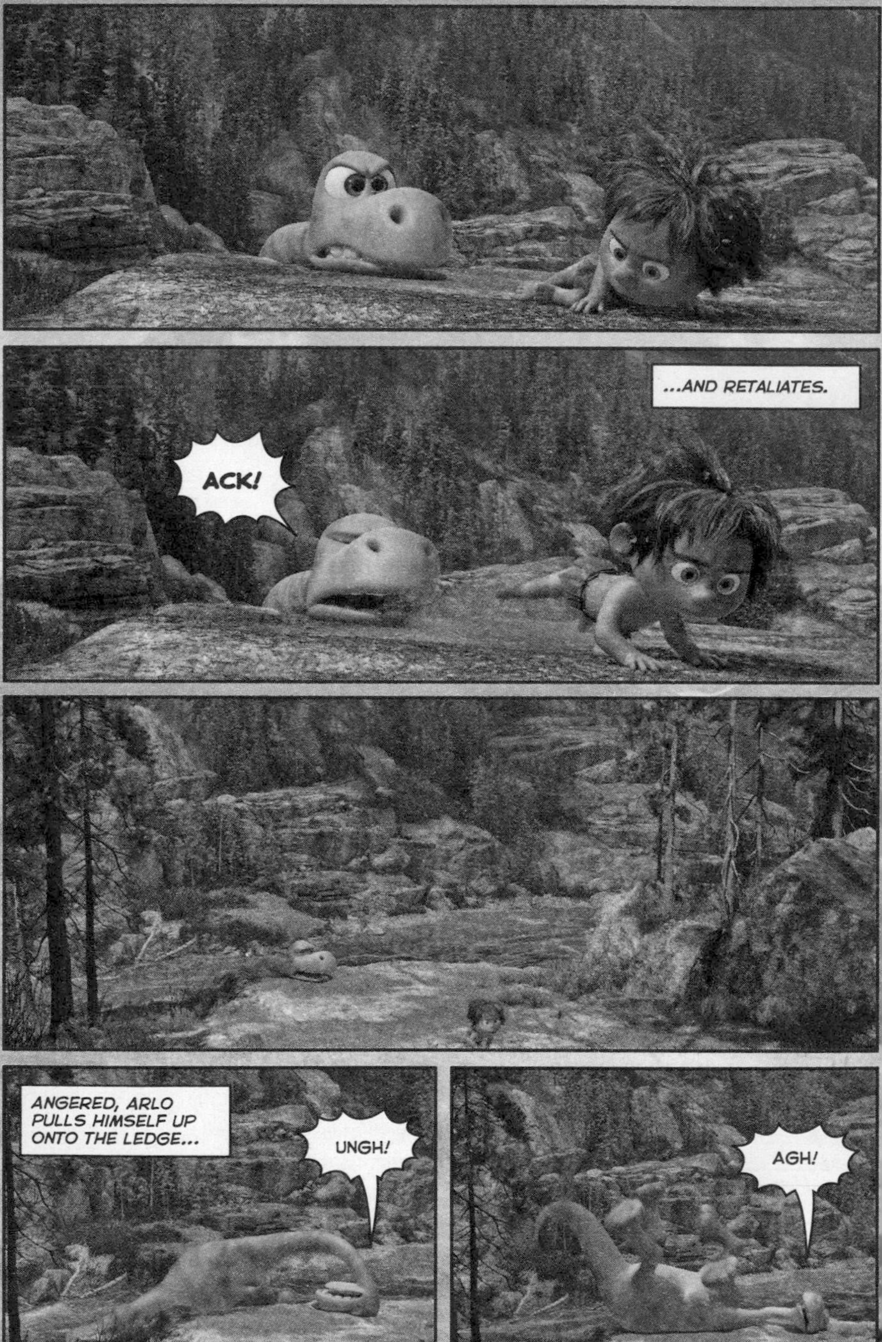
...AND RETALIATES.
ACK!
ANGERED, ARLO PULLS HIMSELF UP ONTO THE LEDGE...
UNGH!
AGH!

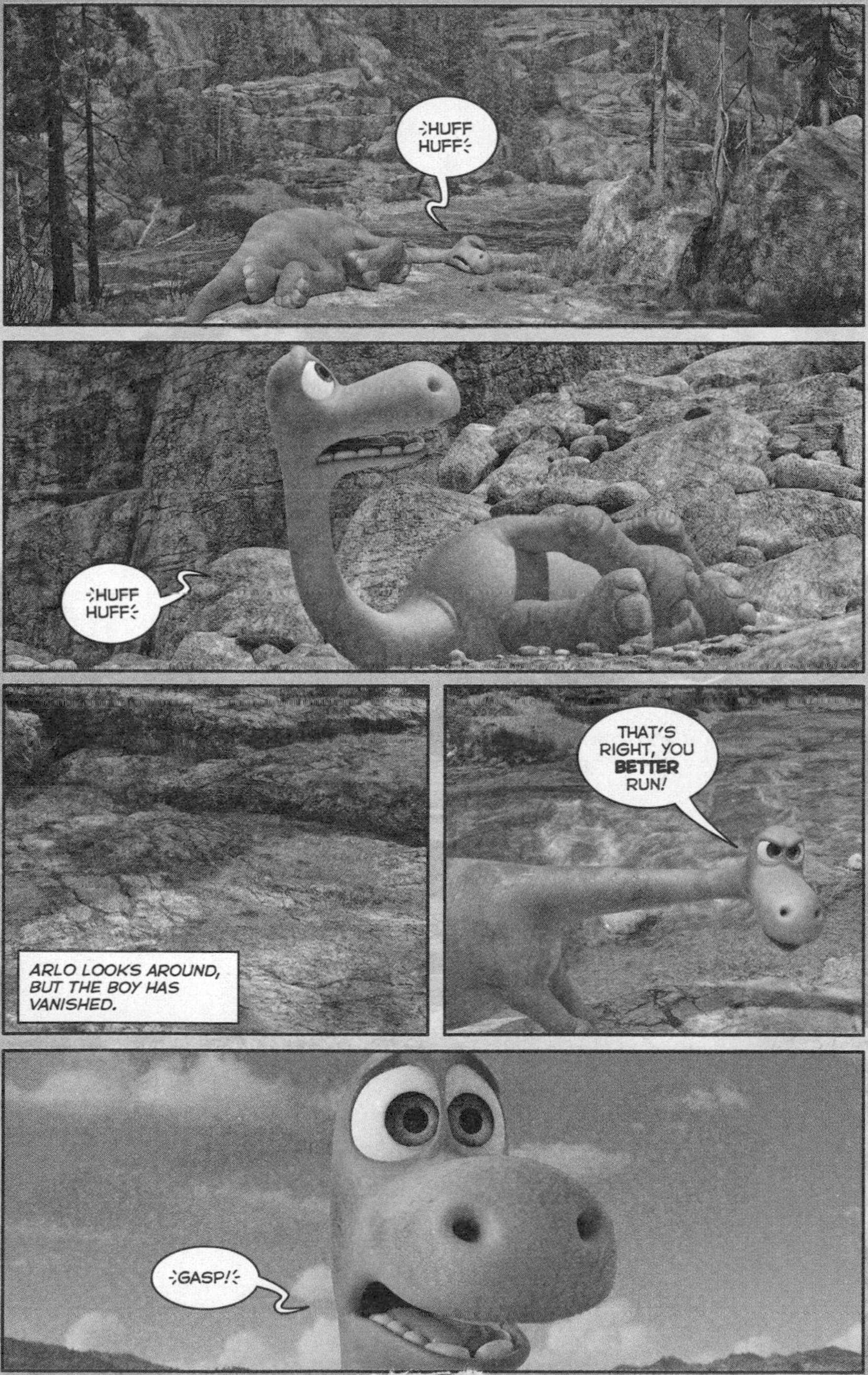
HUFF HUFF
HUFF HUFF
ARLO LOOKS AROUND, BUT THE BOY HAS VANISHED.
THAT'S RIGHT, YOU **BETTER** RUN!
GASP!

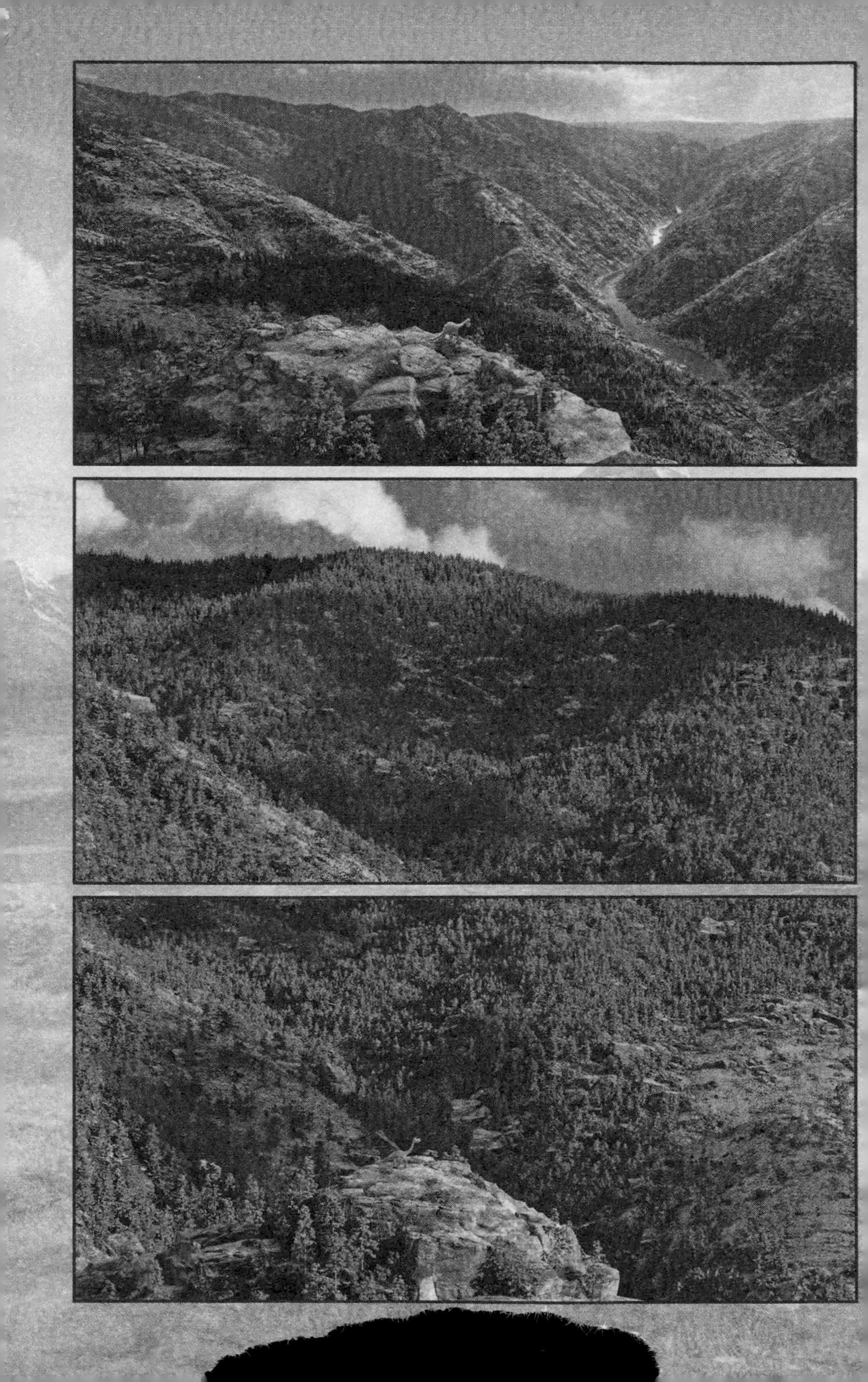

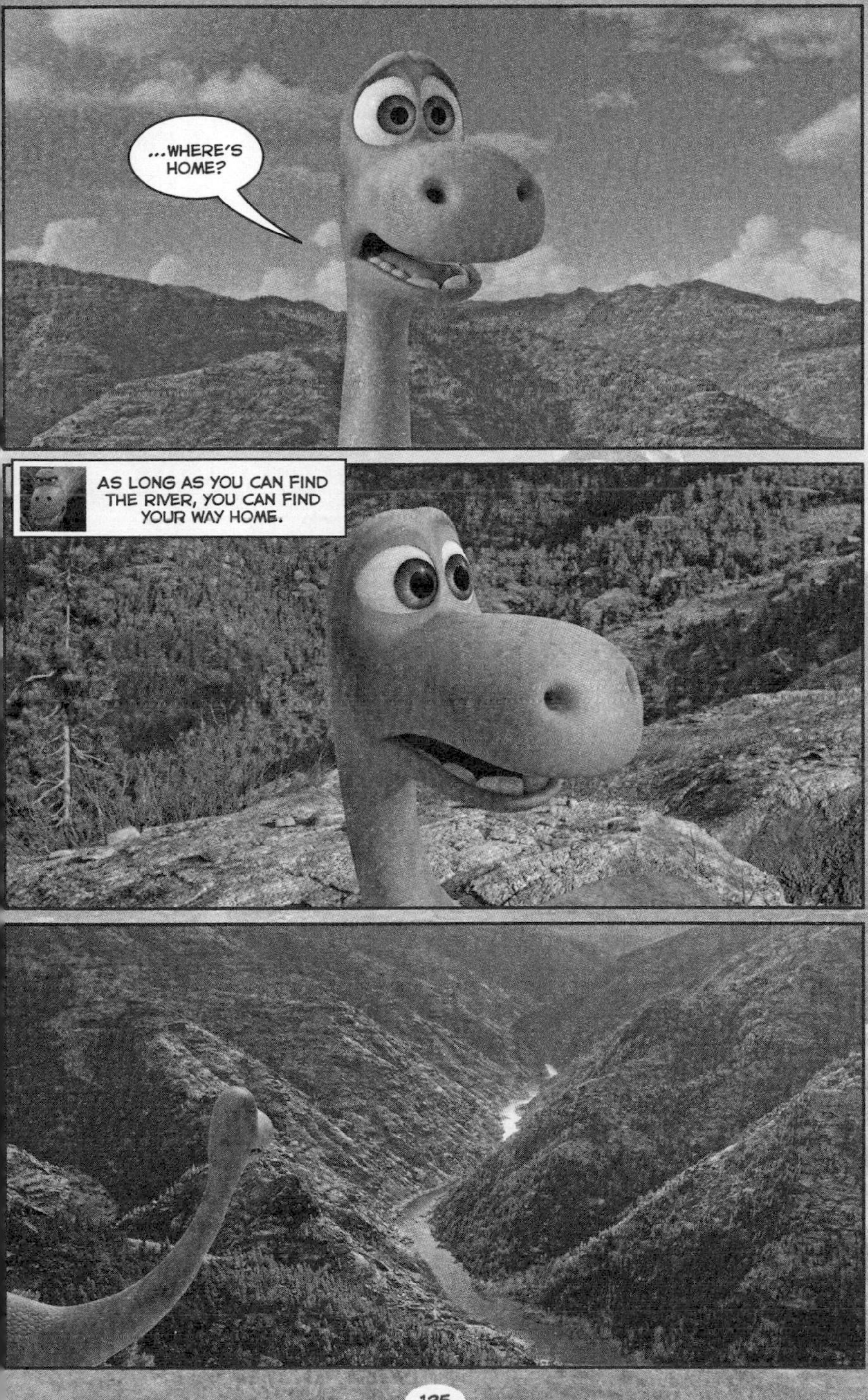
...WHERE'S HOME?
AS LONG AS YOU CAN FIND THE RIVER, YOU CAN FIND YOUR WAY HOME.

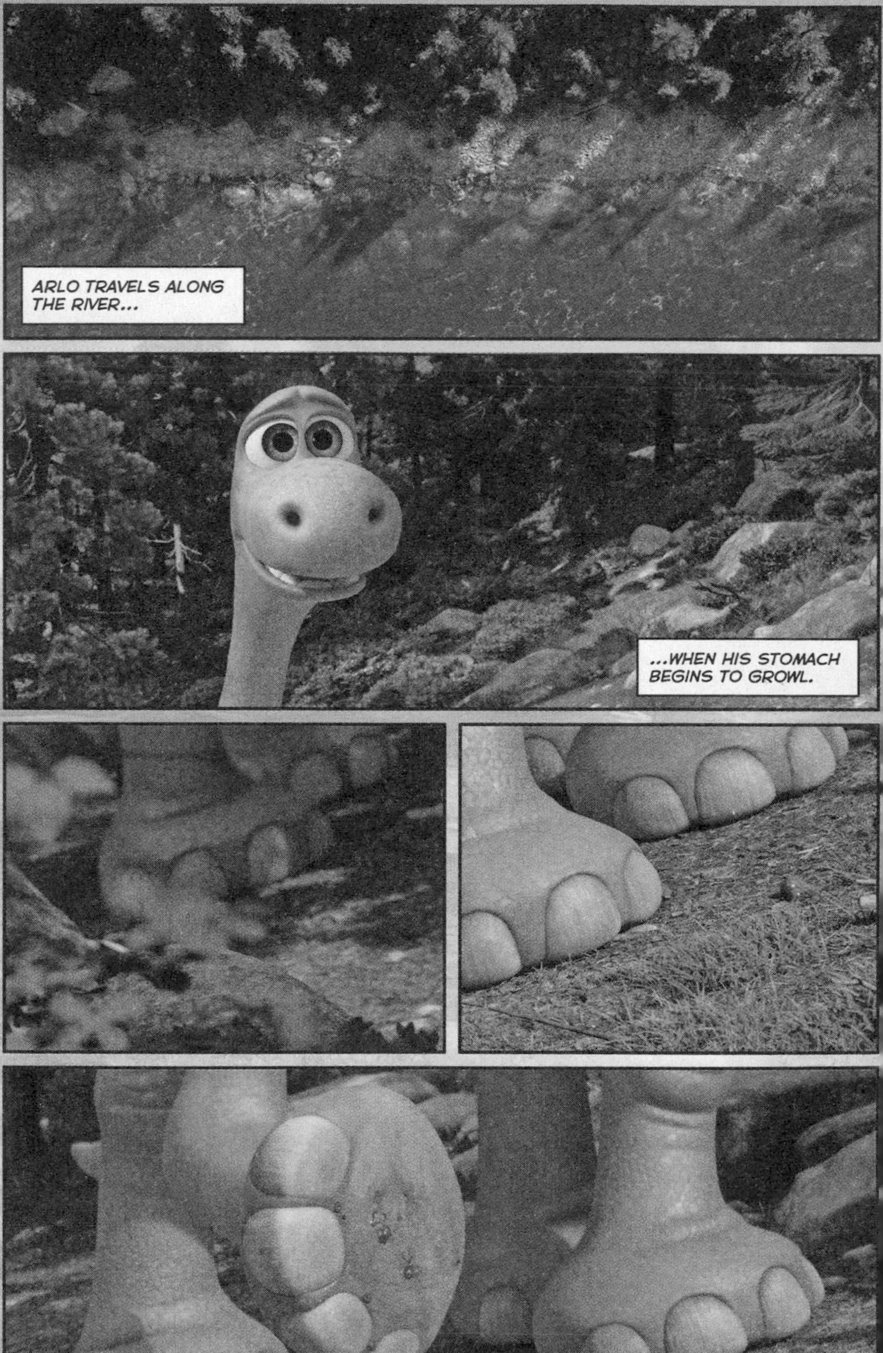
ARLO TRAVELS ALONG THE RIVER...
...WHEN HIS STOMACH BEGINS TO GROWL.

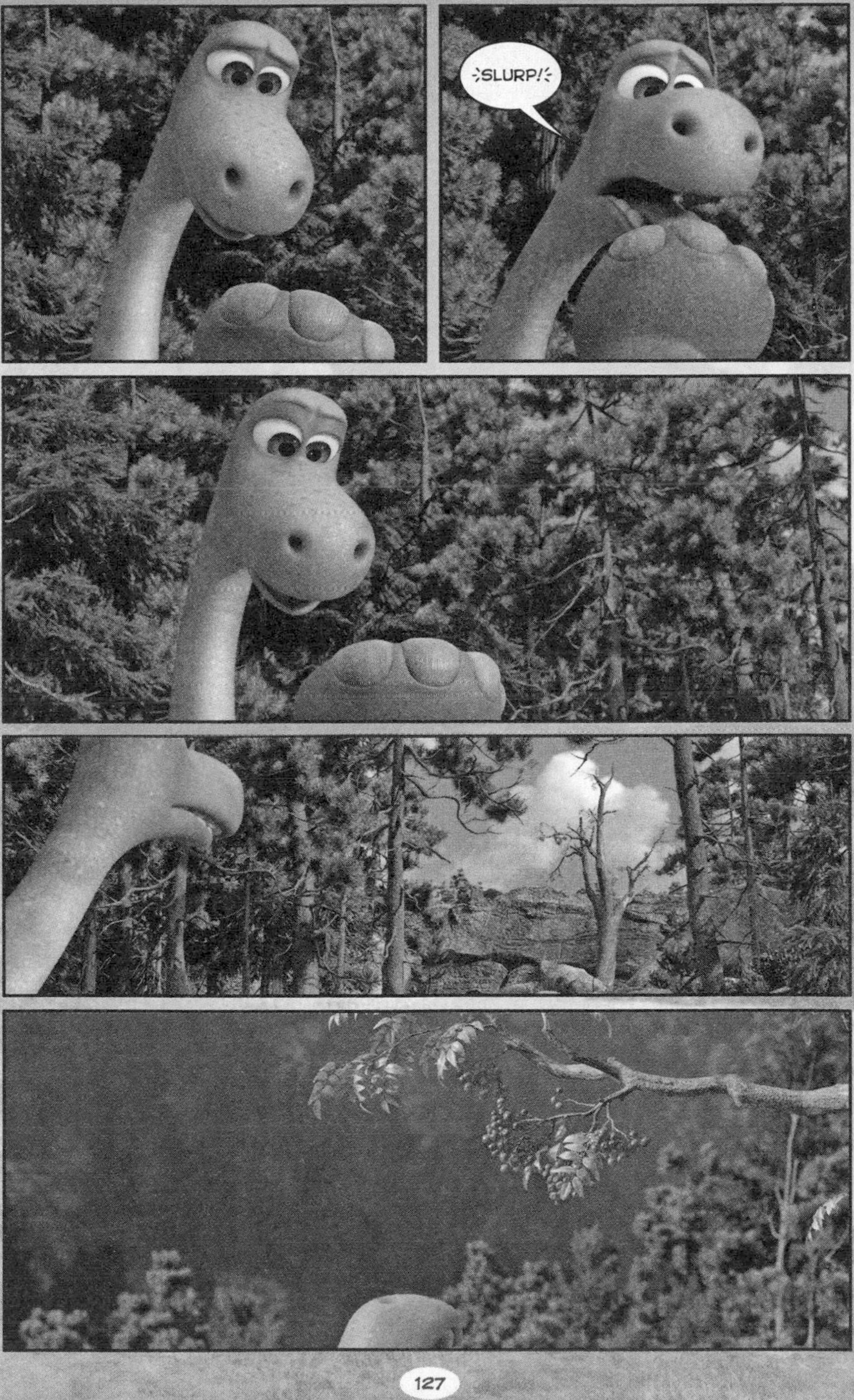
SLURP!

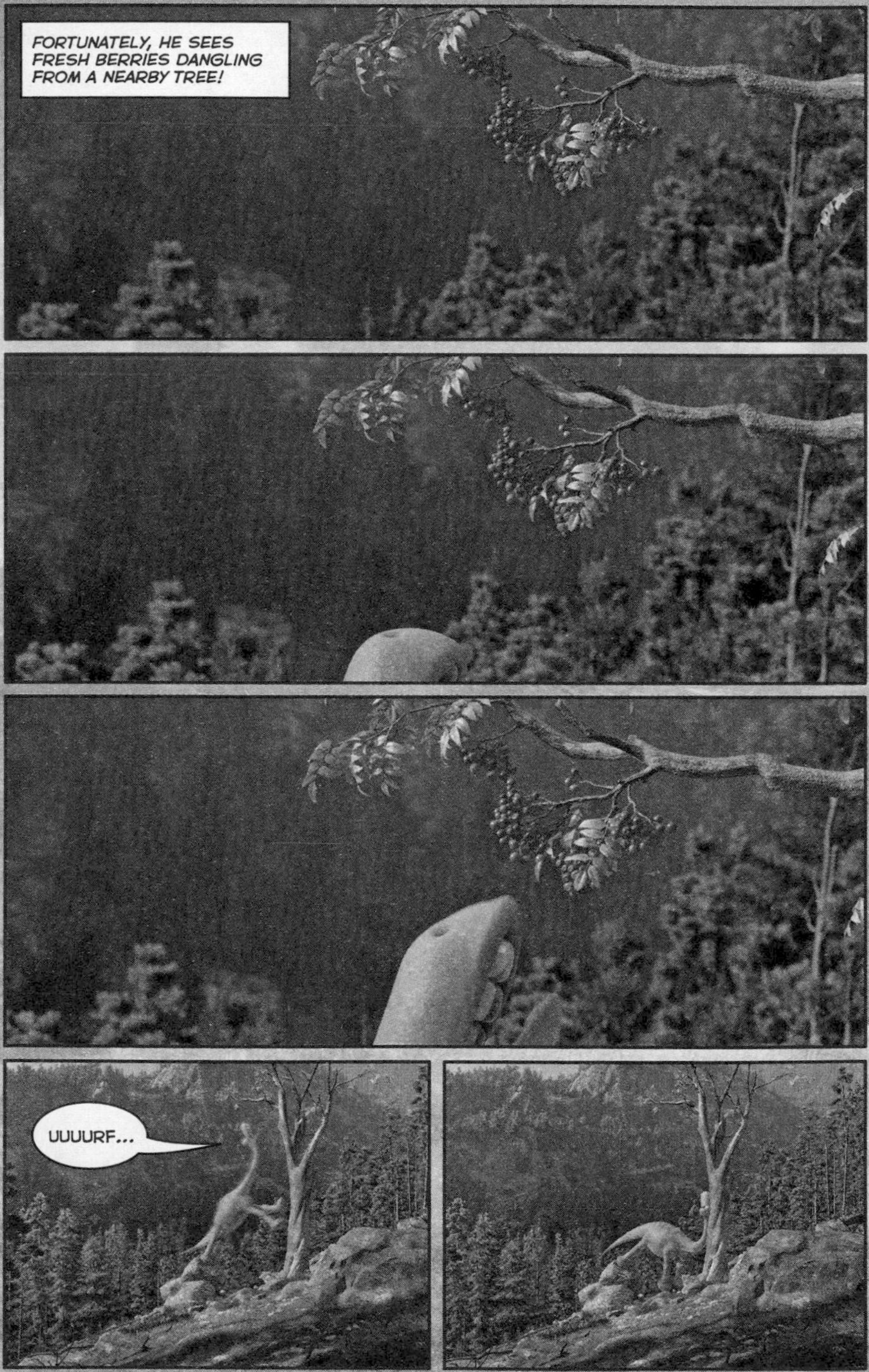
FORTUNATELY, HE SEES FRESH BERRIES DANGLING FROM A NEARBY TREE!
UUUURF...

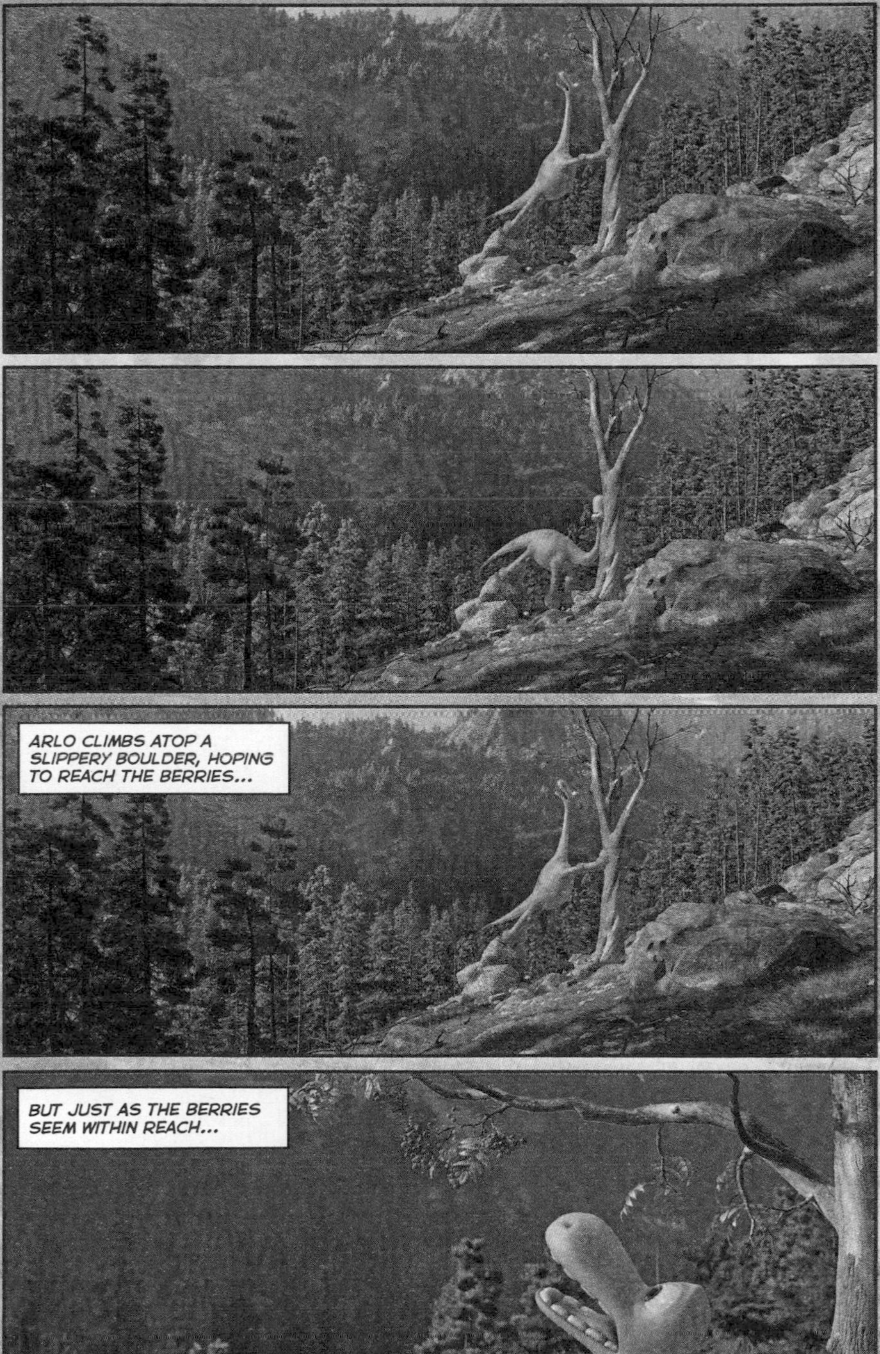
ARLO CLIMBS ATOP A SLIPPERY BOULDER, HOPING TO REACH THE BERRIES...
BUT JUST AS THE BERRIES SEEM WITHIN REACH...

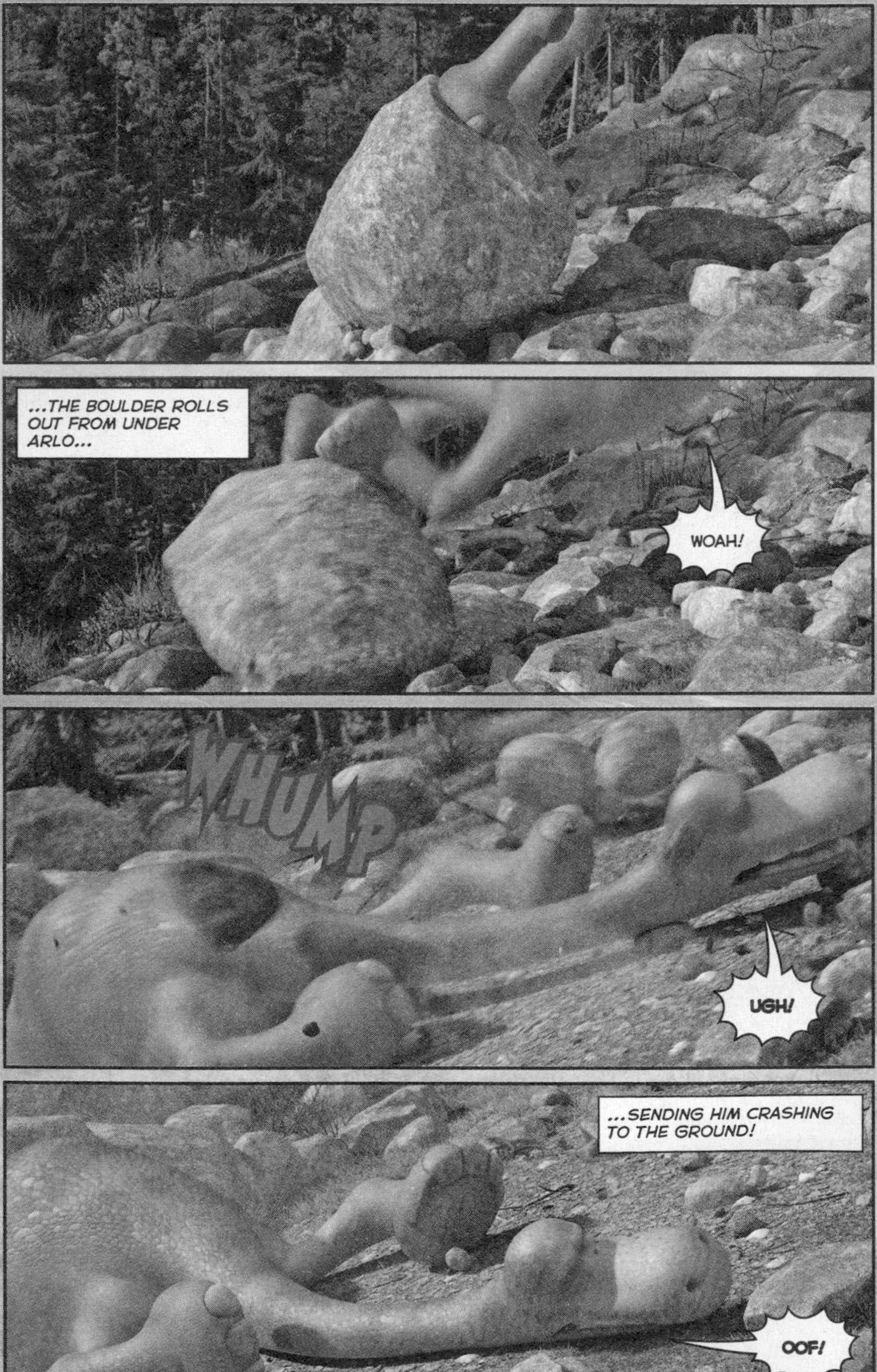
...THE BOULDER ROLLS OUT FROM UNDER ARLO...
WOAH!
WHUMP
UGH!
...SENDING HIM CRASHING TO THE GROUND!
OOF!

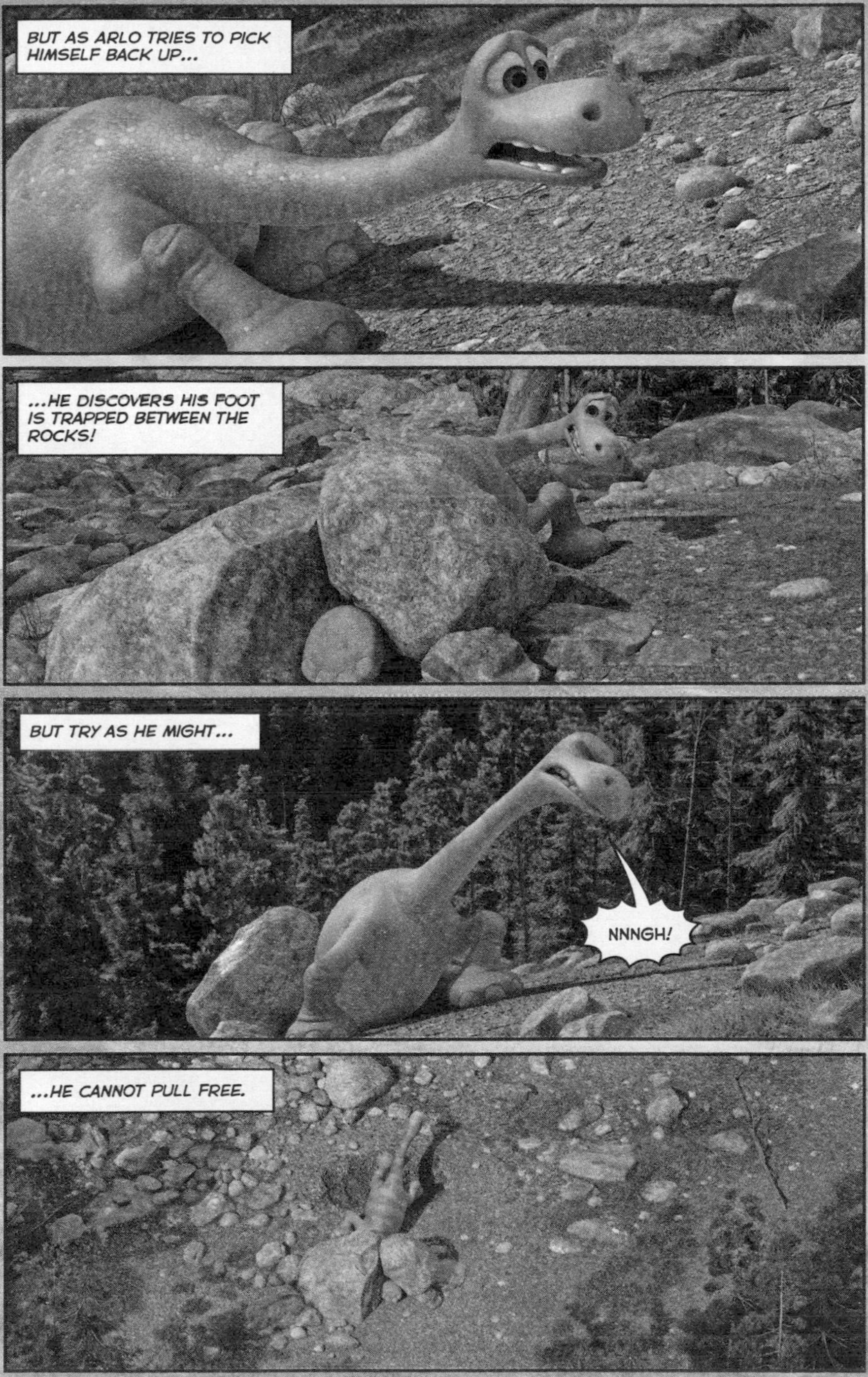
BUT AS ARLO TRIES TO PICK HIMSELF BACK UP...
...HE DISCOVERS HIS FOOT IS TRAPPED BETWEEN THE ROCKS!
BUT TRY AS HE MIGHT...
NNNGH!
...HE CANNOT PULL FREE.

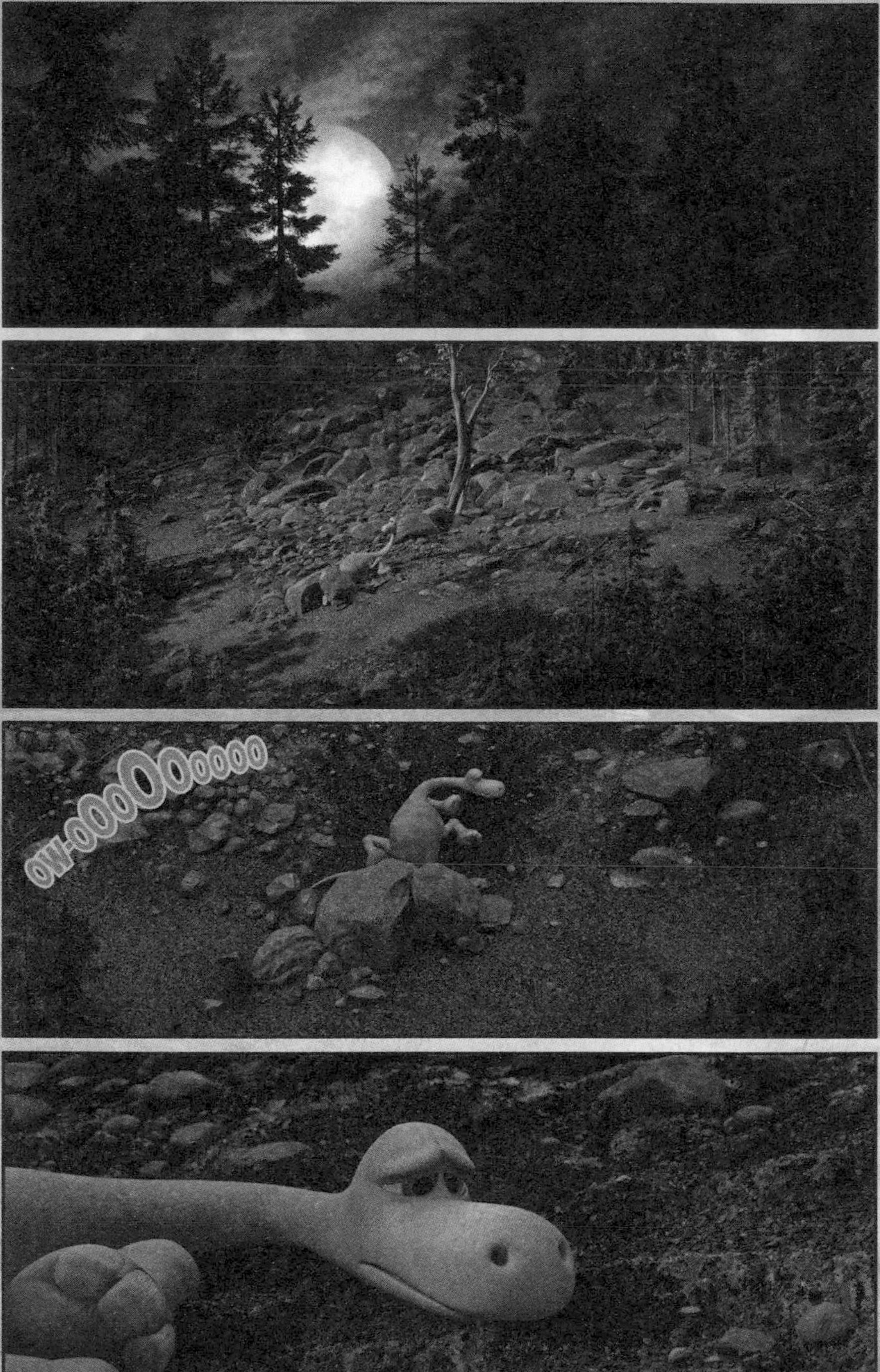
OW-oOOOOooooo

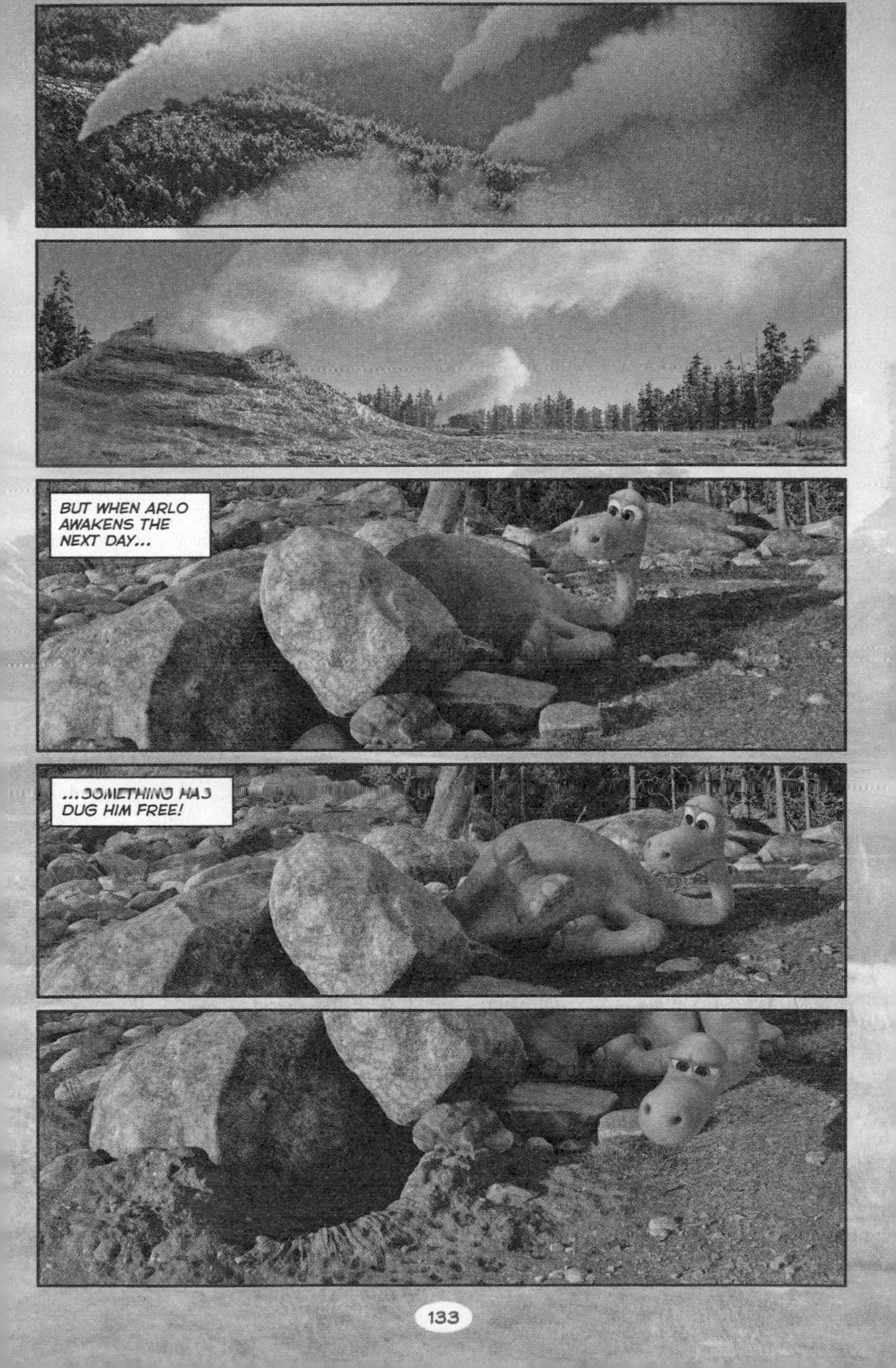
BUT WHEN ARLO AWAKENS THE NEXT DAY...
...SOMETHING HAS DUG HIM FREE!

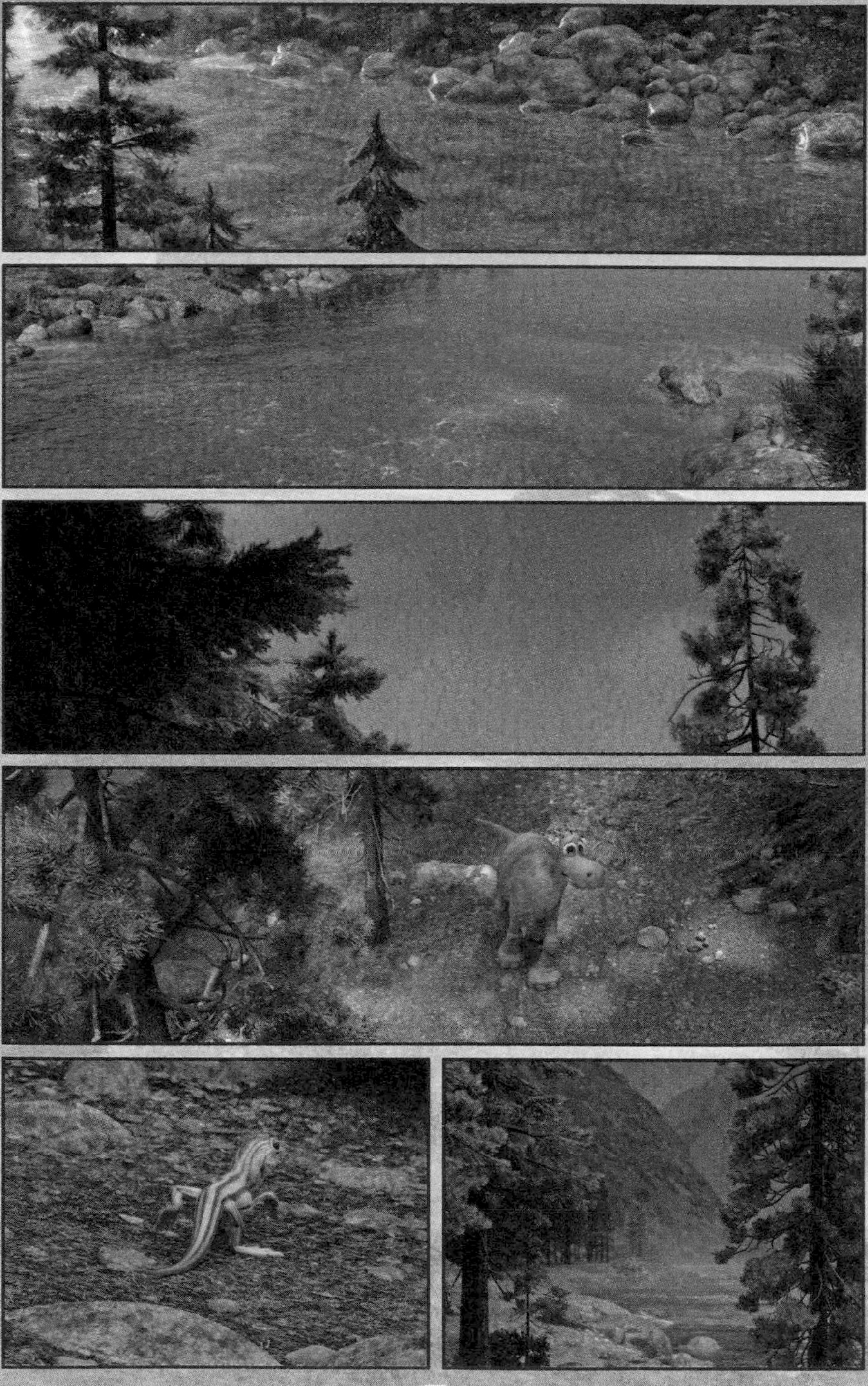

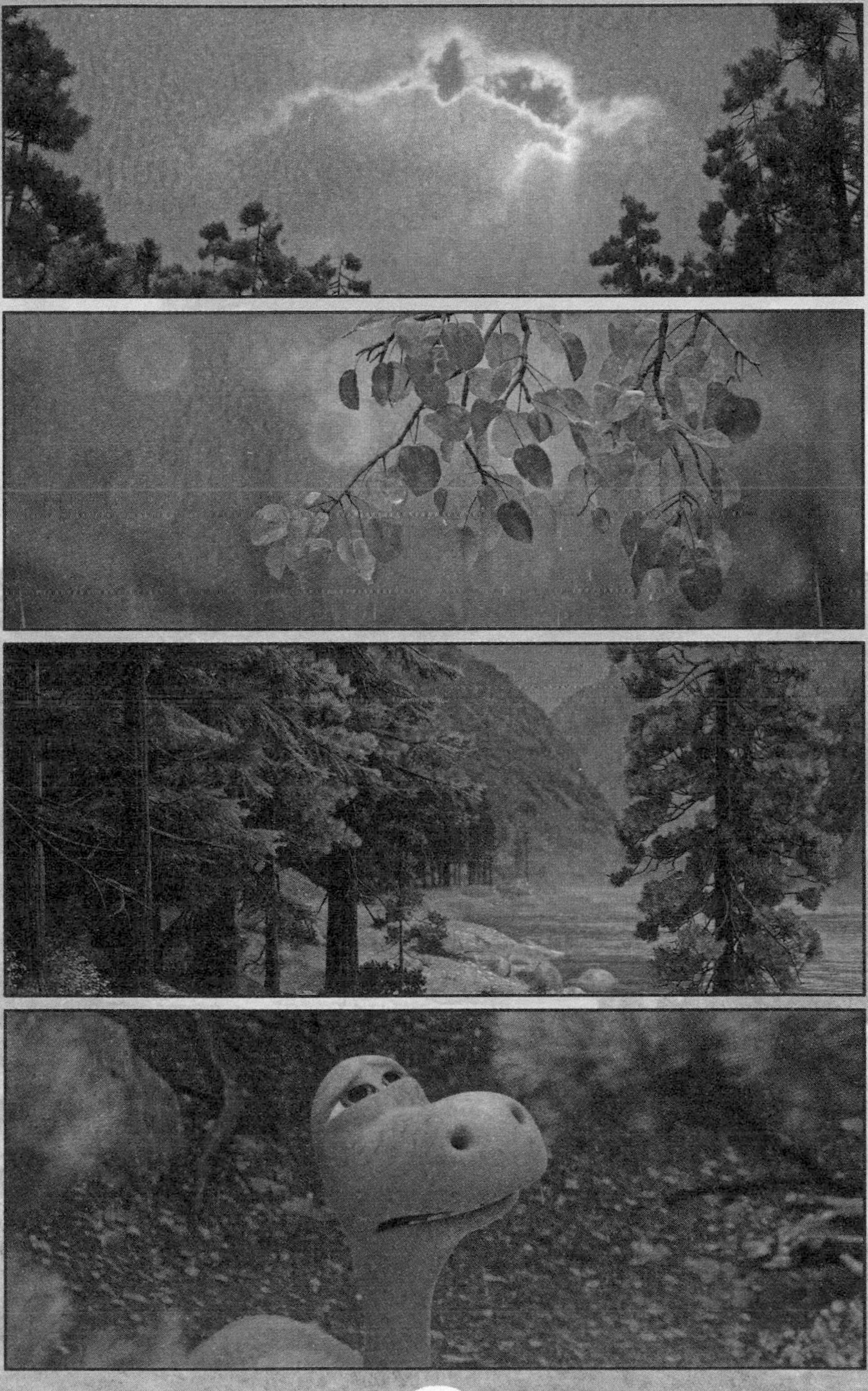

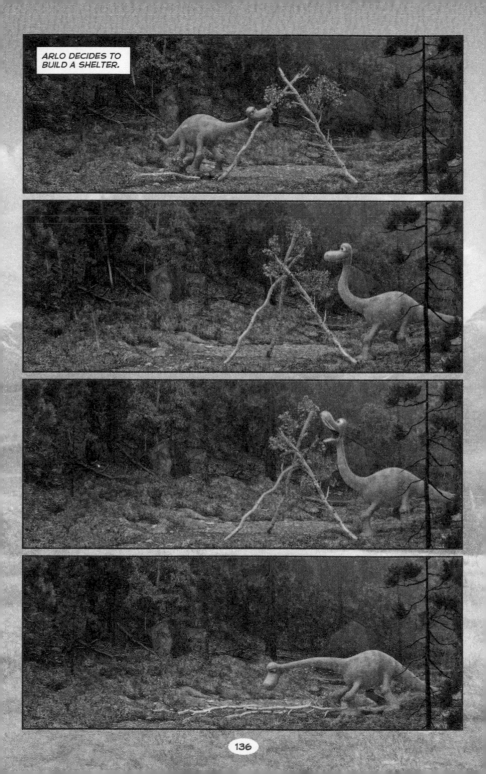

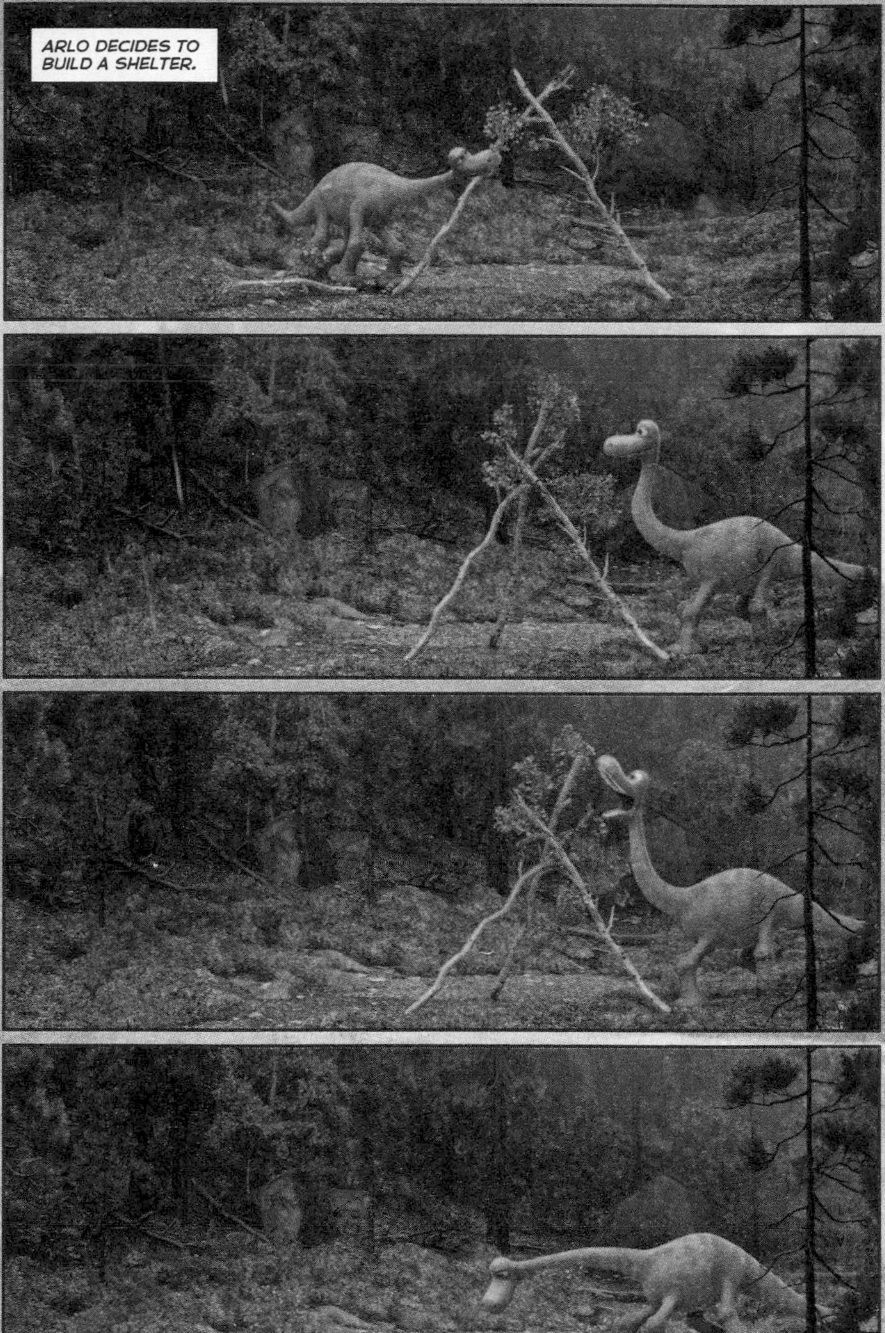
ARLO DECIDES TO
BUILD A SHELTER.

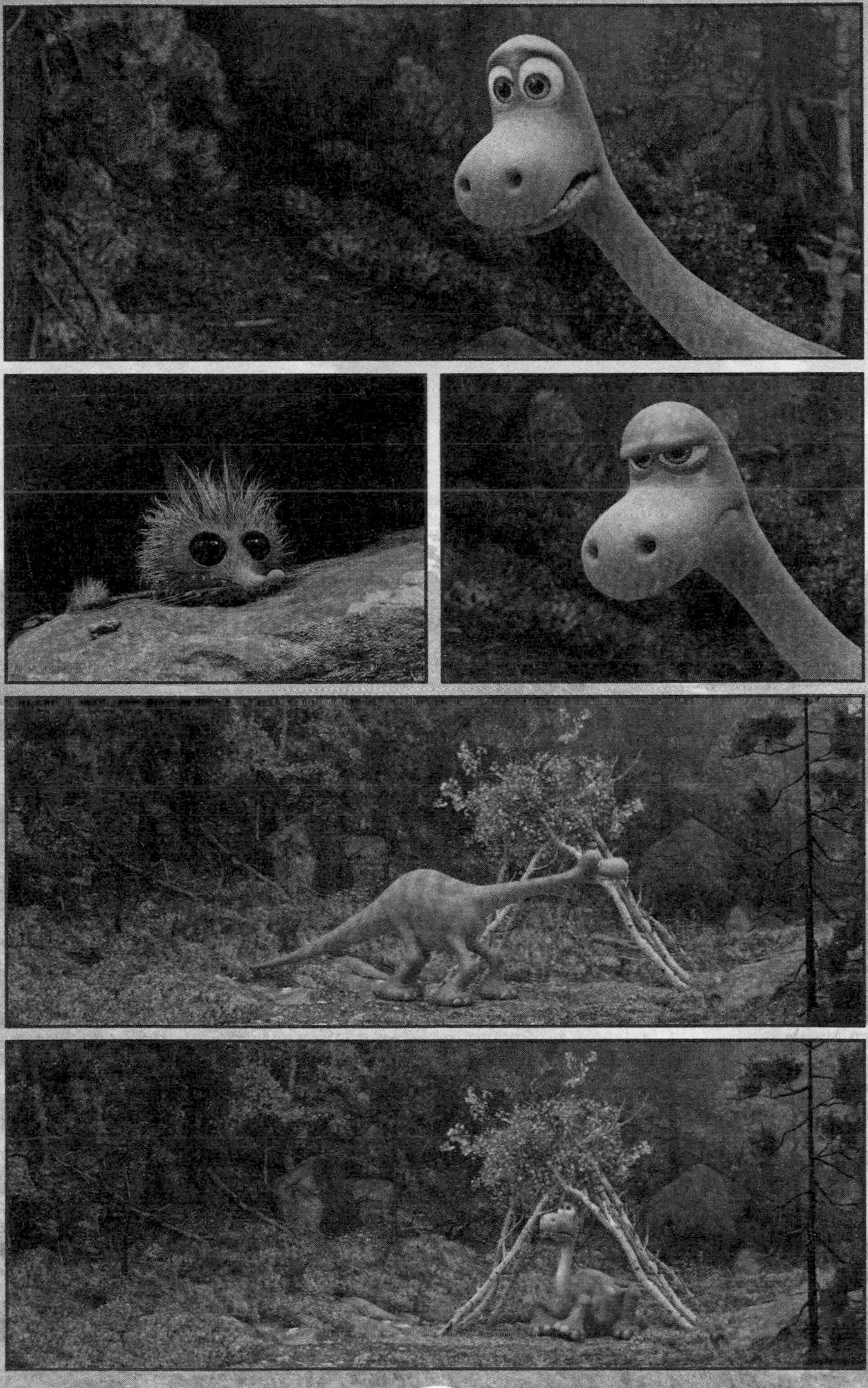

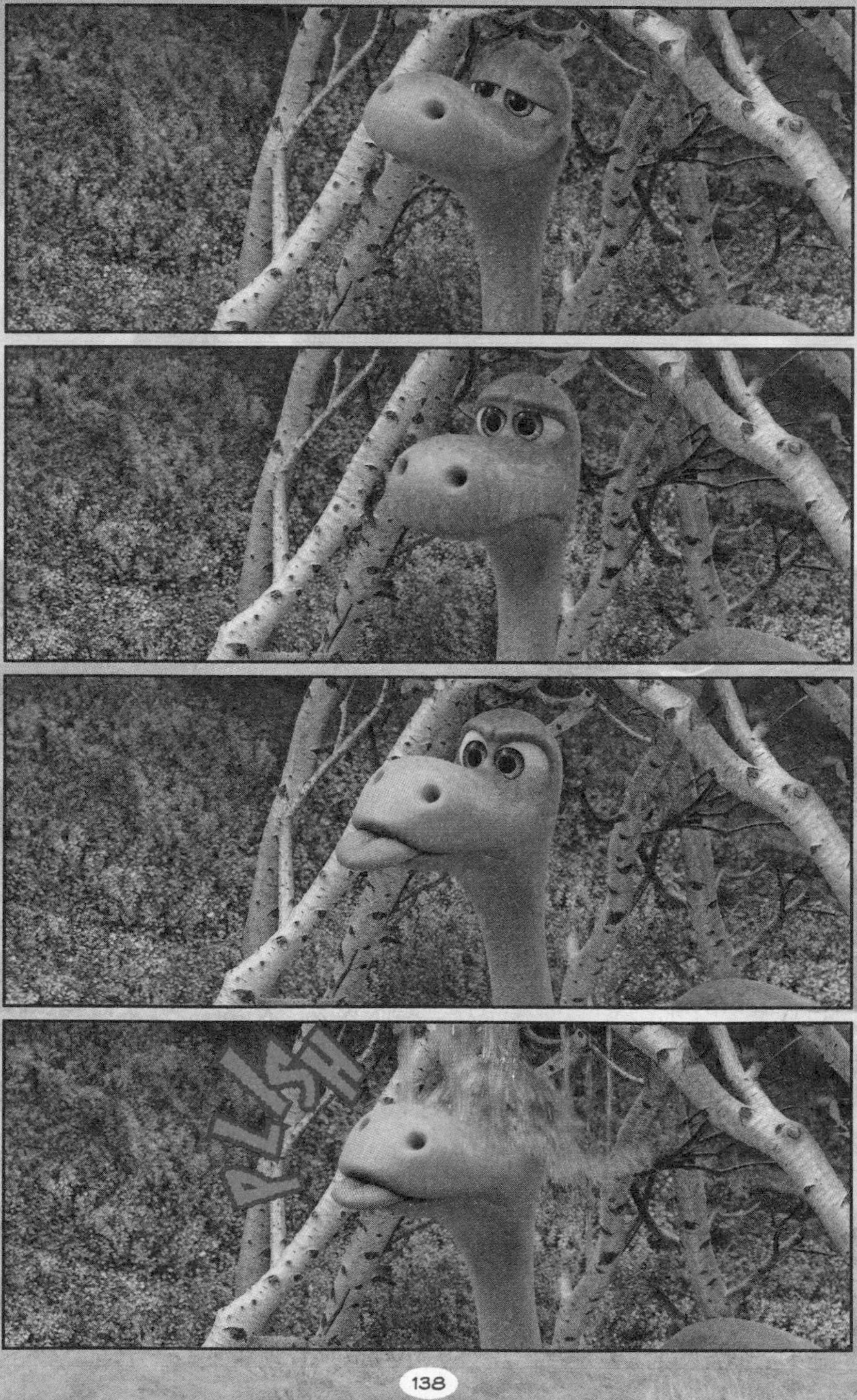
PLISH

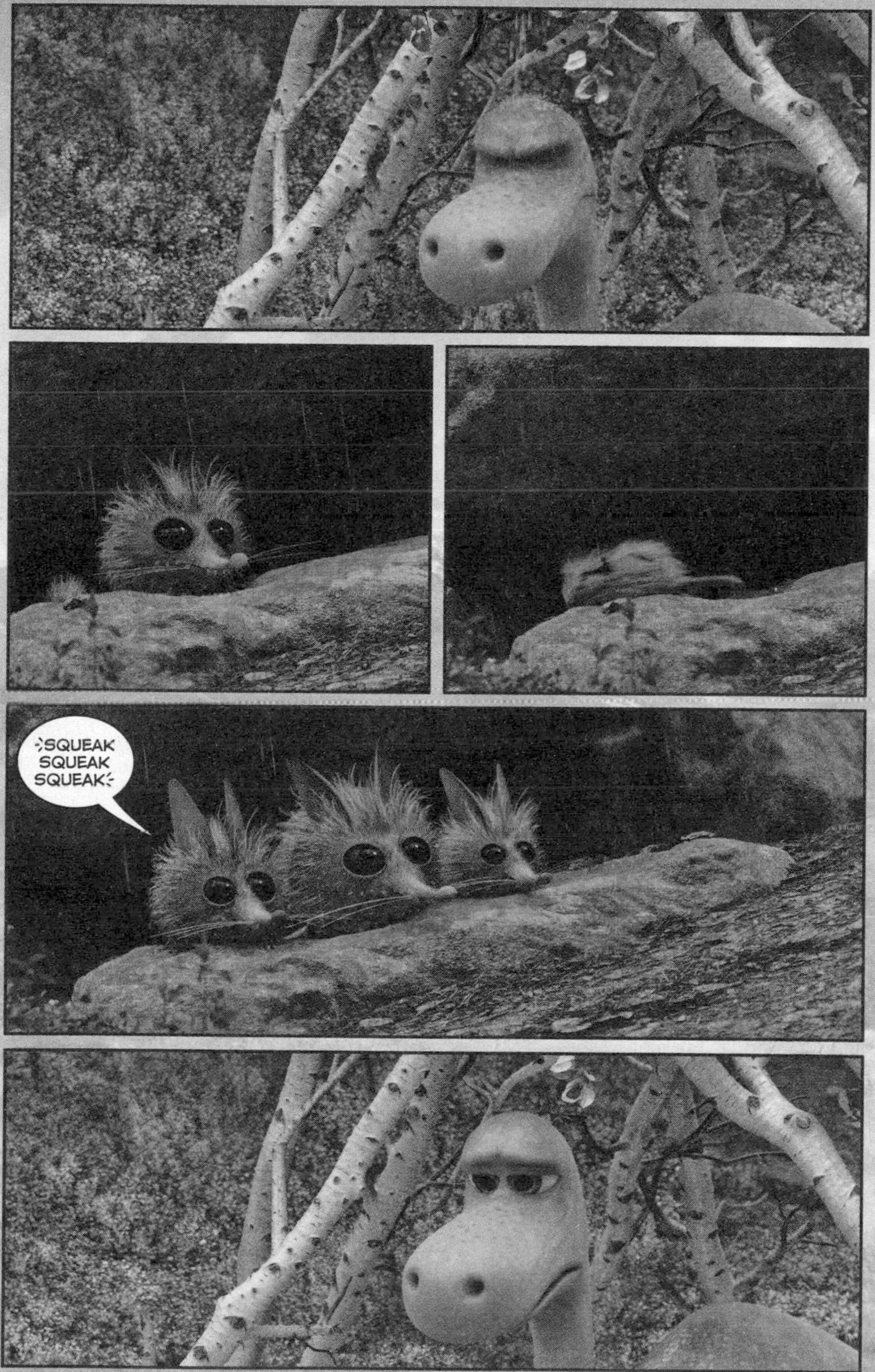
SQUEAK SQUEAK SQUEAK

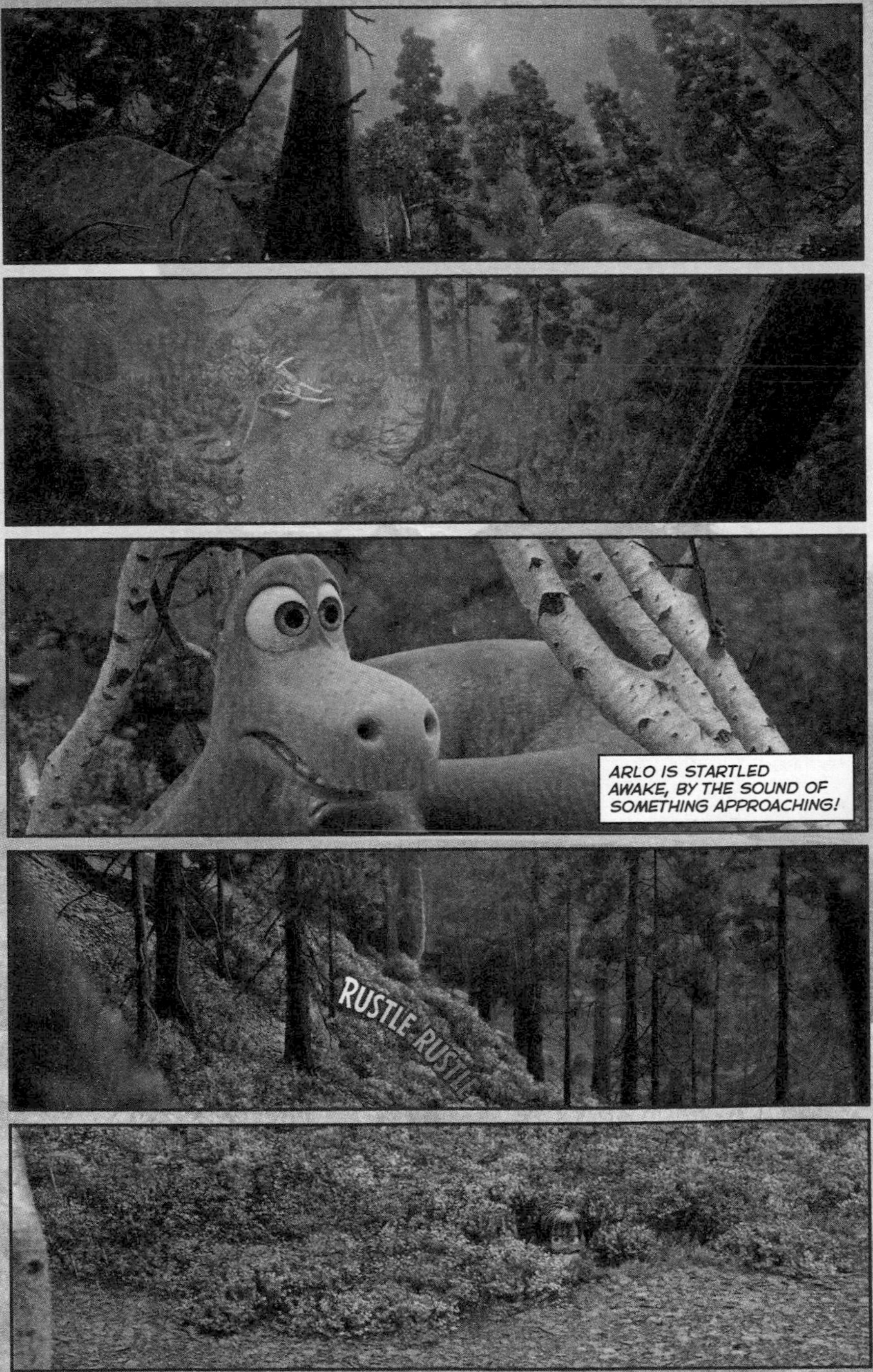
ARLO IS STARTLED AWAKE, BY THE SOUND OF SOMETHING APPROACHING!
RUSTLE RUSTLE

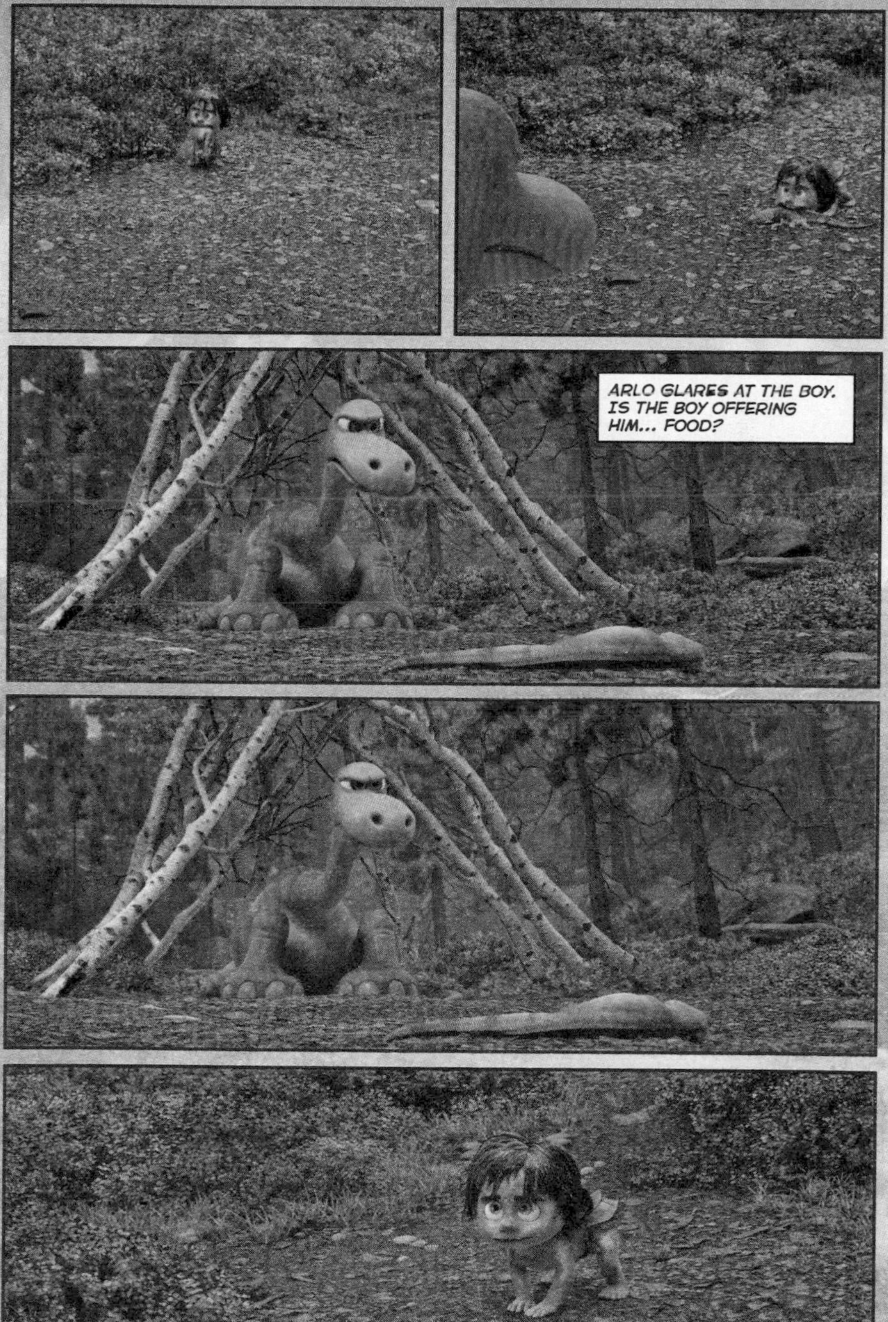
ARLO GLARES AT THE BOY. IS THE BOY OFFERING HIM... FOOD?

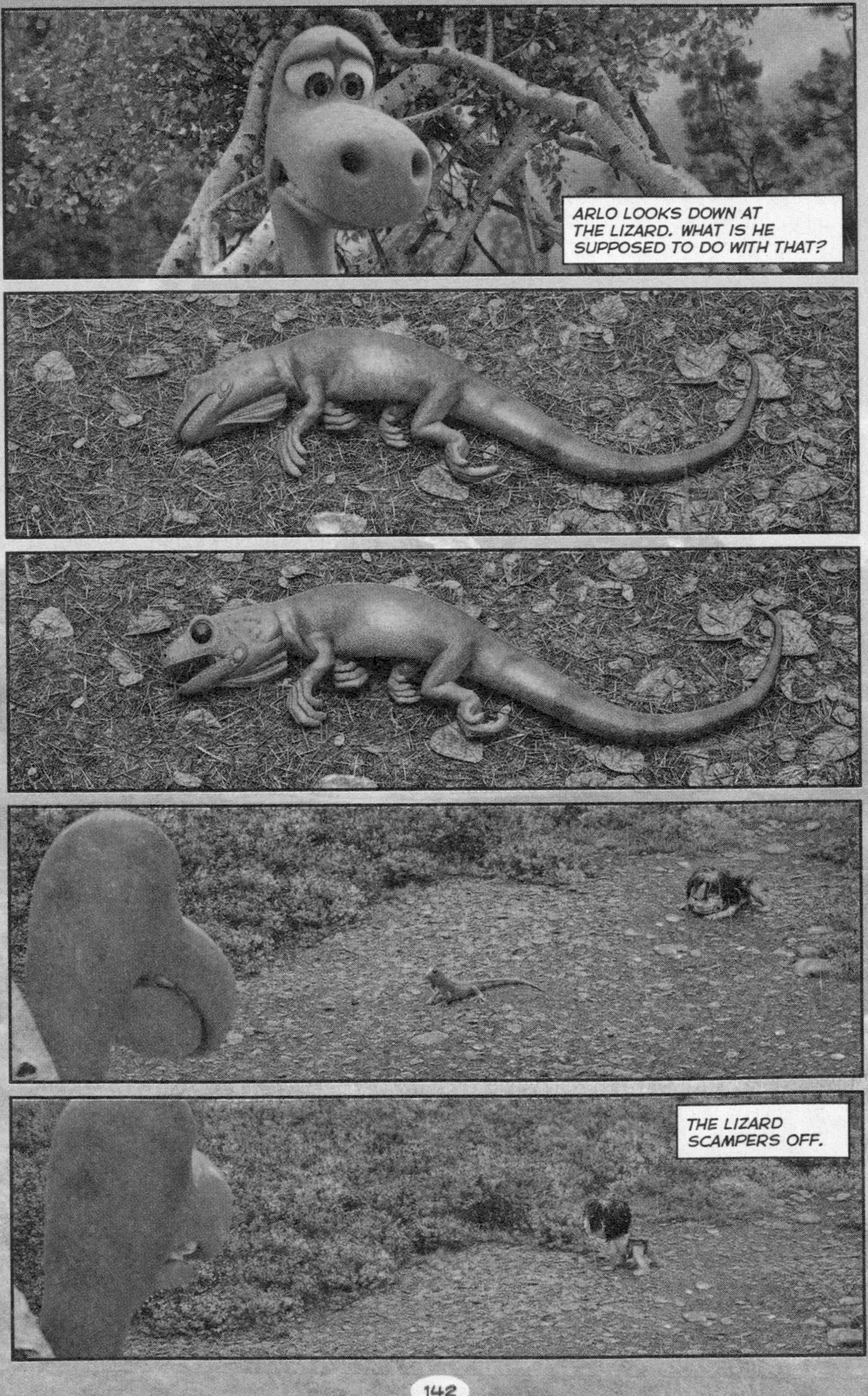
ARLO LOOKS DOWN AT THE LIZARD. WHAT IS HE SUPPOSED TO DO WITH THAT?
THE LIZARD SCAMPERS OFF.

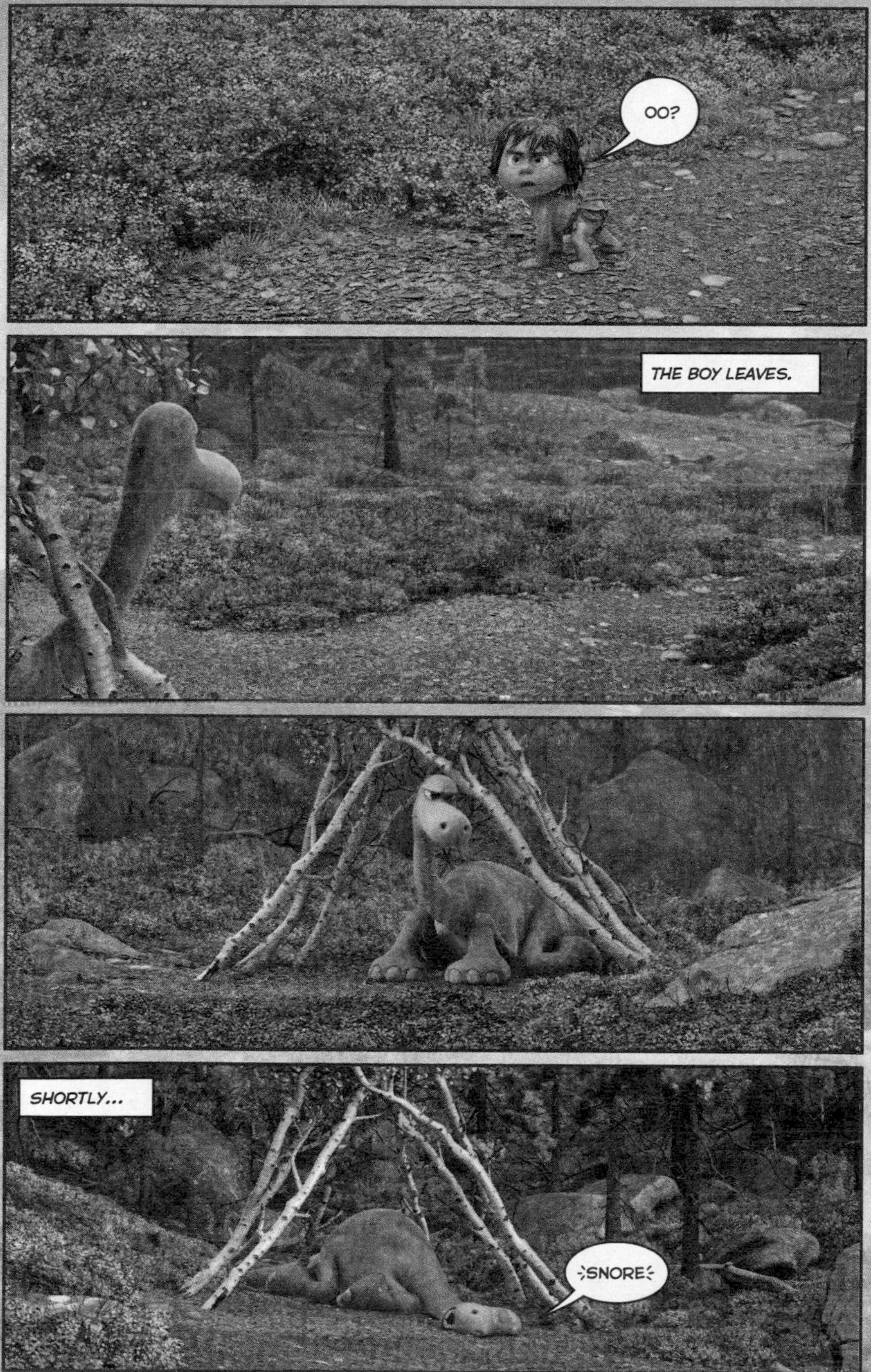
OO?
THE BOY LEAVES.
SHORTLY...
SNORE

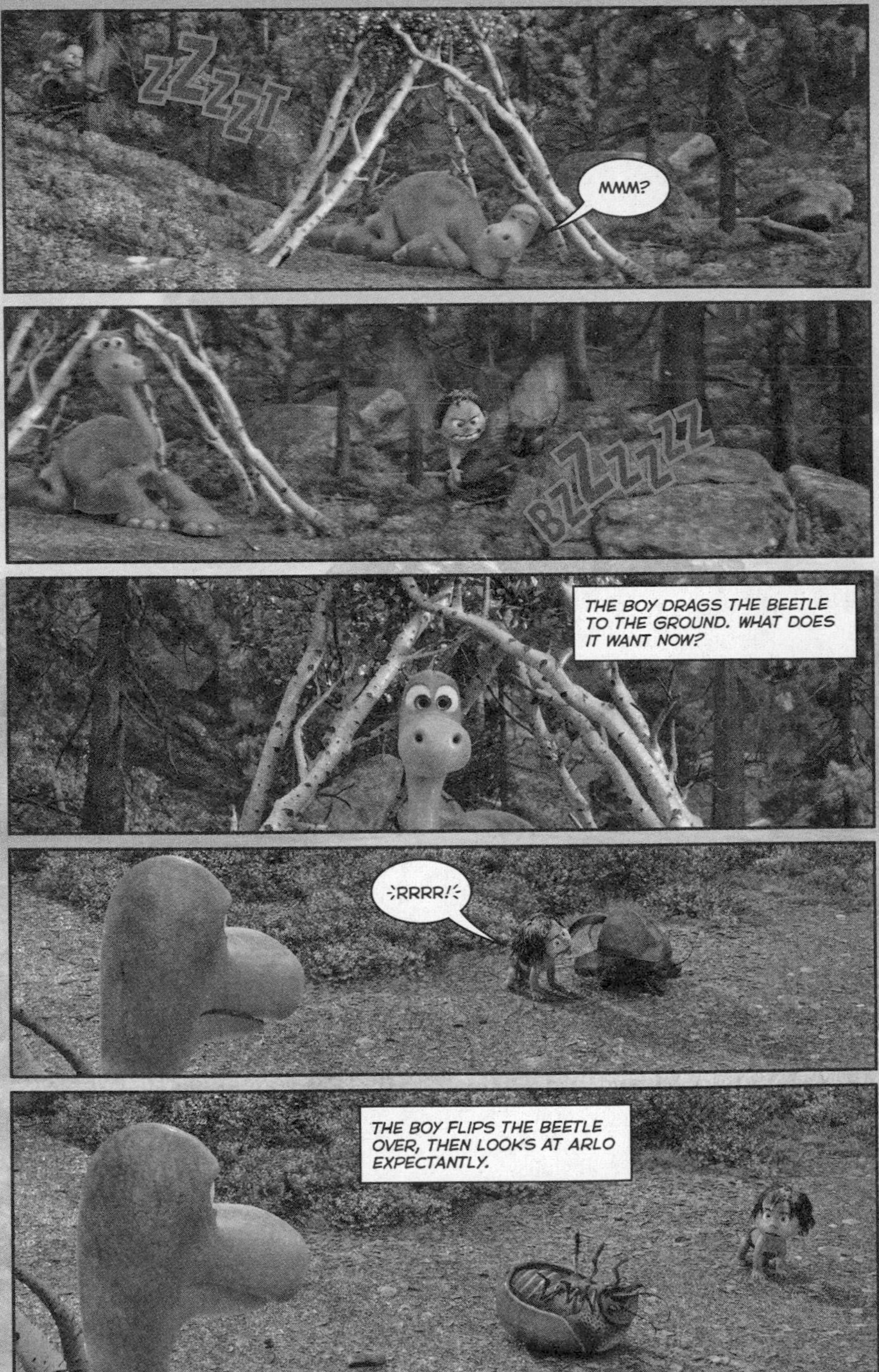
ZZZZZ
MMM?
BZZZZZZ
THE BOY DRAGS THE BEETLE TO THE GROUND. WHAT DOES IT WANT NOW?
RRRR!
THE BOY FLIPS THE BEETLE OVER, THEN LOOKS AT ARLO EXPECTANTLY.

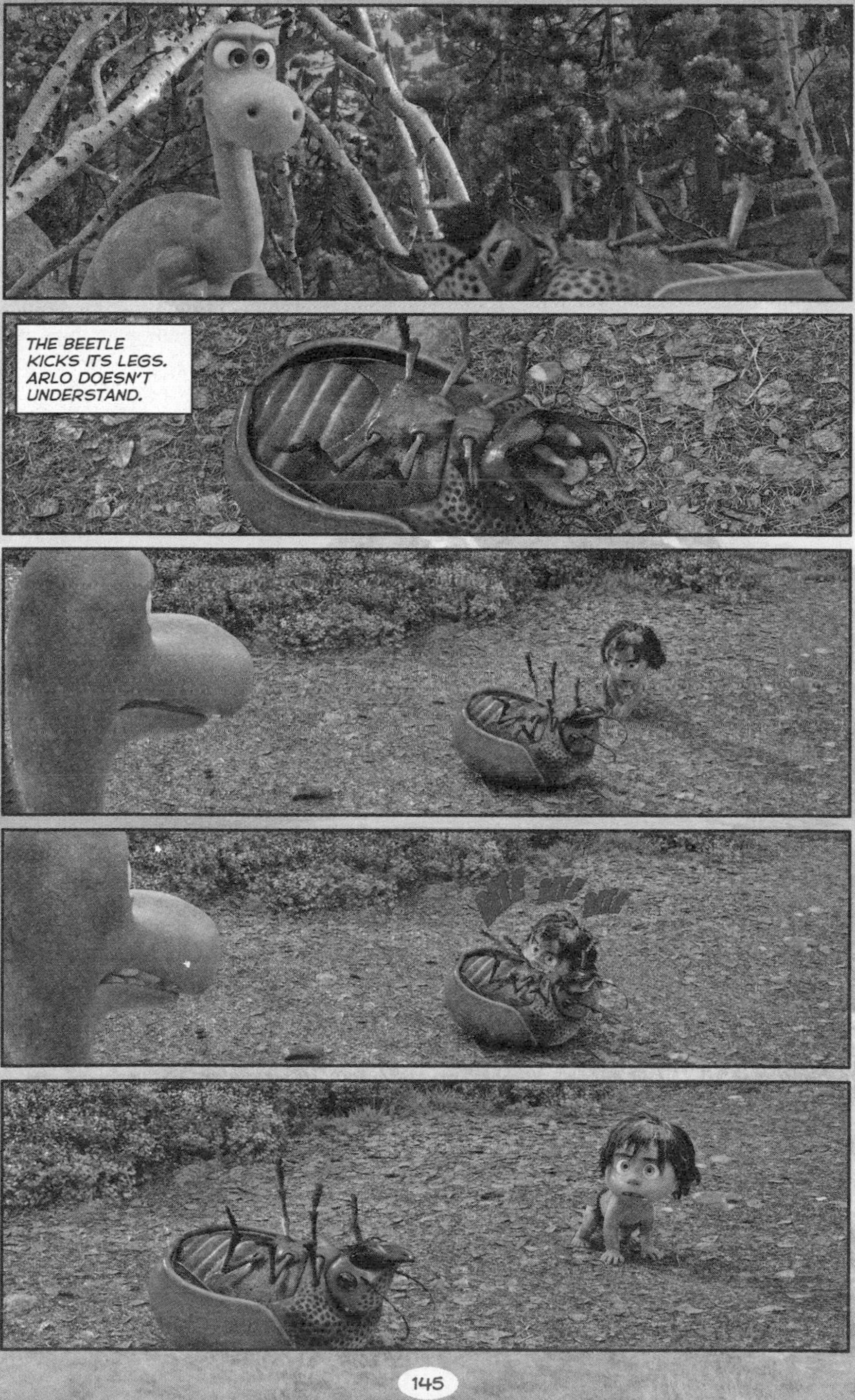
THE BEETLE KICKS ITS LEGS. ARLO DOESN'T UNDERSTAND.

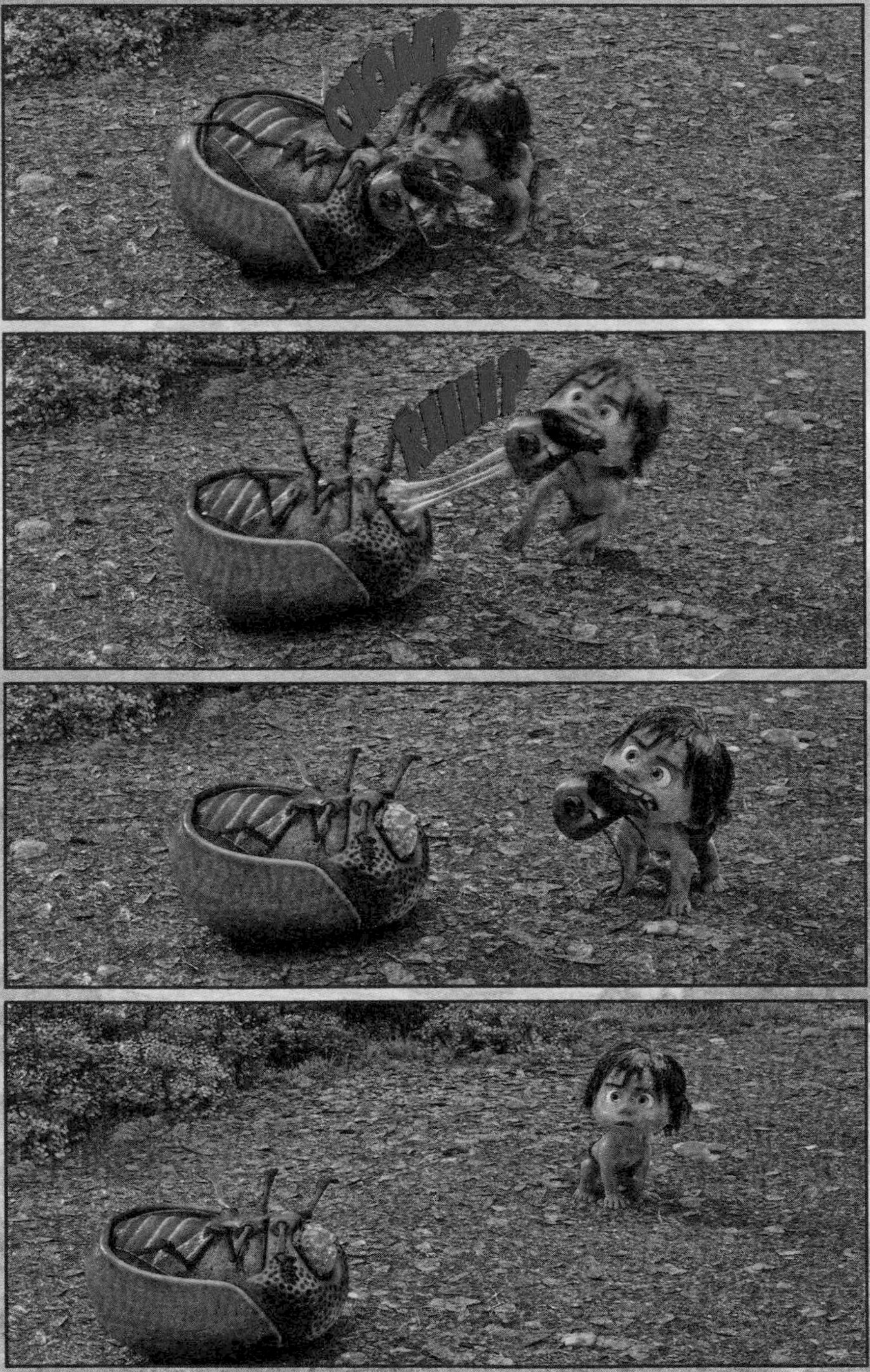
CHOMP
RIIIIP

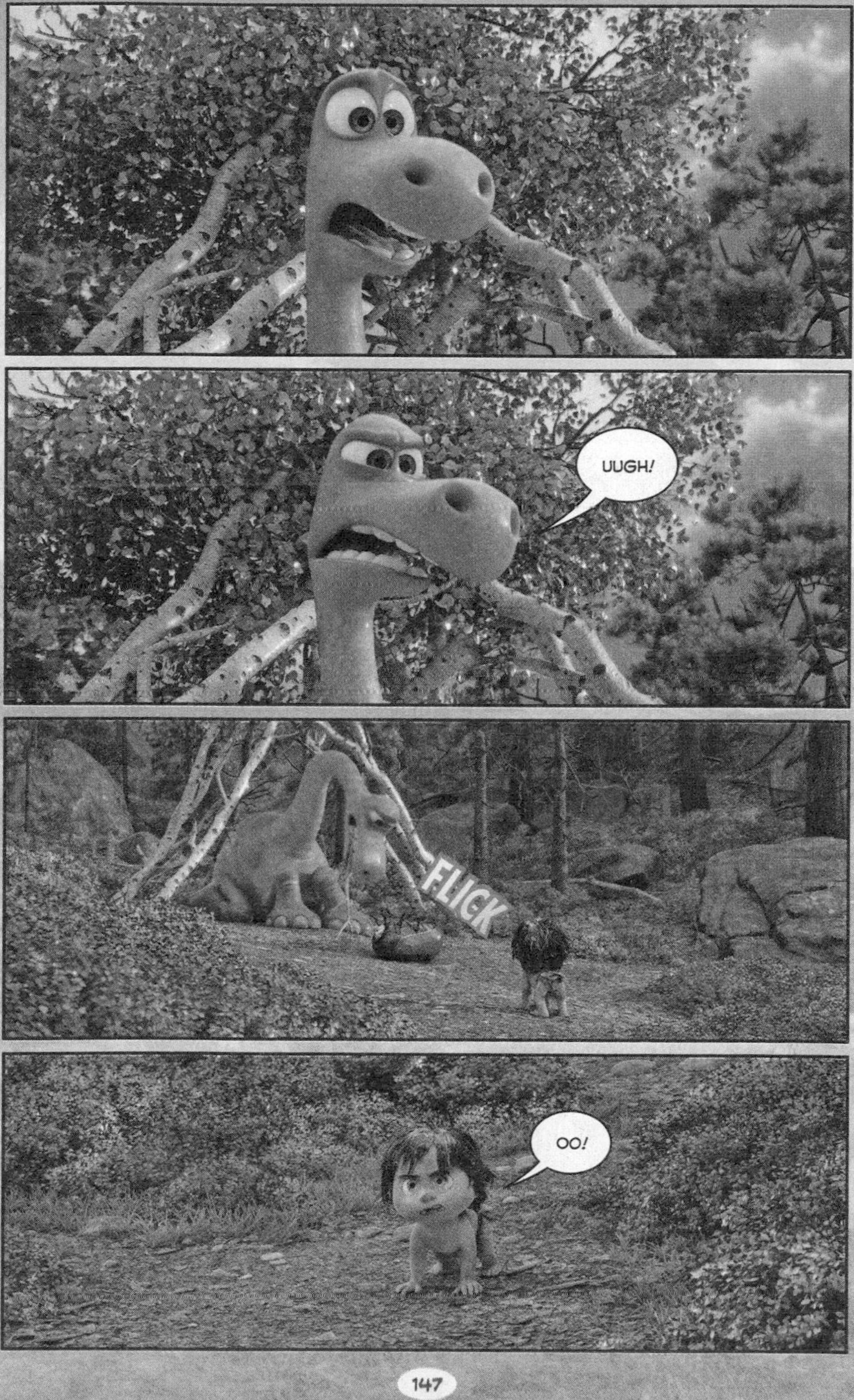
UUGH!
FLICK
OO!

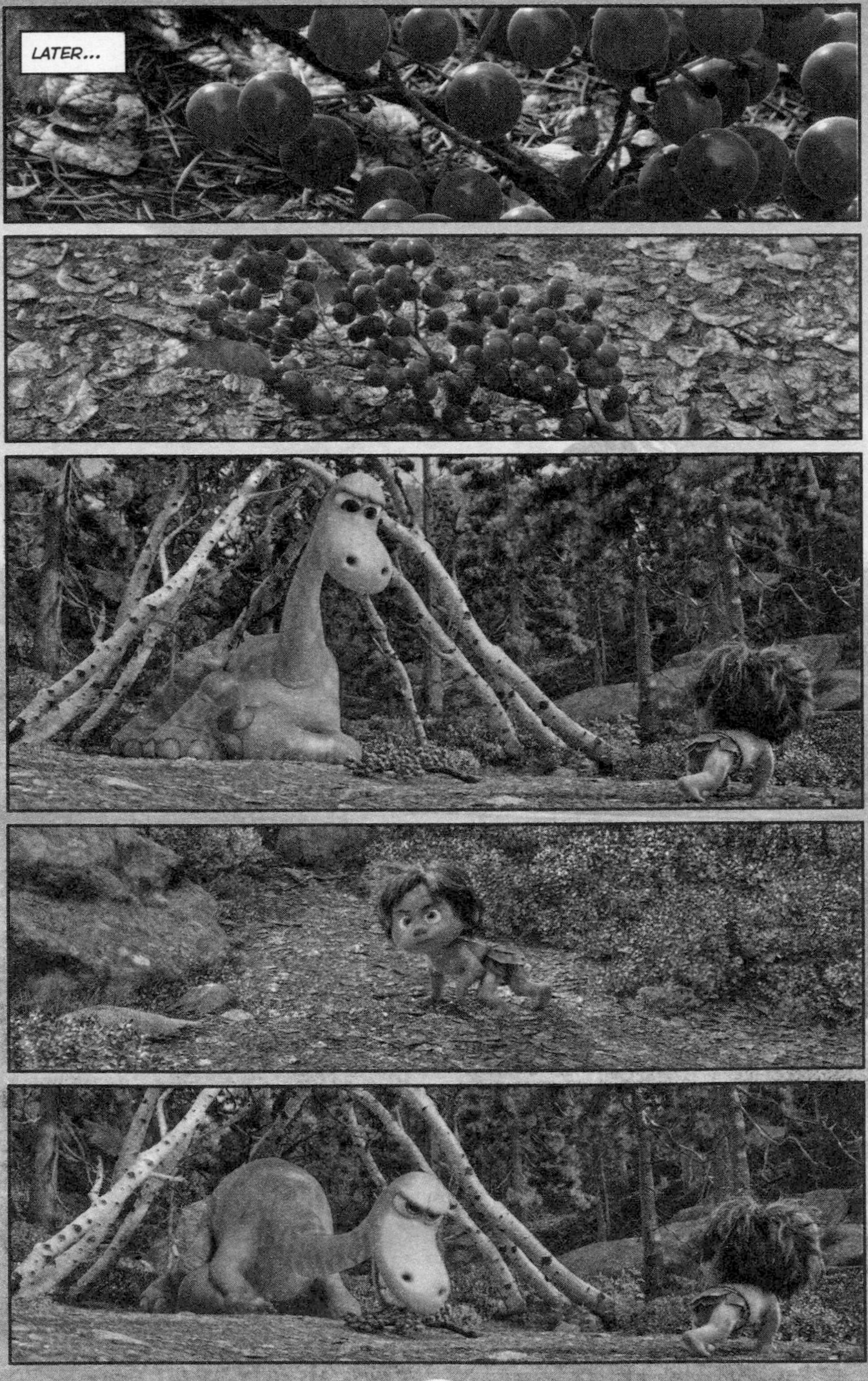
LATER...

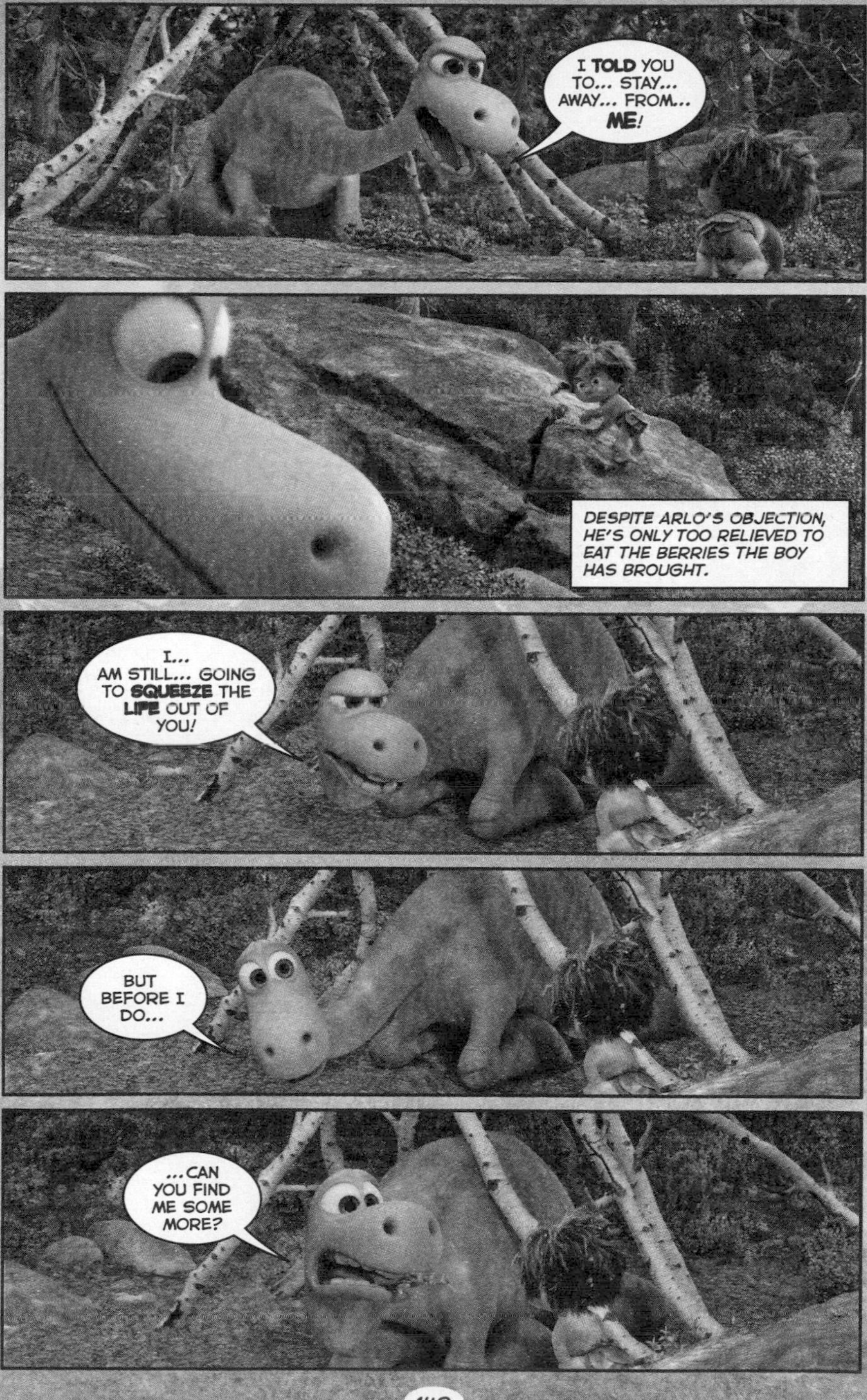
I TOLD YOU TO... STAY... AWAY... FROM... ME!
DESPITE ARLO'S OBJECTION, HE'S ONLY TOO RELIEVED TO EAT THE BERRIES THE BOY HAS BROUGHT.
I... AM STILL... GOING TO SQUEEZE THE LIFE OUT OF YOU!
BUT BEFORE I DO...
...CAN YOU FIND ME SOME MORE?

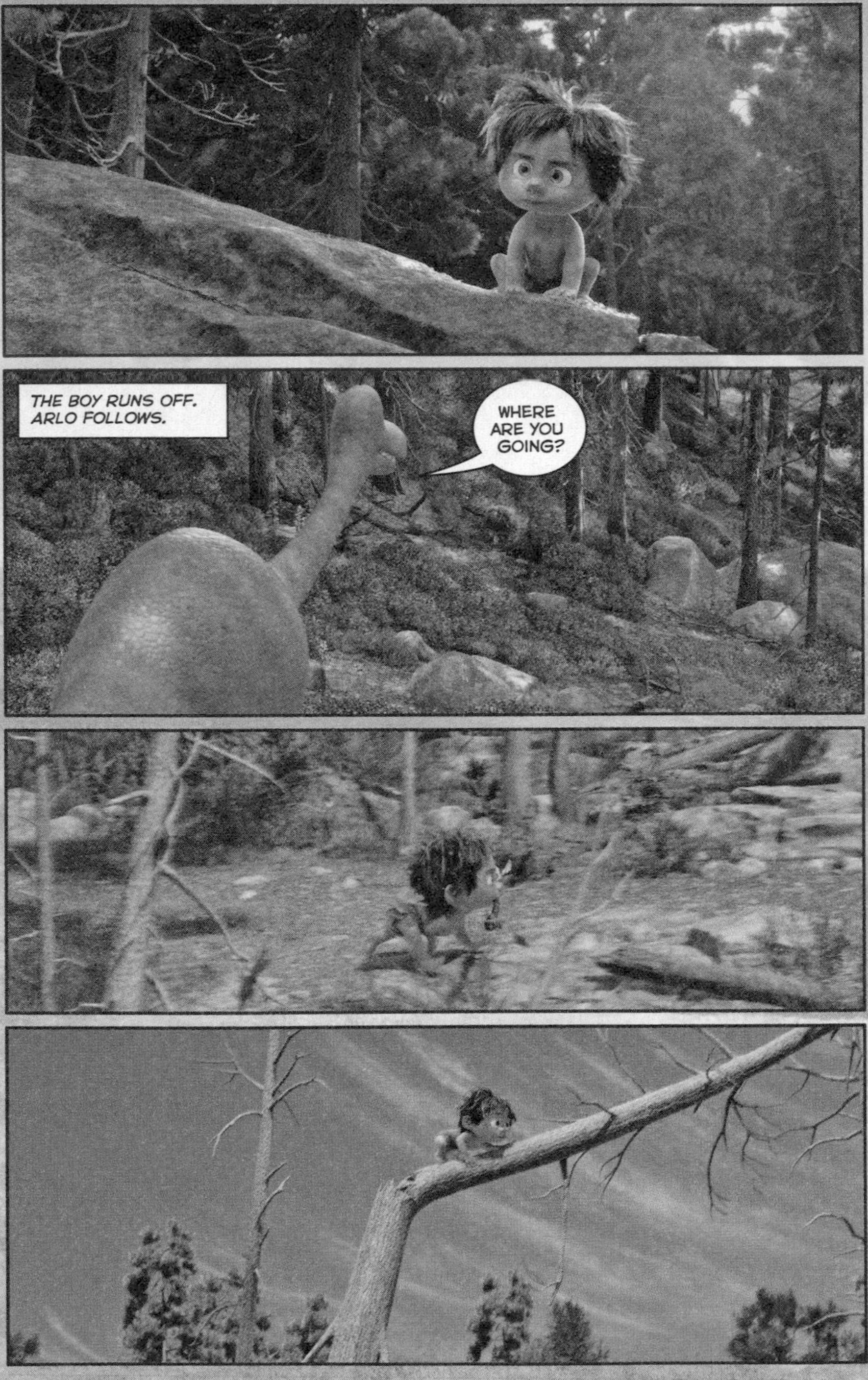
THE BOY RUNS OFF. ARLO FOLLOWS.
WHERE ARE YOU GOING?

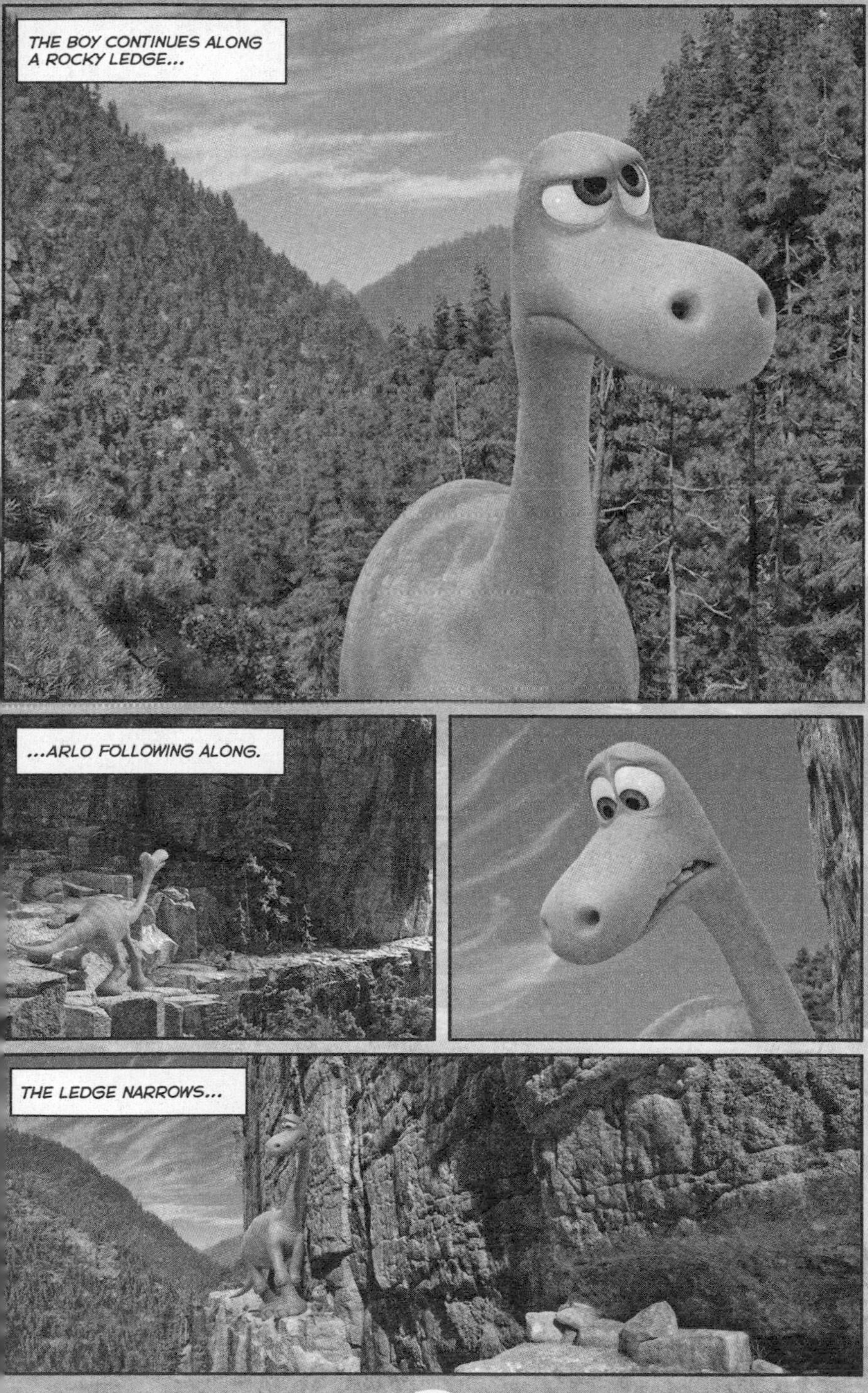
THE BOY CONTINUES ALONG A ROCKY LEDGE...
...ARLO FOLLOWING ALONG.
THE LEDGE NARROWS...

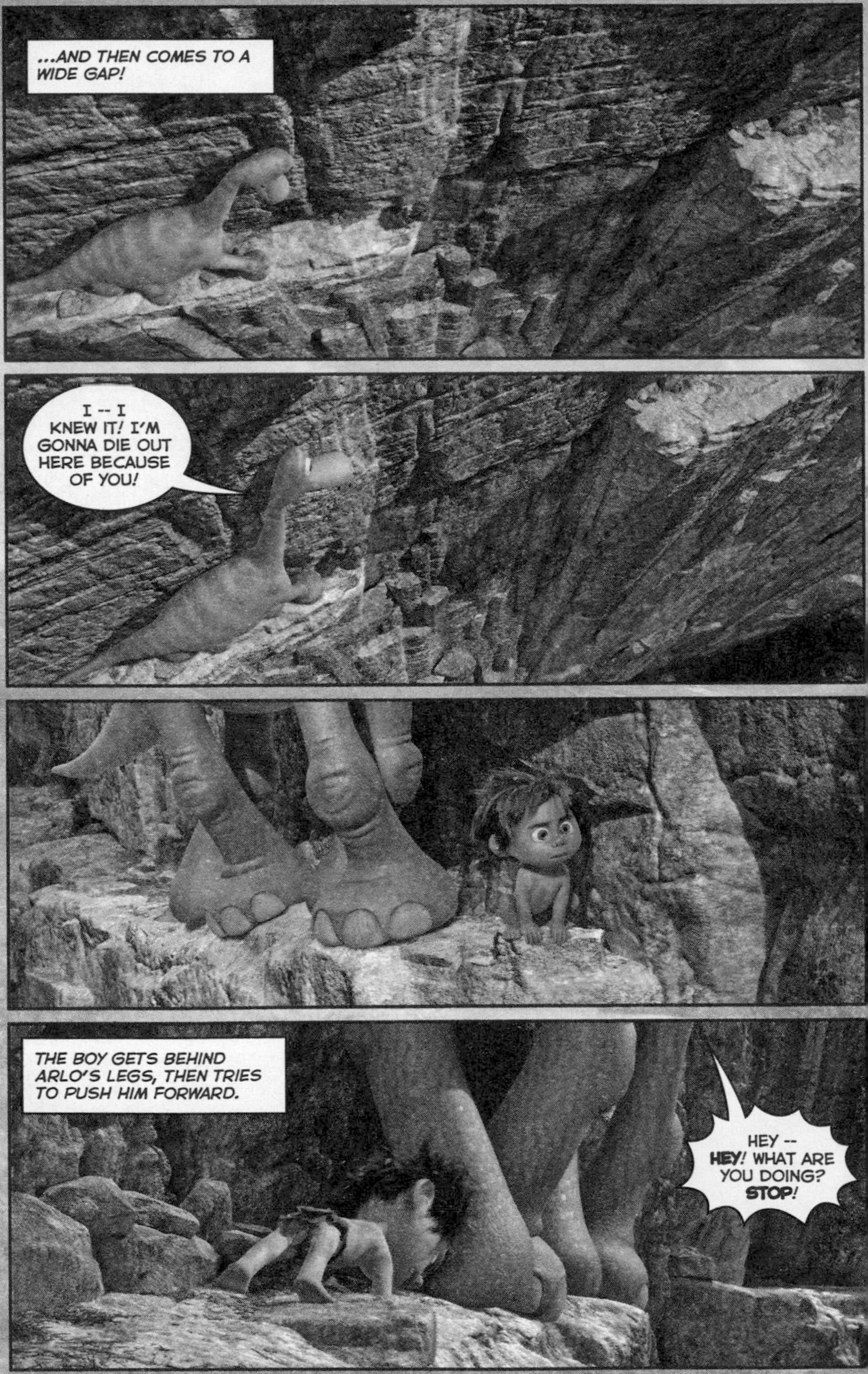
...AND THEN COMES TO A WIDE GAP!
I -- I KNEW IT! I'M GONNA DIE OUT HERE BECAUSE OF YOU!
THE BOY GETS BEHIND ARLO'S LEGS, THEN TRIES TO PUSH HIM FORWARD.
HEY -- HEY! WHAT ARE YOU DOING? STOP!

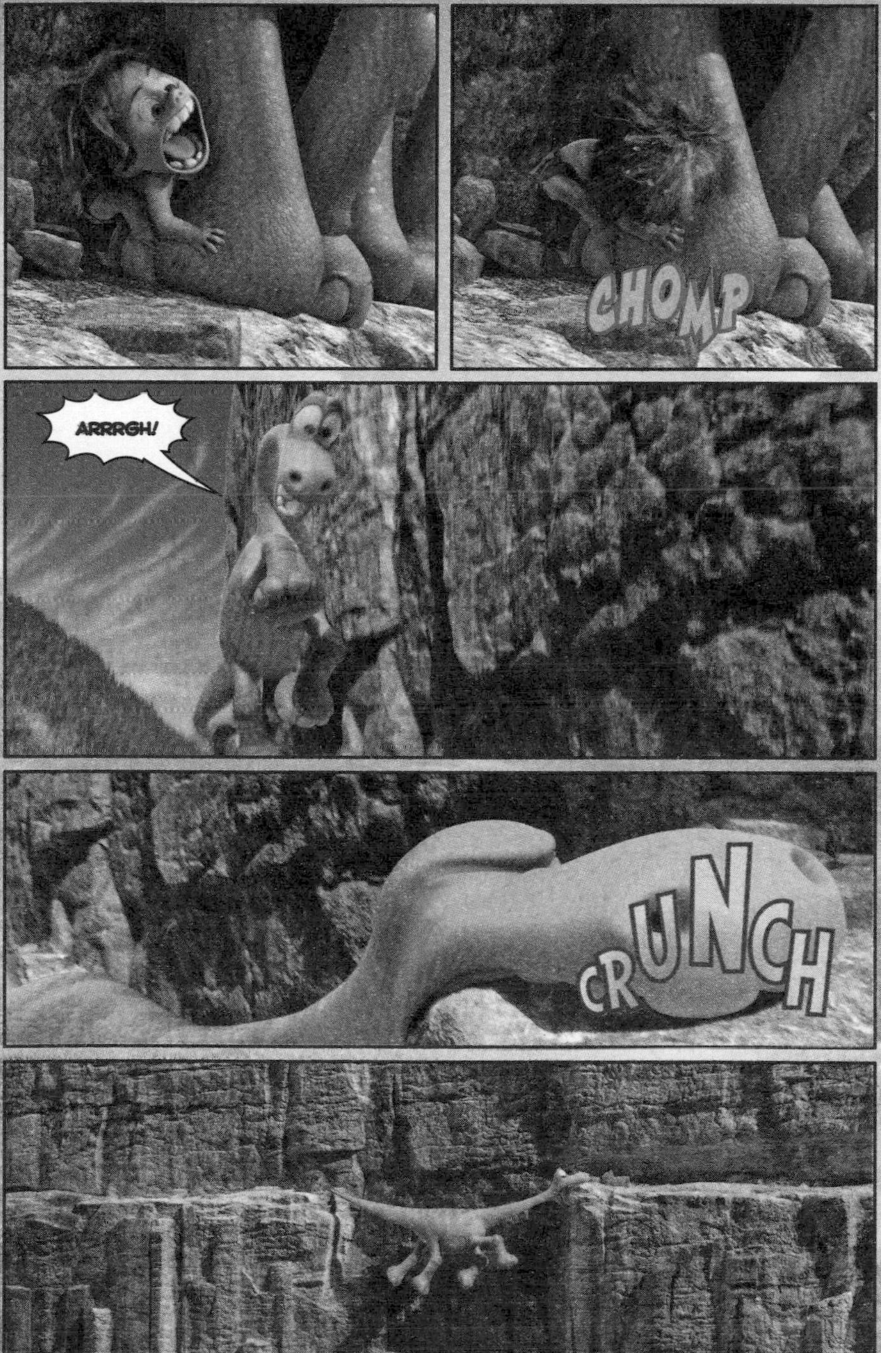
CHOMP
ARRRGH!
CRUNCH

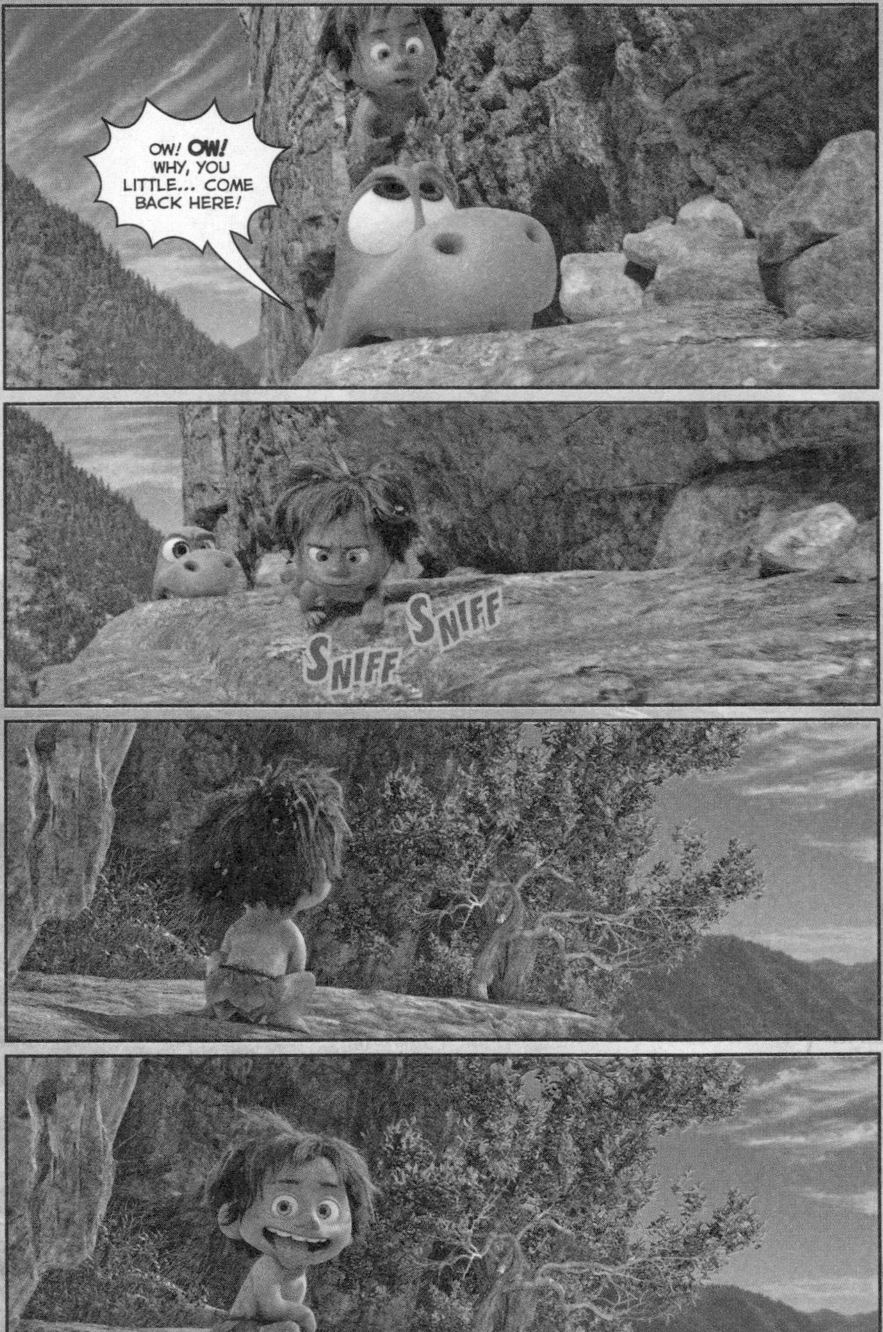
OW! OW! WHY, YOU LITTLE... COME BACK HERE!
SNIFF
SNIFF

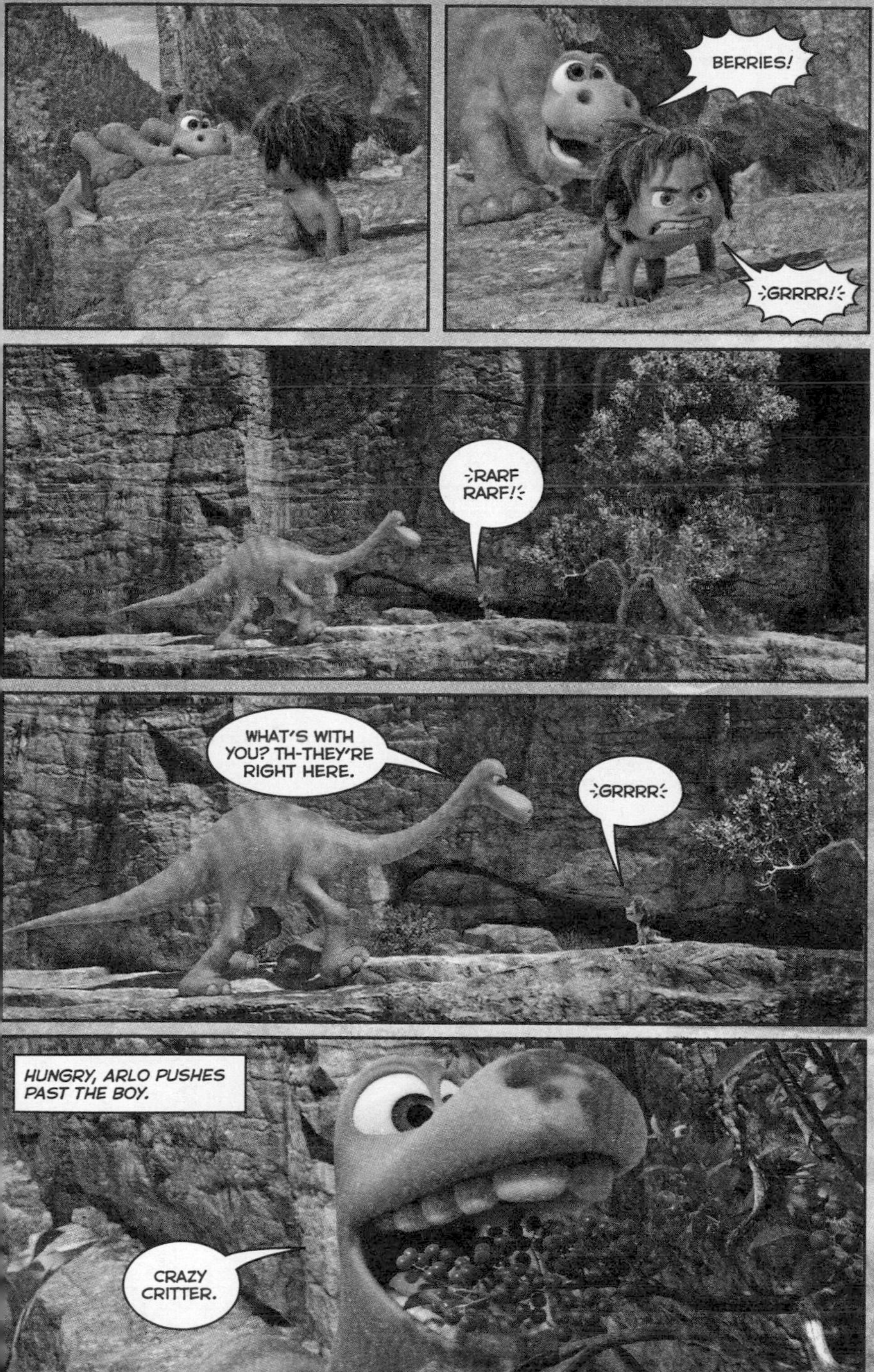
BERRIES!
GRRRR!
RARF RARF!
WHAT'S WITH YOU? TH-THEY'RE RIGHT HERE.
GRRRR
HUNGRY, ARLO PUSHES PAST THE BOY.
CRAZY CRITTER.

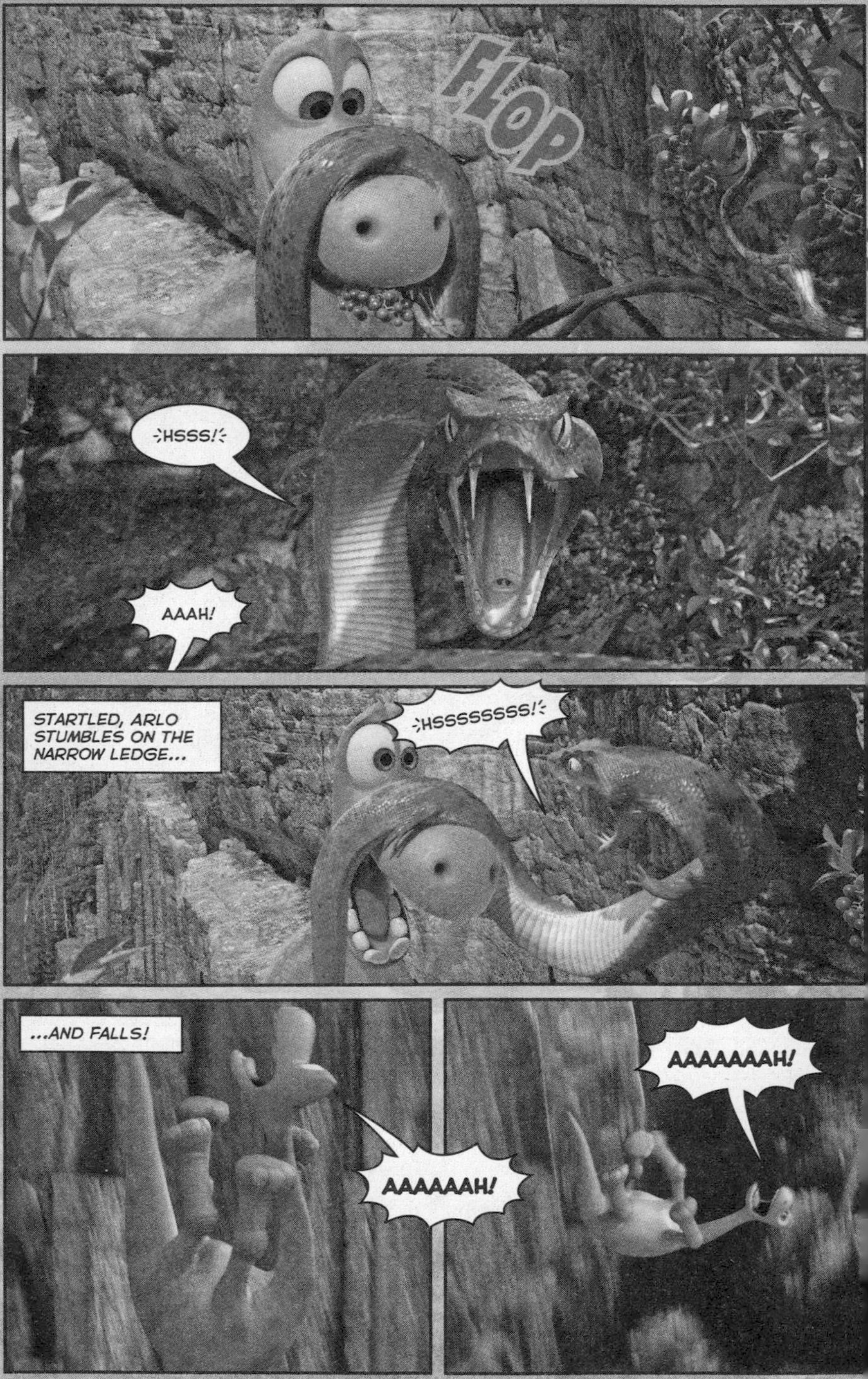
FLOP
HSSS!
AAAH!
STARTLED, ARLO STUMBLES ON THE NARROW LEDGE...
HSSSSSSSS!
...AND FALLS!
AAAAAAH!
AAAAAAAH!

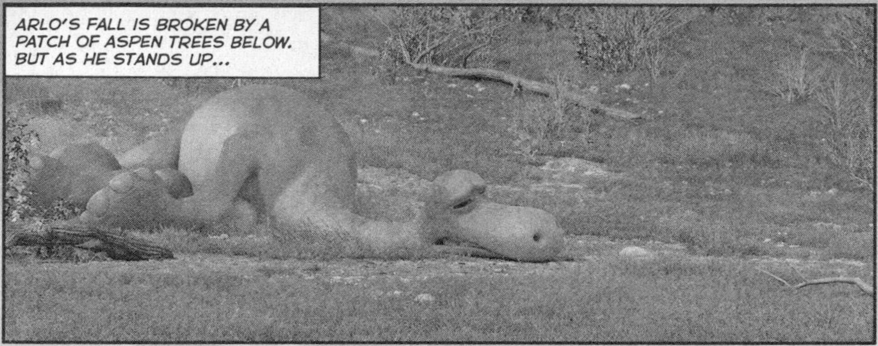
ARLO'S FALL IS BROKEN BY A PATCH OF ASPEN TREES BELOW. BUT AS HE STANDS UP...

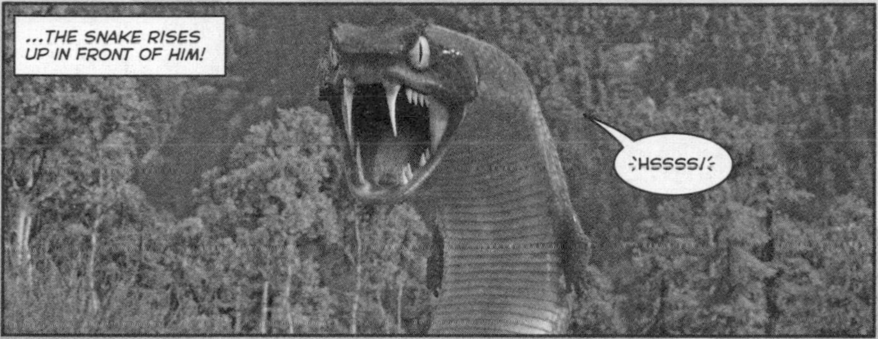
...THE SNAKE RISES UP IN FRONT OF HIM!
HSSSS!

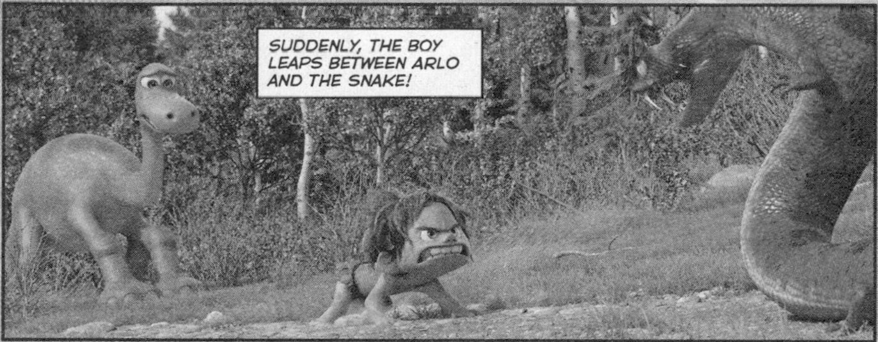
SUDDENLY, THE BOY LEAPS BETWEEN ARLO AND THE SNAKE!

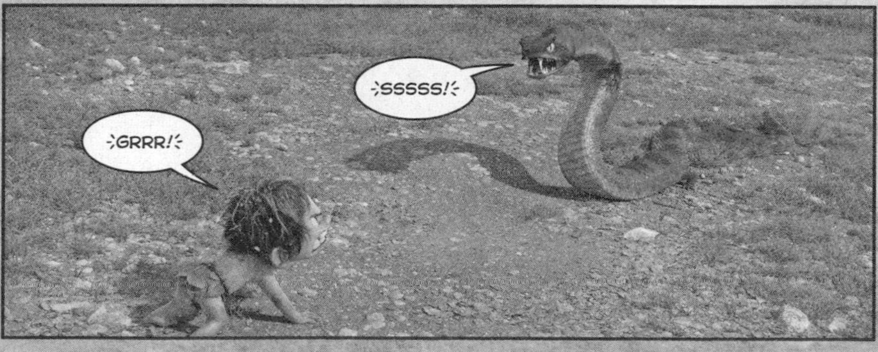
SSSSS!
GRRR!

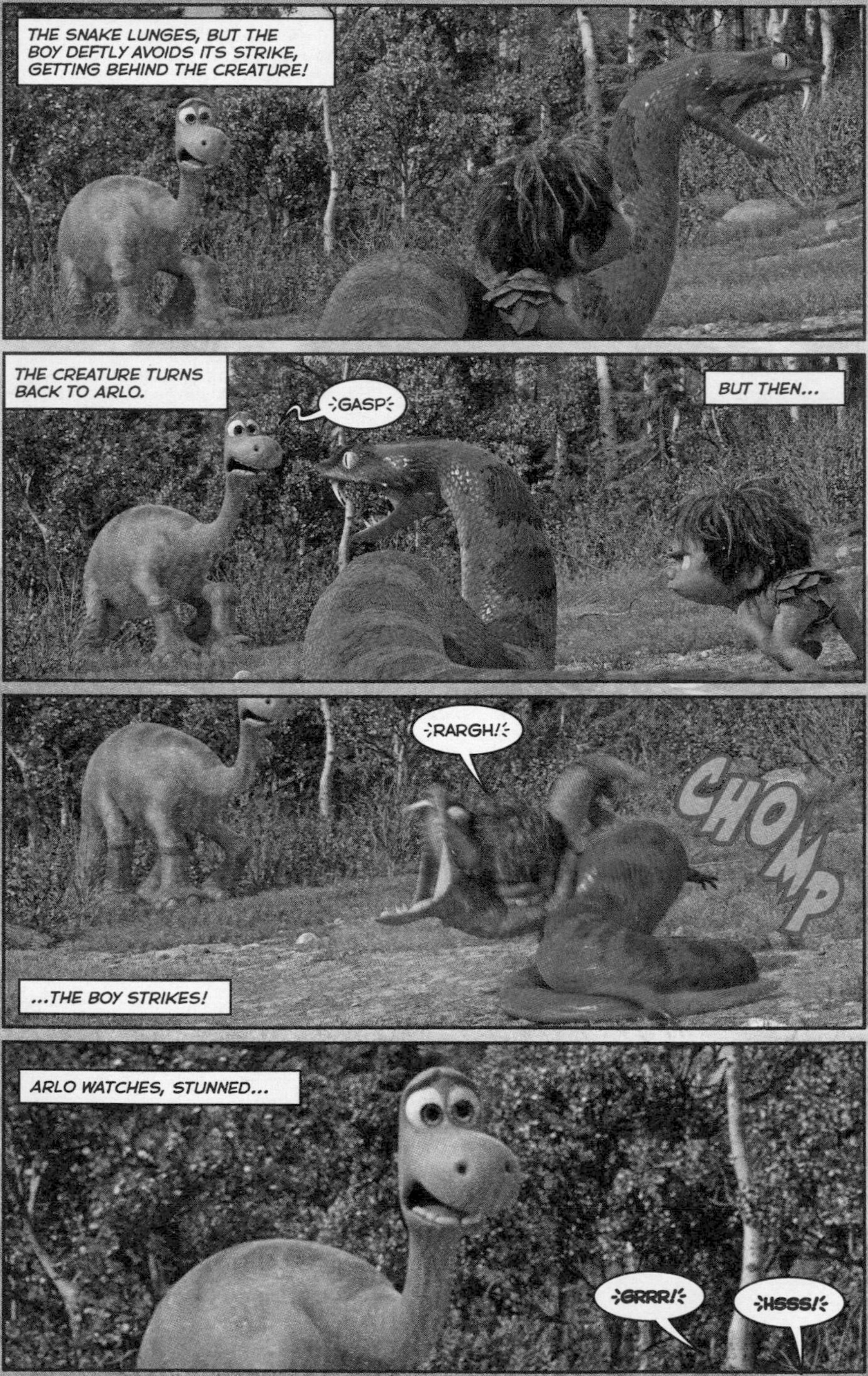
THE SNAKE LUNGES, BUT THE BOY DEFTLY AVOIDS ITS STRIKE, GETTING BEHIND THE CREATURE!
THE CREATURE TURNS BACK TO ARLO.
GASP
BUT THEN...
RARGH!
CHOMP
...THE BOY STRIKES!
ARLO WATCHES, STUNNED...
GRRR!
HSSS!

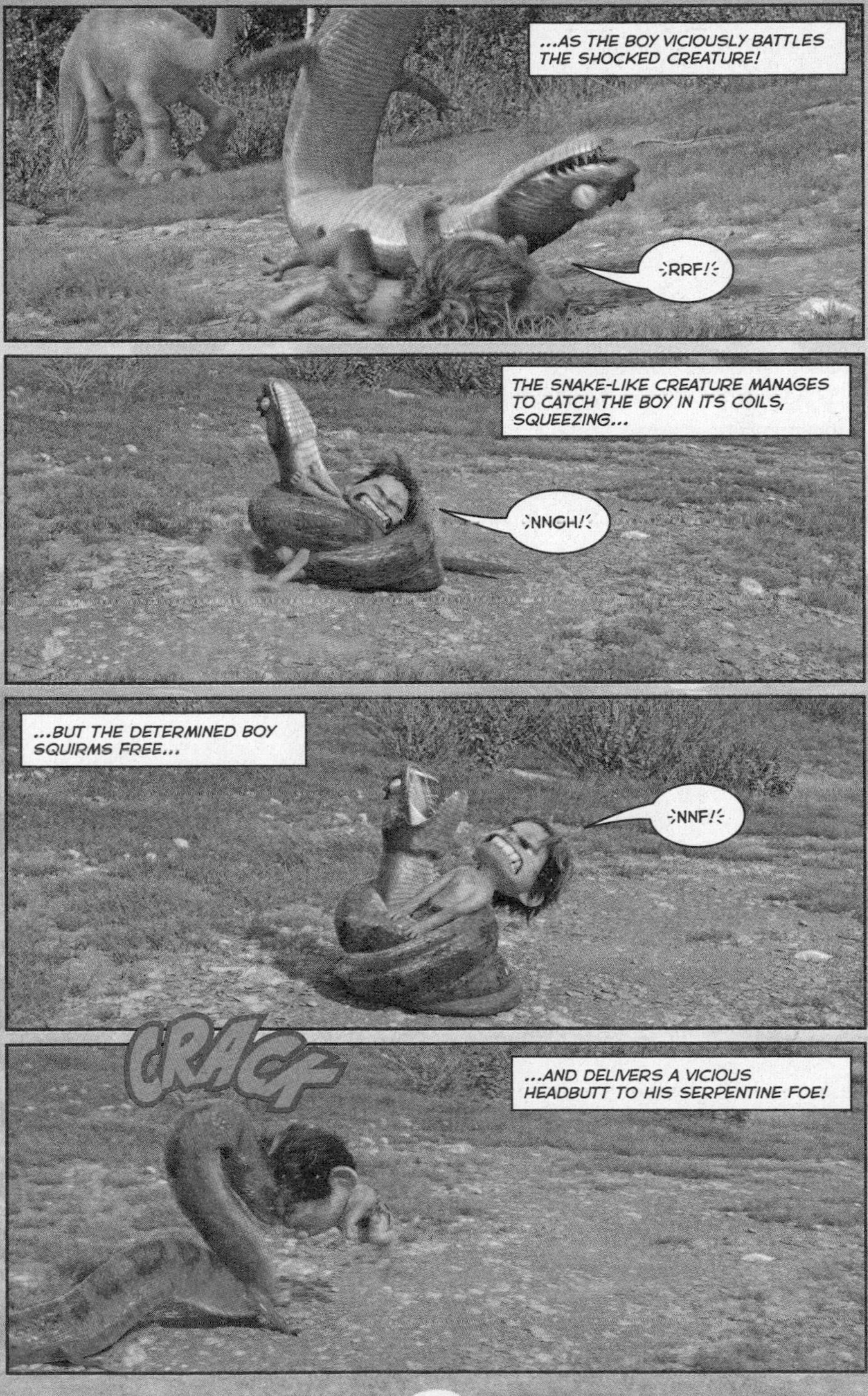
...AS THE BOY VICIOUSLY BATTLES THE SHOCKED CREATURE!
RRF!
THE SNAKE-LIKE CREATURE MANAGES TO CATCH THE BOY IN ITS COILS, SQUEEZING...
NNGH!
...BUT THE DETERMINED BOY SQUIRMS FREE...
NNF!
CRACK
...AND DELIVERS A VICIOUS HEADBUTT TO HIS SERPENTINE FOE!

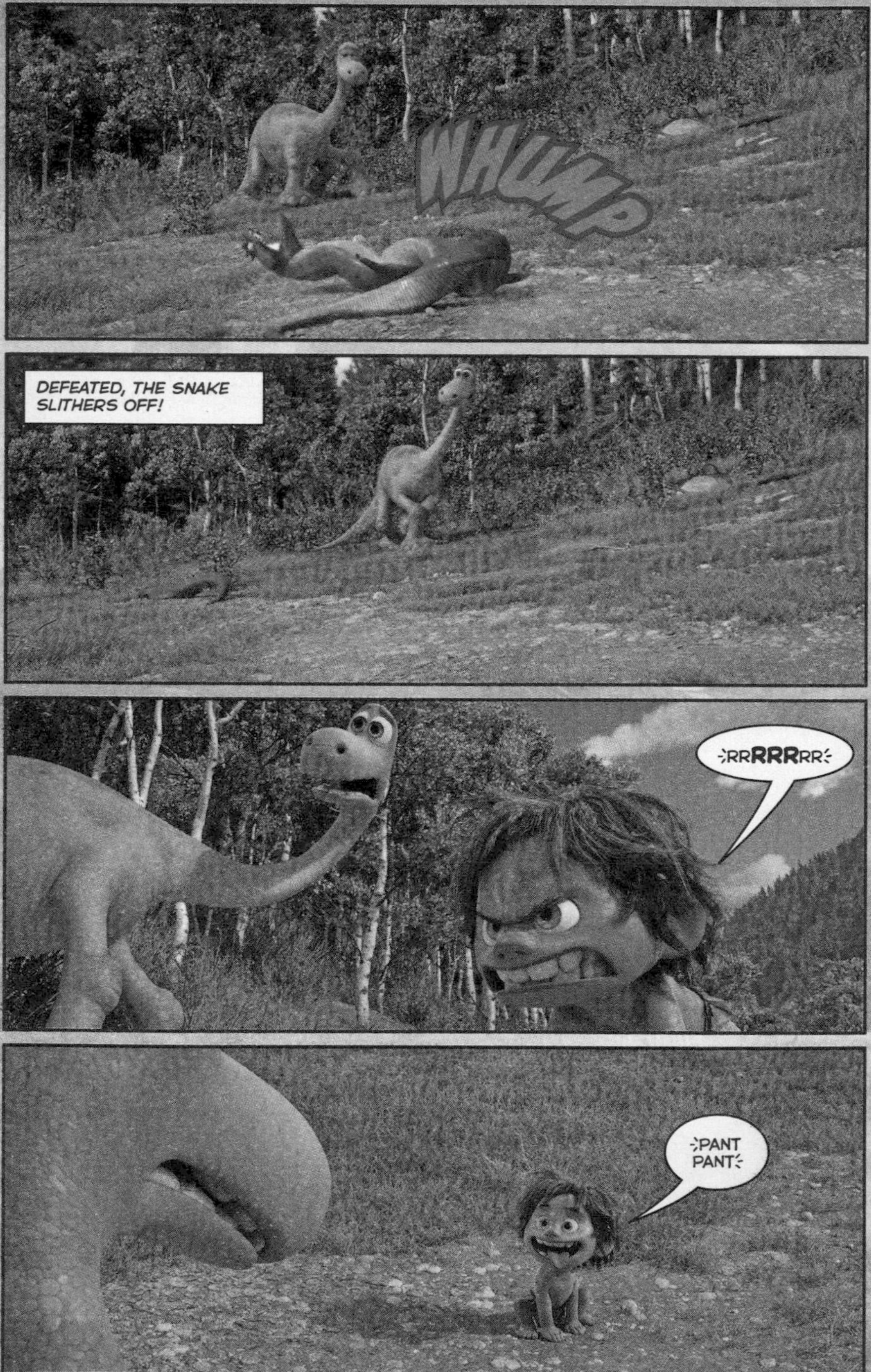
WHUMP
DEFEATED, THE SNAKE SLITHERS OFF!
RRRRRRR
PANT PANT

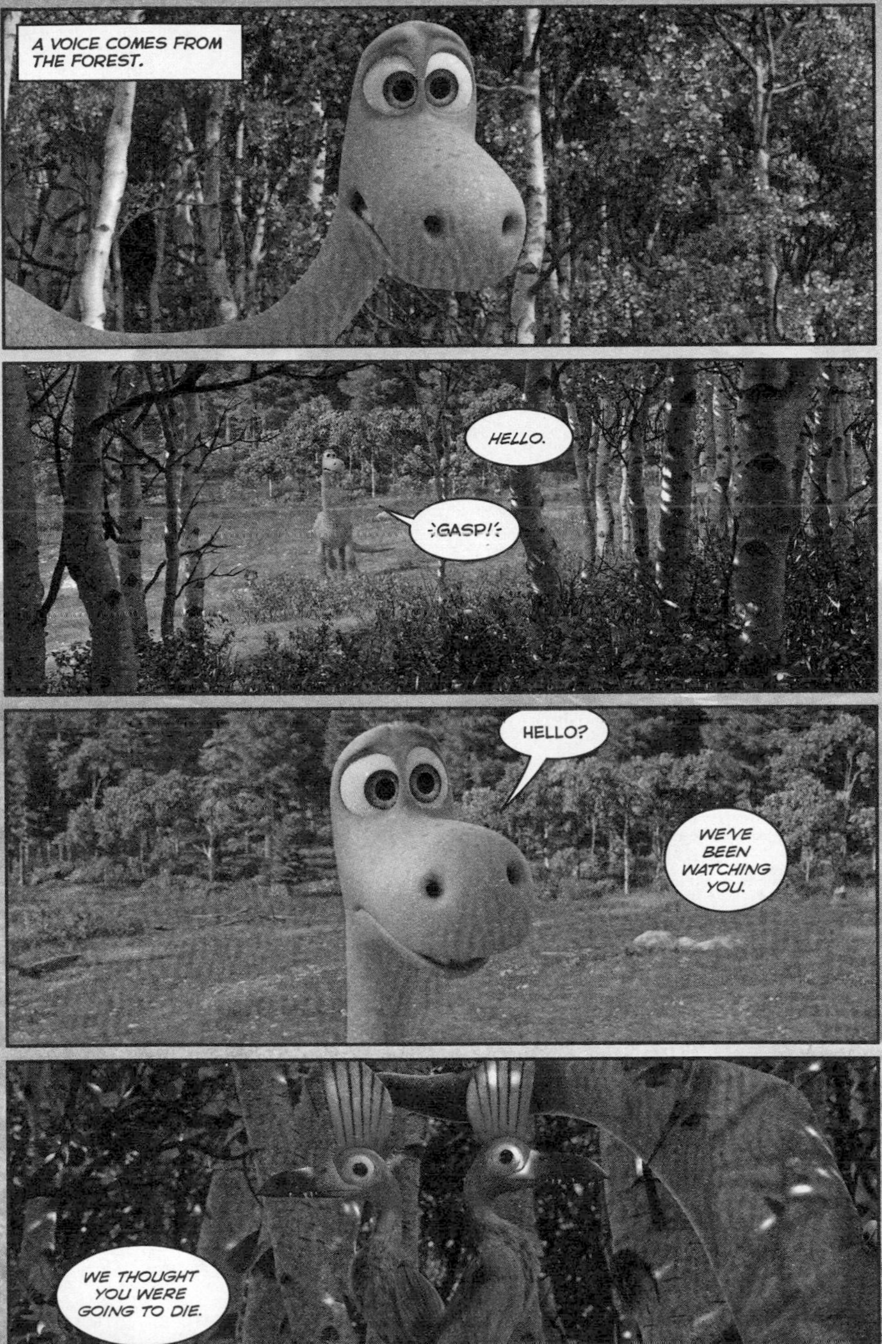
A VOICE COMES FROM THE FOREST.
HELLO.
GASP!
HELLO?
WE'VE BEEN WATCHING YOU.
WE THOUGHT YOU WERE GOING TO DIE.

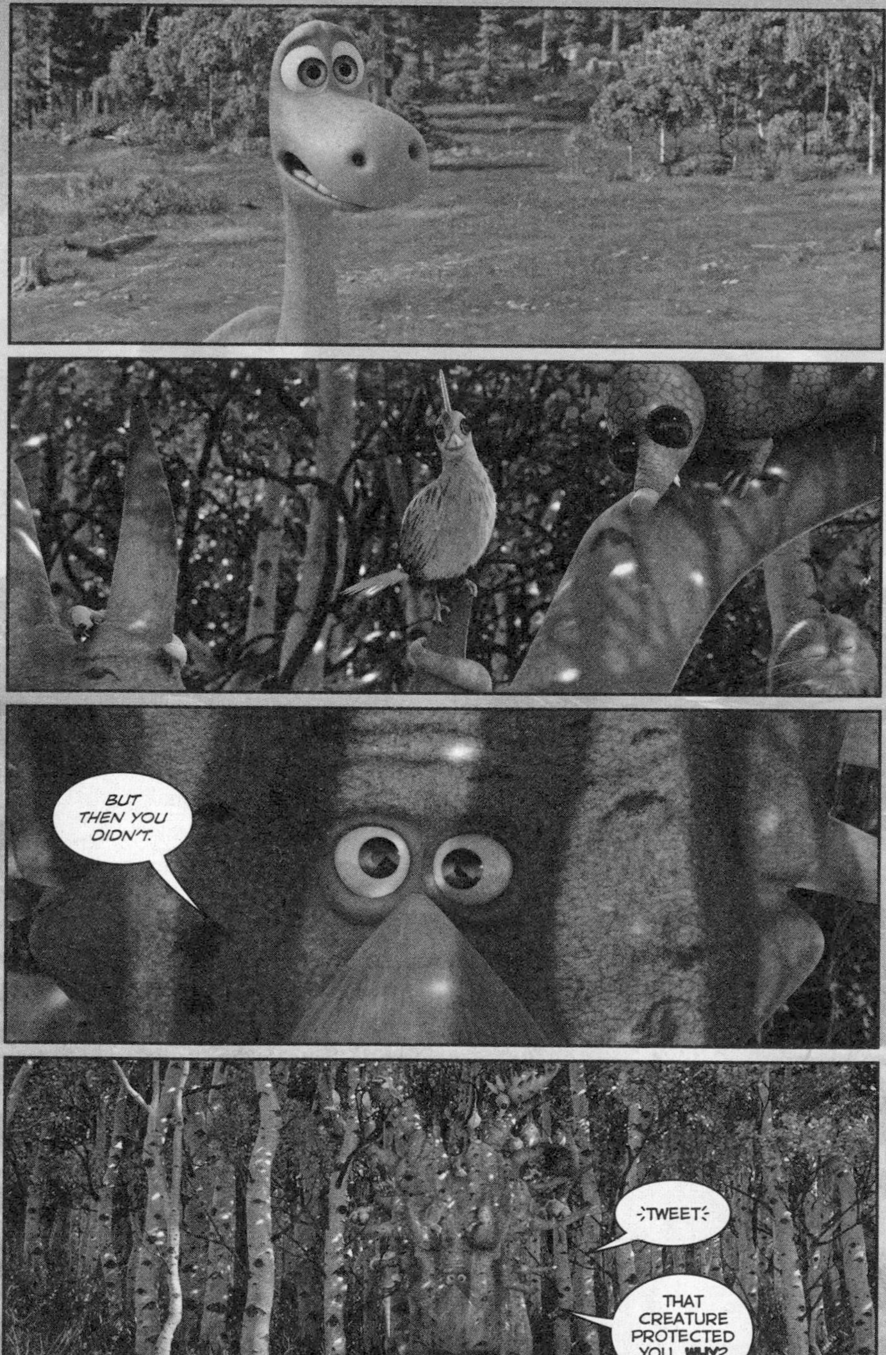
BUT THEN YOU DIDN'T.
TWEET
THAT CREATURE PROTECTED YOU. WHY?

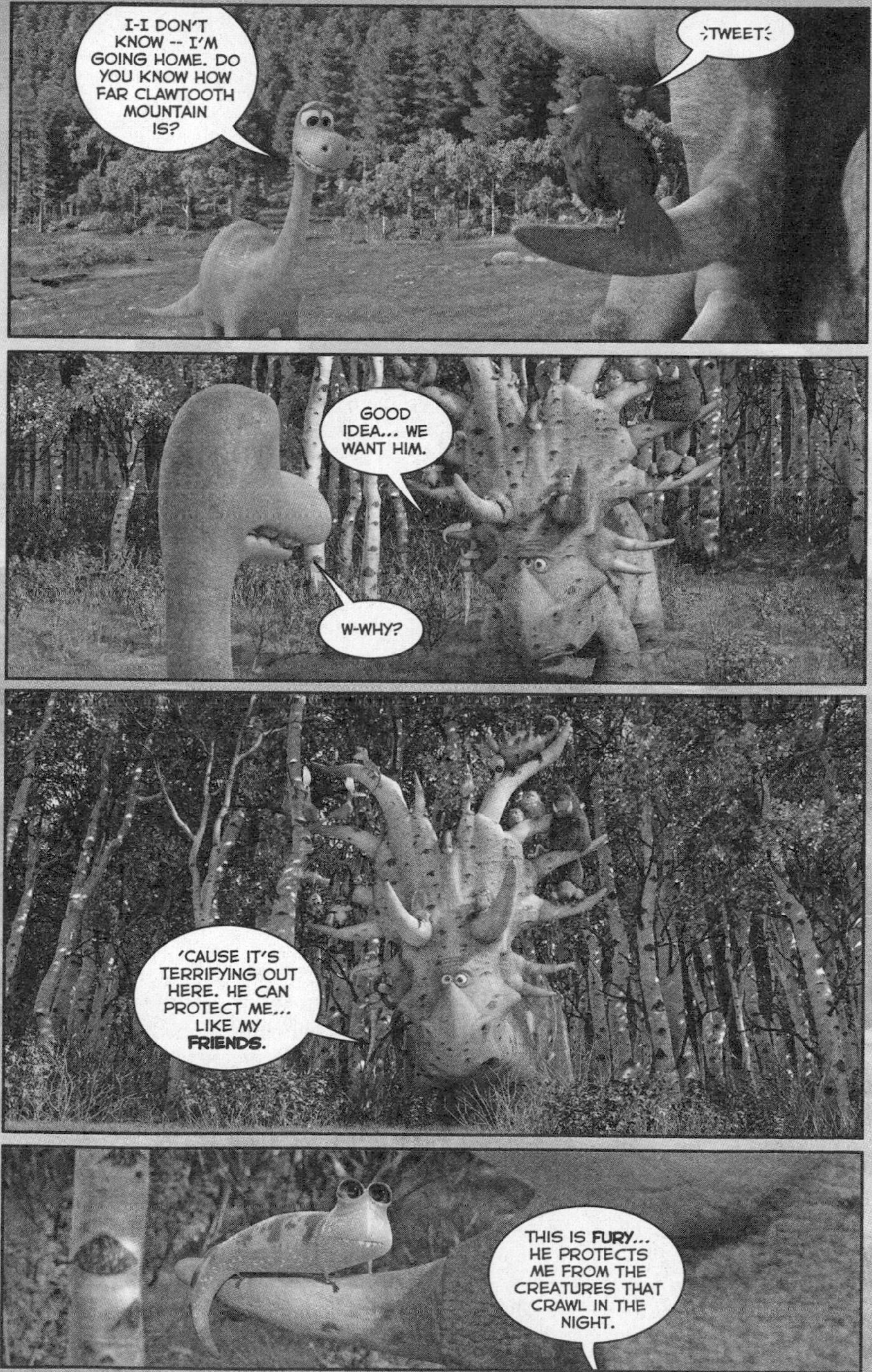
I-I DON'T KNOW -- I'M GOING HOME. DO YOU KNOW HOW FAR CLAWTOOTH MOUNTAIN IS?
TWEET
GOOD IDEA... WE WANT HIM.
W-WHY?
'CAUSE IT'S TERRIFYING OUT HERE. HE CAN PROTECT ME... LIKE MY **FRIENDS**.
THIS IS **FURY**... HE PROTECTS ME FROM THE CREATURES THAT CRAWL IN THE NIGHT.

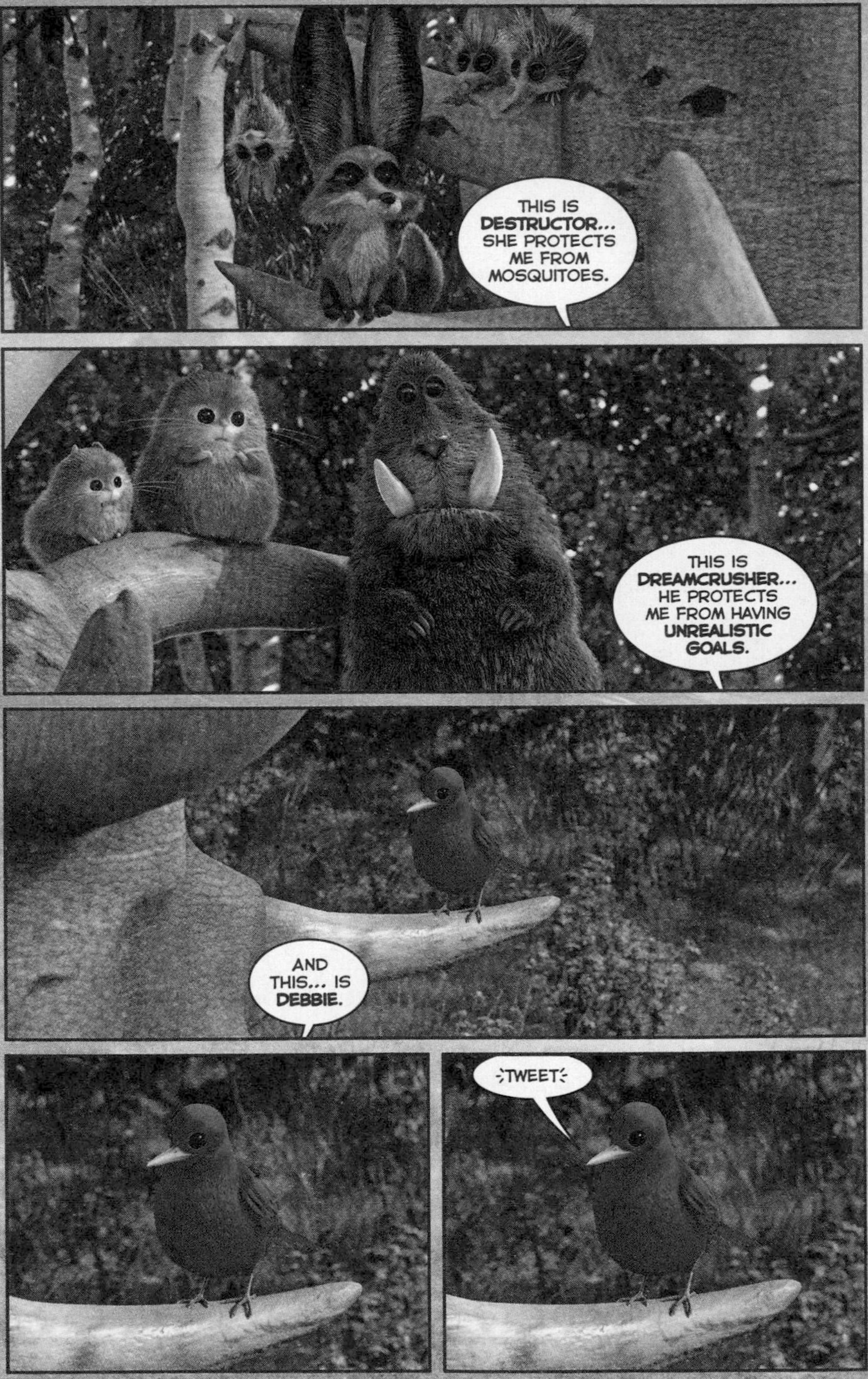
THIS IS **DESTRUCTOR...** SHE PROTECTS ME FROM MOSQUITOES.
THIS IS **DREAMCRUSHER...** HE PROTECTS ME FROM HAVING **UNREALISTIC GOALS.**
AND THIS... IS **DEBBIE.**
TWEET

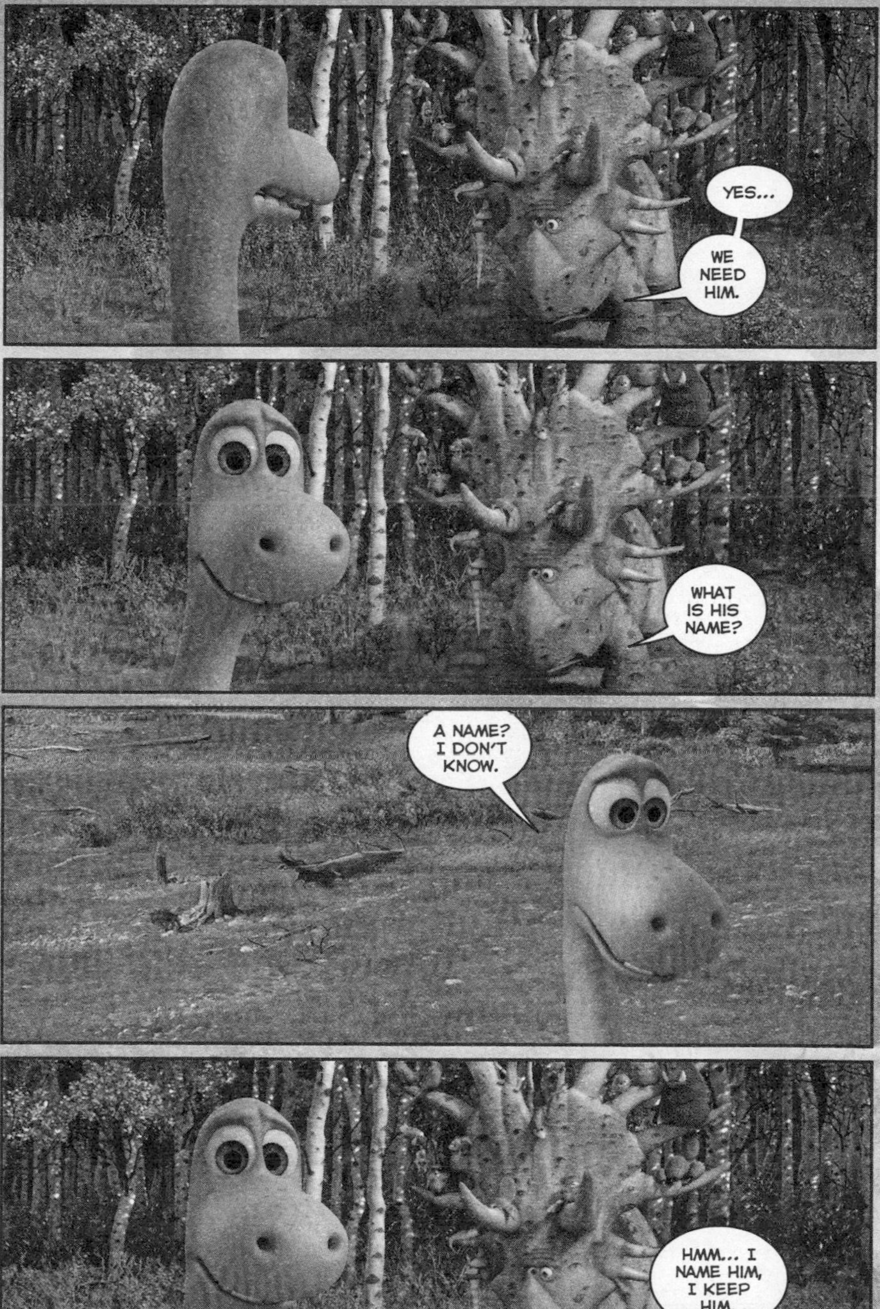
YES...
WE NEED HIM.
WHAT IS HIS NAME?
A NAME? I DON'T KNOW.
HMM... I NAME HIM, I KEEP HIM.

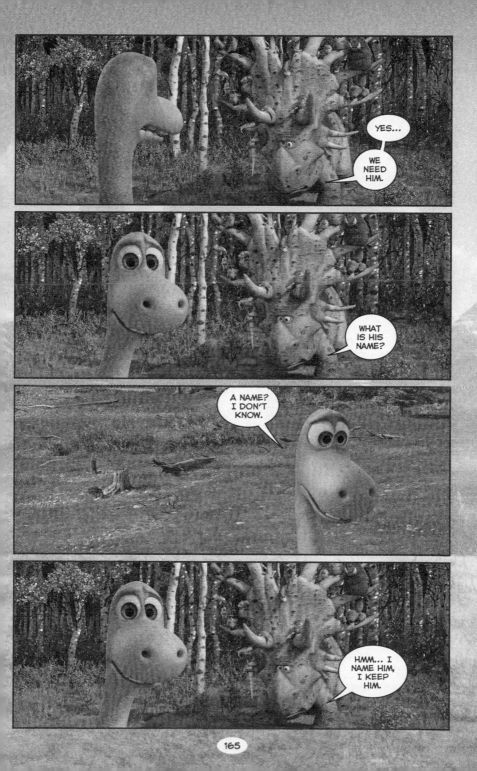

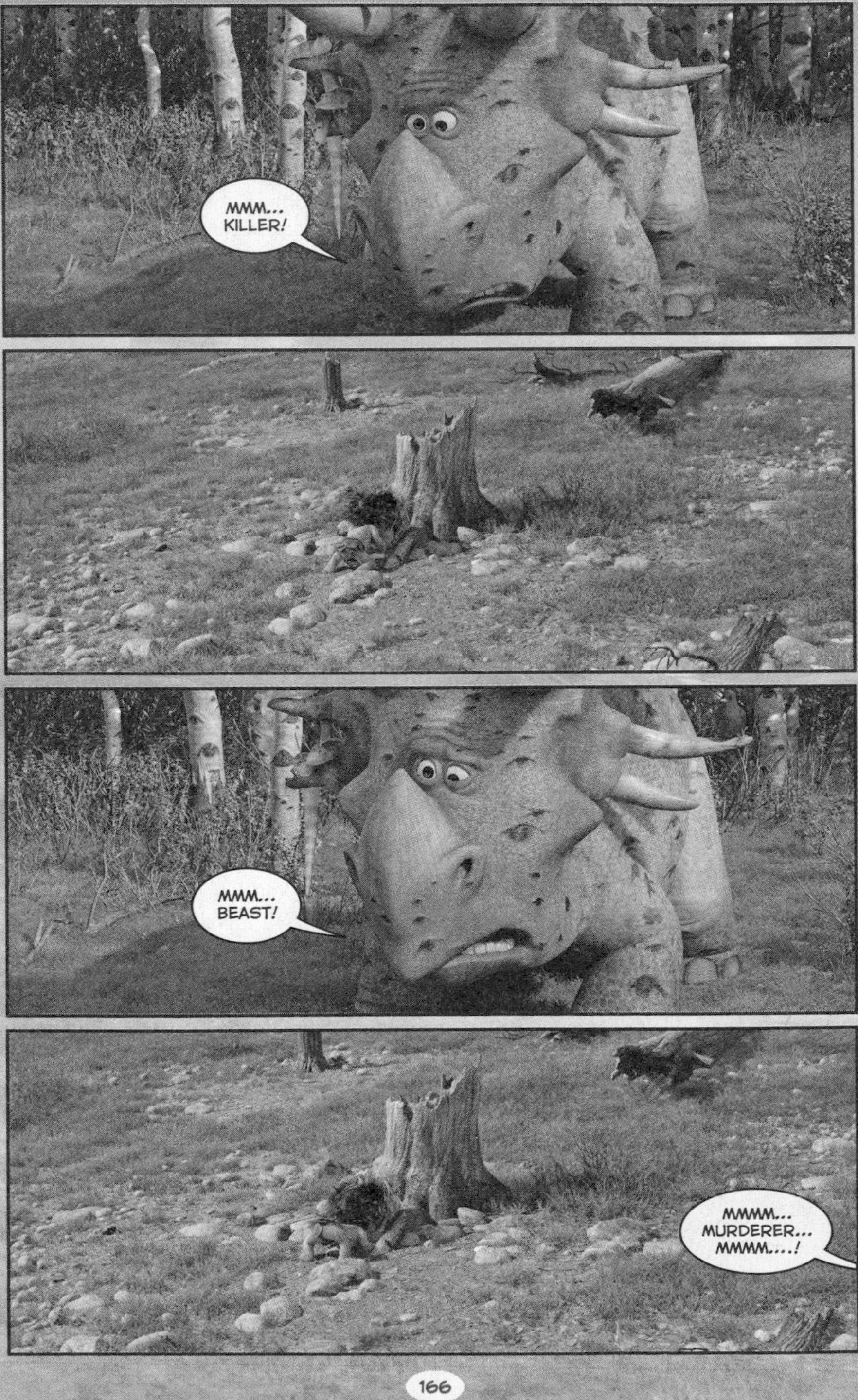
MMM...
KILLER!
MMM...
BEAST!
MMMM...
MURDERER...
MMMM....!

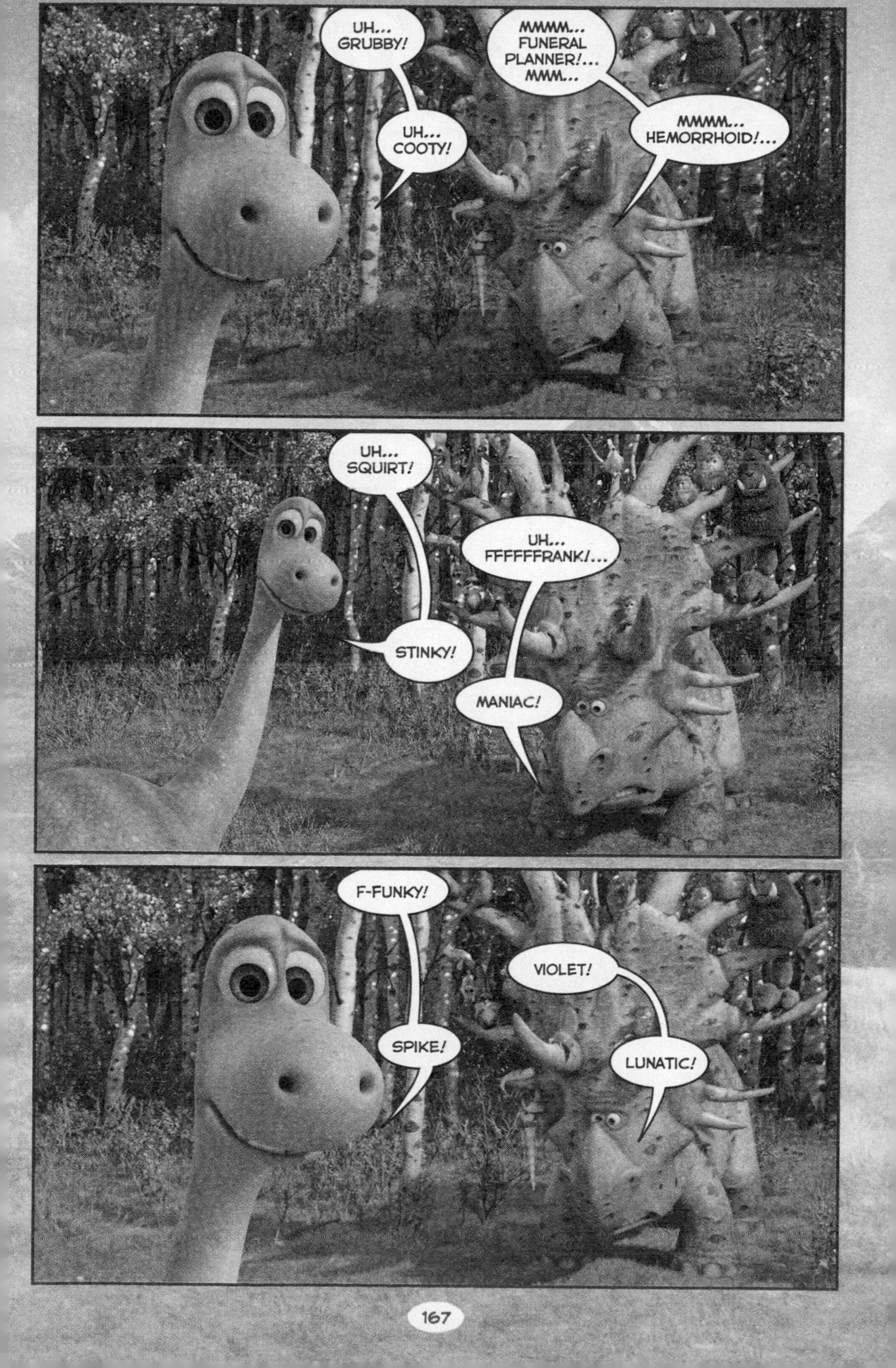
UH... GRUBBY!
MMMM... FUNERAL PLANNER!... MMM...
UH... COOTY!
MMMM... HEMORRHOID!...
UH... SQUIRT!
UH... FFFFFFRANK!...
STINKY!
MANIAC!
F-FUNKY!
VIOLET!
SPIKE!
LUNATIC!

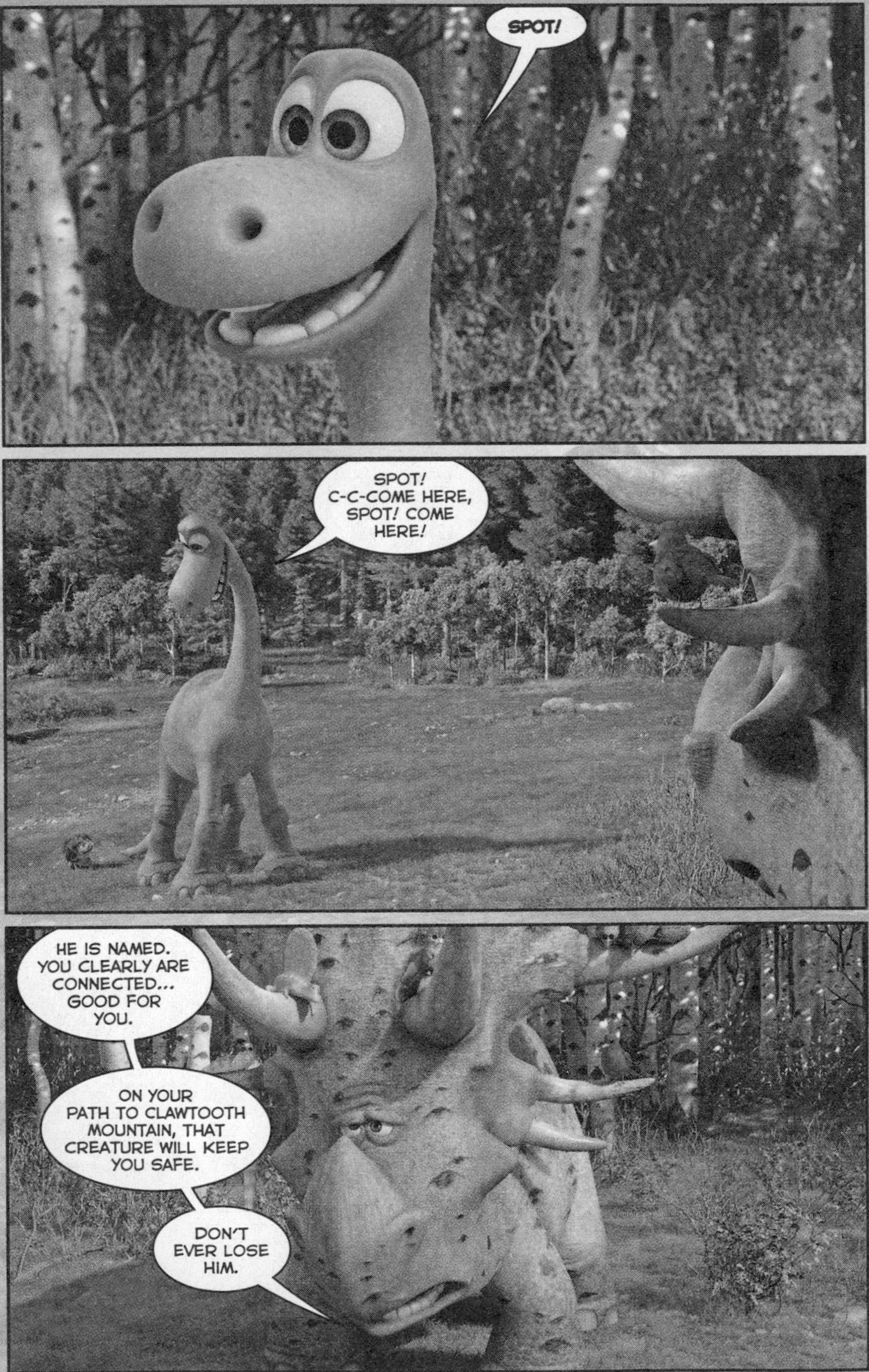
SPOT!
SPOT! C-C-COME HERE, SPOT! COME HERE!
HE IS NAMED. YOU CLEARLY ARE CONNECTED... GOOD FOR YOU.
ON YOUR PATH TO CLAWTOOTH MOUNTAIN, THAT CREATURE WILL KEEP YOU SAFE.
DON'T EVER LOSE HIM.

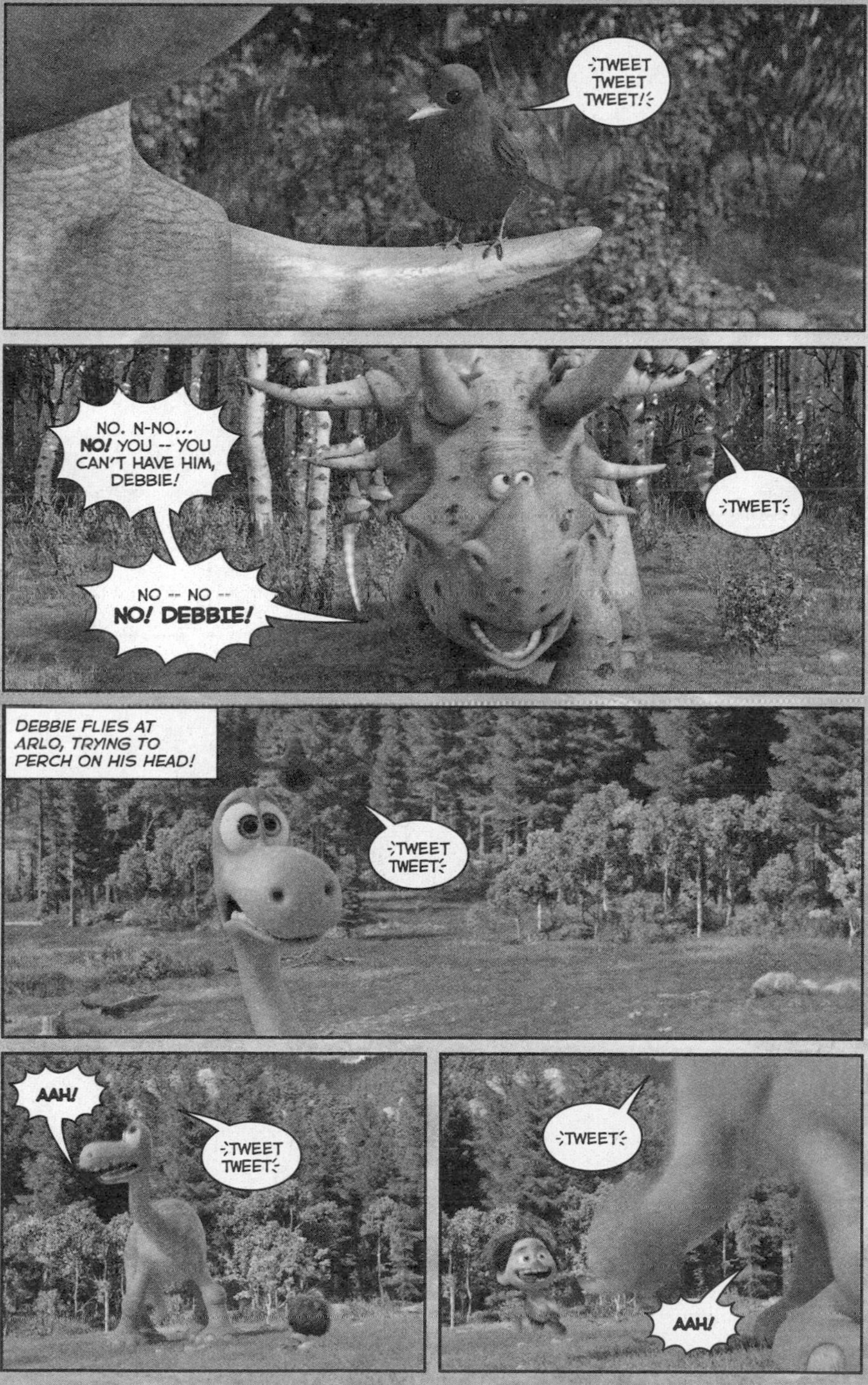
TWEET TWEET TWEET!
NO. N-NO... NO! YOU -- YOU CAN'T HAVE HIM, DEBBIE!
NO -- NO -- NO! DEBBIE!
TWEET
DEBBIE FLIES AT ARLO, TRYING TO PERCH ON HIS HEAD!
TWEET TWEET
AAH!
TWEET TWEET
TWEET
AAH!

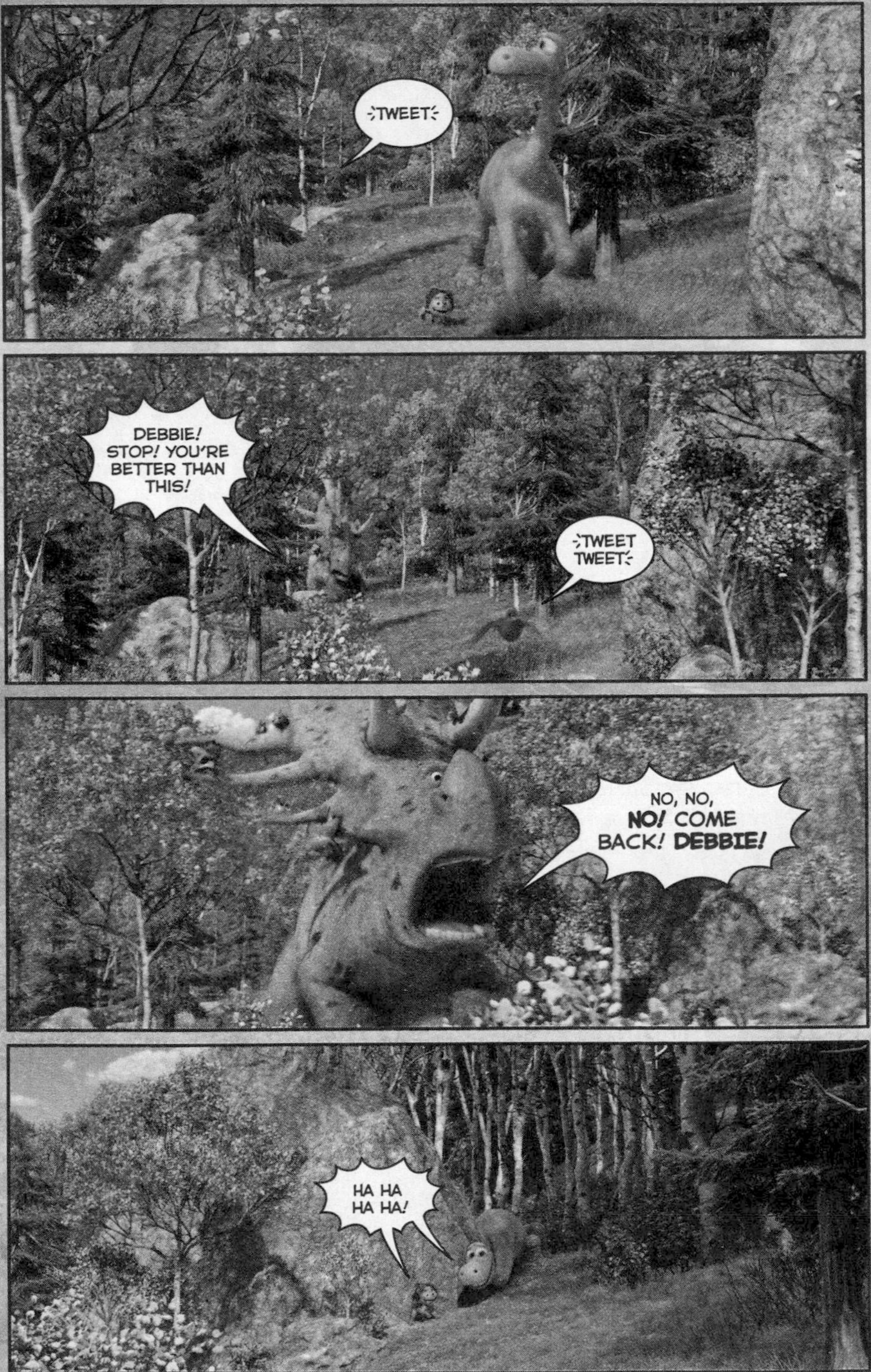
TWEET
DEBBIE! STOP! YOU'RE BETTER THAN THIS!
TWEET TWEET
NO, NO, **NO!** COME BACK! **DEBBIE!**
HA HA HA HA!

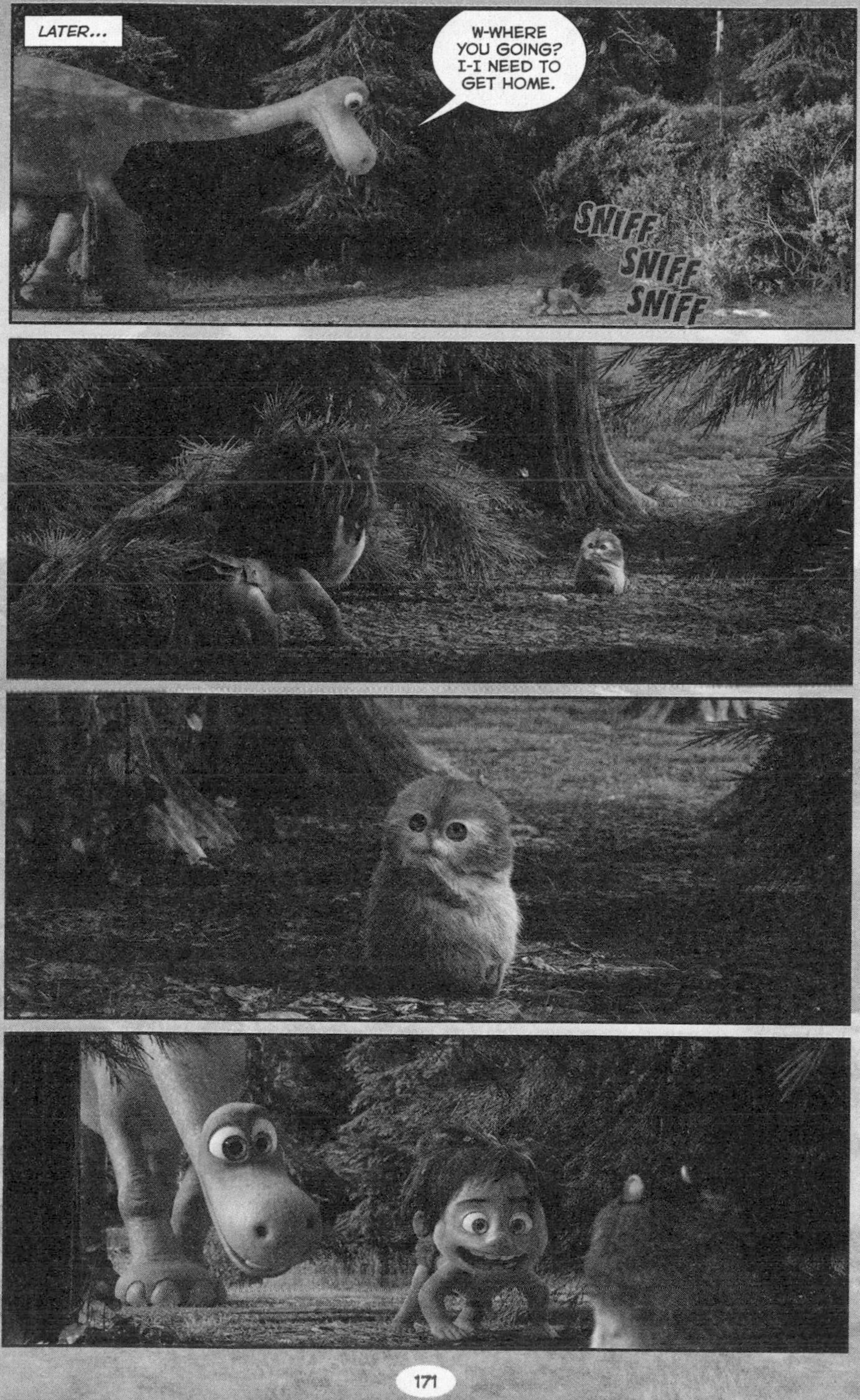
LATER...
W-WHERE YOU GOING? I-I NEED TO GET HOME.
SNIFF SNIFF SNIFF

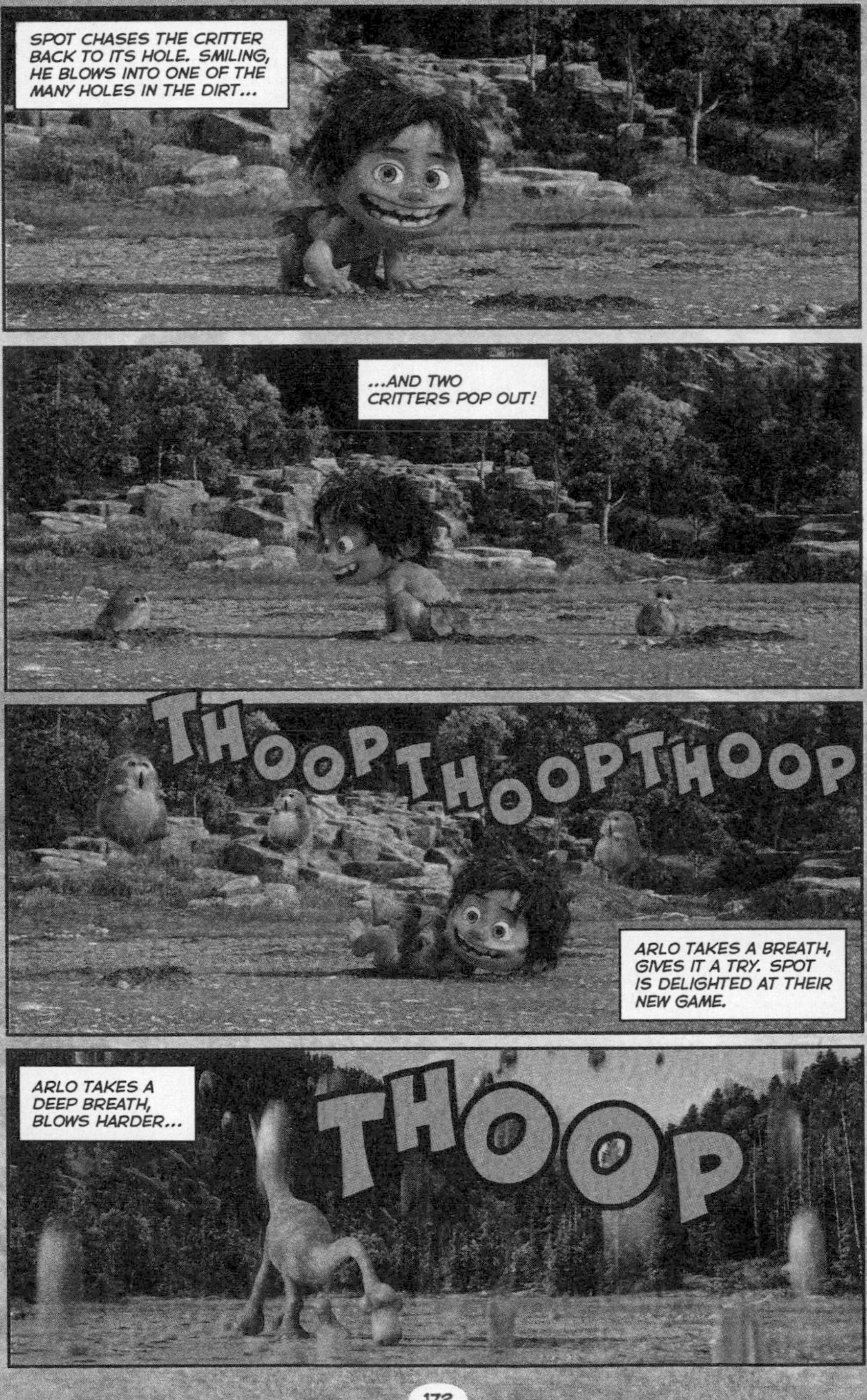
SPOT CHASES THE CRITTER BACK TO ITS HOLE. SMILING, HE BLOWS INTO ONE OF THE MANY HOLES IN THE DIRT...
...AND TWO CRITTERS POP OUT!
THOOP THOOP THOOP
ARLO TAKES A BREATH, GIVES IT A TRY. SPOT IS DELIGHTED AT THEIR NEW GAME.
ARLO TAKES A DEEP BREATH, BLOWS HARDER...
THOOP

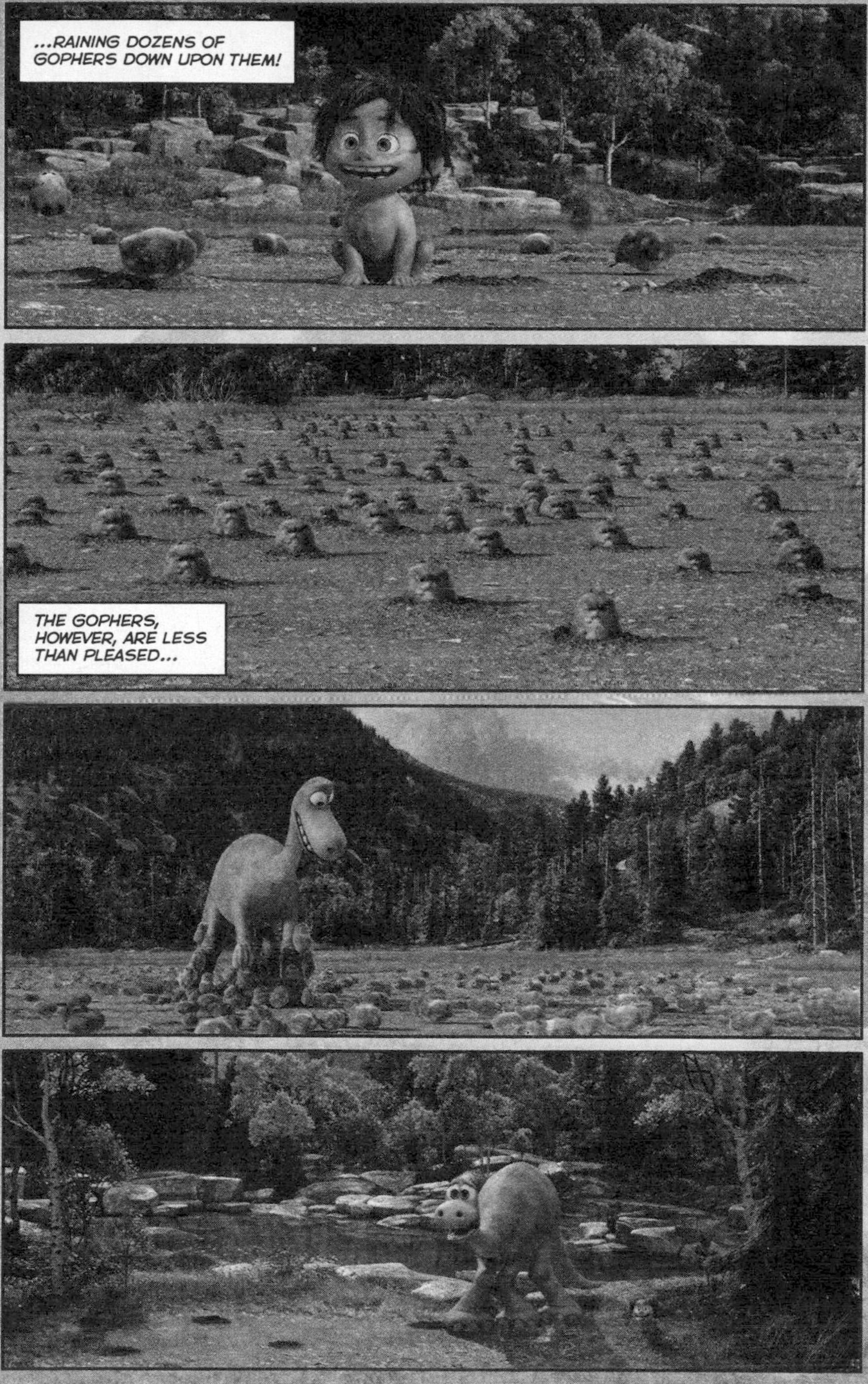
...RAINING DOZENS OF GOPHERS DOWN UPON THEM!
THE GOPHERS, HOWEVER, ARE LESS THAN PLEASED...

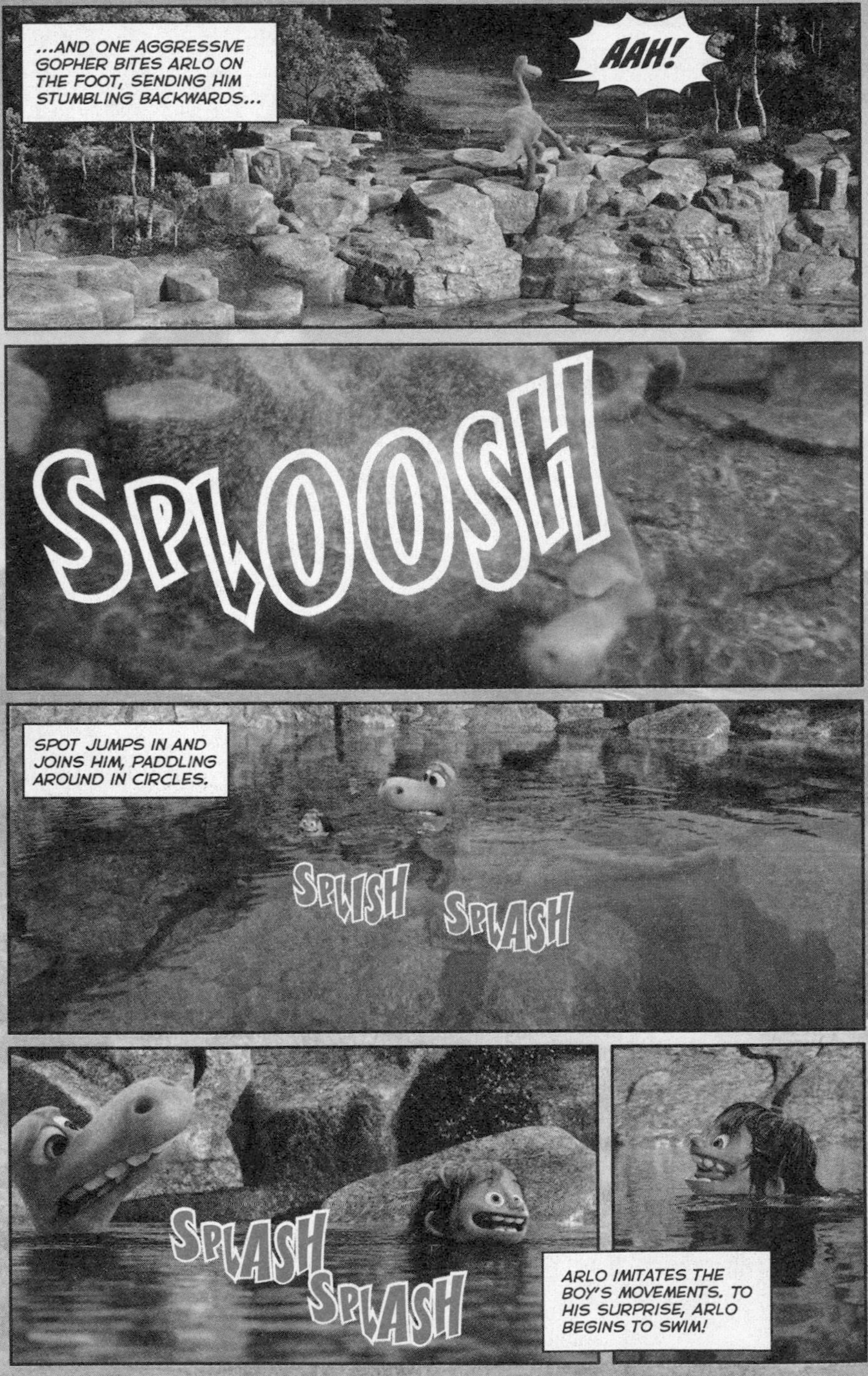
...AND ONE AGGRESSIVE GOPHER BITES ARLO ON THE FOOT, SENDING HIM STUMBLING BACKWARDS...
AAH!
SPLOOSH
SPOT JUMPS IN AND JOINS HIM, PADDLING AROUND IN CIRCLES.
SPLISH
SPLASH
SPLASH
SPLASH
ARLO IMITATES THE BOY'S MOVEMENTS. TO HIS SURPRISE, ARLO BEGINS TO SWIM!

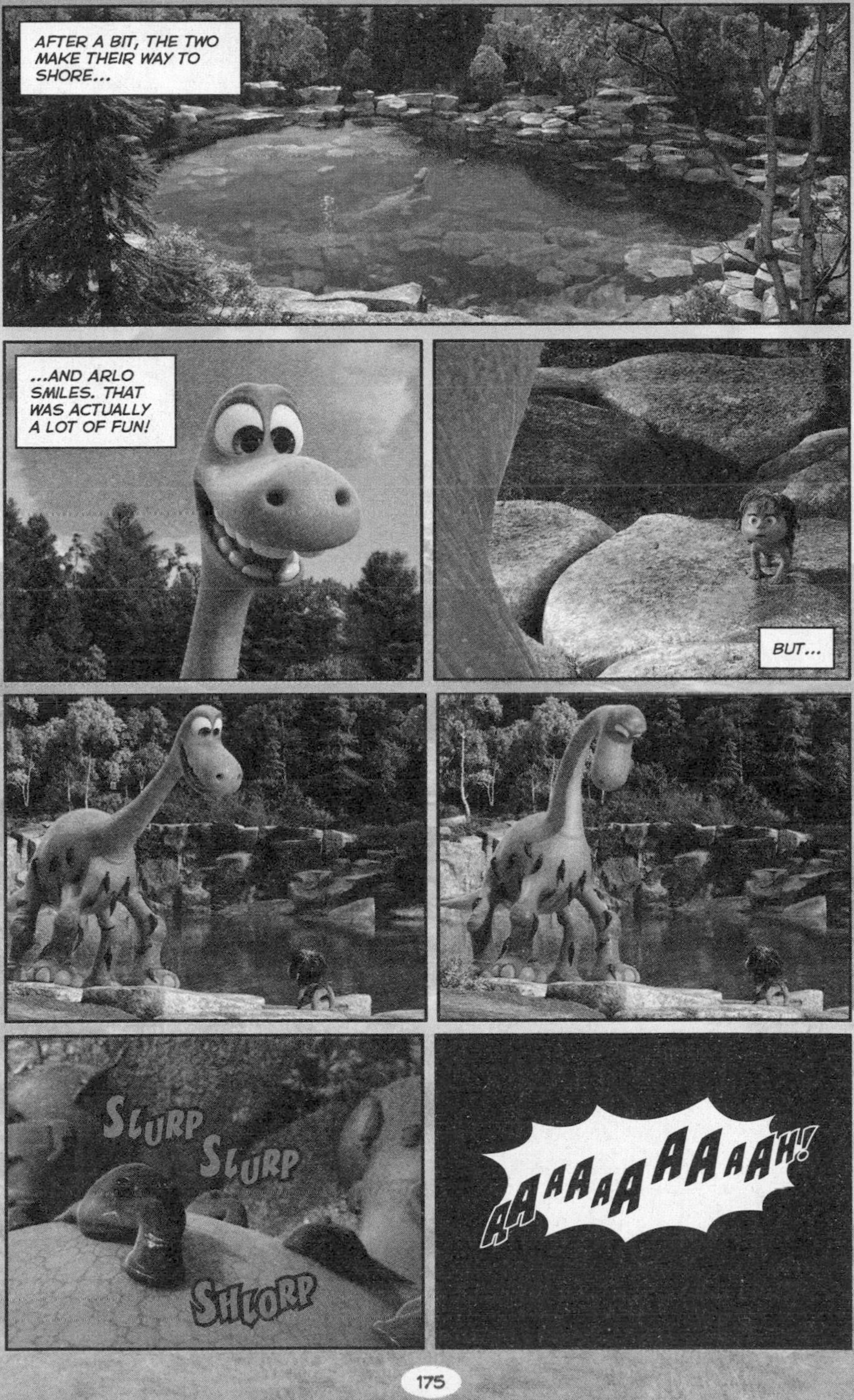

AFTER A BIT, THE TWO MAKE THEIR WAY TO SHORE...
...AND ARLO SMILES. THAT WAS ACTUALLY A LOT OF FUN!
BUT...
SLURP
SLURP
SHLORP
AAAAAAAAAAH!

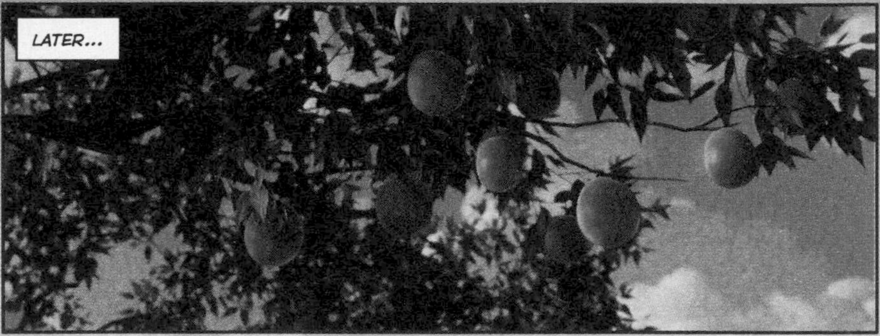
LATER...

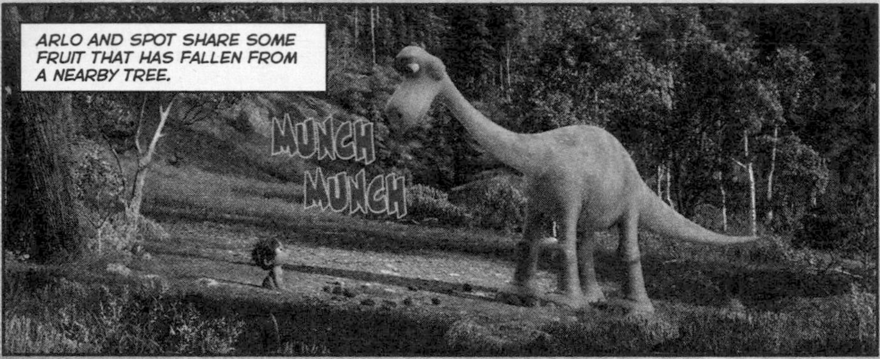
ARLO AND SPOT SHARE SOME FRUIT THAT HAS FALLEN FROM A NEARBY TREE.
MUNCH
MUNCH

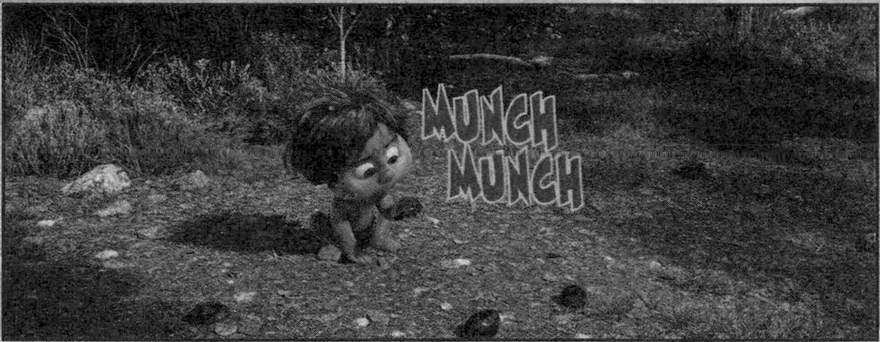
MUNCH
MUNCH

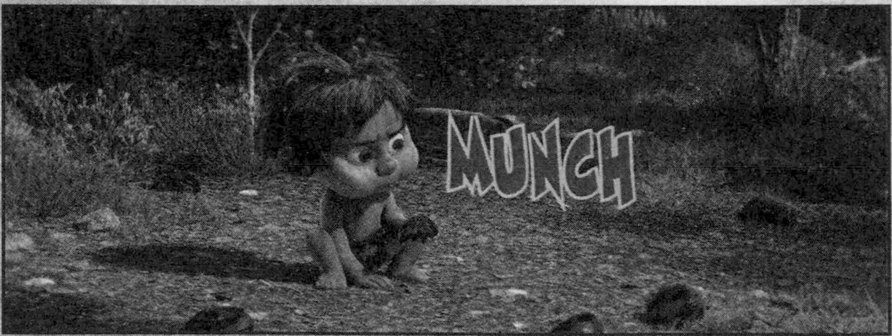
MUNCH

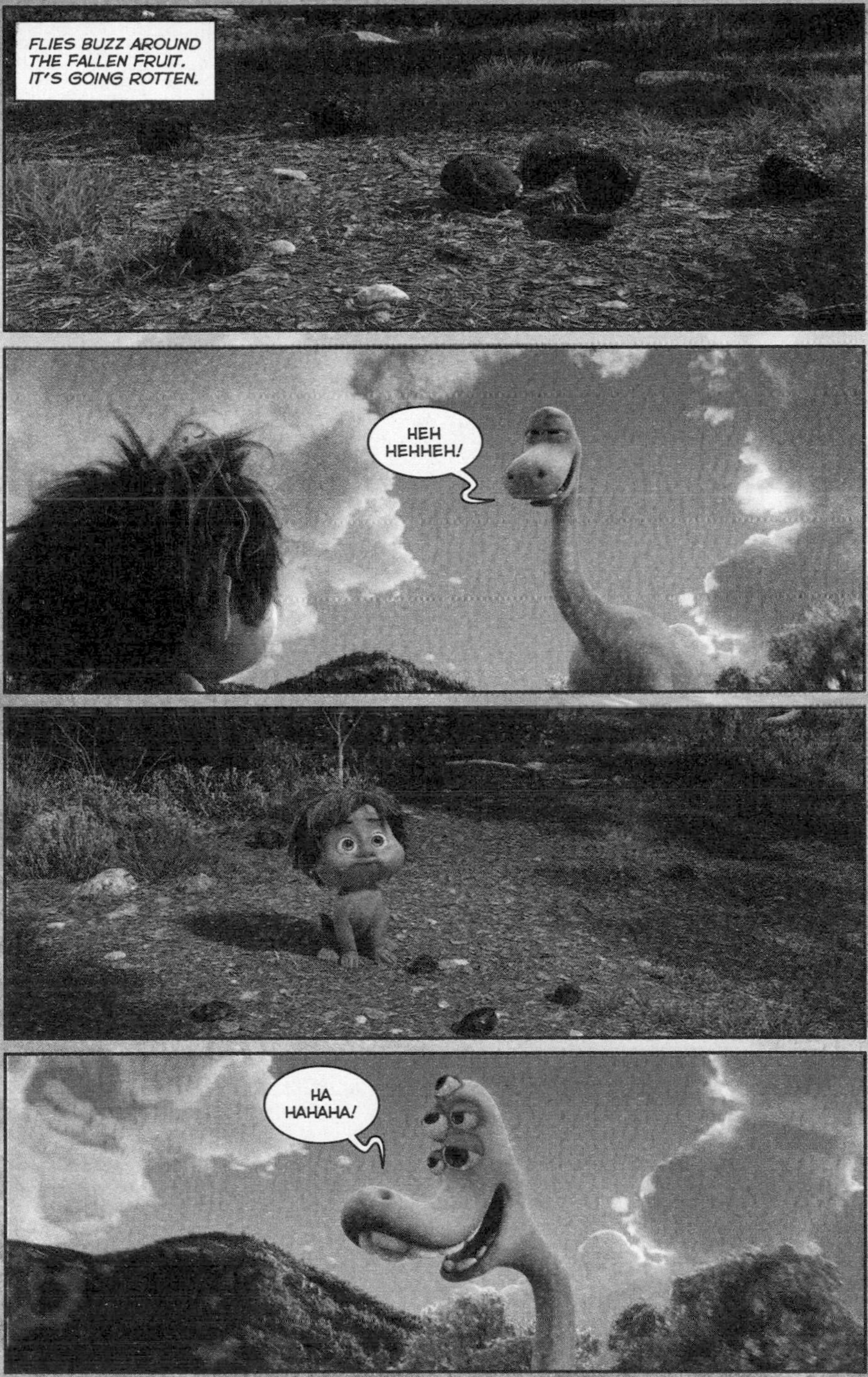
FLIES BUZZ AROUND THE FALLEN FRUIT. IT'S GOING ROTTEN.
HEH HEHHEH!
HA HAHAHA!

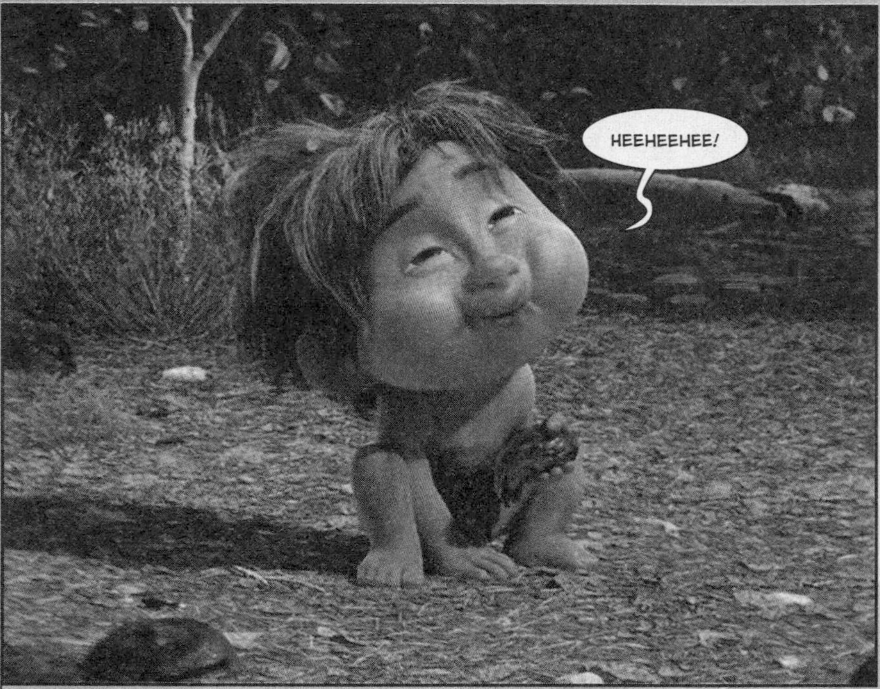
HEEHEEHEE!

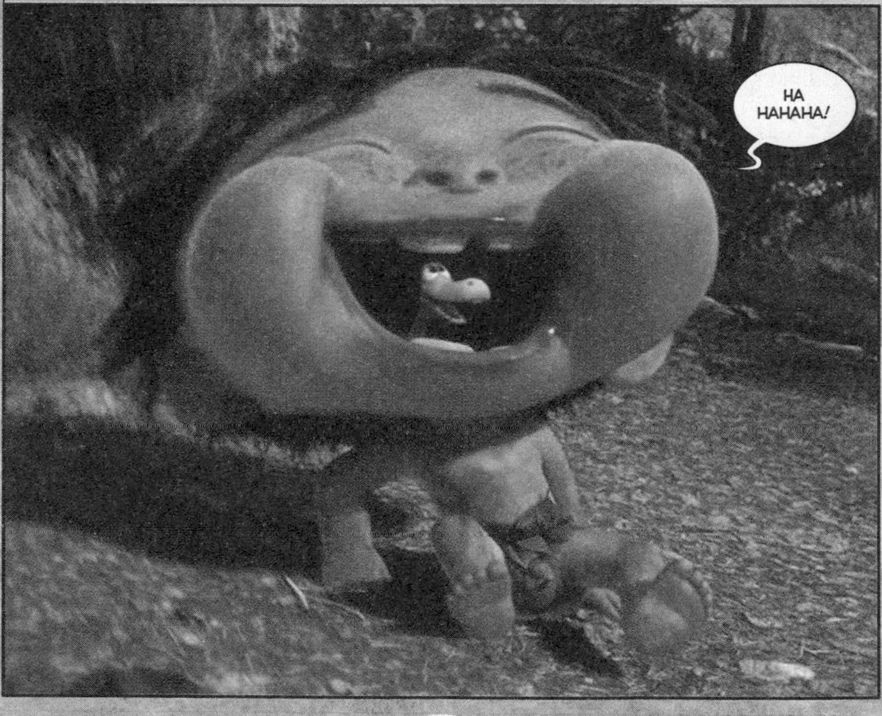
HA
HAHAHA!

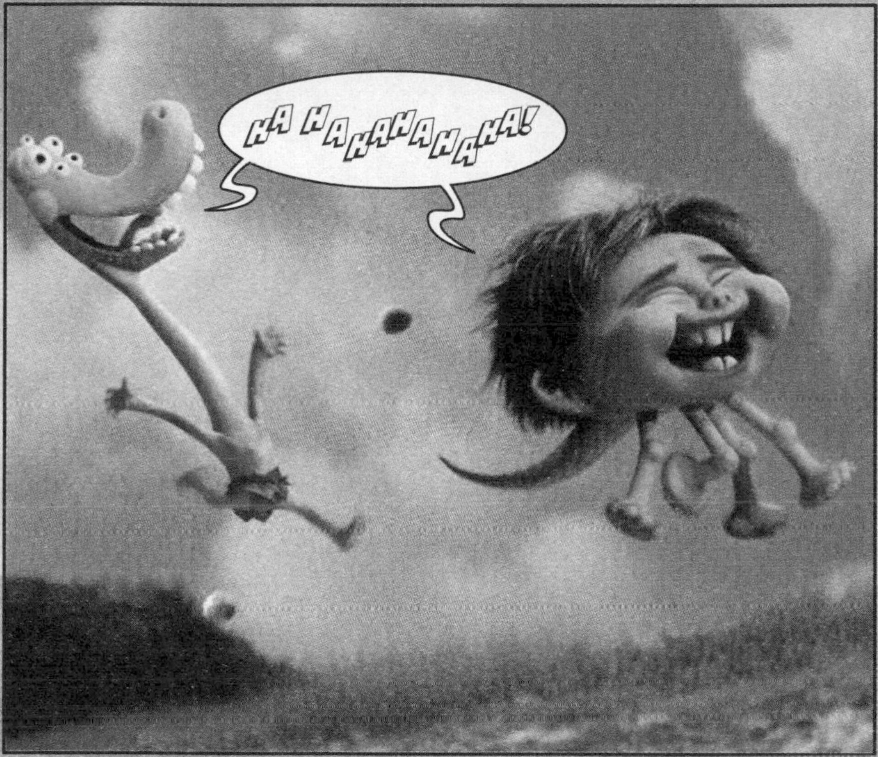
HA HAHAHAHAHAHA!

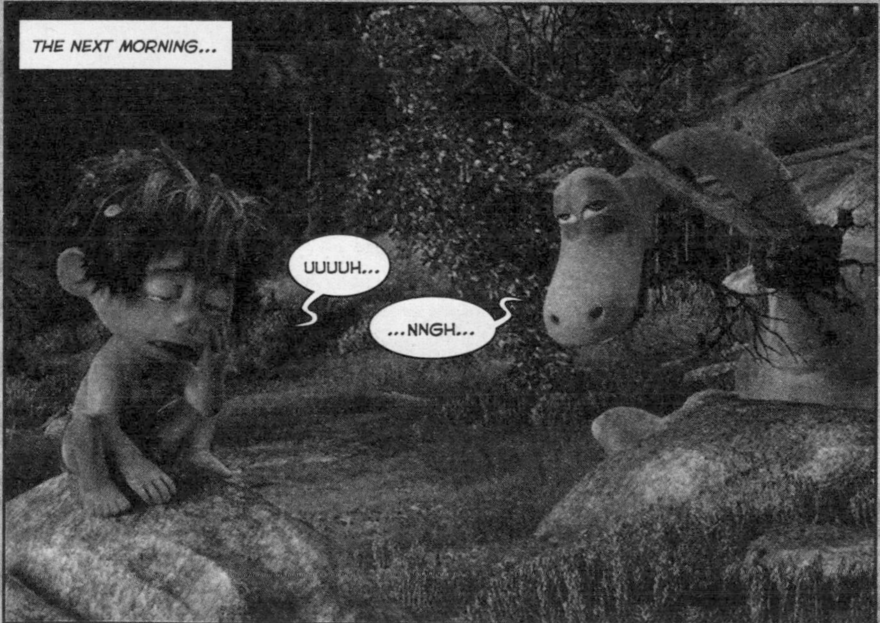
THE NEXT MORNING...
UUUUH...
...NNGH...

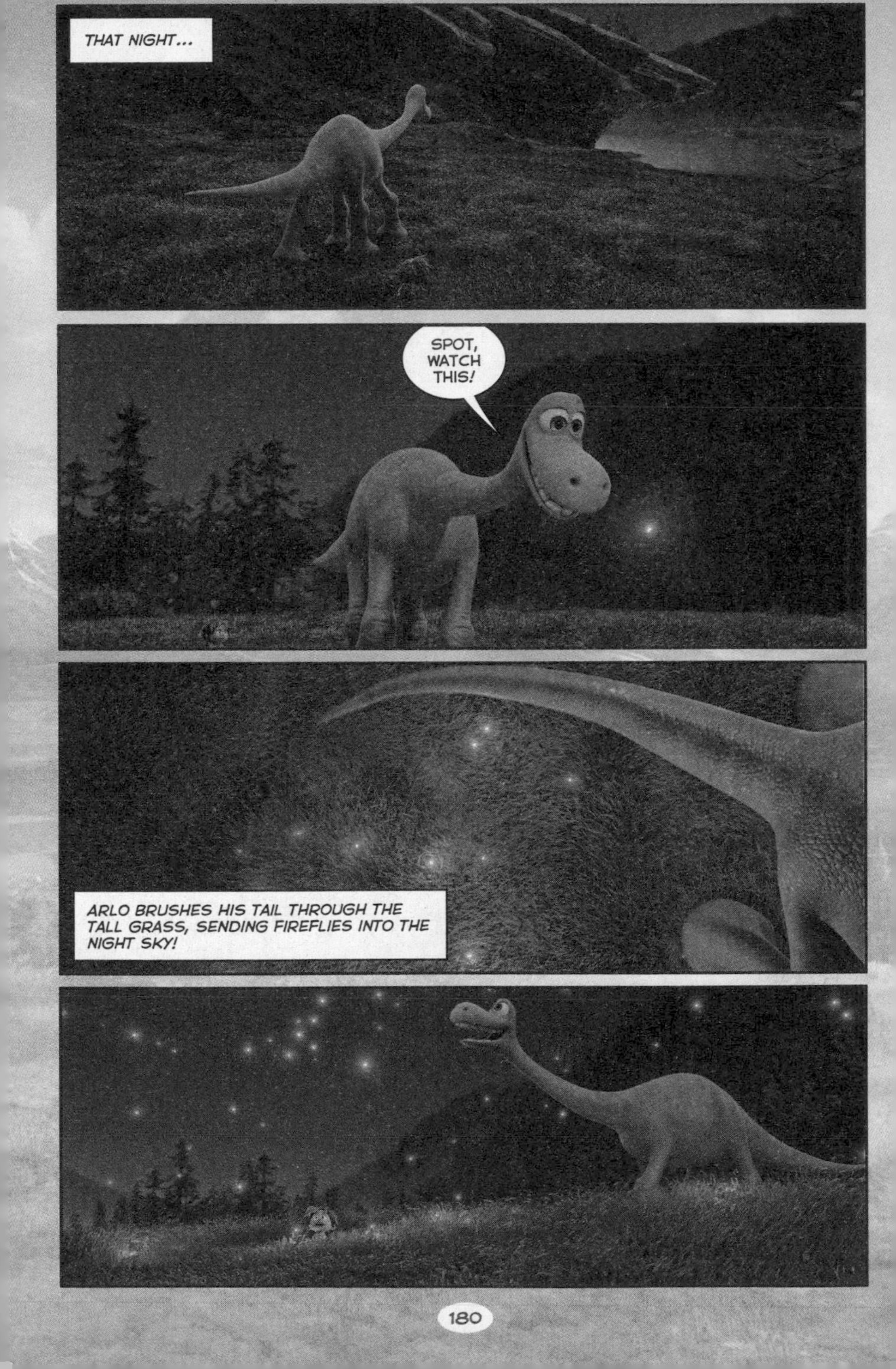
THAT NIGHT...
SPOT, WATCH THIS!
ARLO BRUSHES HIS TAIL THROUGH THE TALL GRASS, SENDING FIREFLIES INTO THE NIGHT SKY!

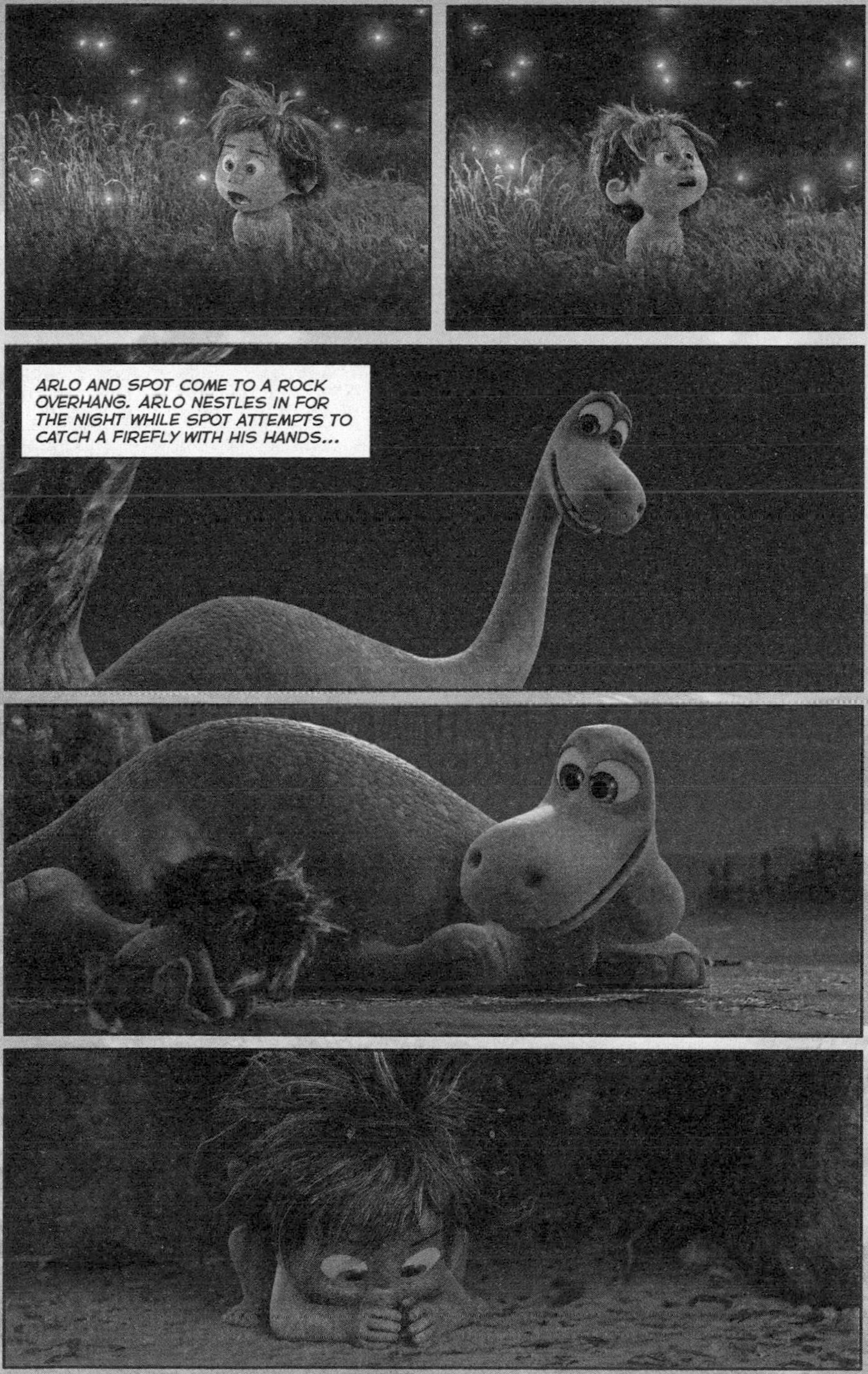
ARLO AND SPOT COME TO A ROCK OVERHANG. ARLO NESTLES IN FOR THE NIGHT WHILE SPOT ATTEMPTS TO CATCH A FIREFLY WITH HIS HANDS...

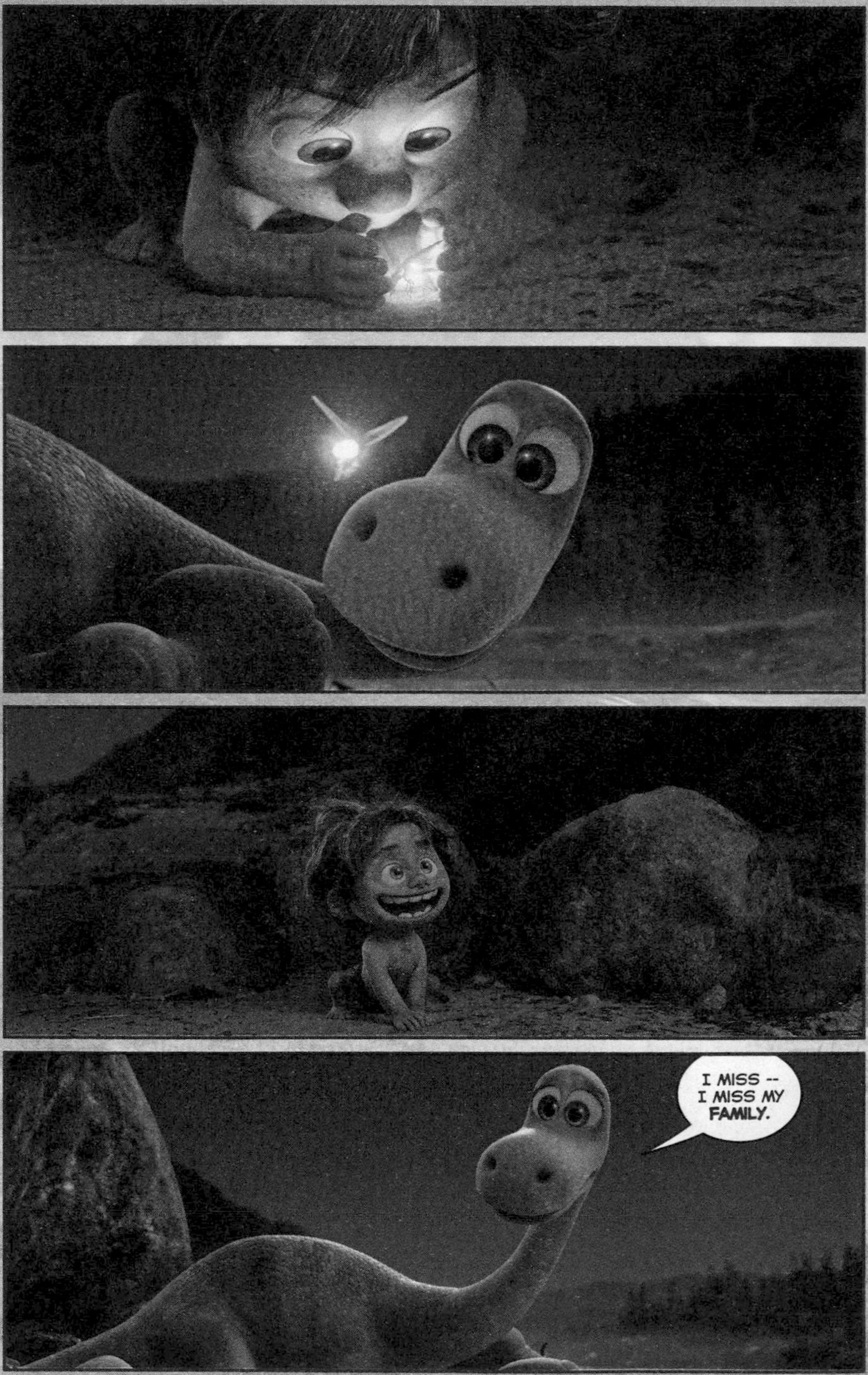
I MISS --
I MISS MY
FAMILY.

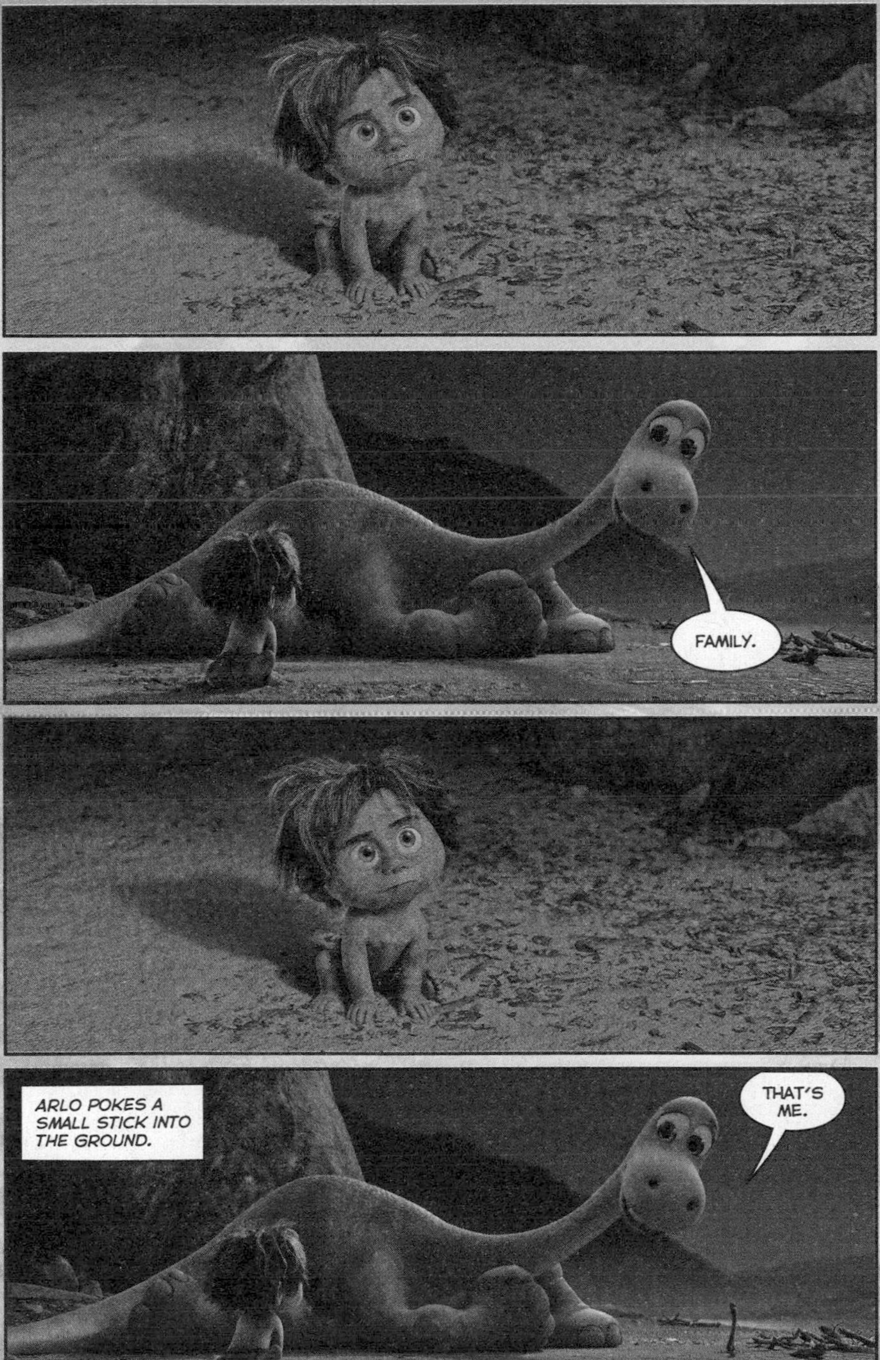
FAMILY.
ARLO POKES A SMALL STICK INTO THE GROUND.
THAT'S ME.

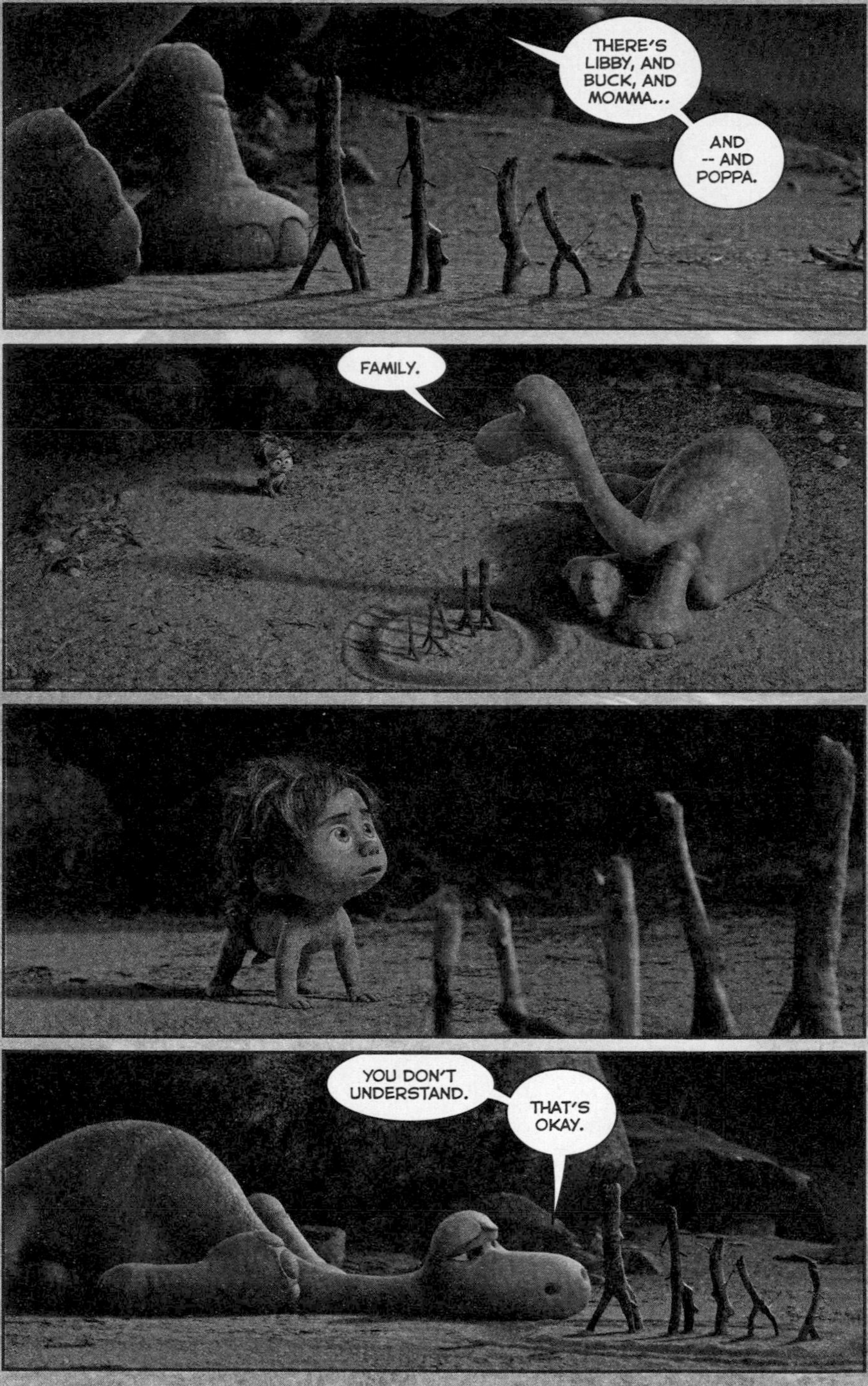
THERE'S LIBBY, AND BUCK, AND MOMMA...
AND -- AND POPPA.
FAMILY.
YOU DON'T UNDERSTAND.
THAT'S OKAY.

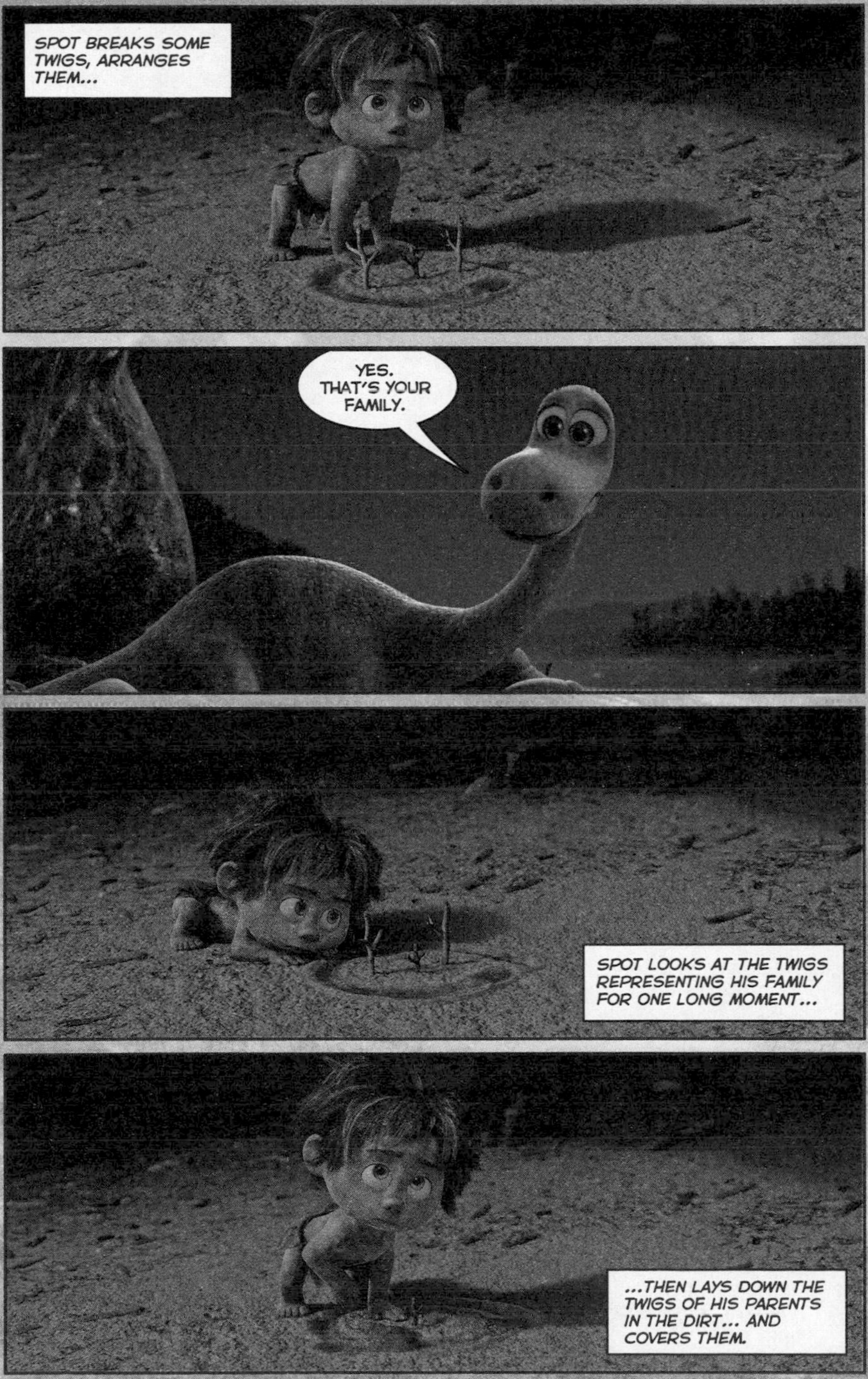
SPOT BREAKS SOME TWIGS, ARRANGES THEM...
YES. THAT'S YOUR FAMILY.
SPOT LOOKS AT THE TWIGS REPRESENTING HIS FAMILY FOR ONE LONG MOMENT...
...THEN LAYS DOWN THE TWIGS OF HIS PARENTS IN THE DIRT... AND COVERS THEM.

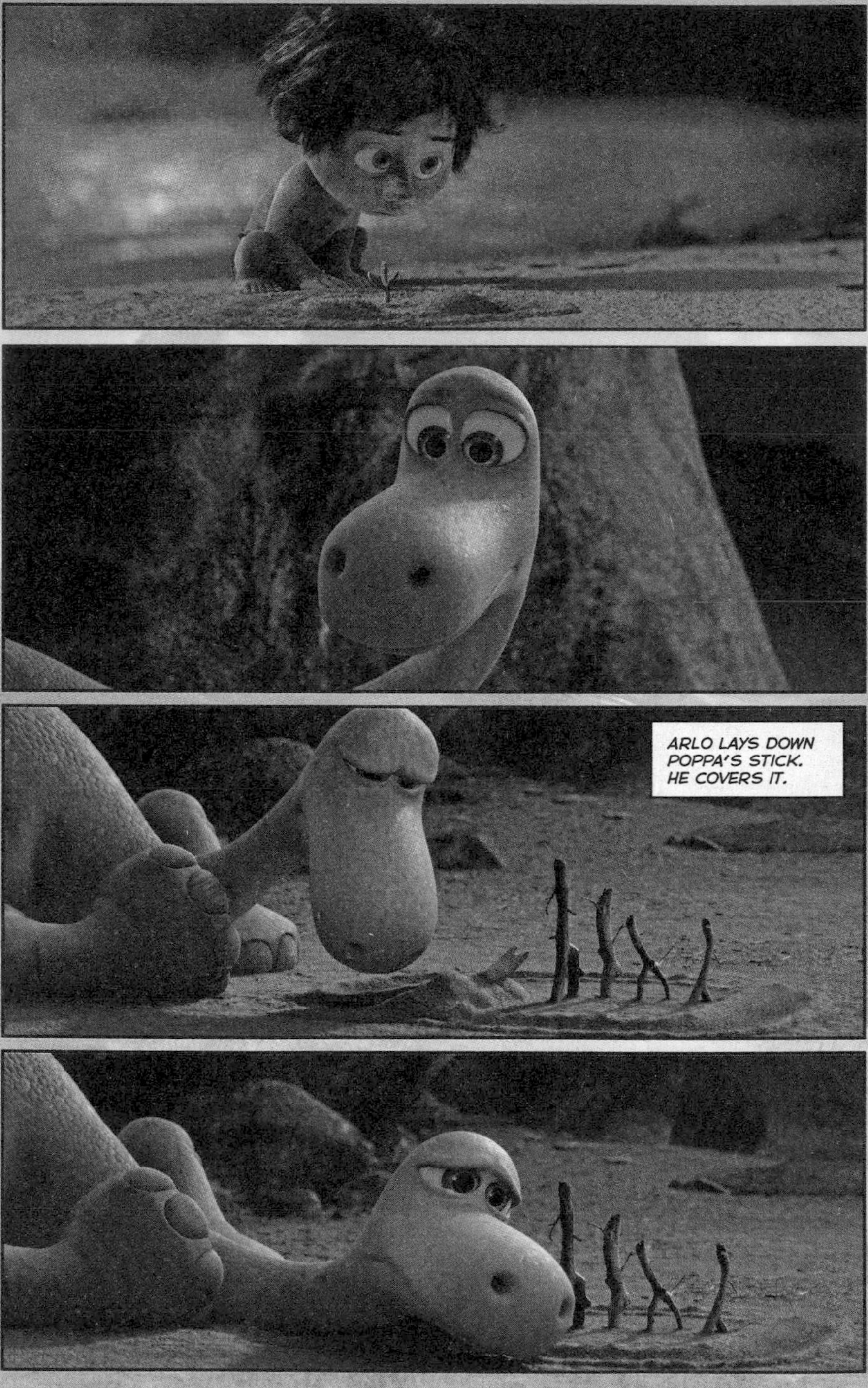
ARLO LAYS DOWN
POPPA'S STICK.
HE COVERS IT.

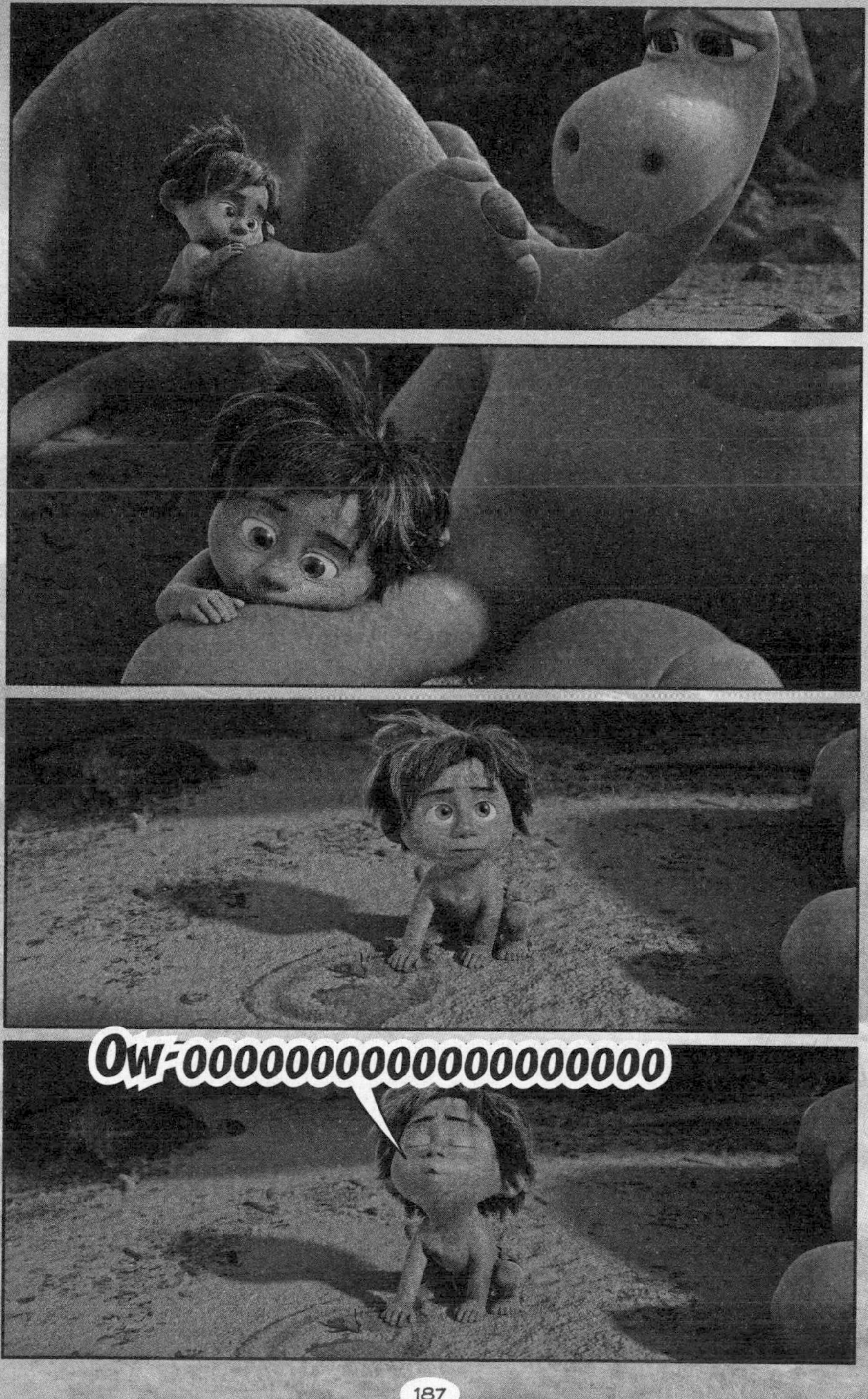

OW-OOOOOOOOOOOOOOOOOOO

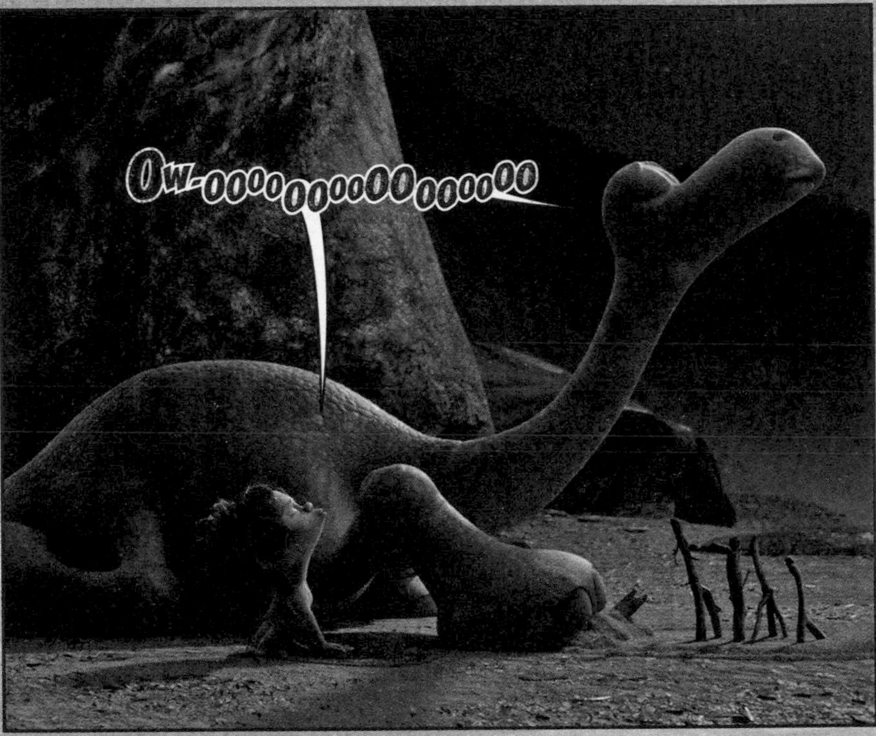
Ow-oooooooooooooooo

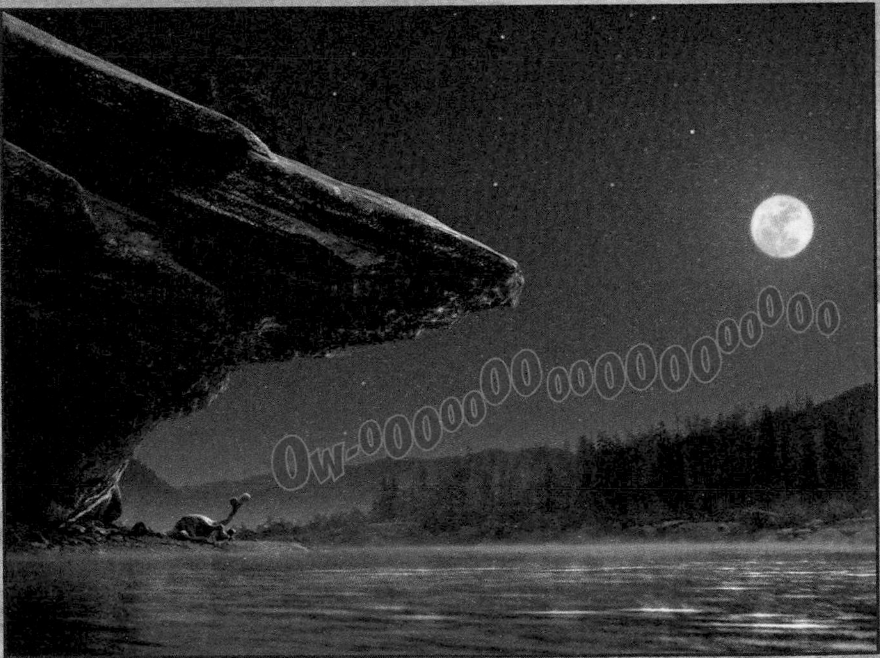
Ow-oooooooooooooooooo

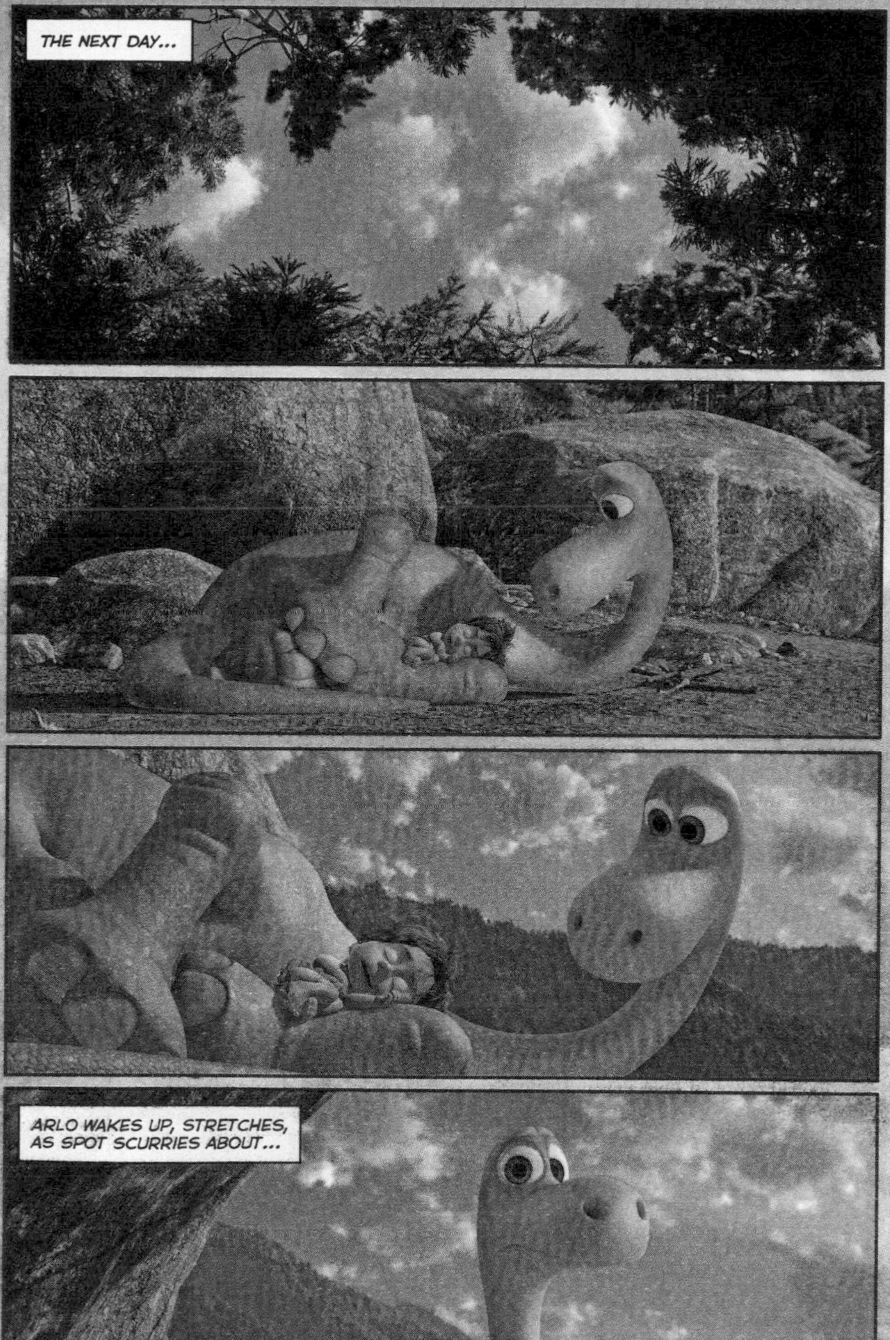
THE NEXT DAY...
ARLO WAKES UP, STRETCHES, AS SPOT SCURRIES ABOUT...

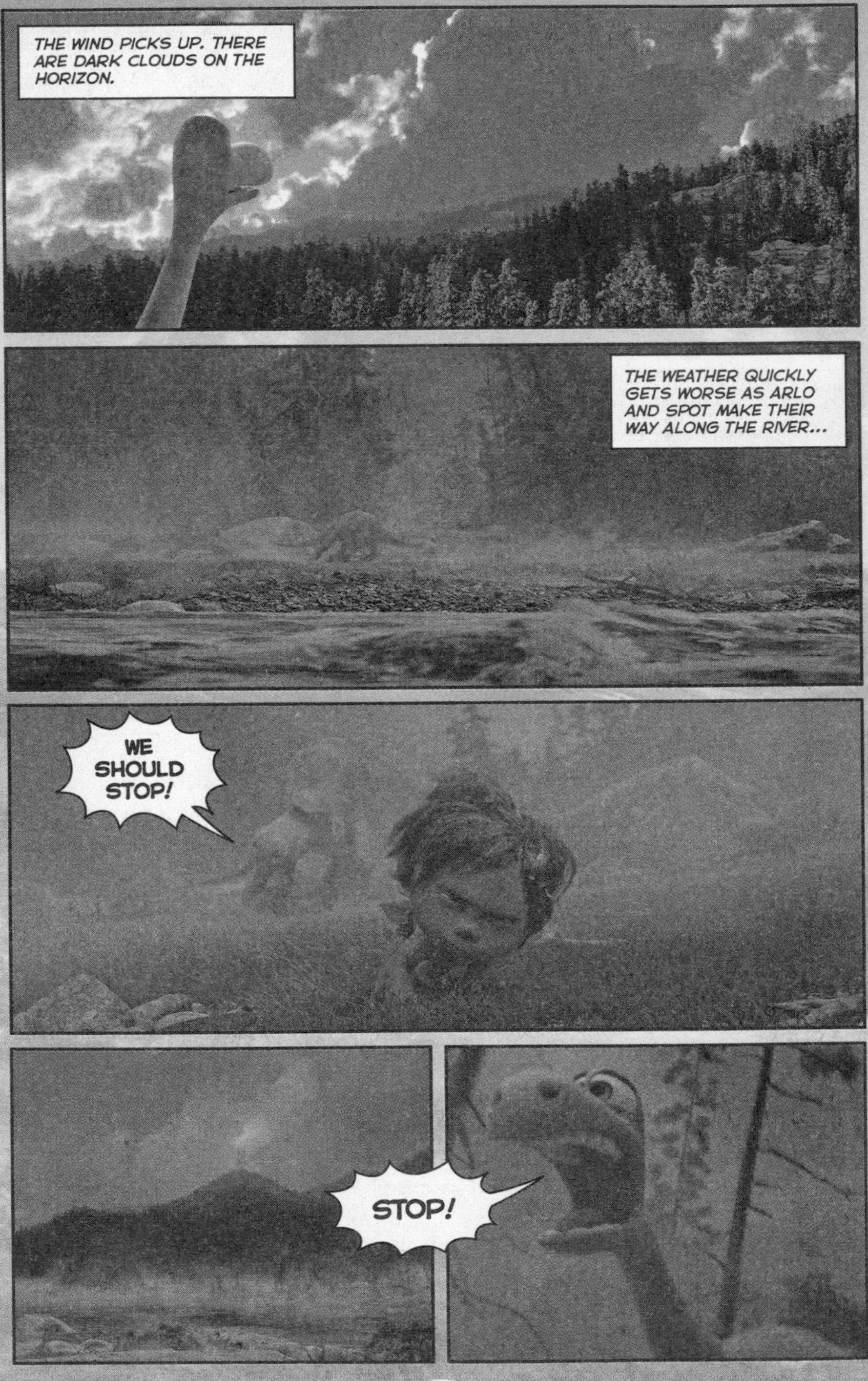
THE WIND PICKS UP. THERE ARE DARK CLOUDS ON THE HORIZON.
THE WEATHER QUICKLY GETS WORSE AS ARLO AND SPOT MAKE THEIR WAY ALONG THE RIVER...
WE SHOULD STOP!
STOP!

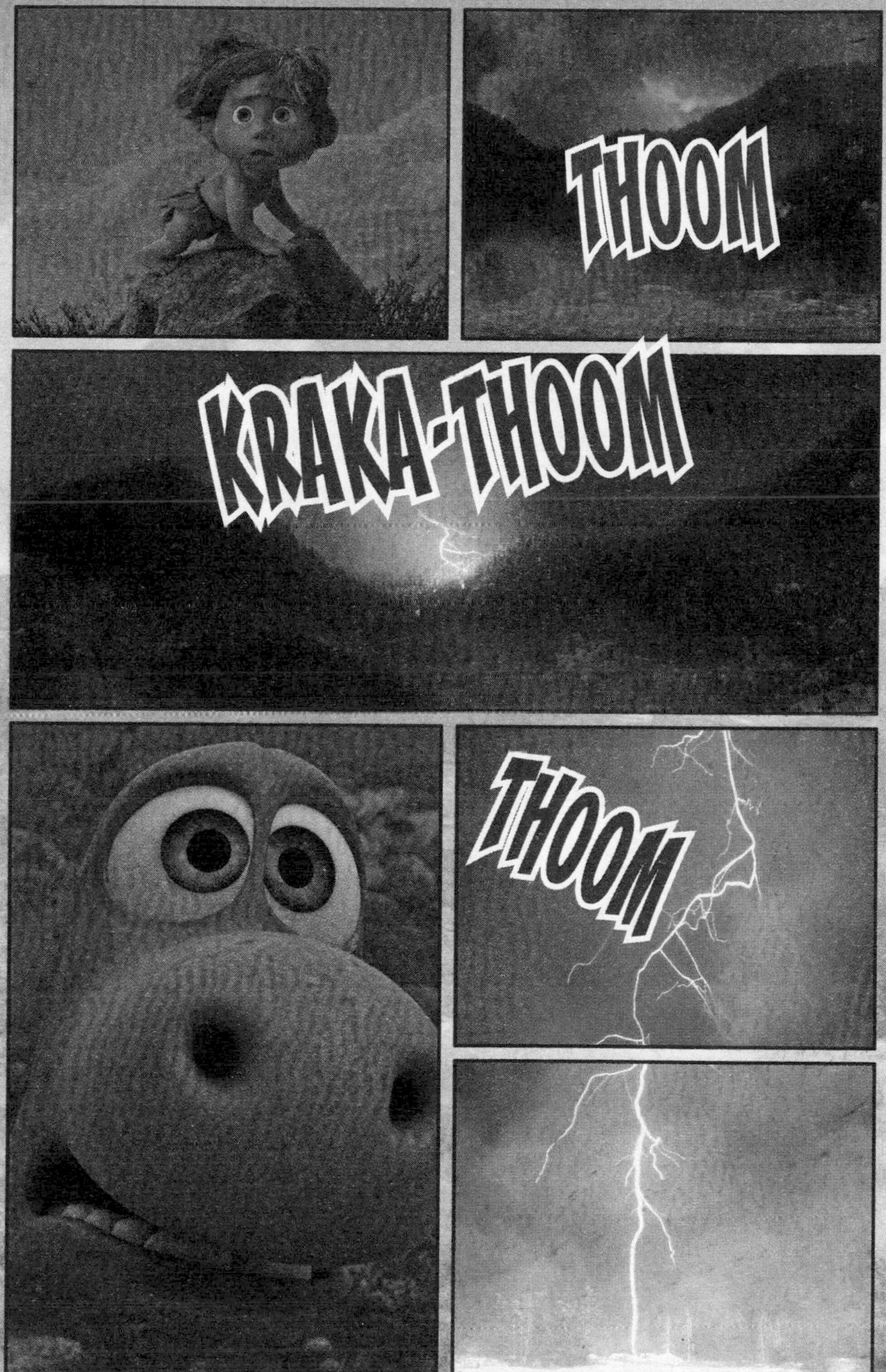
THOOM
KRAKA-THOOM
THOOM

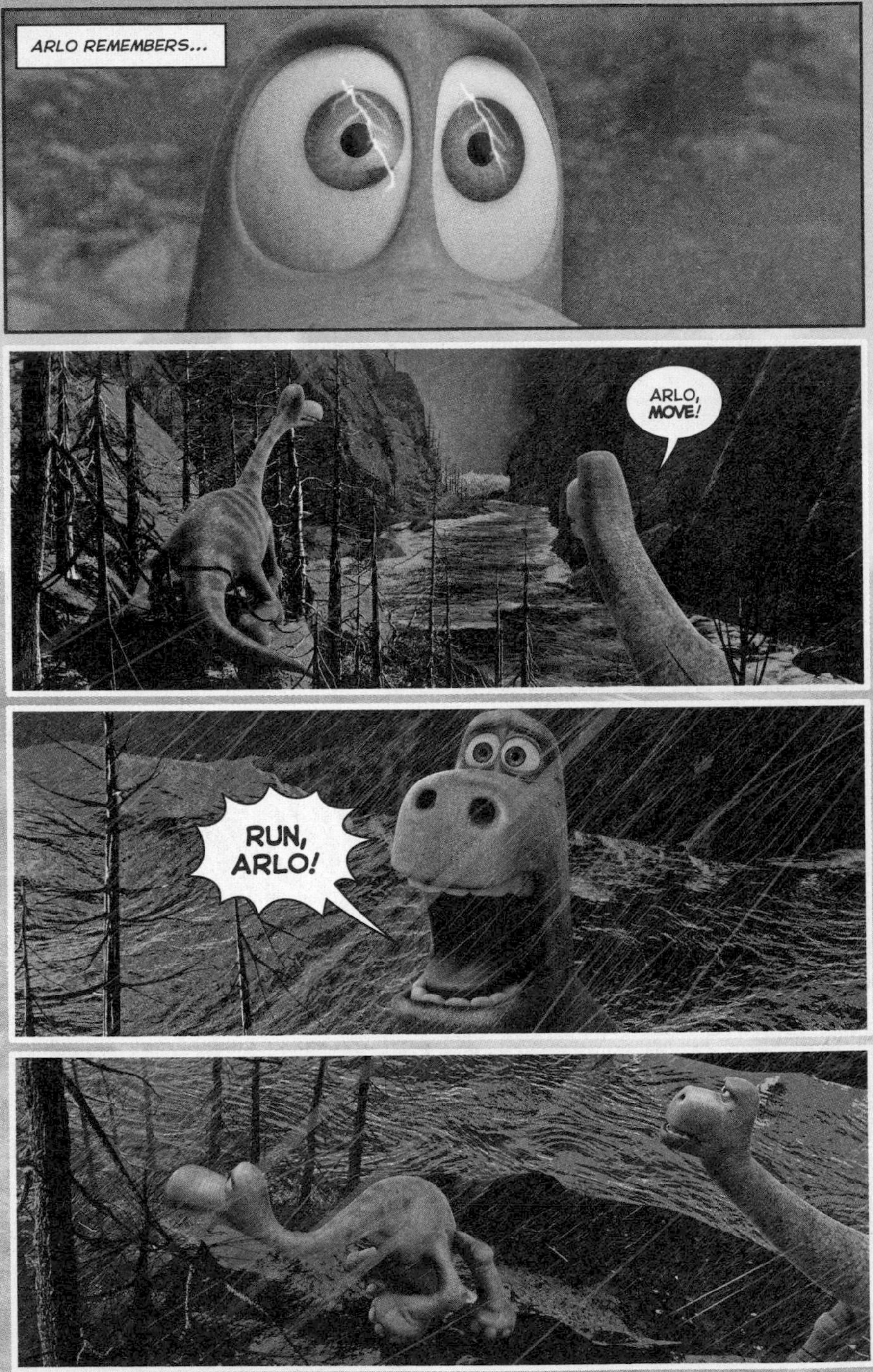
ARLO REMEMBERS...
ARLO, MOVE!
RUN, ARLO!

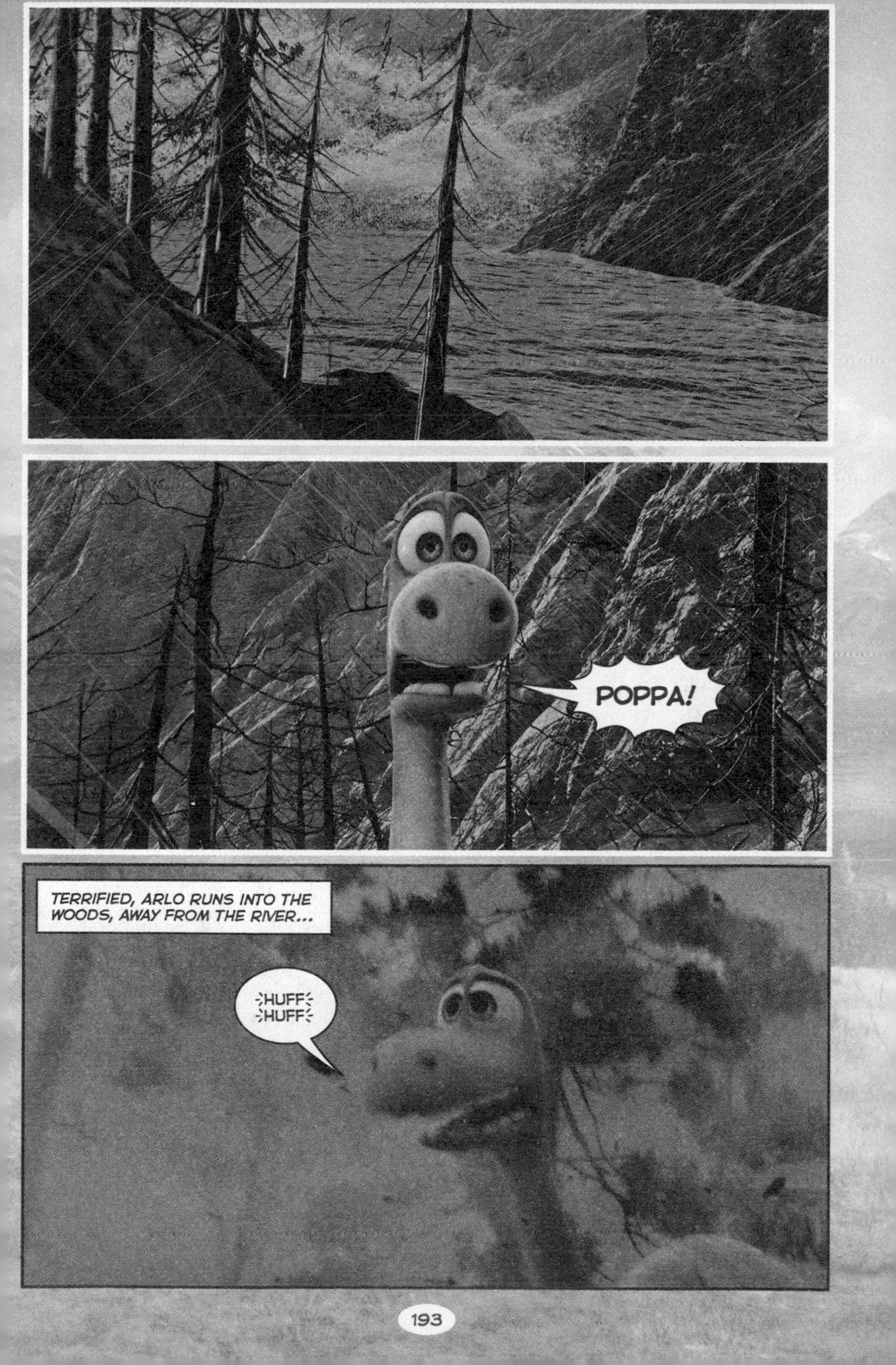
POPPA!
TERRIFIED, ARLO RUNS INTO THE WOODS, AWAY FROM THE RIVER...
HUFF HUFF

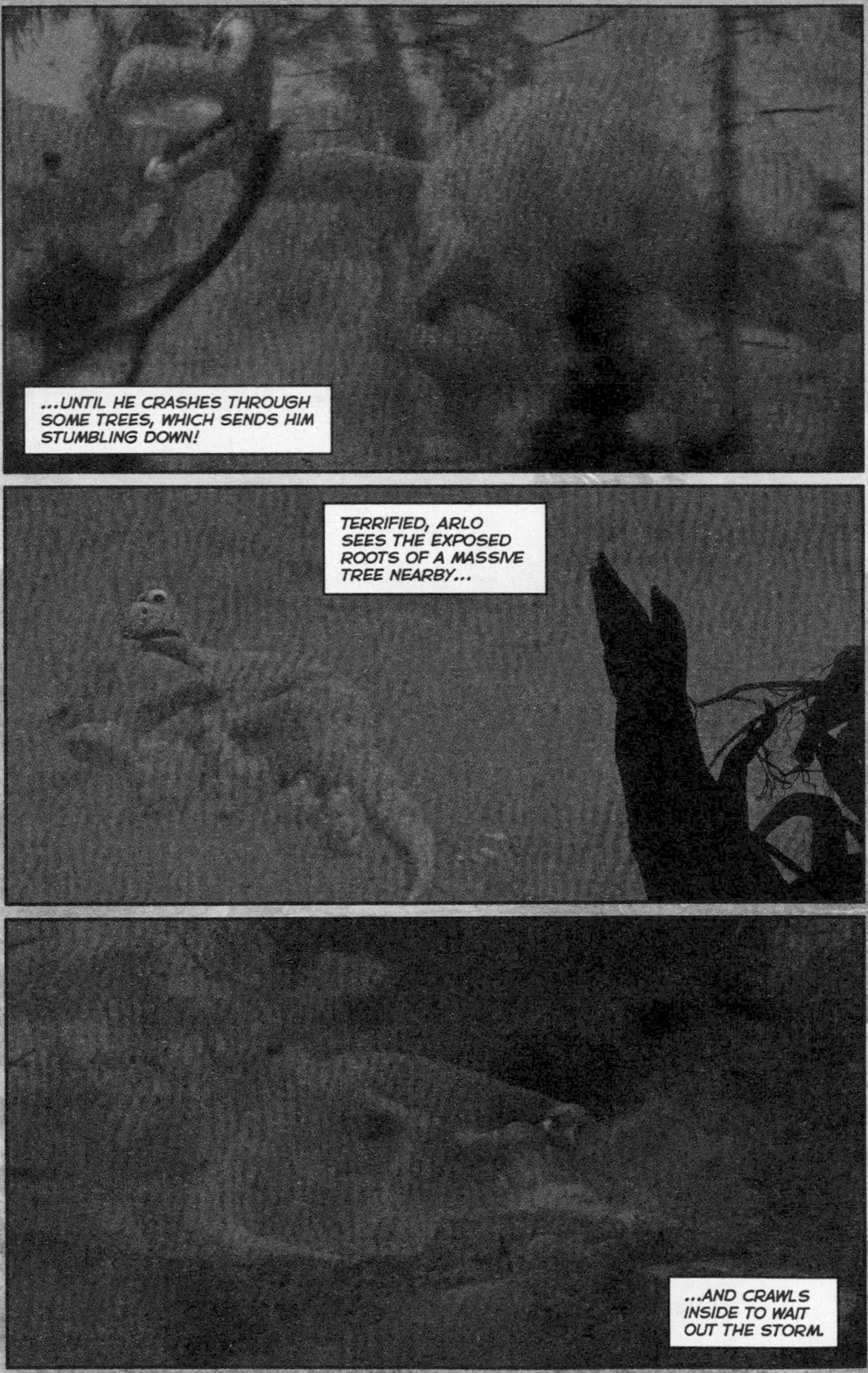
...UNTIL HE CRASHES THROUGH SOME TREES, WHICH SENDS HIM STUMBLING DOWN!
TERRIFIED, ARLO SEES THE EXPOSED ROOTS OF A MASSIVE TREE NEARBY...
...AND CRAWLS INSIDE TO WAIT OUT THE STORM.

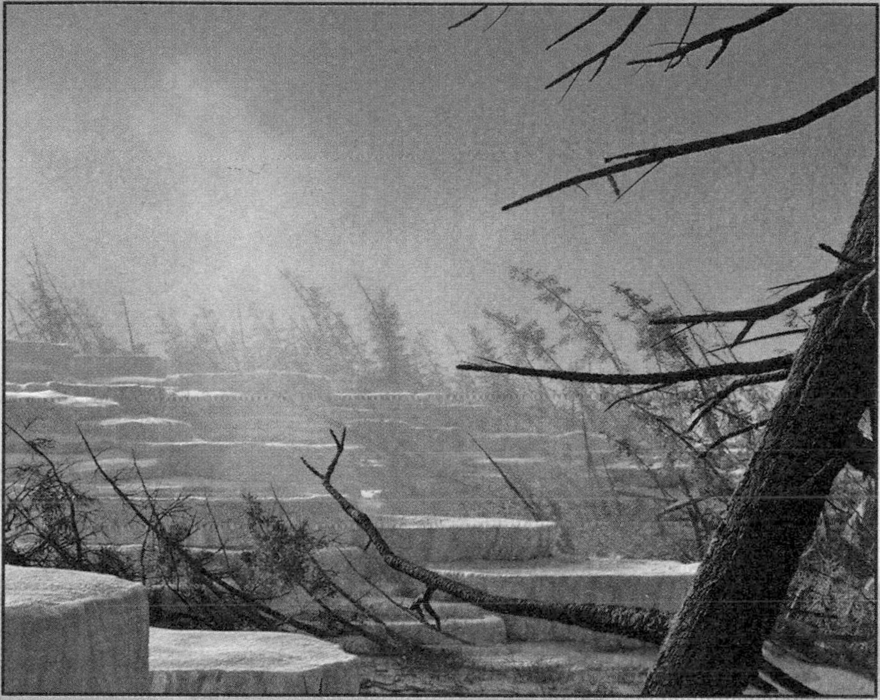

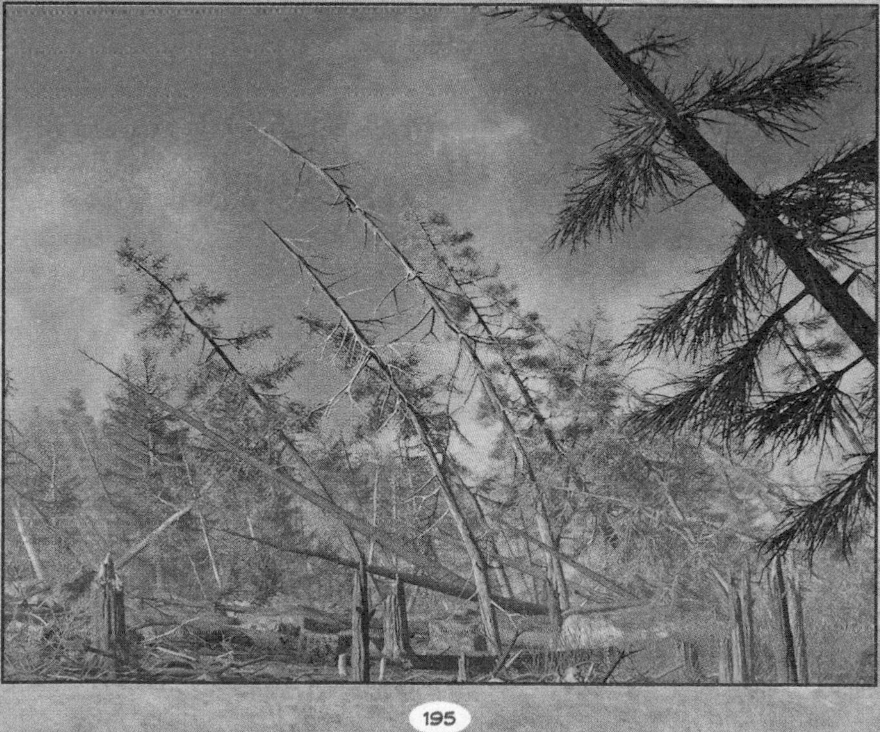

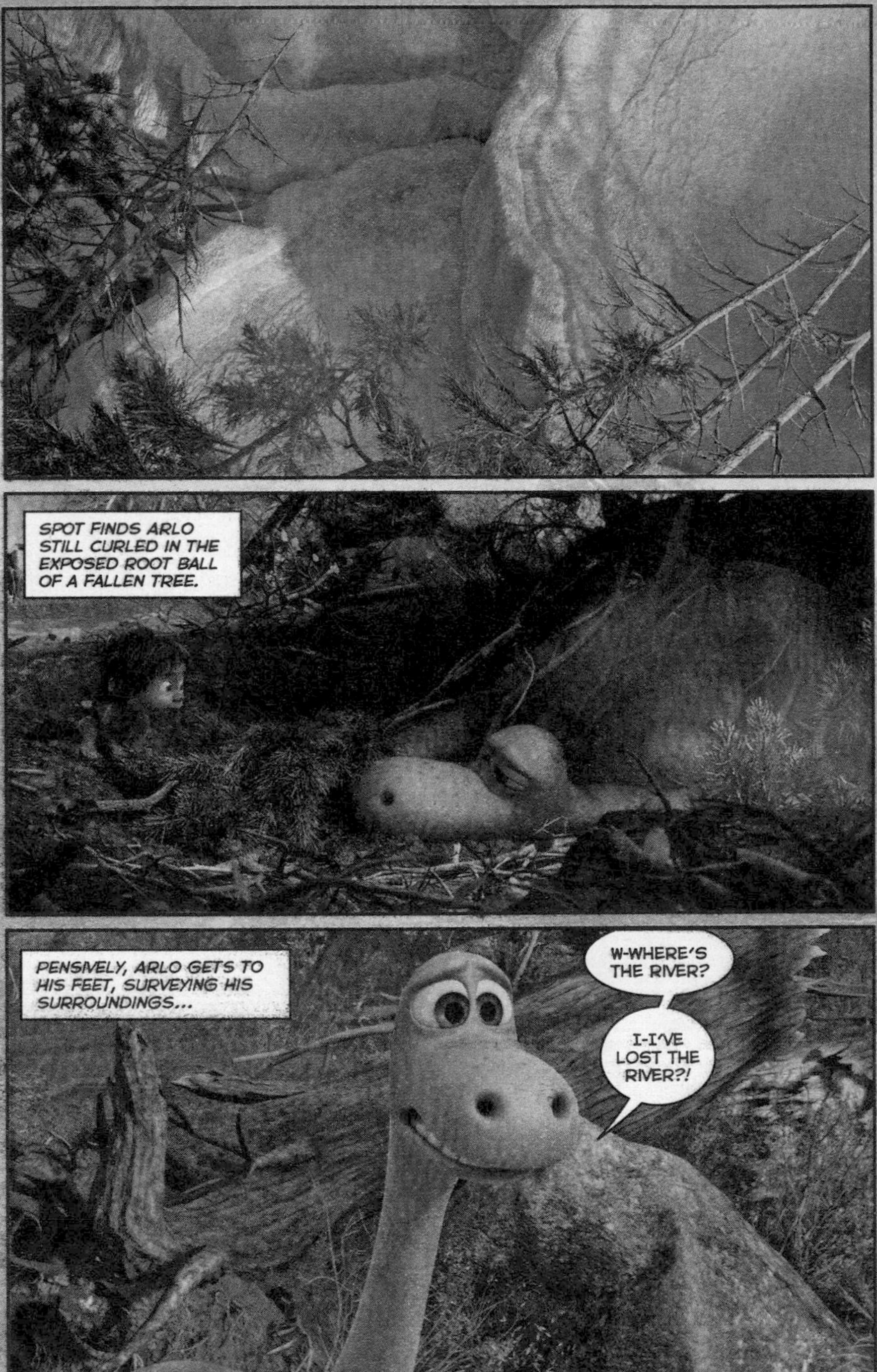
SPOT FINDS ARLO STILL CURLED IN THE EXPOSED ROOT BALL OF A FALLEN TREE.
PENSIVELY, ARLO GETS TO HIS FEET, SURVEYING HIS SURROUNDINGS...
W-WHERE'S THE RIVER?
I-I'VE LOST THE RIVER?!

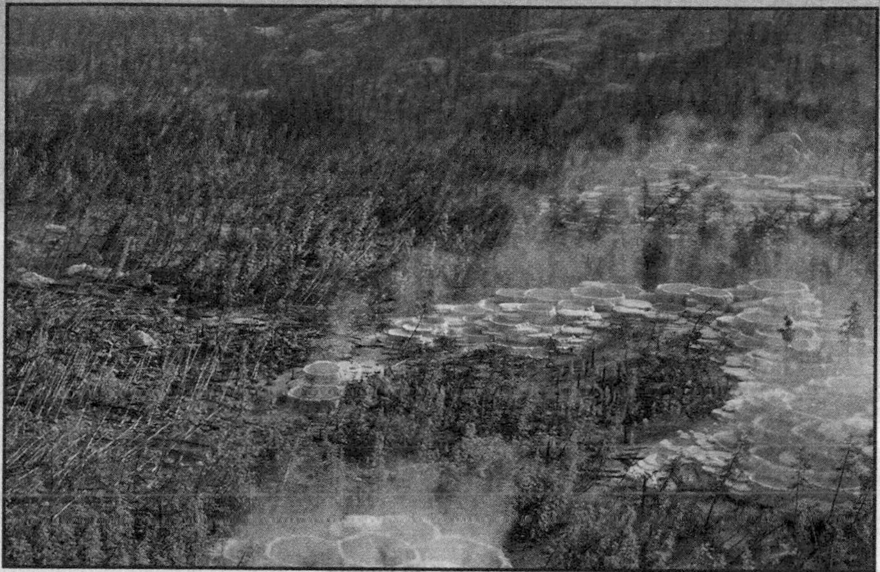

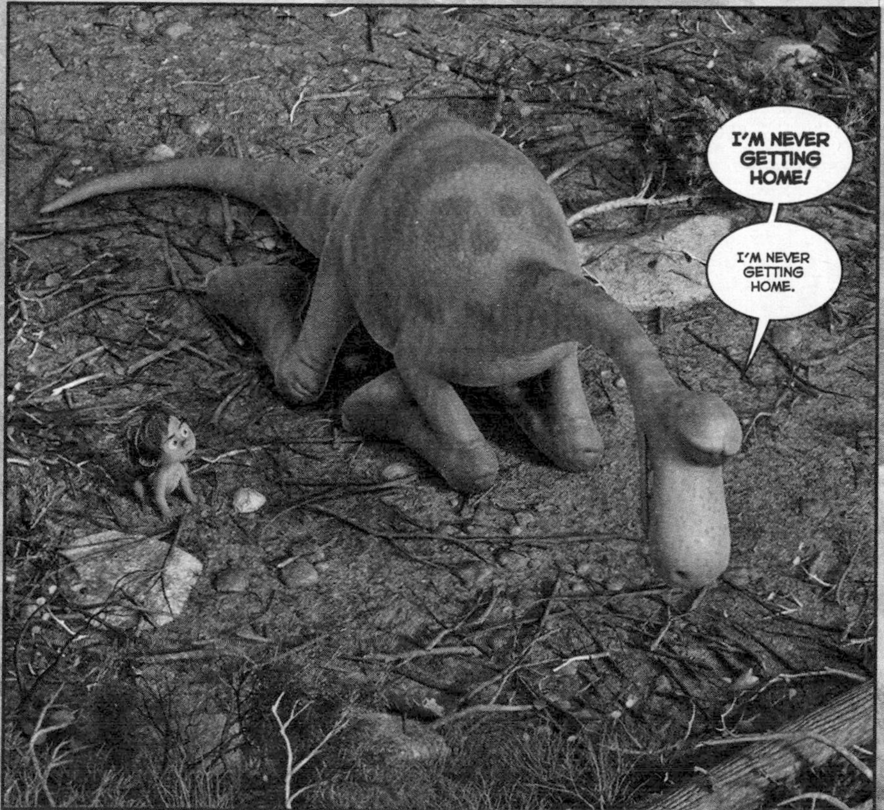

I'M NEVER GETTING HOME!
I'M NEVER GETTING HOME.

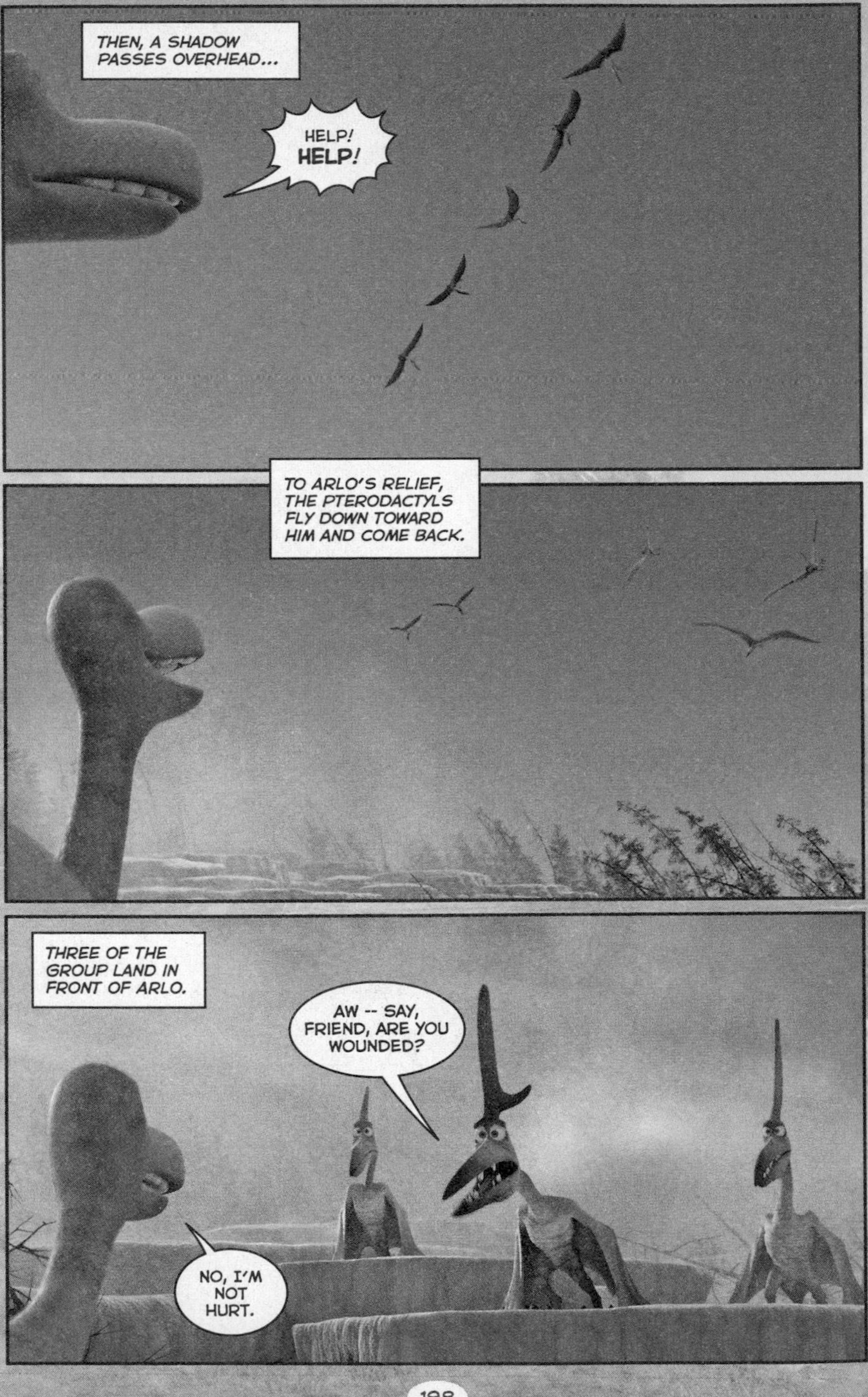
THEN, A SHADOW PASSES OVERHEAD...
HELP! HELP!
TO ARLO'S RELIEF, THE PTERODACTYLS FLY DOWN TOWARD HIM AND COME BACK.
THREE OF THE GROUP LAND IN FRONT OF ARLO.
AW -- SAY, FRIEND, ARE YOU WOUNDED?
NO, I'M NOT HURT.

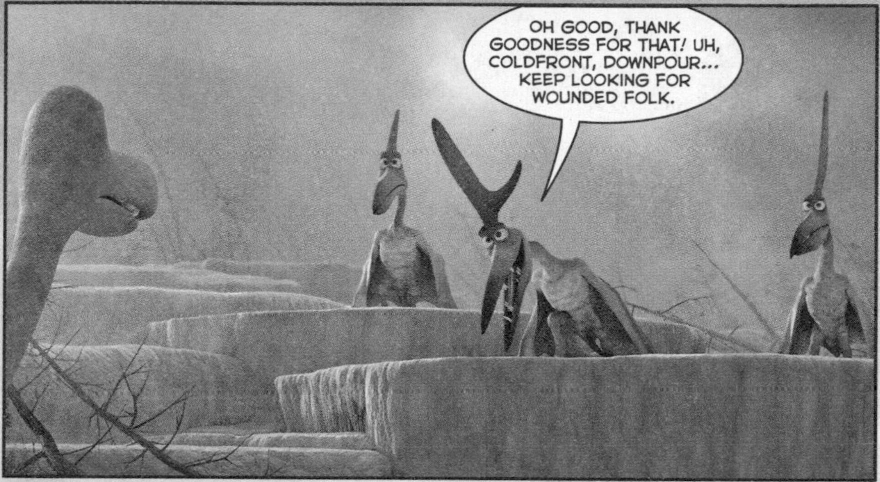
OH GOOD, THANK GOODNESS FOR THAT! UH, COLDFRONT, DOWNPOUR... KEEP LOOKING FOR WOUNDED FOLK.

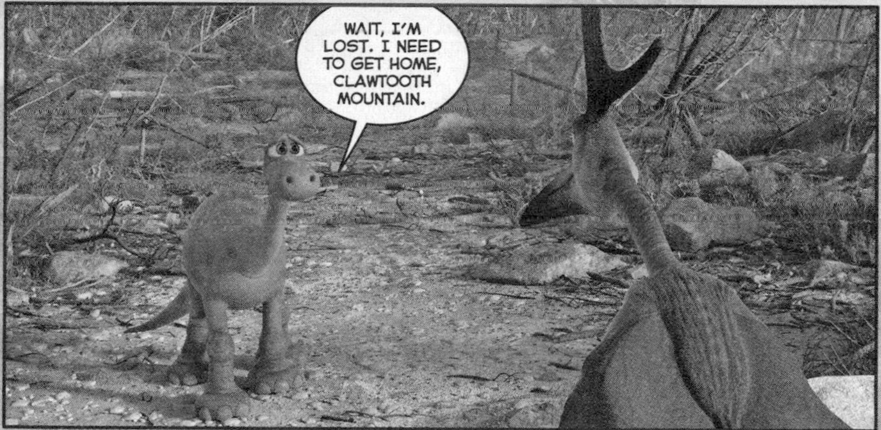
WAIT, I'M LOST. I NEED TO GET HOME, CLAWTOOTH MOUNTAIN.

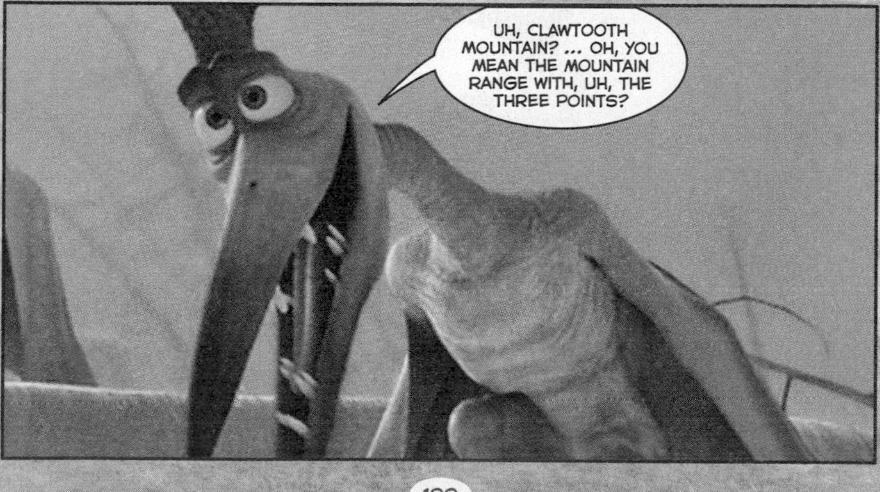
UH, CLAWTOOTH MOUNTAIN? ... OH, YOU MEAN THE MOUNTAIN RANGE WITH, UH, THE THREE POINTS?

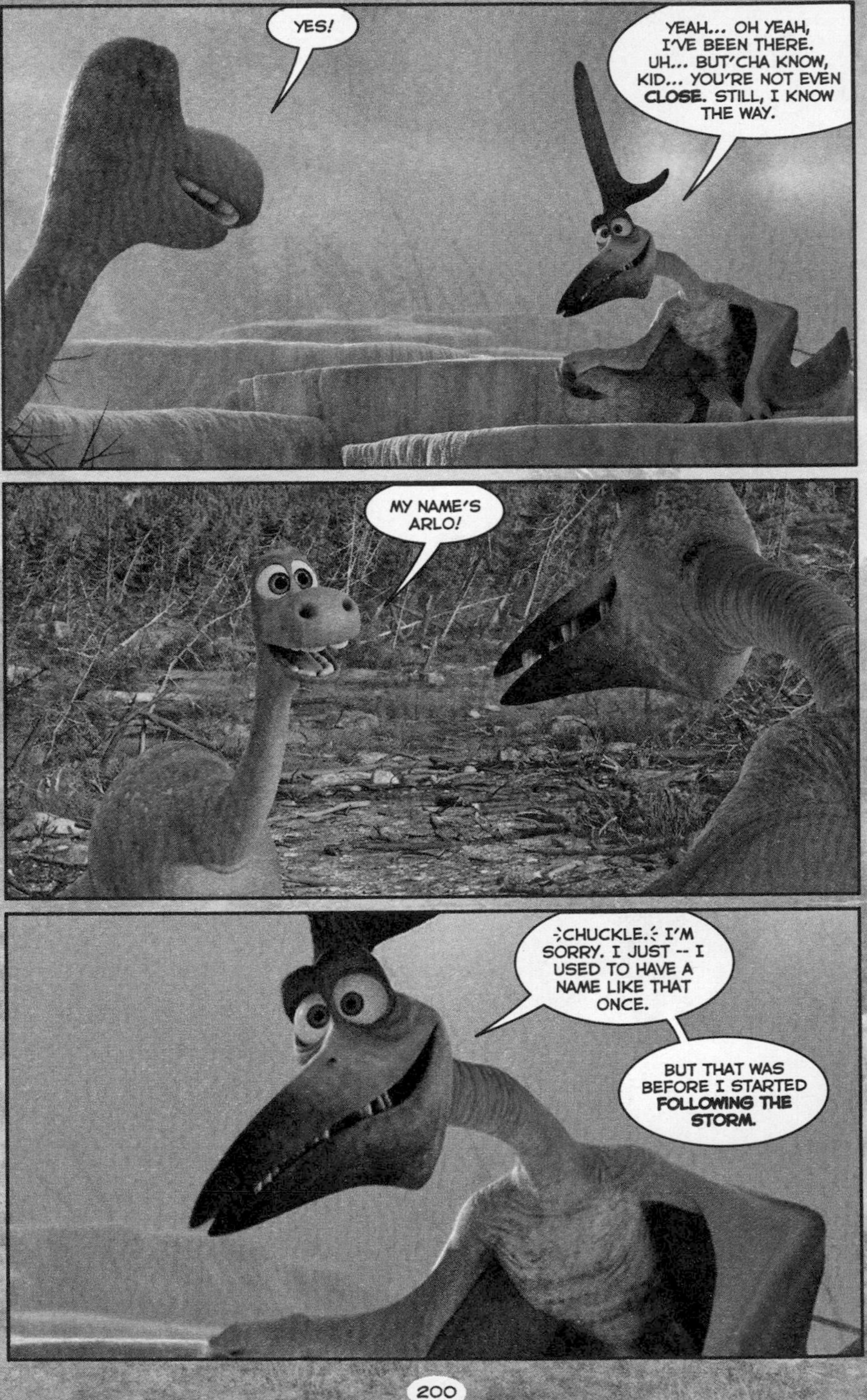
YES!
YEAH... OH YEAH, I'VE BEEN THERE. UH... BUT'CHA KNOW, KID... YOU'RE NOT EVEN **CLOSE**. STILL, I KNOW THE WAY.
MY NAME'S ARLO!
CHUCKLE. I'M SORRY. I JUST -- I USED TO HAVE A NAME LIKE THAT ONCE.
BUT THAT WAS BEFORE I STARTED **FOLLOWING THE STORM.**

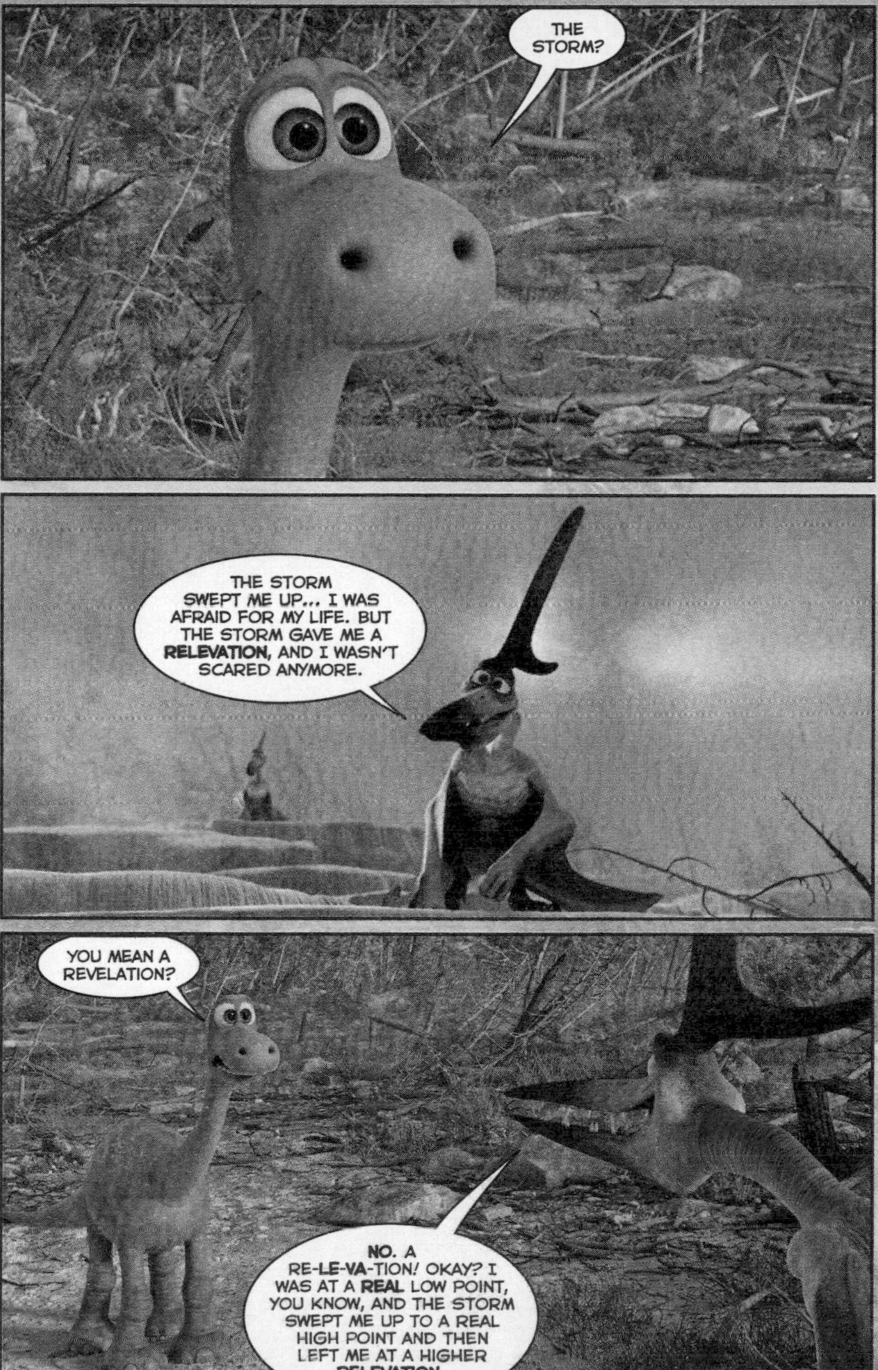
THE STORM?
THE STORM SWEPT ME UP... I WAS AFRAID FOR MY LIFE. BUT THE STORM GAVE ME A **RELEVATION**, AND I WASN'T SCARED ANYMORE.
YOU MEAN A REVELATION?
NO. A RE-**LE**-**VA**-TION! OKAY? I WAS AT A **REAL** LOW POINT, YOU KNOW, AND THE STORM SWEPT ME UP TO A REAL HIGH POINT AND THEN LEFT ME AT A HIGHER **RELEVATION.**

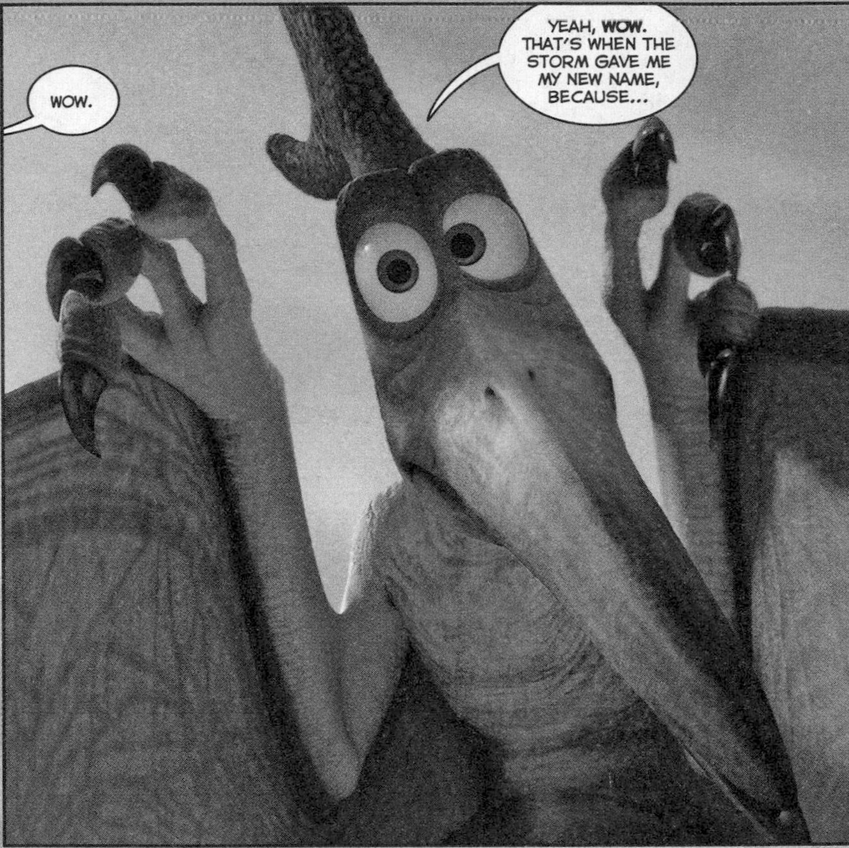
WOW.
YEAH, WOW. THAT'S WHEN THE STORM GAVE ME MY NEW NAME, BECAUSE...

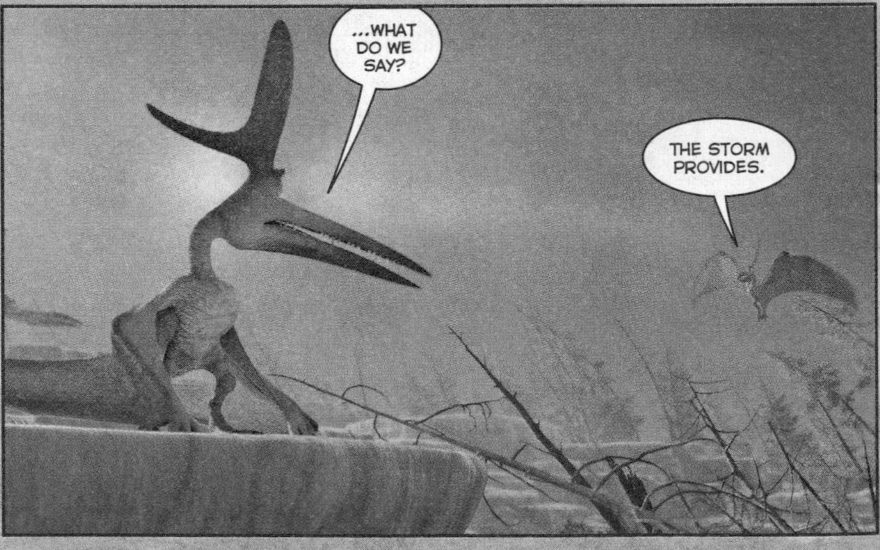
...WHAT DO WE SAY?
THE STORM PROVIDES.

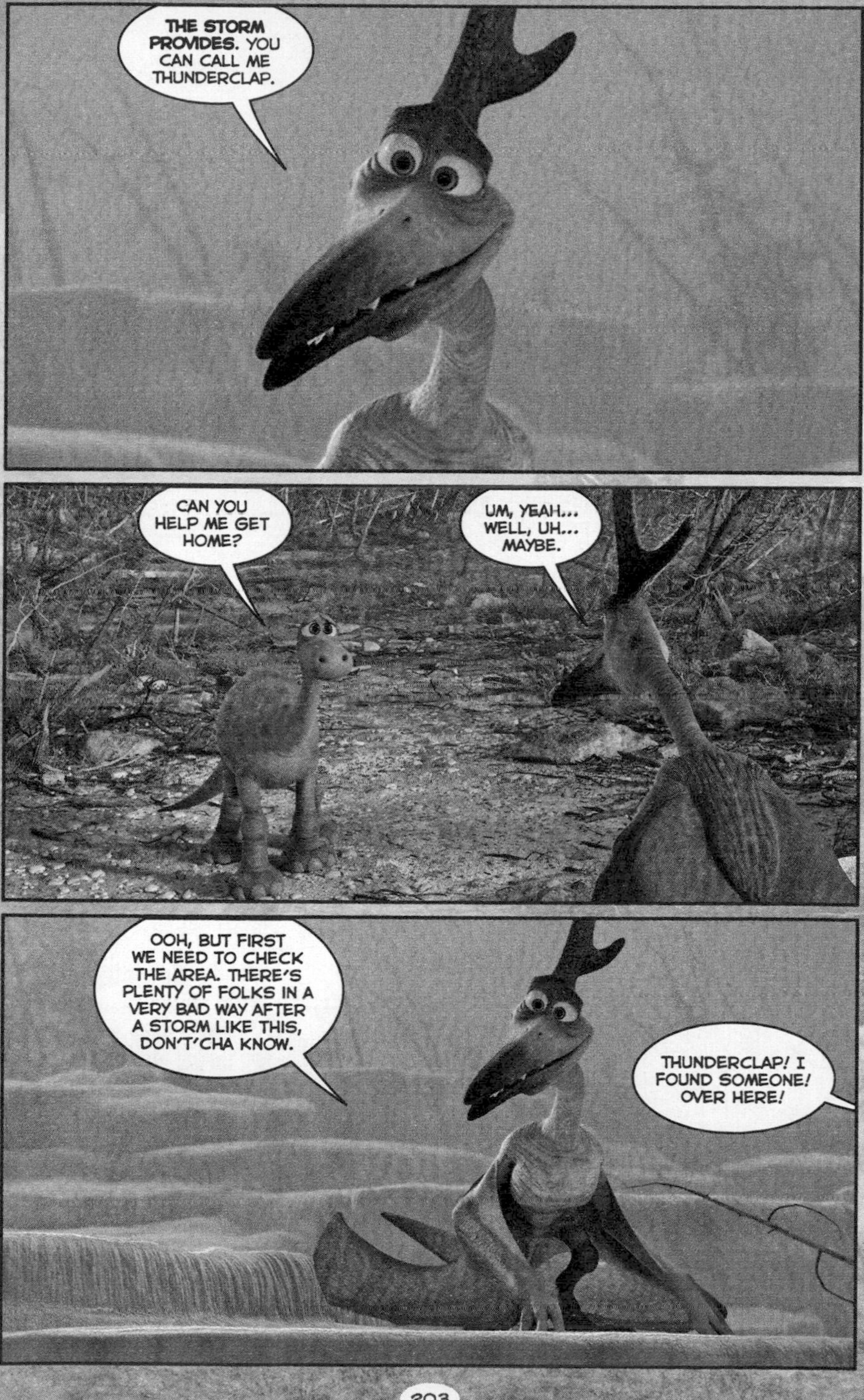
THE STORM PROVIDES. YOU CAN CALL ME THUNDERCLAP.
CAN YOU HELP ME GET HOME?
UM, YEAH... WELL, UH... MAYBE.
OOH, BUT FIRST WE NEED TO CHECK THE AREA. THERE'S PLENTY OF FOLKS IN A VERY BAD WAY AFTER A STORM LIKE THIS, DON'T'CHA KNOW.
THUNDERCLAP! I FOUND SOMEONE! OVER HERE!

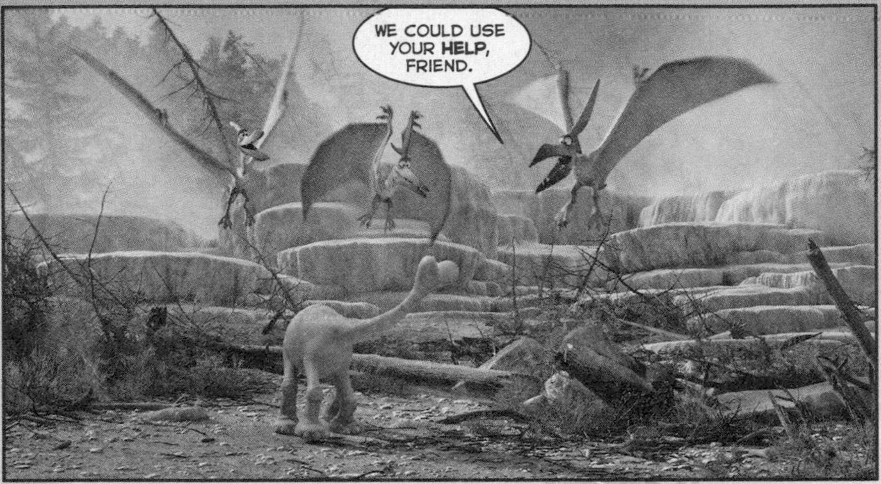
WE COULD USE YOUR **HELP**, FRIEND.

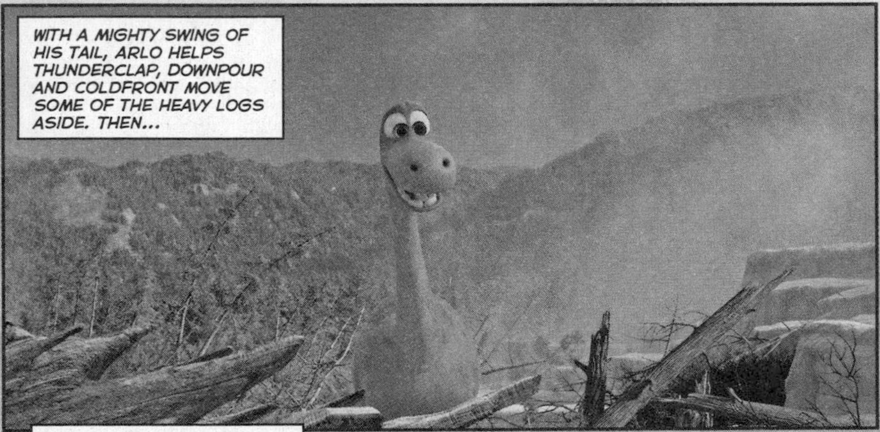
WITH A MIGHTY SWING OF HIS TAIL, ARLO HELPS THUNDERCLAP, DOWNPOUR AND COLDFRONT MOVE SOME OF THE HEAVY LOGS ASIDE. THEN...

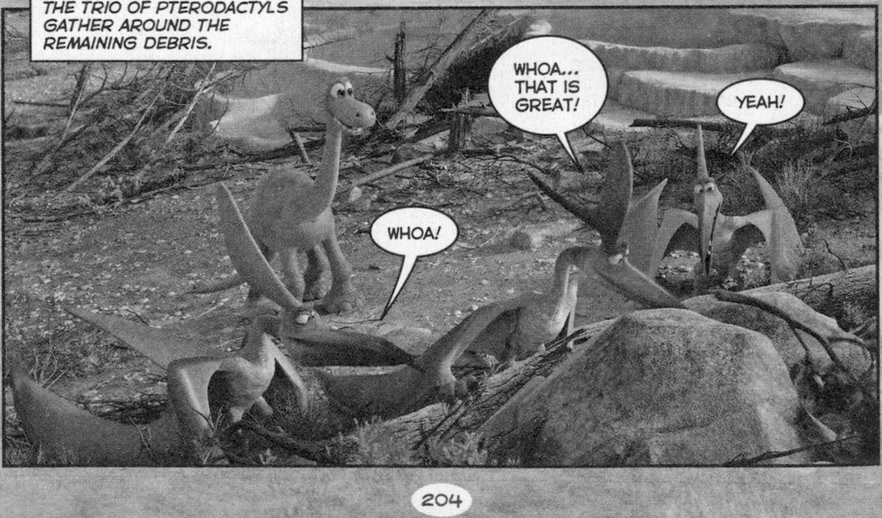
THE TRIO OF PTERODACTYLS GATHER AROUND THE REMAINING DEBRIS.
WHOA... THAT IS GREAT!
YEAH!
WHOA!

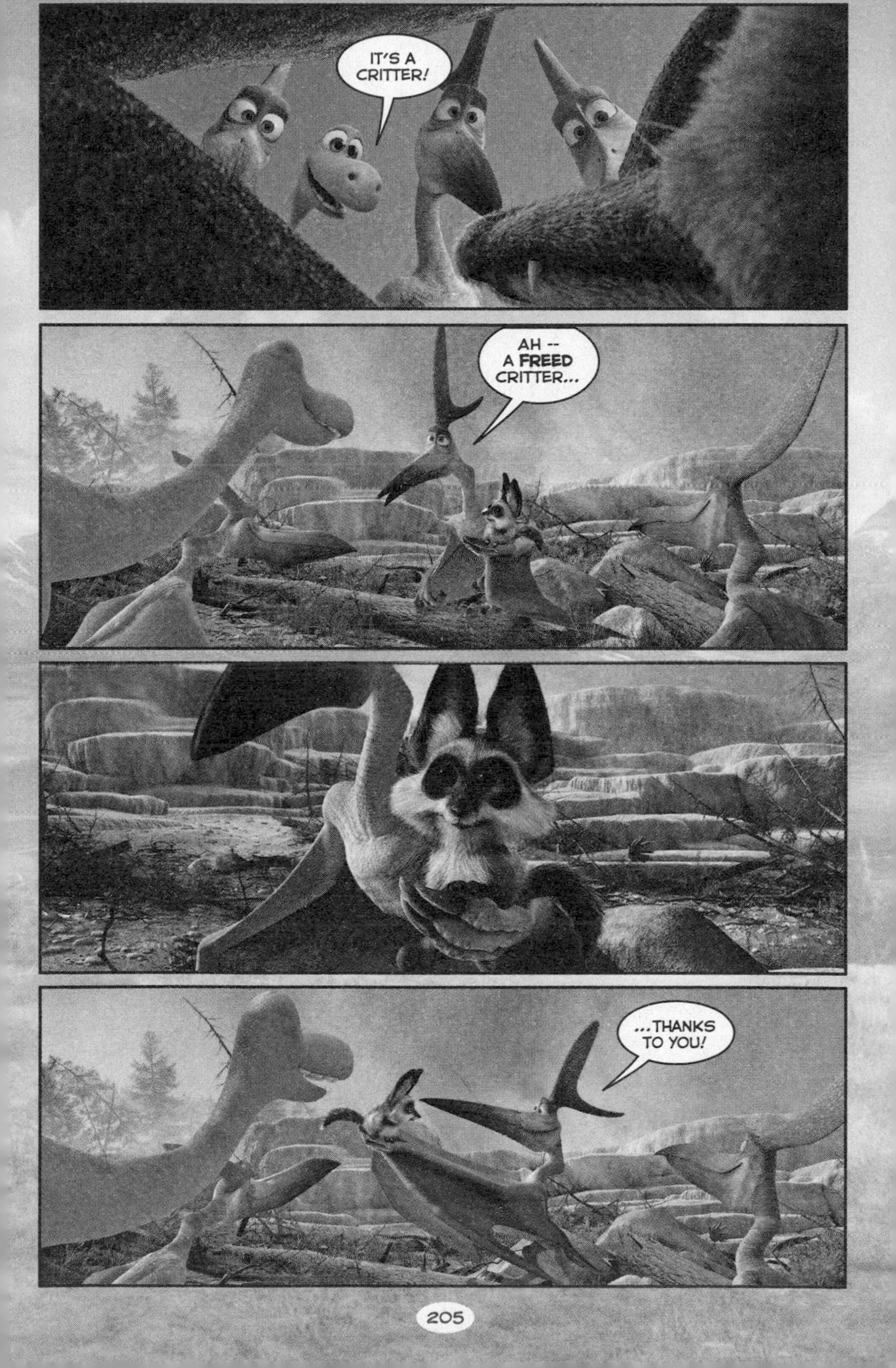
IT'S A CRITTER!
AH -- A **FREED** CRITTER...
...THANKS TO YOU!

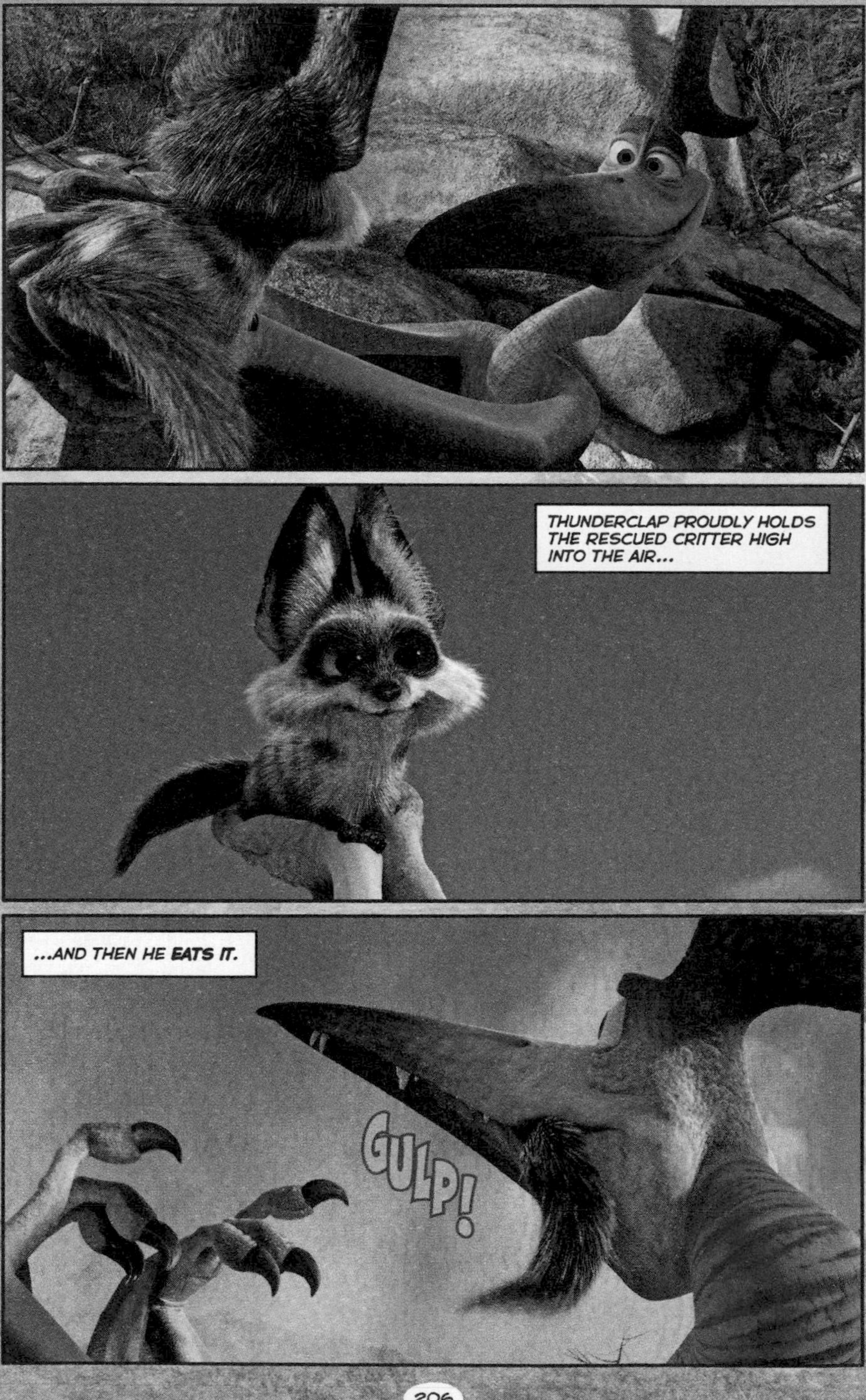
THUNDERCLAP PROUDLY HOLDS THE RESCUED CRITTER HIGH INTO THE AIR...
...AND THEN HE EATS IT.
GULP!

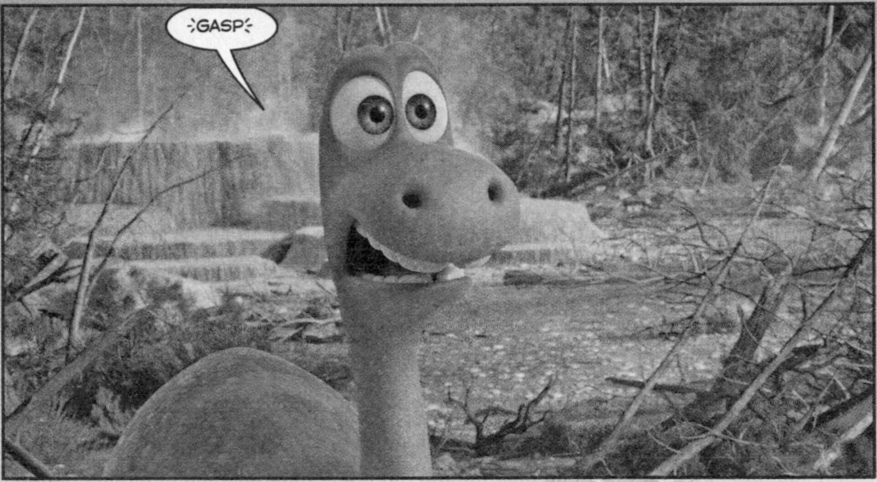
GASP

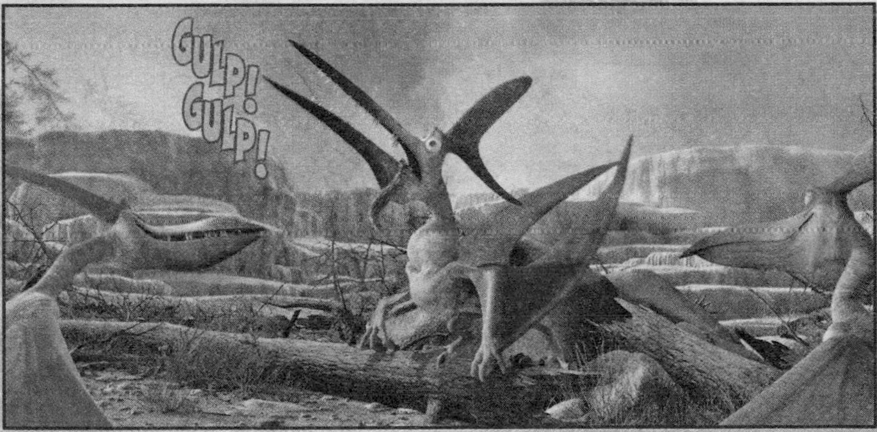
GULP! GULP!

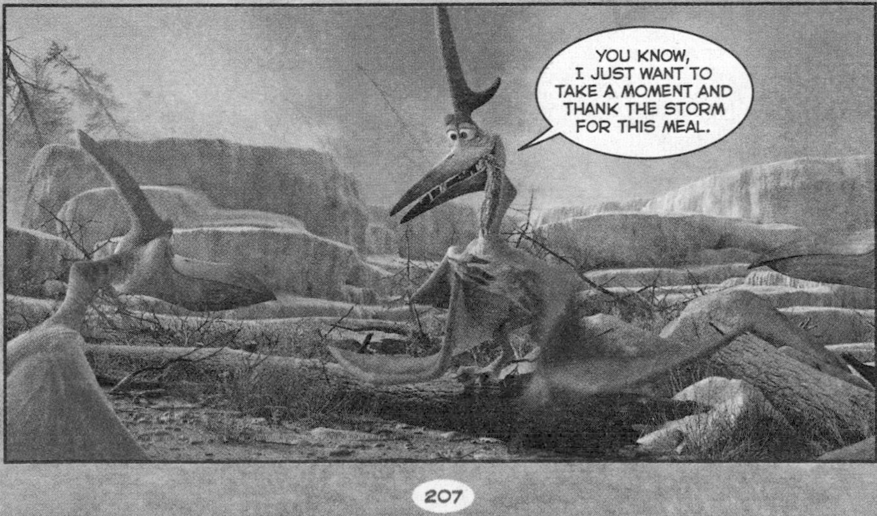
YOU KNOW, I JUST WANT TO TAKE A MOMENT AND THANK THE STORM FOR THIS MEAL.

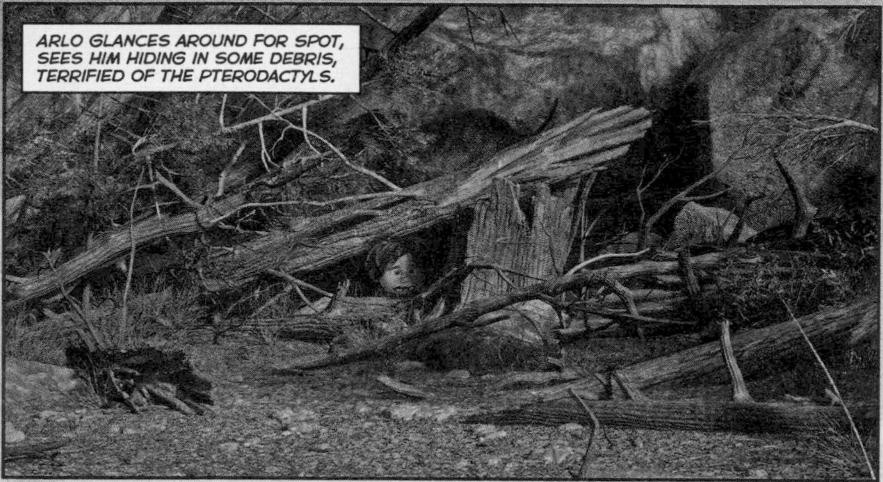
ARLO GLANCES AROUND FOR SPOT, SEES HIM HIDING IN SOME DEBRIS, TERRIFIED OF THE PTERODACTYLS.

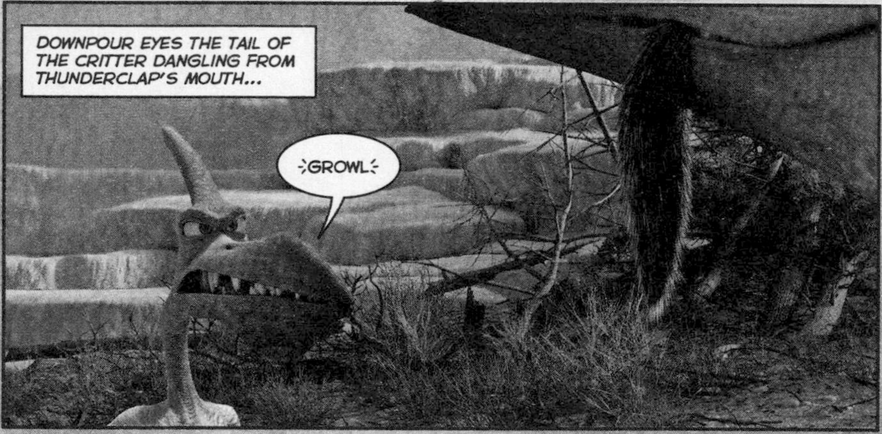
DOWNPOUR EYES THE TAIL OF THE CRITTER DANGLING FROM THUNDERCLAP'S MOUTH...
GROWL

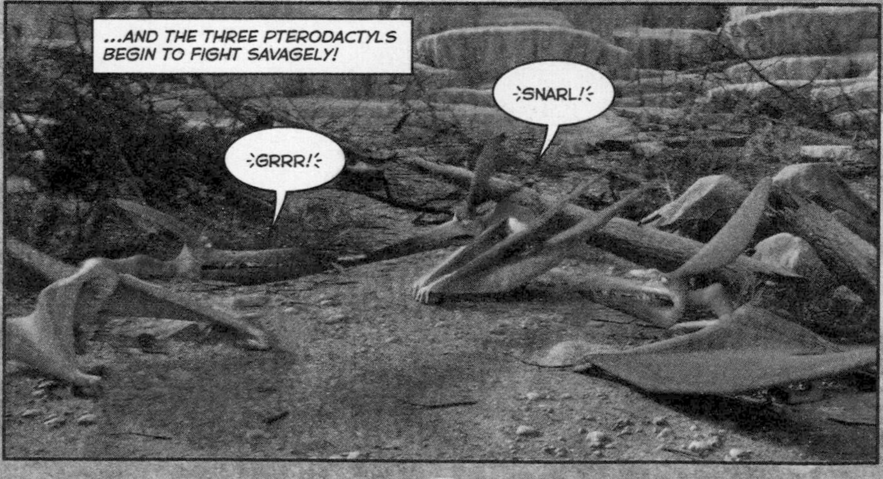
...AND THE THREE PTERODACTYLS BEGIN TO FIGHT SAVAGELY!
SNARL!
GRRR!

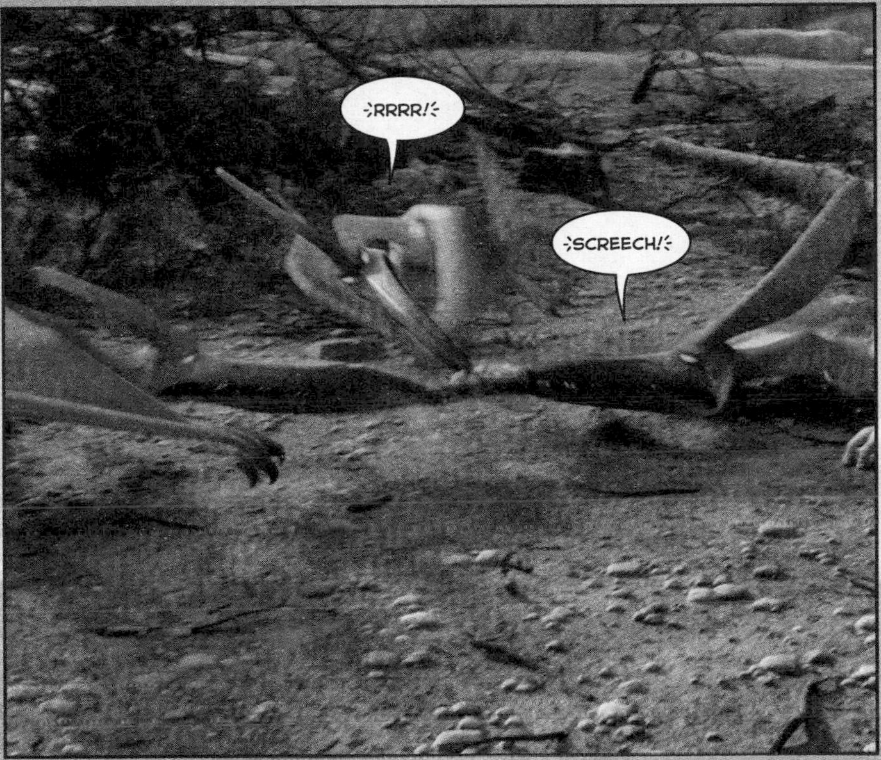
RRRR!
SCREECH!

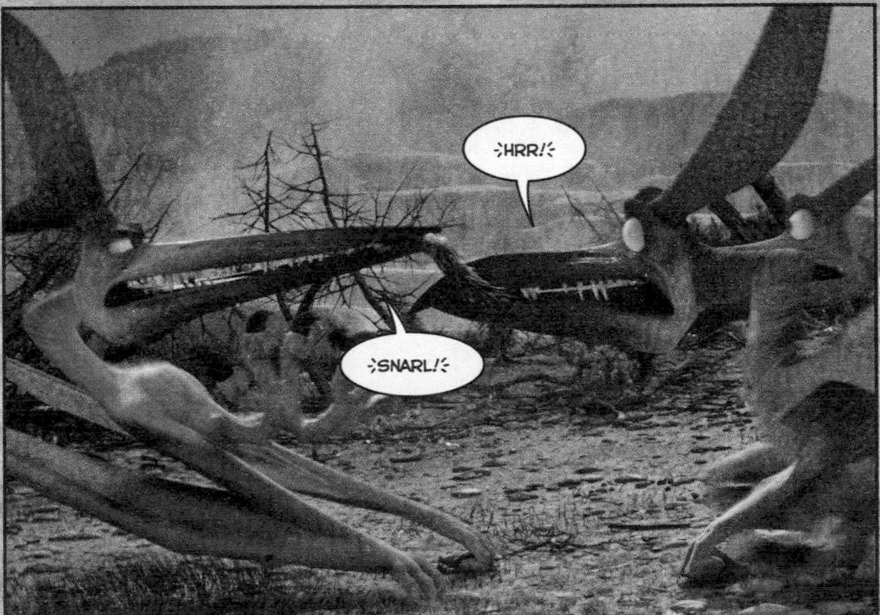
HRR!
SNARL!

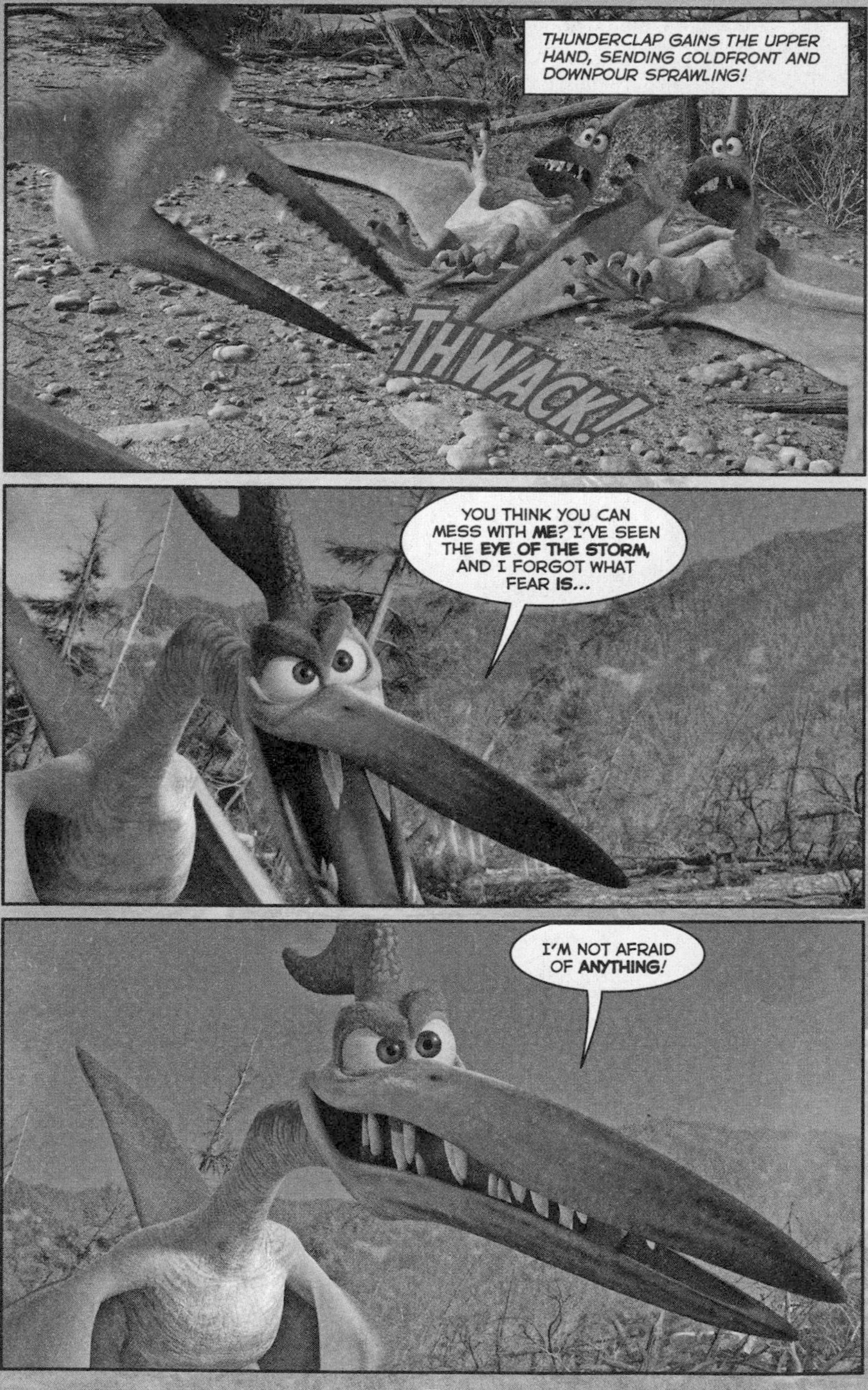
THUNDERCLAP GAINS THE UPPER HAND, SENDING COLDFRONT AND DOWNPOUR SPRAWLING!
THWACK!
YOU THINK YOU CAN MESS WITH ME? I'VE SEEN THE EYE OF THE STORM, AND I FORGOT WHAT FEAR IS...
I'M NOT AFRAID OF ANYTHING!

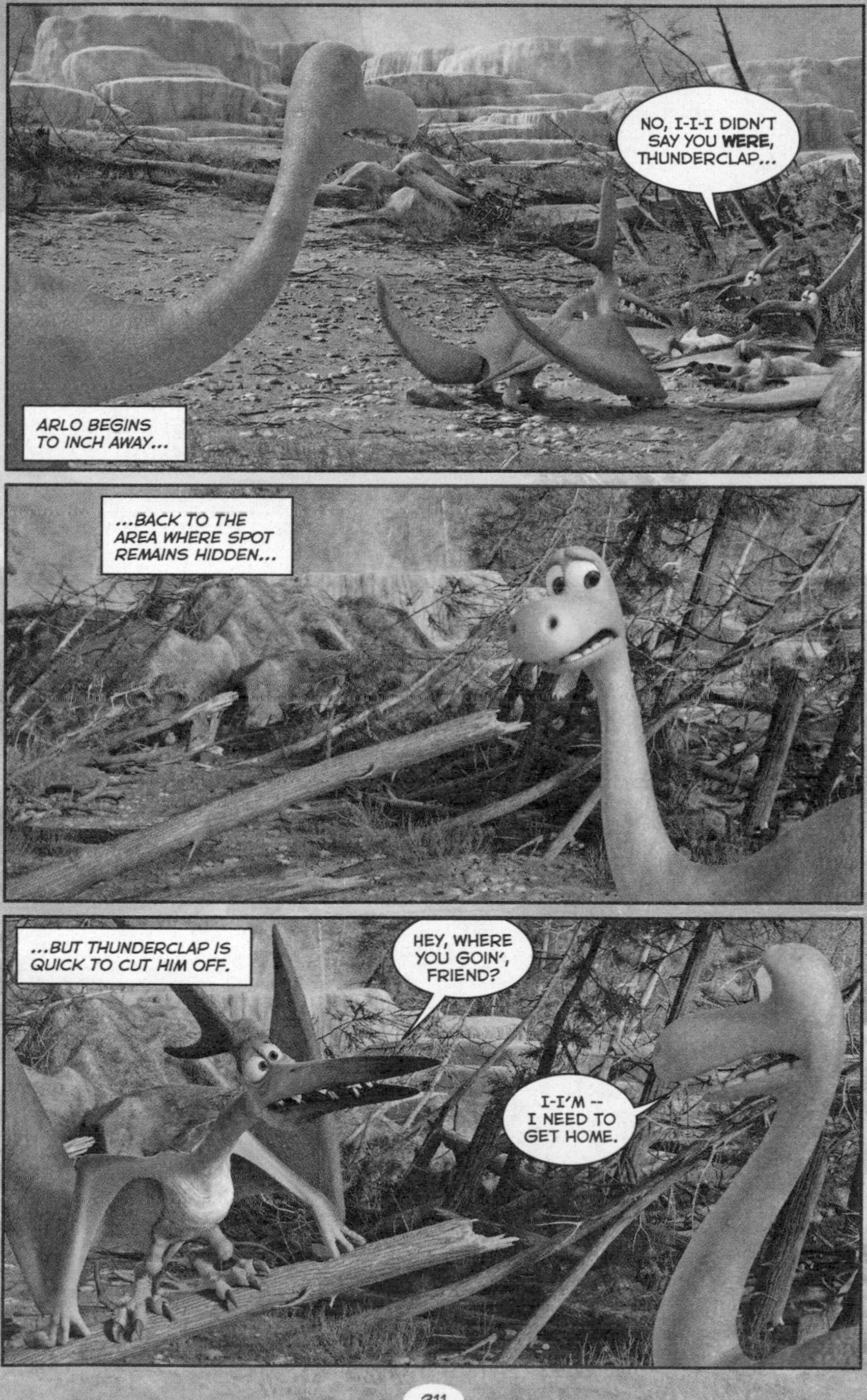
NO, I-I-I DIDN'T SAY YOU **WERE**, THUNDERCLAP...
ARLO BEGINS TO INCH AWAY...
...BACK TO THE AREA WHERE SPOT REMAINS HIDDEN...
...BUT THUNDERCLAP IS QUICK TO CUT HIM OFF.
HEY, WHERE YOU GOIN', FRIEND?
I-I'M -- I NEED TO GET HOME.

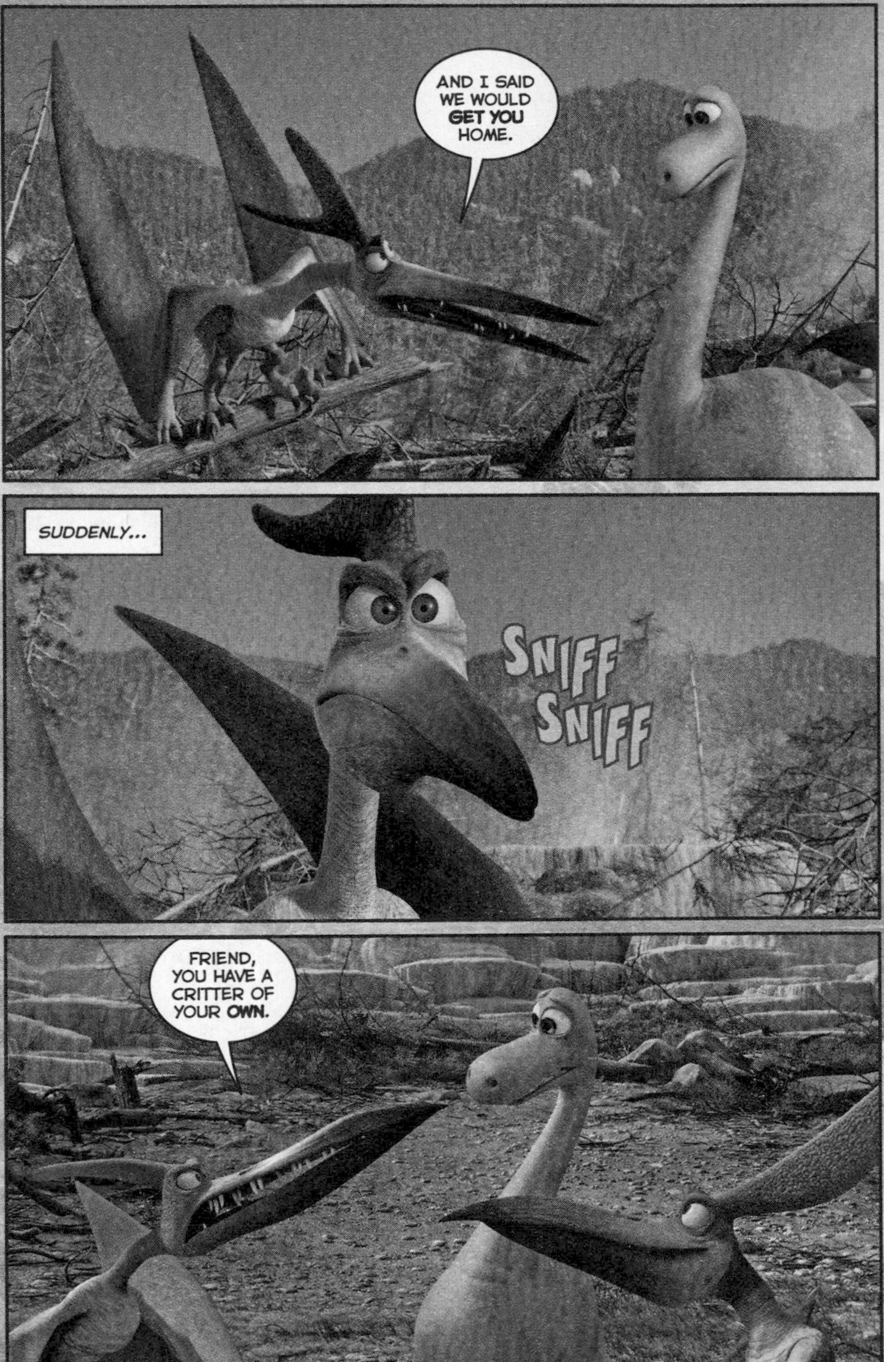
AND I SAID WE WOULD GET YOU HOME.
SUDDENLY...
SNIFF SNIFF
FRIEND, YOU HAVE A CRITTER OF YOUR OWN.

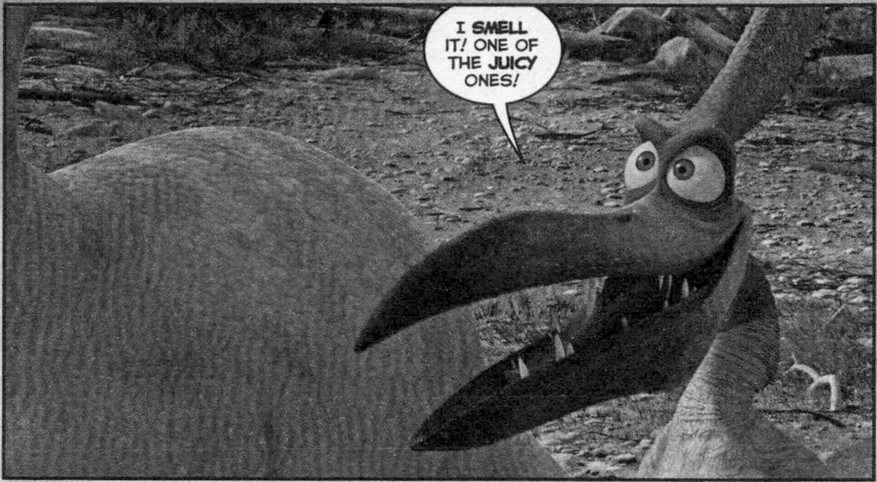
I SMELL IT! ONE OF THE JUICY ONES!

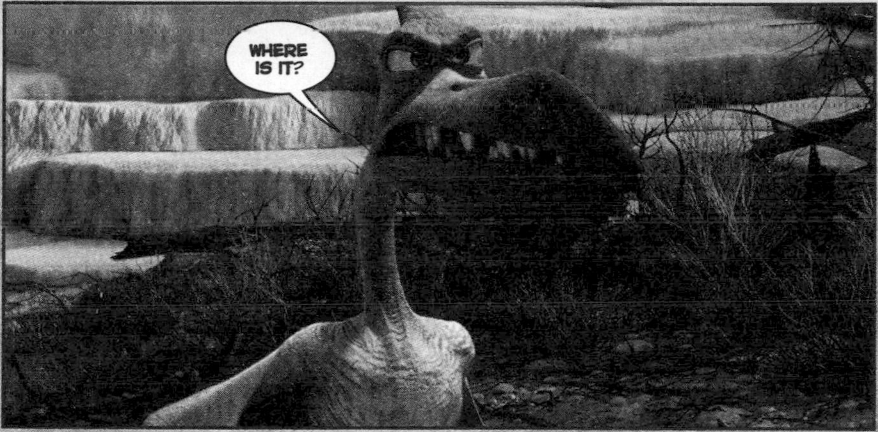
WHERE IS IT?

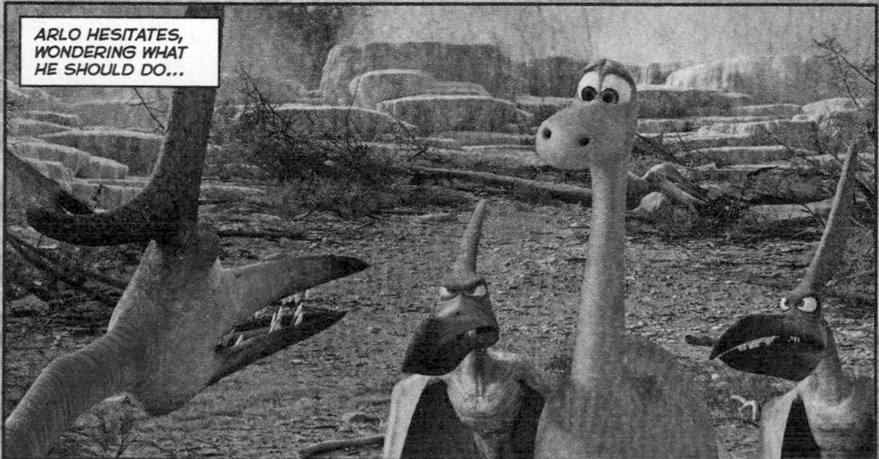
ARLO HESITATES, WONDERING WHAT HE SHOULD DO...

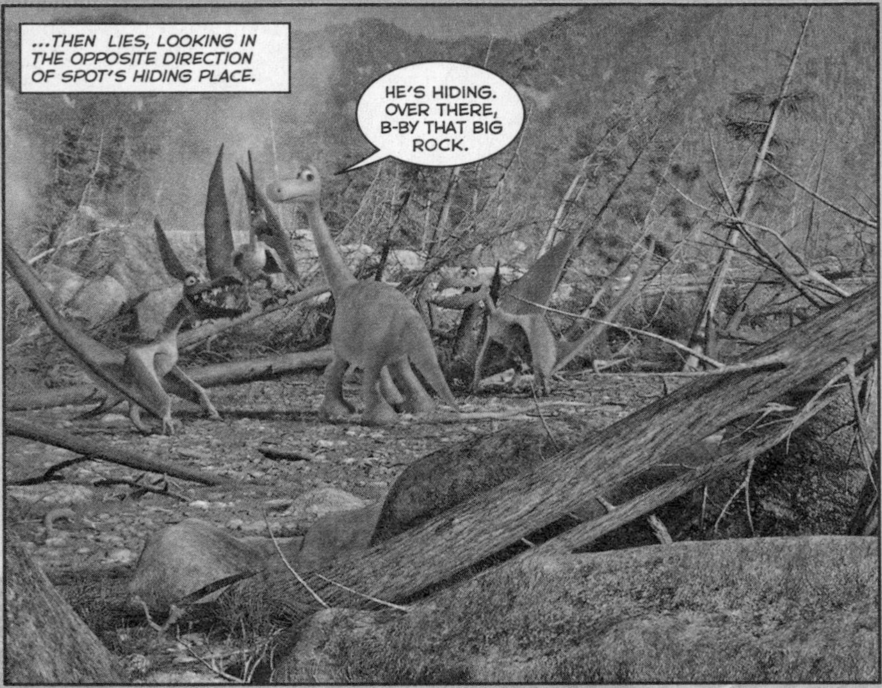
...THEN LIES, LOOKING IN THE OPPOSITE DIRECTION OF SPOT'S HIDING PLACE.
HE'S HIDING. OVER THERE, B-BY THAT BIG ROCK.

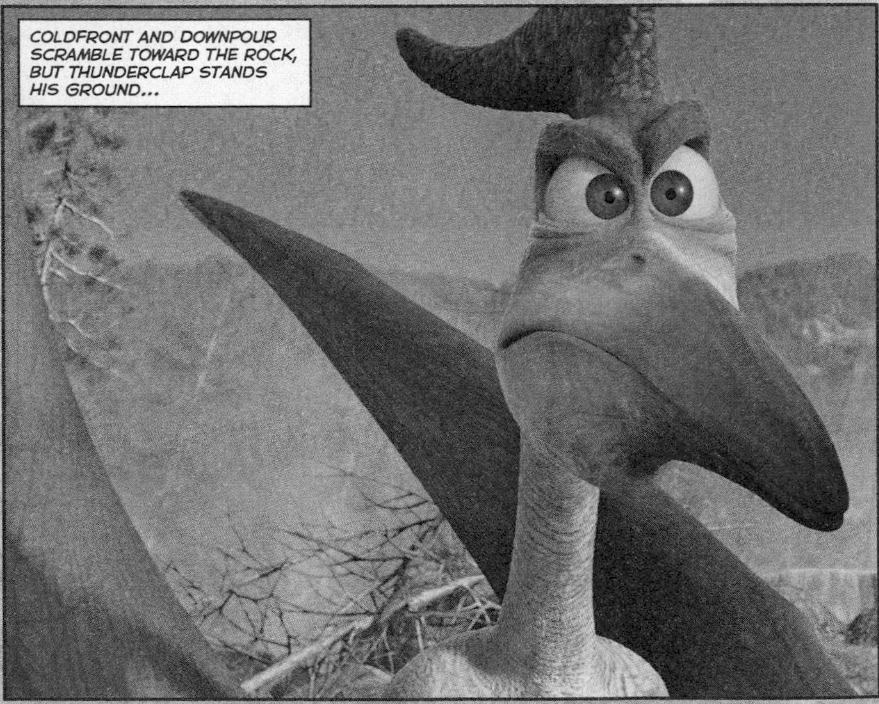
COLDFRONT AND DOWNPOUR SCRAMBLE TOWARD THE ROCK, BUT THUNDERCLAP STANDS HIS GROUND...

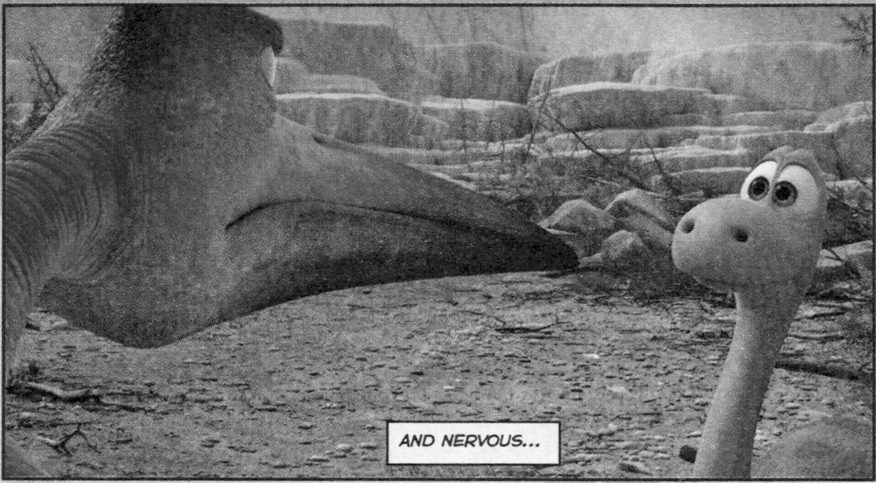
AND NERVOUS...

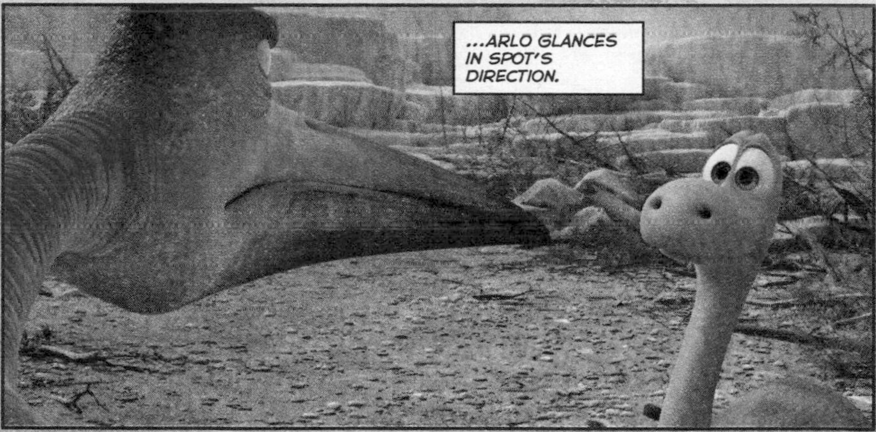
...ARLO GLANCES IN SPOT'S DIRECTION.

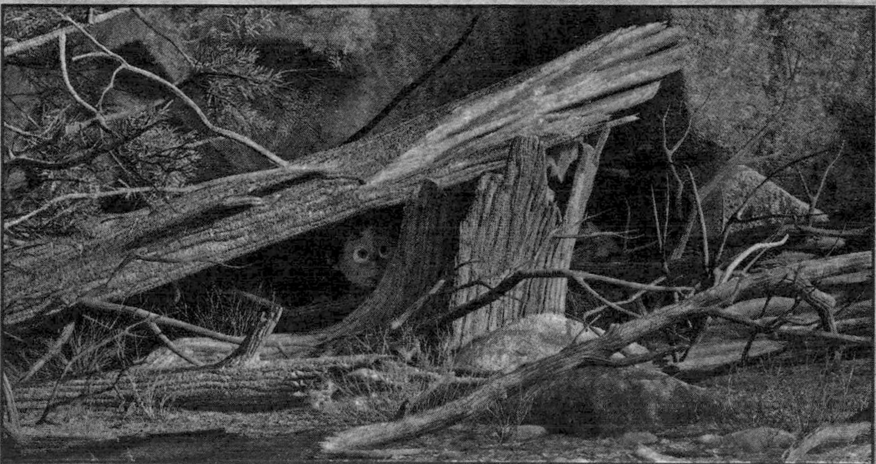

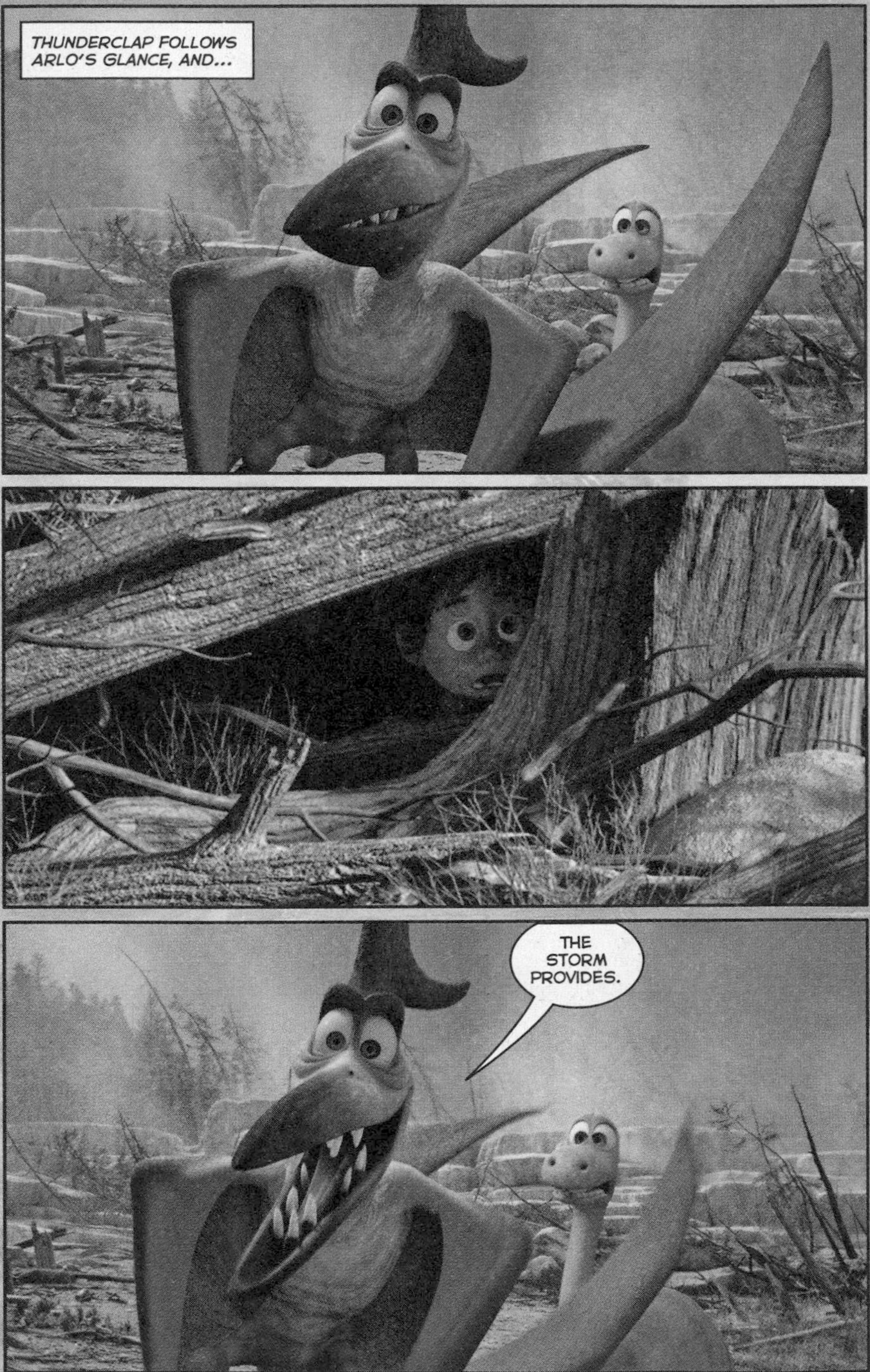
THUNDERCLAP FOLLOWS ARLO'S GLANCE, AND...
THE STORM PROVIDES.

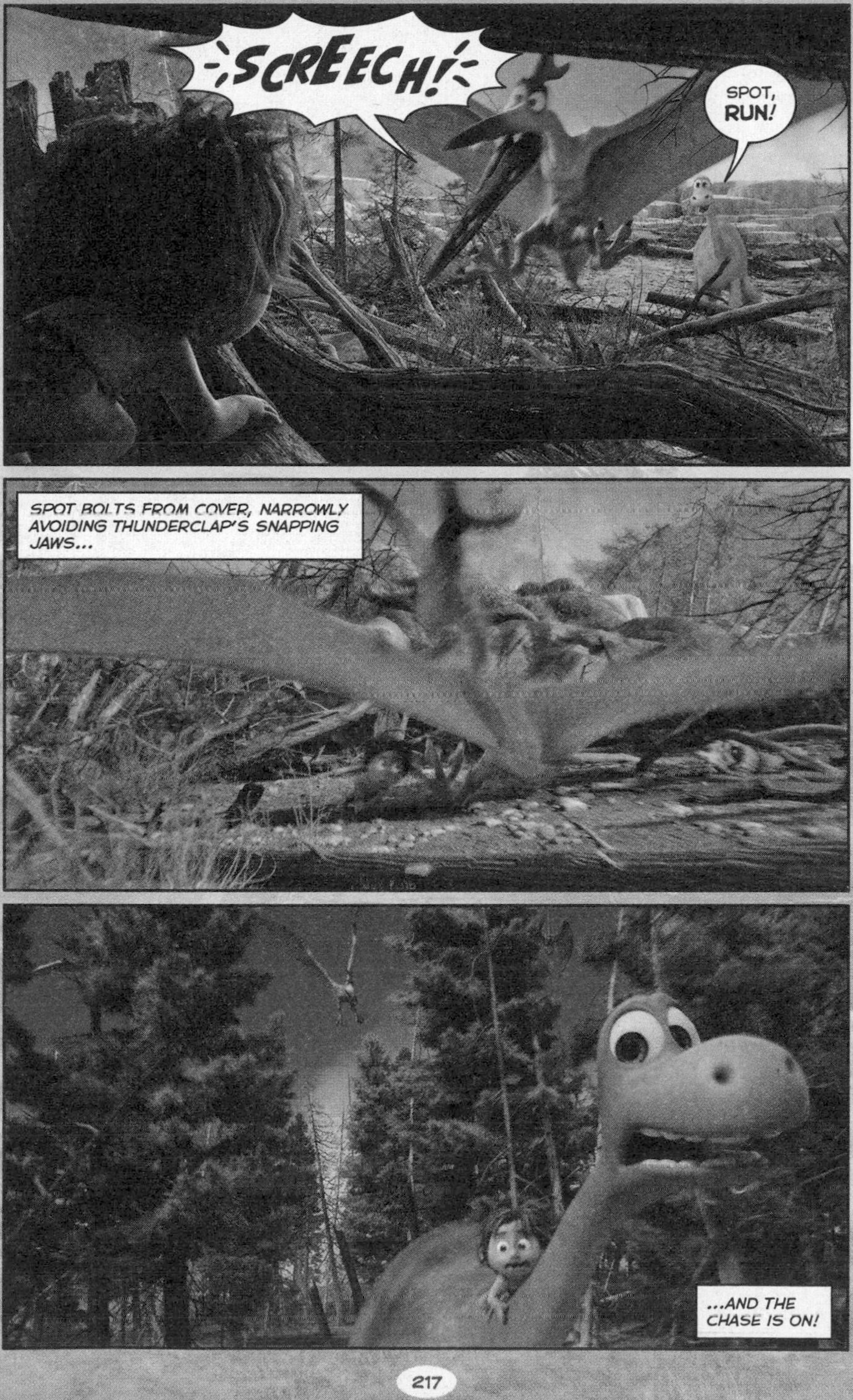
SCREECH!
SPOT, RUN!
SPOT BOLTS FROM COVER, NARROWLY AVOIDING THUNDERCLAP'S SNAPPING JAWS...
...AND THE CHASE IS ON!

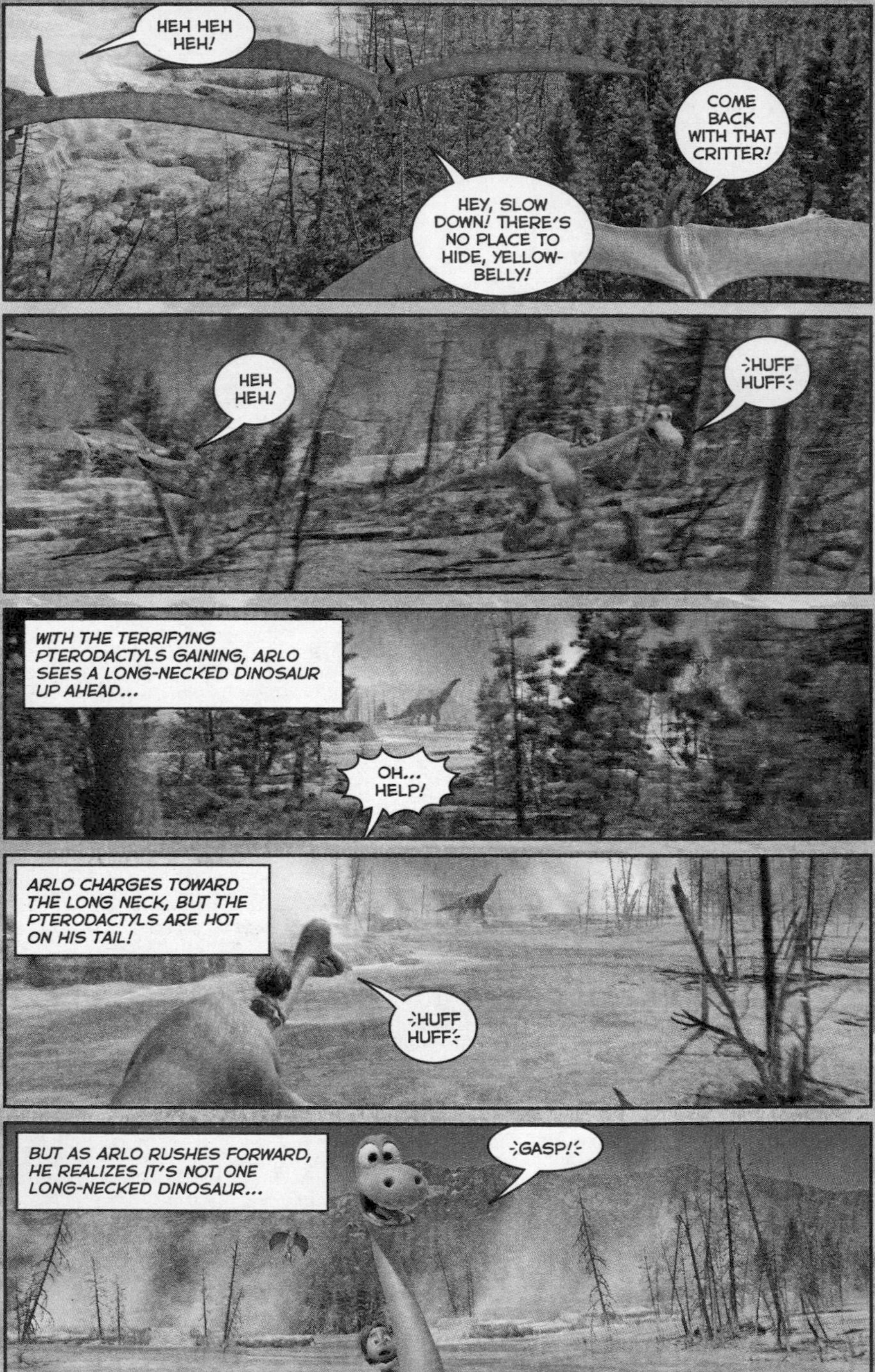
HEH HEH
HEH!
COME BACK WITH THAT CRITTER!
HEY, SLOW DOWN! THERE'S NO PLACE TO HIDE, YELLOW-BELLY!
HEH HEH!
HUFF HUFF
WITH THE TERRIFYING PTERODACTYLS GAINING, ARLO SEES A LONG-NECKED DINOSAUR UP AHEAD...
OH... HELP!
ARLO CHARGES TOWARD THE LONG NECK, BUT THE PTERODACTYLS ARE HOT ON HIS TAIL!
HUFF HUFF
BUT AS ARLO RUSHES FORWARD, HE REALIZES IT'S NOT ONE LONG-NECKED DINOSAUR...
GASP!

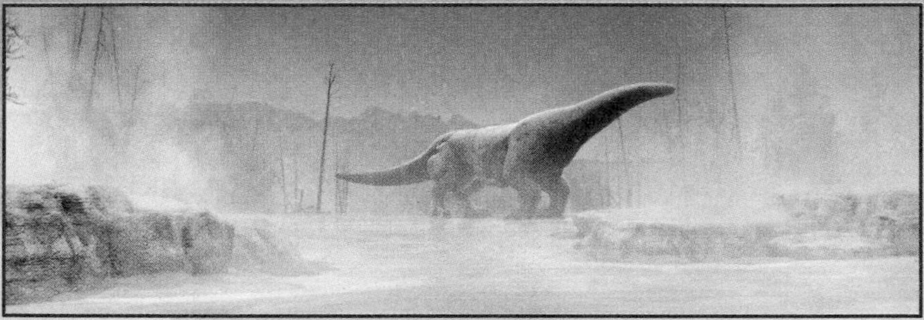

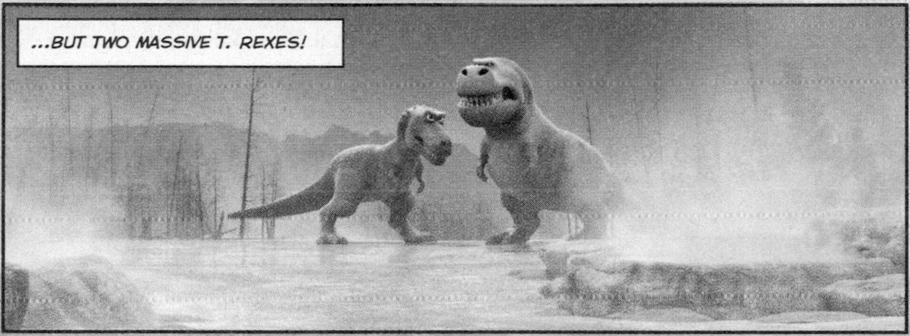
...BUT TWO MASSIVE T. REXES!

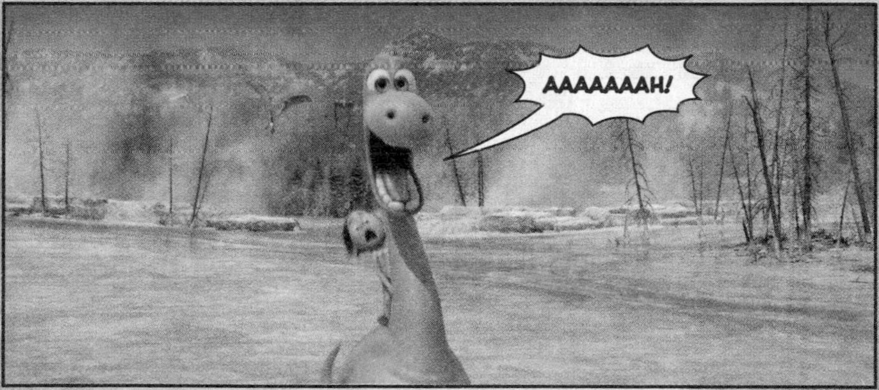
AAAAAAAH!

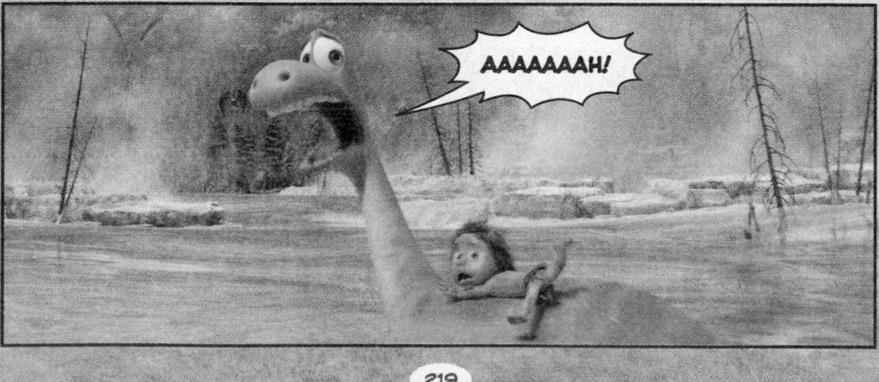
AAAAAAAH!

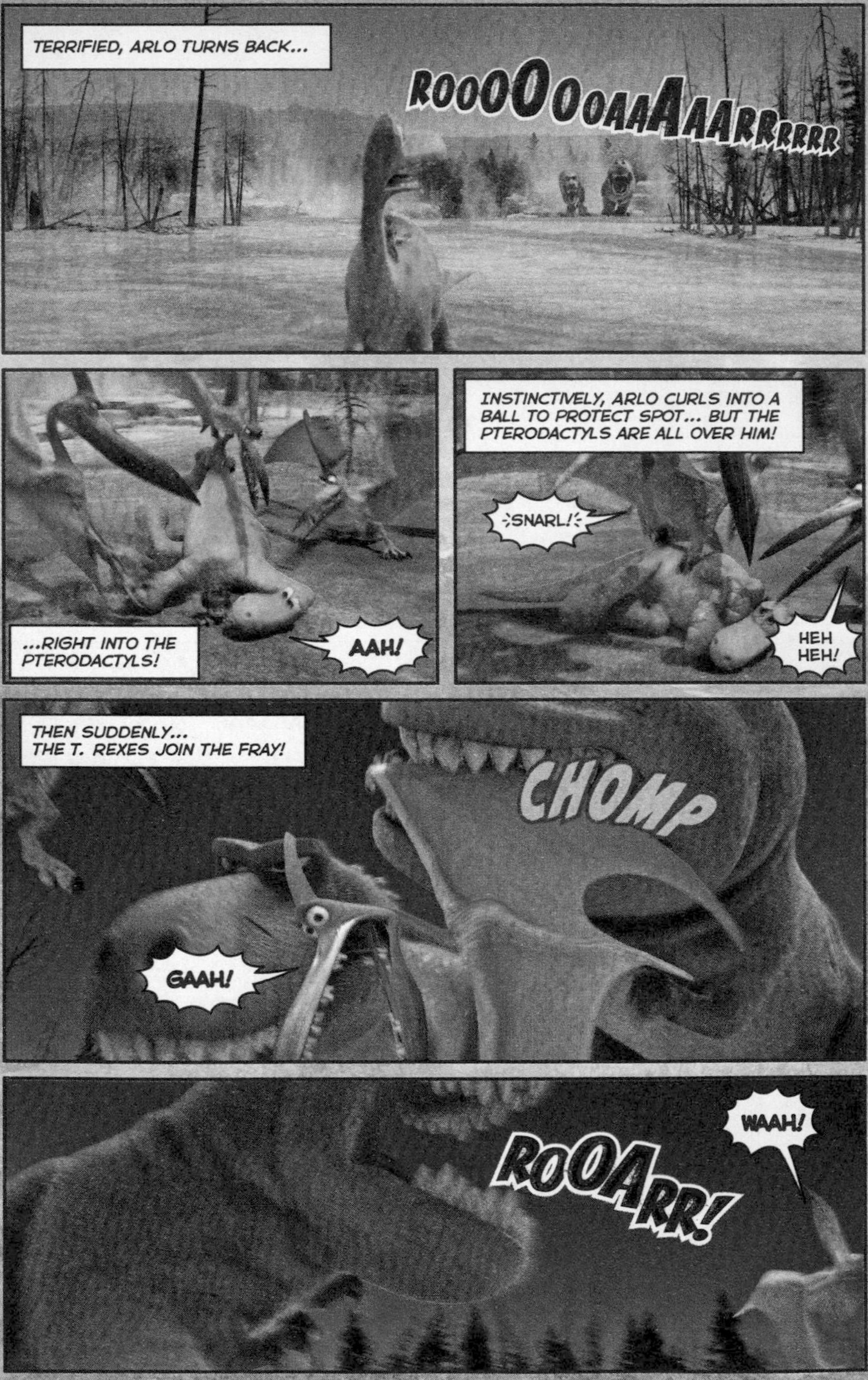

TERRIFIED, ARLO TURNS BACK...
ROOOOOOAAAAAARRRRRR
...RIGHT INTO THE PTERODACTYLS!
AAH!
INSTINCTIVELY, ARLO CURLS INTO A BALL TO PROTECT SPOT... BUT THE PTERODACTYLS ARE ALL OVER HIM!
SNARL!
HEH HEH!
THEN SUDDENLY... THE T. REXES JOIN THE FRAY!
CHOMP
GAAH!
ROOARR!
WAAH!

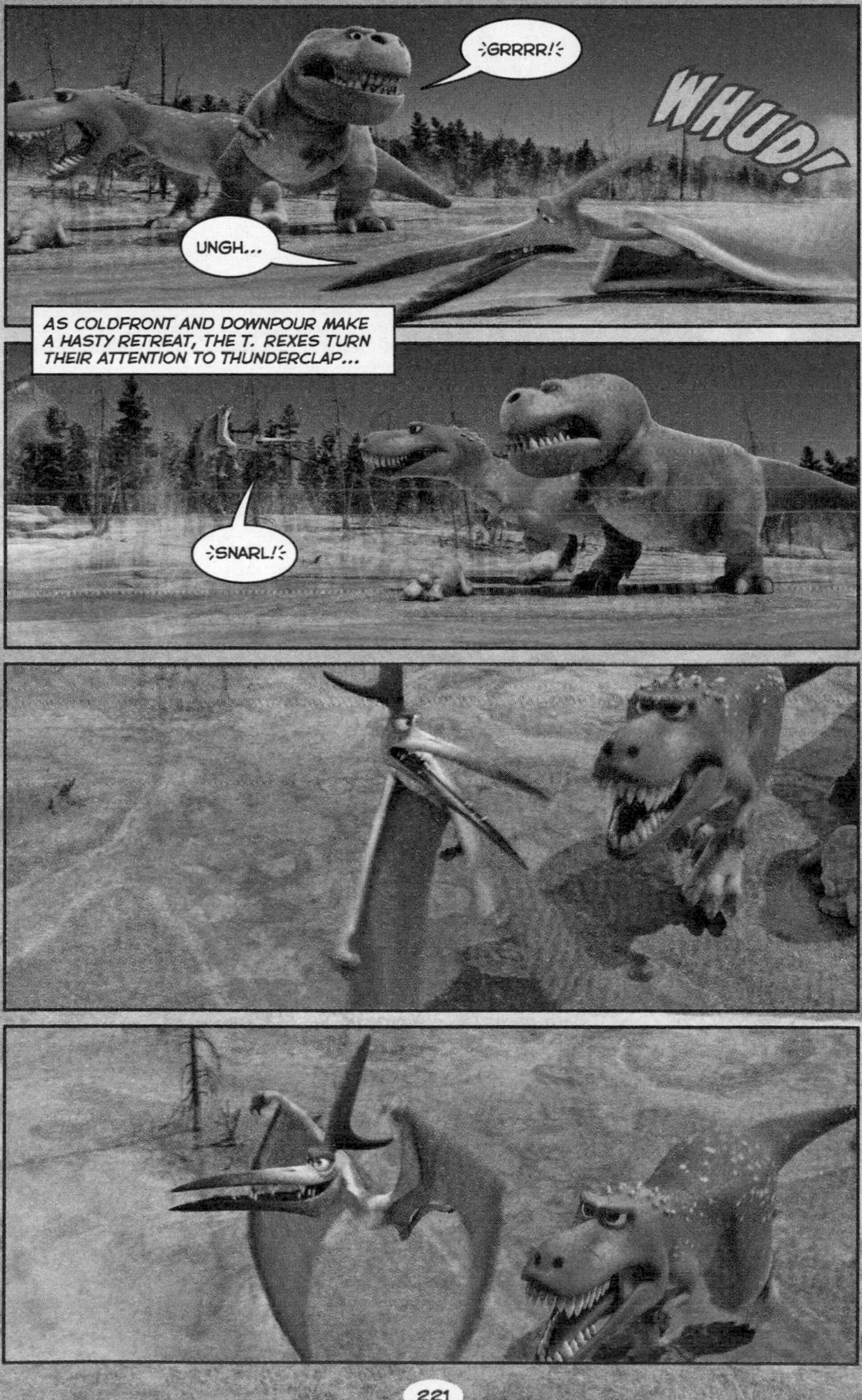
GRRRR!
WHUD!
UNGH...
AS COLDFRONT AND DOWNPOUR MAKE A HASTY RETREAT, THE T. REXES TURN THEIR ATTENTION TO THUNDERCLAP...
SNARL!

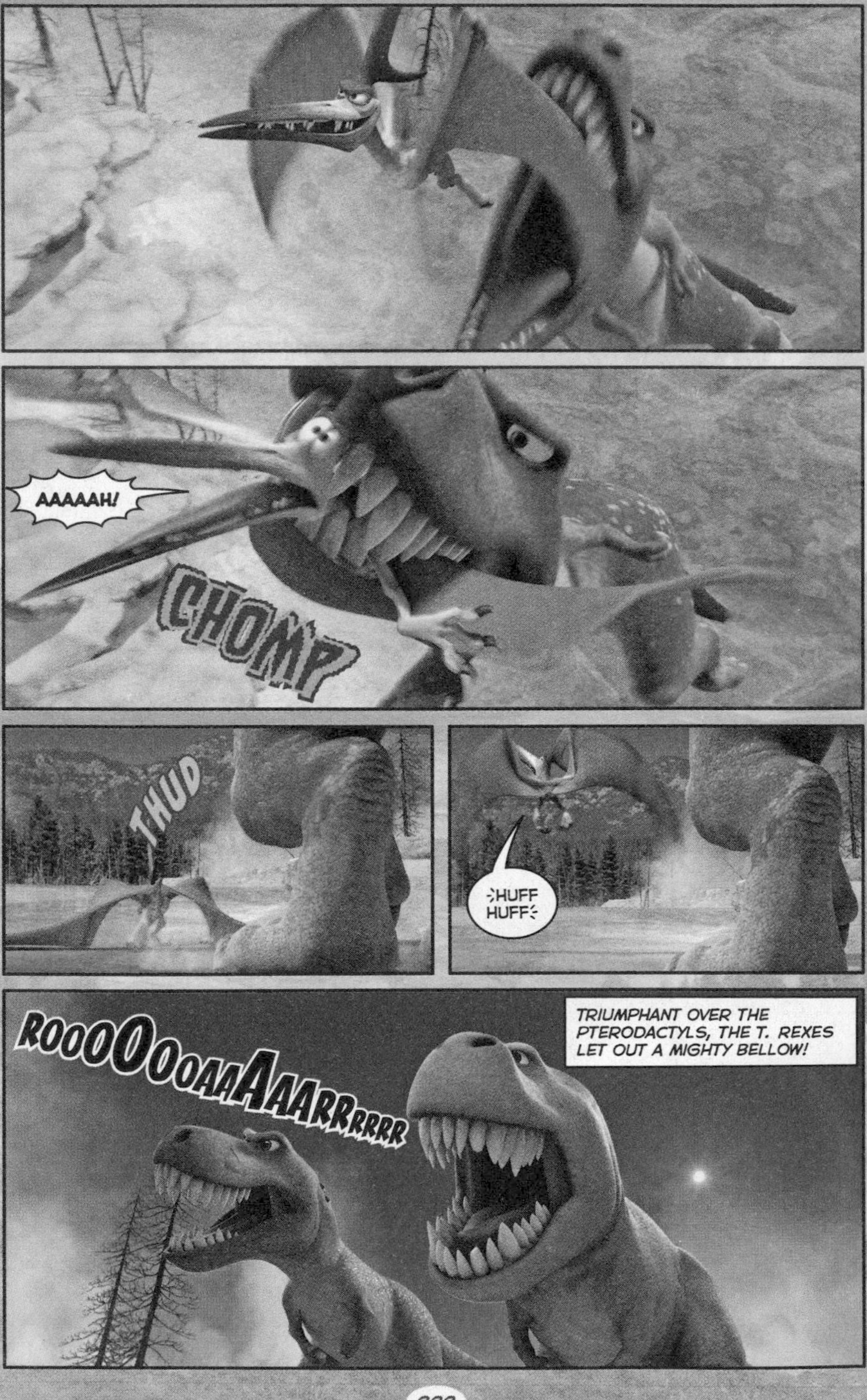
AAAAAH!
CHOMP
THUD
HUFF HUFF
ROOOOOOOAAAAAARRRRRR
TRIUMPHANT OVER THE PTERODACTYLS, THE T. REXES LET OUT A MIGHTY BELLOW!

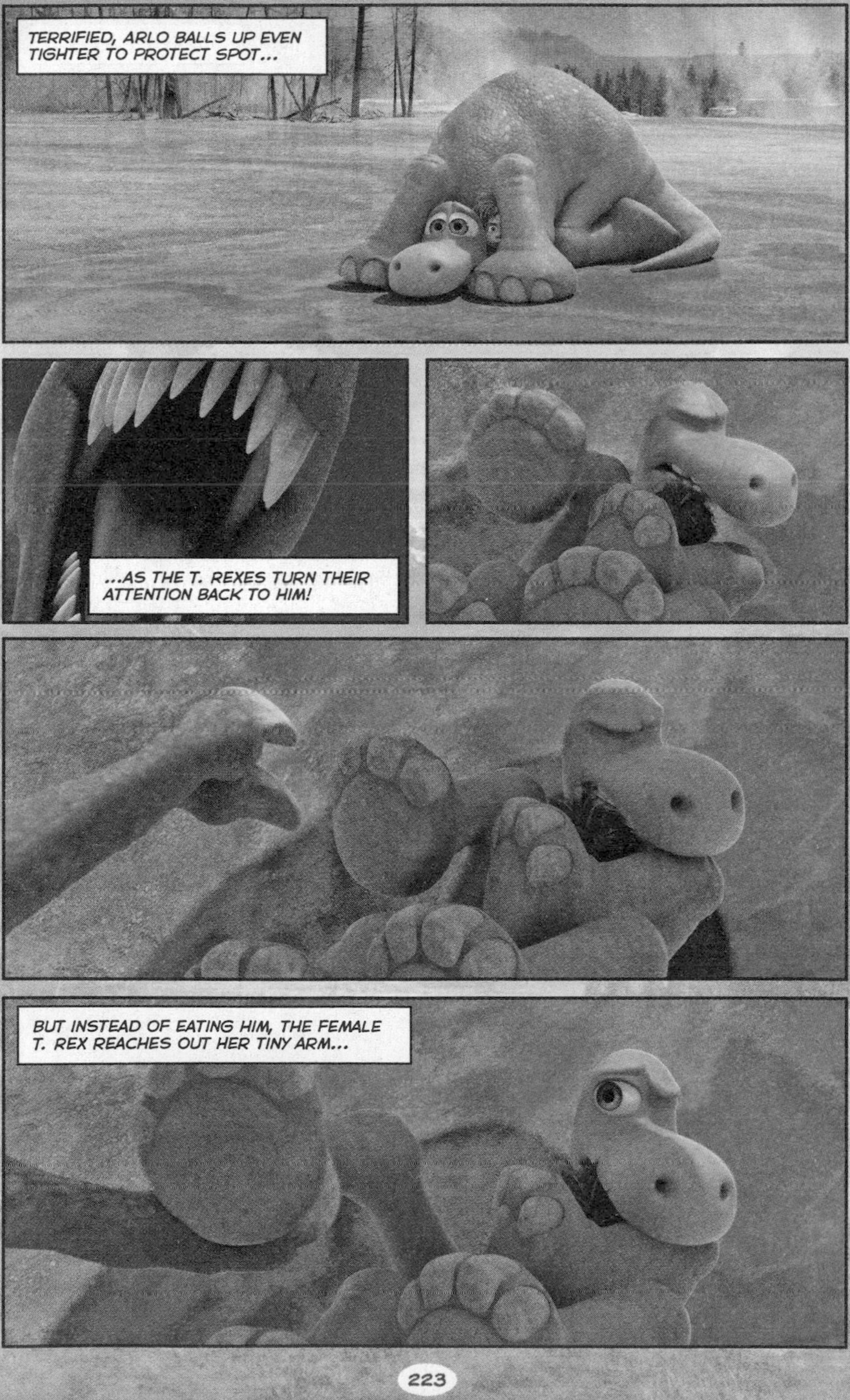
TERRIFIED, ARLO BALLS UP EVEN TIGHTER TO PROTECT SPOT...
...AS THE T. REXES TURN THEIR ATTENTION BACK TO HIM!
BUT INSTEAD OF EATING HIM, THE FEMALE T. REX REACHES OUT HER TINY ARM...

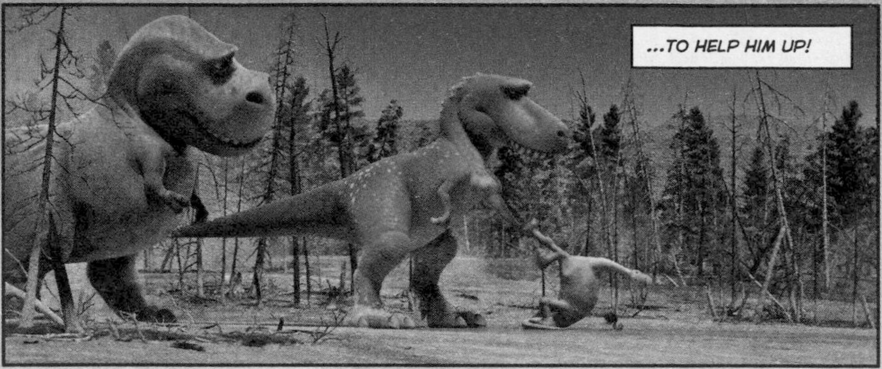
...TO HELP HIM UP!

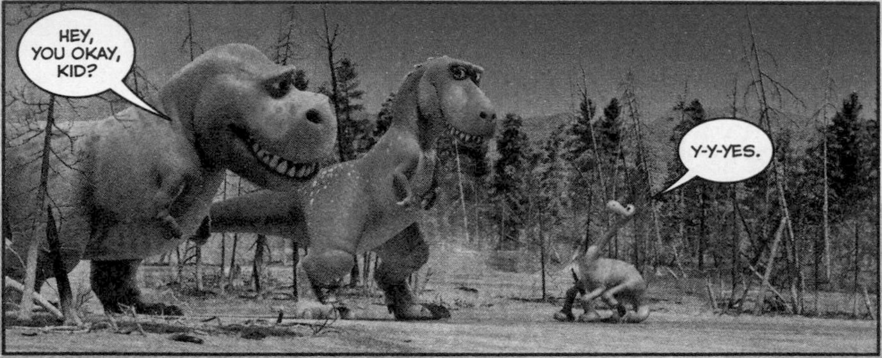
HEY, YOU OKAY, KID?
Y-Y-YES.

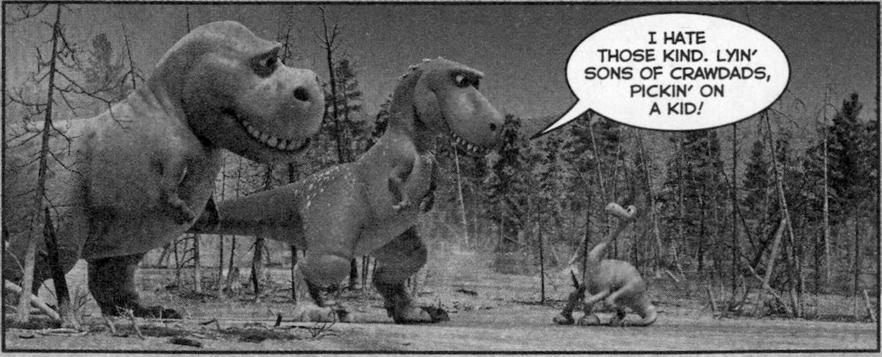
I HATE THOSE KIND. LYIN' SONS OF CRAWDADS, PICKIN' ON A KID!

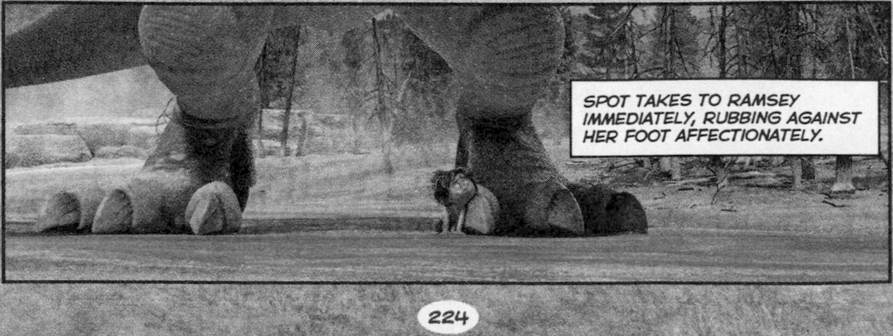
SPOT TAKES TO RAMSEY IMMEDIATELY, RUBBING AGAINST HER FOOT AFFECTIONATELY.

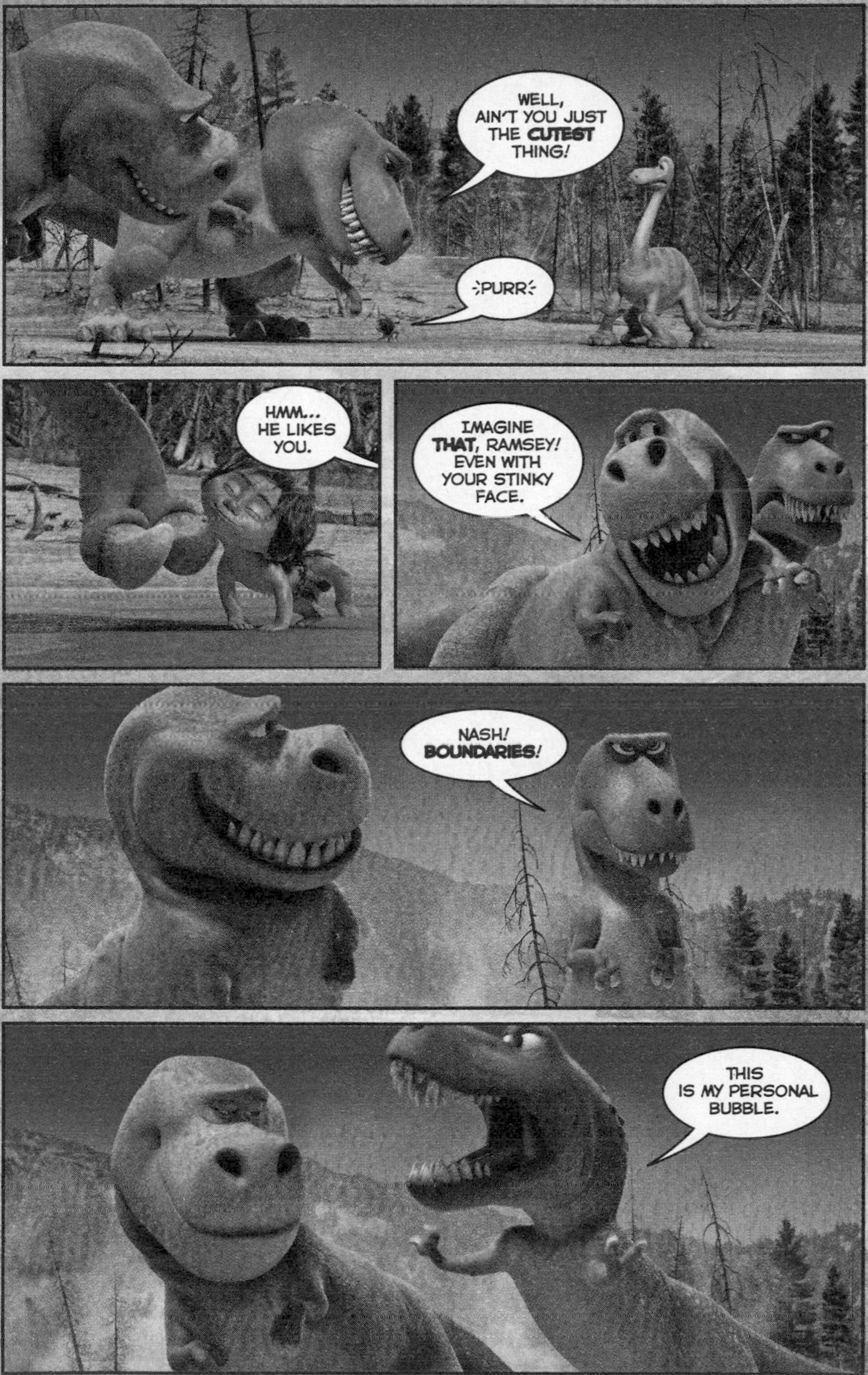
WELL, AIN'T YOU JUST THE **CUTEST** THING!
PURR
HMM... HE LIKES YOU.
IMAGINE **THAT**, RAMSEY! EVEN WITH YOUR STINKY FACE.
NASH! **BOUNDARIES**!
THIS IS MY PERSONAL BUBBLE.

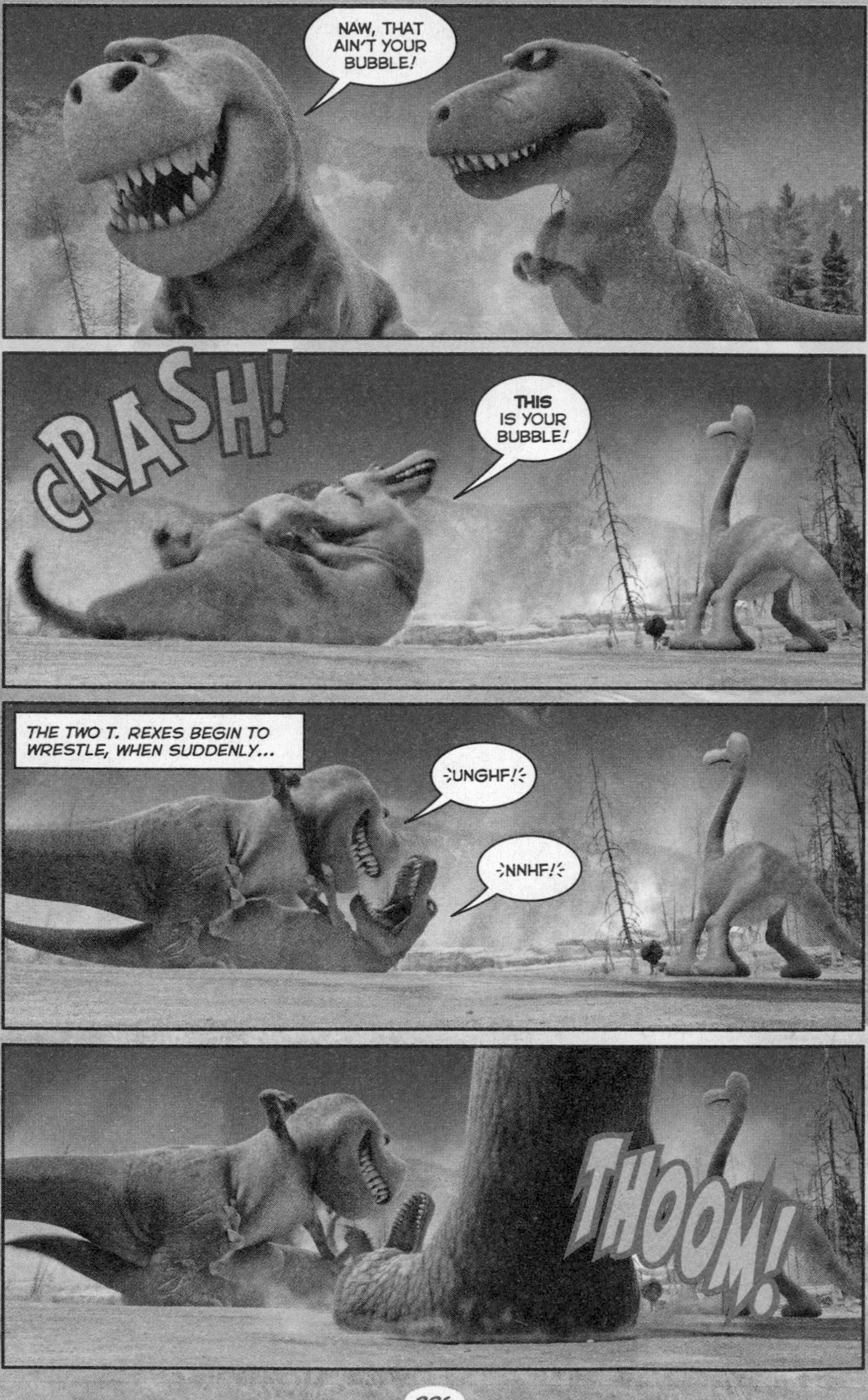
NAW, THAT AIN'T YOUR BUBBLE!
CRASH!
THIS IS YOUR BUBBLE!
THE TWO T. REXES BEGIN TO WRESTLE, WHEN SUDDENLY...
UNGHF!
NNHF!
THOOM!

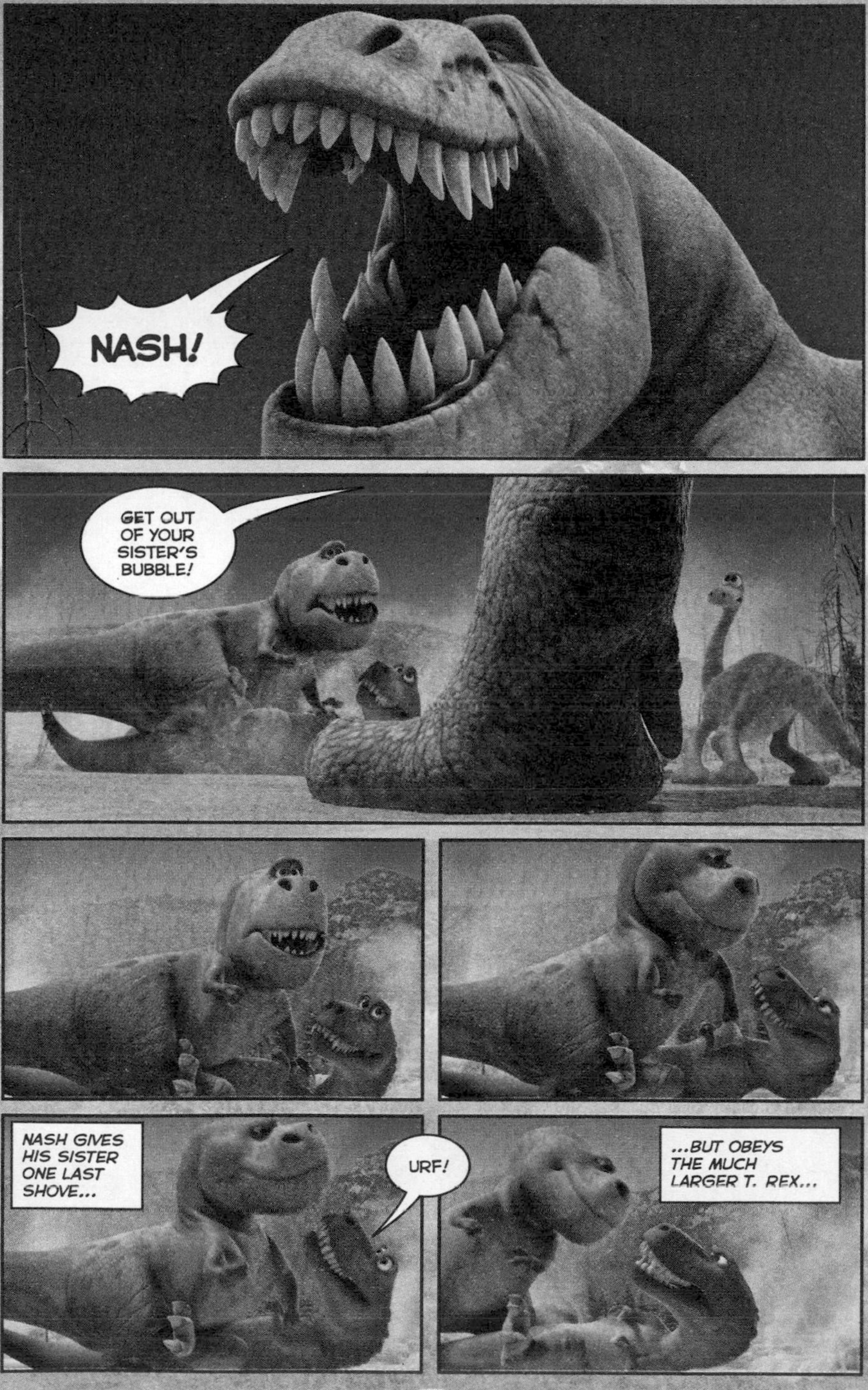
NASH!
GET OUT OF YOUR SISTER'S BUBBLE!
NASH GIVES HIS SISTER ONE LAST SHOVE...
URF!
...BUT OBEYS THE MUCH LARGER T. REX...

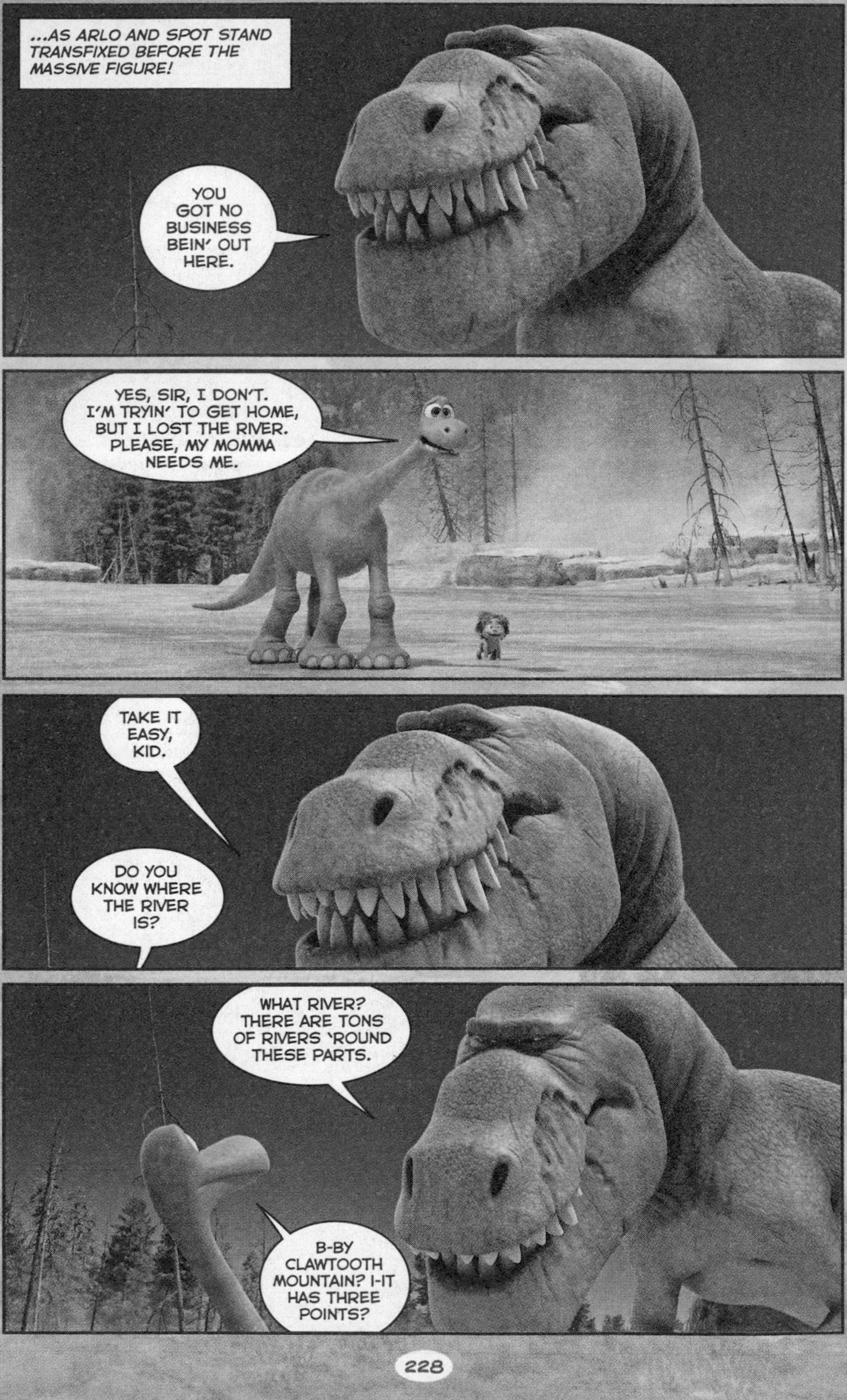
...AS ARLO AND SPOT STAND TRANSFIXED BEFORE THE MASSIVE FIGURE!
YOU GOT NO BUSINESS BEIN' OUT HERE.
YES, SIR, I DON'T. I'M TRYIN' TO GET HOME, BUT I LOST THE RIVER. PLEASE, MY MOMMA NEEDS ME.
TAKE IT EASY, KID.
DO YOU KNOW WHERE THE RIVER IS?
WHAT RIVER? THERE ARE TONS OF RIVERS 'ROUND THESE PARTS.
B-BY CLAWTOOTH MOUNTAIN? I-IT HAS THREE POINTS?

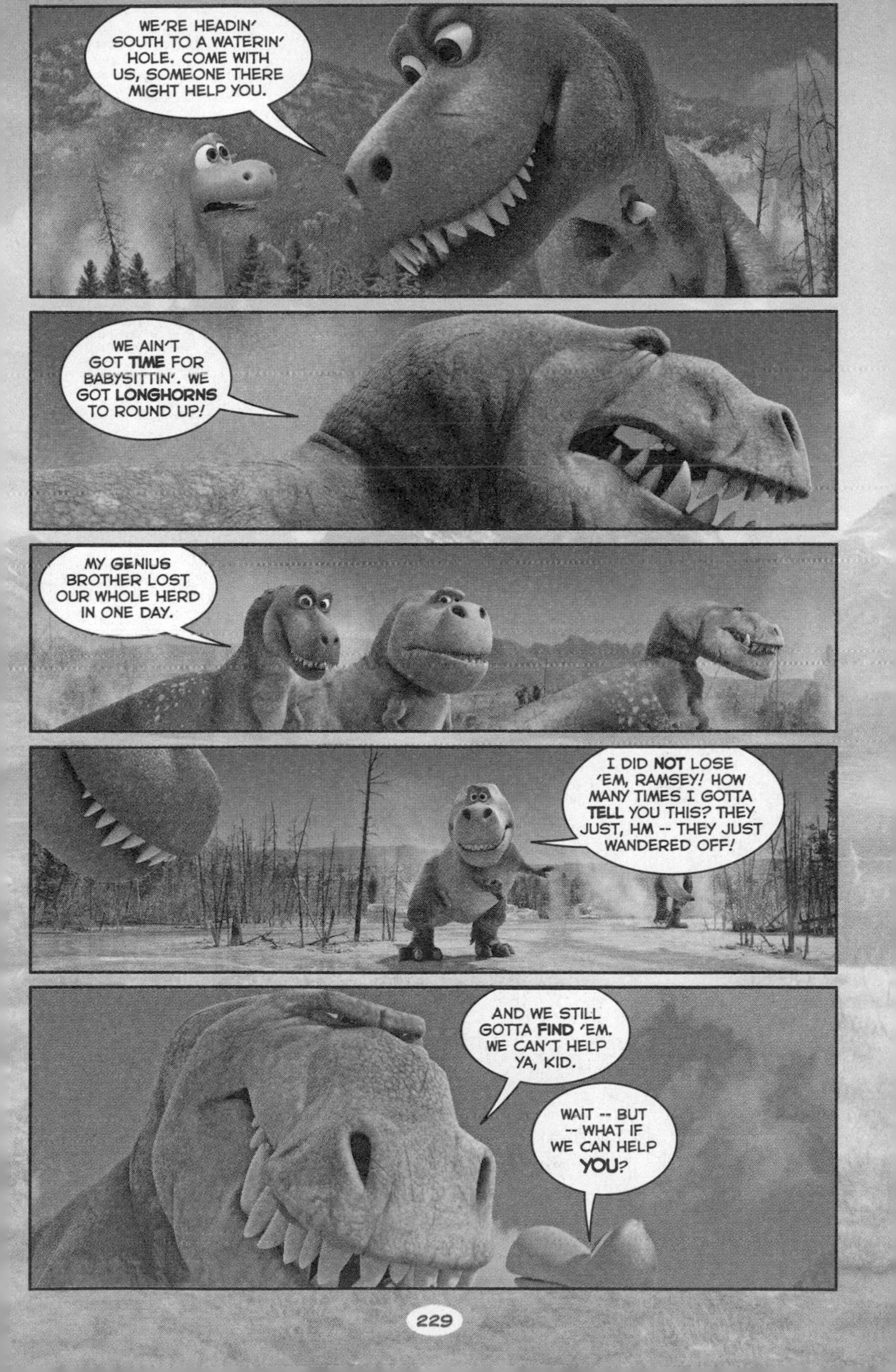
WE'RE HEADIN' SOUTH TO A WATERIN' HOLE. COME WITH US, SOMEONE THERE MIGHT HELP YOU.
WE AIN'T GOT **TIME** FOR BABYSITTIN'. WE GOT **LONGHORNS** TO ROUND UP!
MY GENIUS BROTHER LOST OUR WHOLE HERD IN ONE DAY.
I DID **NOT** LOSE 'EM, RAMSEY! HOW MANY TIMES I GOTTA **TELL** YOU THIS? THEY JUST, HM -- THEY JUST WANDERED OFF!
AND WE STILL GOTTA **FIND** 'EM. WE CAN'T HELP YA, KID.
WAIT -- BUT -- WHAT IF WE CAN HELP **YOU**?

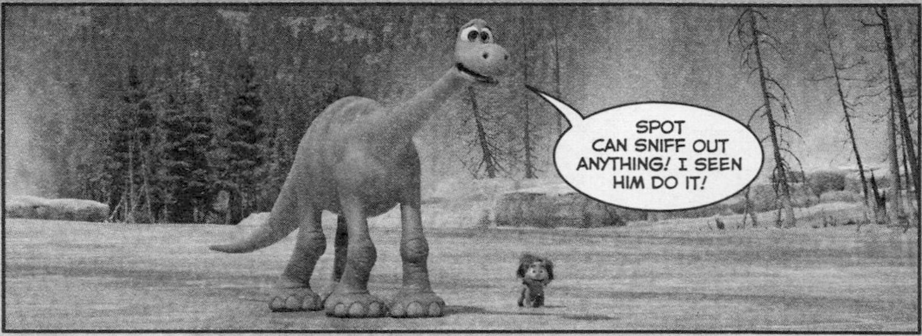
SPOT CAN SNIFF OUT ANYTHING! I SEEN HIM DO IT!

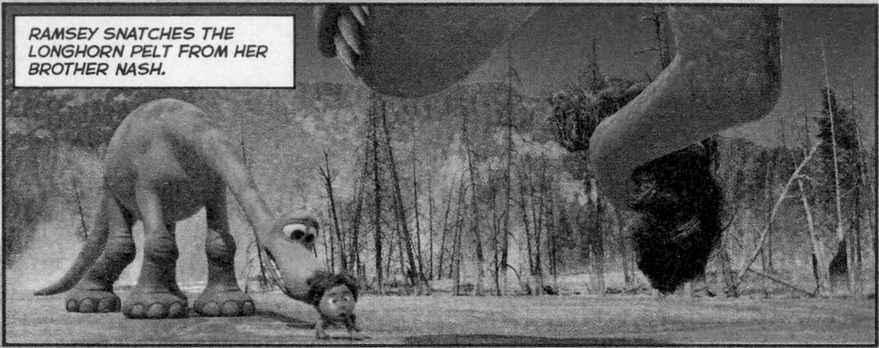
RAMSEY SNATCHES THE LONGHORN PELT FROM HER BROTHER NASH.

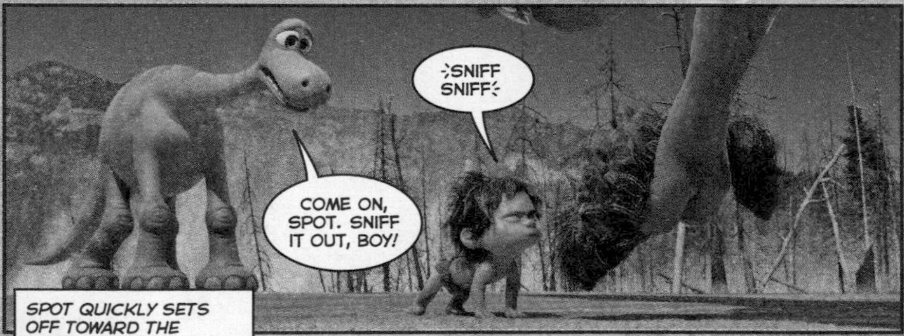
SNIFF SNIFF
COME ON, SPOT. SNIFF IT OUT, BOY!

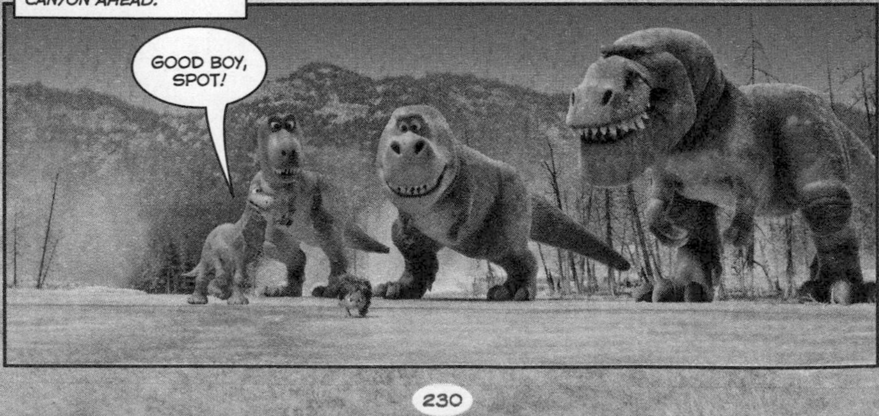
SPOT QUICKLY SETS OFF TOWARD THE CANYON AHEAD.
GOOD BOY, SPOT!

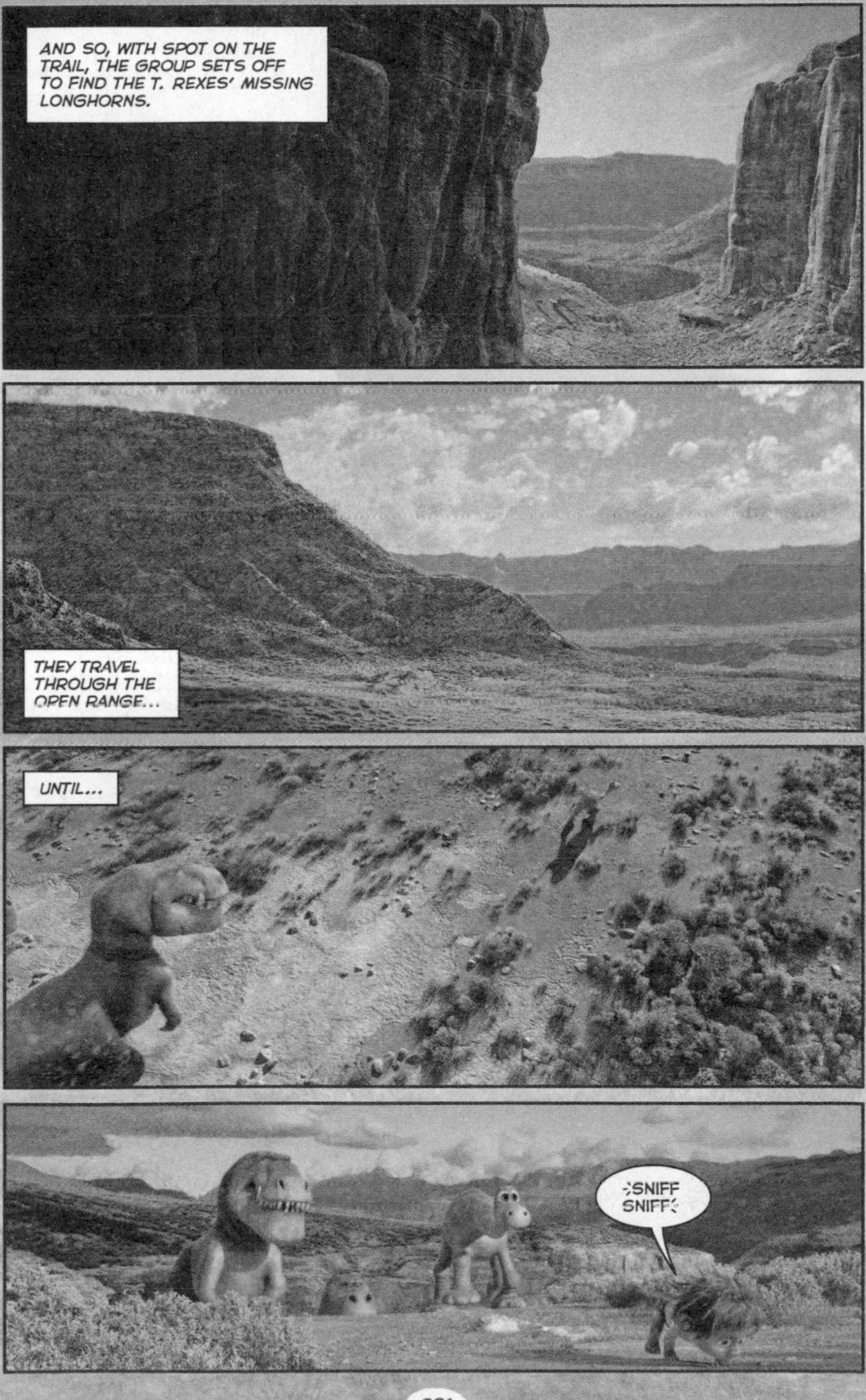
AND SO, WITH SPOT ON THE TRAIL, THE GROUP SETS OFF TO FIND THE T. REXES' MISSING LONGHORNS.
THEY TRAVEL THROUGH THE OPEN RANGE...
UNTIL...
SNIFF SNIFF

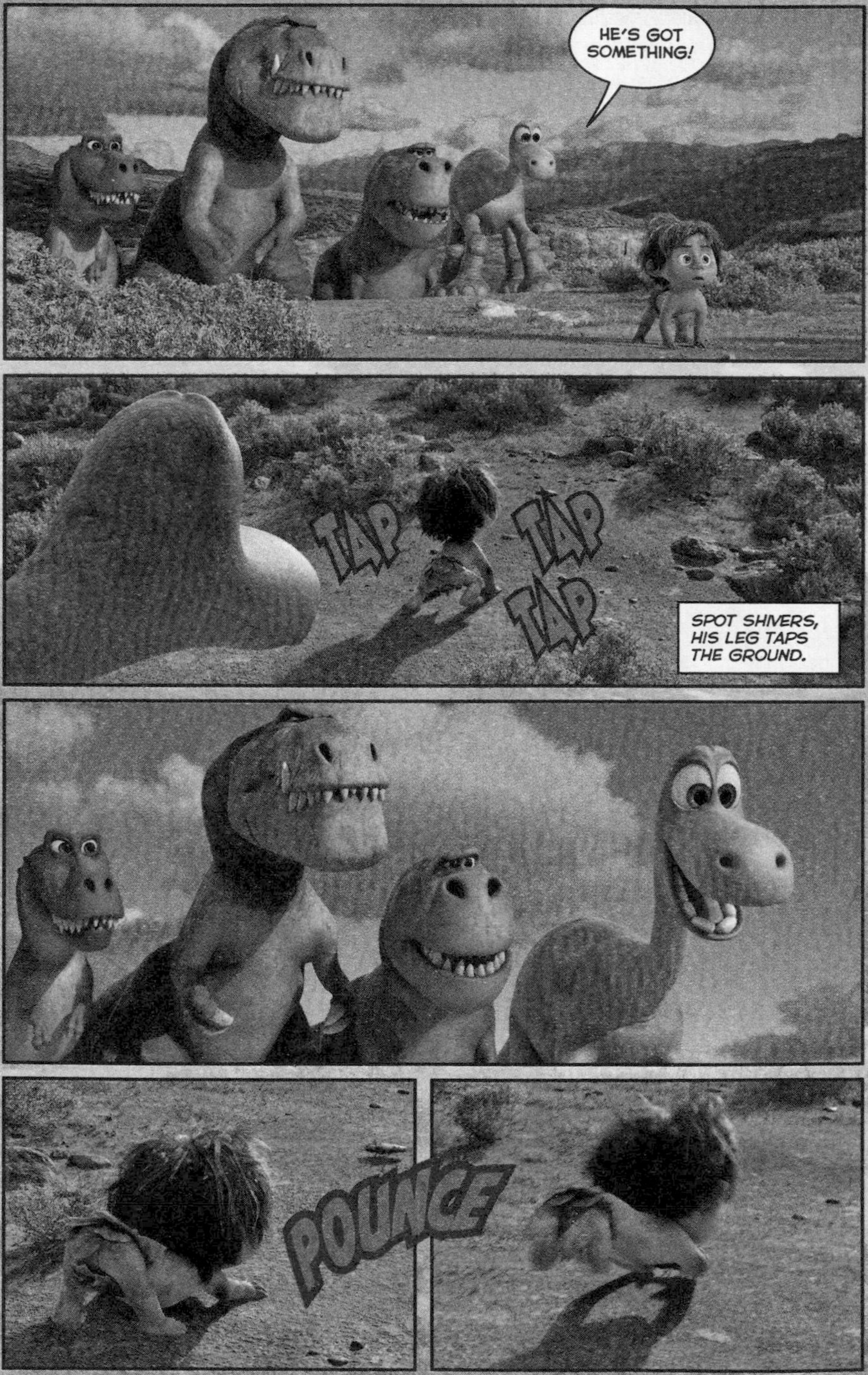
HE'S GOT SOMETHING!
TAP
TAP
TAP
SPOT SHIVERS, HIS LEG TAPS THE GROUND.
POUNCE

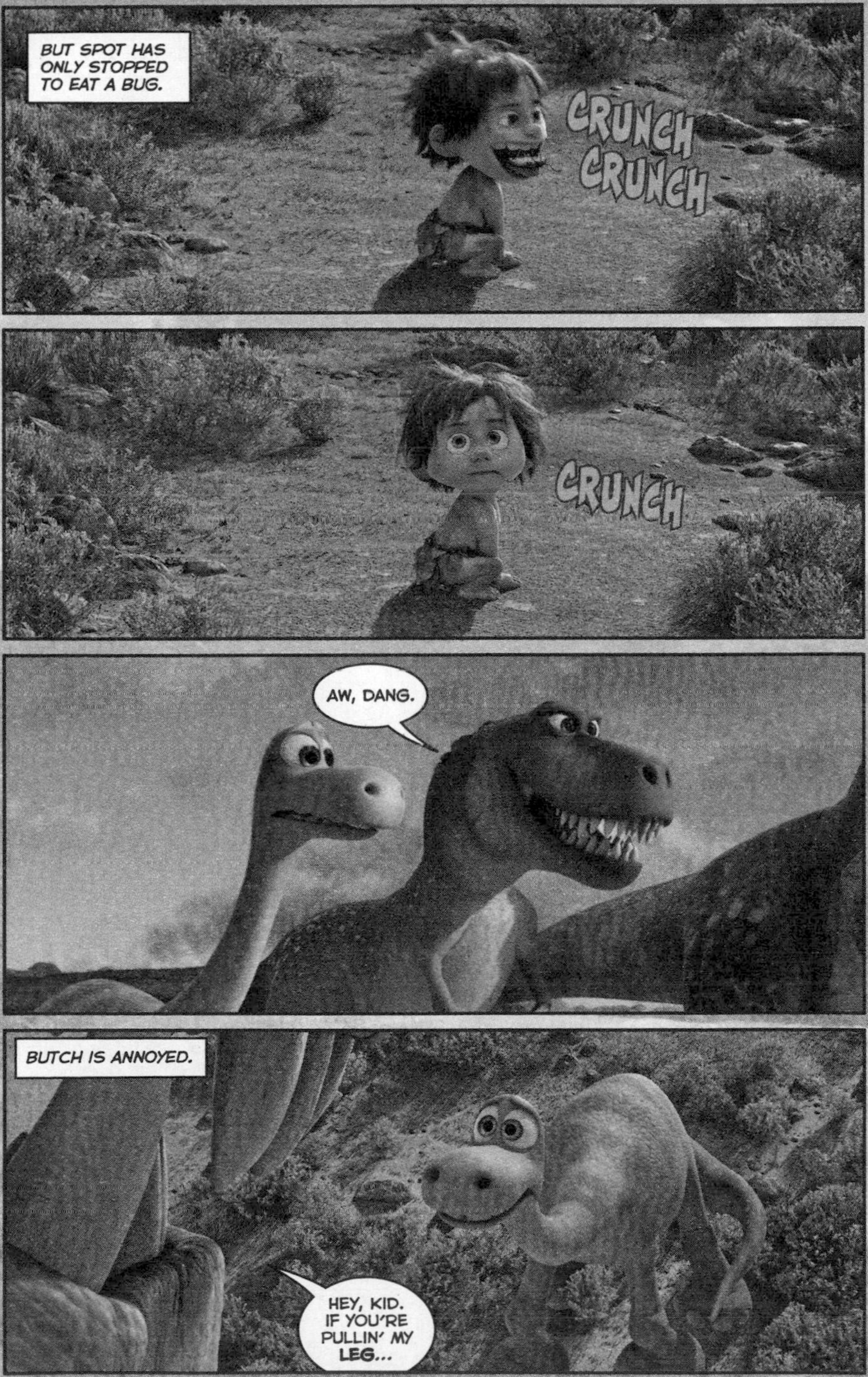
BUT SPOT HAS ONLY STOPPED TO EAT A BUG.
CRUNCH CRUNCH
CRUNCH
AW, DANG.
BUTCH IS ANNOYED.
HEY, KID. IF YOU'RE PULLIN' MY **LEG**...

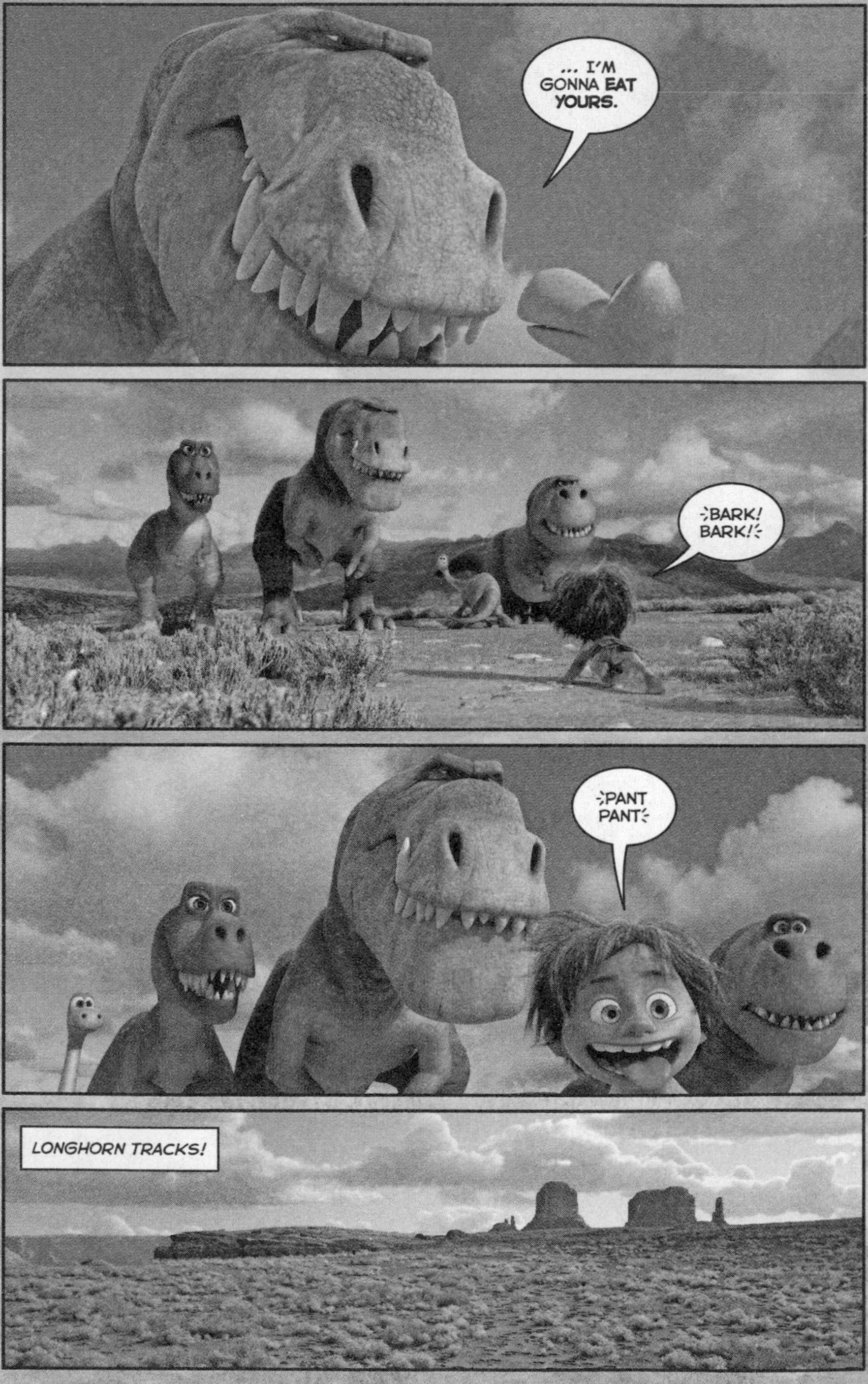
... I'M GONNA EAT YOURS.
BARK! BARK!
PANT PANT
LONGHORN TRACKS!

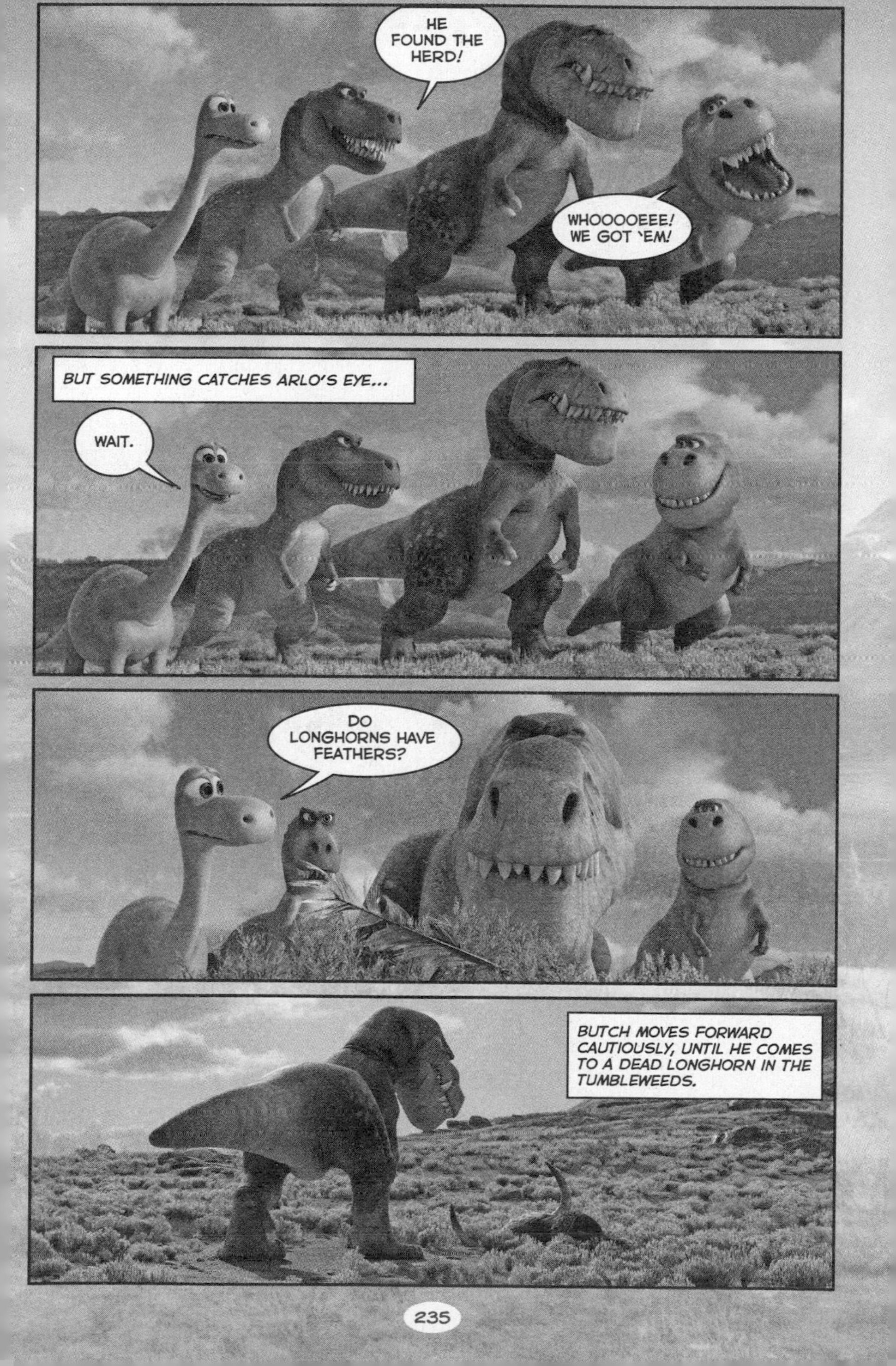
HE FOUND THE HERD!
WHOOOOEEE! WE GOT 'EM!
BUT SOMETHING CATCHES ARLO'S EYE...
WAIT.
DO LONGHORNS HAVE FEATHERS?
BUTCH MOVES FORWARD CAUTIOUSLY, UNTIL HE COMES TO A DEAD LONGHORN IN THE TUMBLEWEEDS.

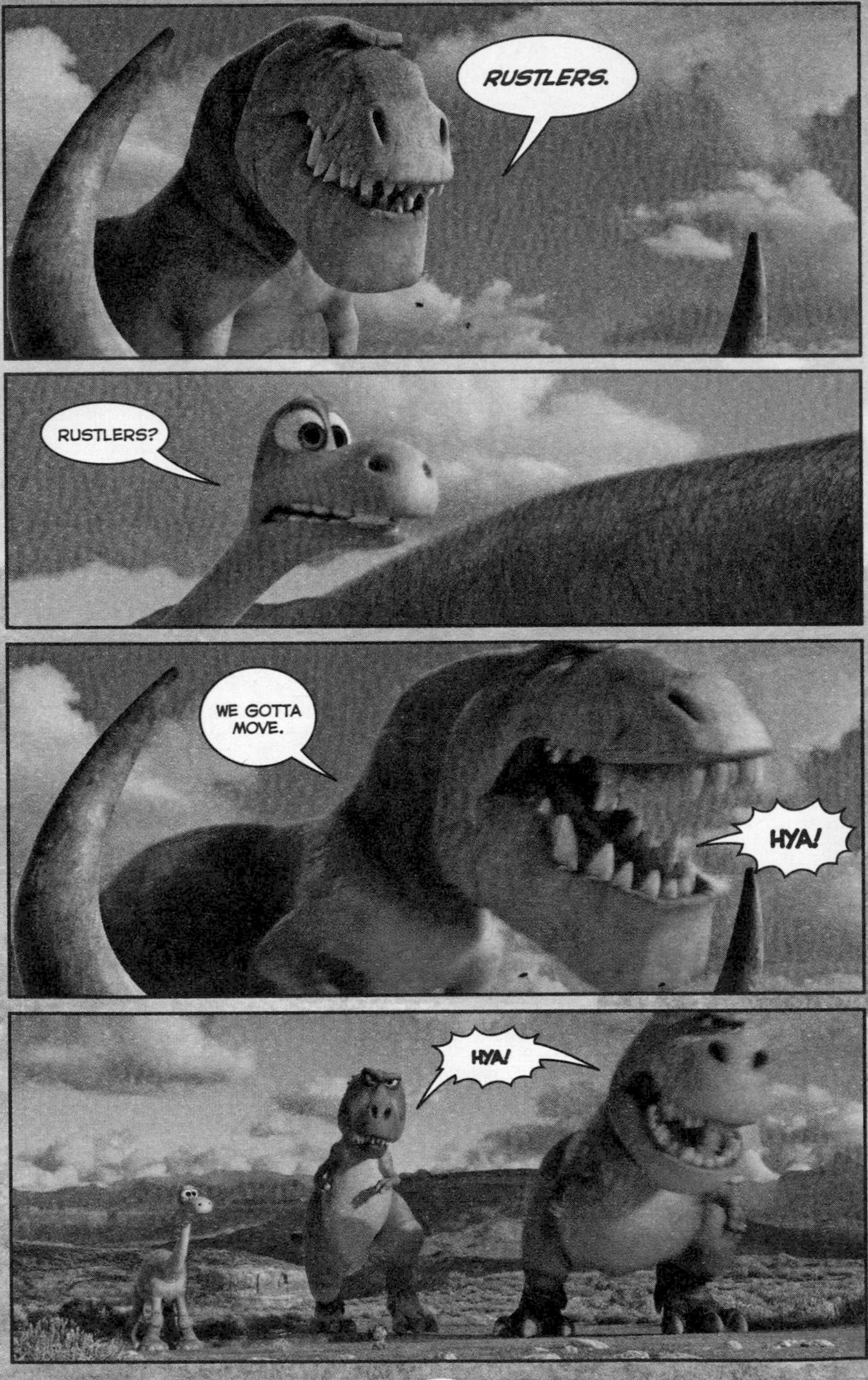
RUSTLERS.
RUSTLERS?
WE GOTTA MOVE.
HYA!
HYA!

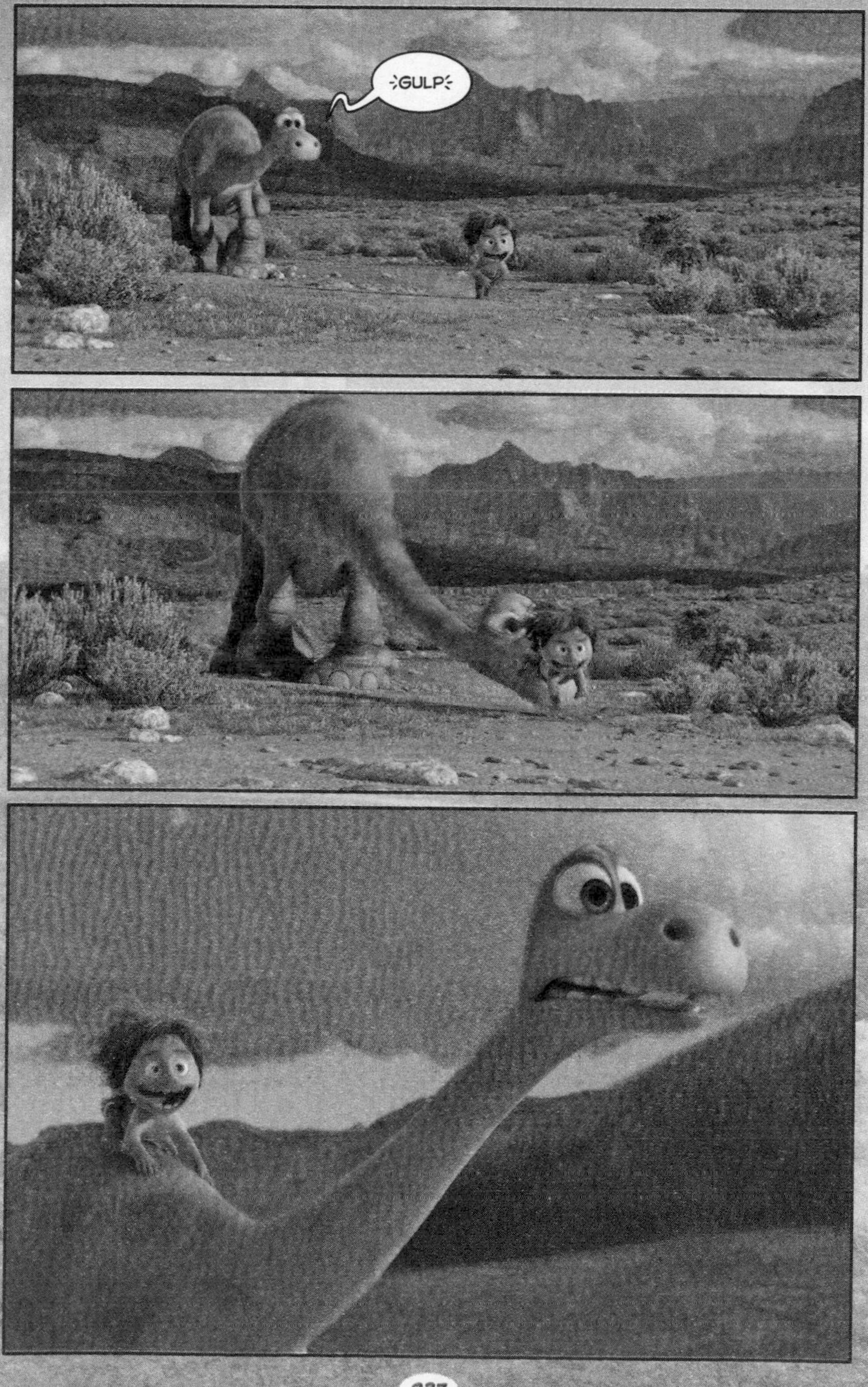
GULP

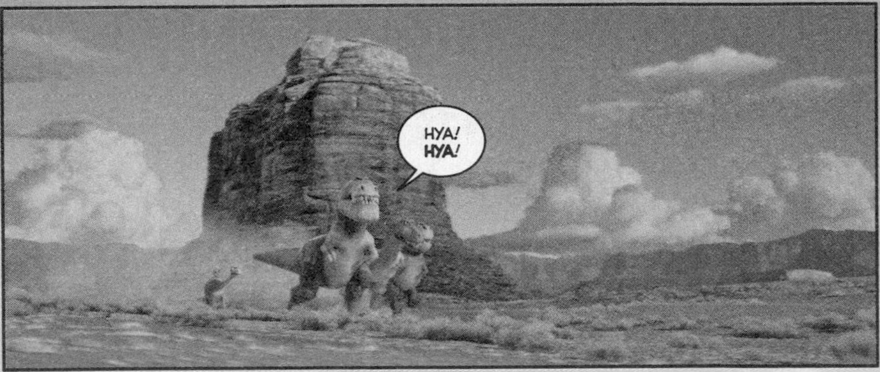
HYA! HYA!

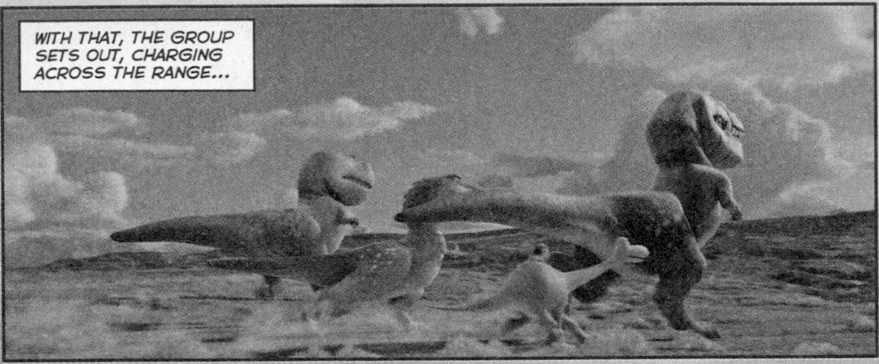
WITH THAT, THE GROUP SETS OUT, CHARGING ACROSS THE RANGE...

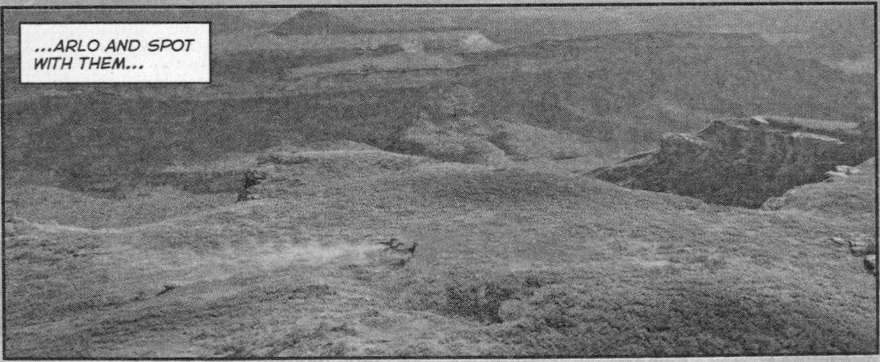
...ARLO AND SPOT WITH THEM...

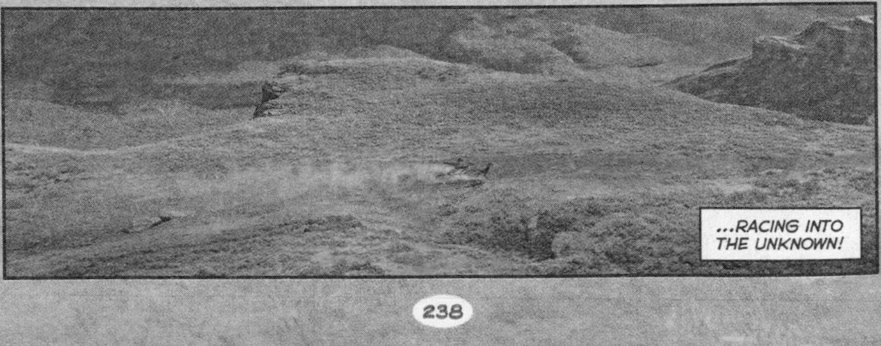
...RACING INTO THE UNKNOWN!

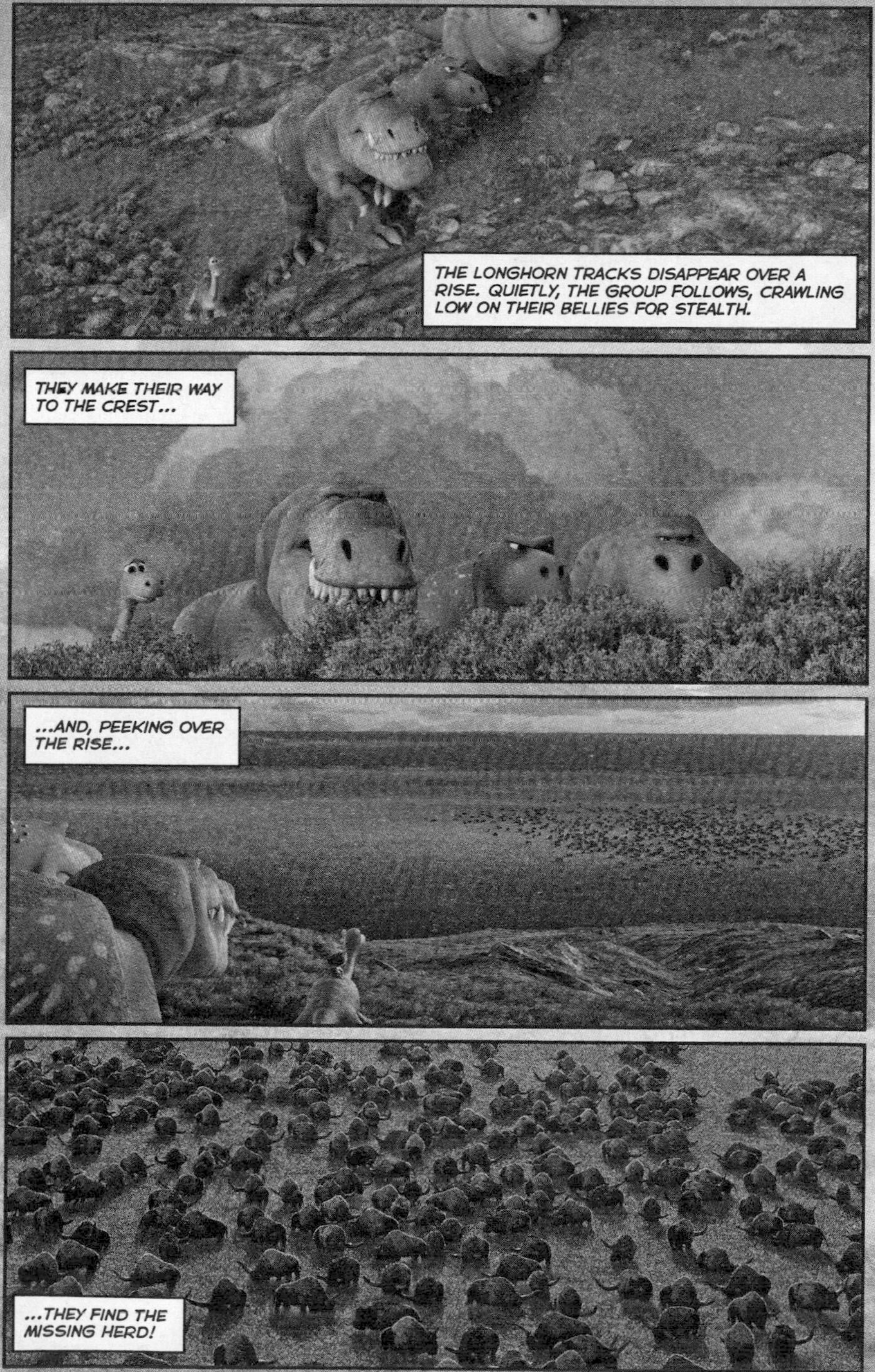
THE LONGHORN TRACKS DISAPPEAR OVER A RISE. QUIETLY, THE GROUP FOLLOWS, CRAWLING LOW ON THEIR BELLIES FOR STEALTH.
THEY MAKE THEIR WAY TO THE CREST...
...AND, PEEKING OVER THE RISE...
...THEY FIND THE MISSING HERD!

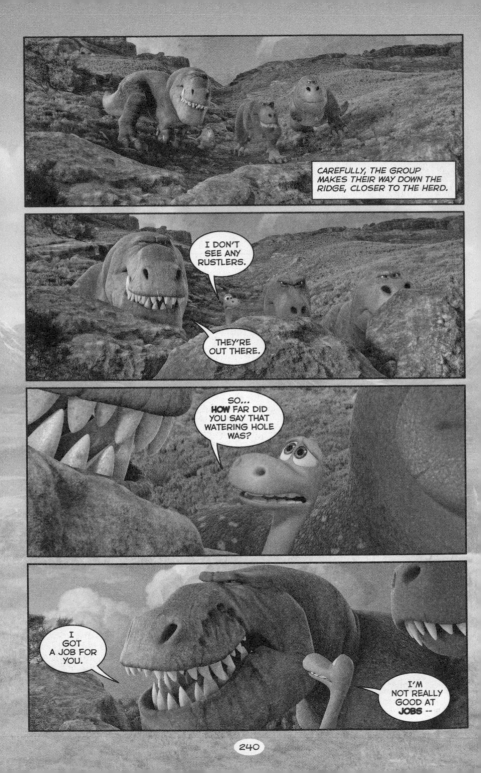

CAREFULLY, THE GROUP MAKES THEIR WAY DOWN THE RIDGE, CLOSER TO THE HERD.

I DON'T SEE ANY RUSTLERS.

THEY'RE OUT THERE.

SO... **HOW** FAR DID YOU SAY THAT WATERING HOLE WAS?

I GOT A JOB FOR YOU.

I'M NOT REALLY GOOD AT **JOBS** --

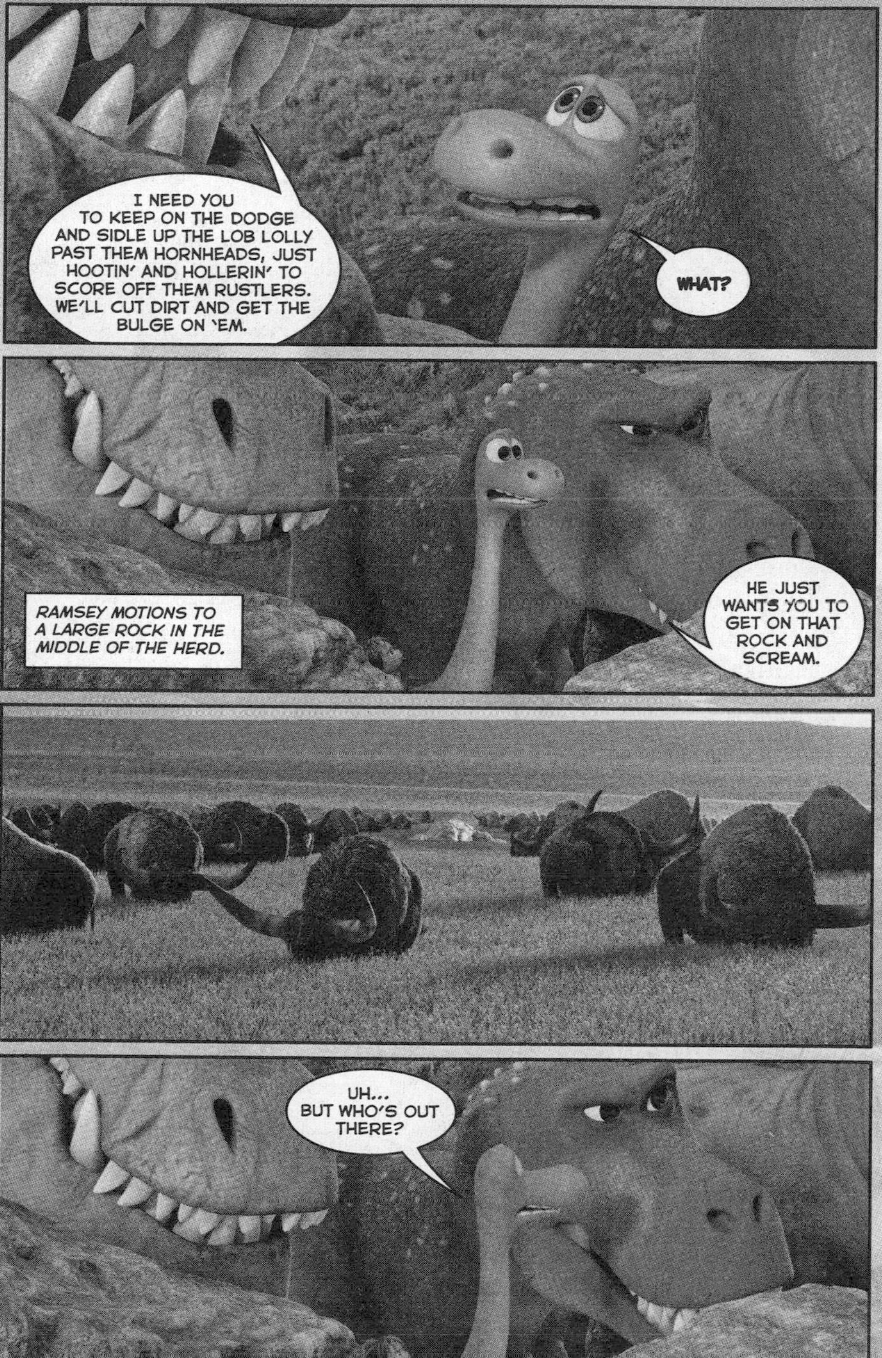
I NEED YOU TO KEEP ON THE DODGE AND SIDLE UP THE LOB LOLLY PAST THEM HORNHEADS, JUST HOOTIN' AND HOLLERIN' TO SCORE OFF THEM RUSTLERS. WE'LL CUT DIRT AND GET THE BULGE ON 'EM.
WHAT?
RAMSEY MOTIONS TO A LARGE ROCK IN THE MIDDLE OF THE HERD.
HE JUST WANTS YOU TO GET ON THAT ROCK AND SCREAM.
UH... BUT WHO'S OUT THERE?

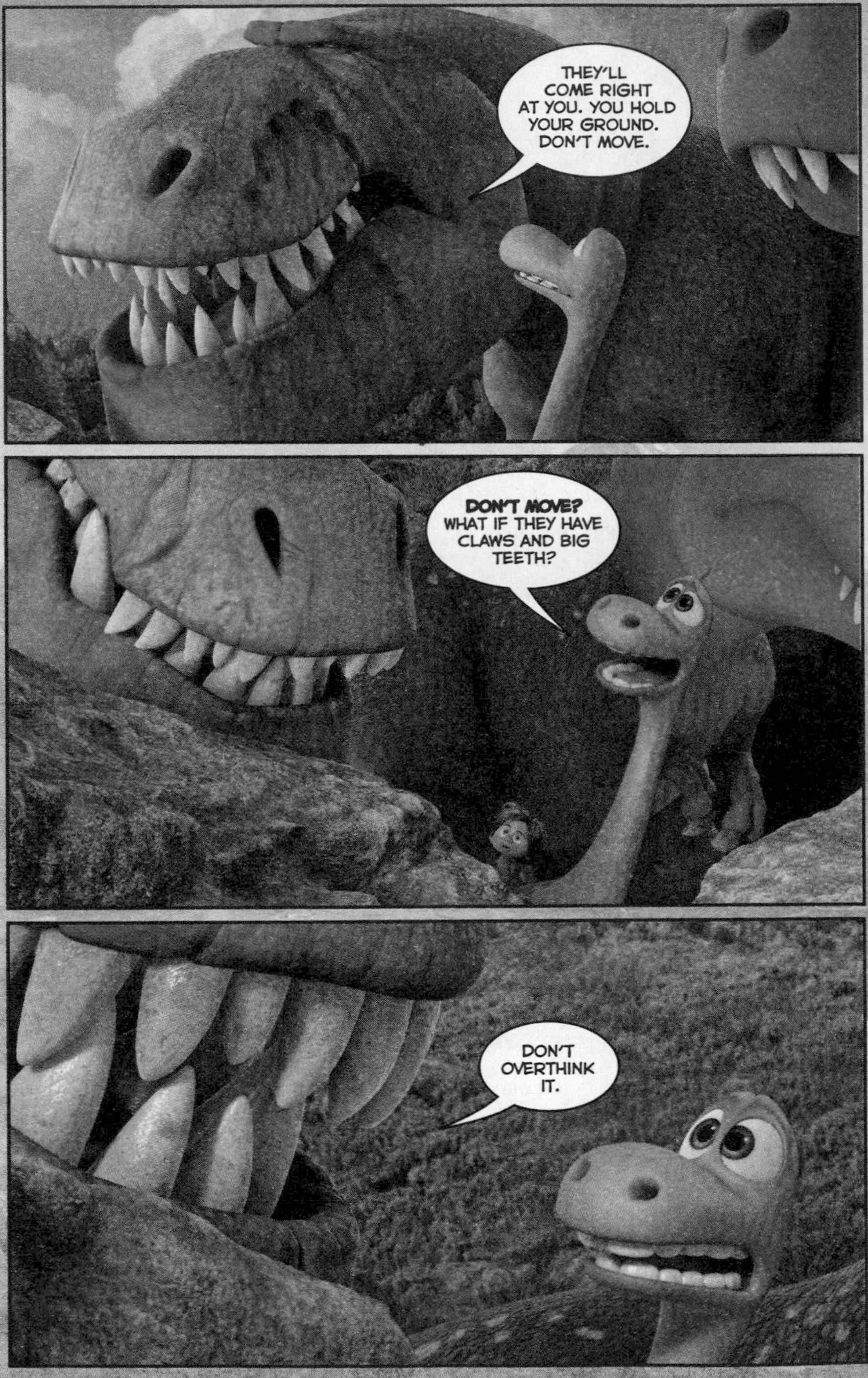
THEY'LL COME RIGHT AT YOU. YOU HOLD YOUR GROUND. DON'T MOVE.
DON'T MOVE? WHAT IF THEY HAVE CLAWS AND BIG TEETH?
DON'T OVERTHINK IT.

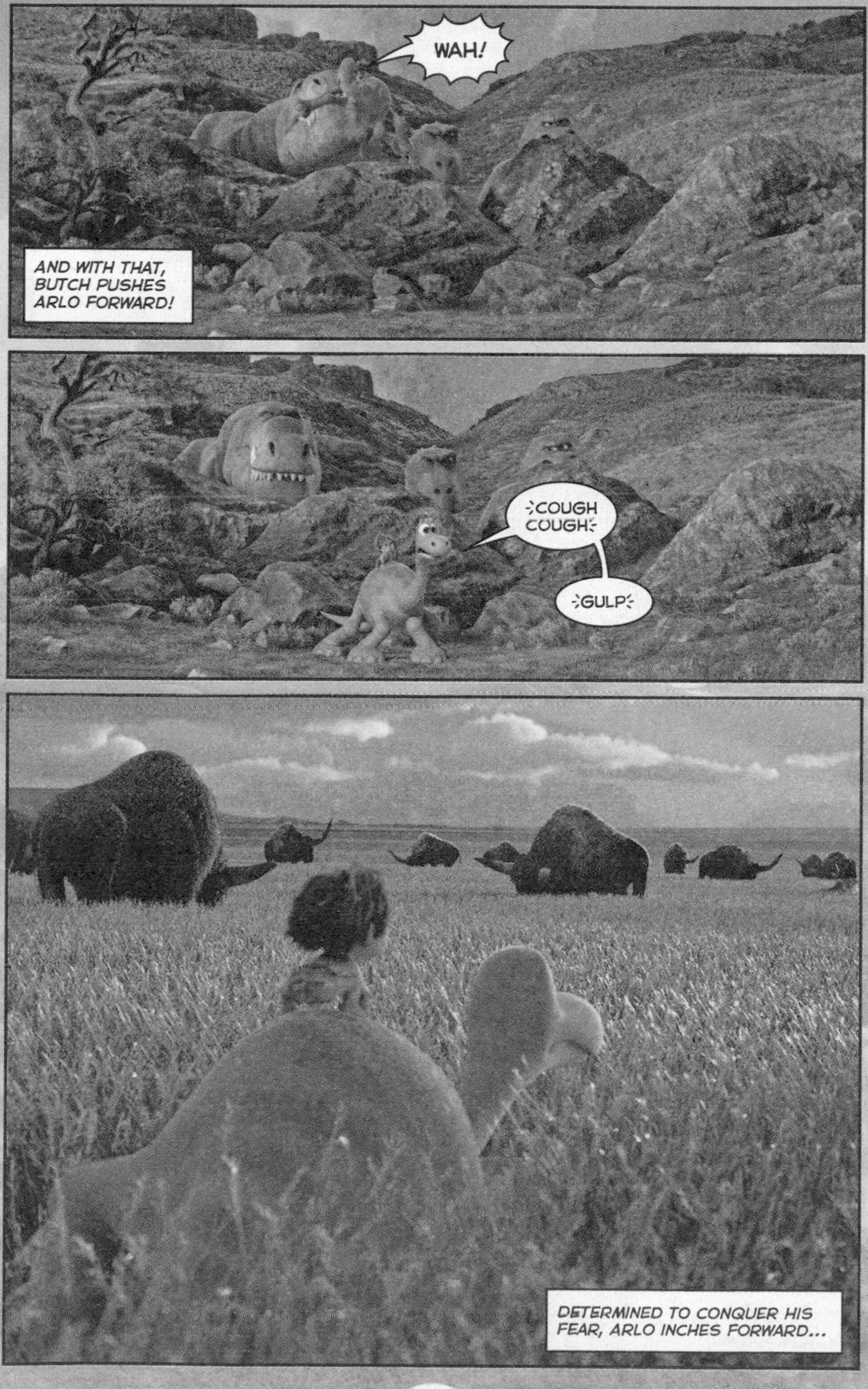
WAH!
AND WITH THAT, BUTCH PUSHES ARLO FORWARD!
COUGH COUGH
GULP
DETERMINED TO CONQUER HIS FEAR, ARLO INCHES FORWARD...

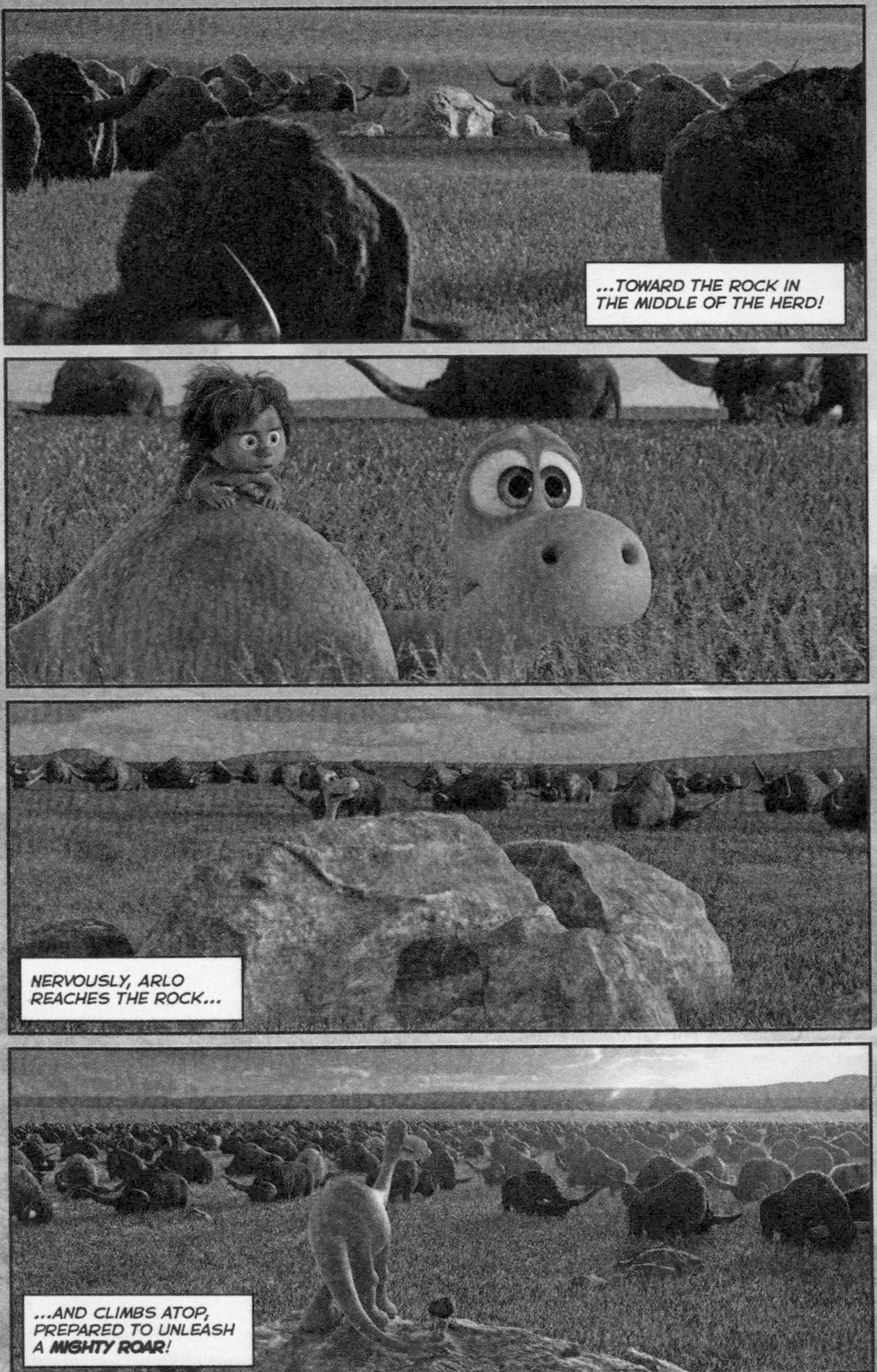
...TOWARD THE ROCK IN THE MIDDLE OF THE HERD!
NERVOUSLY, ARLO REACHES THE ROCK...
...AND CLIMBS ATOP, PREPARED TO UNLEASH A **MIGHTY ROAR**!

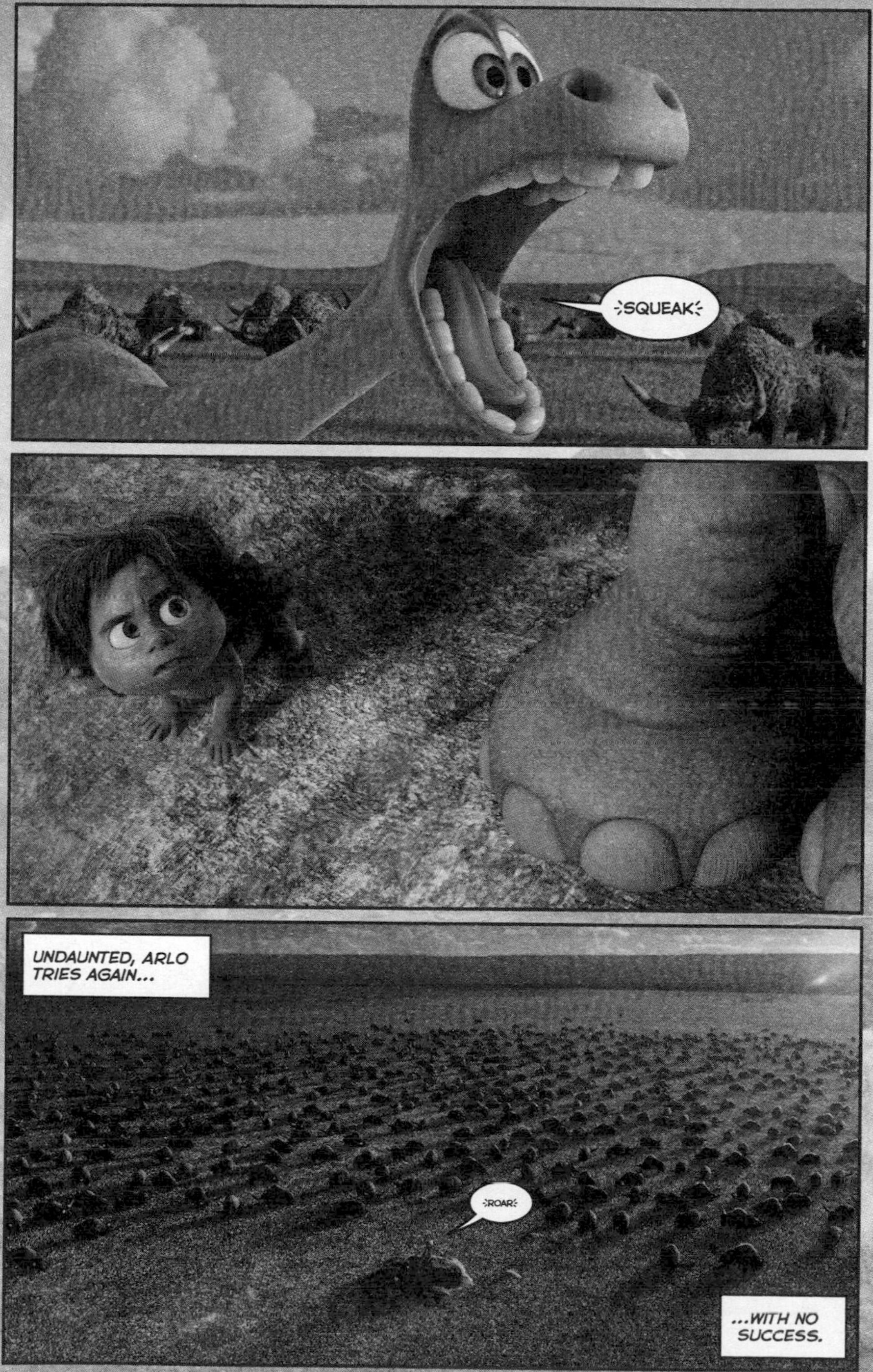
SQUEAK
UNDAUNTED, ARLO TRIES AGAIN...
ROAR
...WITH NO SUCCESS.

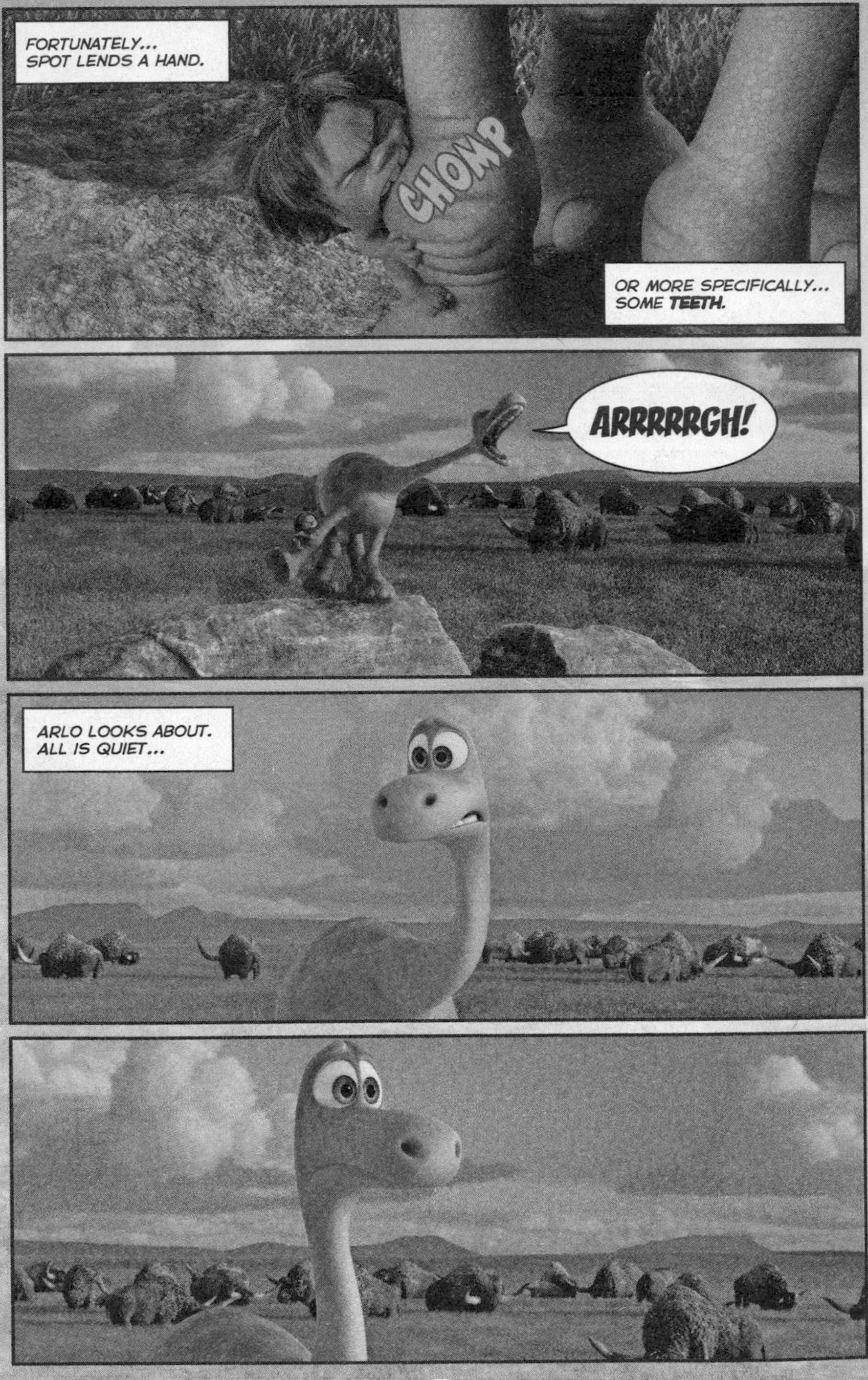
FORTUNATELY...
SPOT LENDS A HAND.
CHOMP
OR MORE SPECIFICALLY...
SOME **TEETH.**
ARRRRRGH!
ARLO LOOKS ABOUT.
ALL IS QUIET...

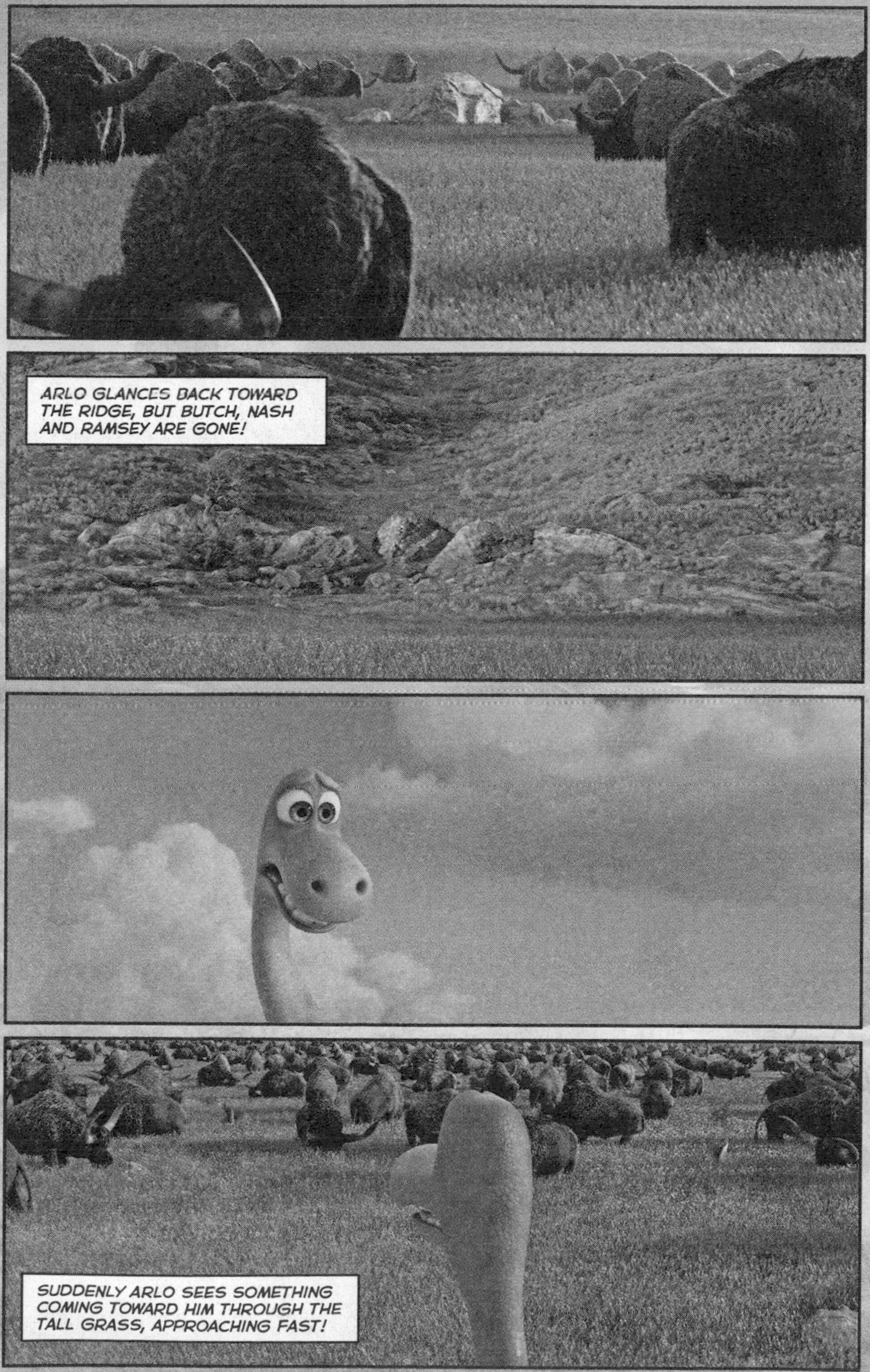
ARLO GLANCES BACK TOWARD THE RIDGE, BUT BUTCH, NASH AND RAMSEY ARE GONE!
SUDDENLY ARLO SEES SOMETHING COMING TOWARD HIM THROUGH THE TALL GRASS, APPROACHING FAST!

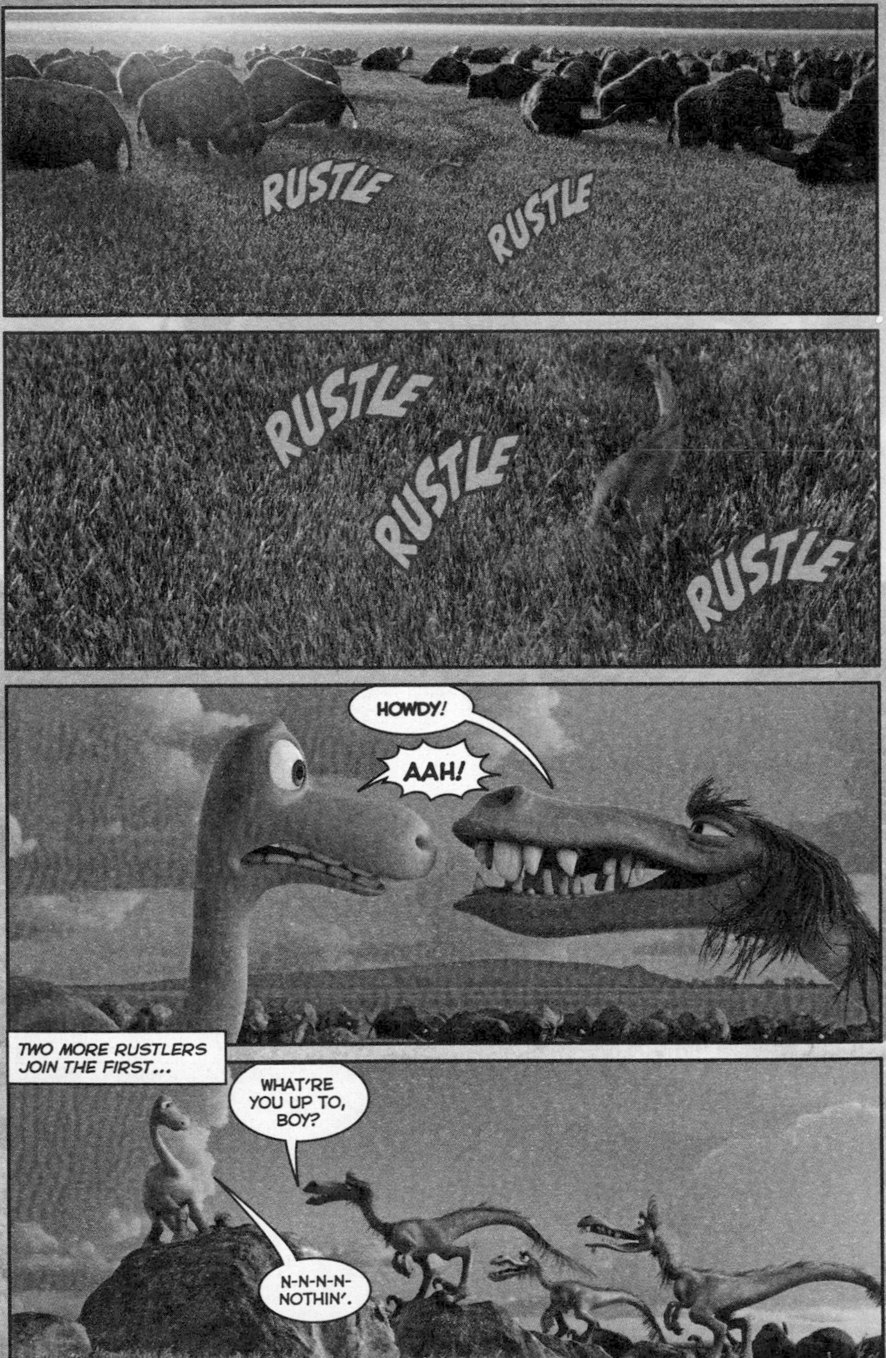
RUSTLE
RUSTLE
RUSTLE
RUSTLE
RUSTLE
HOWDY!
AAH!
TWO MORE RUSTLERS JOIN THE FIRST...
WHAT'RE YOU UP TO, BOY?
N-N-N-N-NOTHIN'.

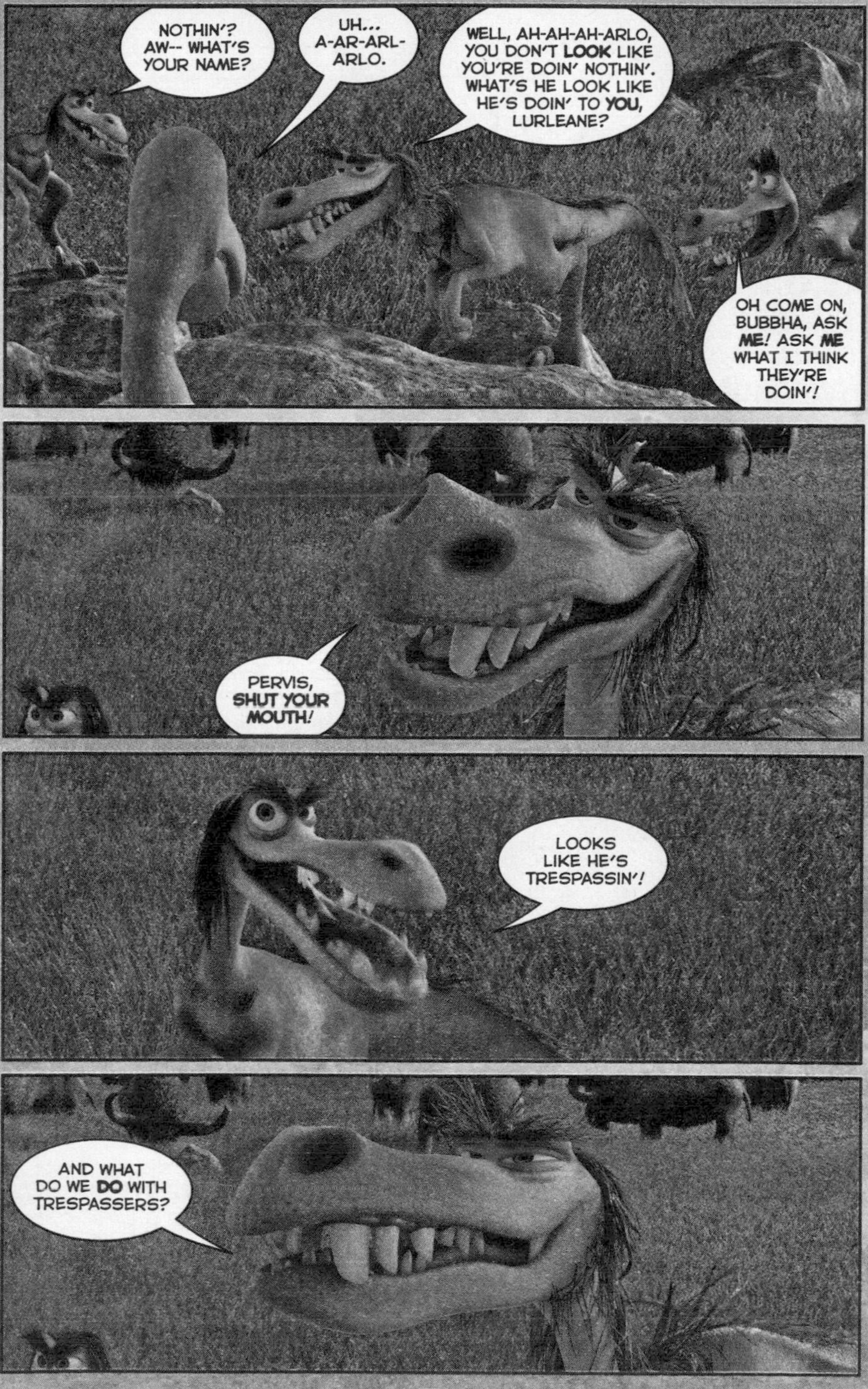
NOTHIN'? AW-- WHAT'S YOUR NAME?
UH... A-AR-ARL-ARLO.
WELL, AH-AH-AH-ARLO, YOU DON'T **LOOK** LIKE YOU'RE DOIN' NOTHIN'. WHAT'S HE LOOK LIKE HE'S DOIN' TO **YOU**, LURLEANE?
OH COME ON, BUBBHA, ASK **ME**! ASK **ME** WHAT I THINK THEY'RE DOIN'!
PERVIS, **SHUT YOUR MOUTH**!
LOOKS LIKE HE'S TRESPASSIN'!
AND WHAT DO WE **DO** WITH TRESPASSERS?

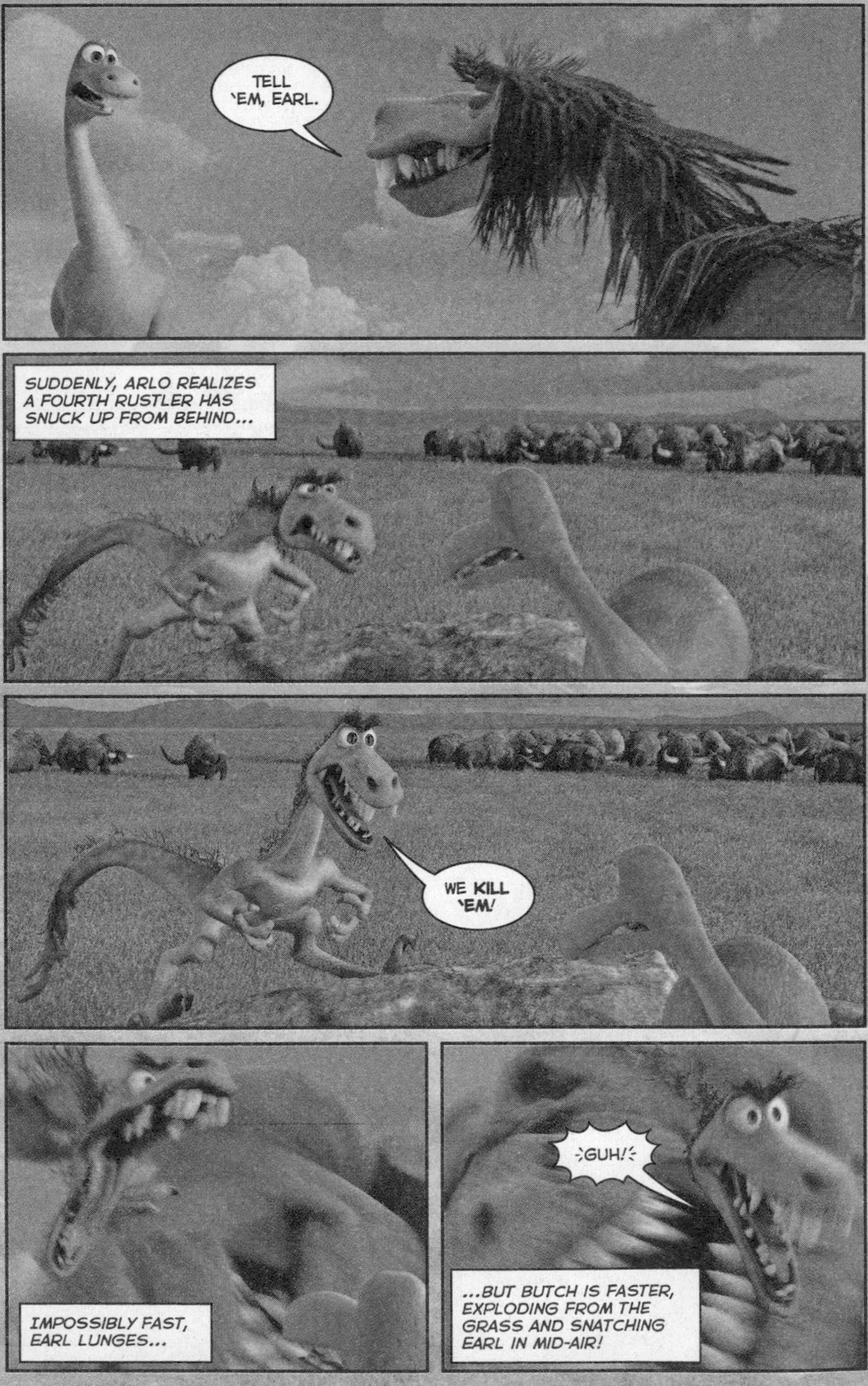
TELL 'EM, EARL.
SUDDENLY, ARLO REALIZES A FOURTH RUSTLER HAS SNUCK UP FROM BEHIND...
WE KILL 'EM!
IMPOSSIBLY FAST, EARL LUNGES...
GUH!
...BUT BUTCH IS FASTER, EXPLODING FROM THE GRASS AND SNATCHING EARL IN MID-AIR!

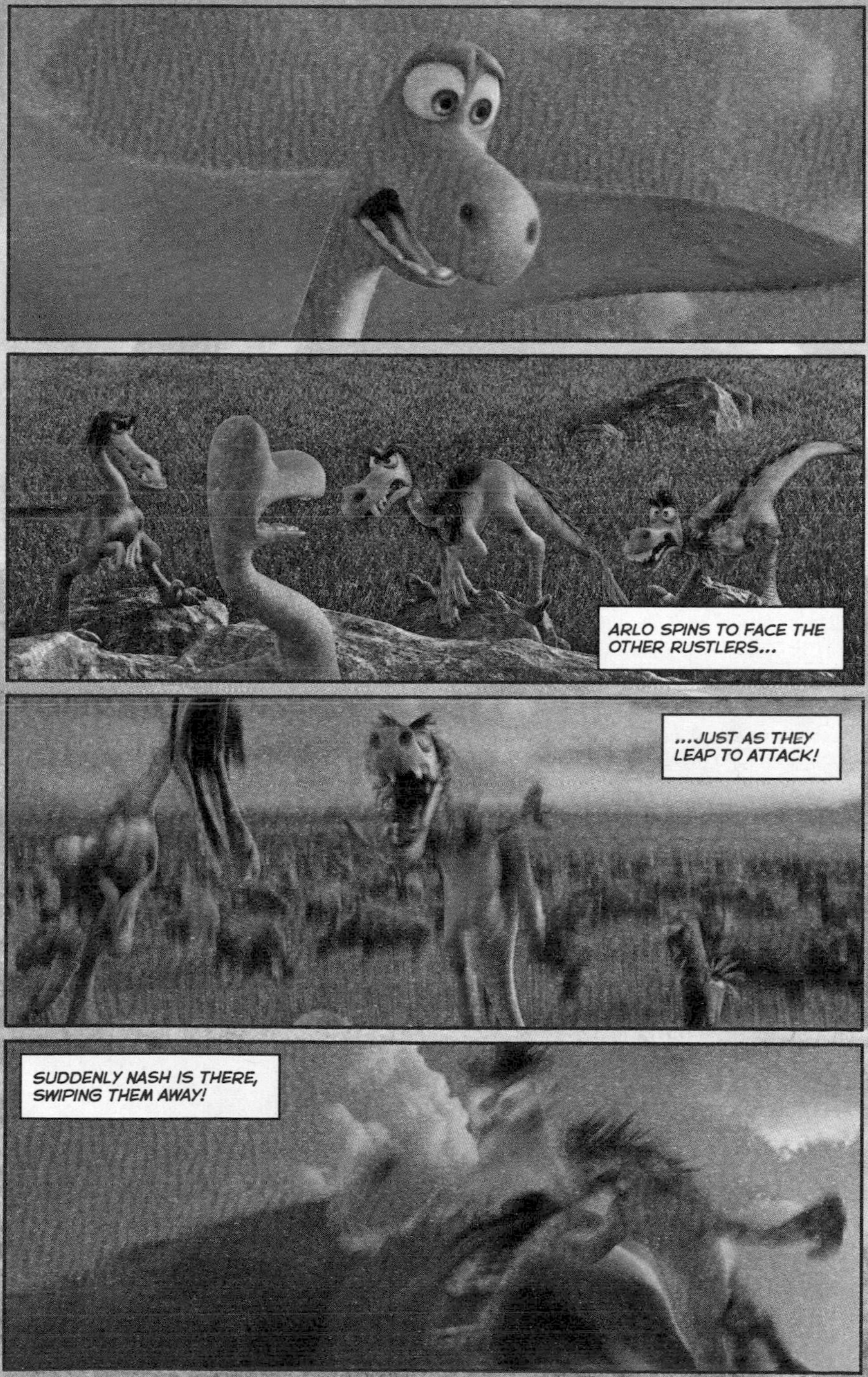
ARLO SPINS TO FACE THE OTHER RUSTLERS...
...JUST AS THEY LEAP TO ATTACK!
SUDDENLY NASH IS THERE, SWIPING THEM AWAY!

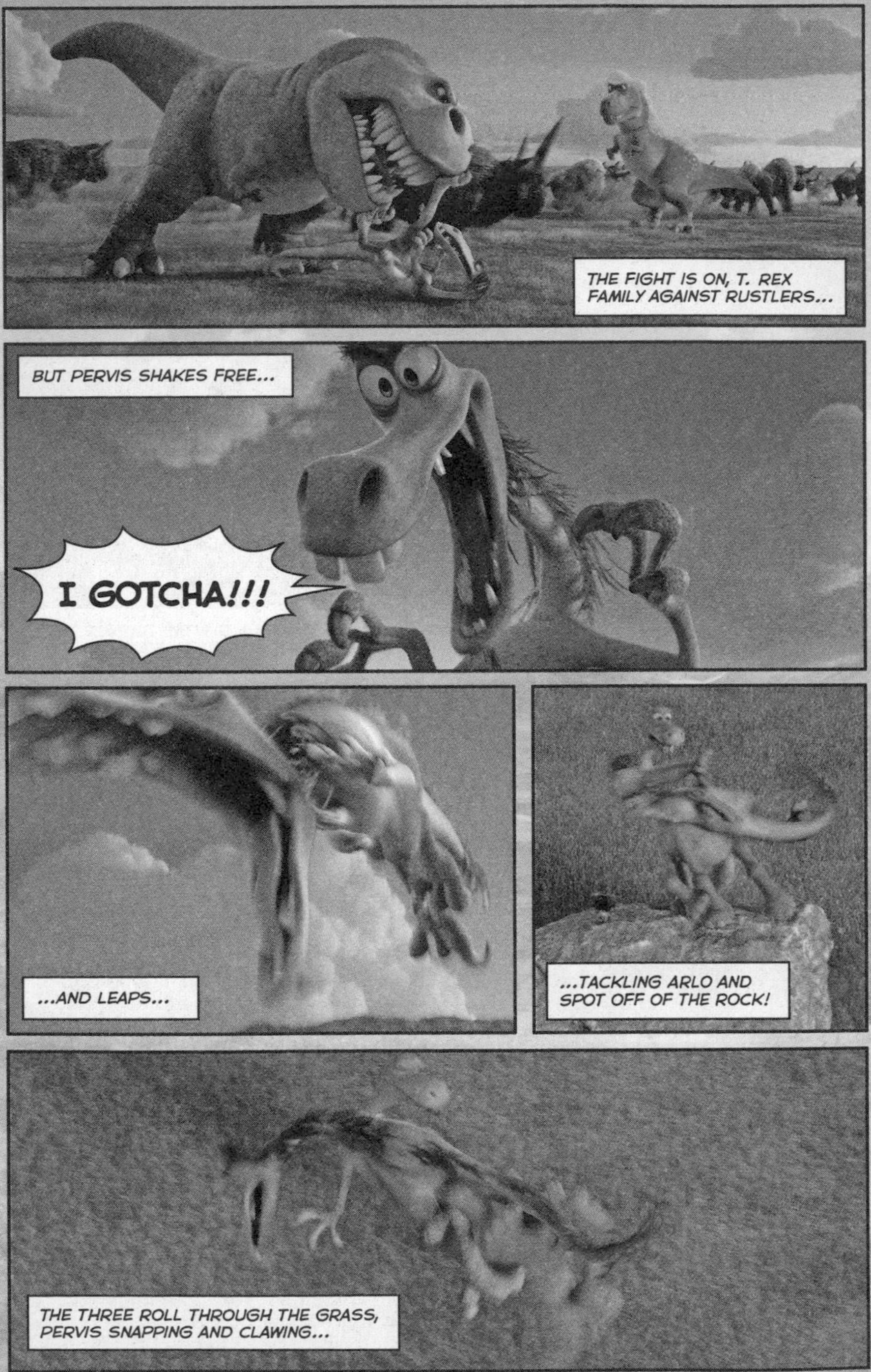
THE FIGHT IS ON, T. REX FAMILY AGAINST RUSTLERS...
BUT PERVIS SHAKES FREE...
I GOTCHA!!!
...AND LEAPS...
...TACKLING ARLO AND SPOT OFF OF THE ROCK!
THE THREE ROLL THROUGH THE GRASS, PERVIS SNAPPING AND CLAWING...

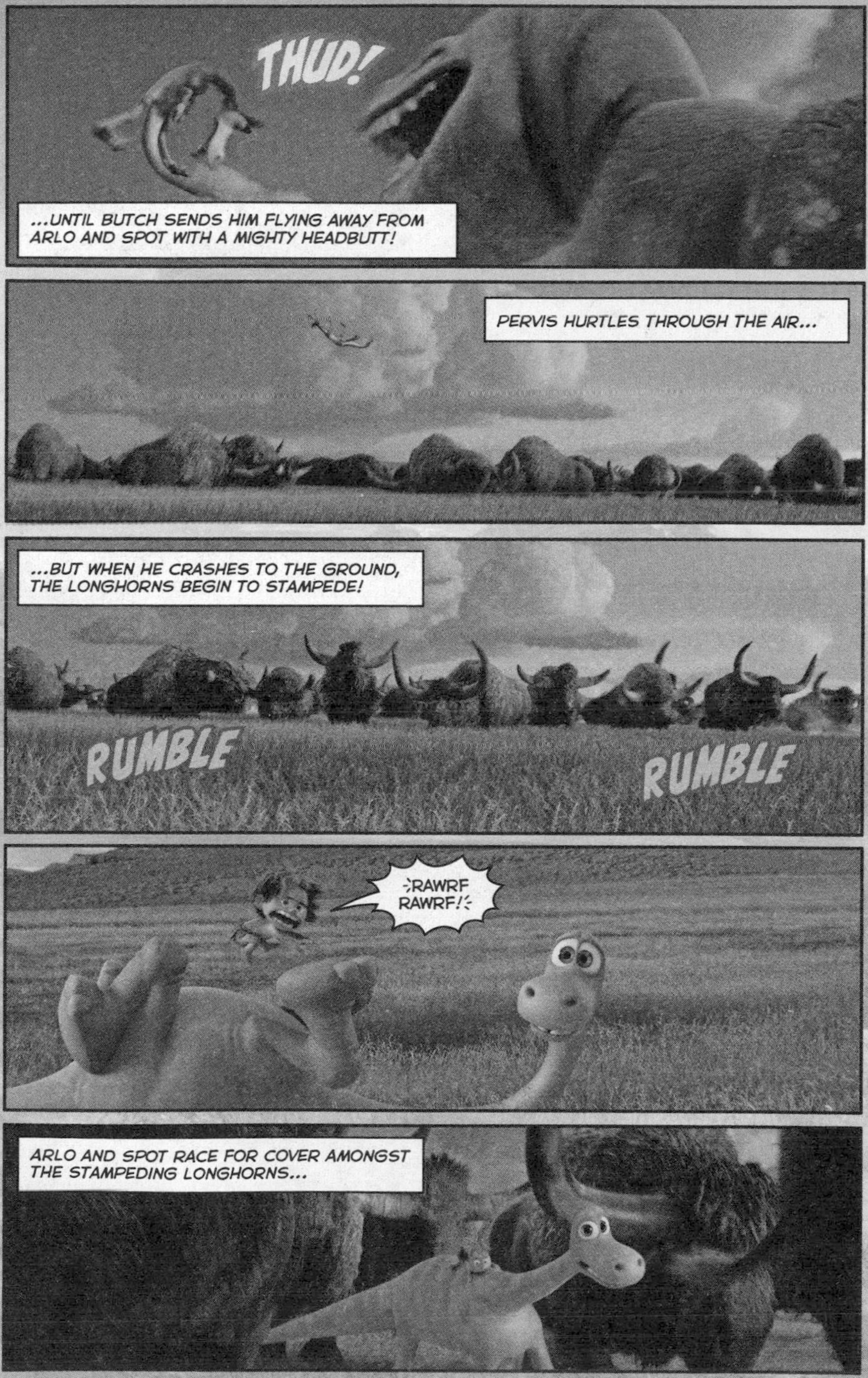
THUD!
...UNTIL BUTCH SENDS HIM FLYING AWAY FROM ARLO AND SPOT WITH A MIGHTY HEADBUTT!
PERVIS HURTLES THROUGH THE AIR...
...BUT WHEN HE CRASHES TO THE GROUND, THE LONGHORNS BEGIN TO STAMPEDE!
RUMBLE
RUMBLE
RAWRF RAWRF!
ARLO AND SPOT RACE FOR COVER AMONGST THE STAMPEDING LONGHORNS...

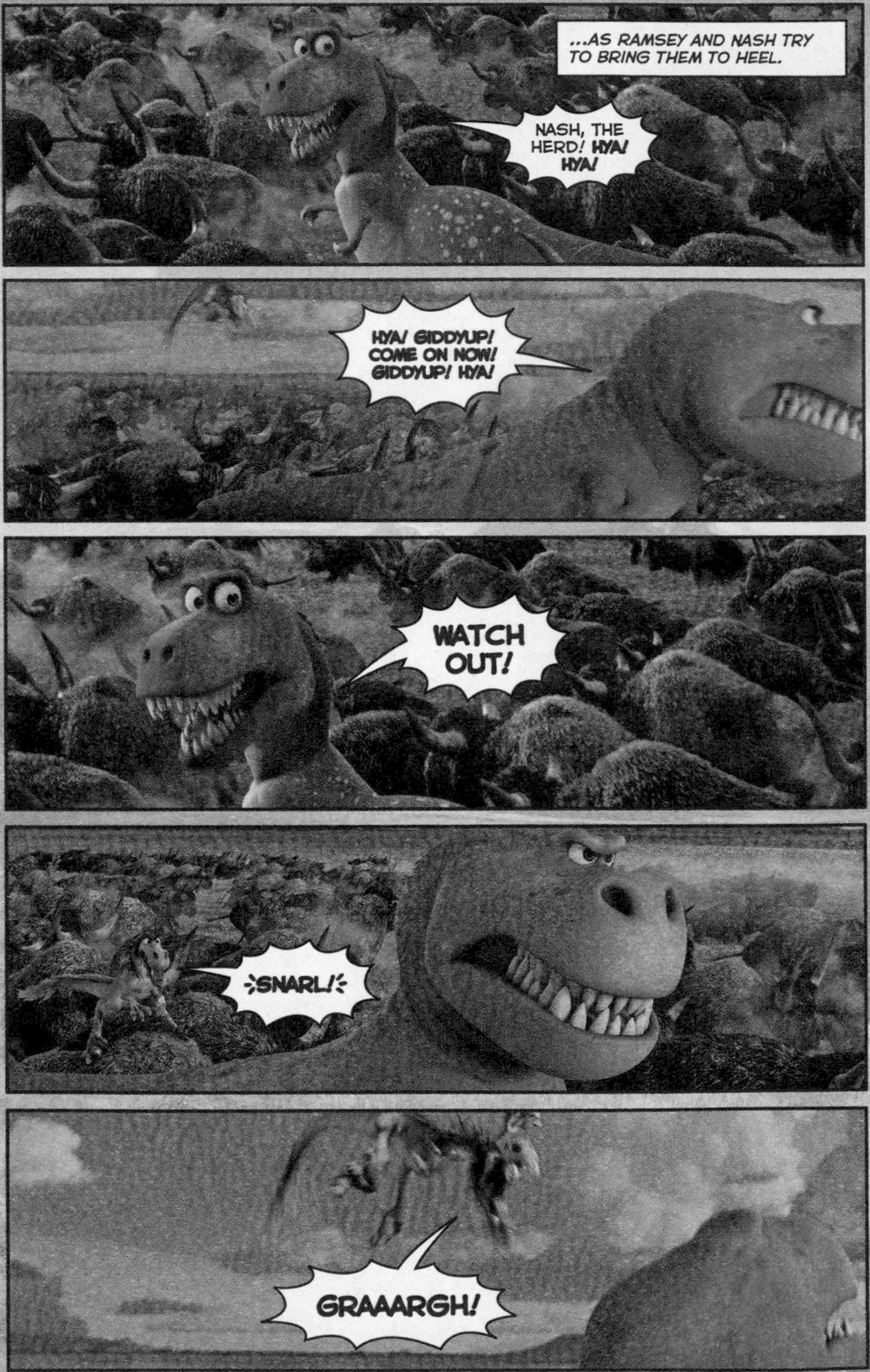
...AS RAMSEY AND NASH TRY TO BRING THEM TO HEEL.
NASH, THE HERD! HYA! HYA!
HYA! GIDDYUP! COME ON NOW! GIDDYUP! HYA!
WATCH OUT!
SNARL!
GRAAARGH!

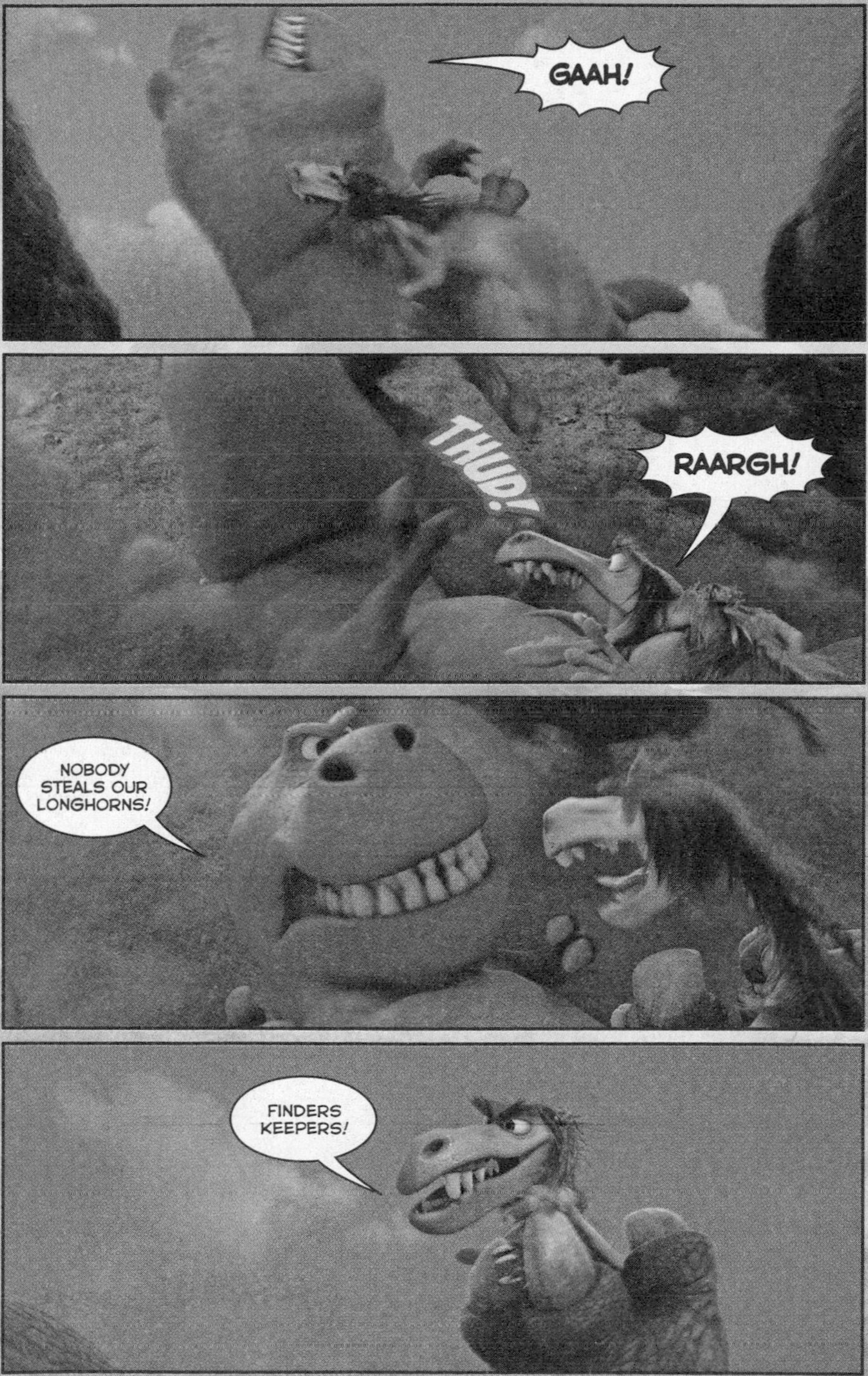
GAAH!
THUD!
RAARGH!
NOBODY STEALS OUR LONGHORNS!
FINDERS KEEPERS!

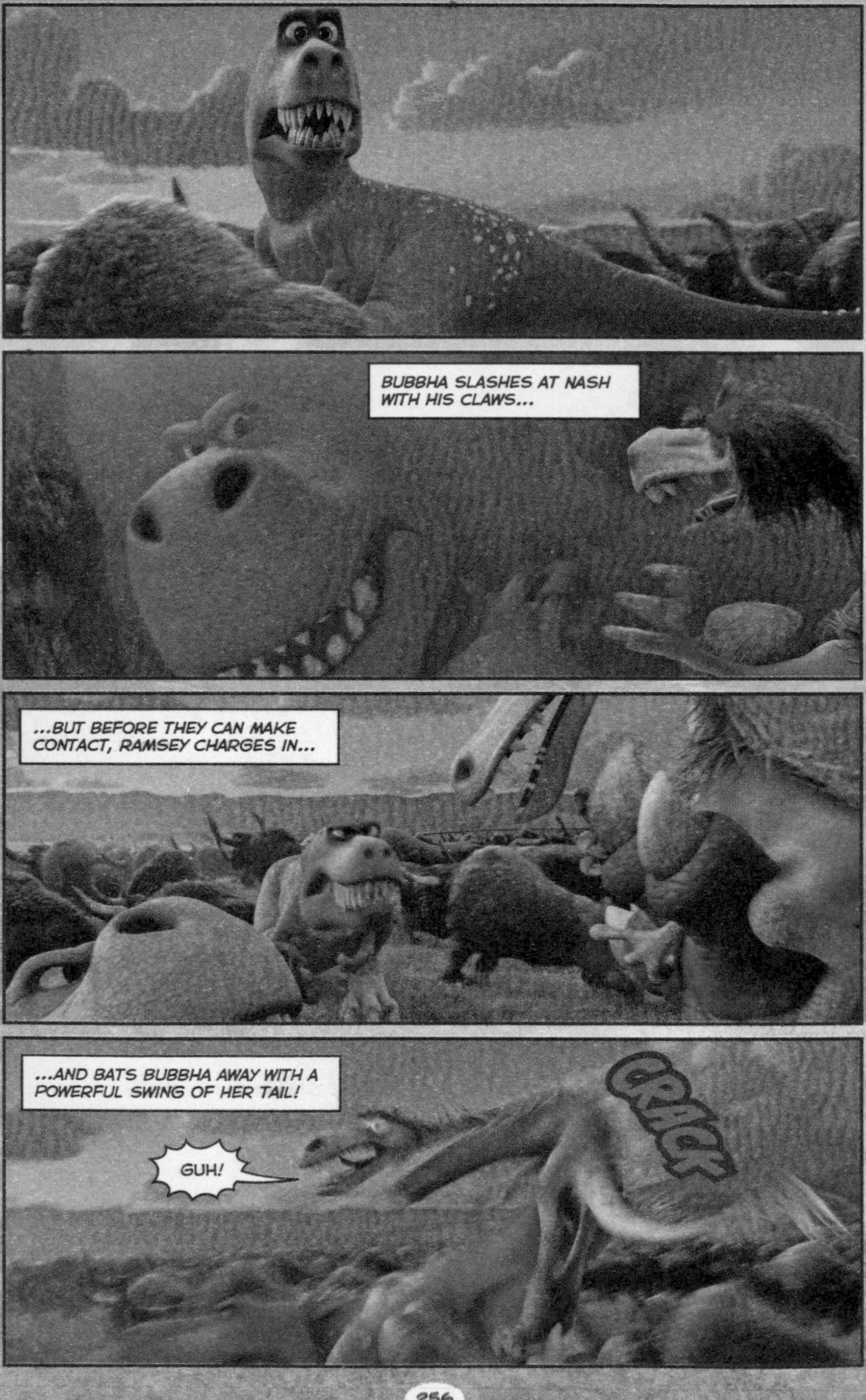
BUBBHA SLASHES AT NASH WITH HIS CLAWS...
...BUT BEFORE THEY CAN MAKE CONTACT, RAMSEY CHARGES IN...
...AND BATS BUBBHA AWAY WITH A POWERFUL SWING OF HER TAIL!
CRACK
GUH!

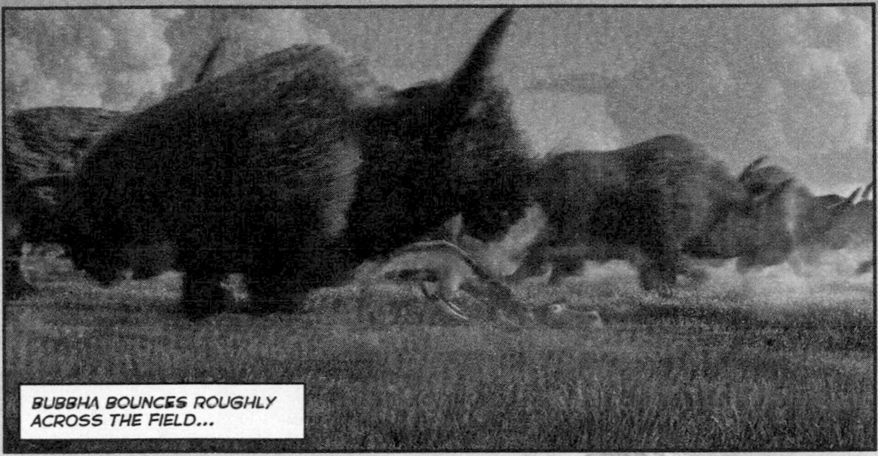
BUBBHA BOUNCES ROUGHLY ACROSS THE FIELD...

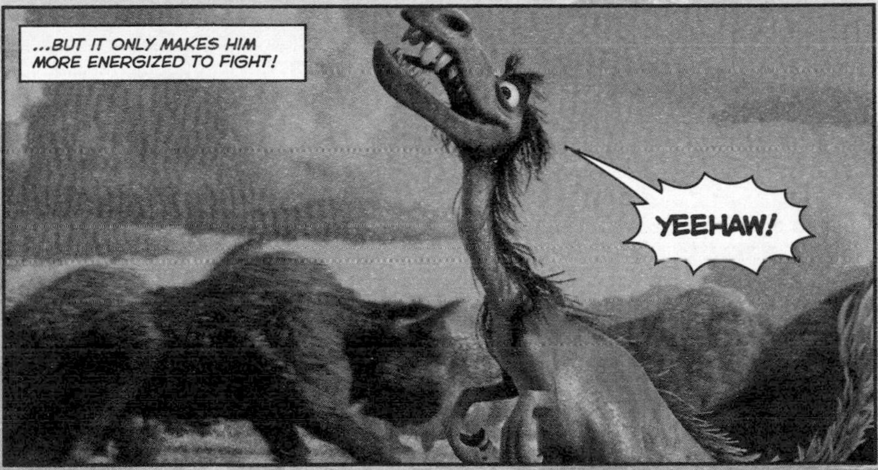
...BUT IT ONLY MAKES HIM MORE ENERGIZED TO FIGHT!
YEEHAW!

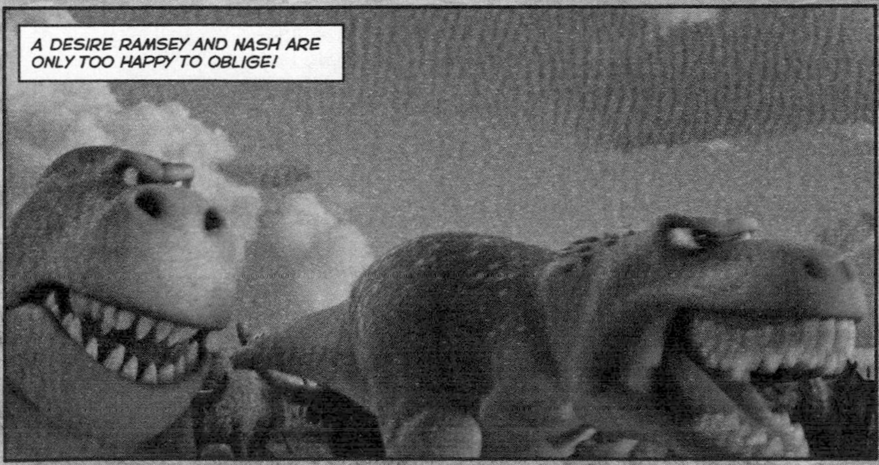
A DESIRE RAMSEY AND NASH ARE ONLY TOO HAPPY TO OBLIGE!

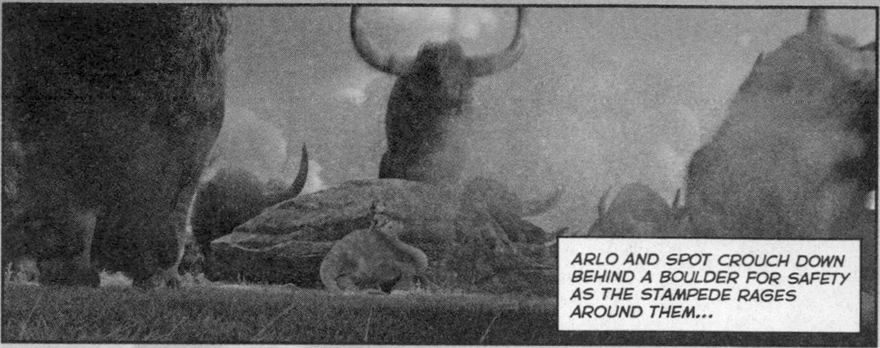
ARLO AND SPOT CROUCH DOWN BEHIND A BOULDER FOR SAFETY AS THE STAMPEDE RAGES AROUND THEM...

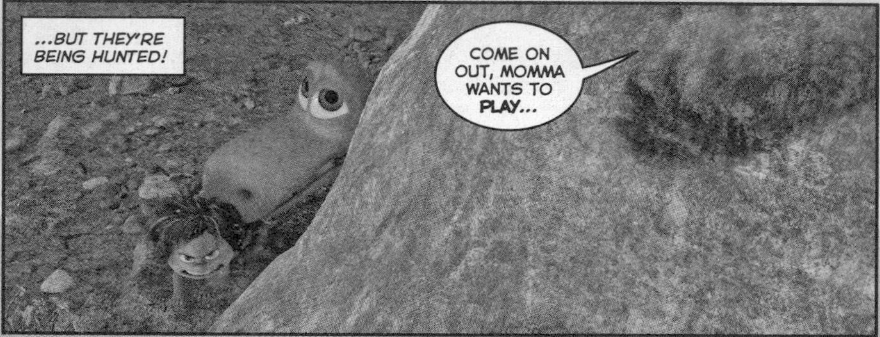
...BUT THEY'RE BEING HUNTED!
COME ON OUT, MOMMA WANTS TO PLAY...

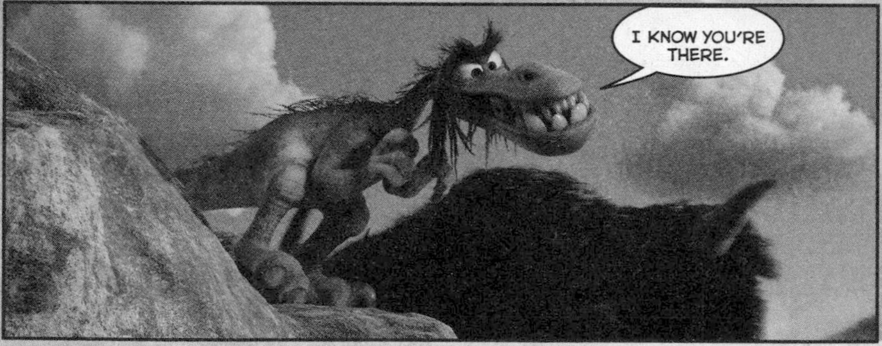
I KNOW YOU'RE THERE.

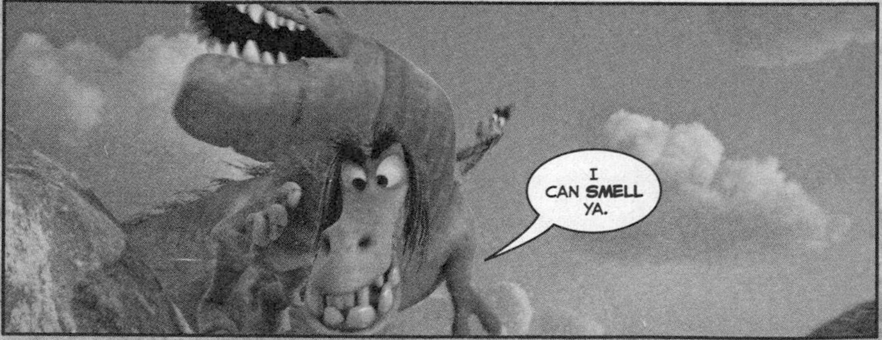
I CAN SMELL YA.

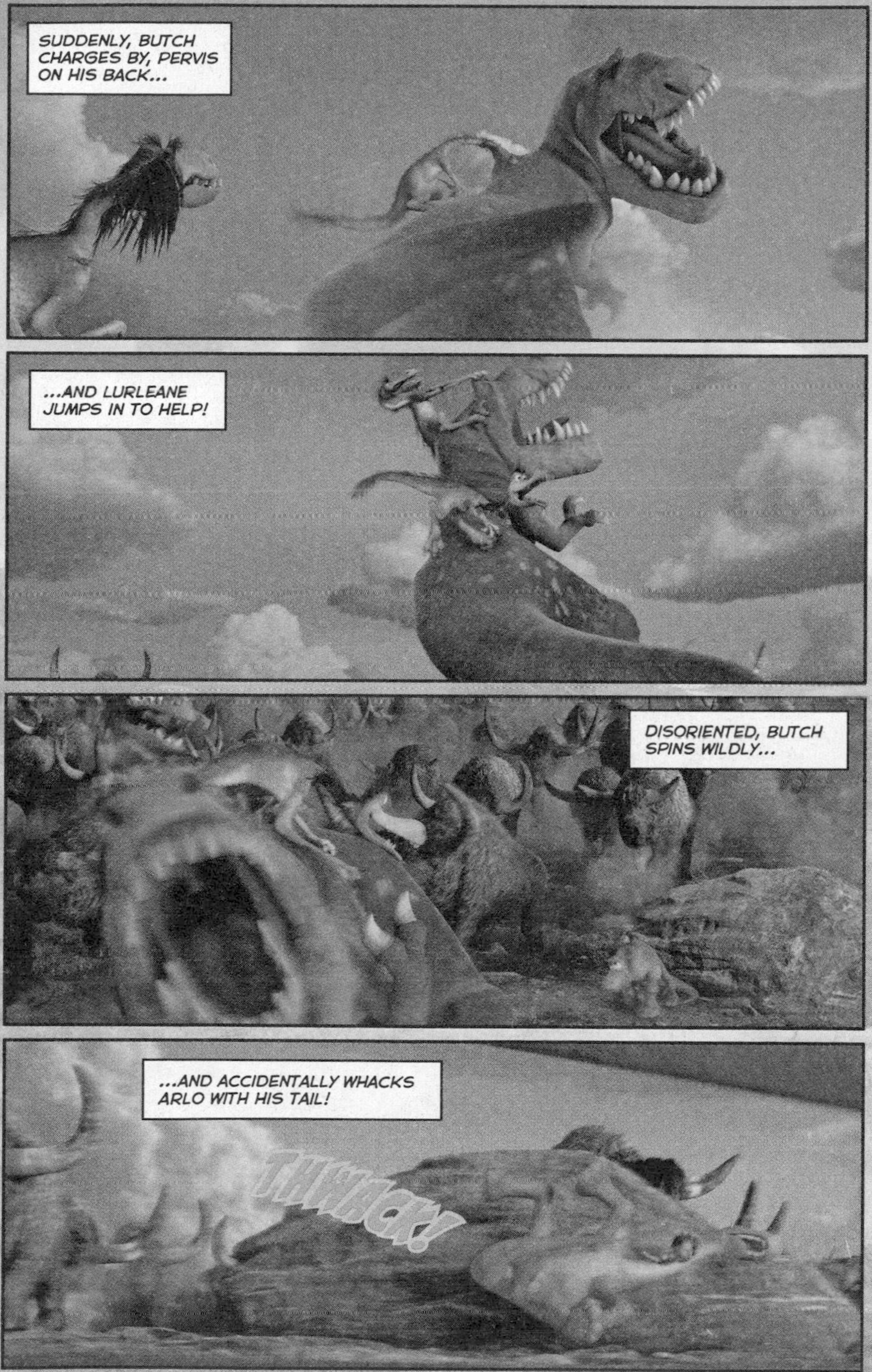
SUDDENLY, BUTCH CHARGES BY, PERVIS ON HIS BACK...
...AND LURLEANE JUMPS IN TO HELP!
DISORIENTED, BUTCH SPINS WILDLY...
...AND ACCIDENTALLY WHACKS ARLO WITH HIS TAIL!
THWACK!

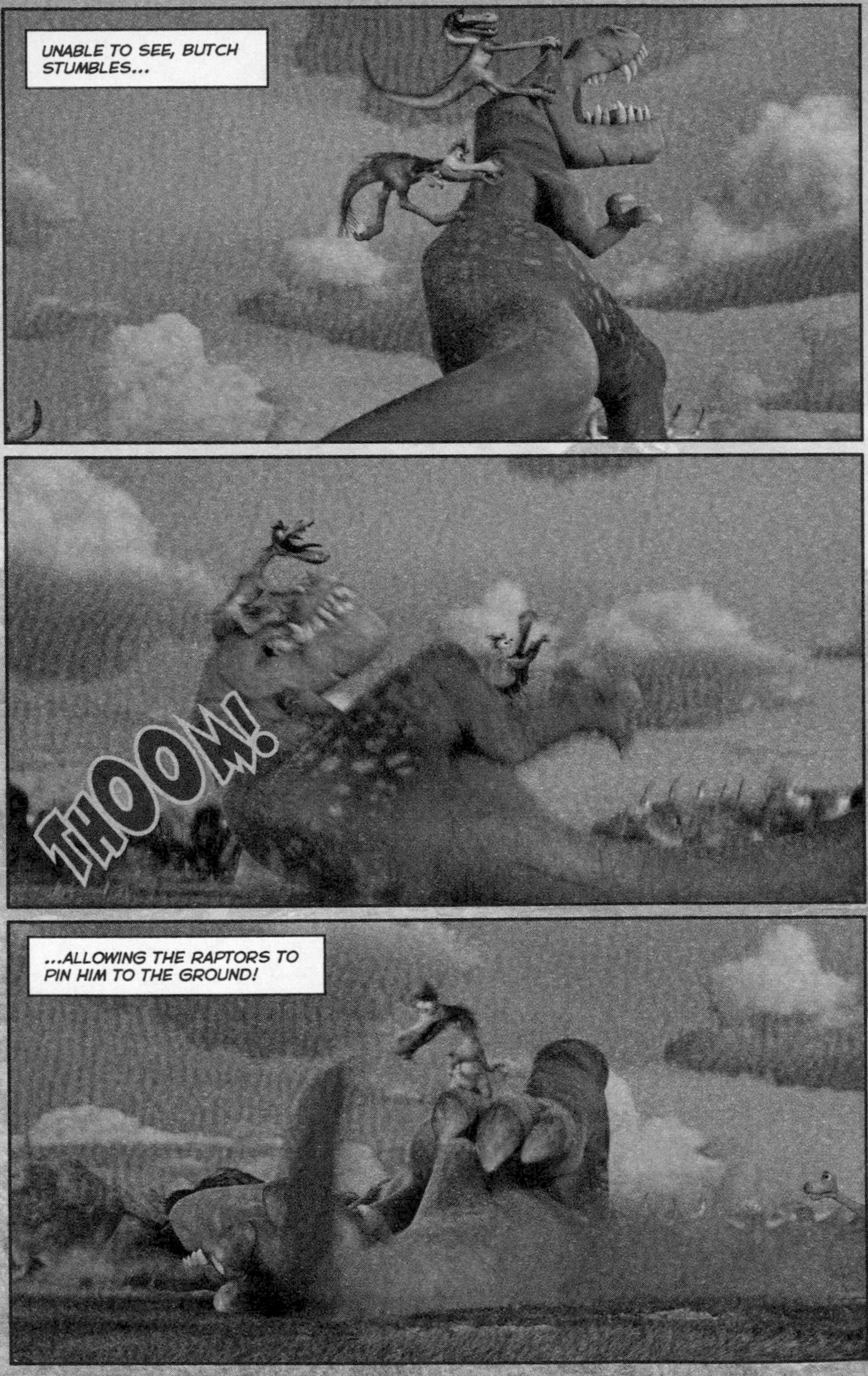
UNABLE TO SEE, BUTCH STUMBLES...
THOOM!
...ALLOWING THE RAPTORS TO PIN HIM TO THE GROUND!

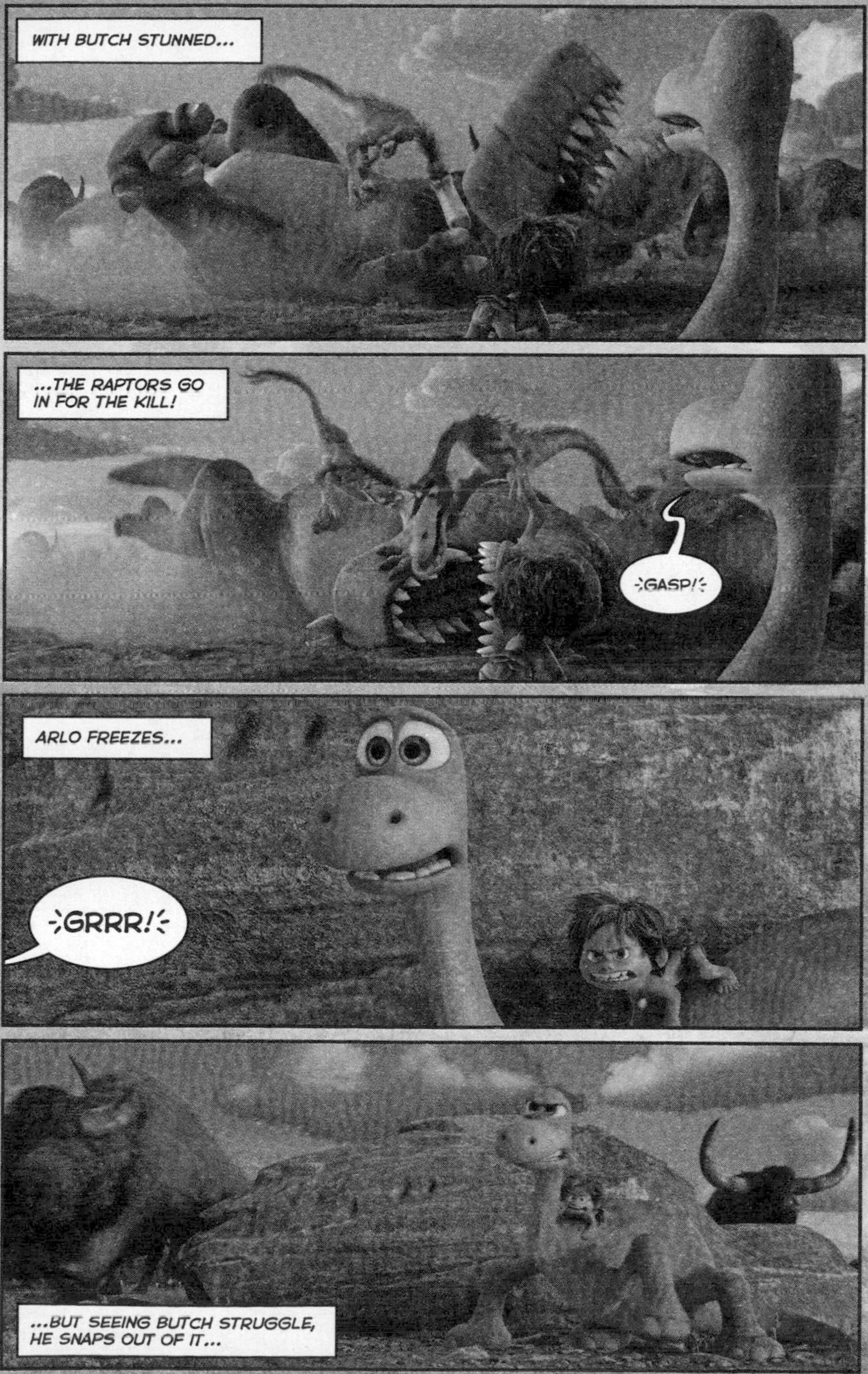
WITH BUTCH STUNNED...
...THE RAPTORS GO IN FOR THE KILL!
GASP!
ARLO FREEZES...
GRRR!
...BUT SEEING BUTCH STRUGGLE, HE SNAPS OUT OF IT...

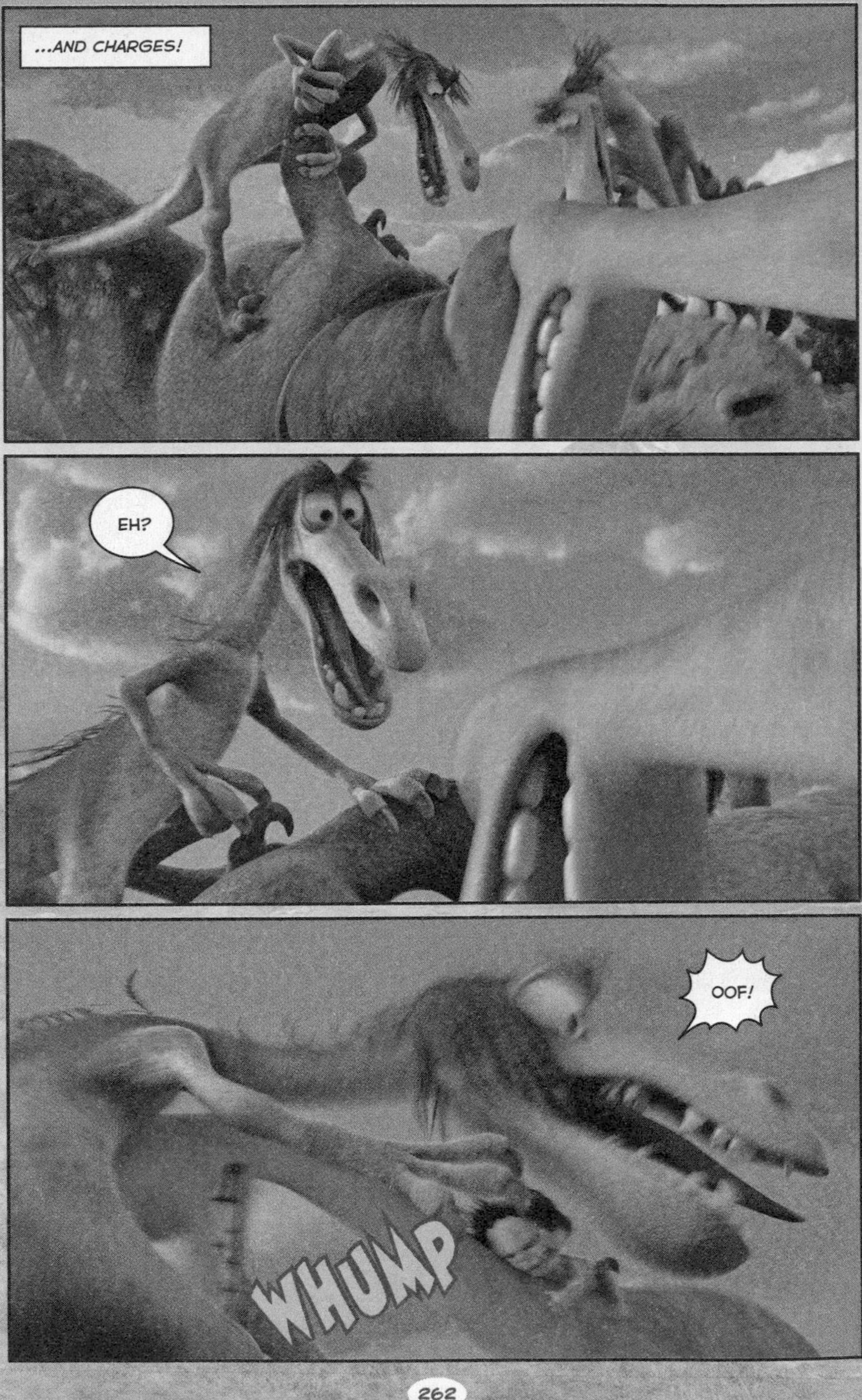
...AND CHARGES!
EH?
OOF!
WHUMP

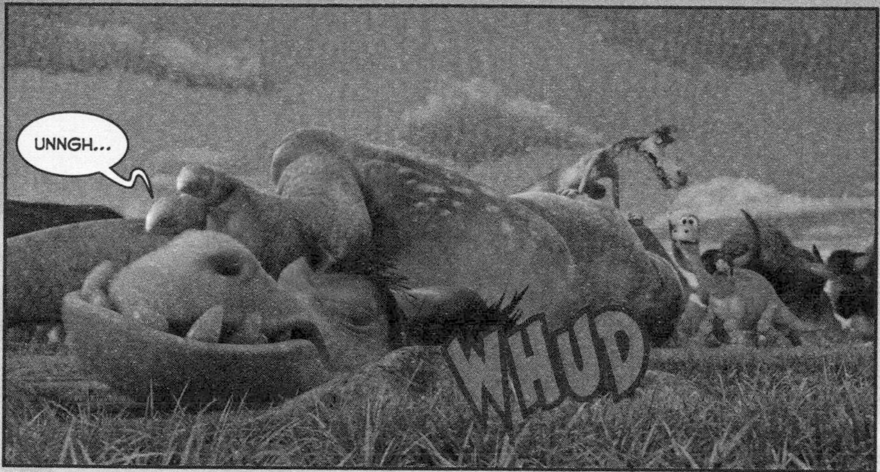
UNNGH...
WHUD

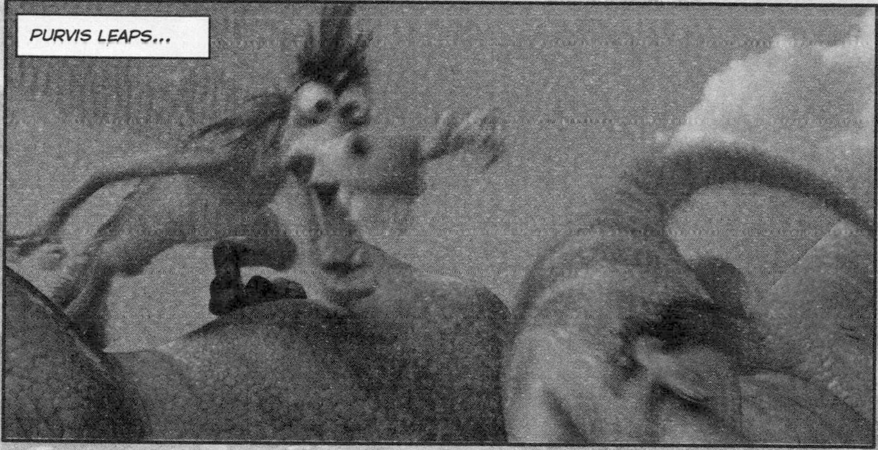
PURVIS LEAPS...

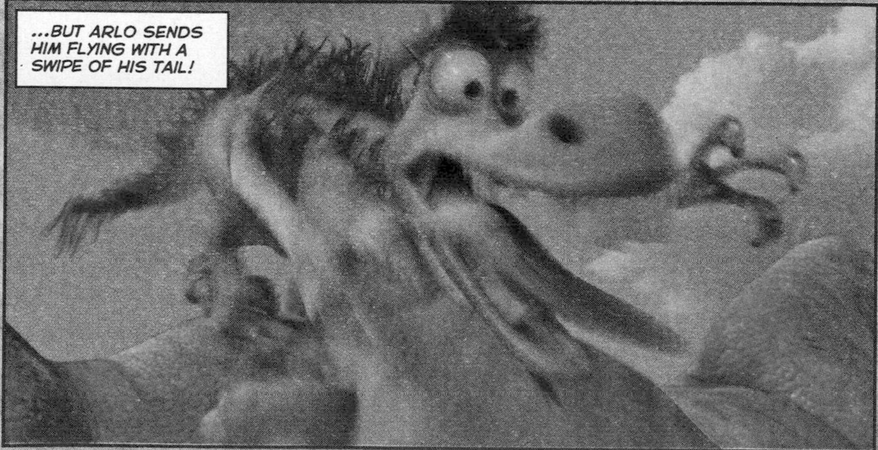
...BUT ARLO SENDS HIM FLYING WITH A SWIPE OF HIS TAIL!

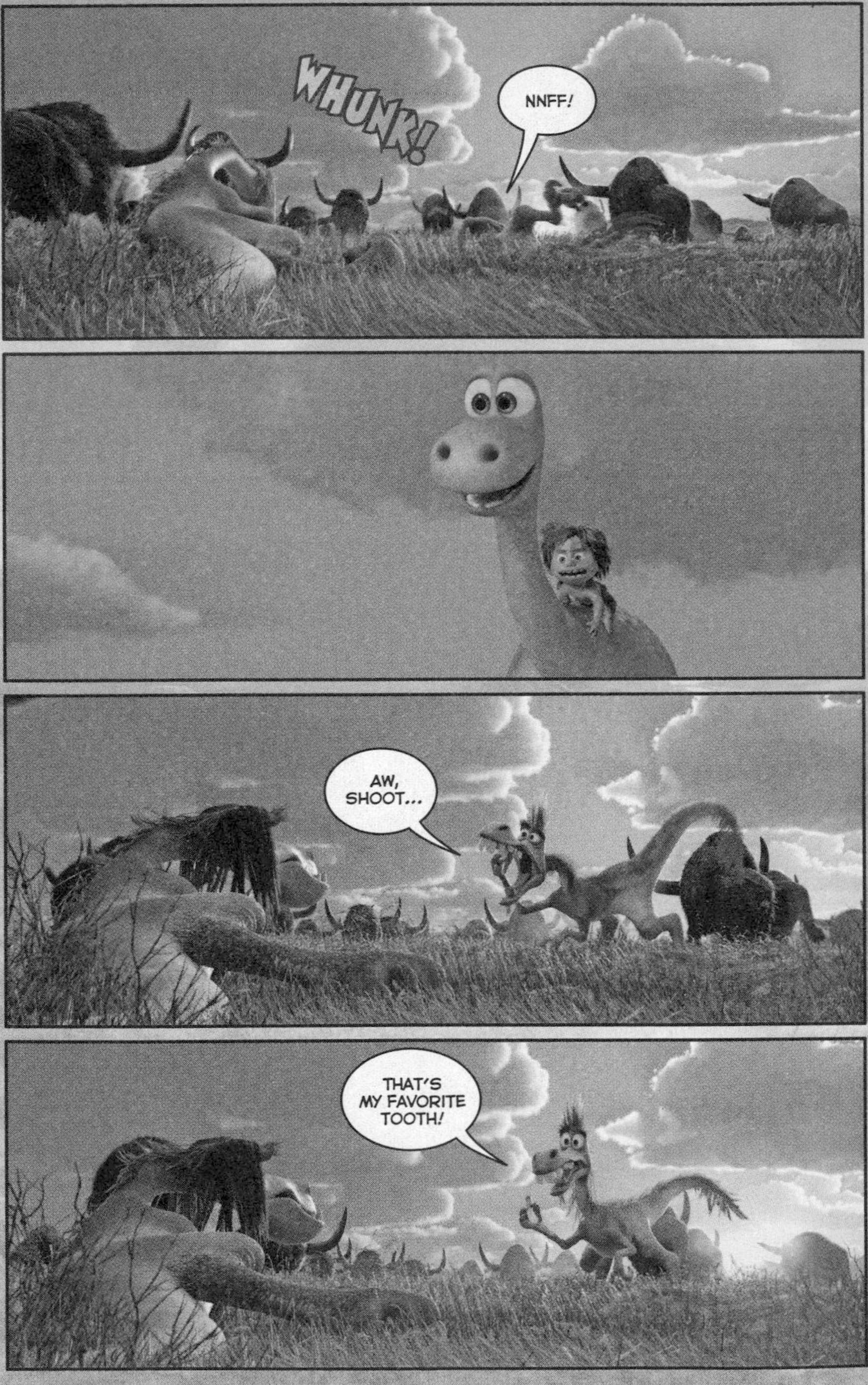
WHUNK!
NNFF!
AW, SHOOT...
THAT'S MY FAVORITE TOOTH!

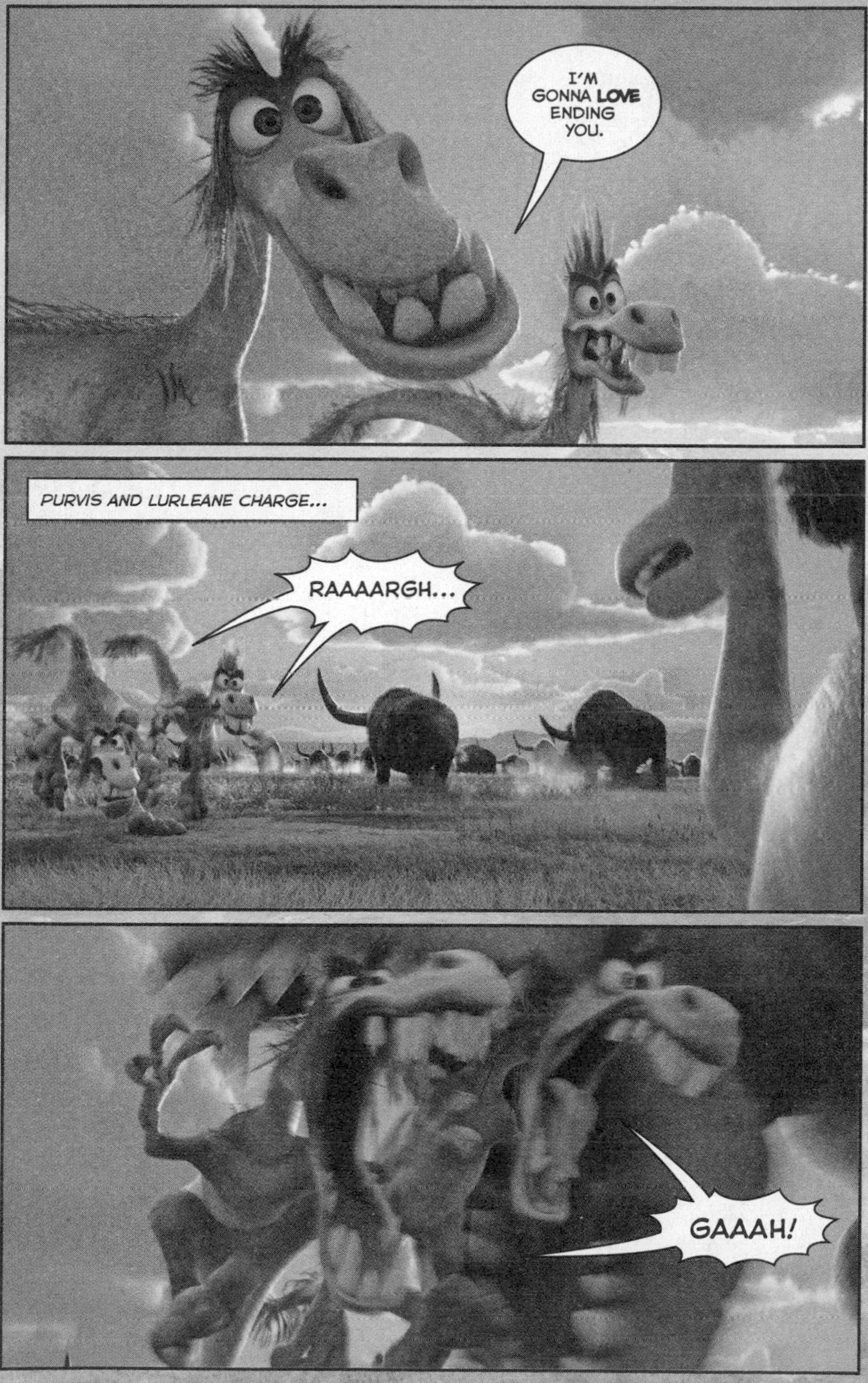
I'M GONNA LOVE ENDING YOU.
PURVIS AND LURLEANE CHARGE...
RAAAARGH...
GAAAH!

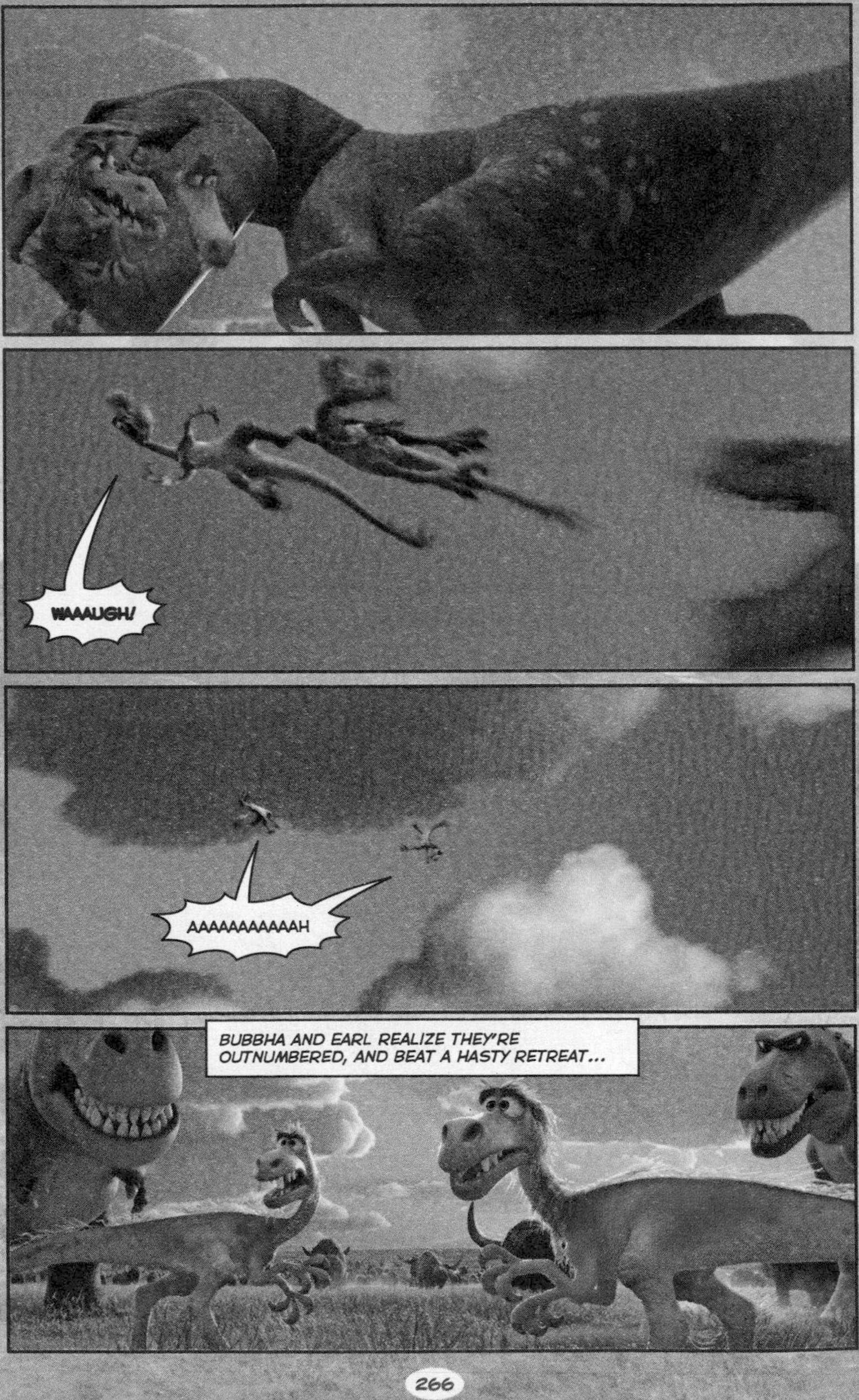
WAAAUGH!
AAAAAAAAAAAH
BUBBHA AND EARL REALIZE THEY'RE OUTNUMBERED, AND BEAT A HASTY RETREAT...

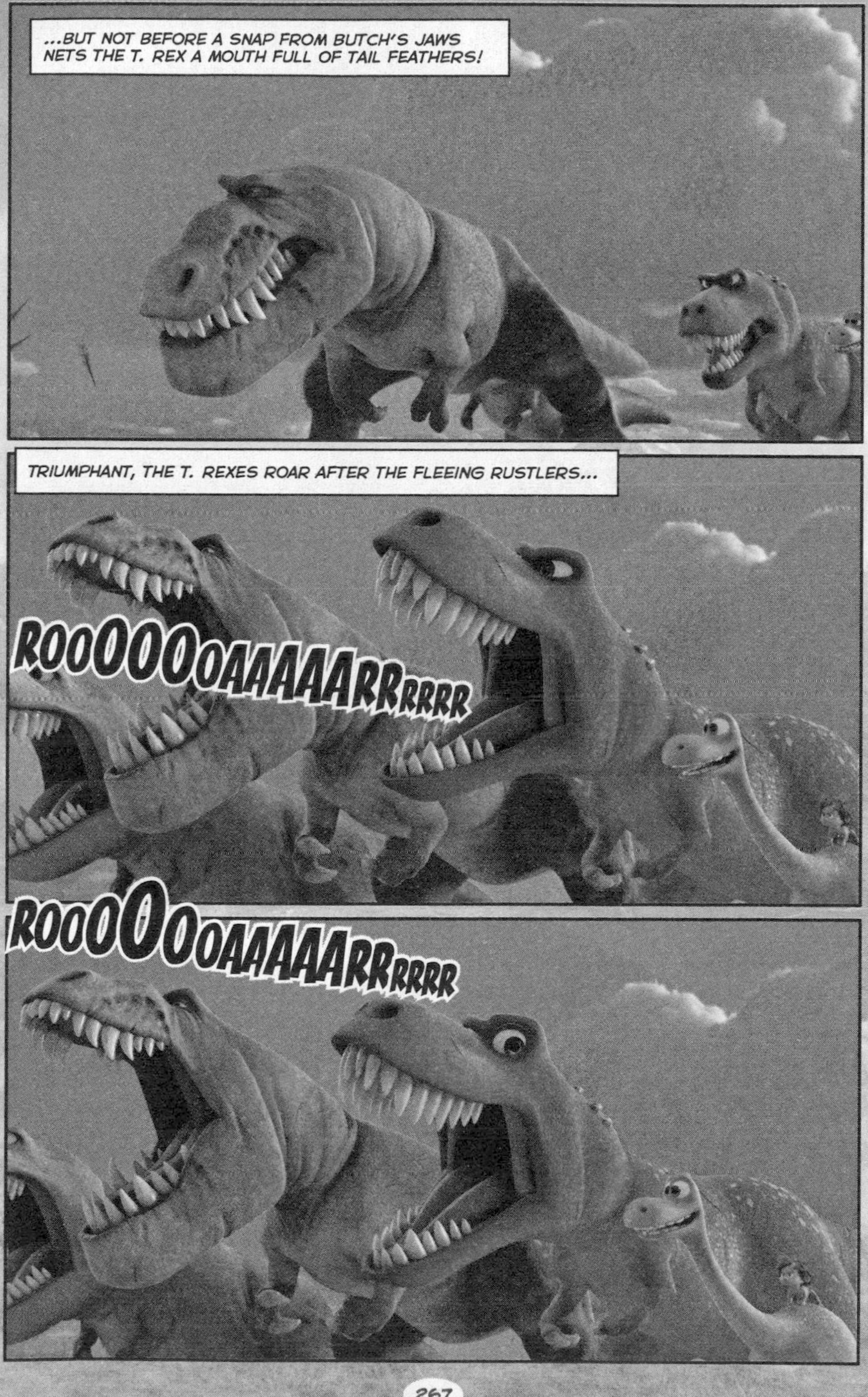
...BUT NOT BEFORE A SNAP FROM BUTCH'S JAWS NETS THE T. REX A MOUTH FULL OF TAIL FEATHERS!
TRIUMPHANT, THE T. REXES ROAR AFTER THE FLEEING RUSTLERS...
ROOOOOOAAAAAARRrrrr
ROOOOOOAAAAAARRrrrr

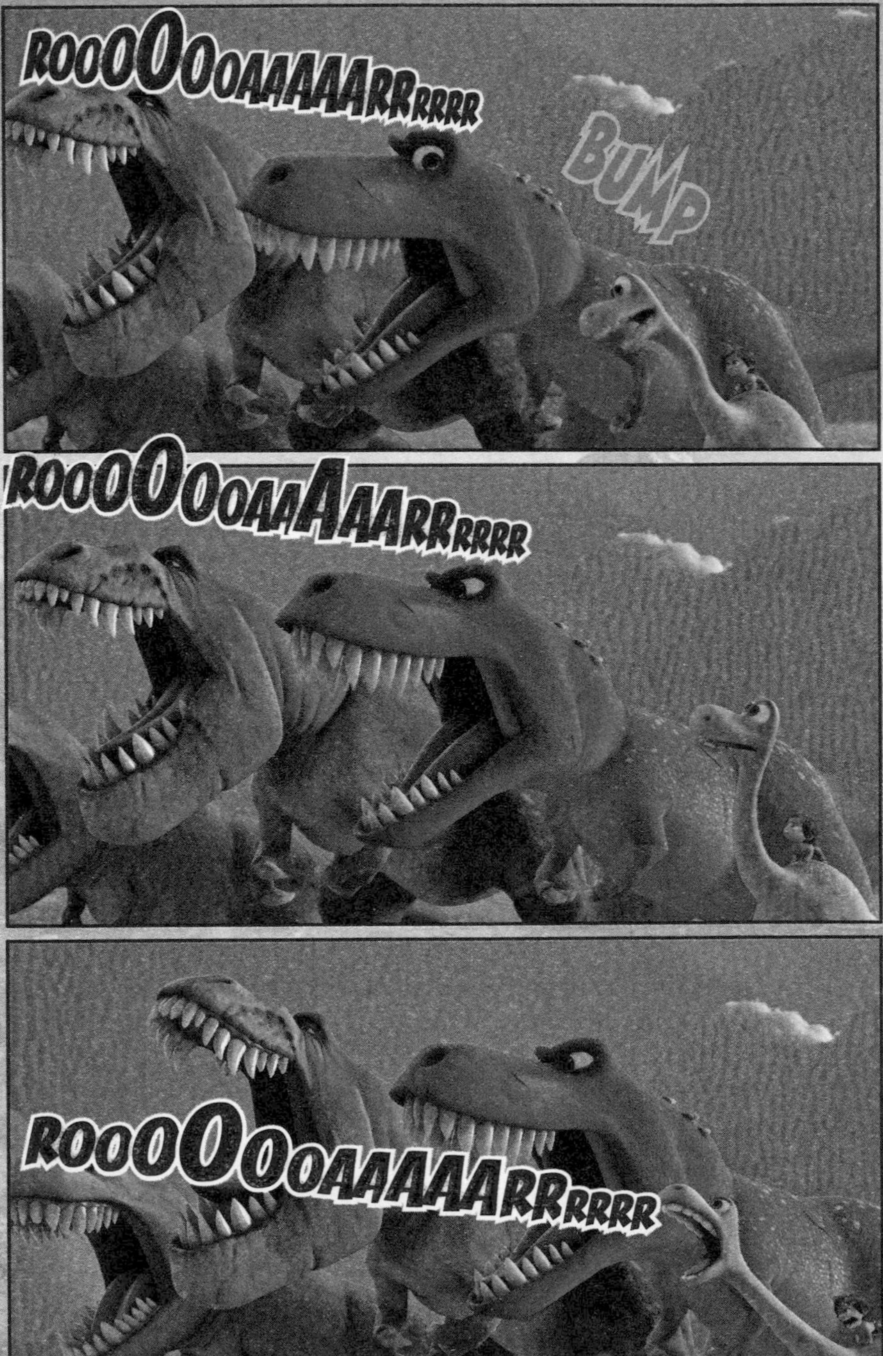
ROOOOOOOAAAAAARRrrrr
BUMP
ROOOOOOOAAAAAARRrrrr
ROOOOOOOAAAAAARRrrrr

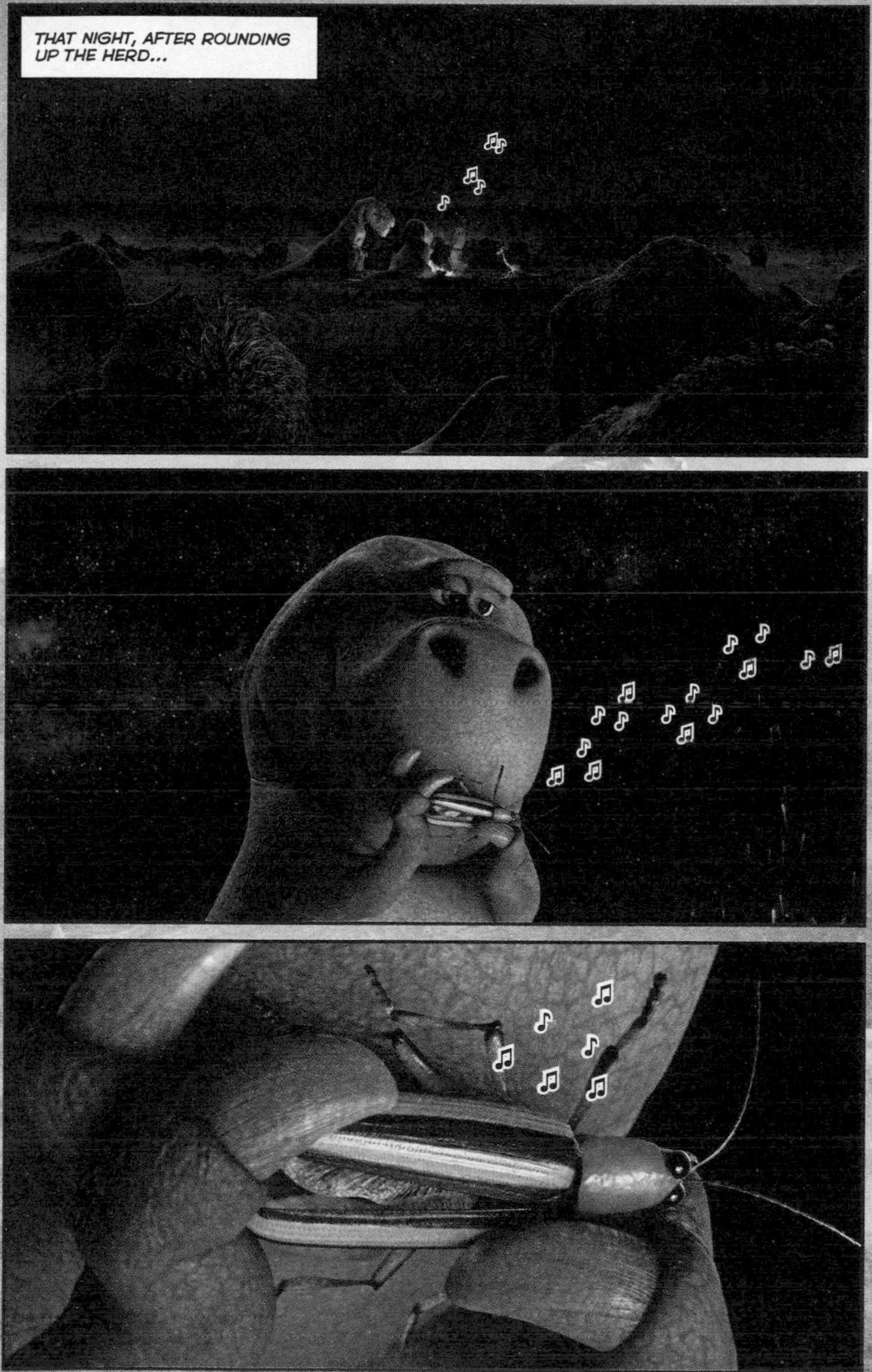
THAT NIGHT, AFTER ROUNDING UP THE HERD...

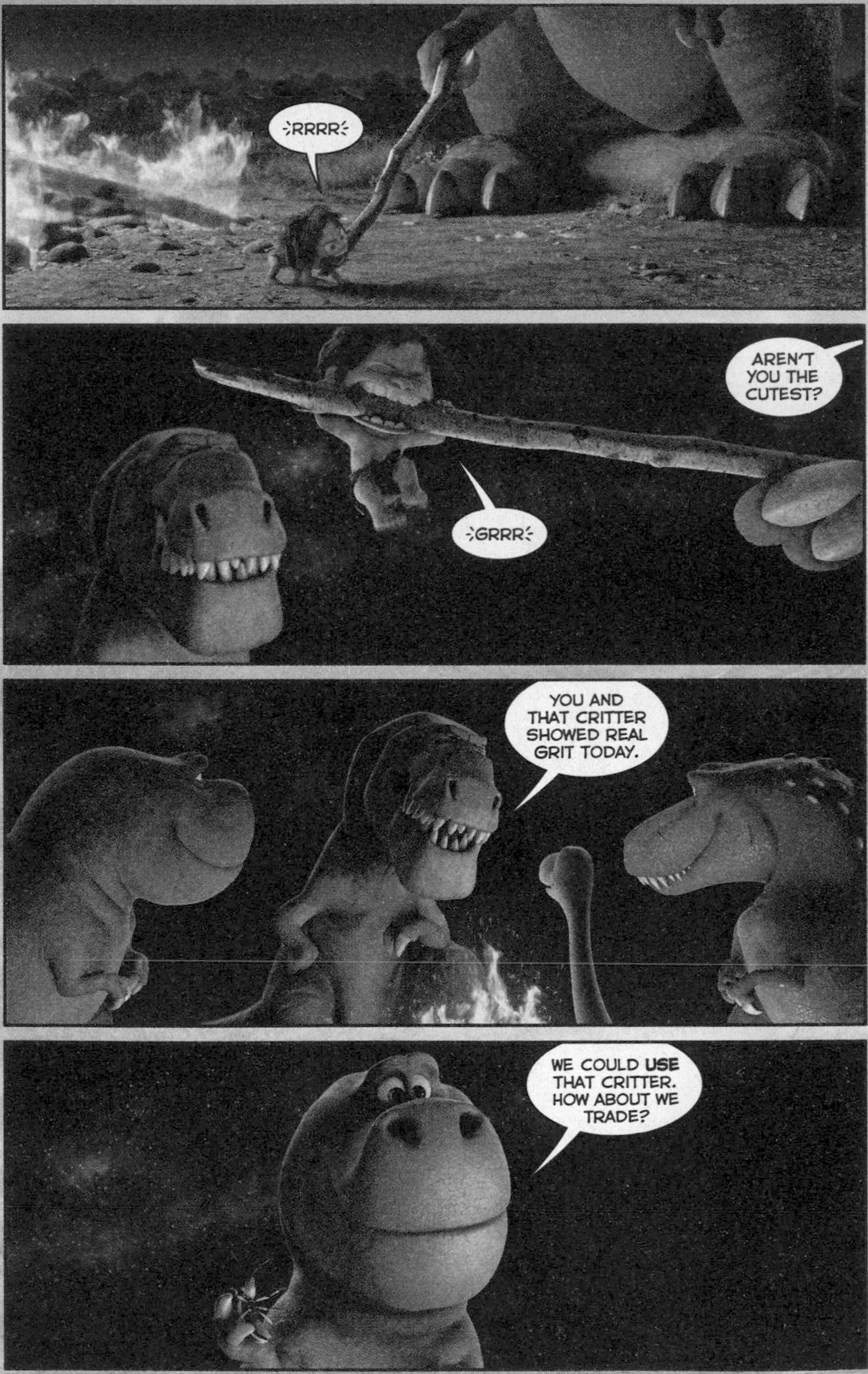
RRRR
AREN'T YOU THE CUTEST?
GRRR
YOU AND THAT CRITTER SHOWED REAL GRIT TODAY.
WE COULD **USE** THAT CRITTER. HOW ABOUT WE TRADE?

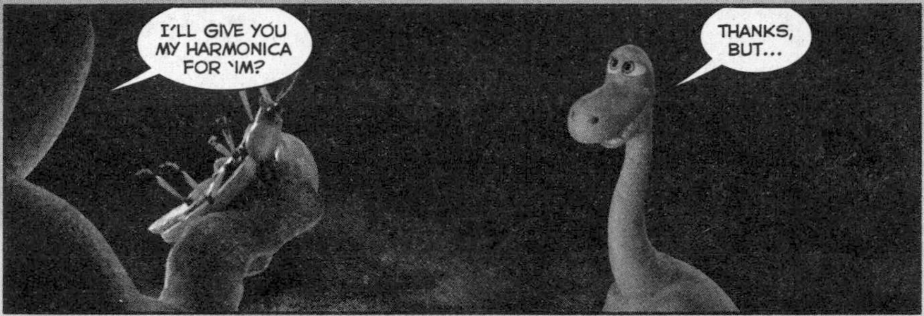
I'LL GIVE YOU MY HARMONICA FOR 'IM?
THANKS, BUT...

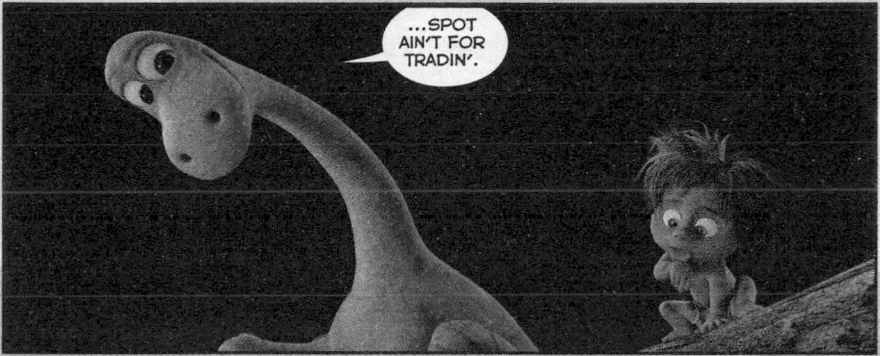
...SPOT AIN'T FOR TRADIN'.

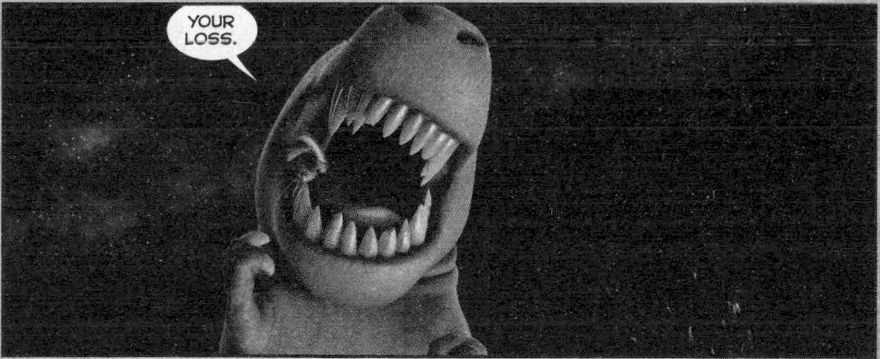
YOUR LOSS.

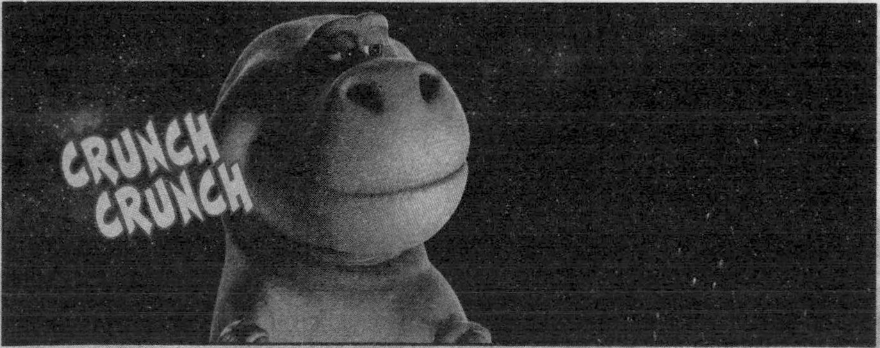
CRUNCH
CRUNCH

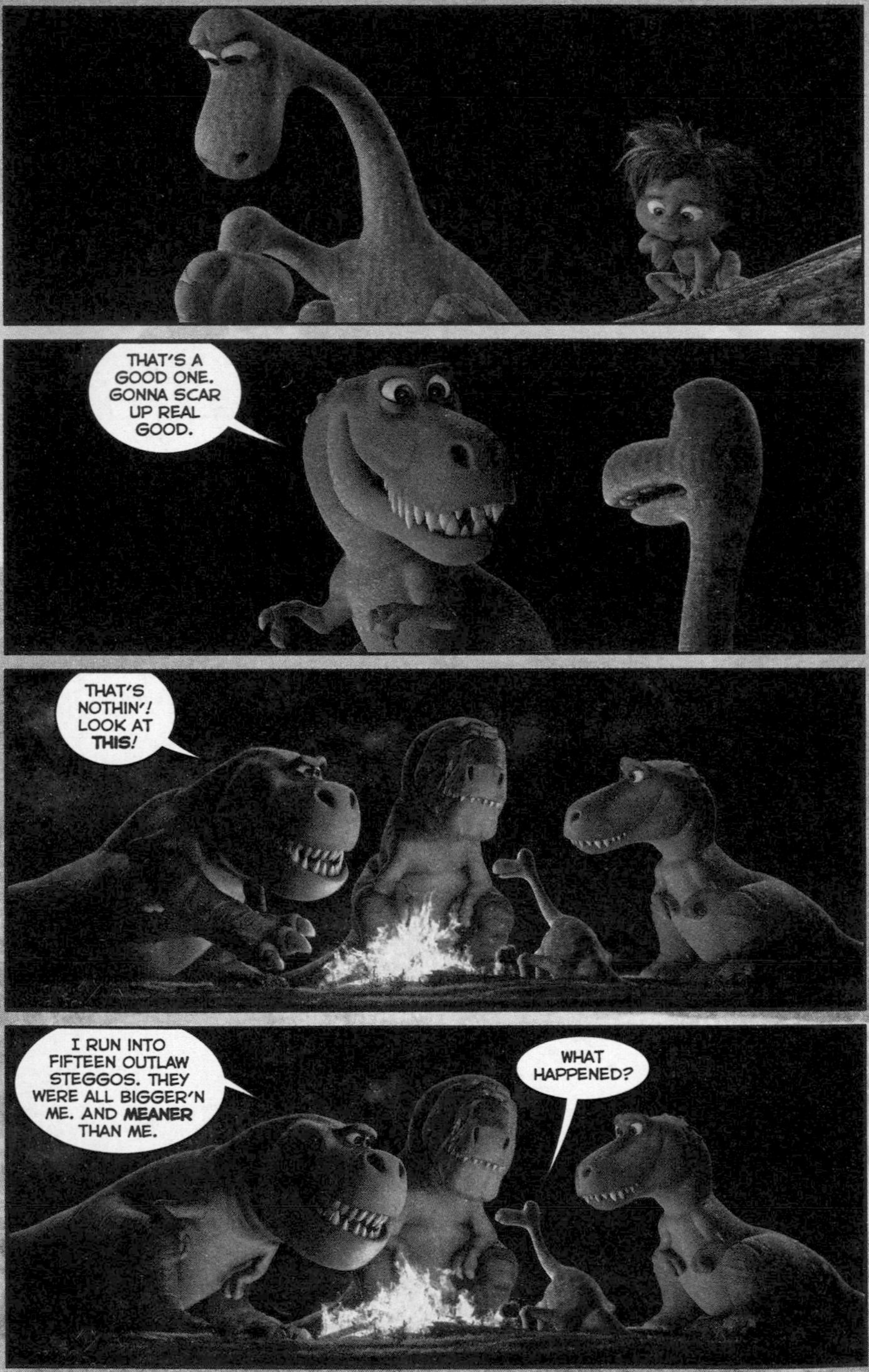
THAT'S A GOOD ONE. GONNA SCAR UP REAL GOOD.
THAT'S NOTHIN'! LOOK AT **THIS**!
I RUN INTO FIFTEEN OUTLAW STEGGOS. THEY WERE ALL BIGGER'N ME. AND **MEANER** THAN ME.
WHAT HAPPENED?

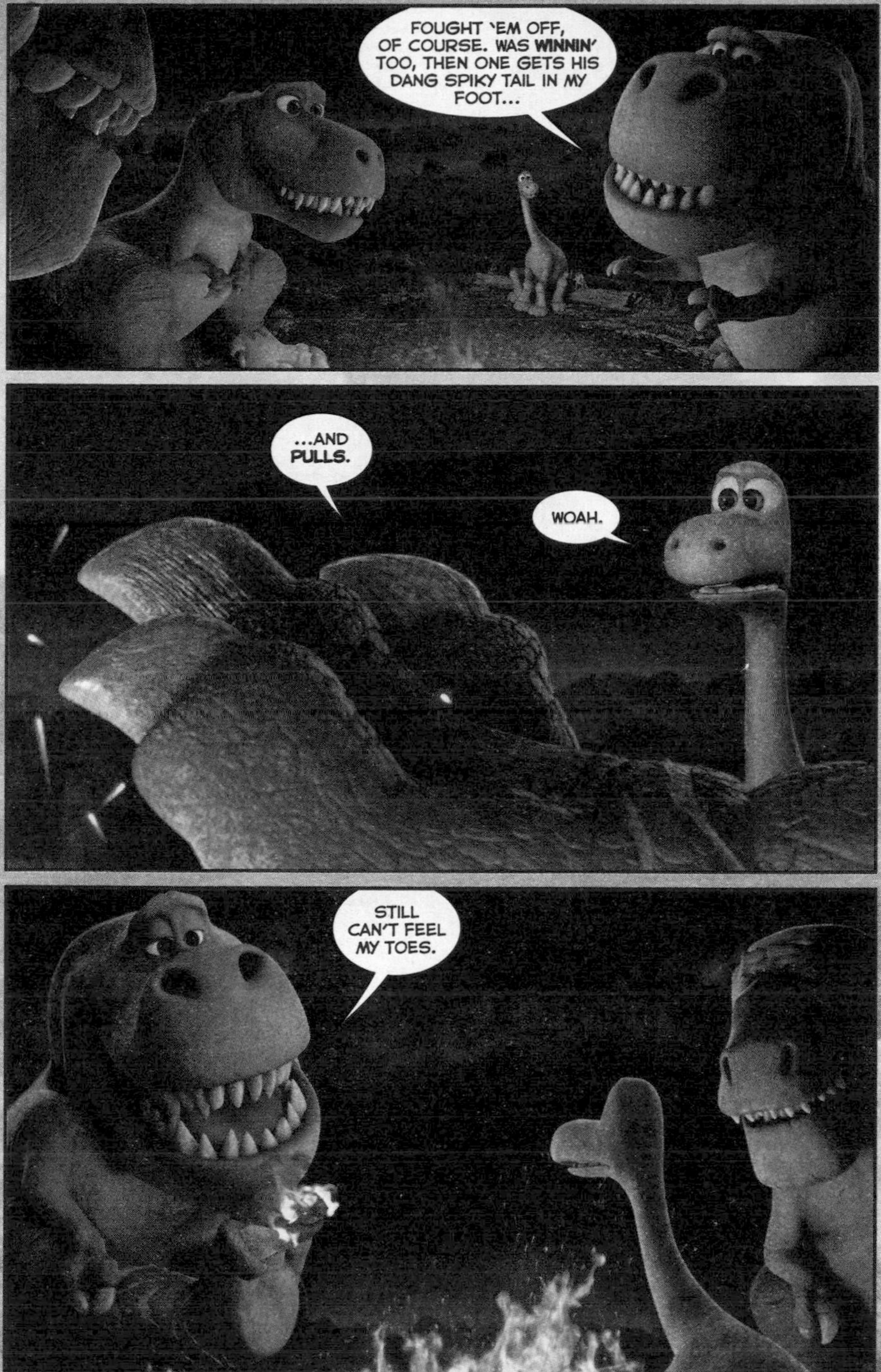
FOUGHT 'EM OFF, OF COURSE. WAS **WINNIN'** TOO, THEN ONE GETS HIS DANG SPIKY TAIL IN MY FOOT...
...AND **PULLS.**
WOAH.
STILL CAN'T FEEL MY TOES.

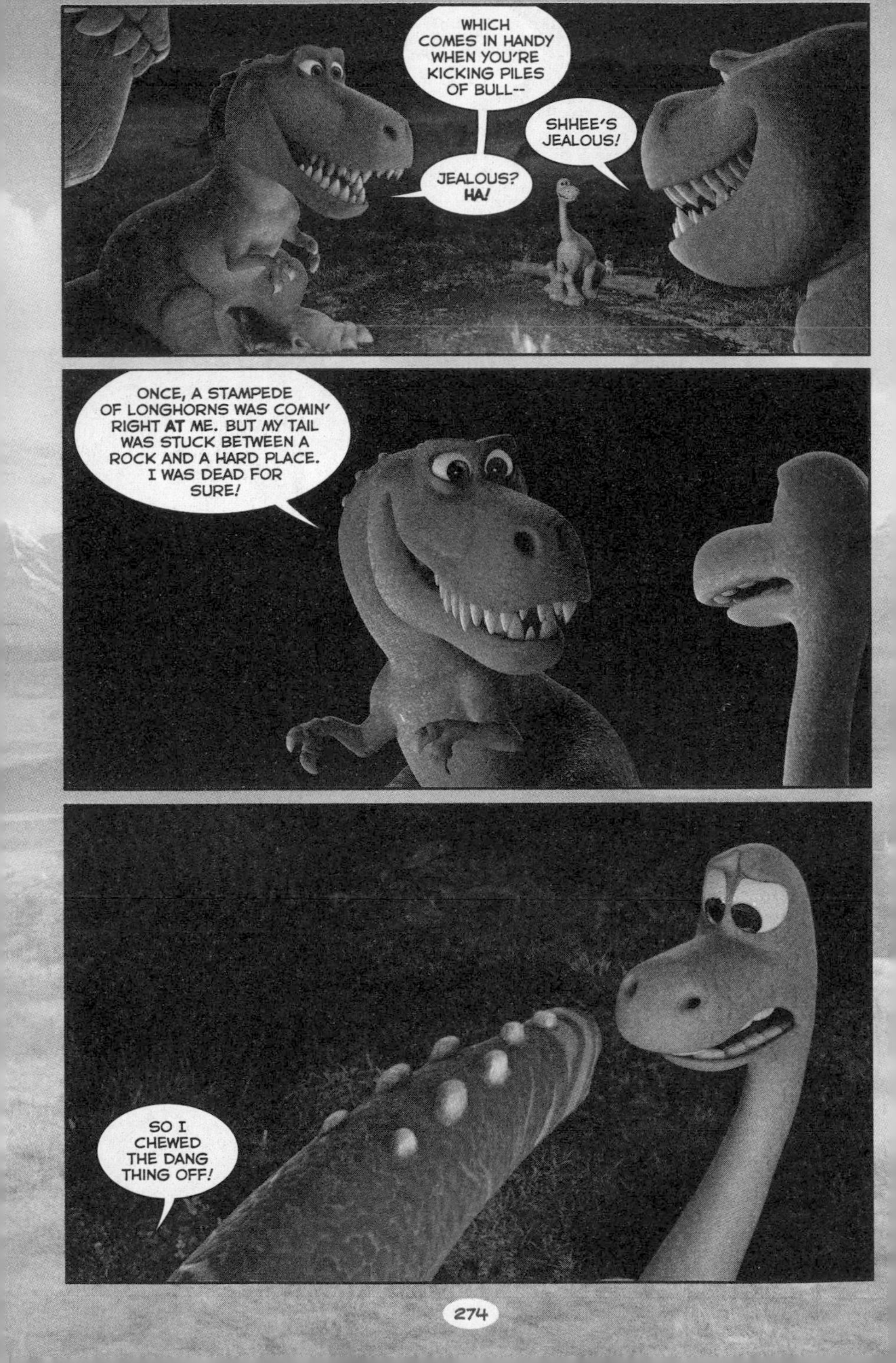
WHICH COMES IN HANDY WHEN YOU'RE KICKING PILES OF BULL--
SHHEE'S JEALOUS!
JEALOUS? HA!
ONCE, A STAMPEDE OF LONGHORNS WAS COMIN' RIGHT AT ME. BUT MY TAIL WAS STUCK BETWEEN A ROCK AND A HARD PLACE. I WAS DEAD FOR SURE!
SO I CHEWED THE DANG THING OFF!

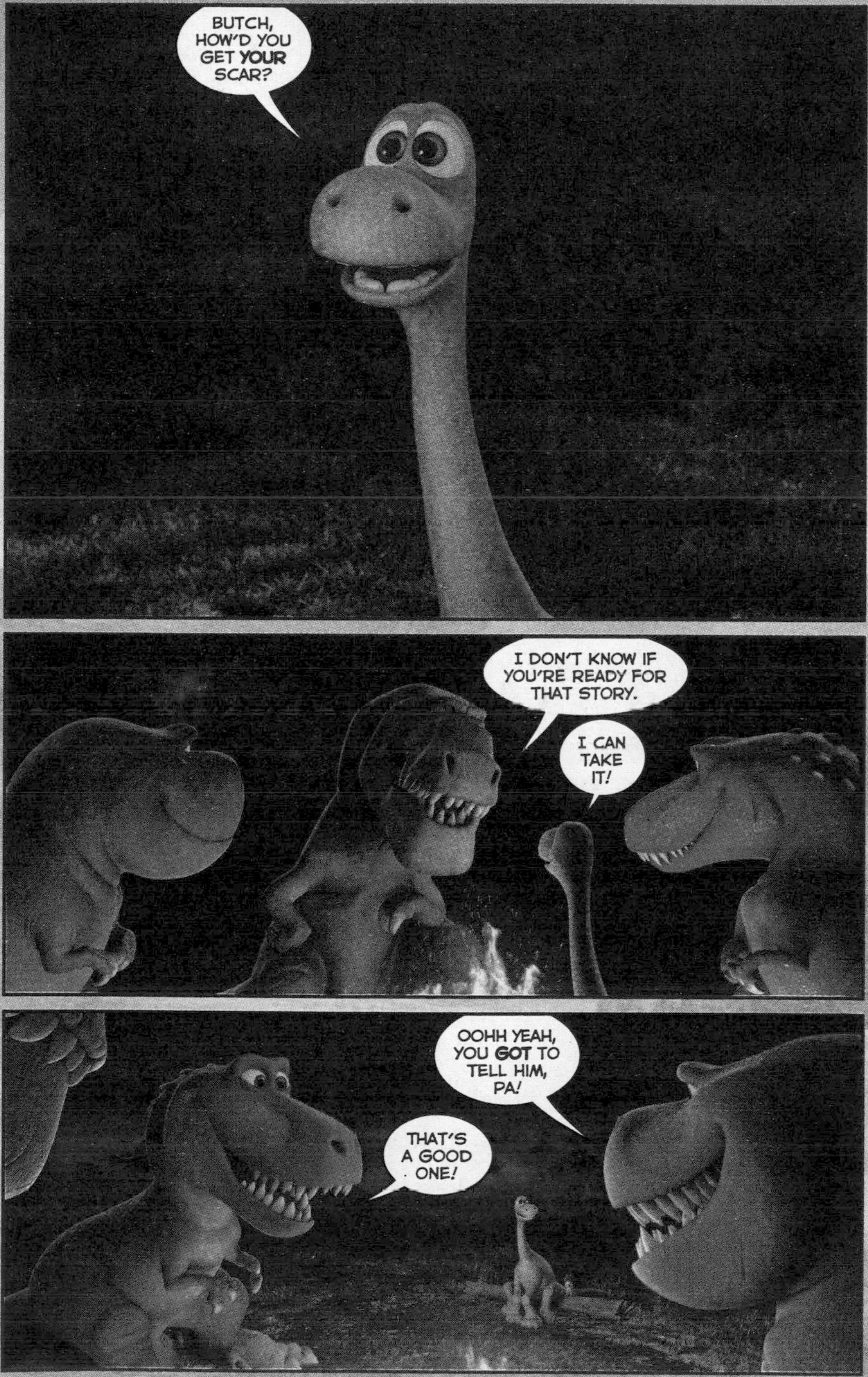
BUTCH, HOW'D YOU GET **YOUR** SCAR?
I DON'T KNOW IF YOU'RE READY FOR THAT STORY.
I CAN TAKE IT!
OOHH YEAH, YOU **GOT** TO TELL HIM, PA!
THAT'S A GOOD ONE!

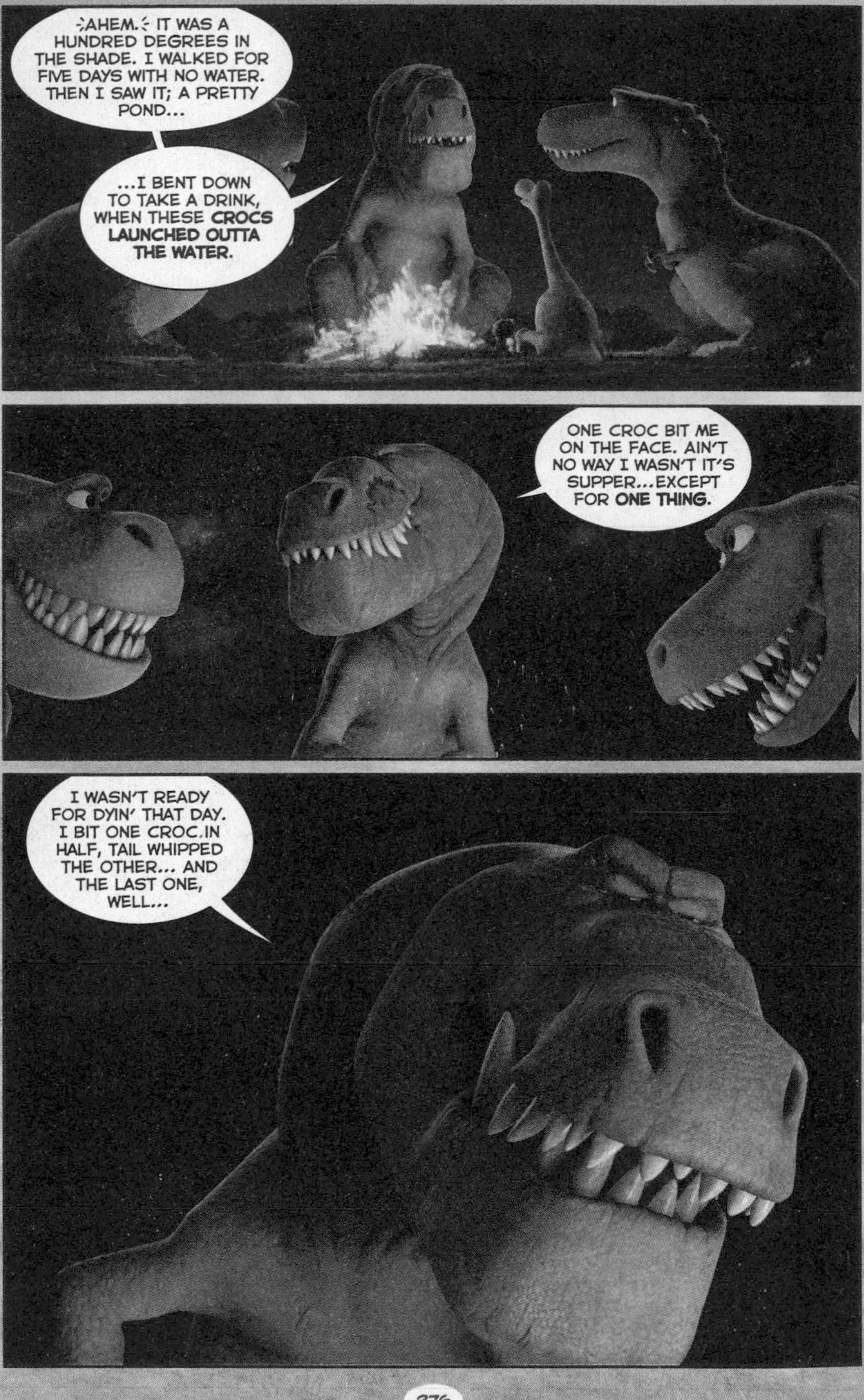
·AHEM.· IT WAS A HUNDRED DEGREES IN THE SHADE. I WALKED FOR FIVE DAYS WITH NO WATER. THEN I SAW IT; A PRETTY POND...
...I BENT DOWN TO TAKE A DRINK, WHEN THESE CROCS LAUNCHED OUTTA THE WATER.
ONE CROC BIT ME ON THE FACE. AIN'T NO WAY I WASN'T IT'S SUPPER...EXCEPT FOR ONE THING.
I WASN'T READY FOR DYIN' THAT DAY. I BIT ONE CROC IN HALF, TAIL WHIPPED THE OTHER... AND THE LAST ONE, WELL...

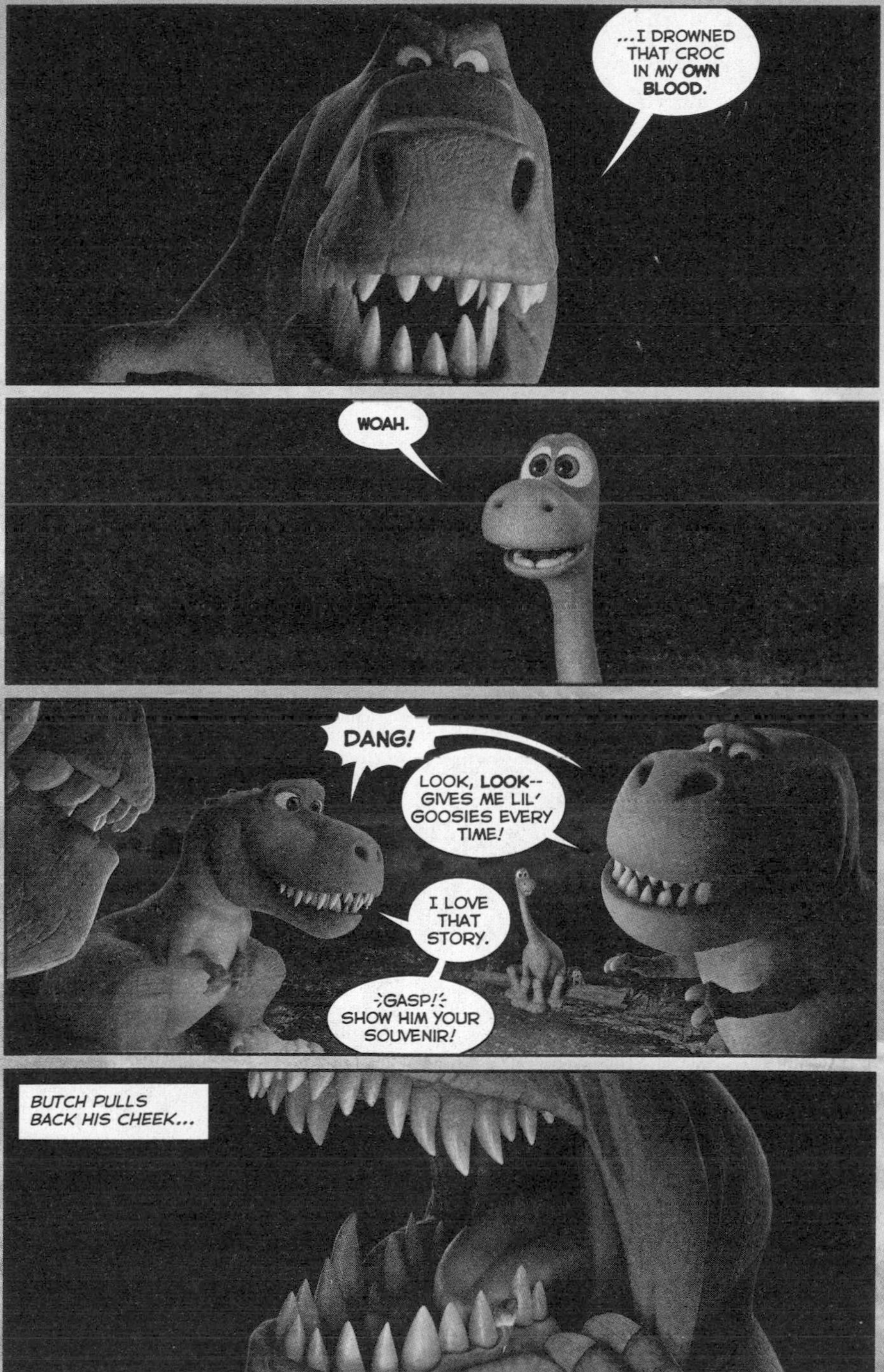
...I DROWNED THAT CROC IN MY **OWN** BLOOD.
WOAH.
DANG!
LOOK, **LOOK**-- GIVES ME LIL' GOOSIES EVERY TIME!
I LOVE THAT STORY.
GASP! SHOW HIM YOUR SOUVENIR!
BUTCH PULLS BACK HIS CHEEK...

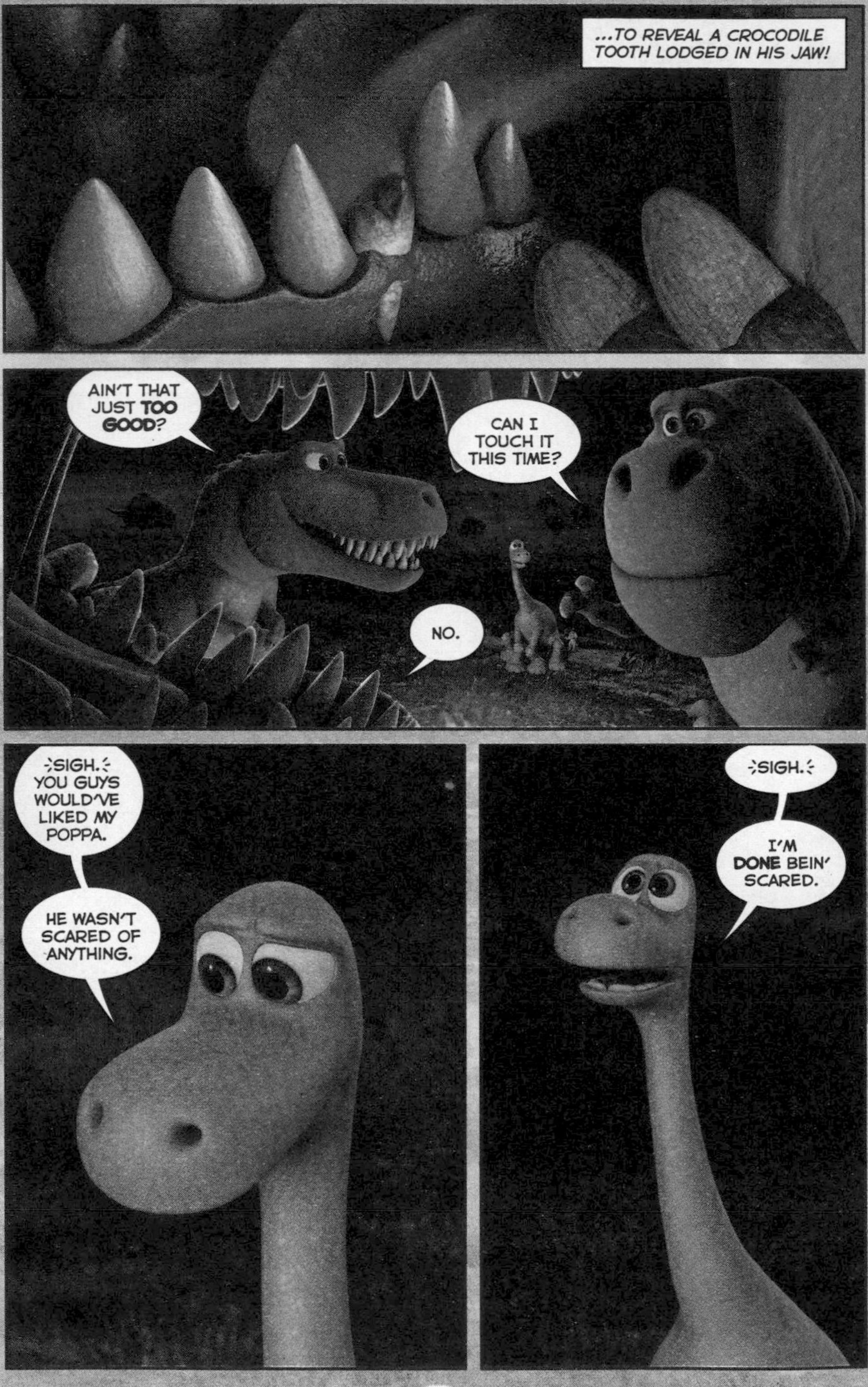
...TO REVEAL A CROCODILE TOOTH LODGED IN HIS JAW!
AIN'T THAT JUST **TOO GOOD**?
CAN I TOUCH IT THIS TIME?
NO.
SIGH.
YOU GUYS WOULD'VE LIKED MY POPPA.
HE WASN'T SCARED OF ANYTHING.
SIGH.
I'M **DONE** BEIN' SCARED.

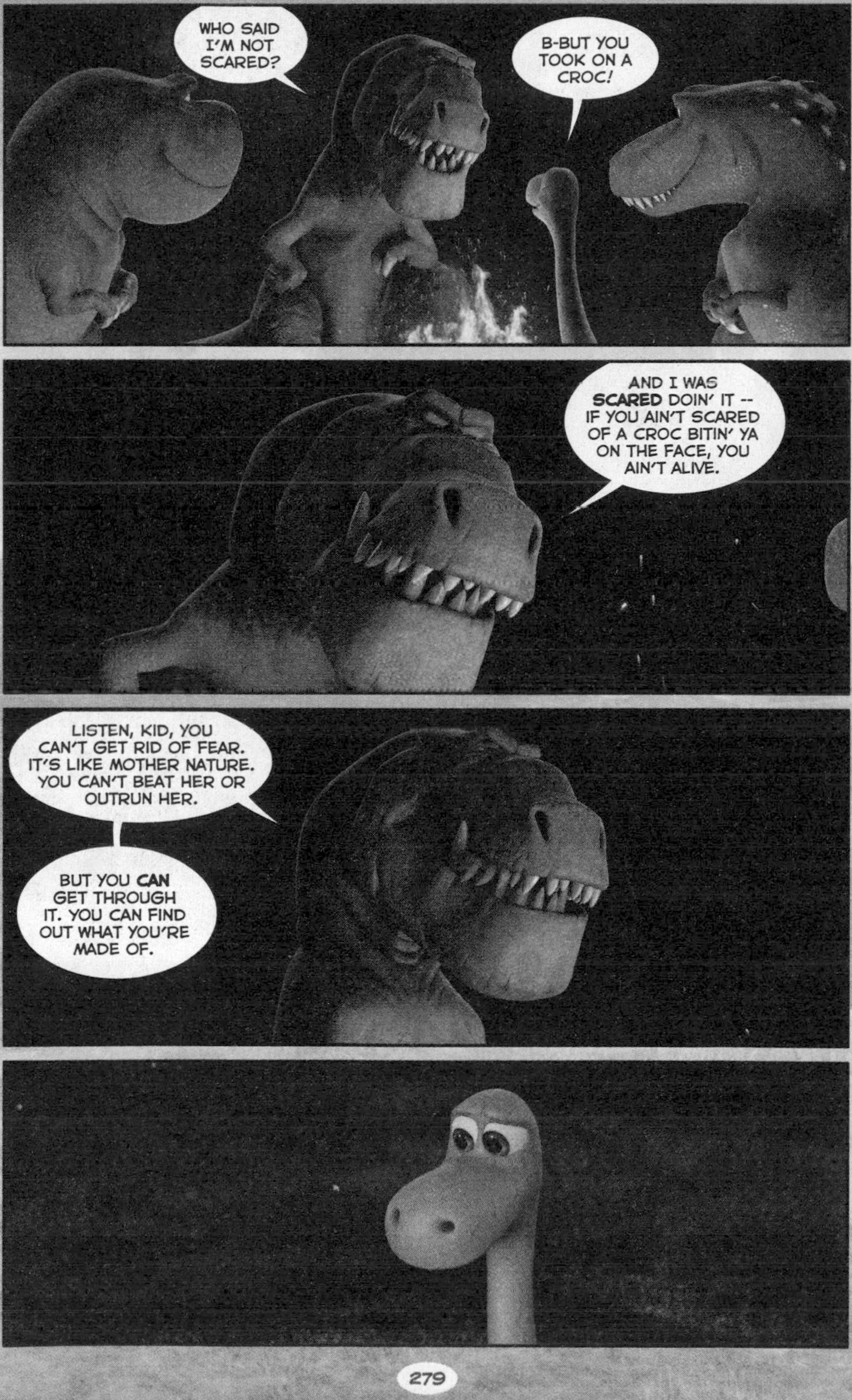
WHO SAID I'M NOT SCARED?
B-BUT YOU TOOK ON A CROC!
AND I WAS **SCARED** DOIN' IT -- IF YOU AIN'T SCARED OF A CROC BITIN' YA ON THE FACE, YOU AIN'T ALIVE.
LISTEN, KID, YOU CAN'T GET RID OF FEAR. IT'S LIKE MOTHER NATURE. YOU CAN'T BEAT HER OR OUTRUN HER.
BUT YOU **CAN** GET THROUGH IT. YOU CAN FIND OUT WHAT YOU'RE MADE OF.

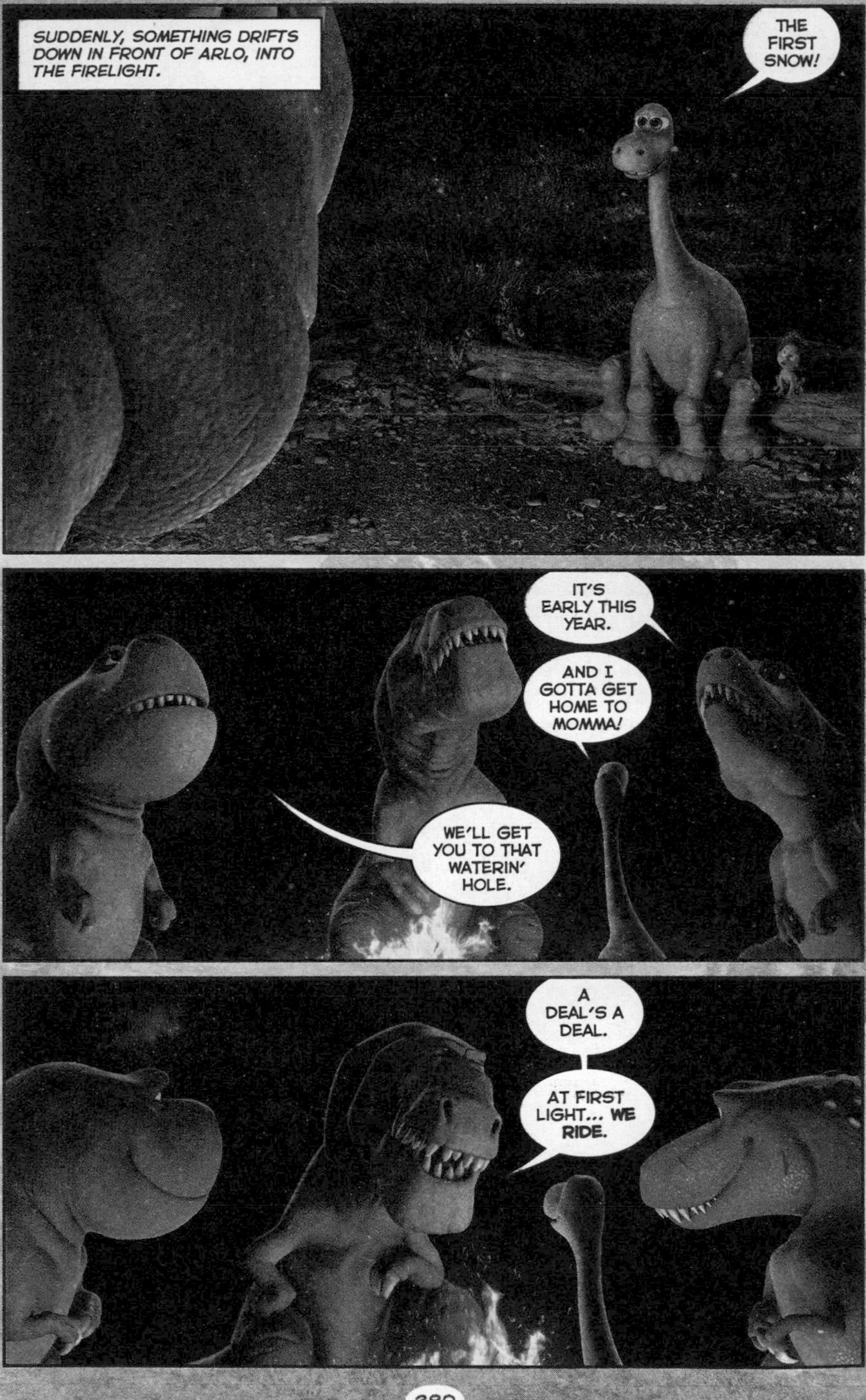
SUDDENLY, SOMETHING DRIFTS DOWN IN FRONT OF ARLO, INTO THE FIRELIGHT.
THE FIRST SNOW!
IT'S EARLY THIS YEAR.
AND I GOTTA GET HOME TO MOMMA!
WE'LL GET YOU TO THAT WATERIN' HOLE.
A DEAL'S A DEAL.
AT FIRST LIGHT... WE RIDE.

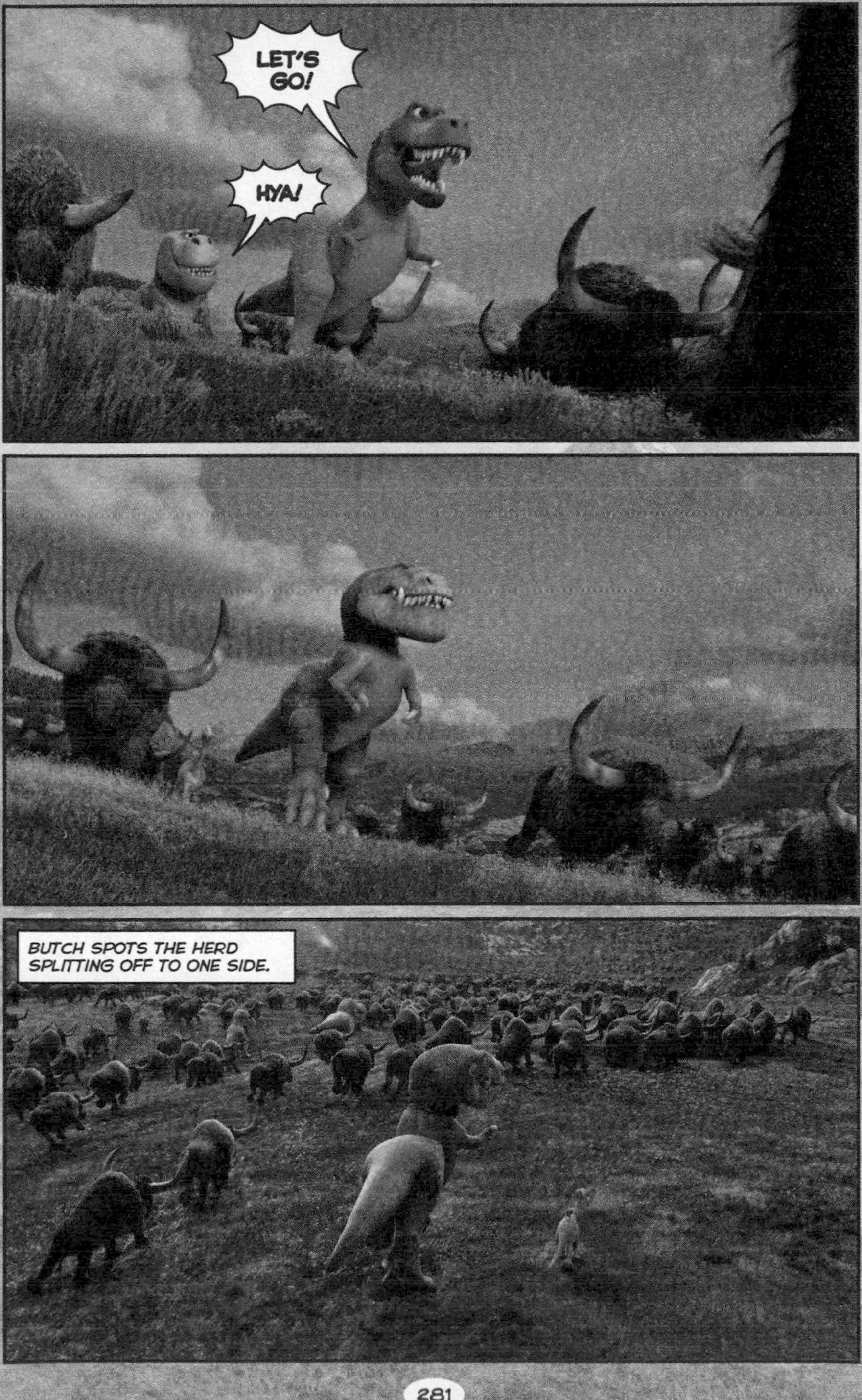
LET'S GO!
HYA!
BUTCH SPOTS THE HERD SPLITTING OFF TO ONE SIDE.

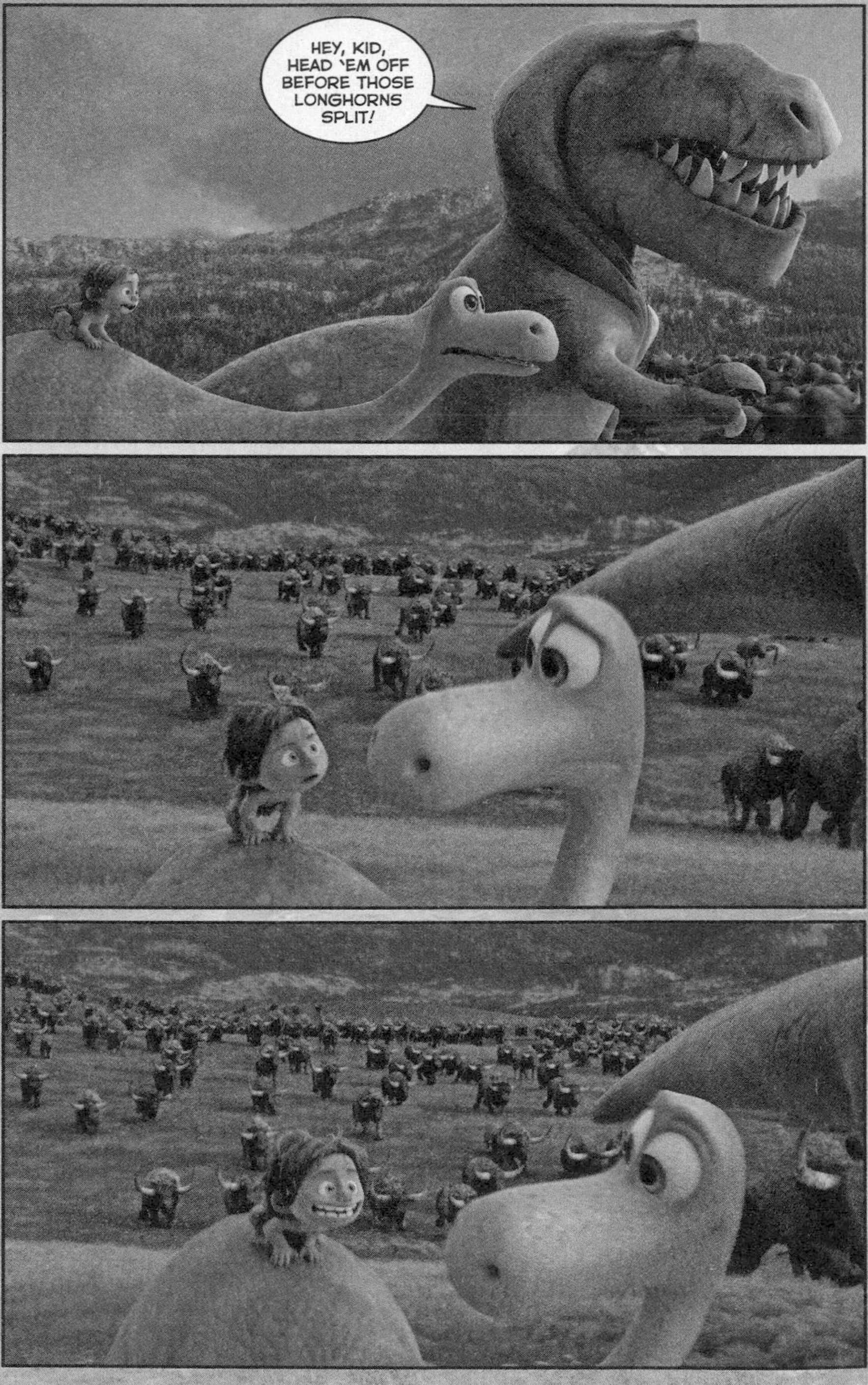
HEY, KID, HEAD 'EM OFF BEFORE THOSE LONGHORNS SPLIT!

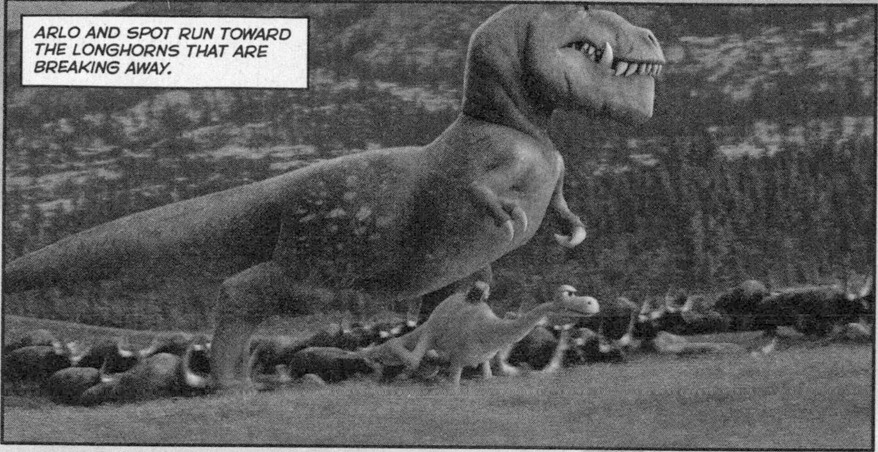
ARLO AND SPOT RUN TOWARD THE LONGHORNS THAT ARE BREAKING AWAY.

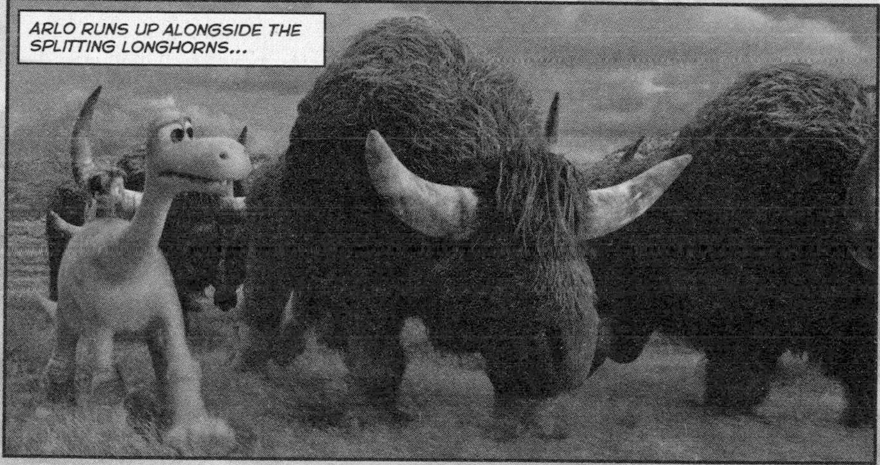
ARLO RUNS UP ALONGSIDE THE SPLITTING LONGHORNS...

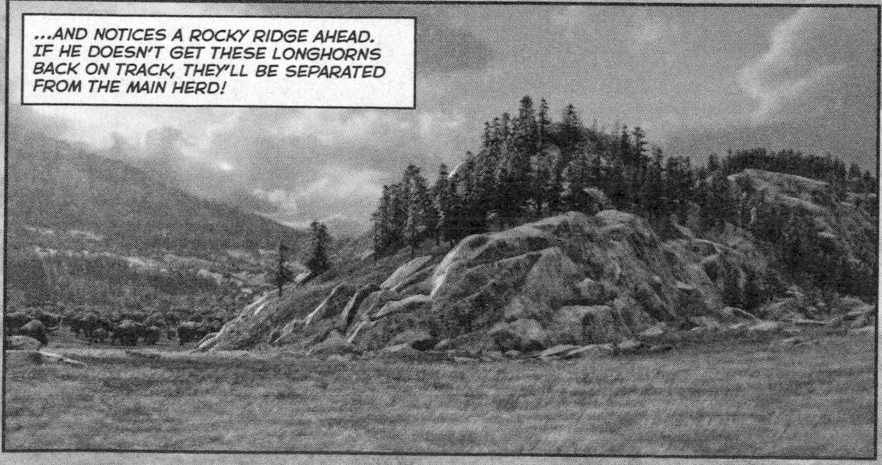
...AND NOTICES A ROCKY RIDGE AHEAD. IF HE DOESN'T GET THESE LONGHORNS BACK ON TRACK, THEY'LL BE SEPARATED FROM THE MAIN HERD!

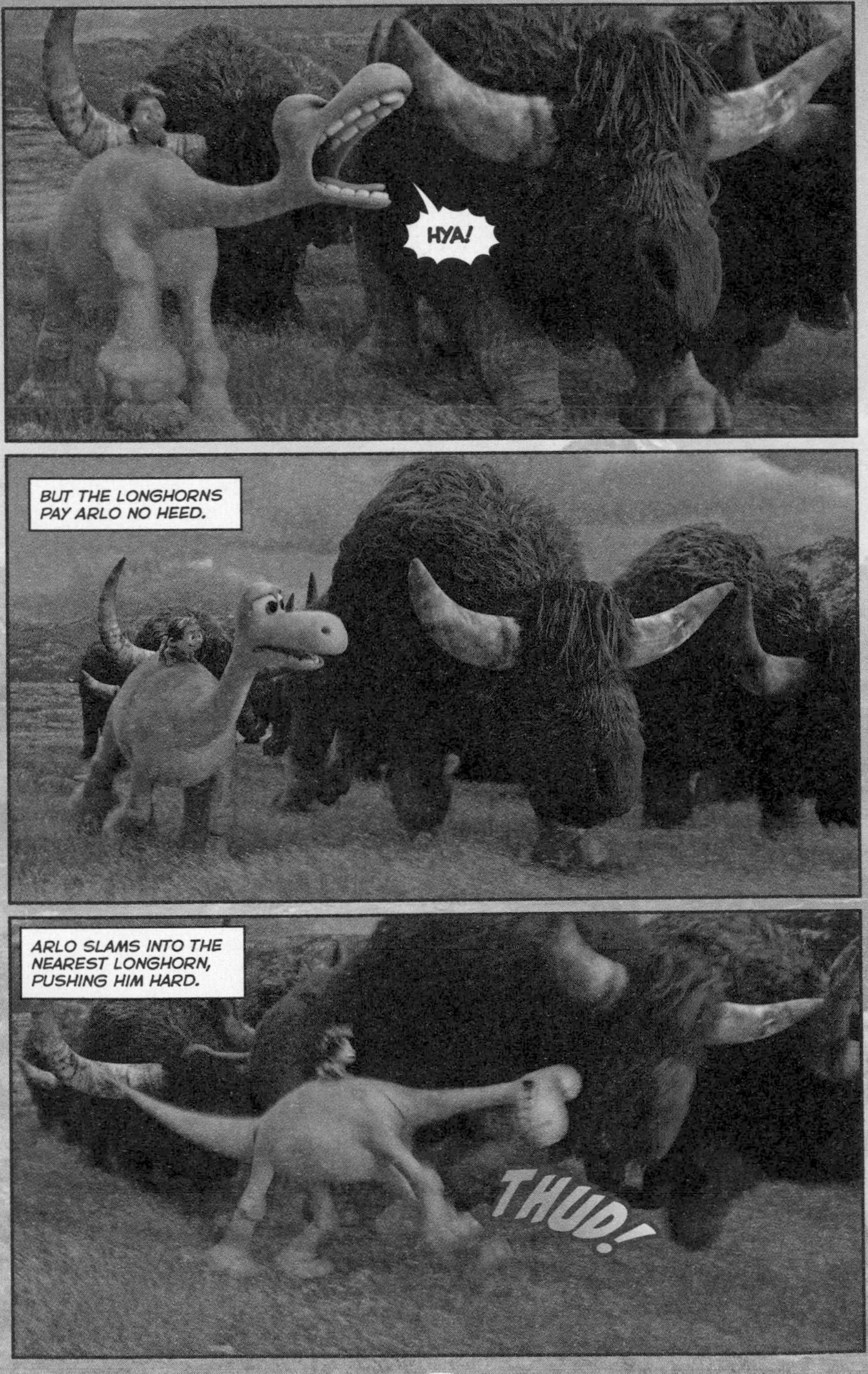
HYA!
BUT THE LONGHORNS PAY ARLO NO HEED.
ARLO SLAMS INTO THE NEAREST LONGHORN, PUSHING HIM HARD.
THUD!

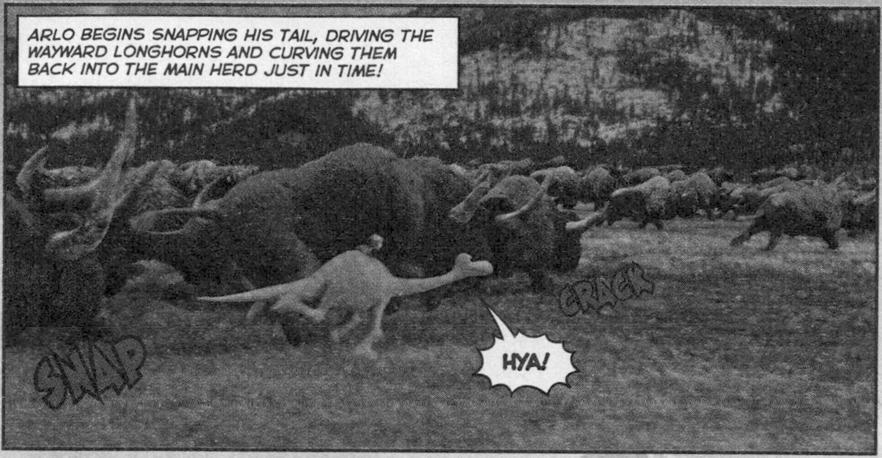
ARLO BEGINS SNAPPING HIS TAIL, DRIVING THE WAYWARD LONGHORNS AND CURVING THEM BACK INTO THE MAIN HERD JUST IN TIME!
SNAP
HYA!
CRACK

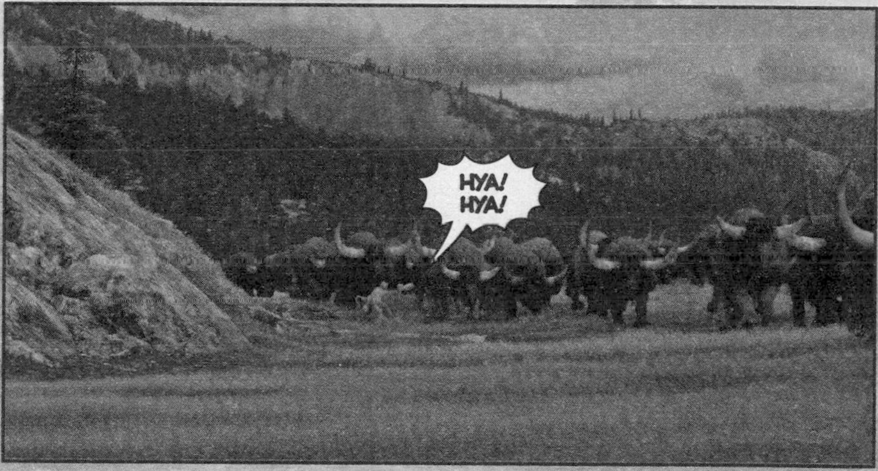
HYA!
HYA!

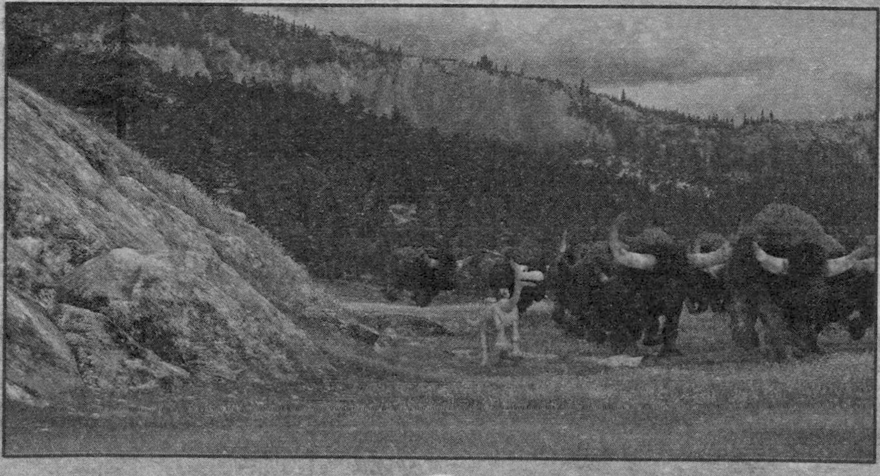

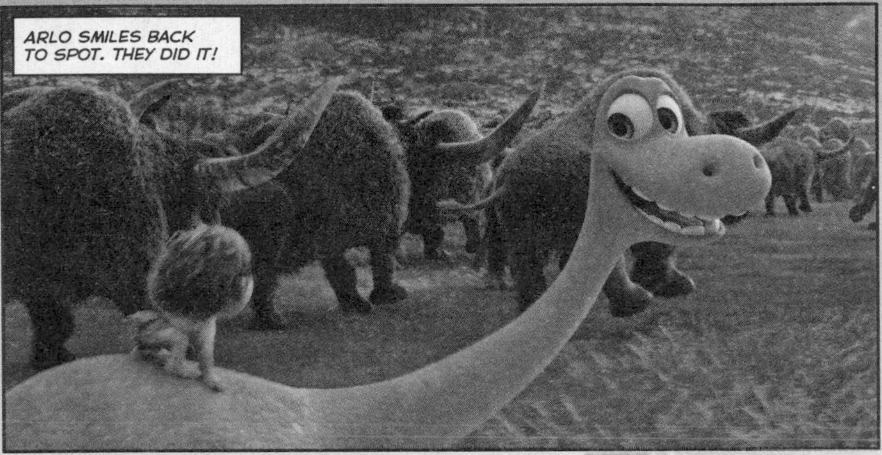
ARLO SMILES BACK TO SPOT. THEY DID IT!

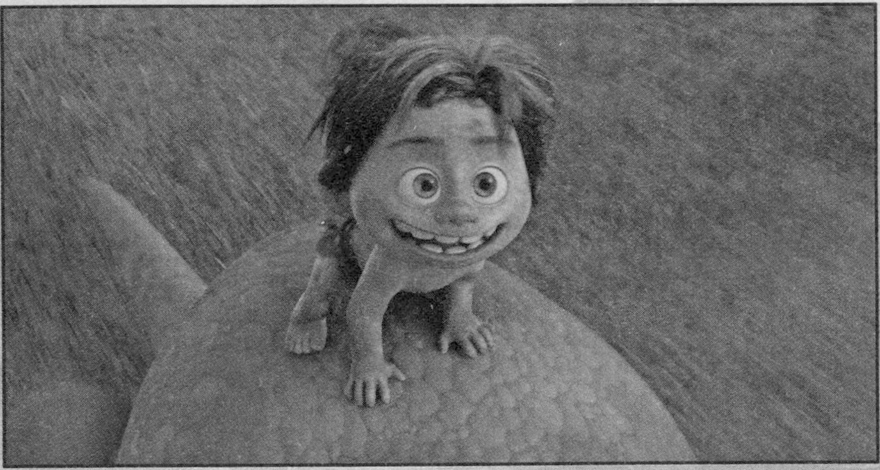

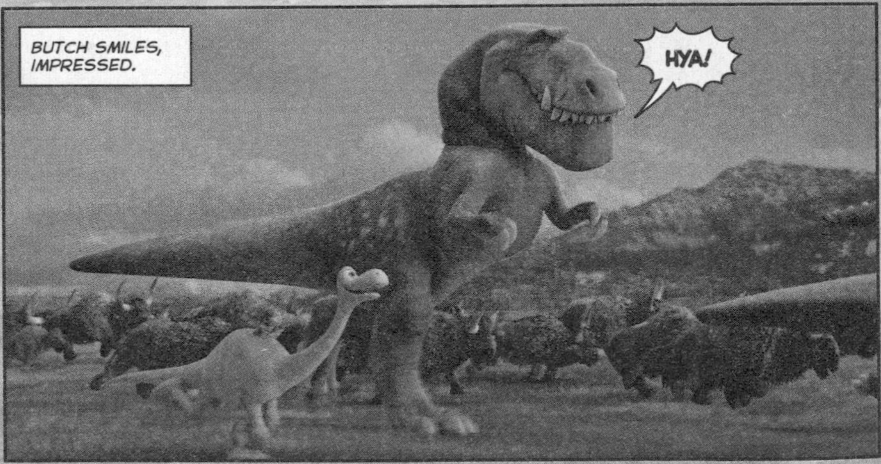
BUTCH SMILES, IMPRESSED.
HYA!

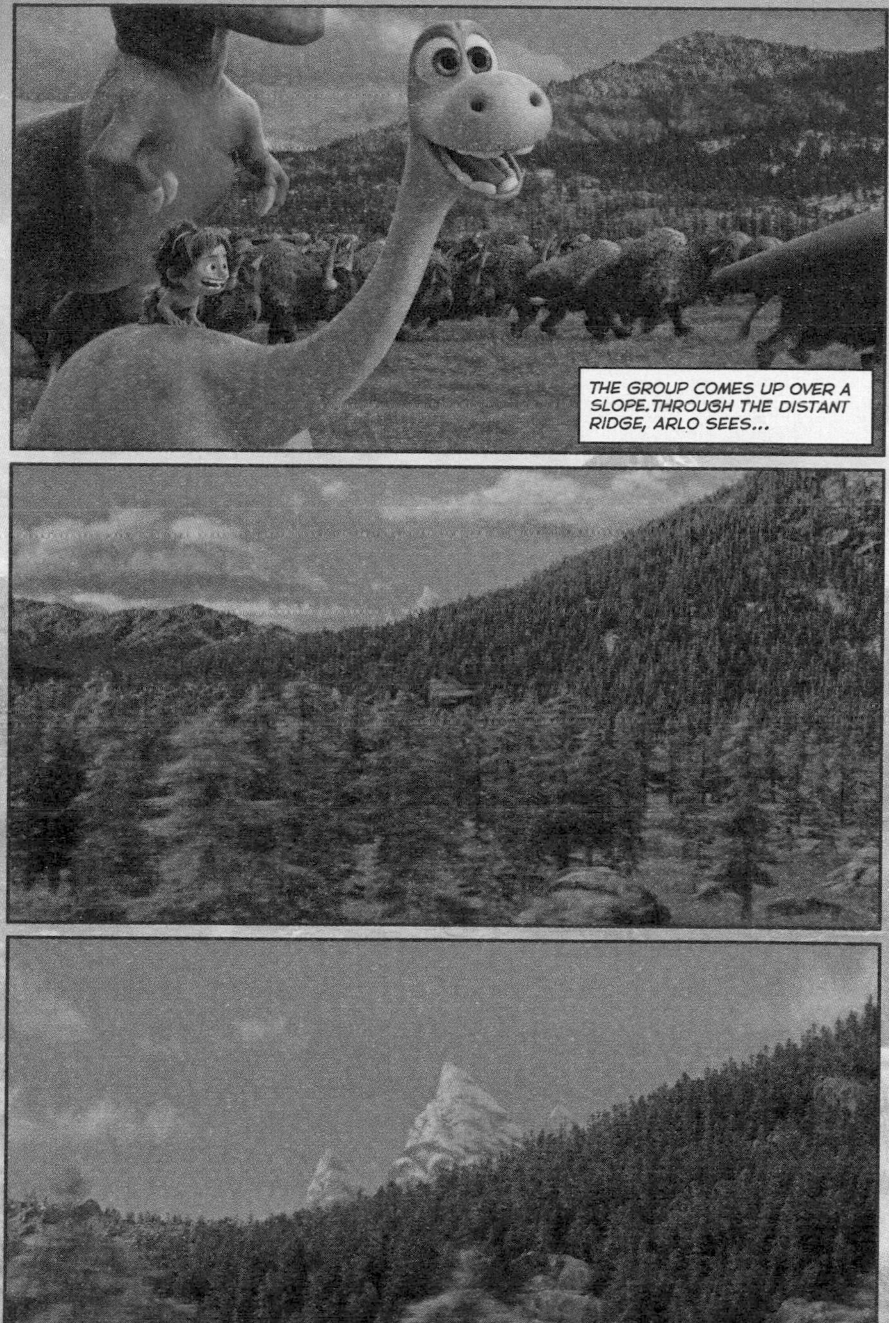
THE GROUP COMES UP OVER A SLOPE. THROUGH THE DISTANT RIDGE, ARLO SEES...

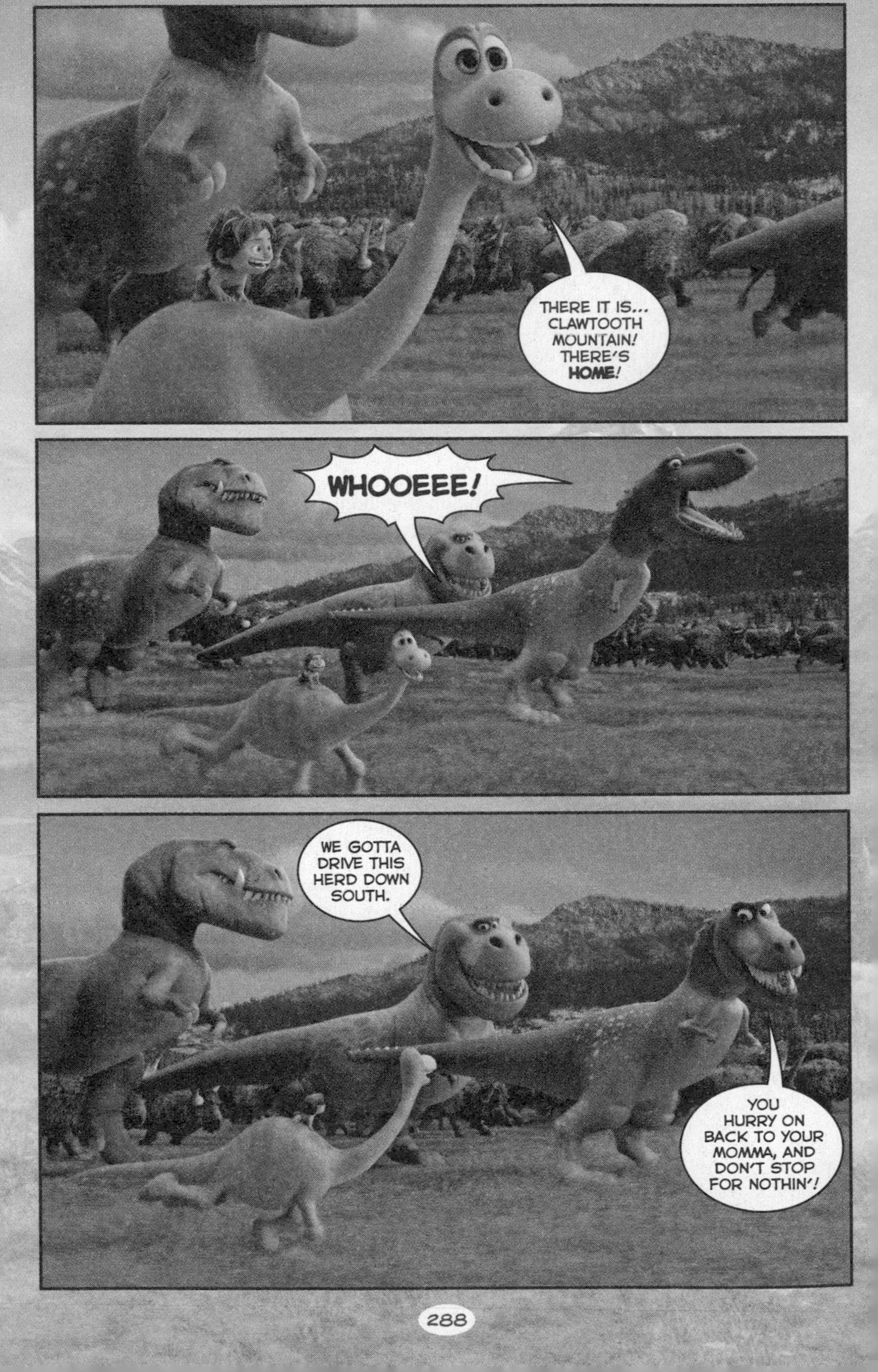
THERE IT IS... CLAWTOOTH MOUNTAIN! THERE'S **HOME**!
WHOOEEE!
WE GOTTA DRIVE THIS HERD DOWN SOUTH.
YOU HURRY ON BACK TO YOUR MOMMA, AND DON'T STOP FOR NOTHIN'!

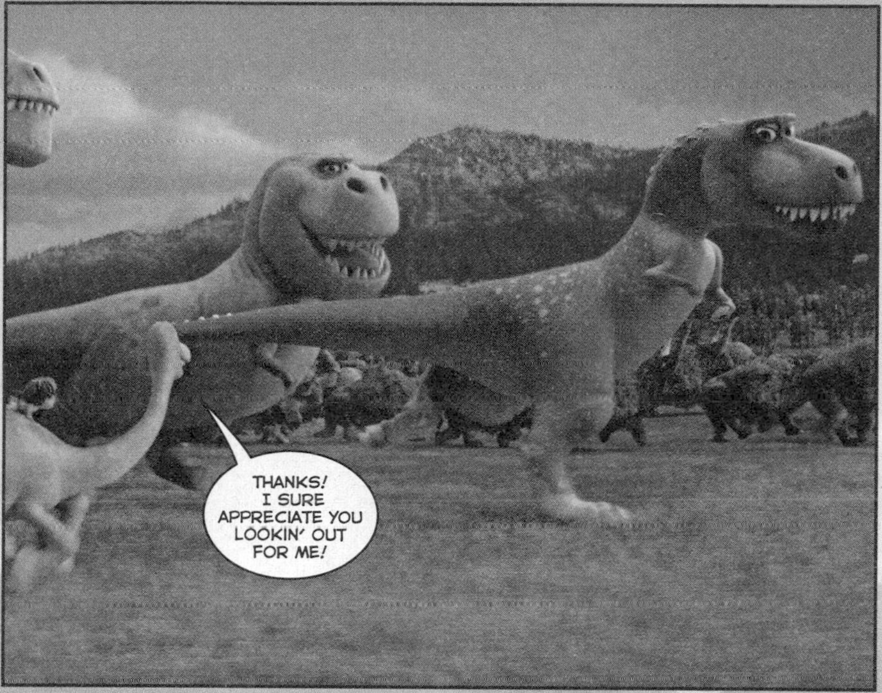
THANKS! I SURE APPRECIATE YOU LOOKIN' OUT FOR ME!

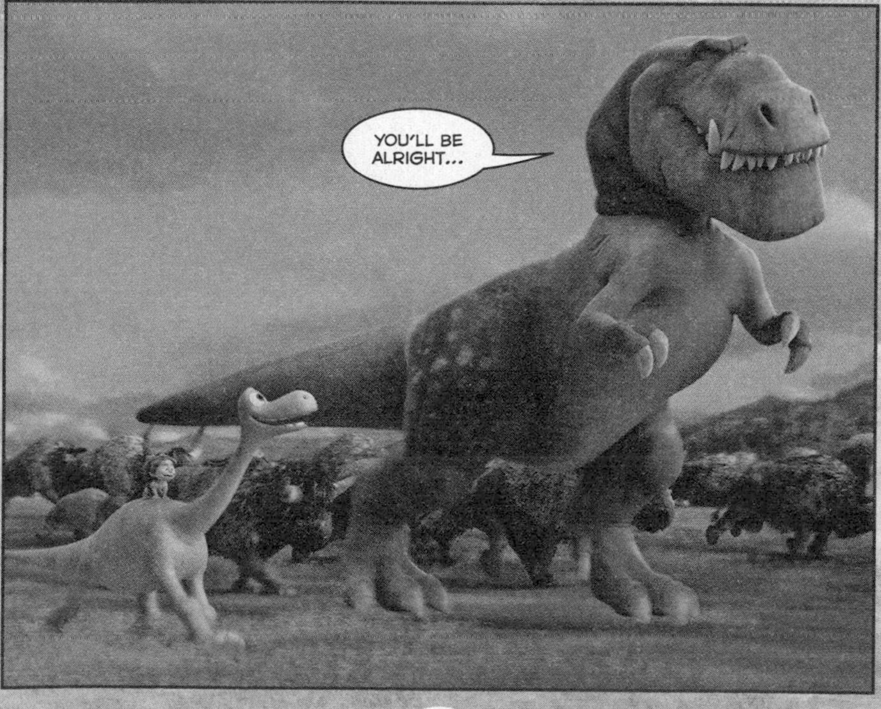
YOU'LL BE ALRIGHT...

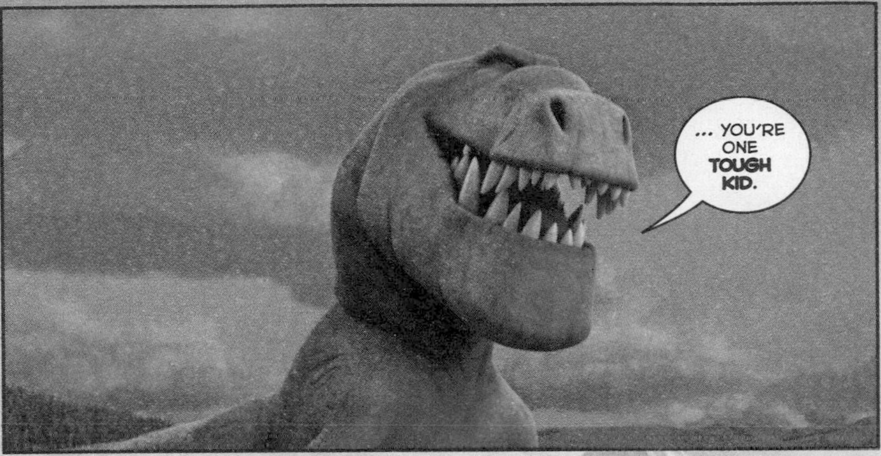
... YOU'RE ONE **TOUGH** KID.

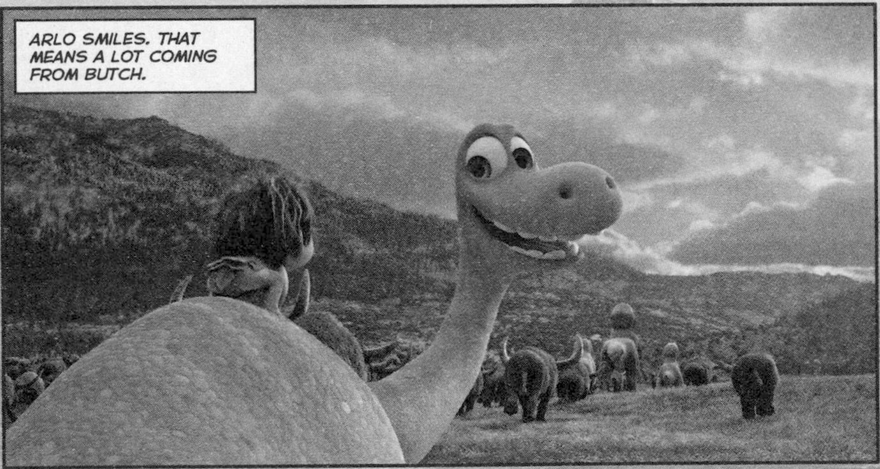
ARLO SMILES. THAT MEANS A LOT COMING FROM BUTCH.

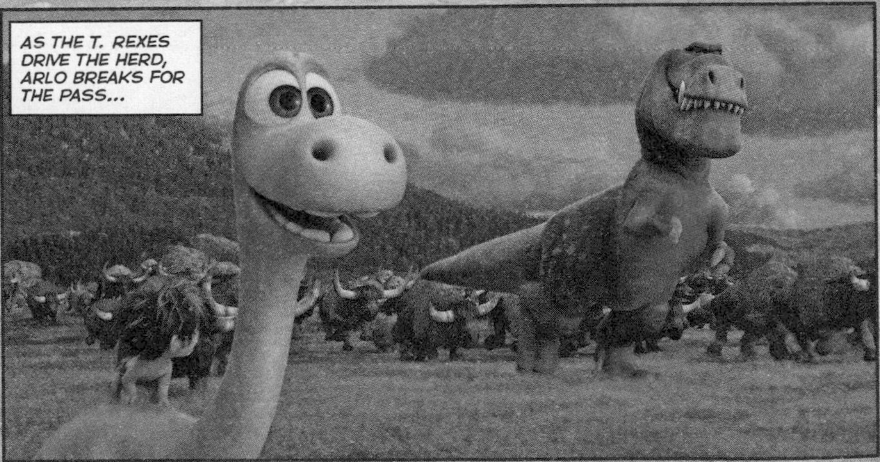
AS THE T. REXES DRIVE THE HERD, ARLO BREAKS FOR THE PASS...

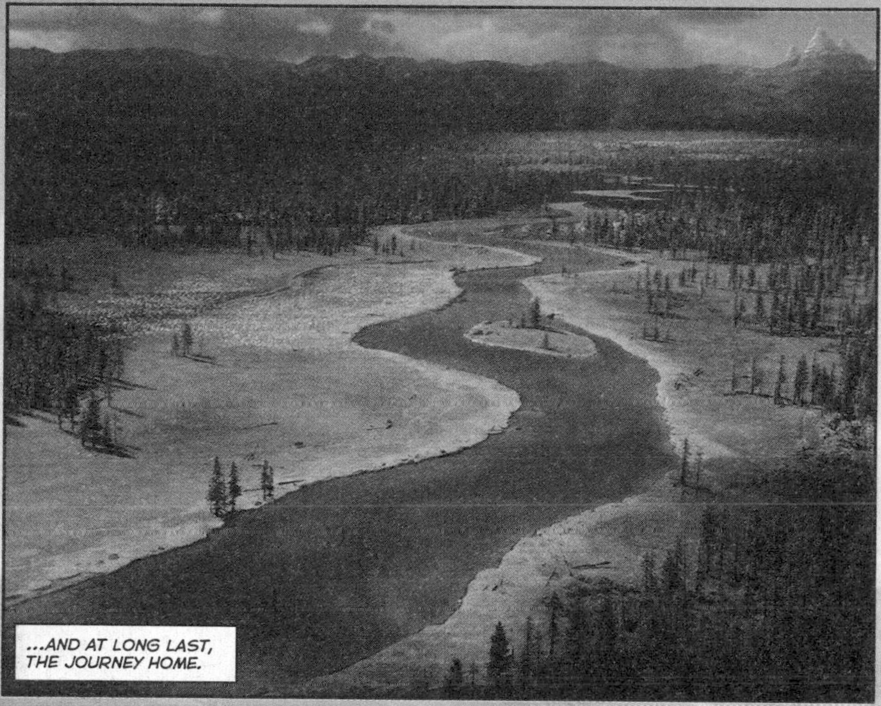
...AND AT LONG LAST,
THE JOURNEY HOME.

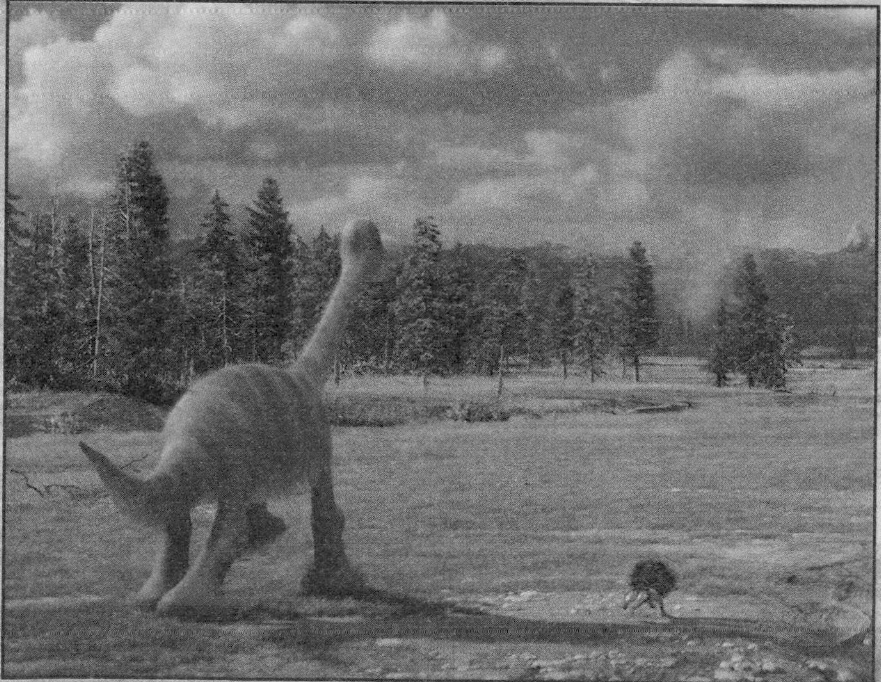

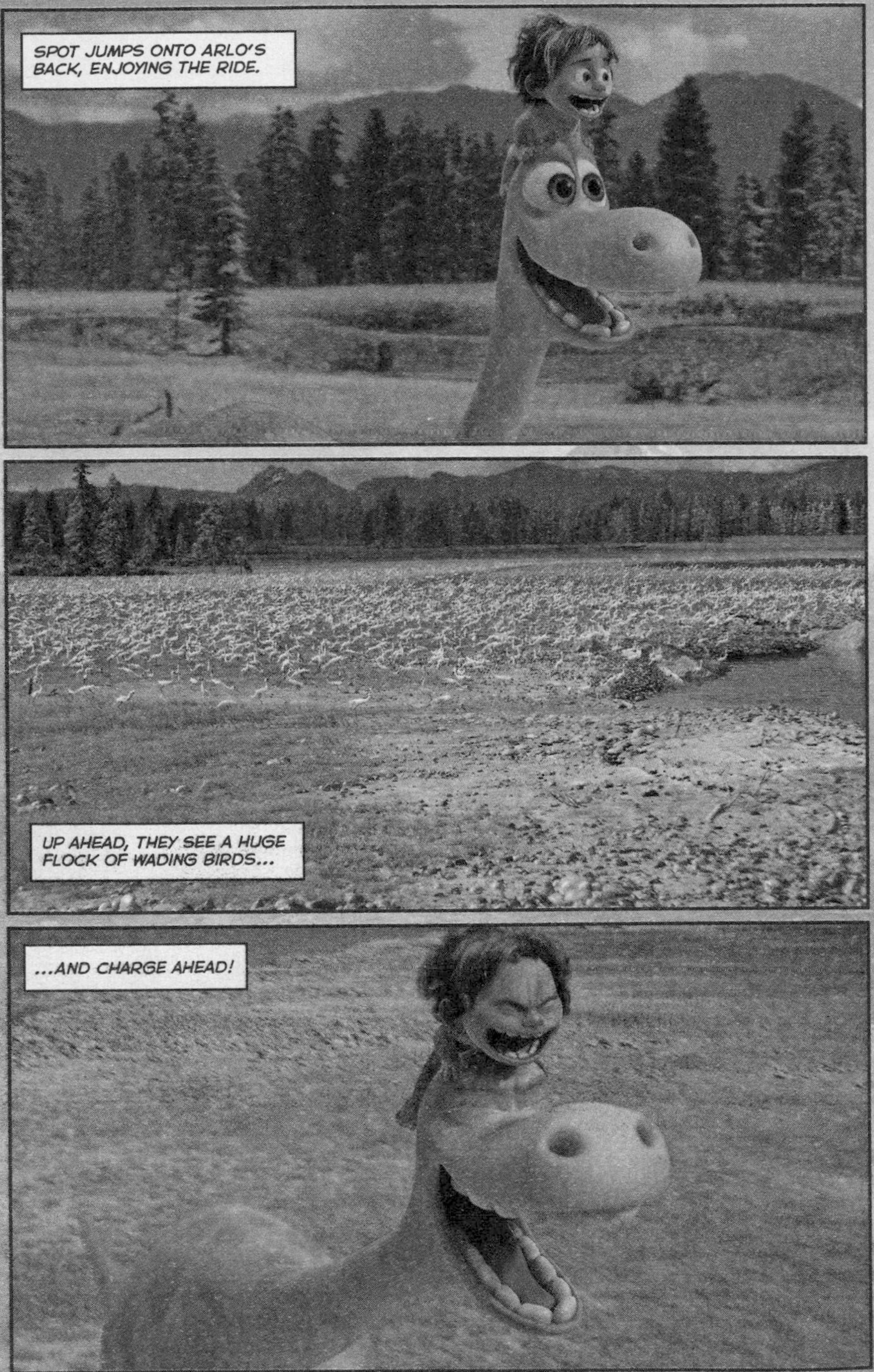
SPOT JUMPS ONTO ARLO'S BACK, ENJOYING THE RIDE.
UP AHEAD, THEY SEE A HUGE FLOCK OF WADING BIRDS...
...AND CHARGE AHEAD!

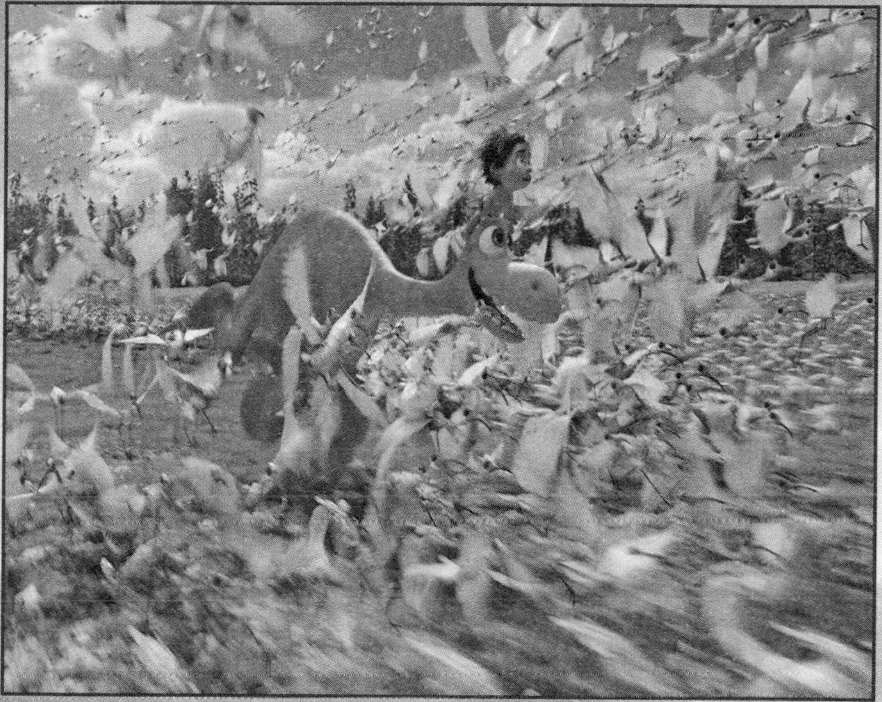

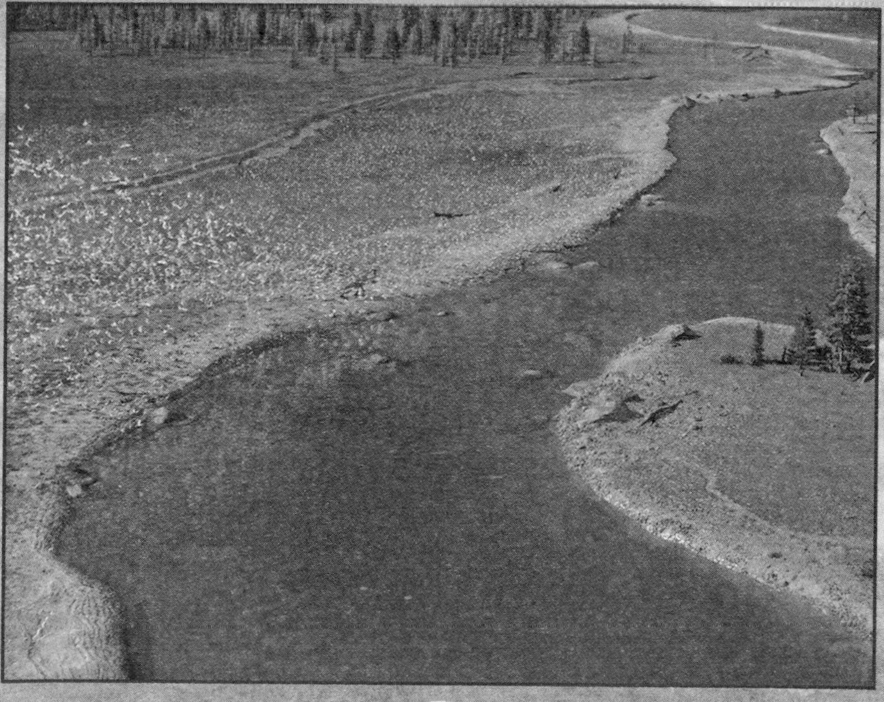

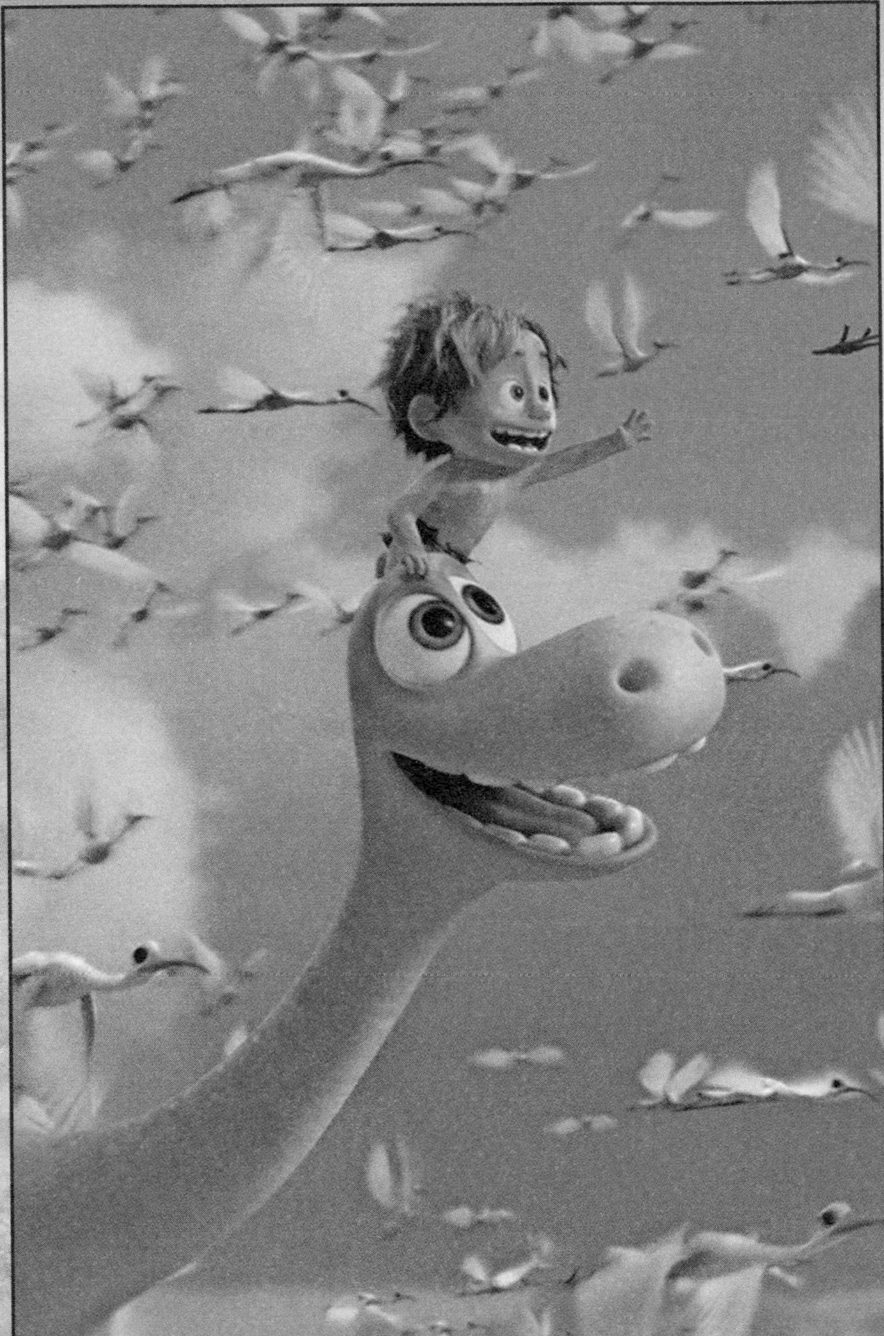

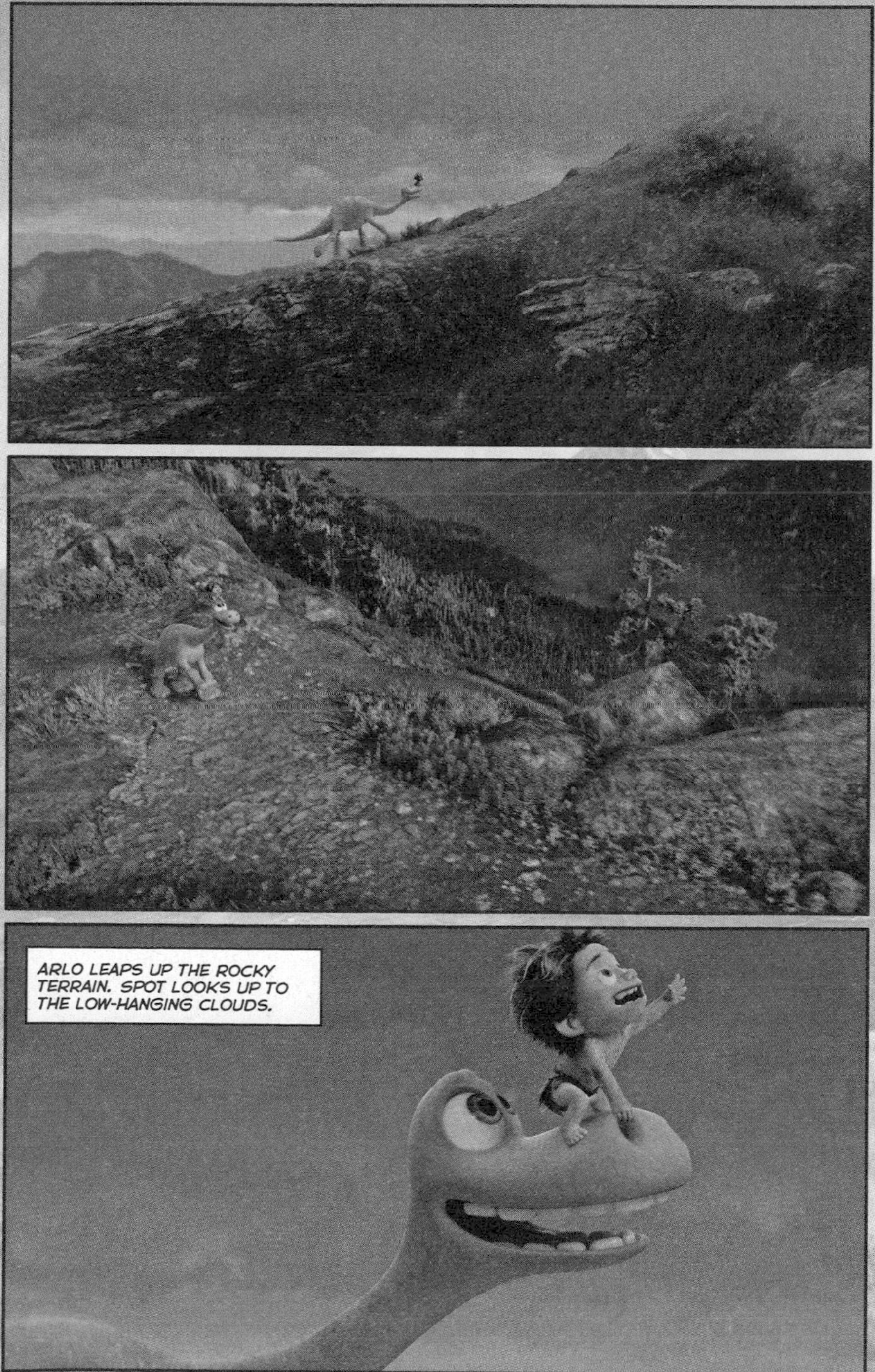
ARLO LEAPS UP THE ROCKY TERRAIN. SPOT LOOKS UP TO THE LOW-HANGING CLOUDS.

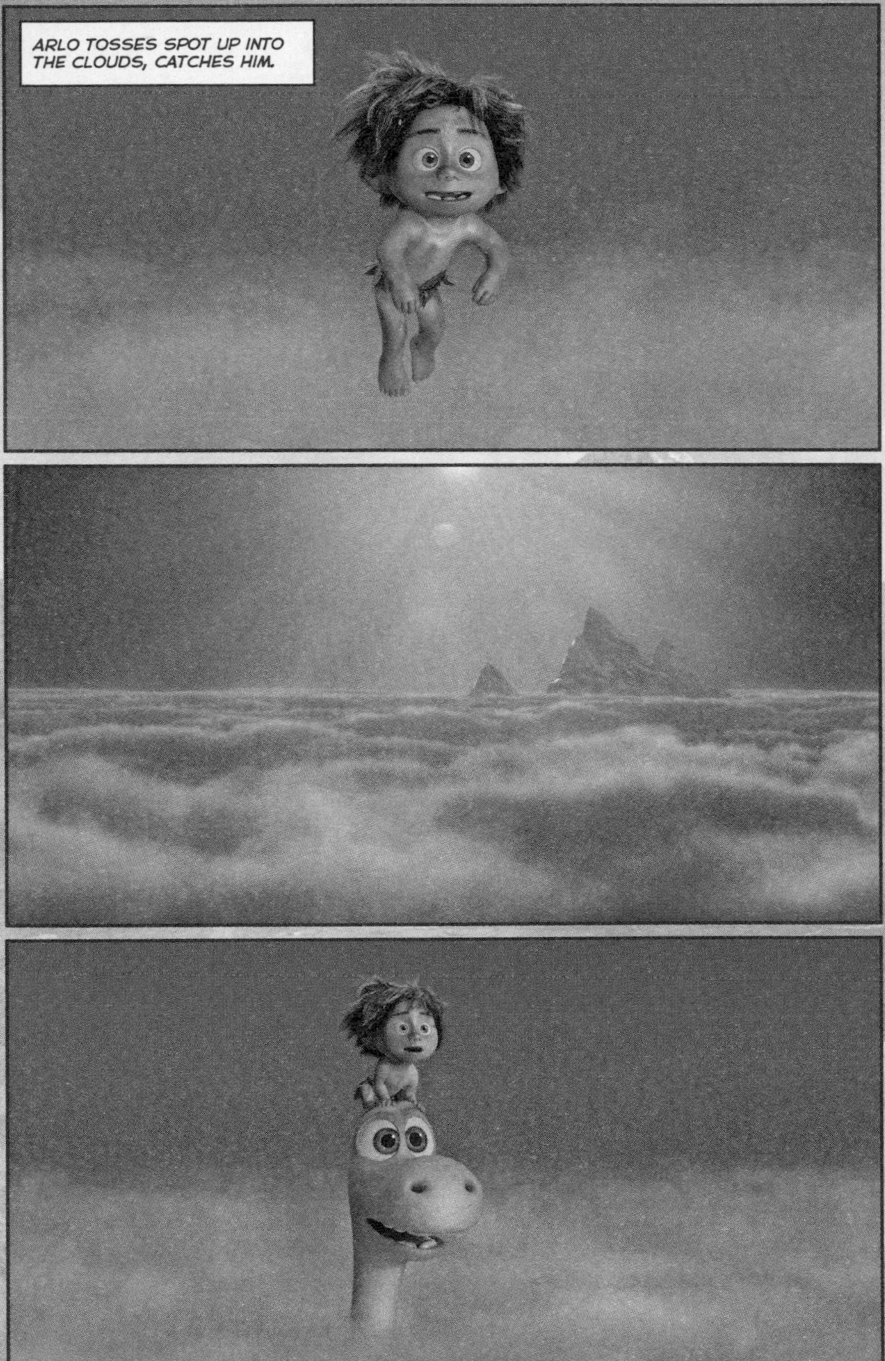
ARLO TOSSES SPOT UP INTO THE CLOUDS, CATCHES HIM.

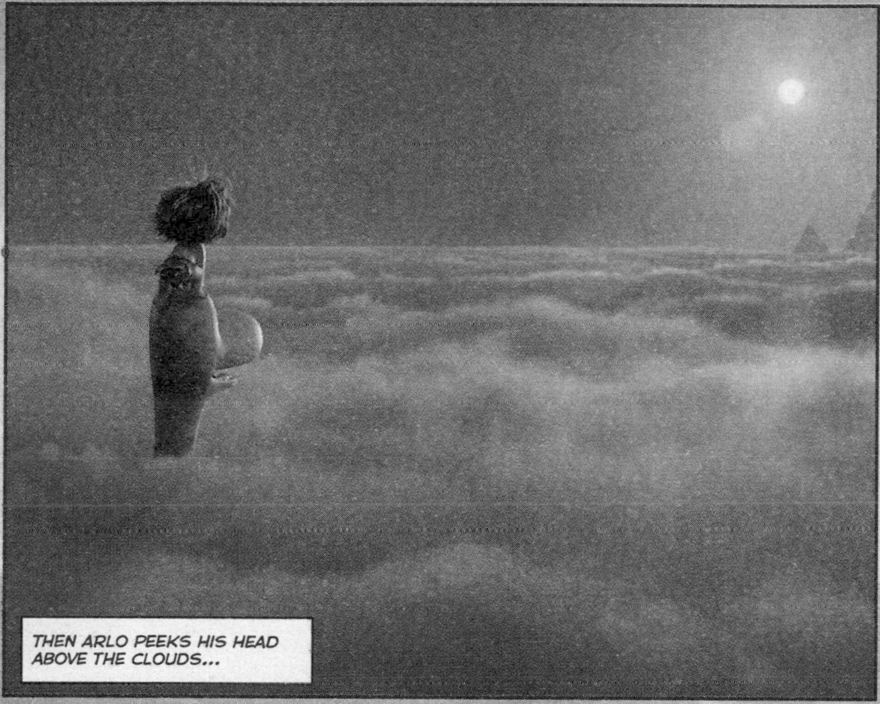
THEN ARLO PEEKS HIS HEAD ABOVE THE CLOUDS...

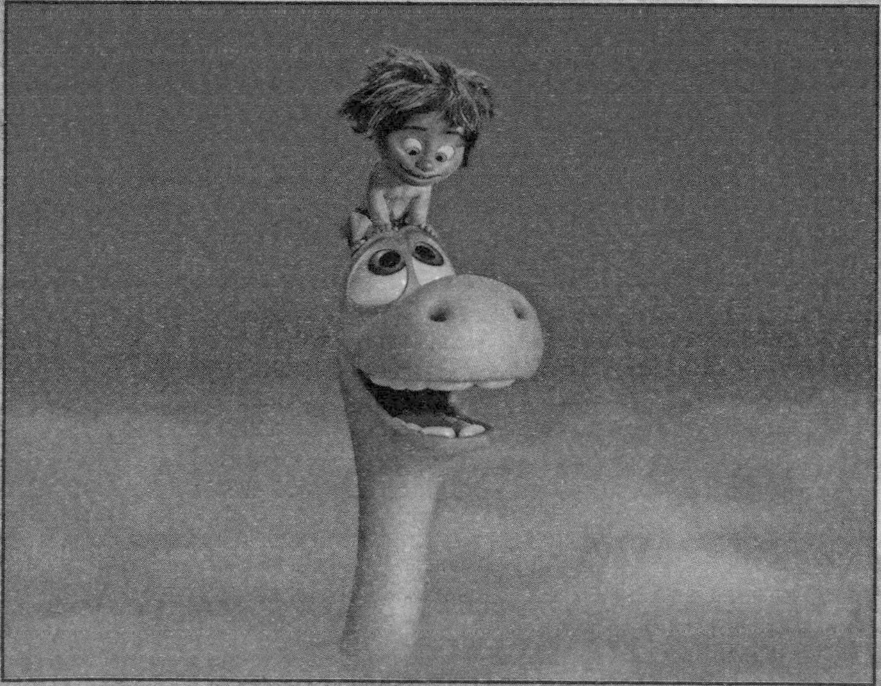

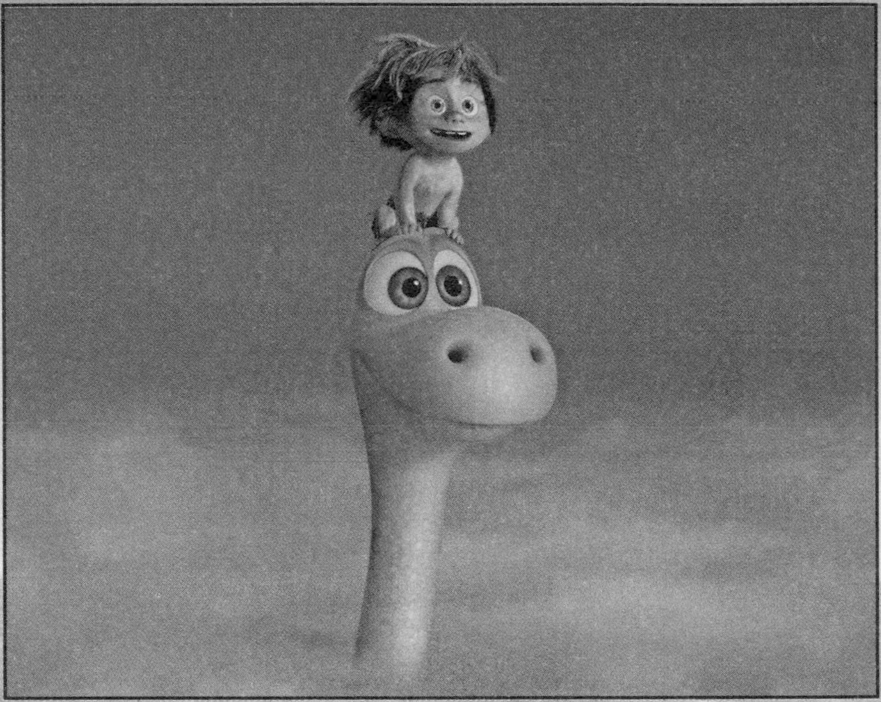

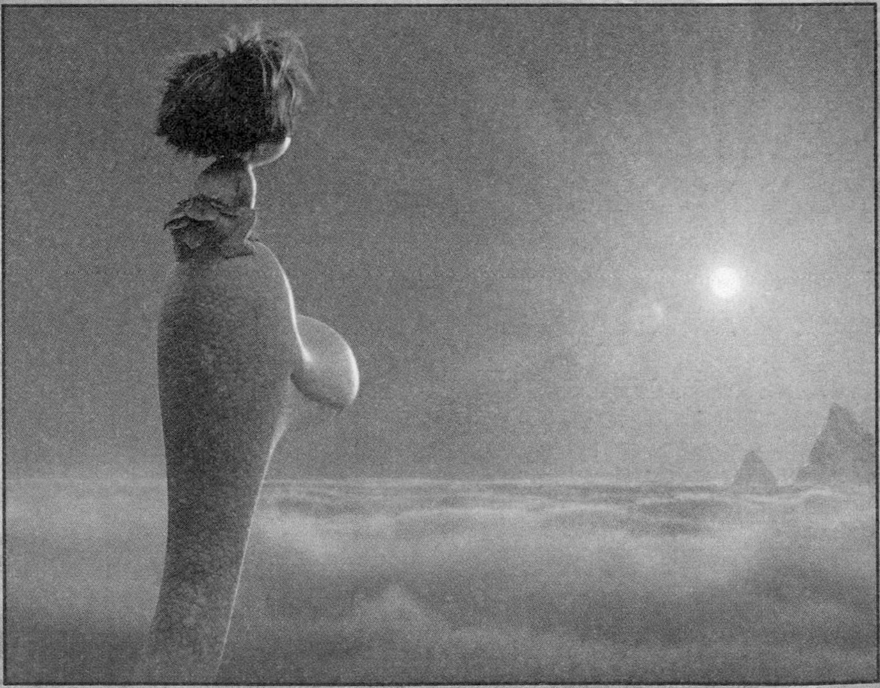

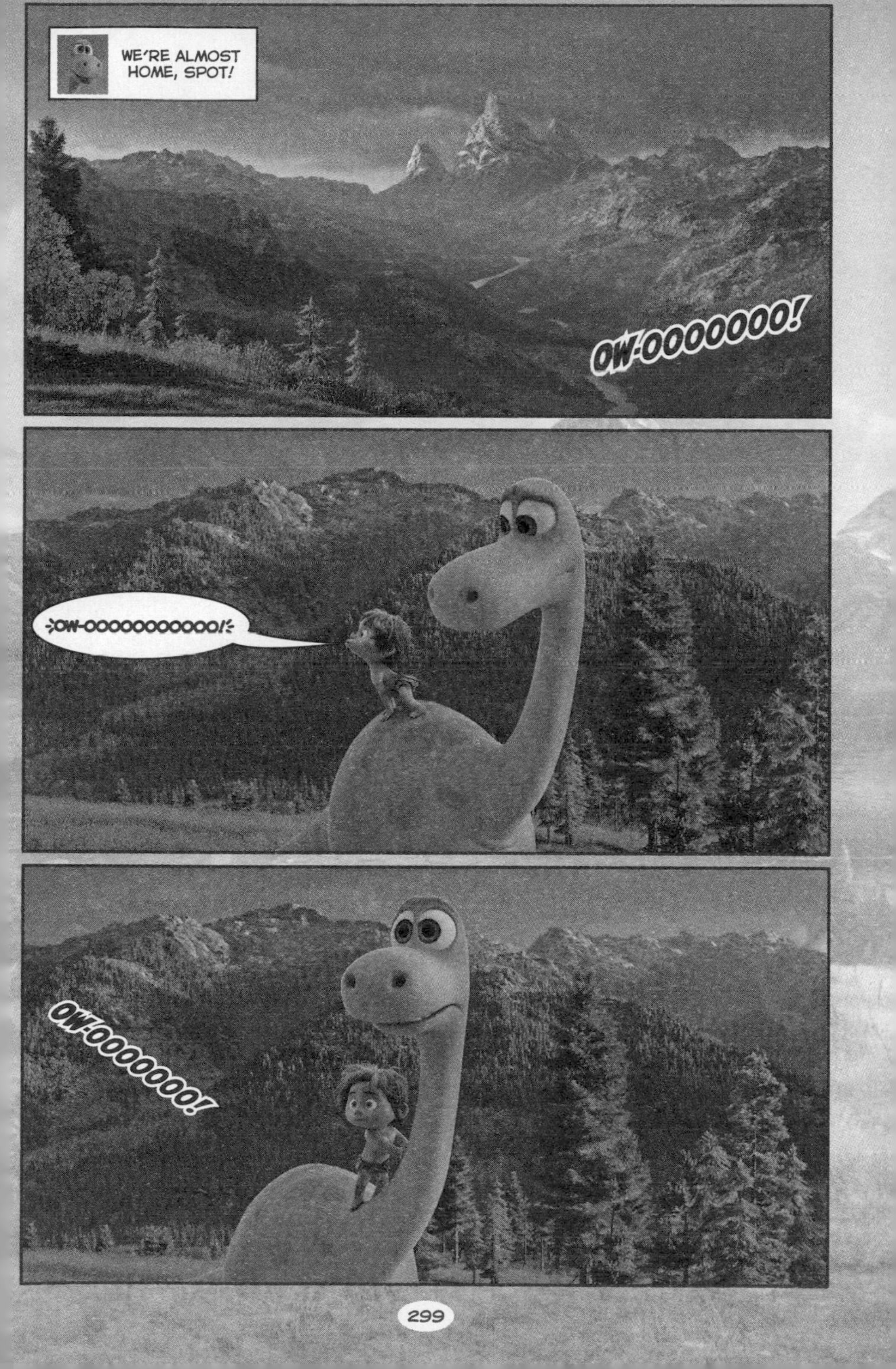
WE'RE ALMOST HOME, SPOT!
OW-OOOOOOO!
OW-OOOOOOOOOOO!
OW-OOOOOOO!

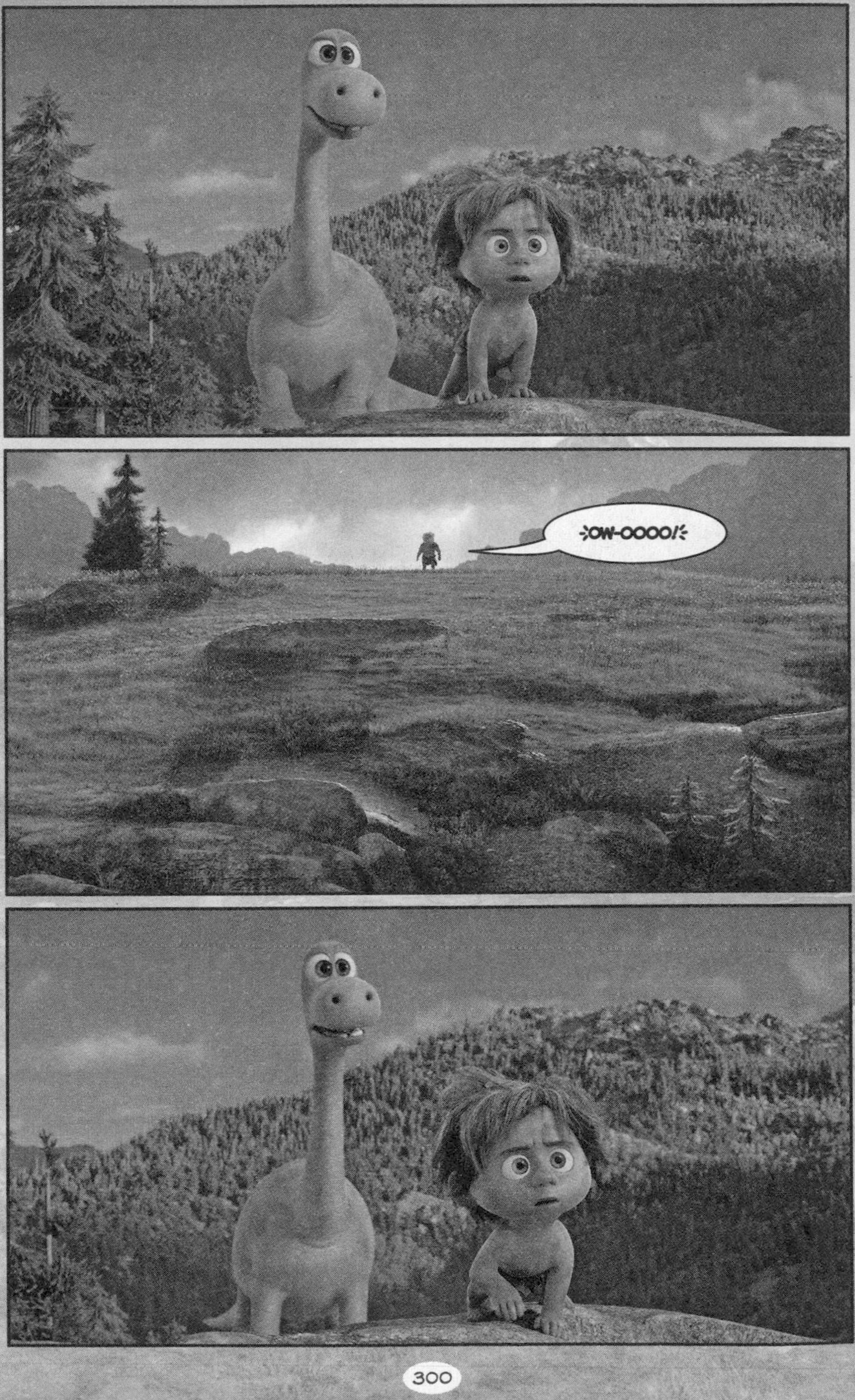
OW-OOOO!

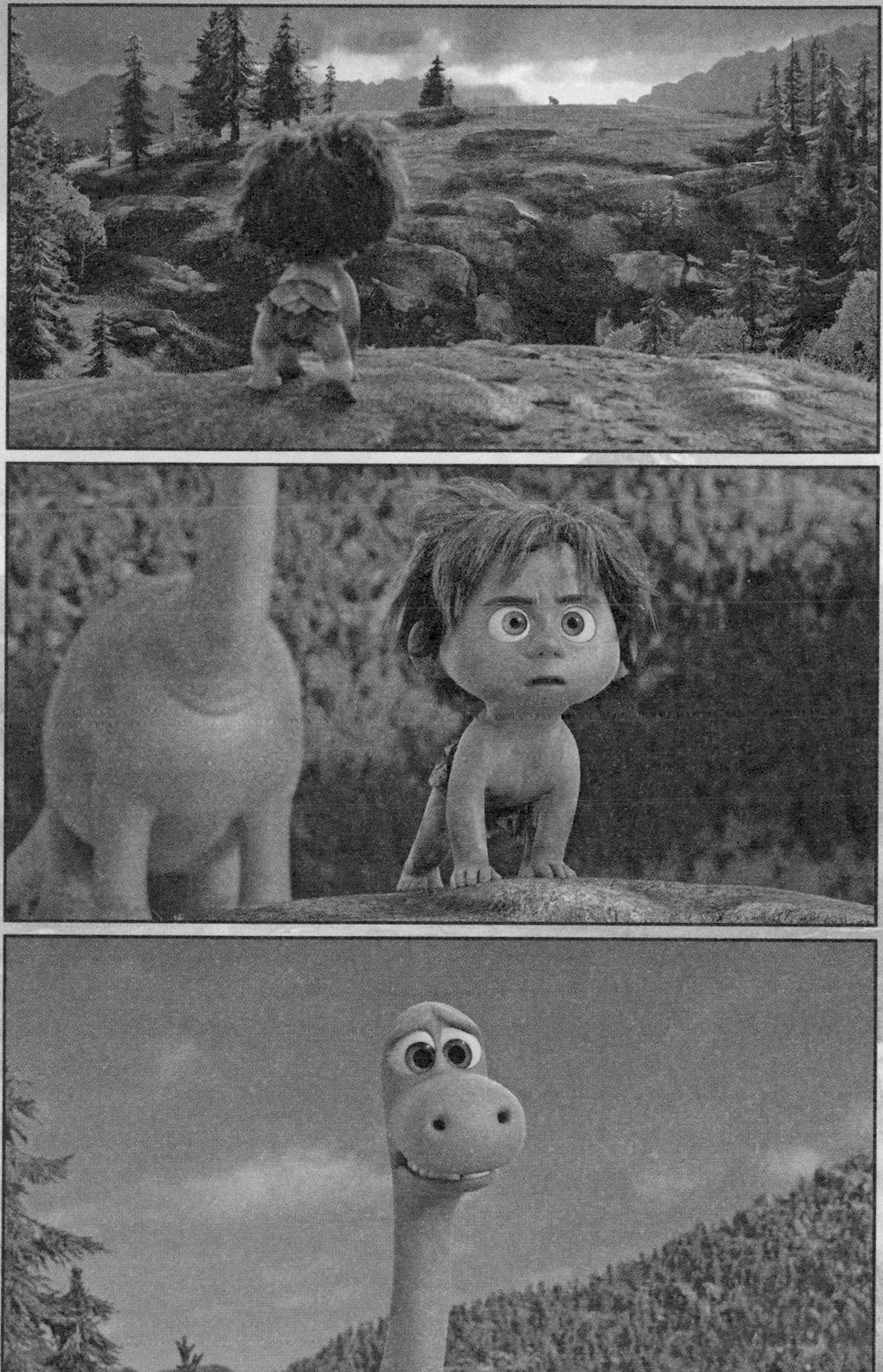

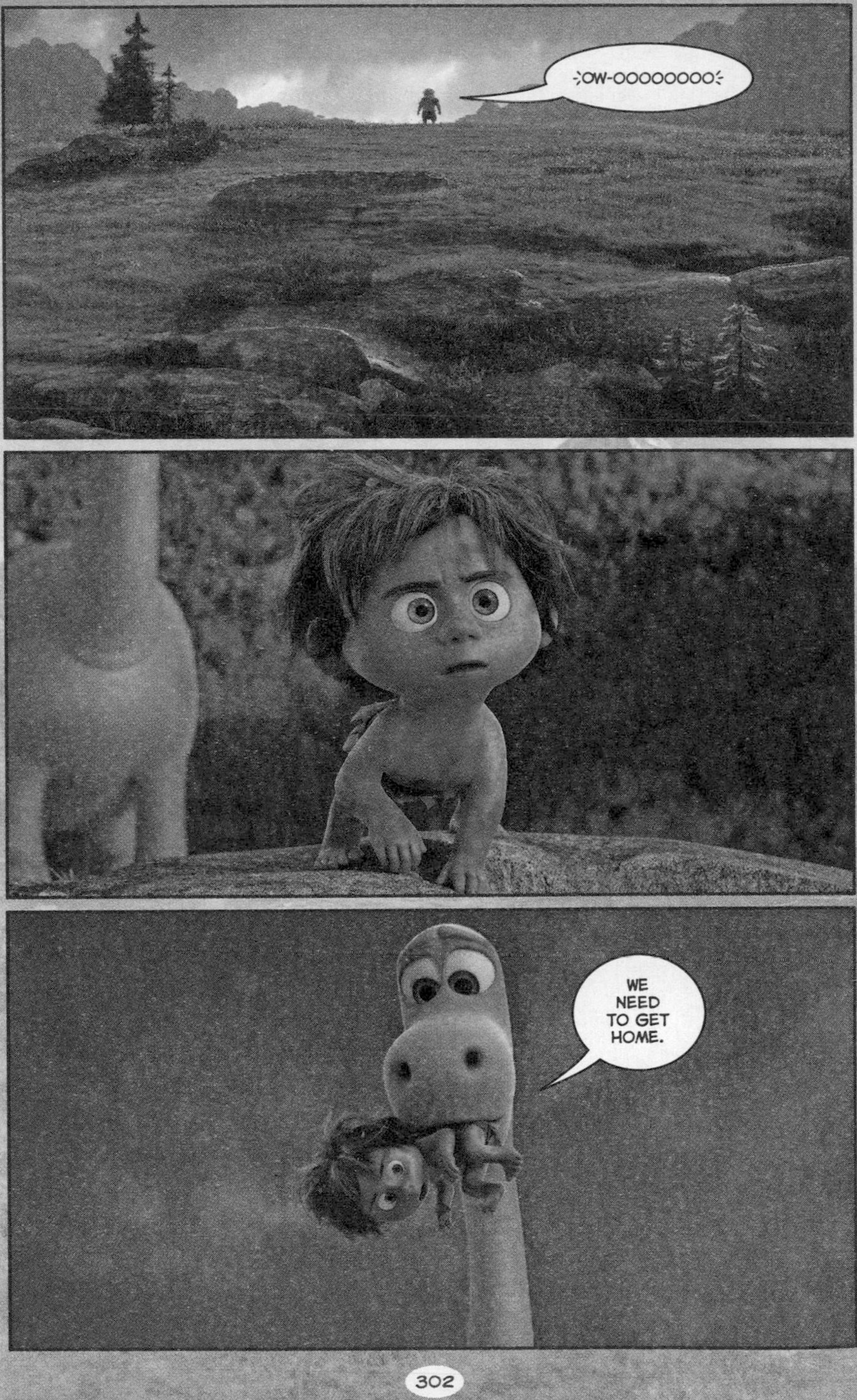
OW-OOOOOOOO
WE NEED TO GET HOME.

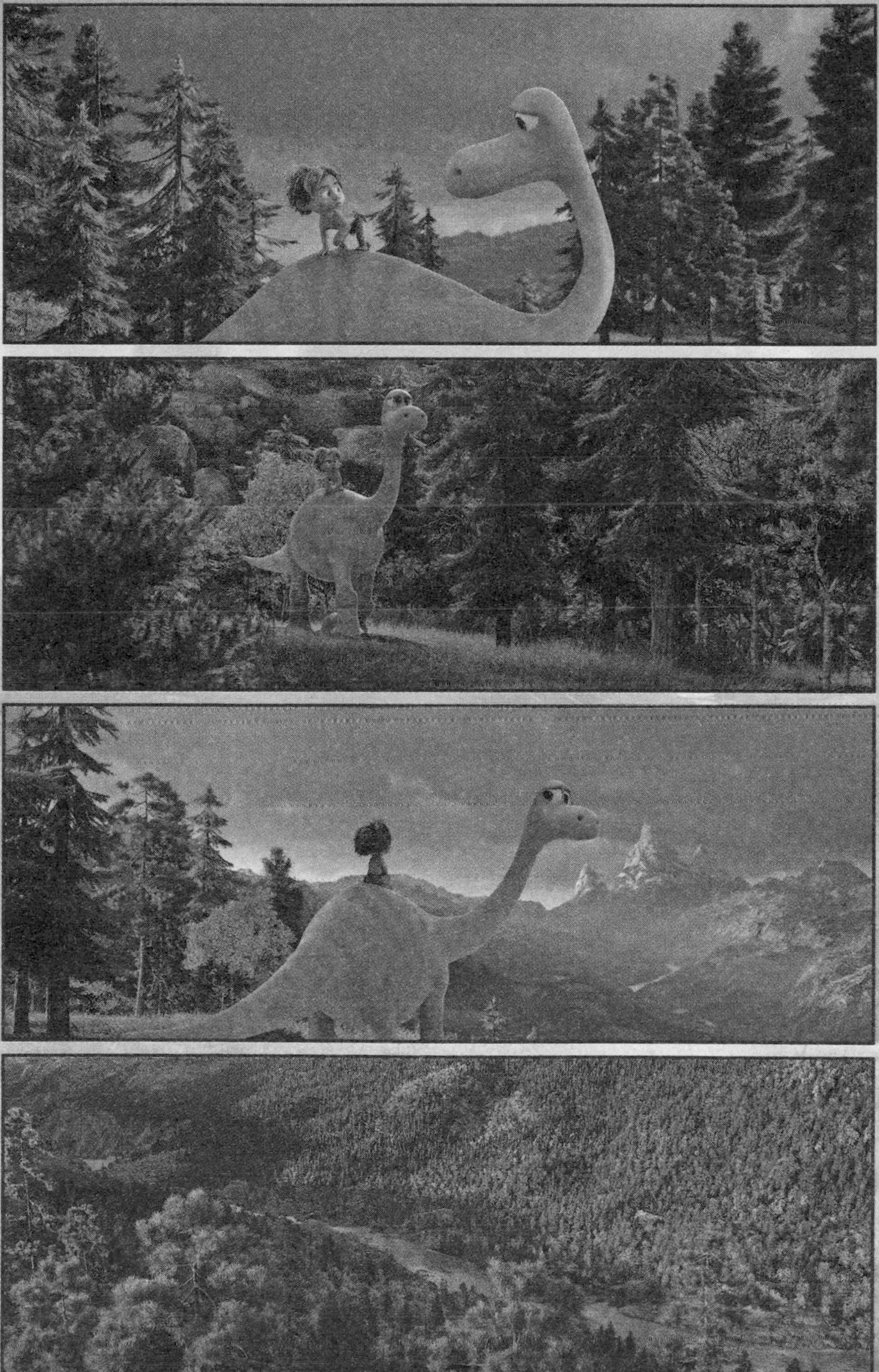

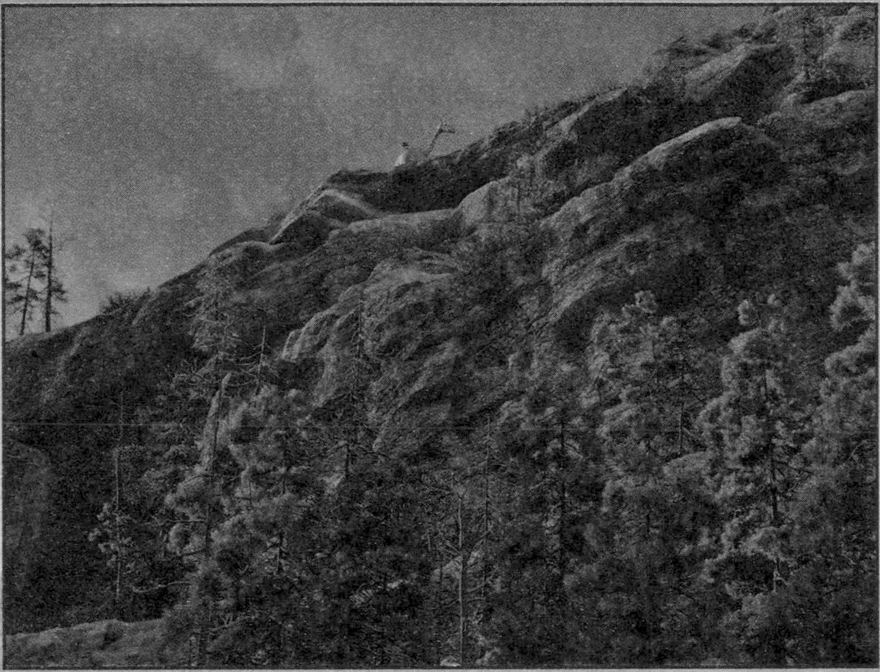

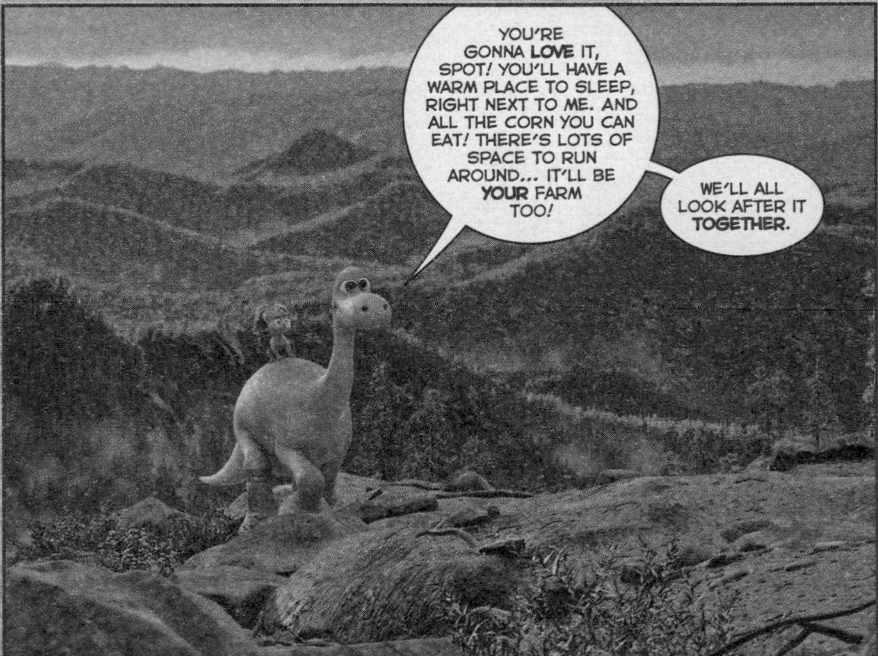
YOU'RE GONNA LOVE IT, SPOT! YOU'LL HAVE A WARM PLACE TO SLEEP, RIGHT NEXT TO ME. AND ALL THE CORN YOU CAN EAT! THERE'S LOTS OF SPACE TO RUN AROUND... IT'LL BE YOUR FARM TOO!
WE'LL ALL LOOK AFTER IT TOGETHER.

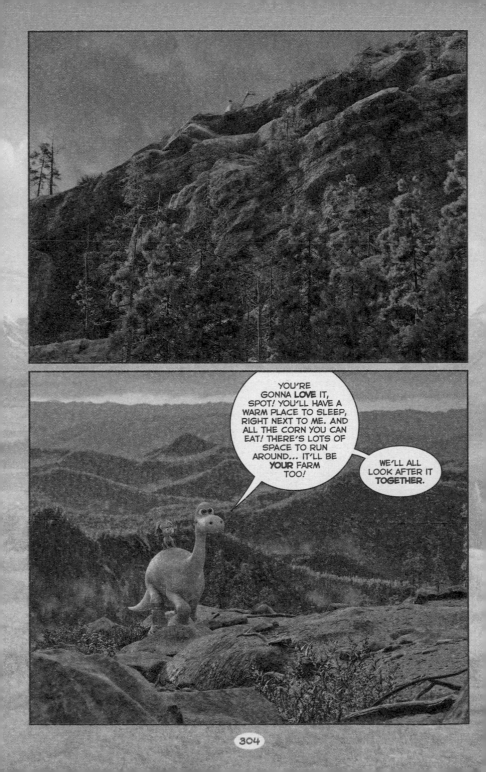

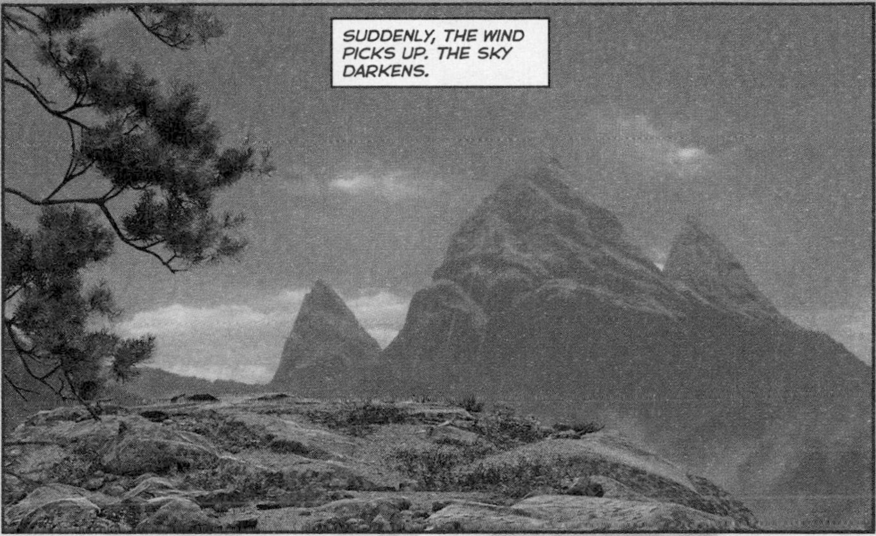
SUDDENLY, THE WIND PICKS UP. THE SKY DARKENS.

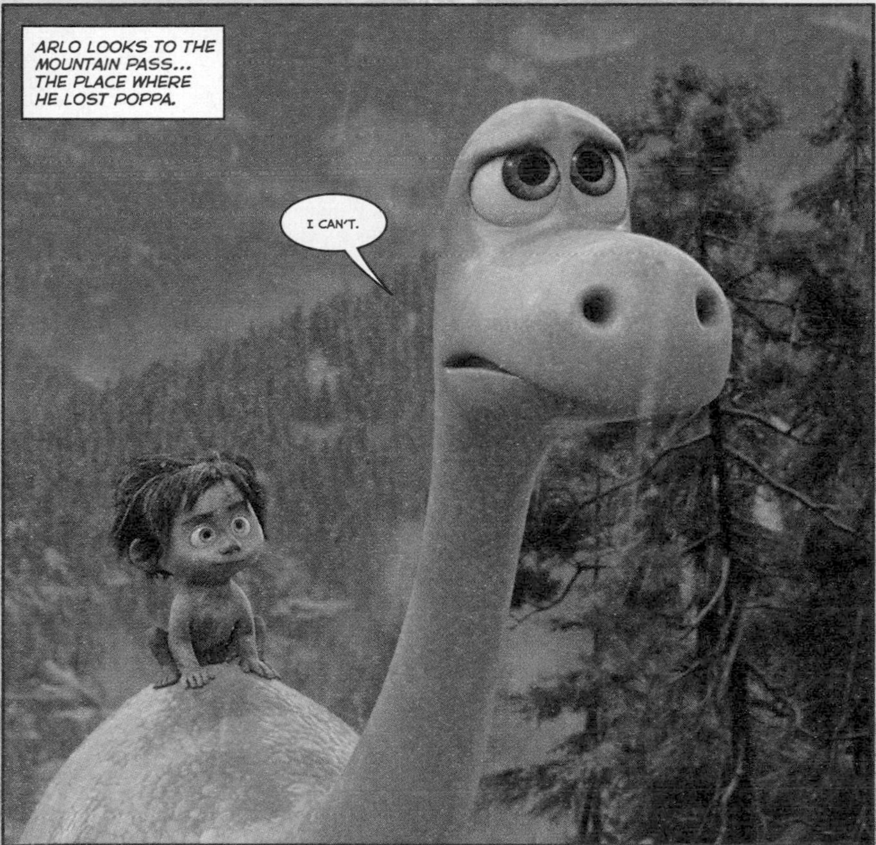
ARLO LOOKS TO THE MOUNTAIN PASS... THE PLACE WHERE HE LOST POPPA.
I CAN'T.

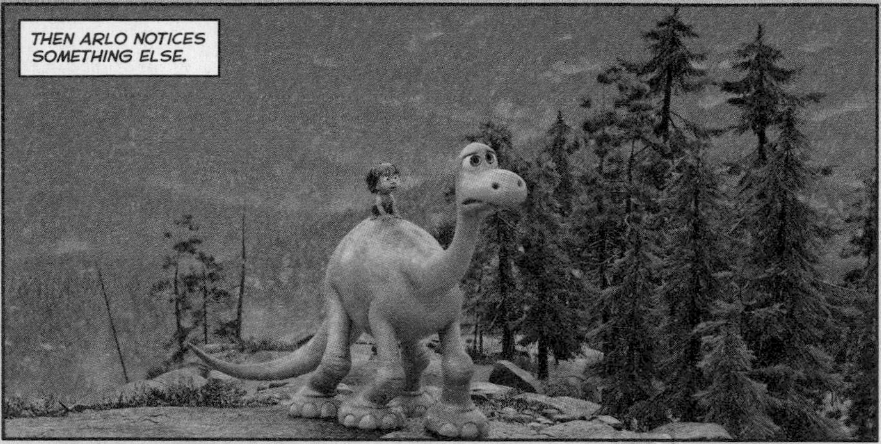
THEN ARLO NOTICES SOMETHING ELSE.

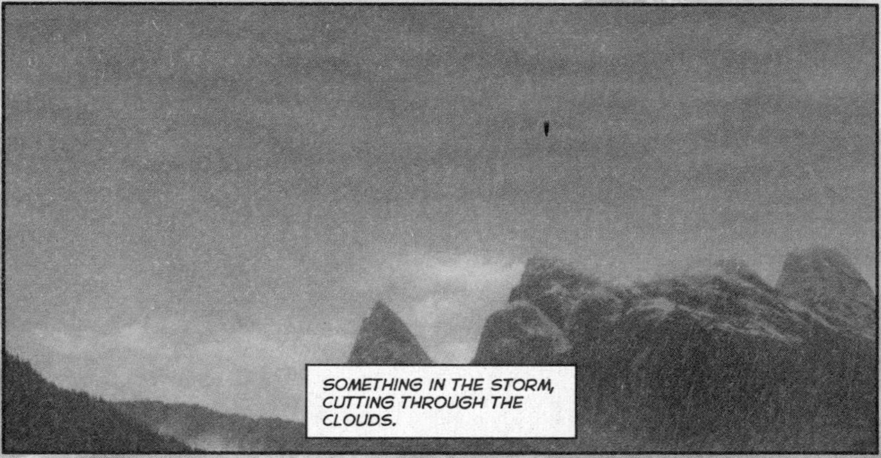
SOMETHING IN THE STORM, CUTTING THROUGH THE CLOUDS.

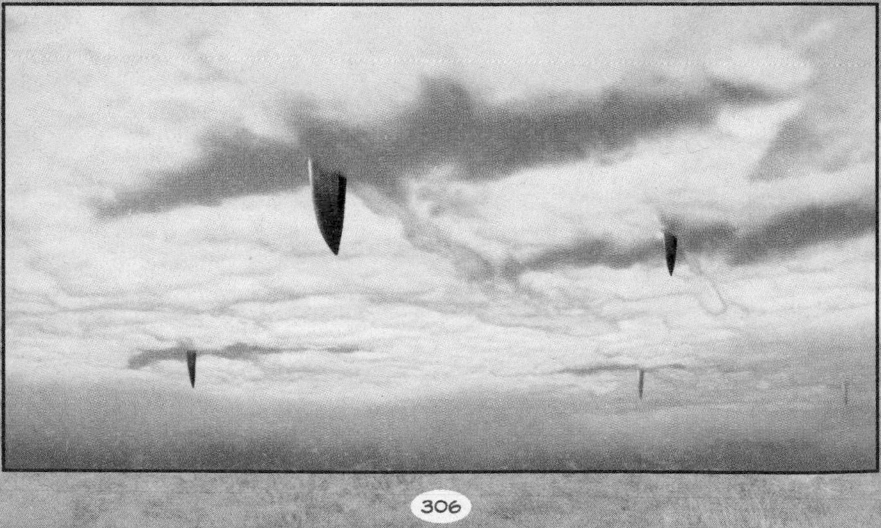

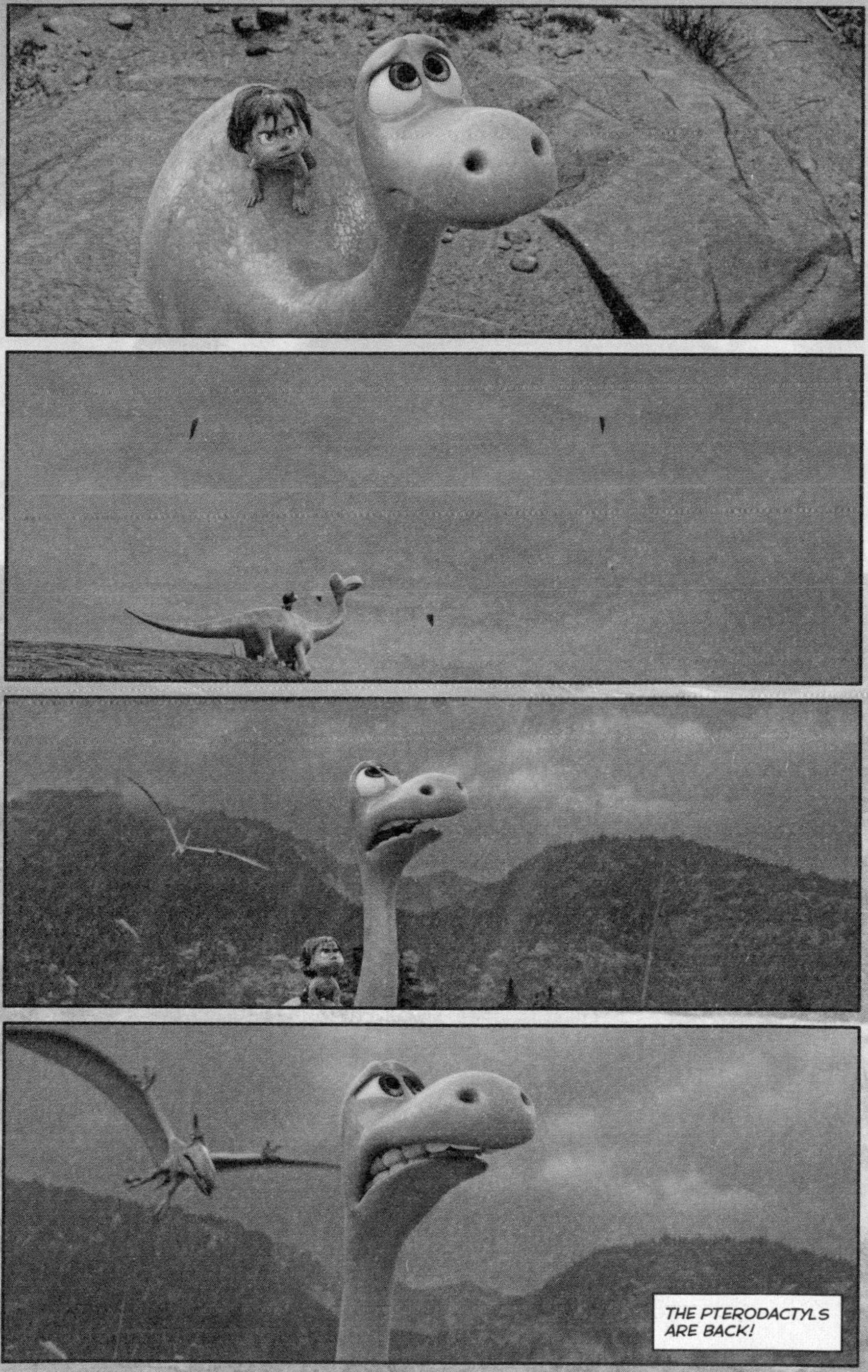
THE PTERODACTYLS
ARE BACK!

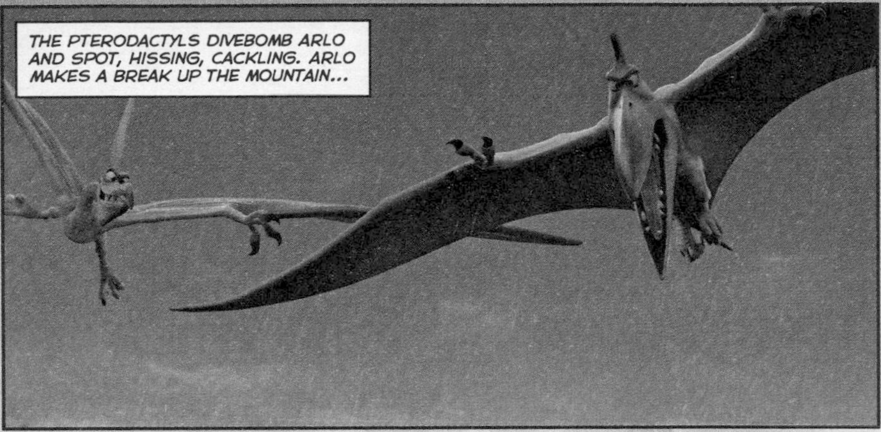
THE PTERODACTYLS DIVEBOMB ARLO AND SPOT, HISSING, CACKLING. ARLO MAKES A BREAK UP THE MOUNTAIN...

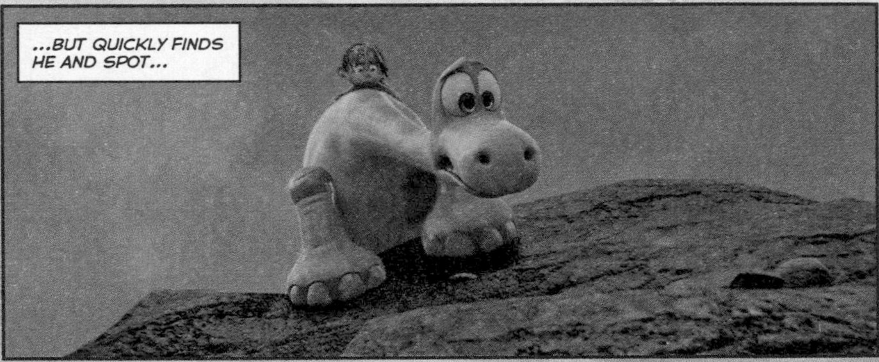
...BUT QUICKLY FINDS HE AND SPOT...

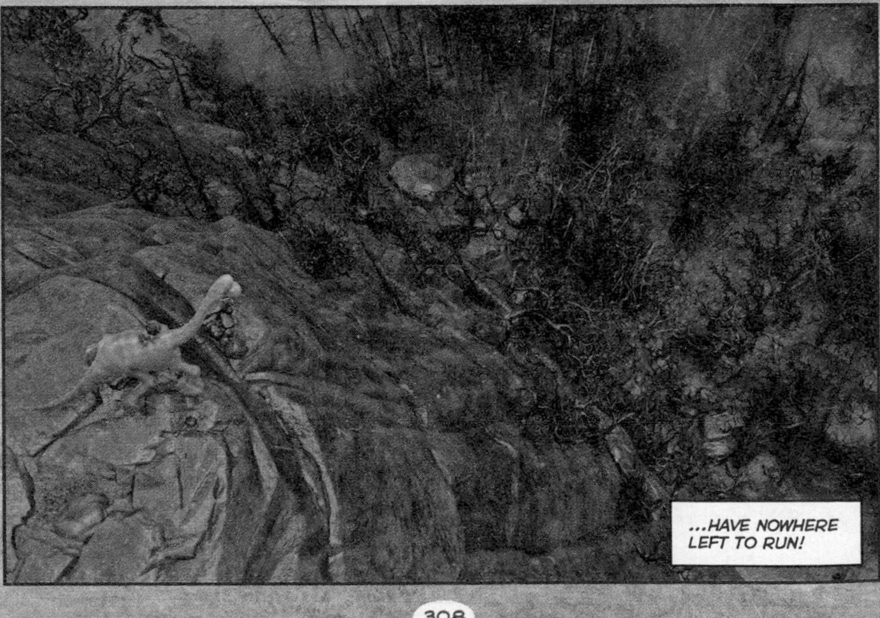
...HAVE NOWHERE LEFT TO RUN!

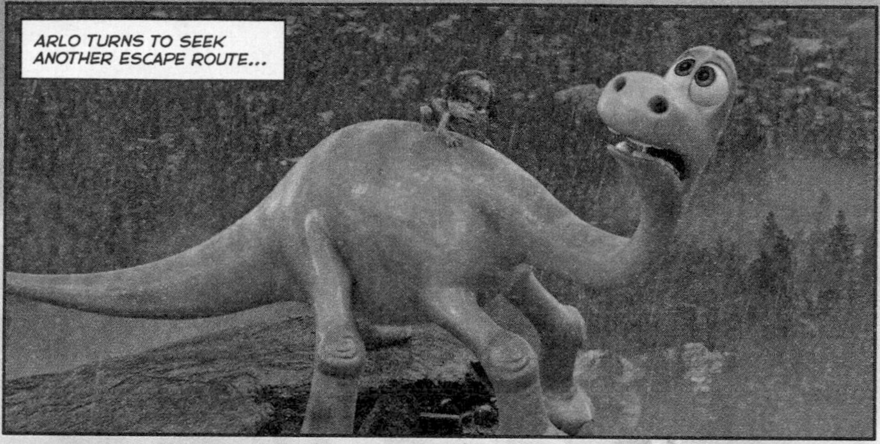
ARLO TURNS TO SEEK ANOTHER ESCAPE ROUTE...

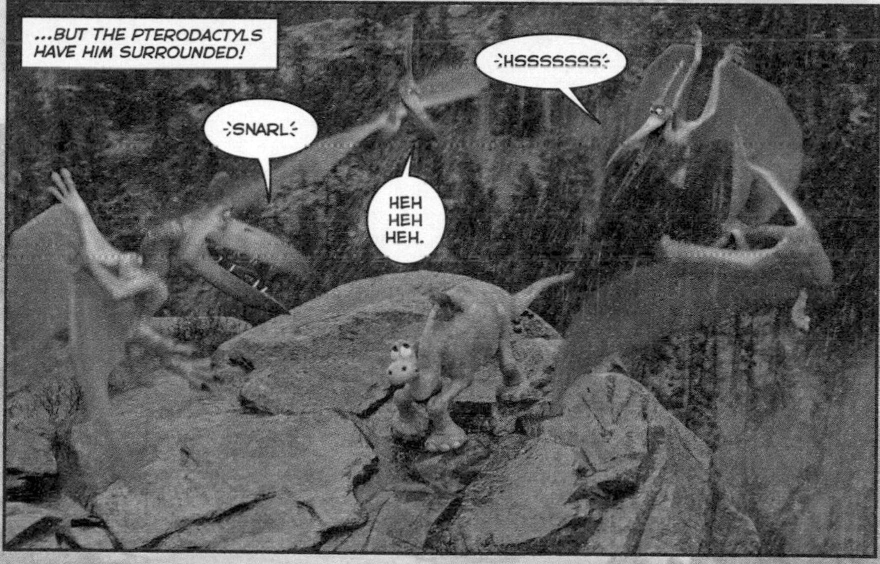
...BUT THE PTERODACTYLS HAVE HIM SURROUNDED!
HSSSSSSS
SNARL
HEH HEH HEH.

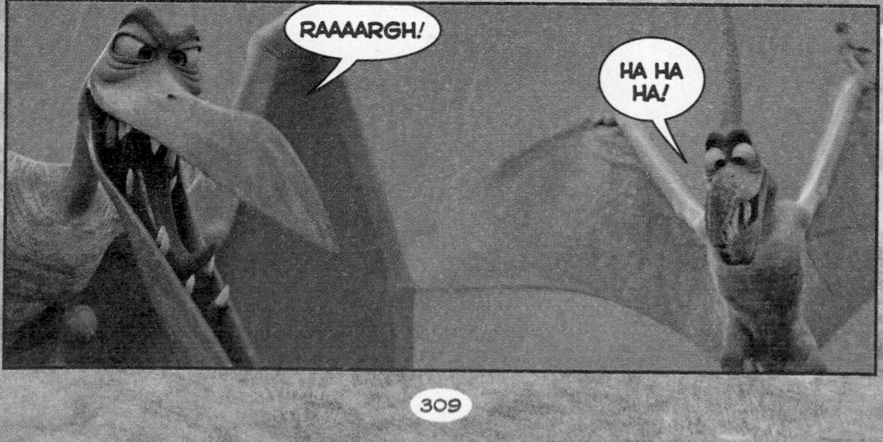
RAAAARGH!
HA HA HA!

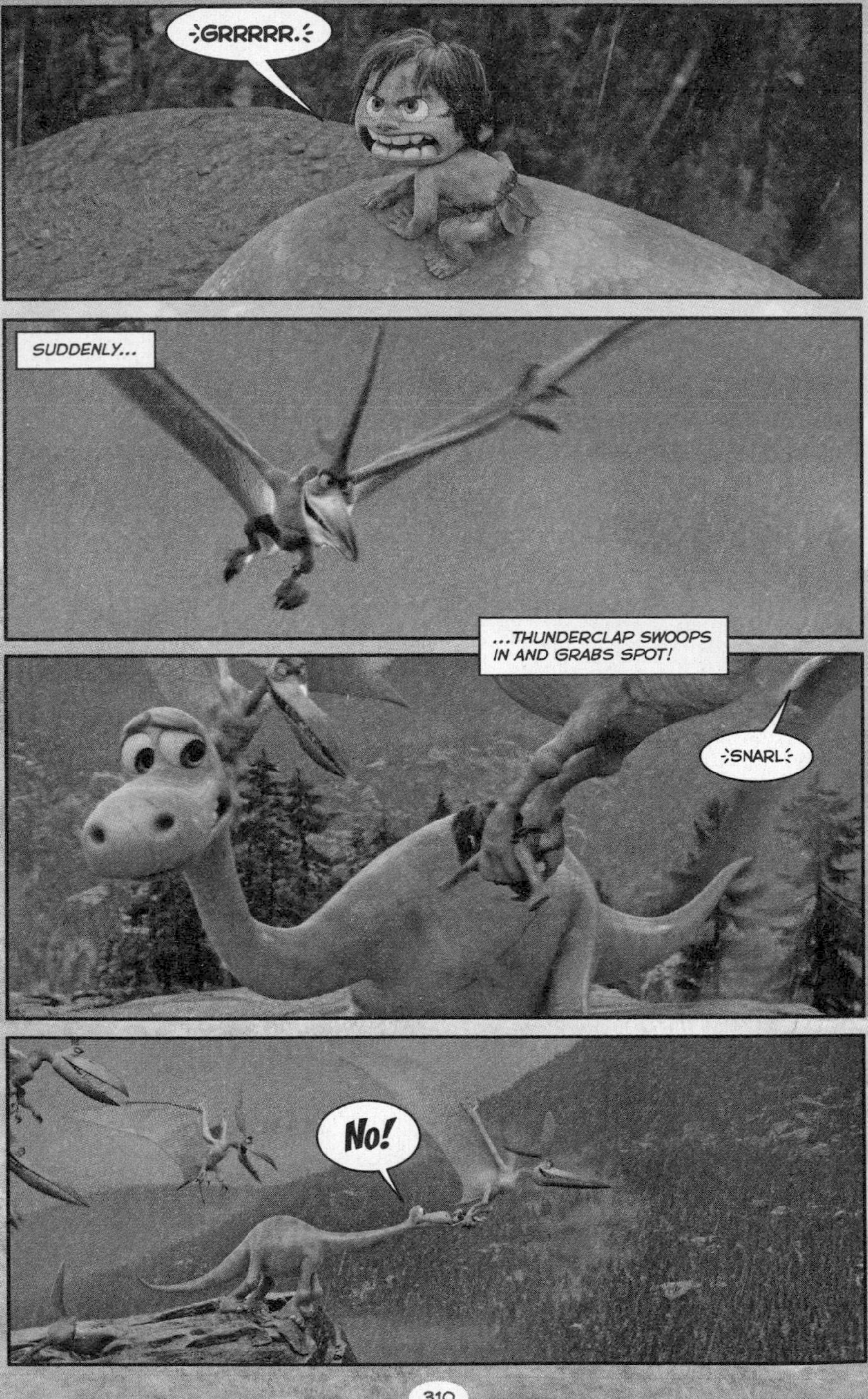
GRRRRR.
SUDDENLY...
...THUNDERCLAP SWOOPS IN AND GRABS SPOT!
SNARL
No!

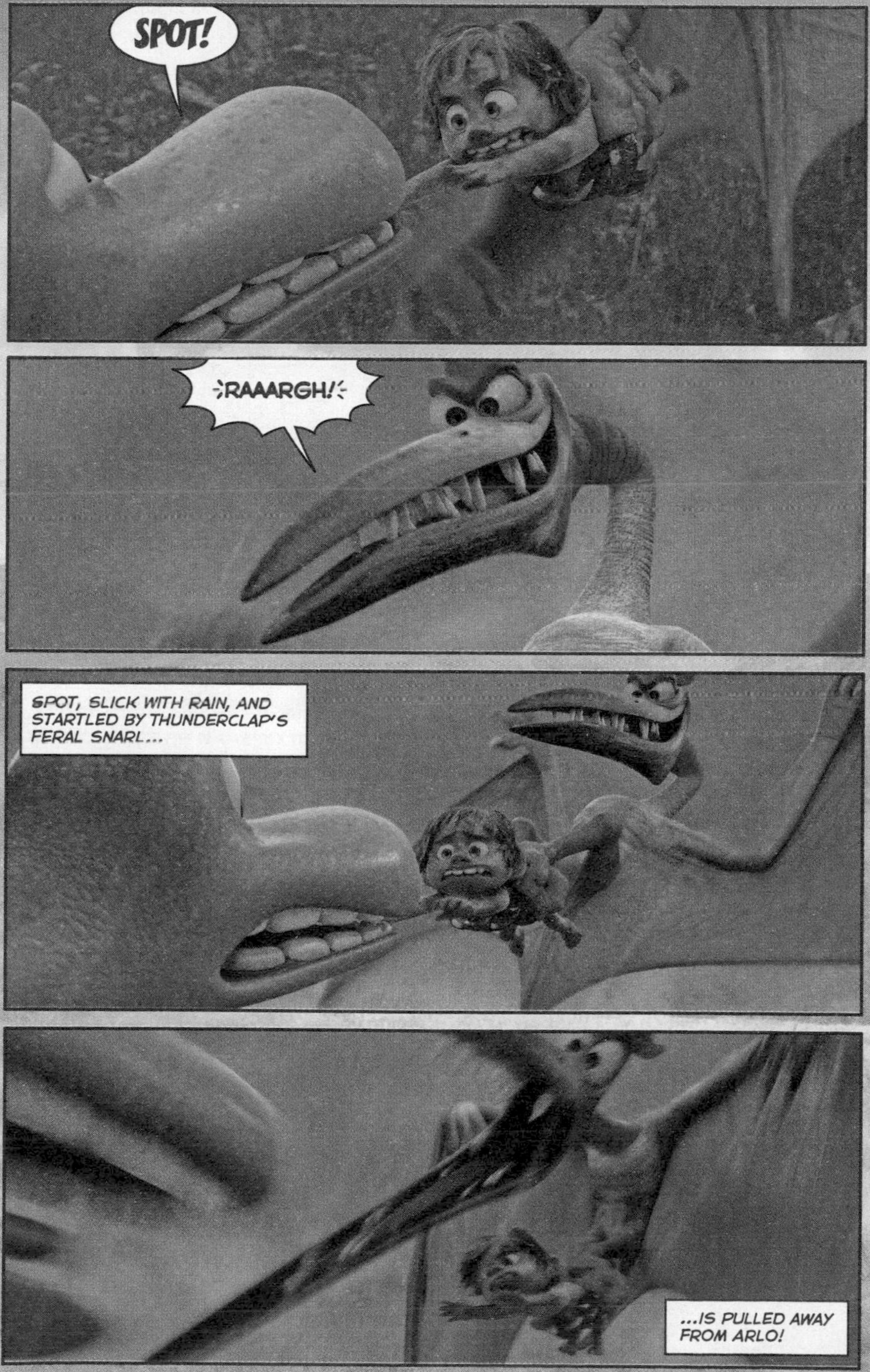
SPOT!
RAAARGH!
SPOT, SLICK WITH RAIN, AND STARTLED BY THUNDERCLAP'S FERAL SNARL...
...IS PULLED AWAY FROM ARLO!

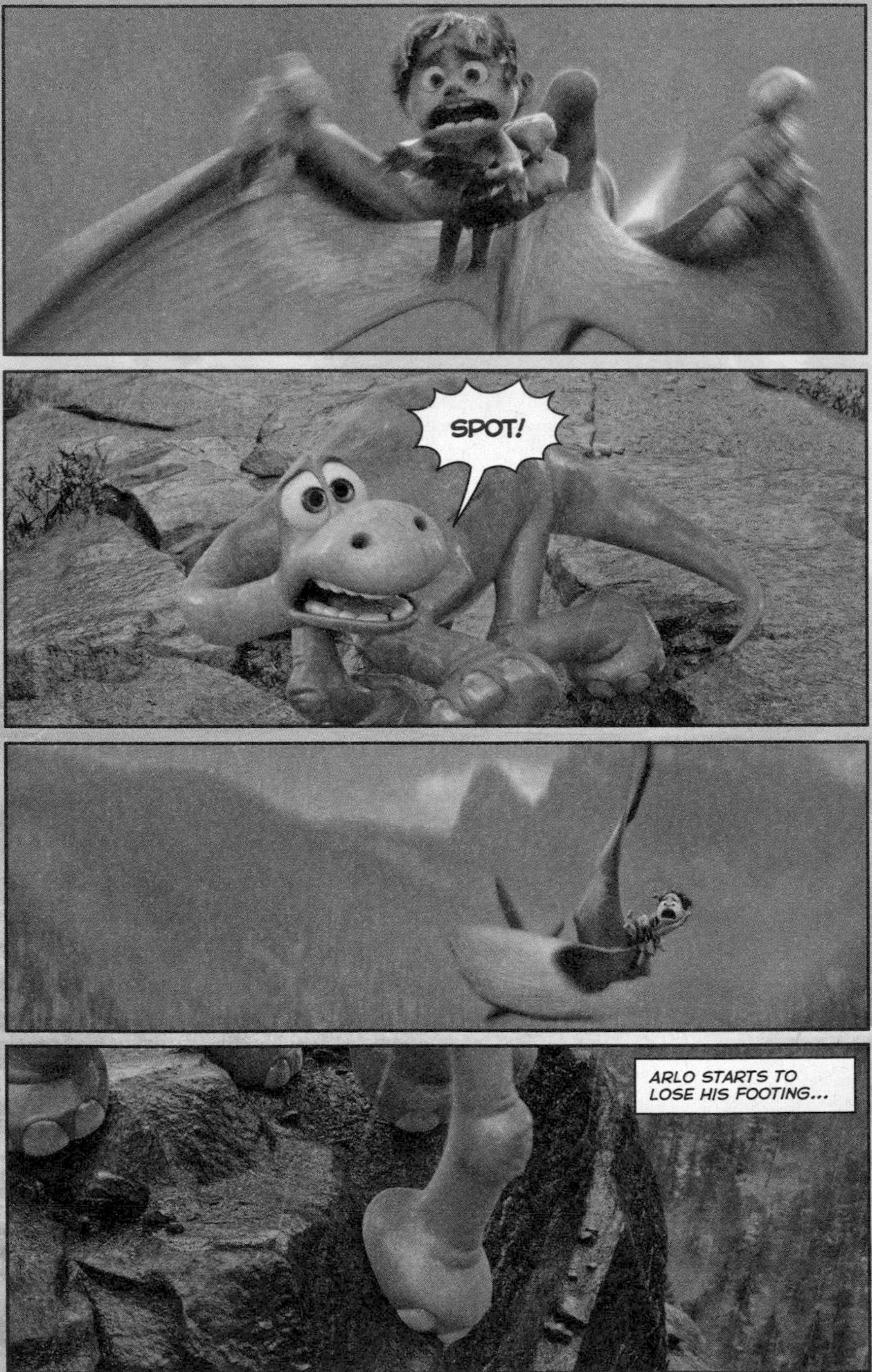
SPOT!
ARLO STARTS TO LOSE HIS FOOTING...

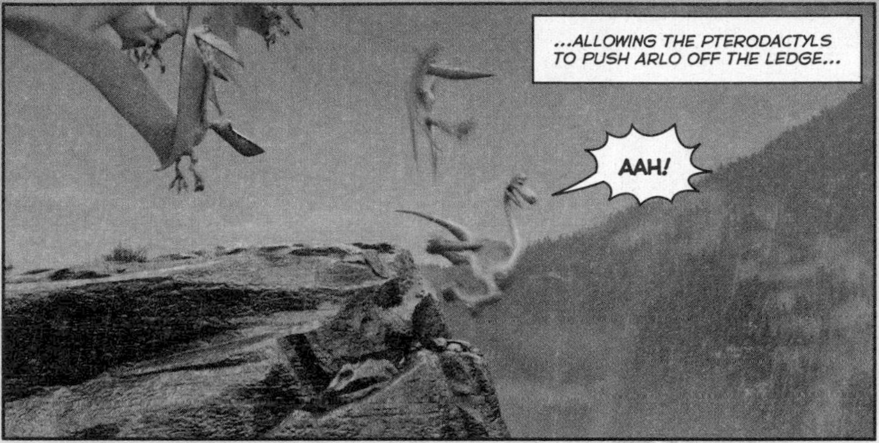
...ALLOWING THE PTERODACTYLS TO PUSH ARLO OFF THE LEDGE...
AAH!

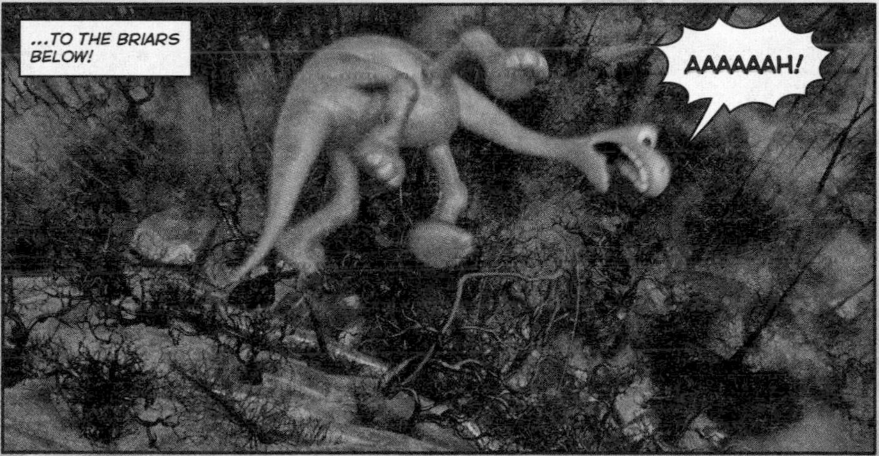
...TO THE BRIARS BELOW!
AAAAAAH!

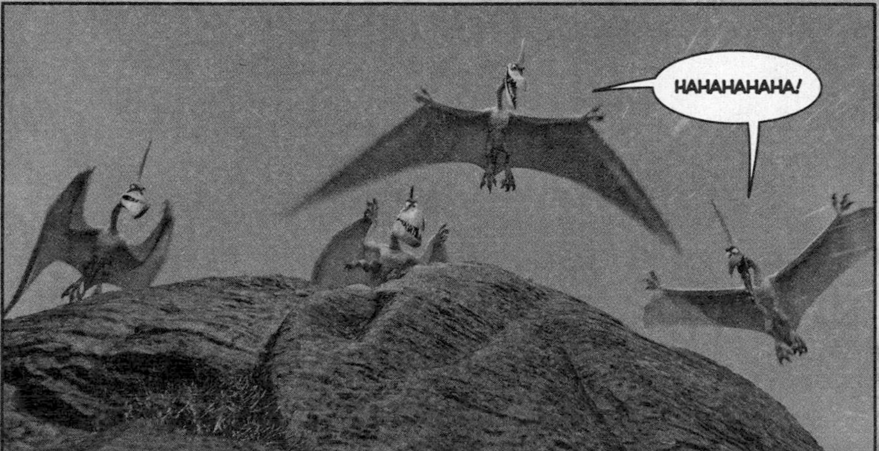
HAHAHAHAHA!

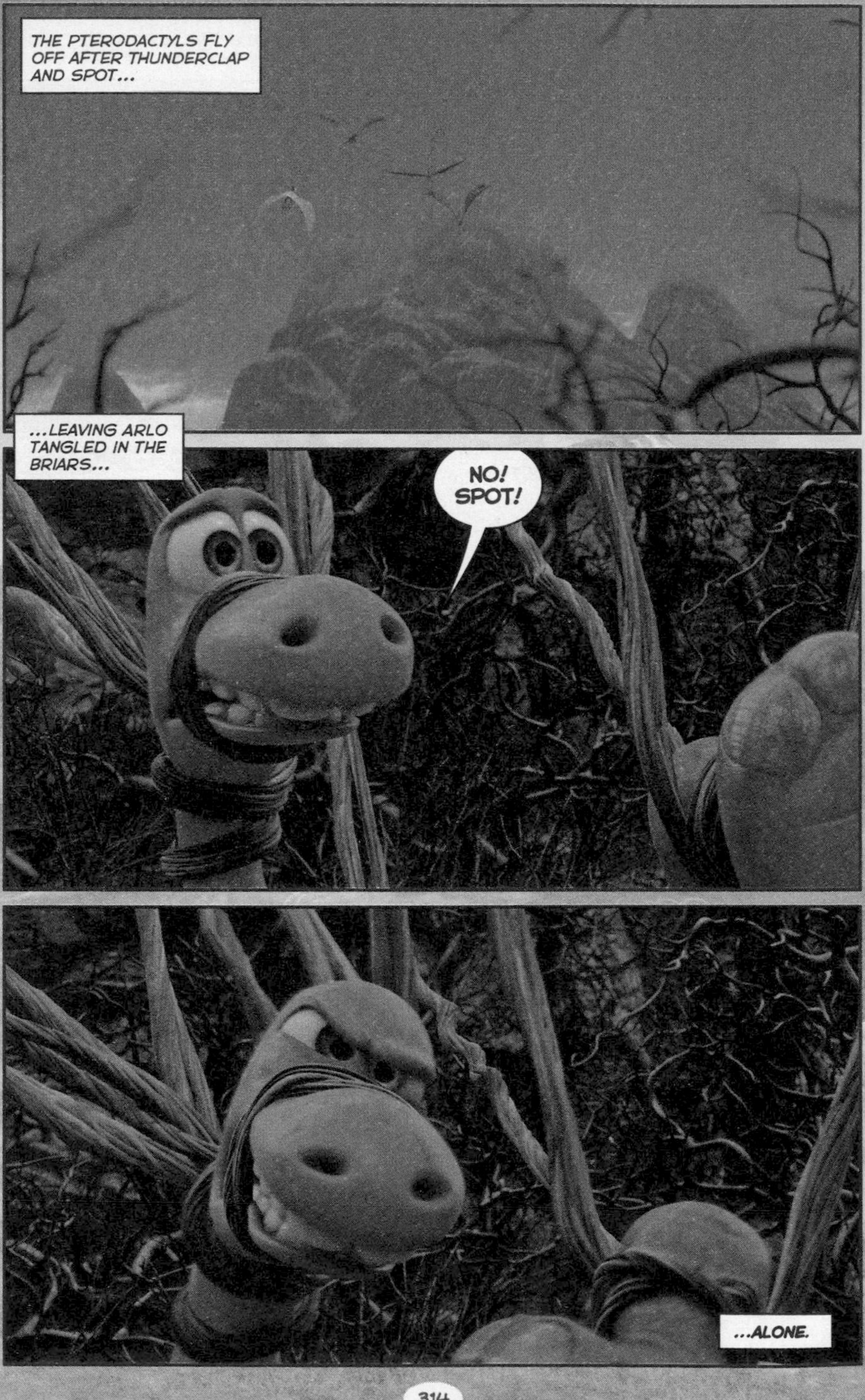
THE PTERODACTYLS FLY OFF AFTER THUNDERCLAP AND SPOT...
...LEAVING ARLO TANGLED IN THE BRIARS...
NO! SPOT!
...ALONE.

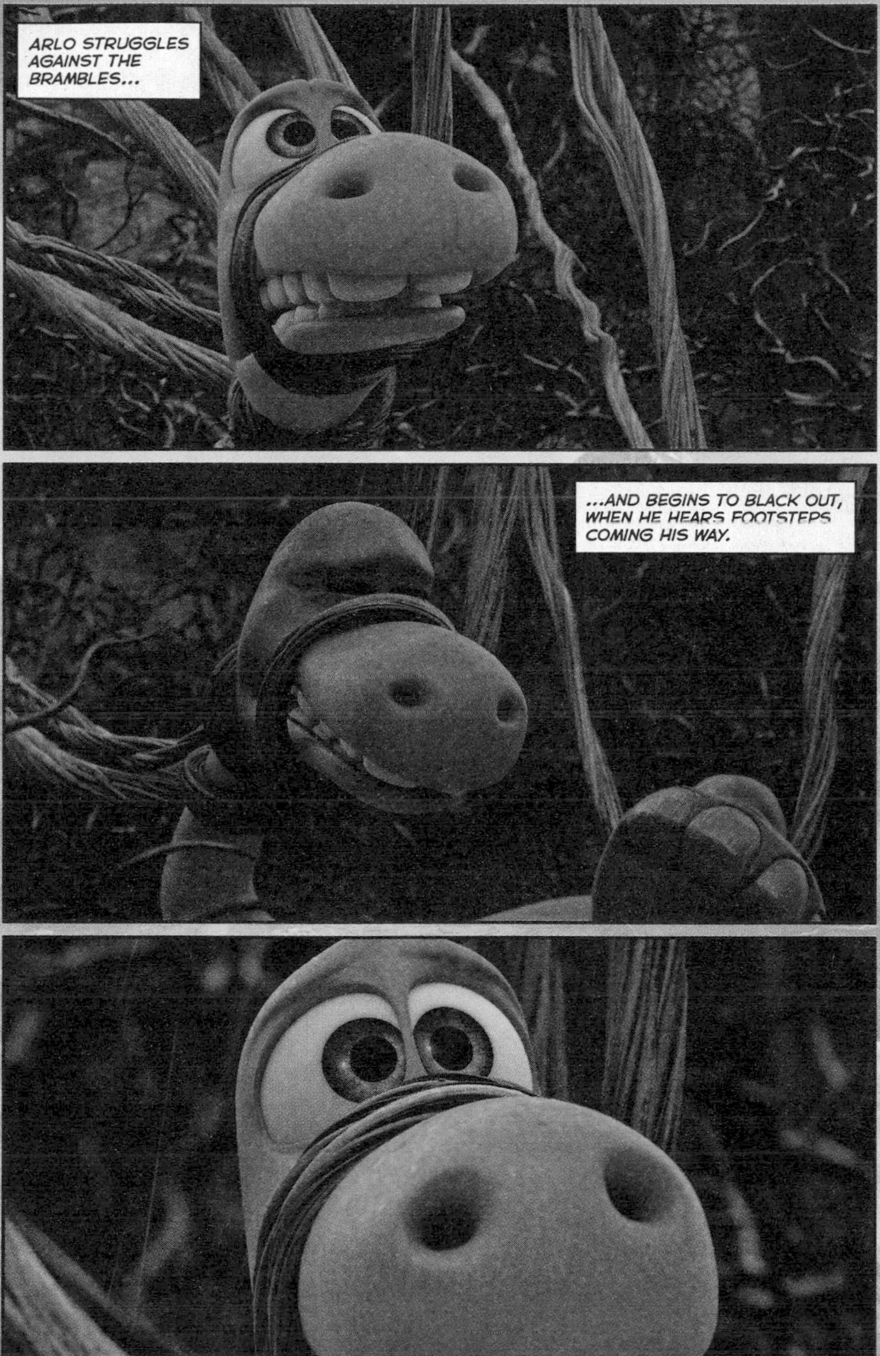
ARLO STRUGGLES AGAINST THE BRAMBLES...
...AND BEGINS TO BLACK OUT, WHEN HE HEARS FOOTSTEPS COMING HIS WAY.

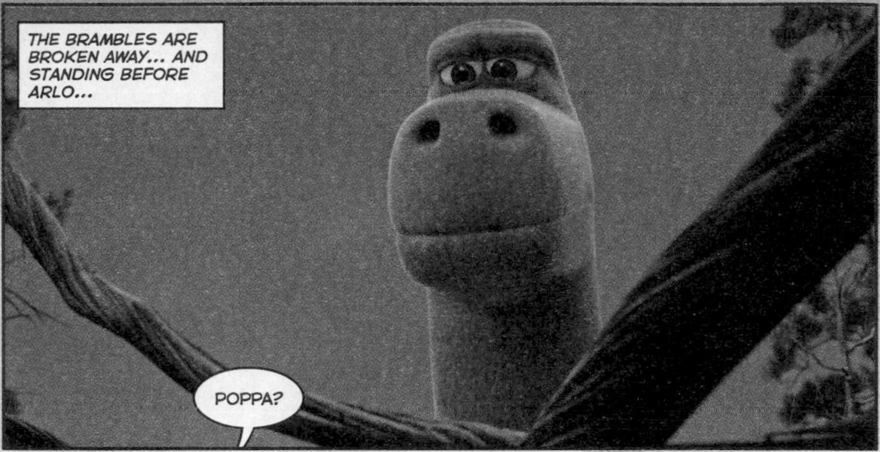
THE BRAMBLES ARE BROKEN AWAY... AND STANDING BEFORE ARLO...
POPPA?

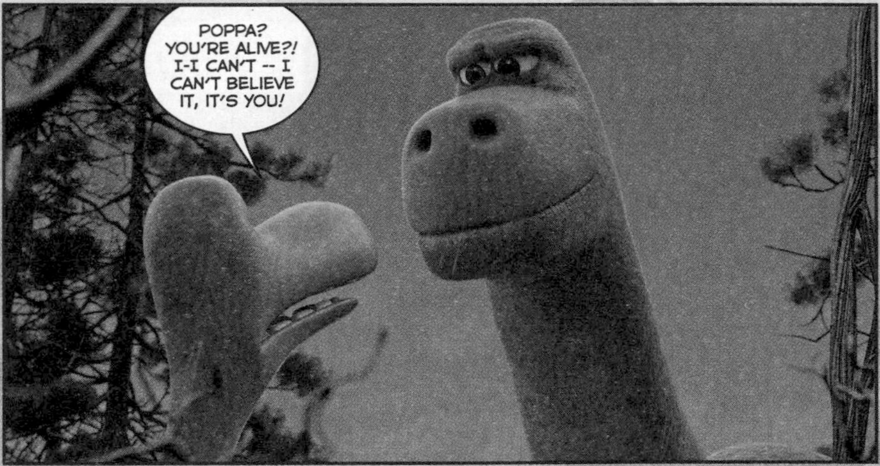
POPPA? YOU'RE ALIVE?! I-I CAN'T -- I CAN'T BELIEVE IT, IT'S YOU!

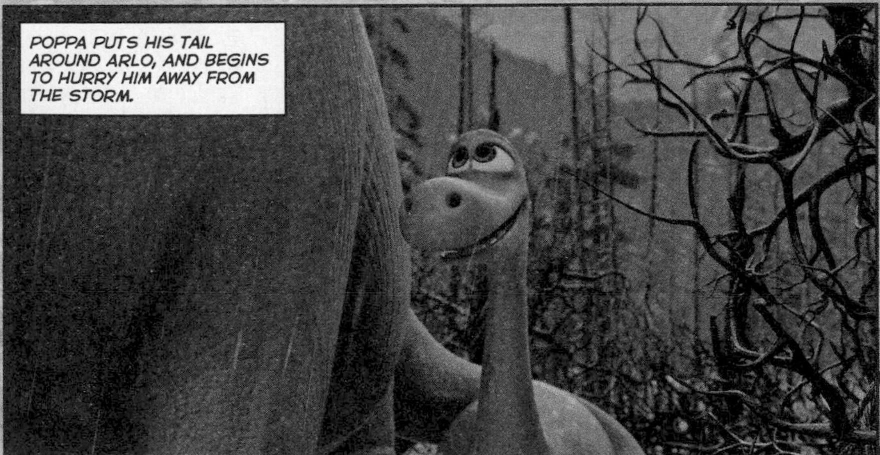
POPPA PUTS HIS TAIL AROUND ARLO, AND BEGINS TO HURRY HIM AWAY FROM THE STORM.

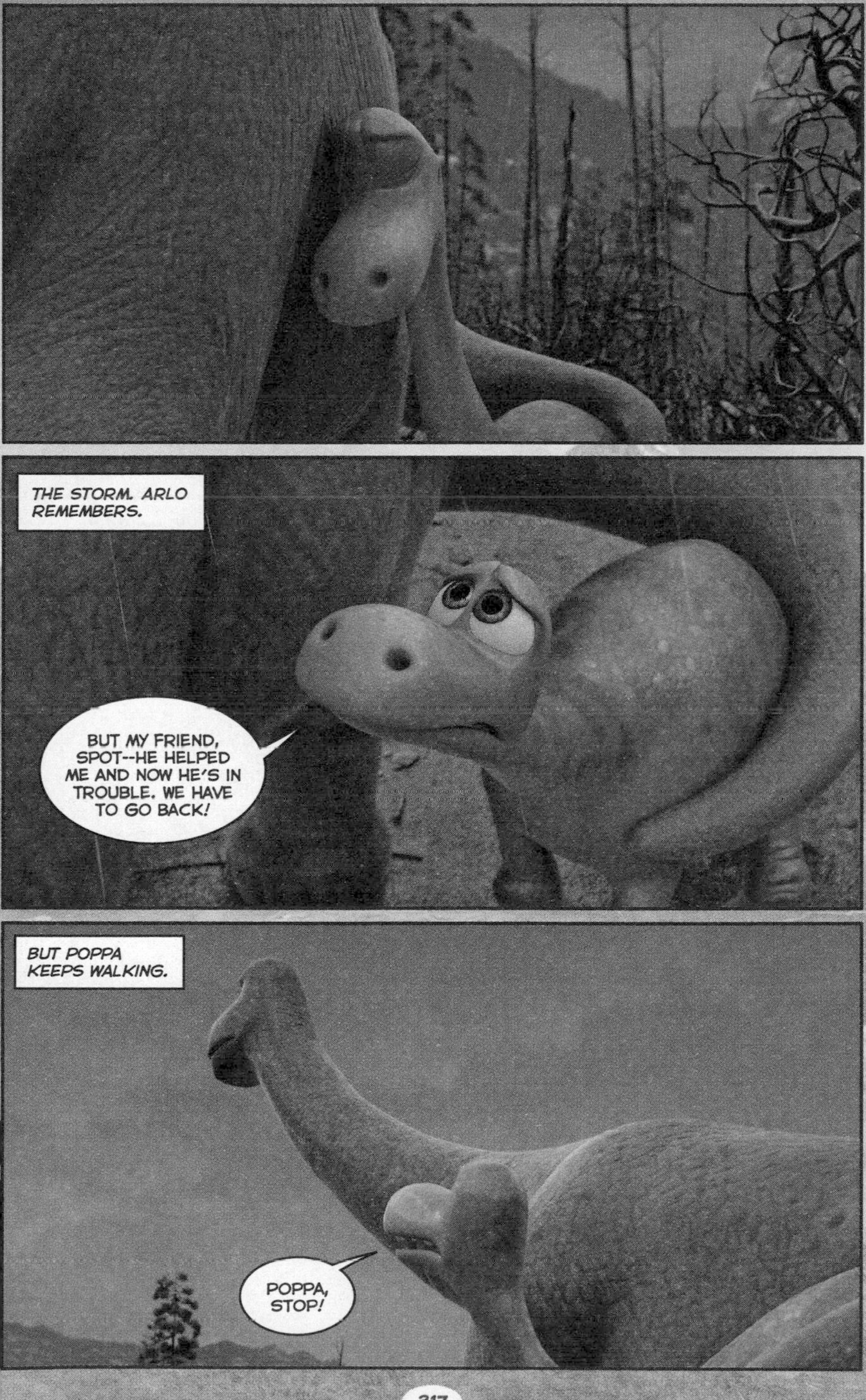
THE STORM. ARLO REMEMBERS.
BUT MY FRIEND, SPOT--HE HELPED ME AND NOW HE'S IN TROUBLE. WE HAVE TO GO BACK!
BUT POPPA KEEPS WALKING.
POPPA, STOP!

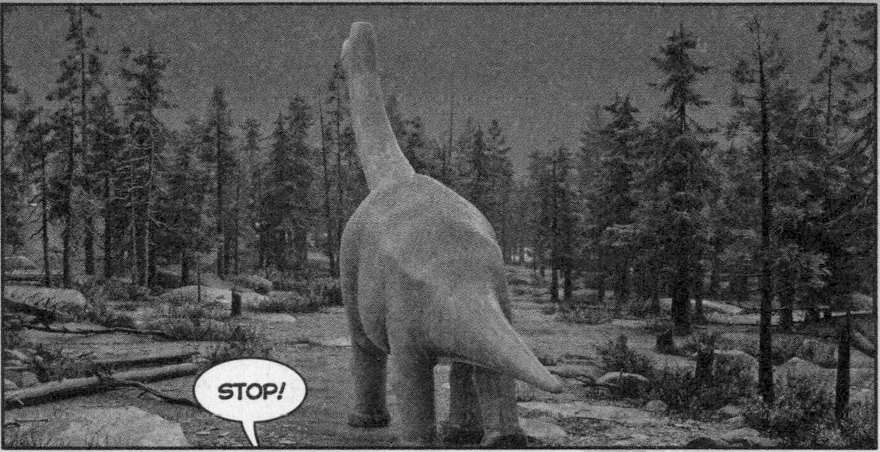
STOP!

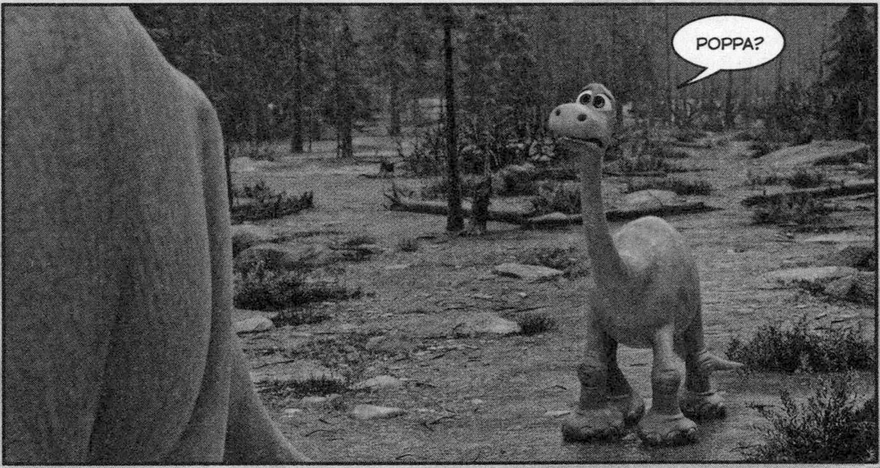
POPPA?

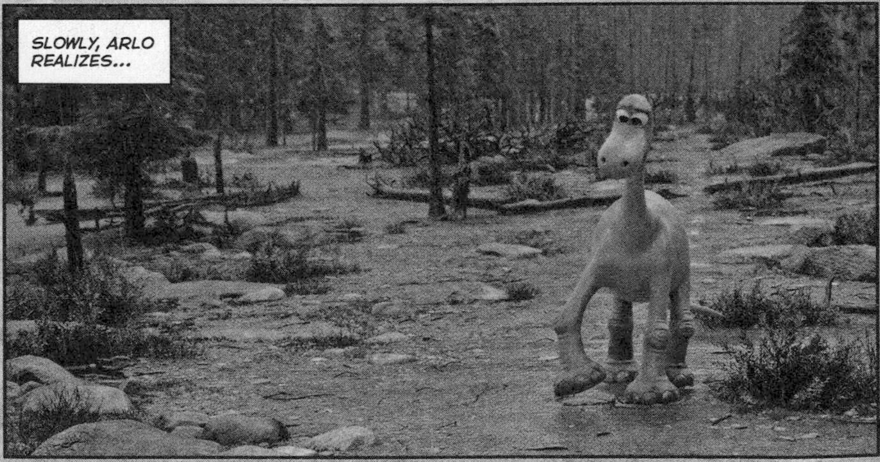
SLOWLY, ARLO
REALIZES...

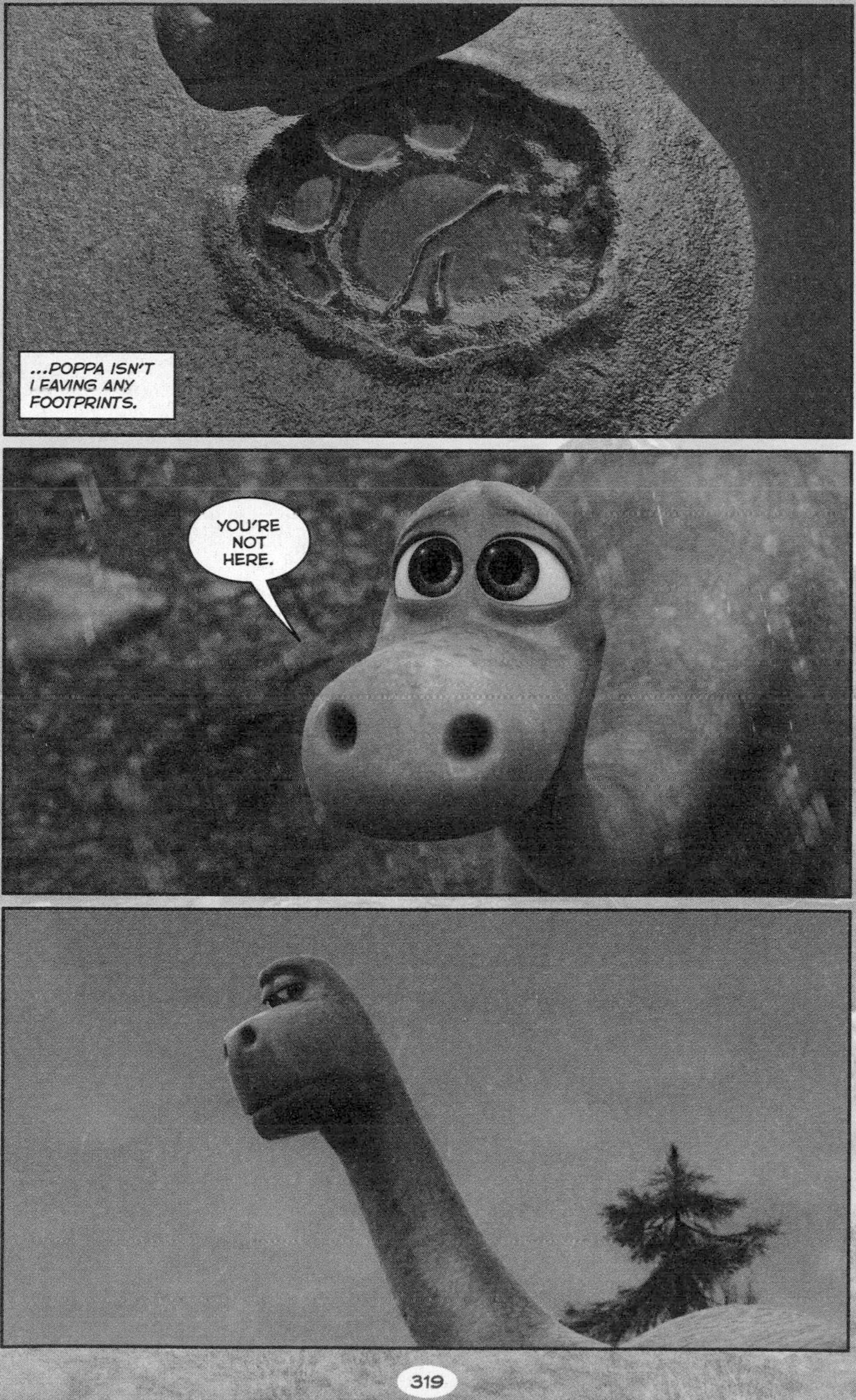
...POPPA ISN'T LEAVING ANY FOOTPRINTS.
YOU'RE NOT HERE.

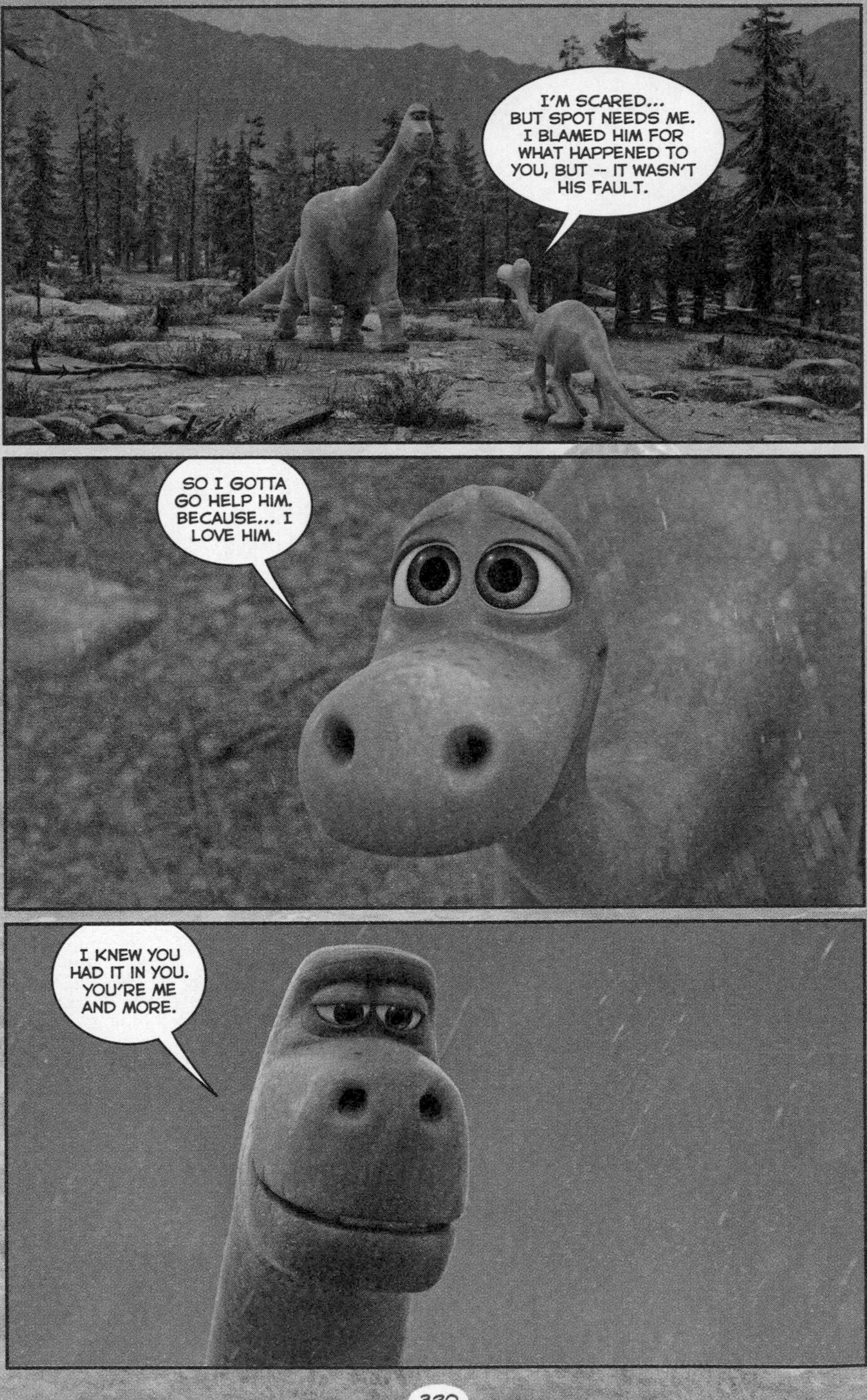
I'M SCARED... BUT SPOT NEEDS ME. I BLAMED HIM FOR WHAT HAPPENED TO YOU, BUT -- IT WASN'T HIS FAULT.
SO I GOTTA GO HELP HIM. BECAUSE... I LOVE HIM.
I KNEW YOU HAD IT IN YOU. YOU'RE ME AND MORE.

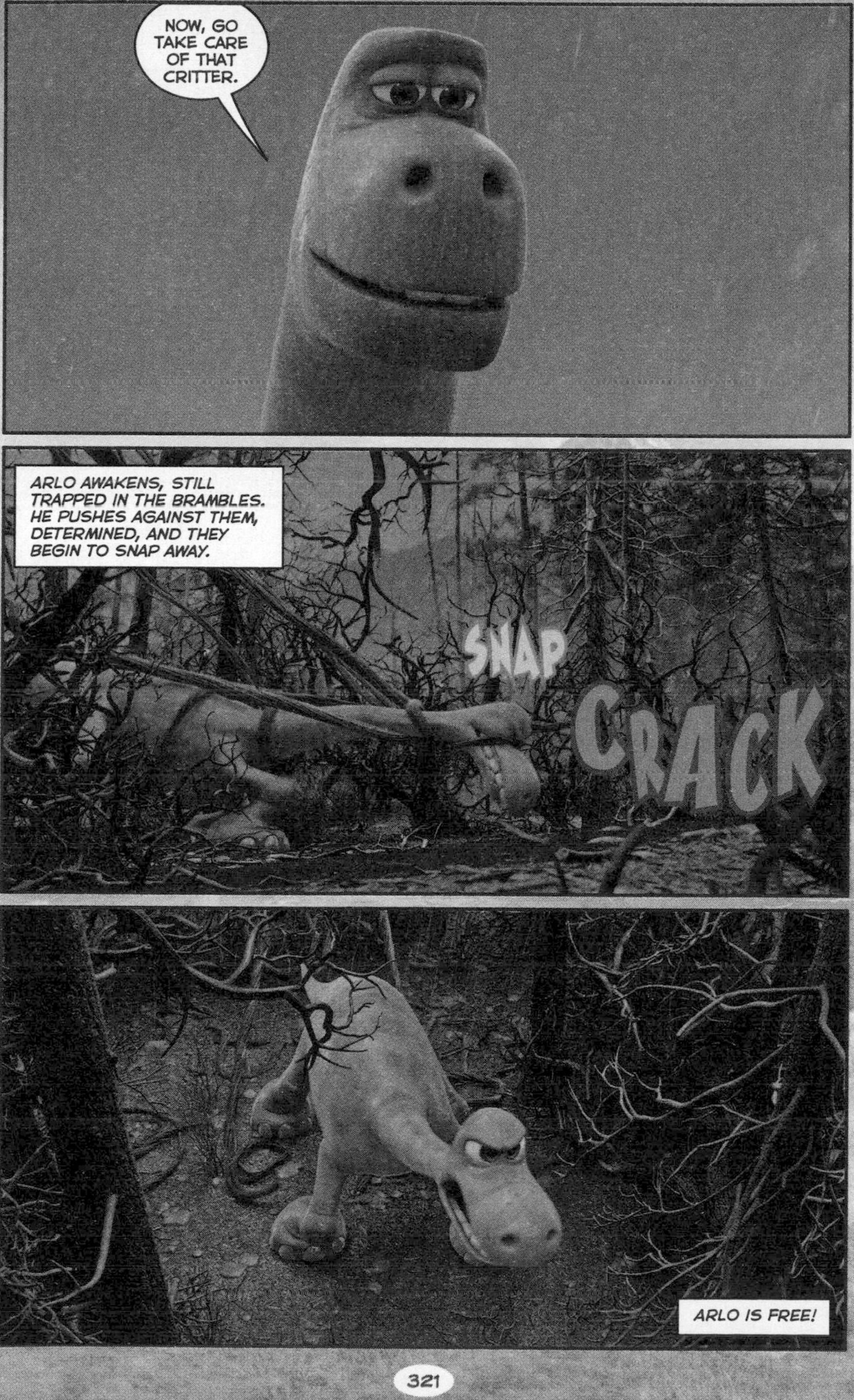
NOW, GO TAKE CARE OF THAT CRITTER.
ARLO AWAKENS, STILL TRAPPED IN THE BRAMBLES. HE PUSHES AGAINST THEM, DETERMINED, AND THEY BEGIN TO SNAP AWAY.
SNAP
CRACK
ARLO IS FREE!

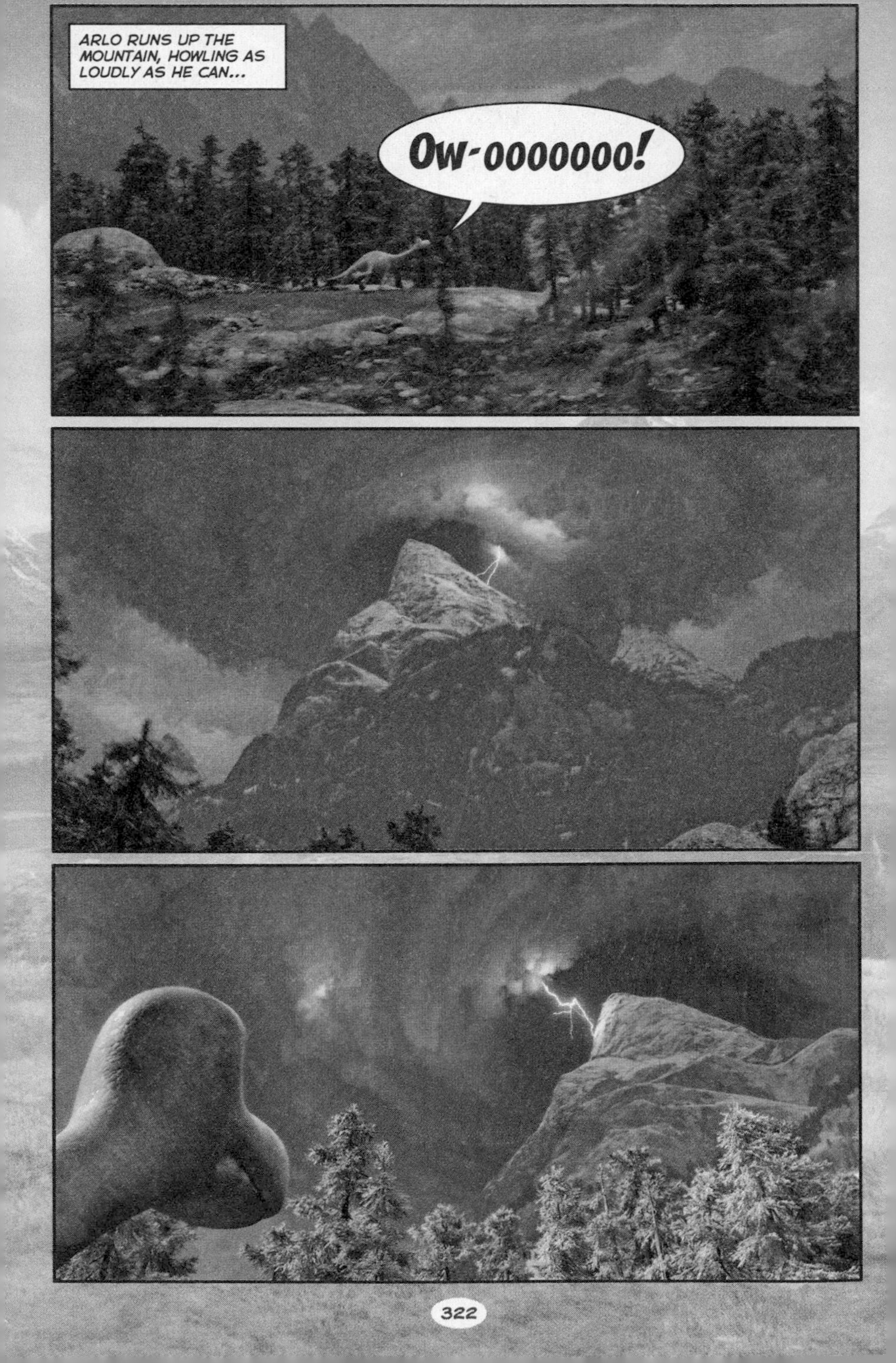
ARLO RUNS UP THE MOUNTAIN, HOWLING AS LOUDLY AS HE CAN...
Ow-0000000!

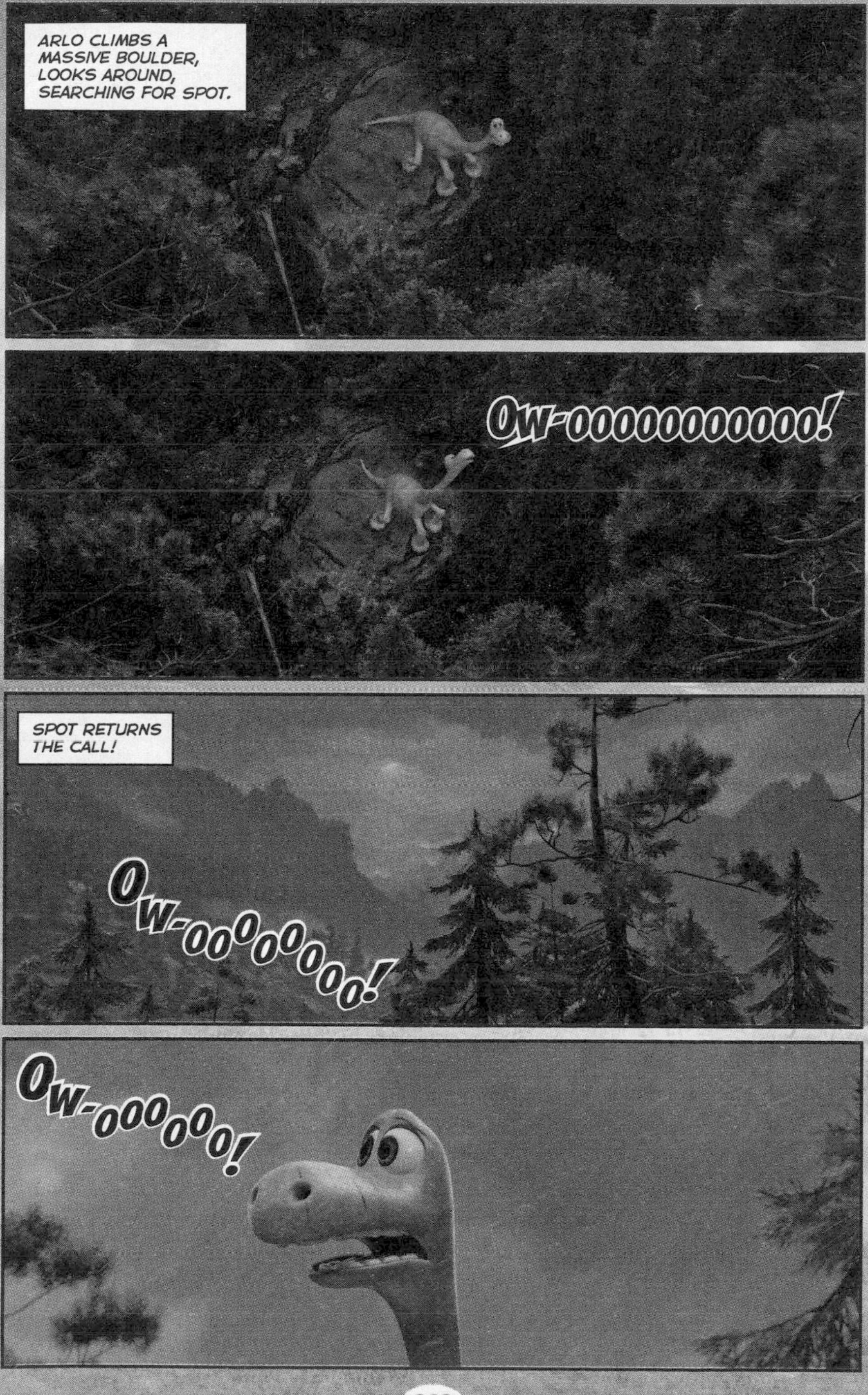
ARLO CLIMBS A MASSIVE BOULDER, LOOKS AROUND, SEARCHING FOR SPOT.
Ow-ooooooooooo!
SPOT RETURNS THE CALL!
Ow-oooooooo!
Ow-oooooo!

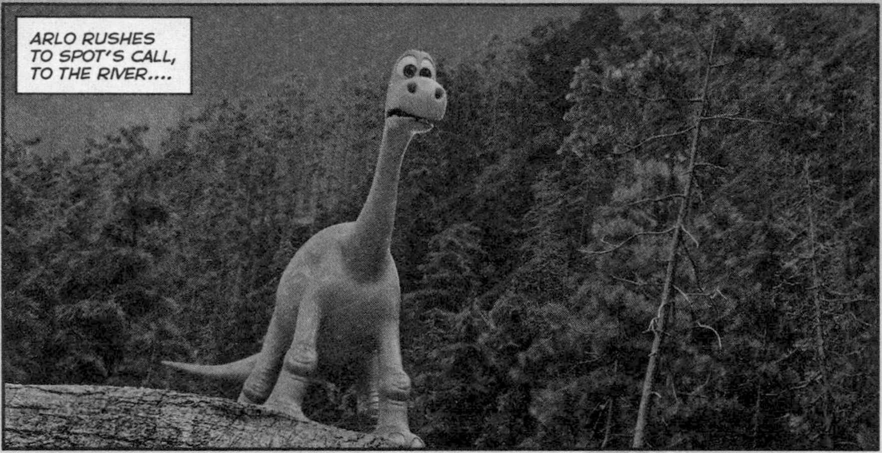
ARLO RUSHES TO SPOT'S CALL, TO THE RIVER....

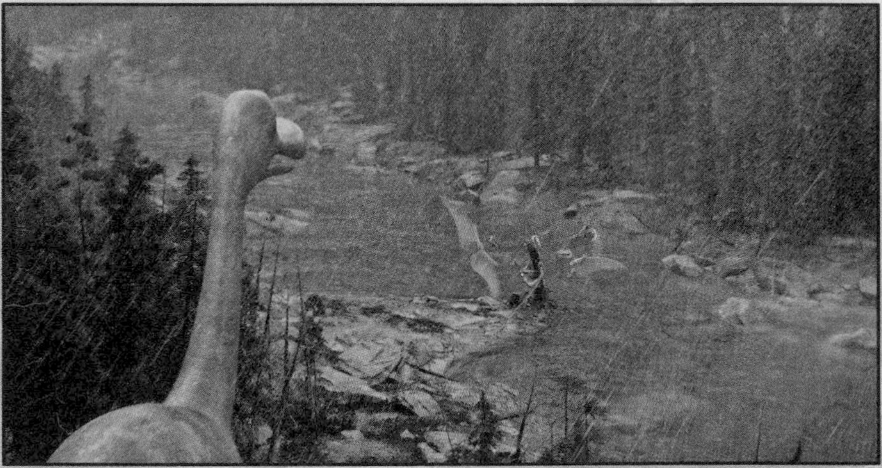

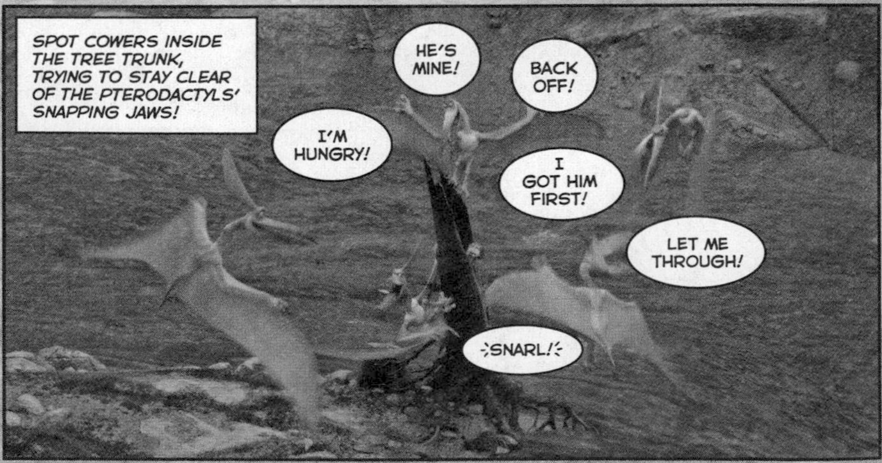
SPOT COWERS INSIDE THE TREE TRUNK, TRYING TO STAY CLEAR OF THE PTERODACTYLS' SNAPPING JAWS!
I'M HUNGRY!
HE'S MINE!
BACK OFF!
I GOT HIM FIRST!
LET ME THROUGH!
SNARL!

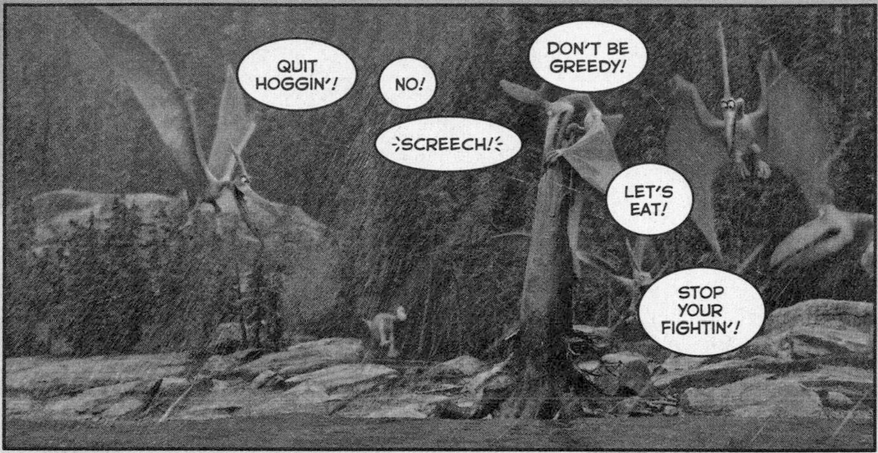
QUIT HOGGIN'!
NO!
DON'T BE GREEDY!
SCREECH!
LET'S EAT!
STOP YOUR FIGHTIN'!

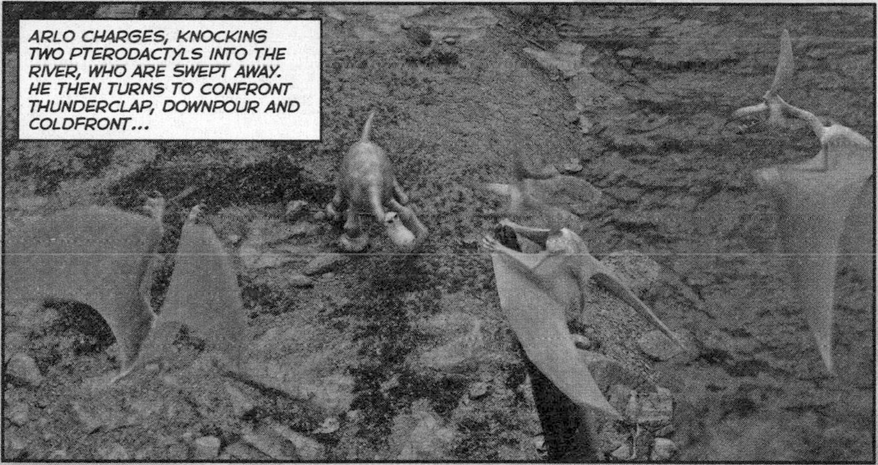
ARLO CHARGES, KNOCKING TWO PTERODACTYLS INTO THE RIVER, WHO ARE SWEPT AWAY. HE THEN TURNS TO CONFRONT THUNDERCLAP, DOWNPOUR AND COLDFRONT...

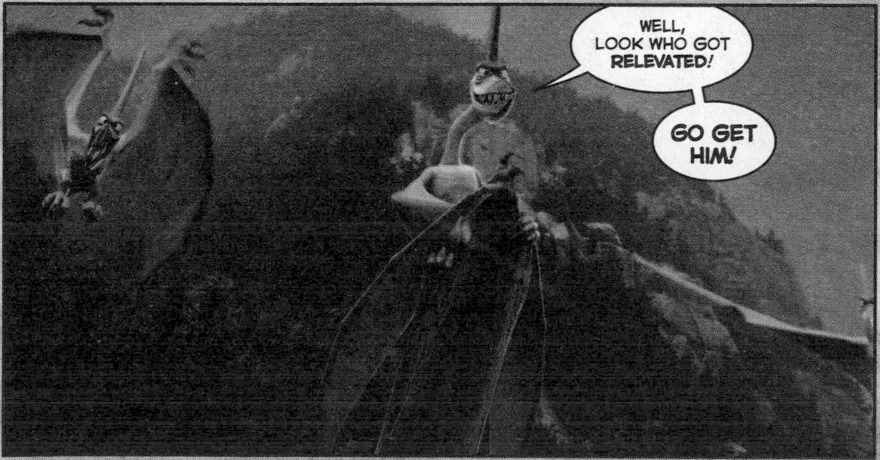
WELL, LOOK WHO GOT **RELEVATED!**
GO GET HIM!

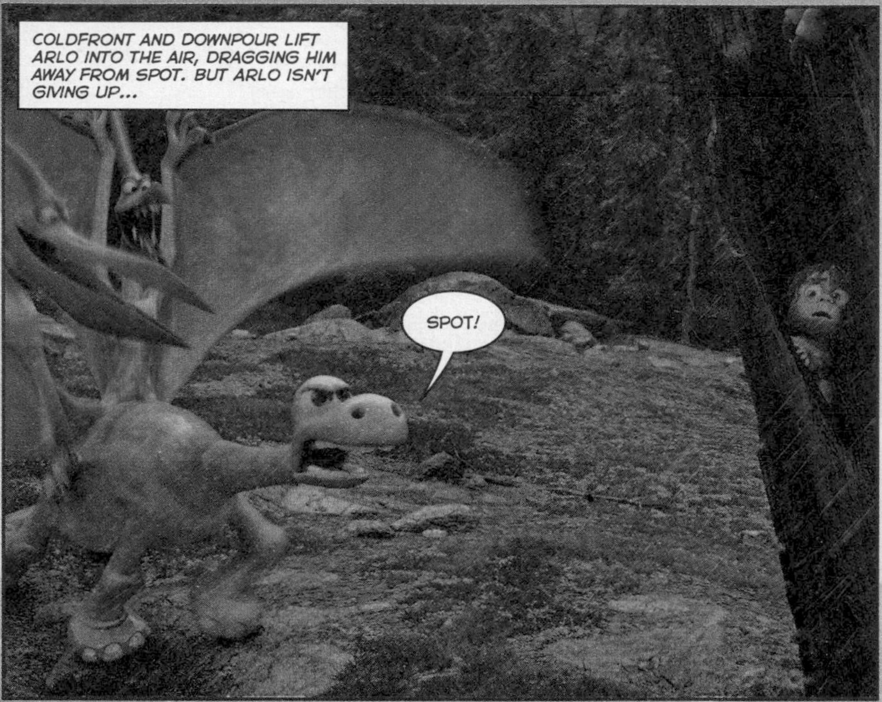
COLDFRONT AND DOWNPOUR LIFT ARLO INTO THE AIR, DRAGGING HIM AWAY FROM SPOT. BUT ARLO ISN'T GIVING UP...
SPOT!

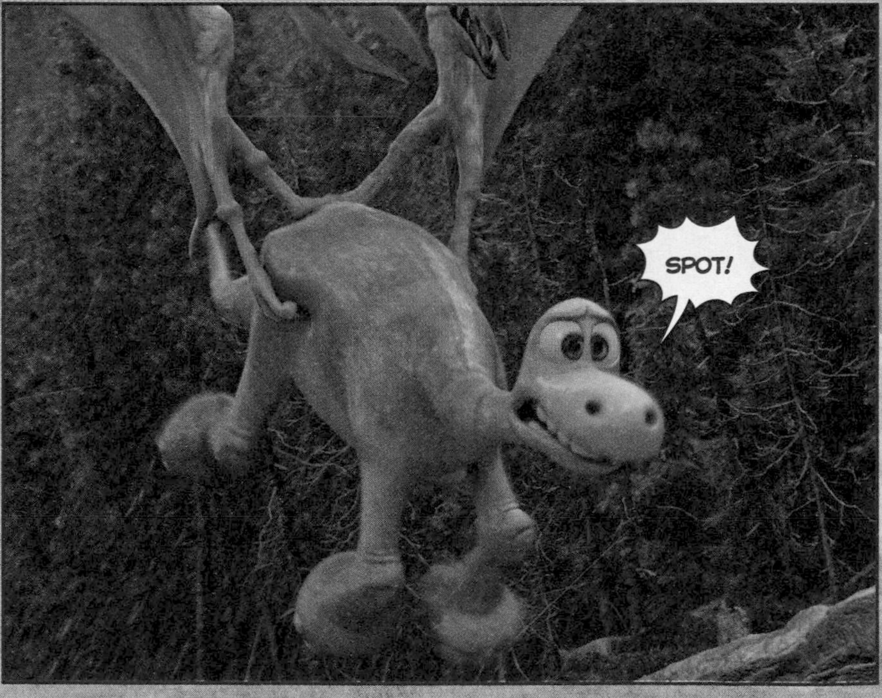
SPOT!

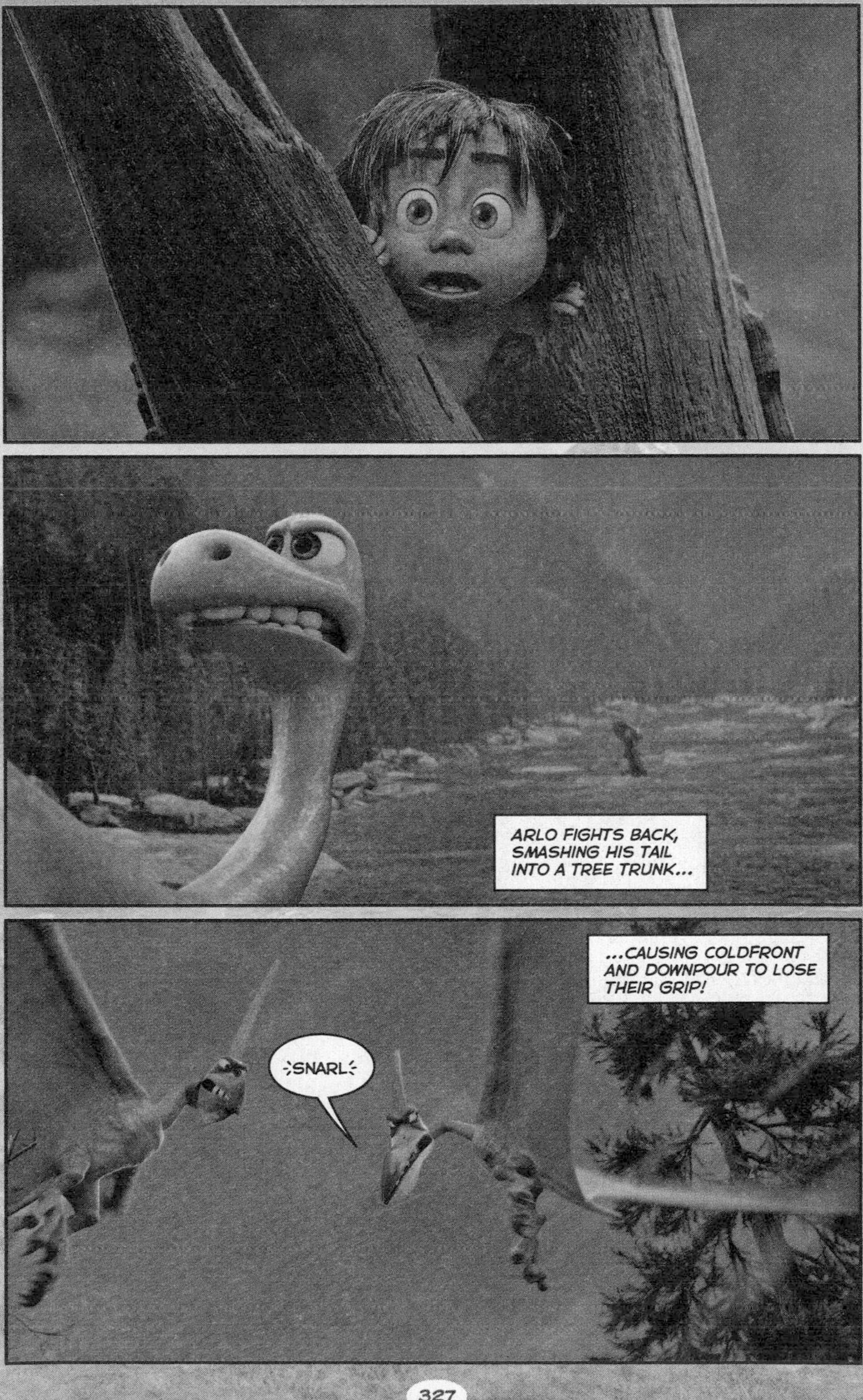
ARLO FIGHTS BACK, SMASHING HIS TAIL INTO A TREE TRUNK...
...CAUSING COLDFRONT AND DOWNPOUR TO LOSE THEIR GRIP!
SNARL

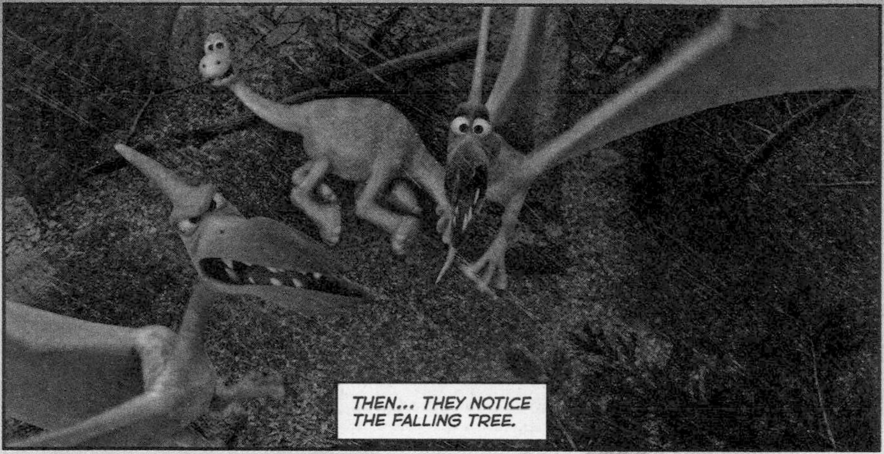
THEN... THEY NOTICE THE FALLING TREE.

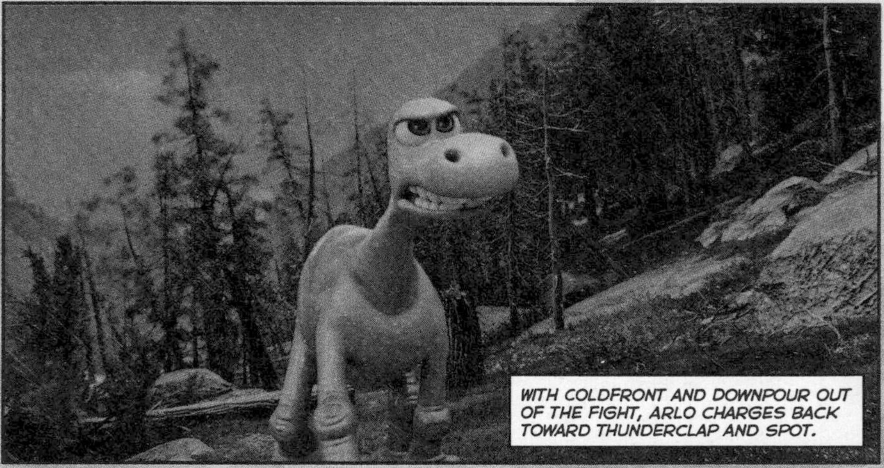
WITH COLDFRONT AND DOWNPOUR OUT OF THE FIGHT, ARLO CHARGES BACK TOWARD THUNDERCLAP AND SPOT.

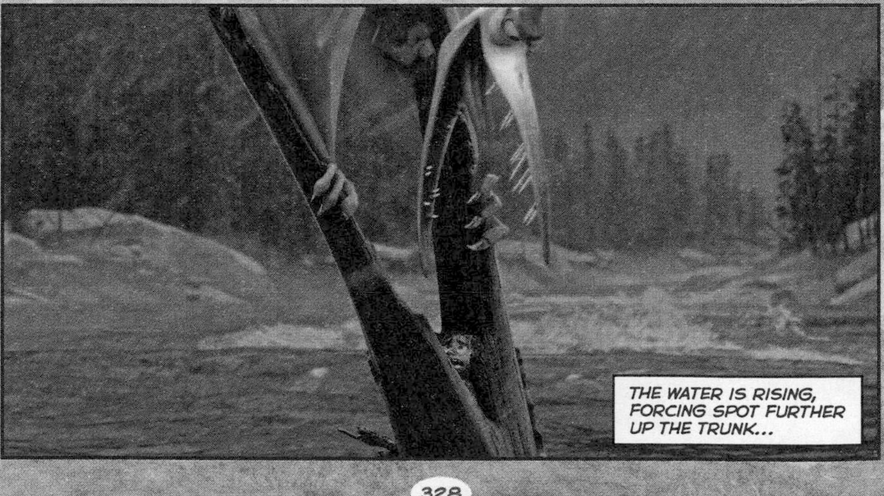
THE WATER IS RISING, FORCING SPOT FURTHER UP THE TRUNK...

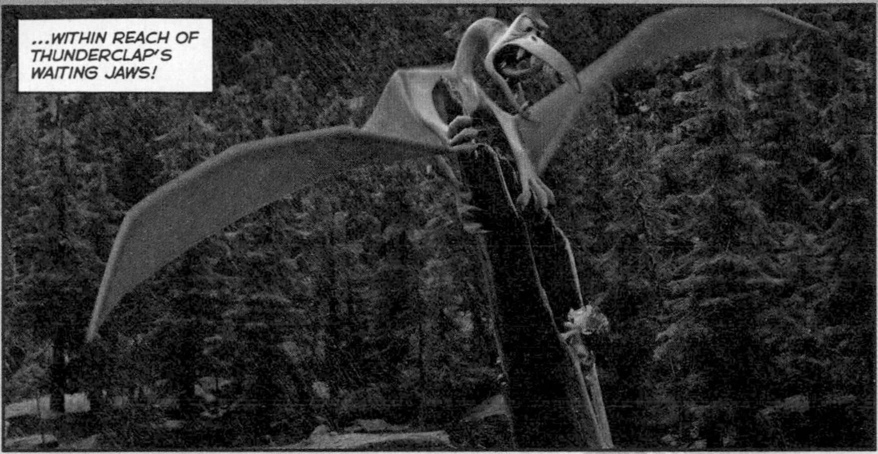
...WITHIN REACH OF THUNDERCLAP'S WAITING JAWS!

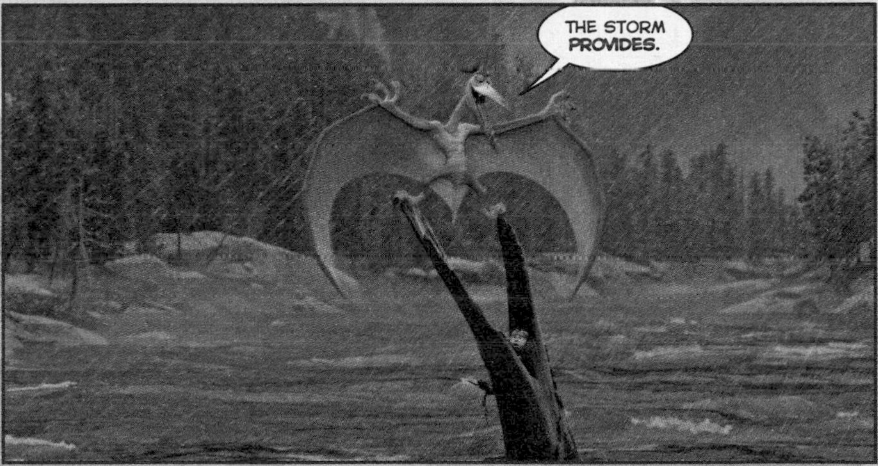
THE STORM PROVIDES.

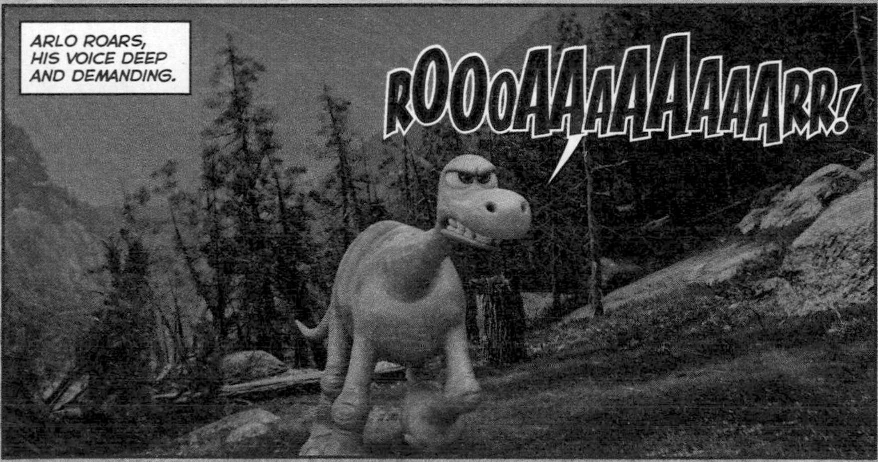
ARLO ROARS, HIS VOICE DEEP AND DEMANDING.
ROOOAAAAAAAARR!

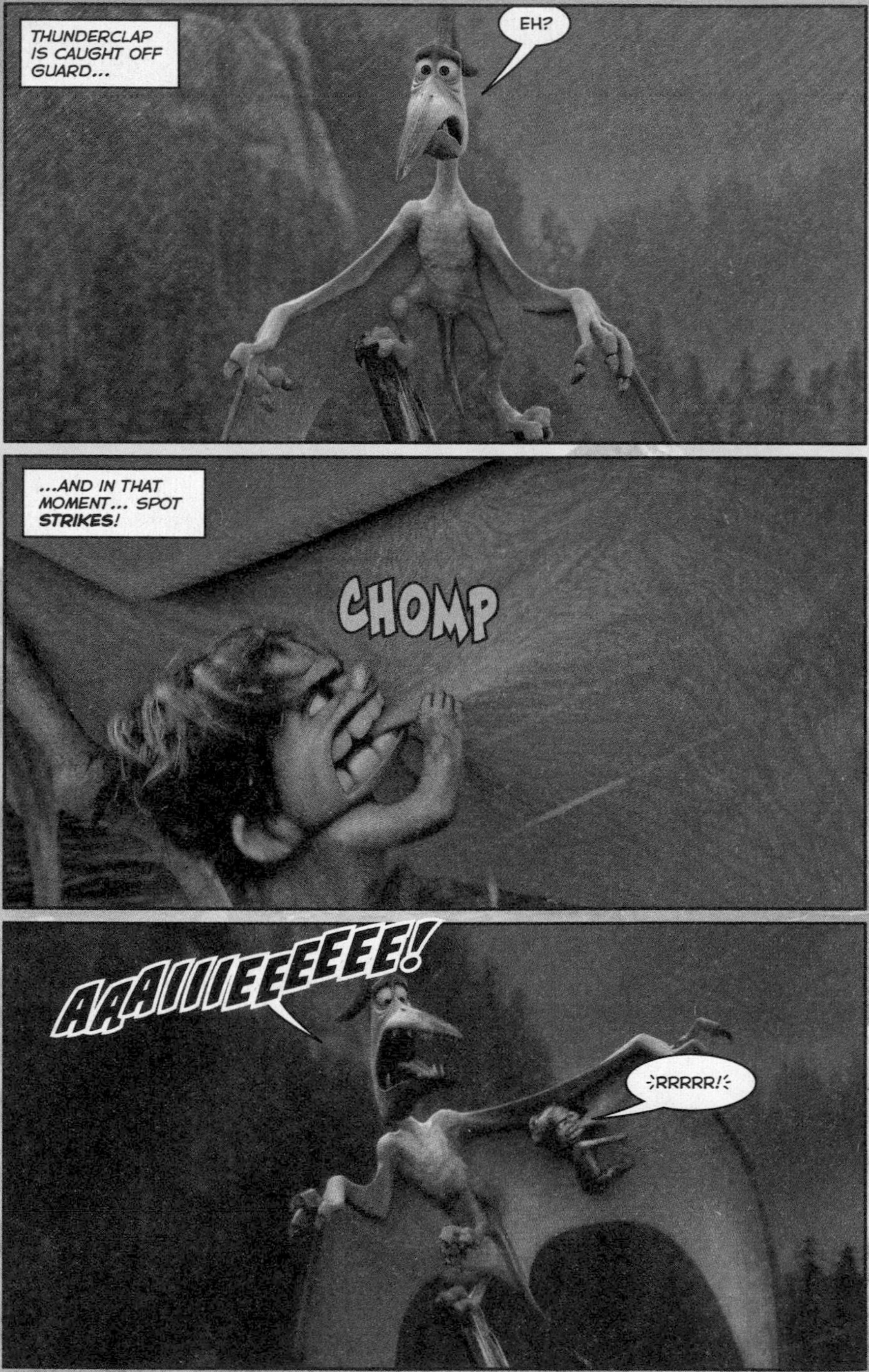
THUNDERCLAP IS CAUGHT OFF GUARD...
EH?
...AND IN THAT MOMENT... SPOT STRIKES!
CHOMP
AAAIIIIEEEEEEE!
RRRRR!

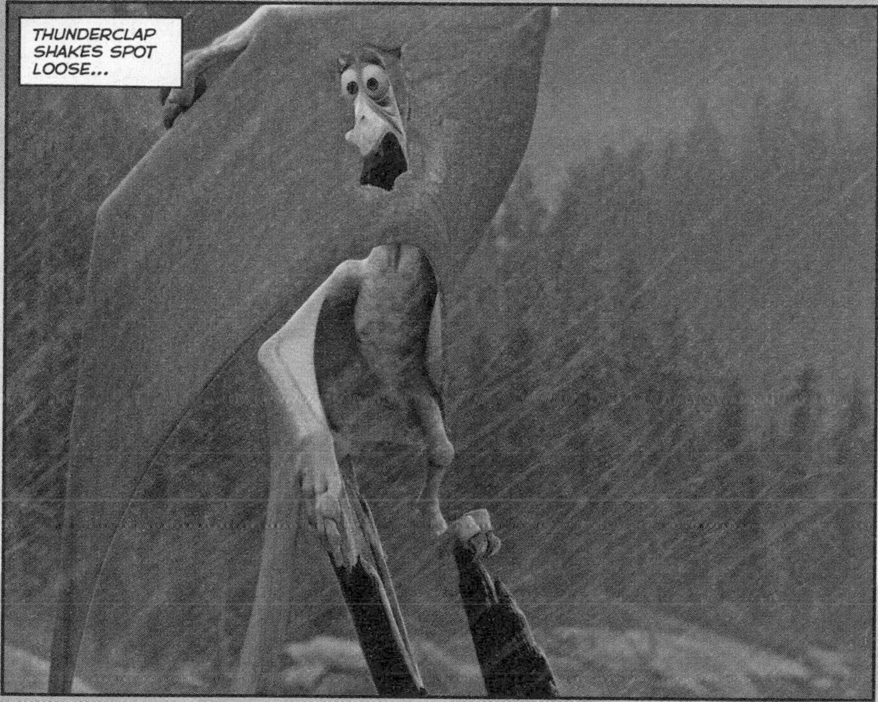
THUNDERCLAP SHAKES SPOT LOOSE...

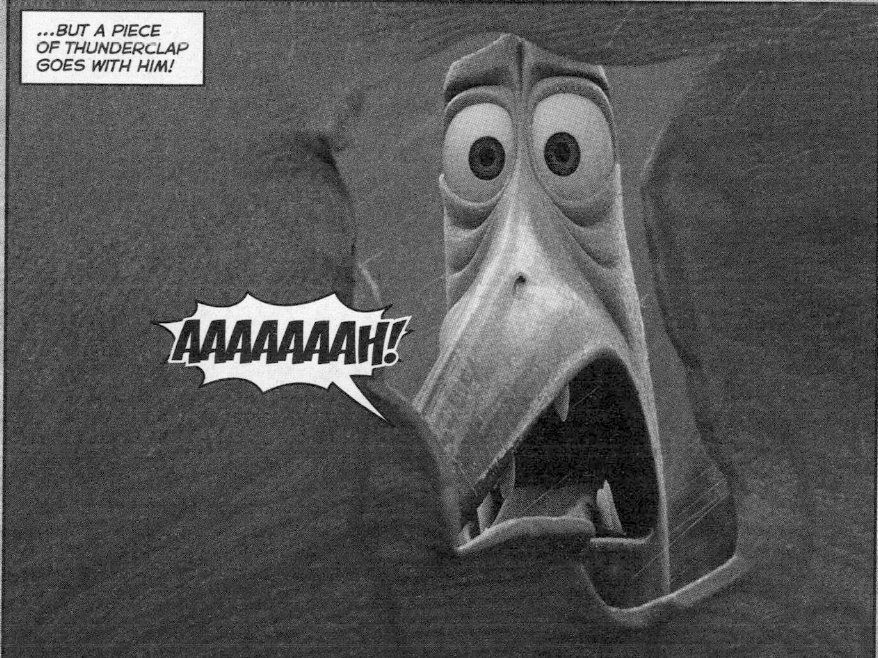
...BUT A PIECE OF THUNDERCLAP GOES WITH HIM!
AAAAAAAH!

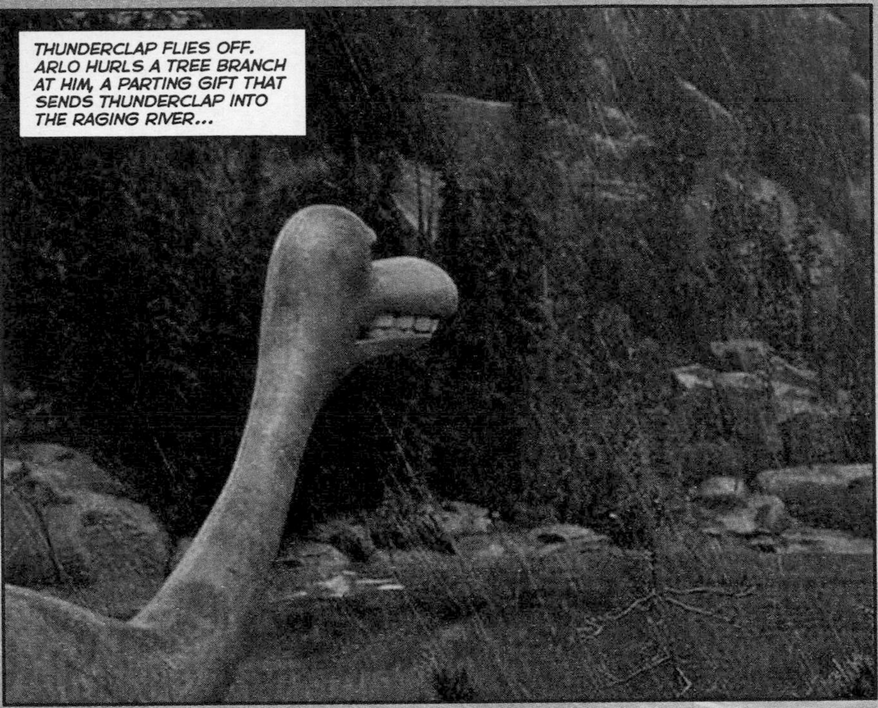
THUNDERCLAP FLIES OFF. ARLO HURLS A TREE BRANCH AT HIM, A PARTING GIFT THAT SENDS THUNDERCLAP INTO THE RAGING RIVER...

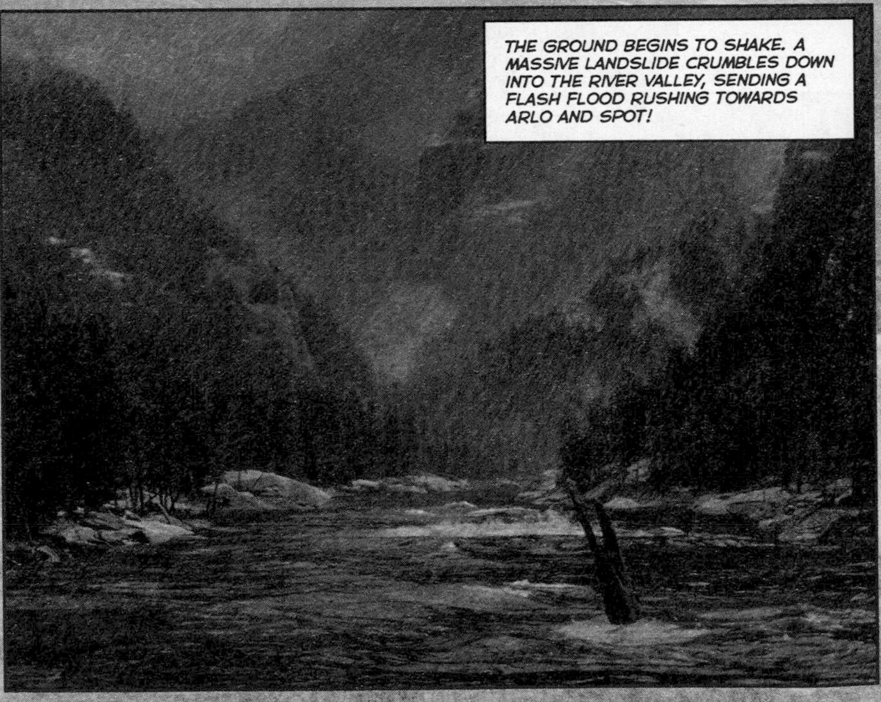
THE GROUND BEGINS TO SHAKE. A MASSIVE LANDSLIDE CRUMBLES DOWN INTO THE RIVER VALLEY, SENDING A FLASH FLOOD RUSHING TOWARDS ARLO AND SPOT!

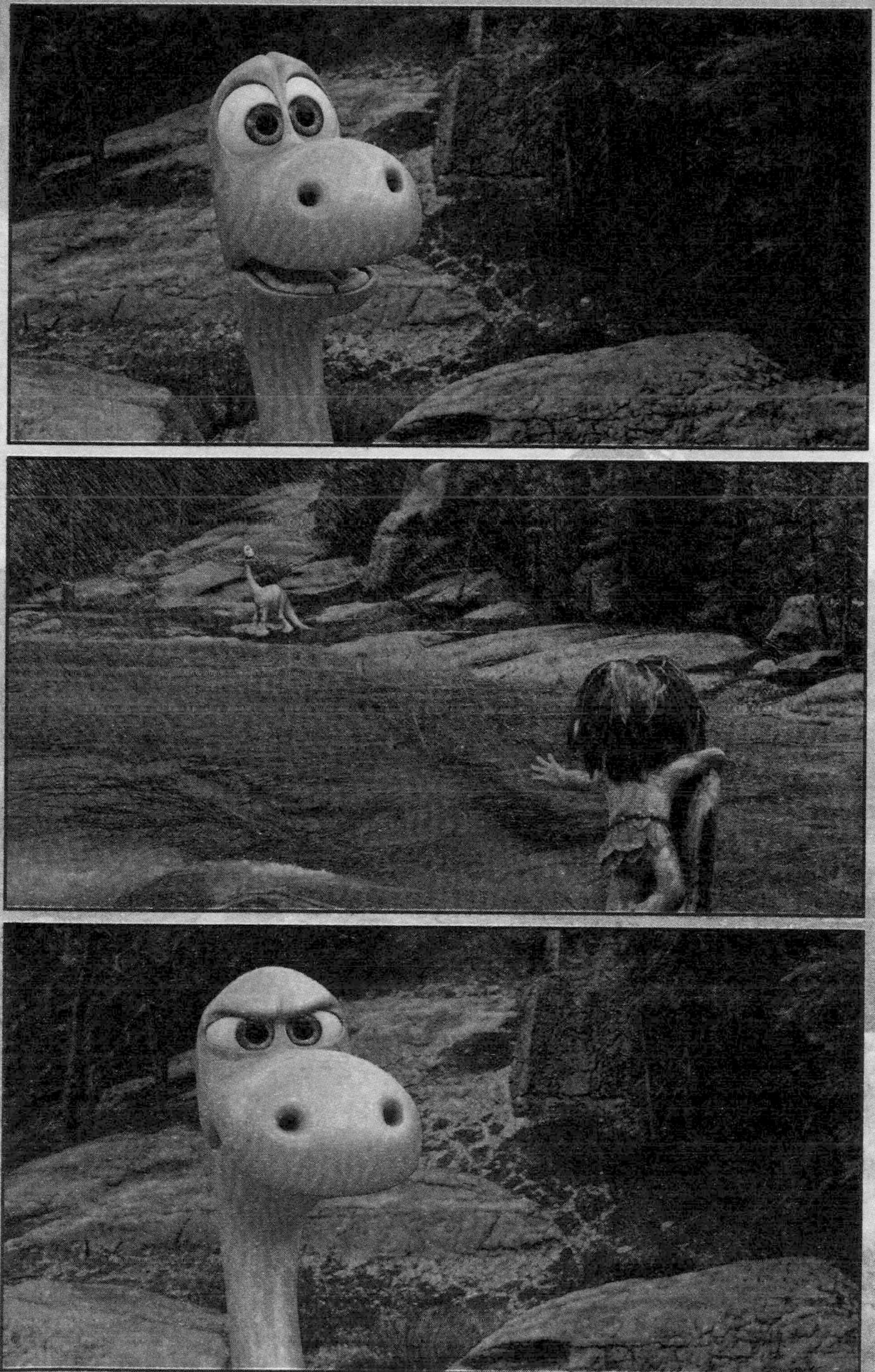

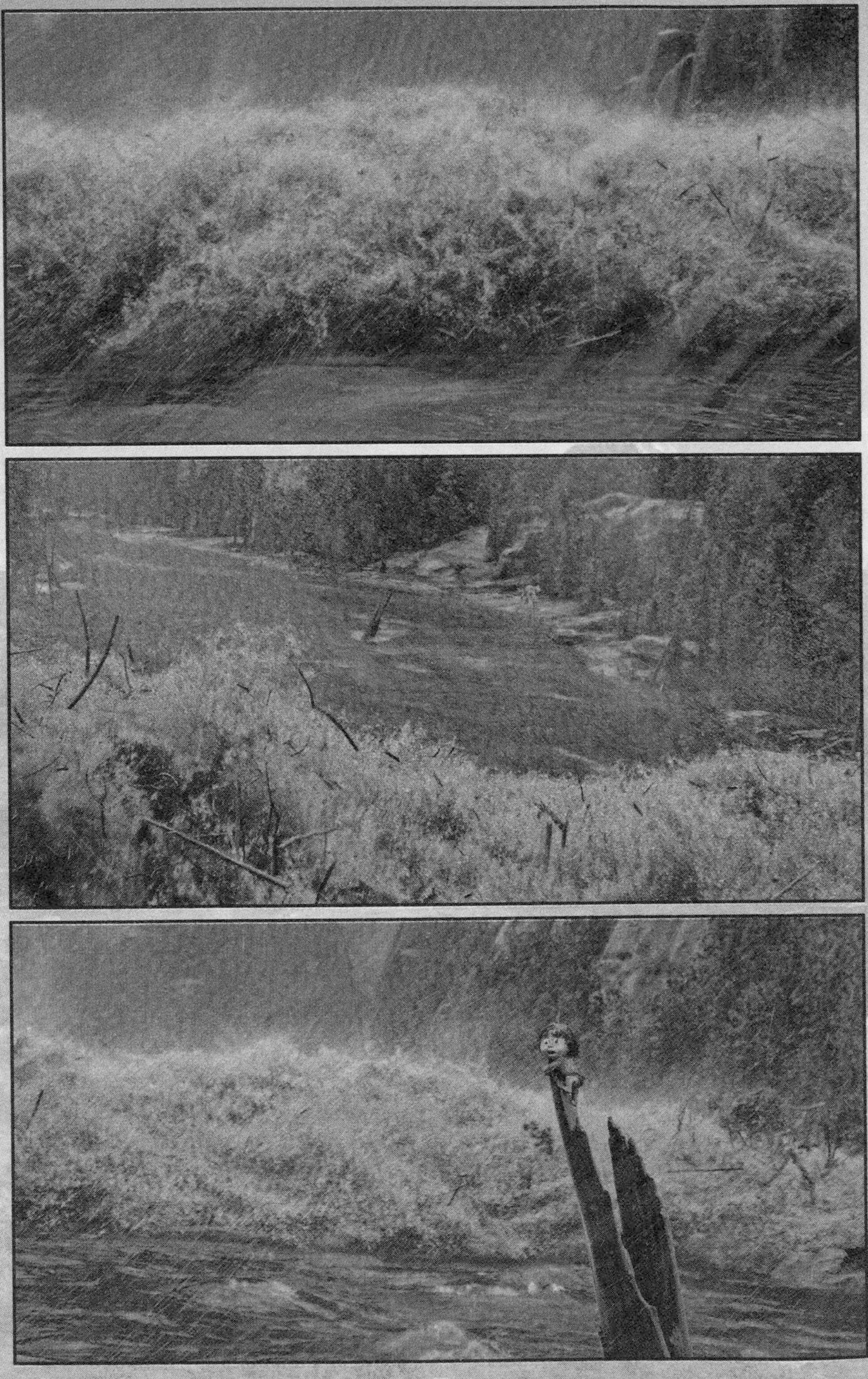

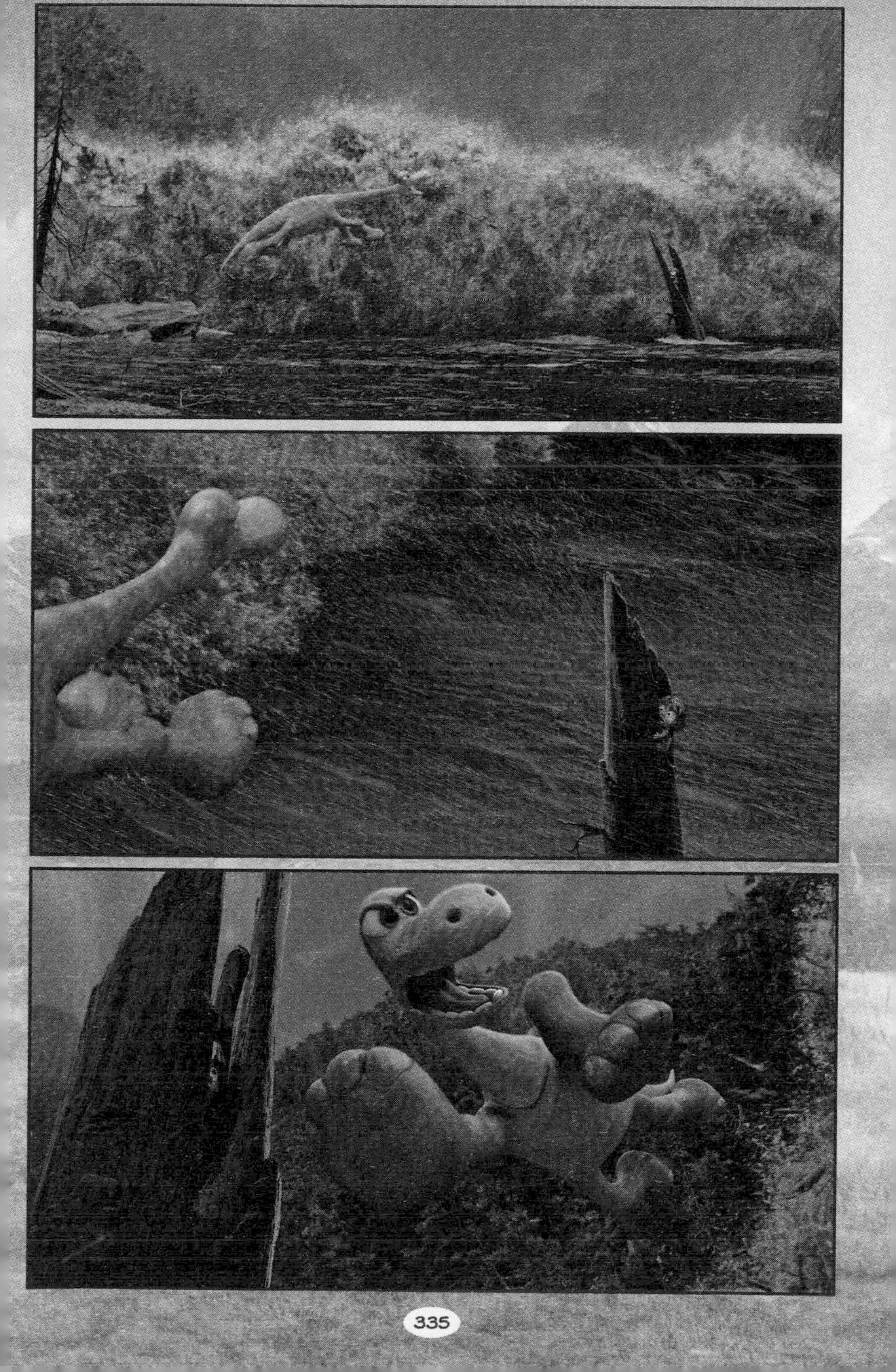

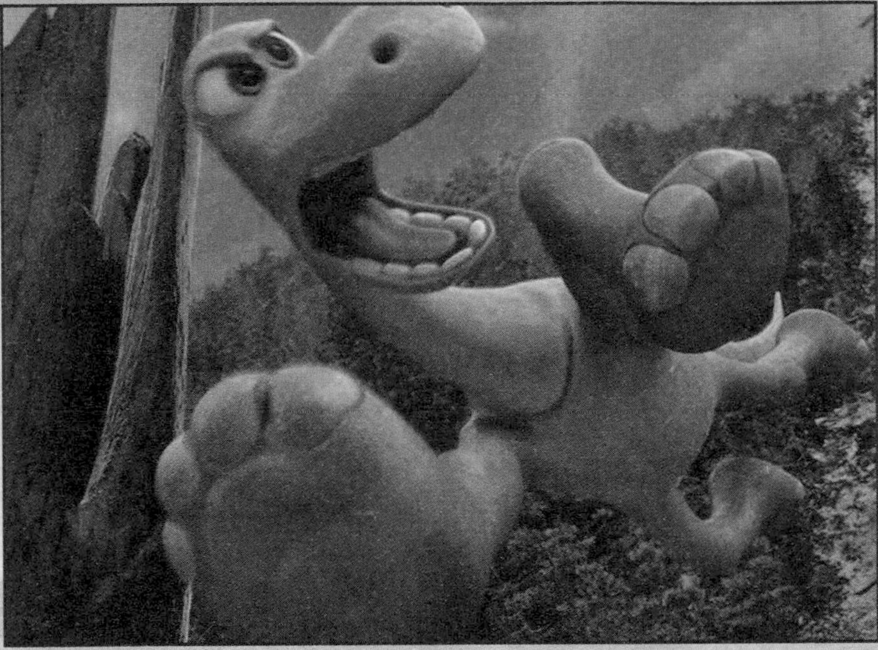

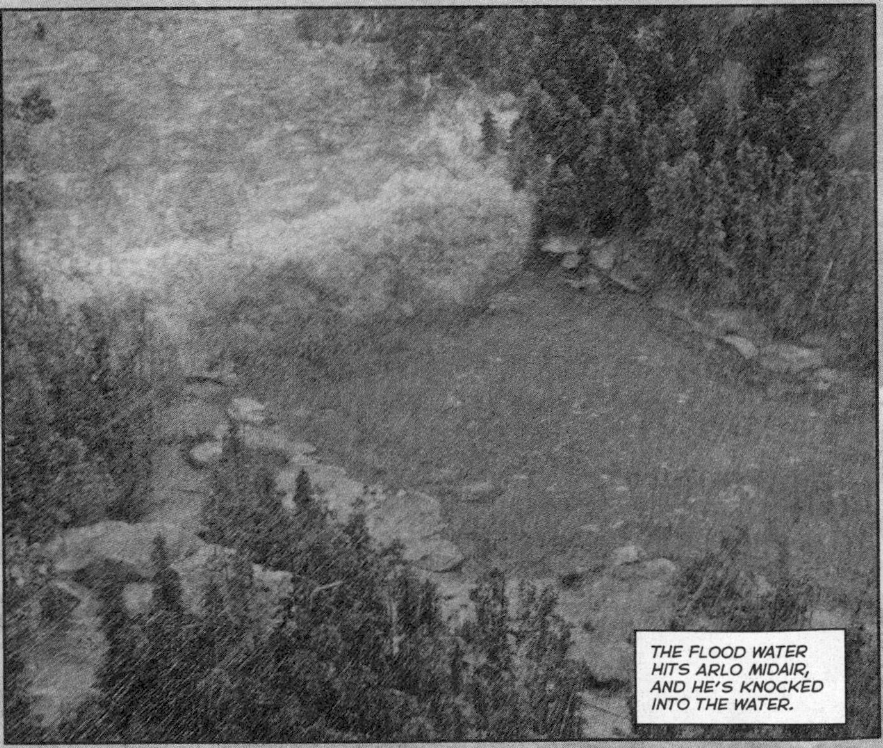
THE FLOOD WATER HITS ARLO MIDAIR, AND HE'S KNOCKED INTO THE WATER.

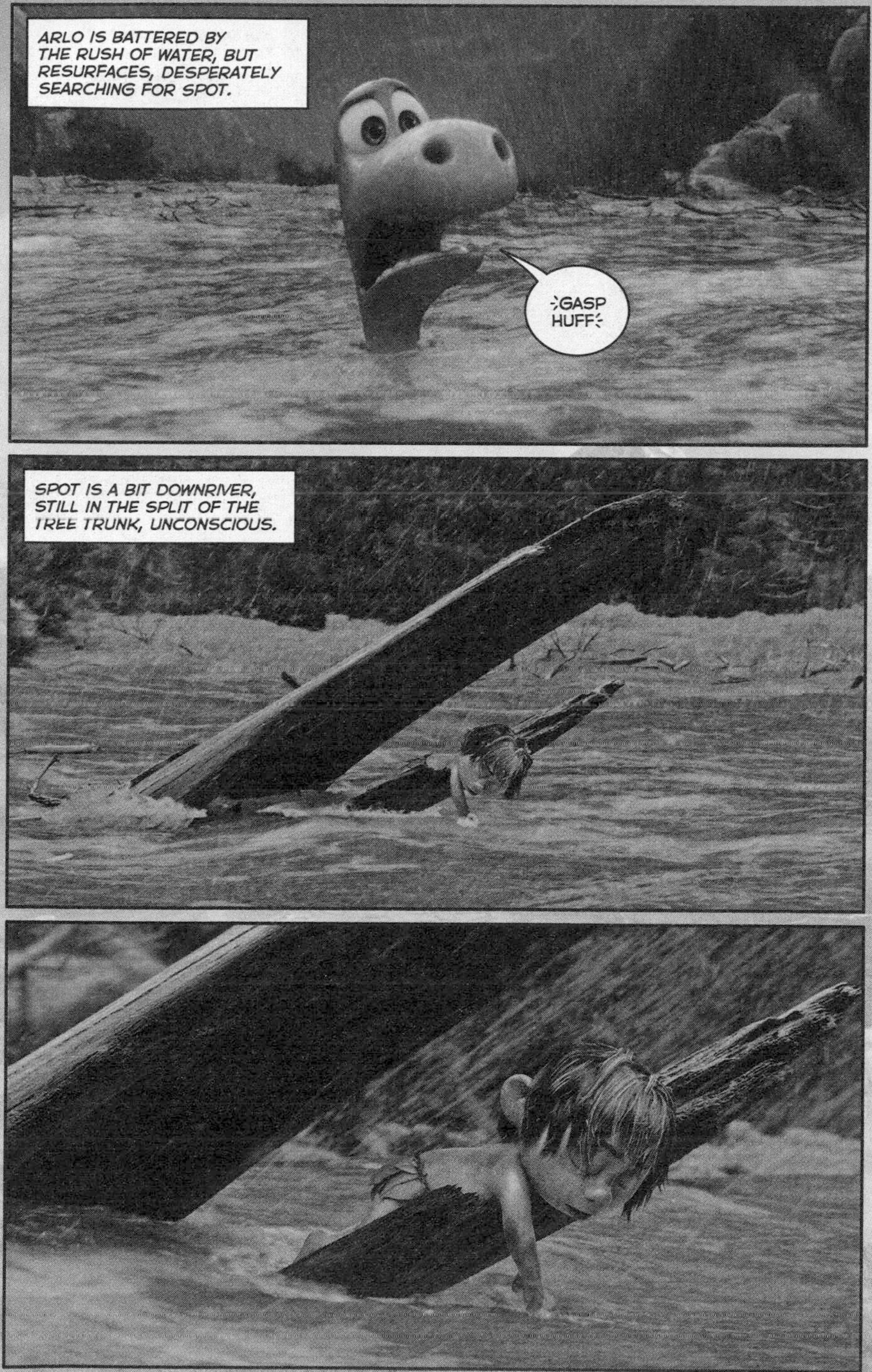
ARLO IS BATTERED BY THE RUSH OF WATER, BUT RESURFACES, DESPERATELY SEARCHING FOR SPOT.
GASP HUFF
SPOT IS A BIT DOWNRIVER, STILL IN THE SPLIT OF THE TREE TRUNK, UNCONSCIOUS.

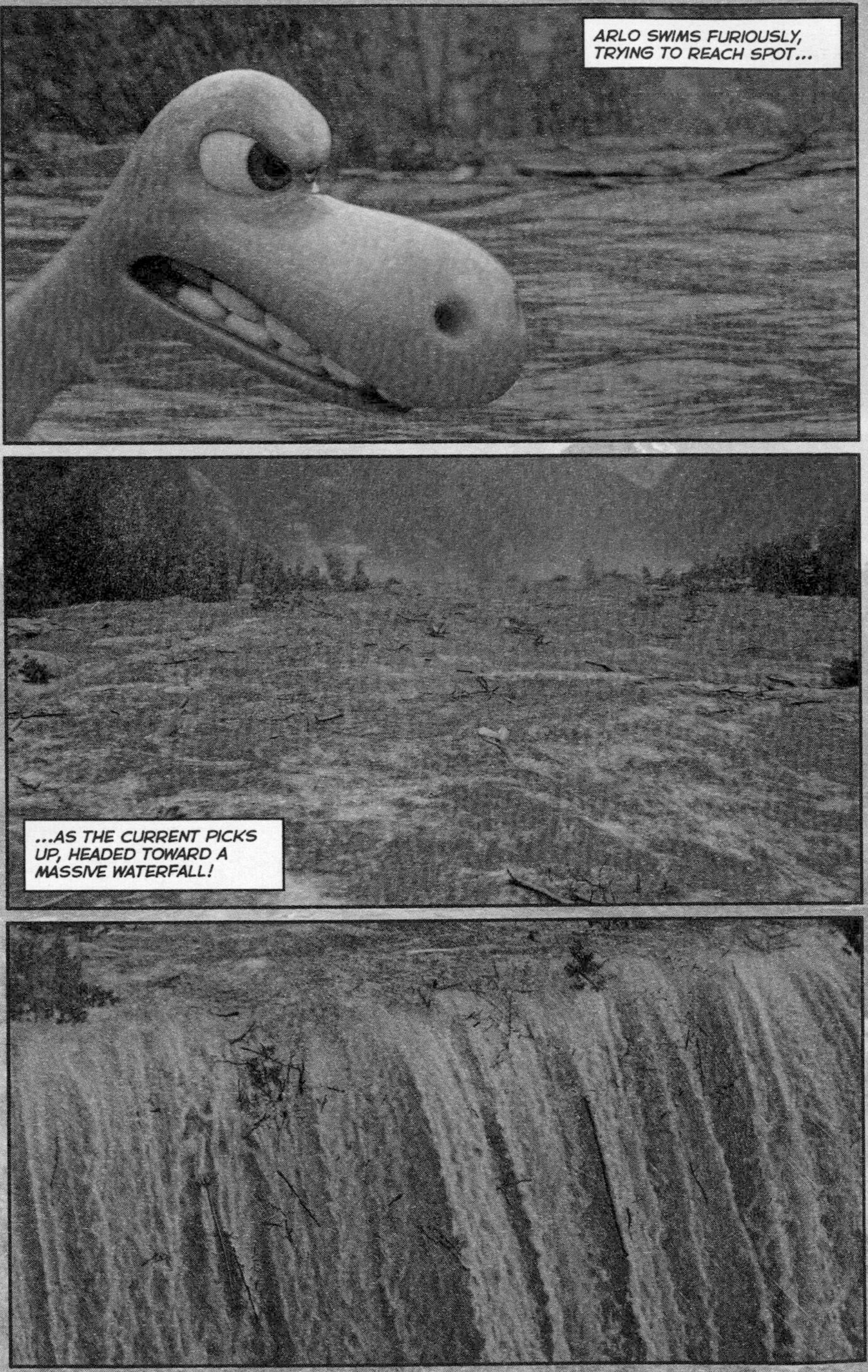
ARLO SWIMS FURIOUSLY, TRYING TO REACH SPOT...
...AS THE CURRENT PICKS UP, HEADED TOWARD A MASSIVE WATERFALL!

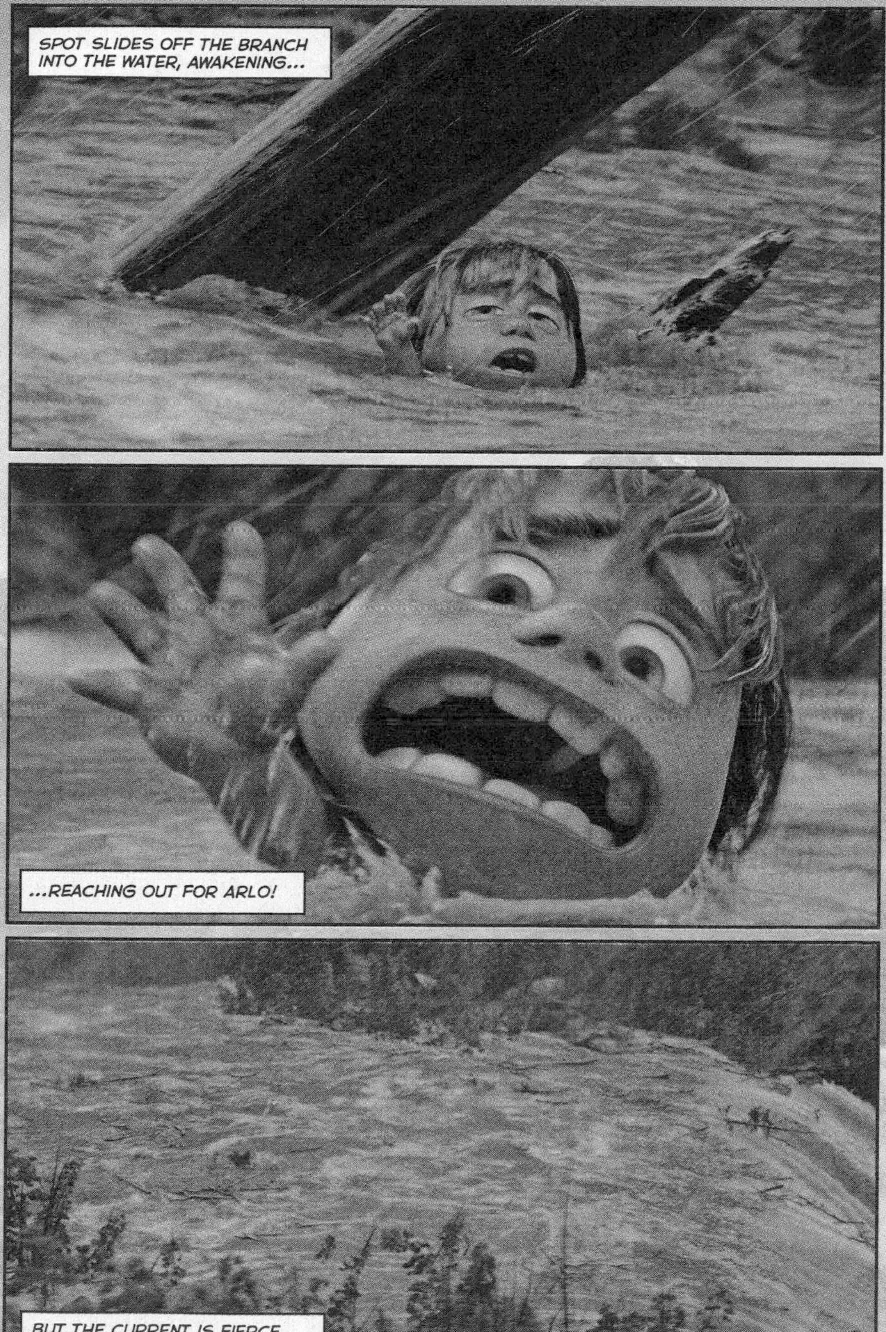
SPOT SLIDES OFF THE BRANCH INTO THE WATER, AWAKENING...
...REACHING OUT FOR ARLO!
BUT THE CURRENT IS FIERCE NOW, THE WATERFALL CLOSE...

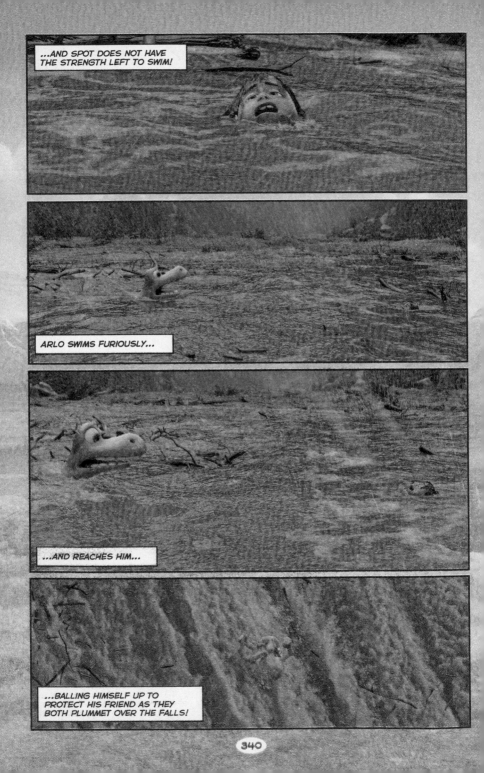

...AND SPOT DOES NOT HAVE THE STRENGTH LEFT TO SWIM!

ARLO SWIMS FURIOUSLY...

...AND REACHES HIM...

...BALLING HIMSELF UP TO PROTECT HIS FRIEND AS THEY BOTH PLUMMET OVER THE FALLS!

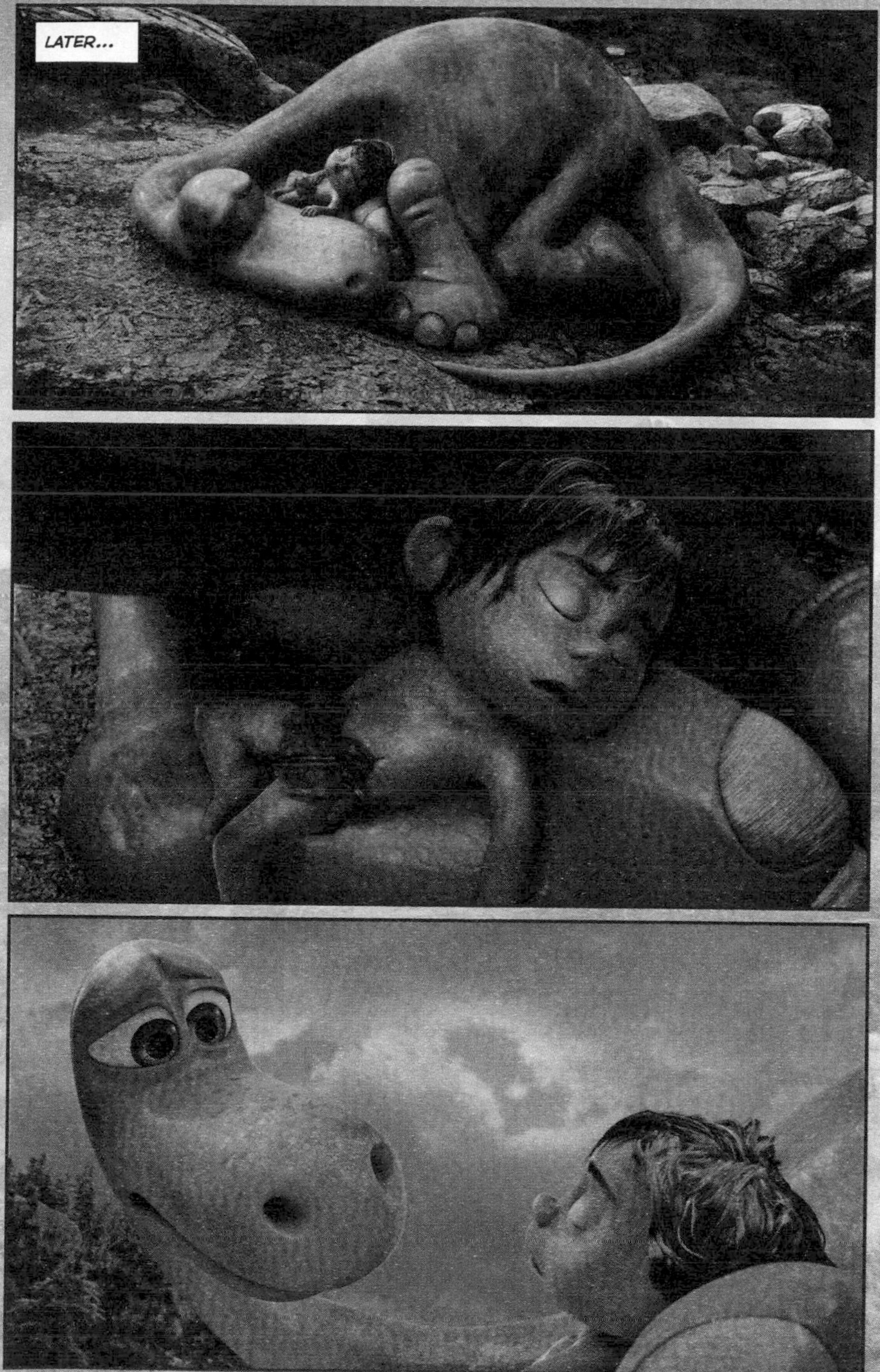
LATER...

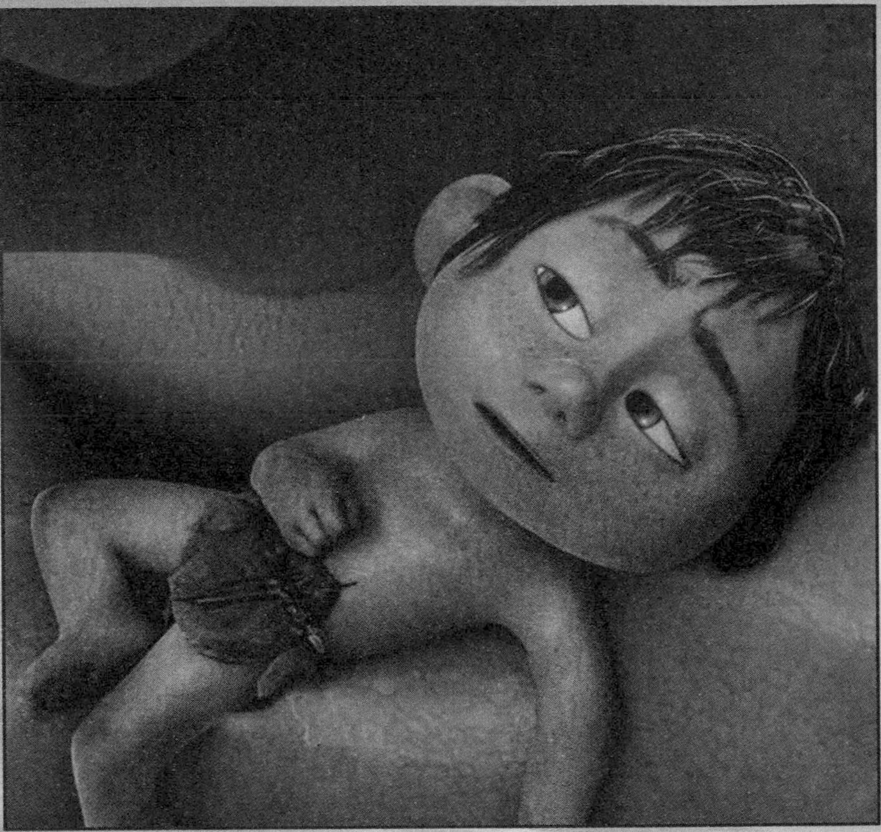

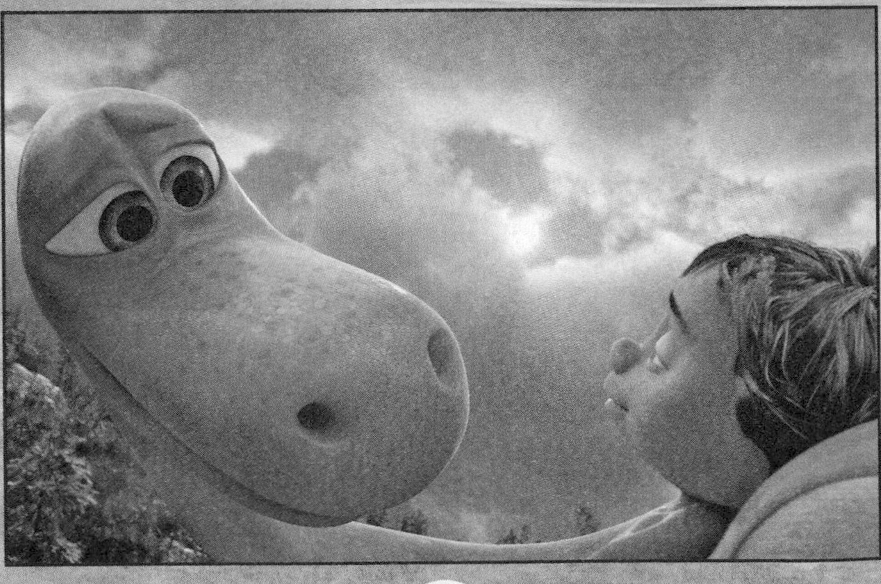

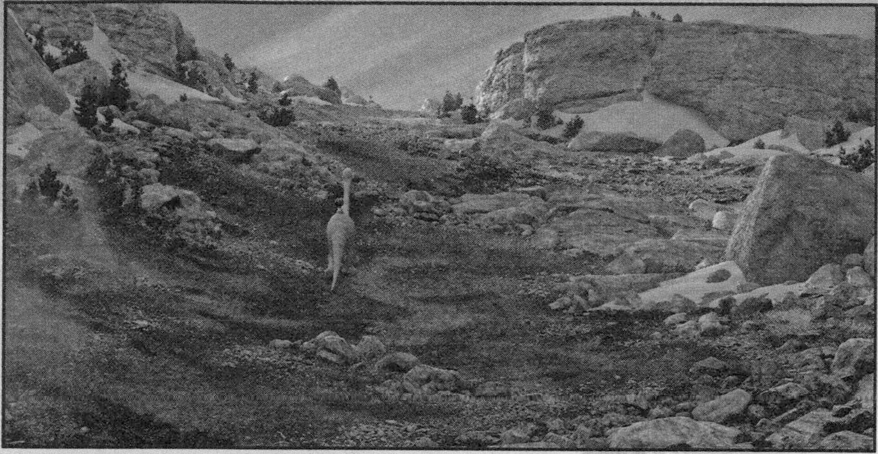

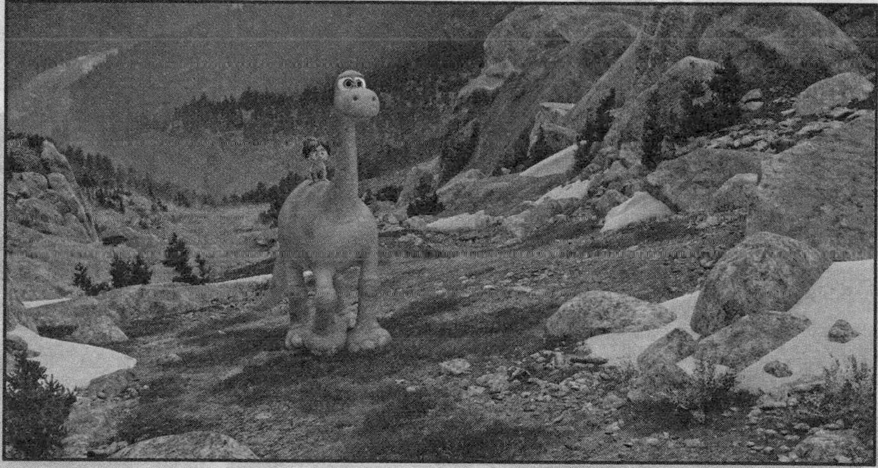

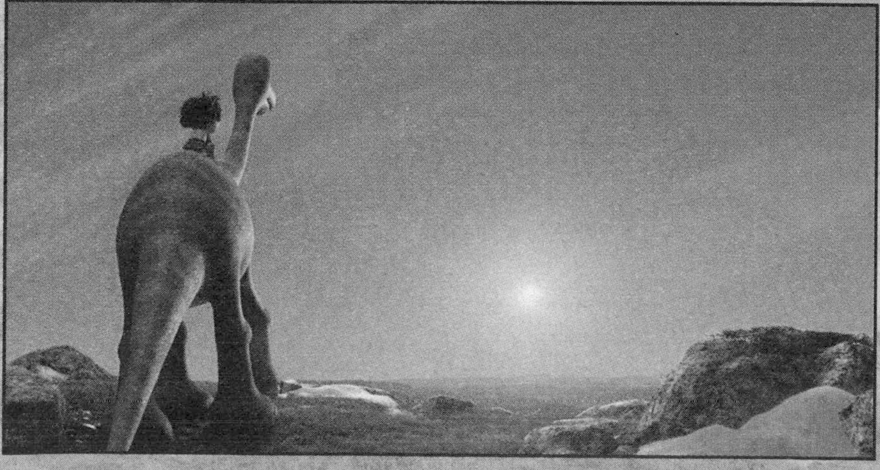

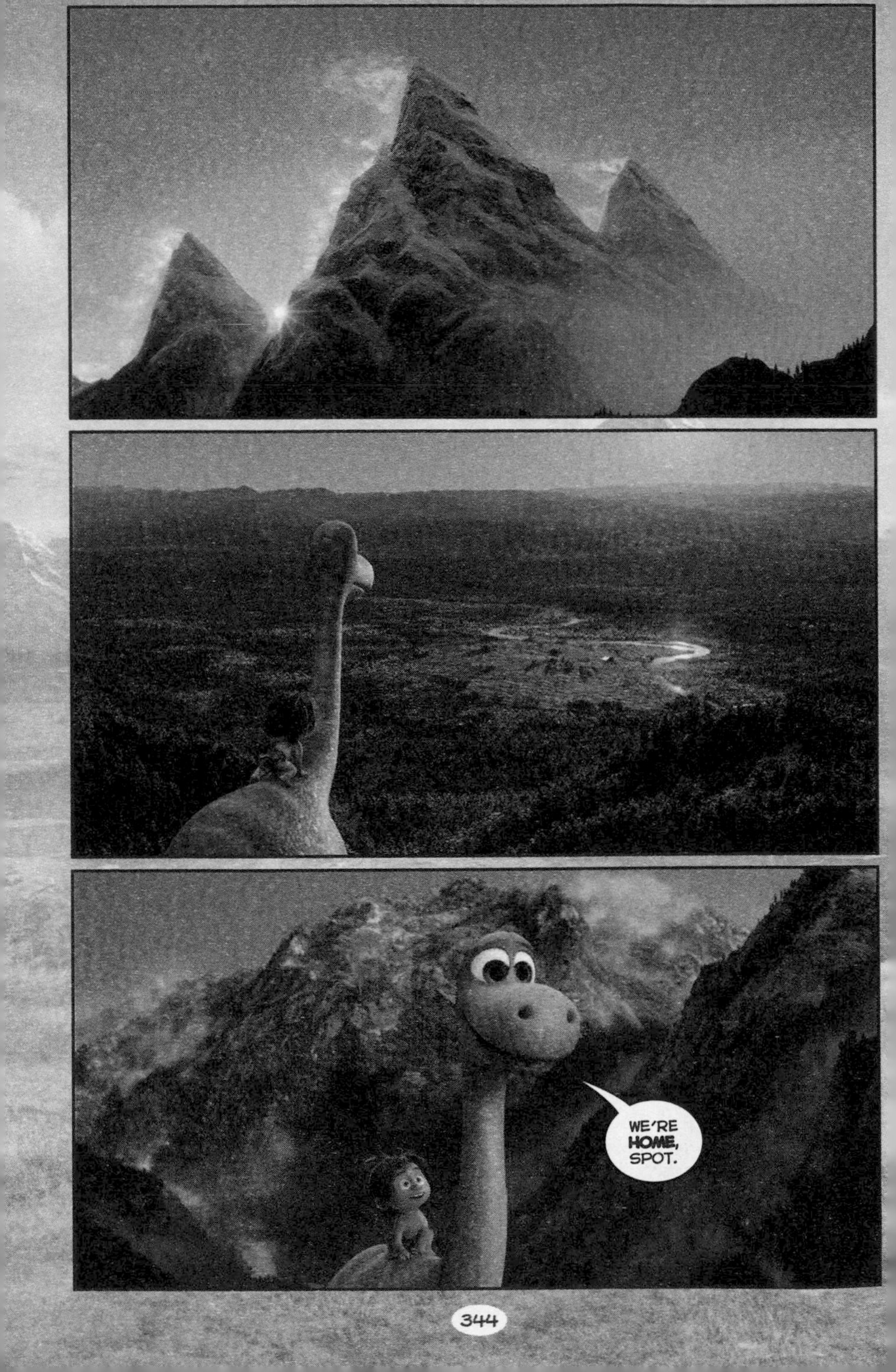
WE'RE **HOME**, SPOT.

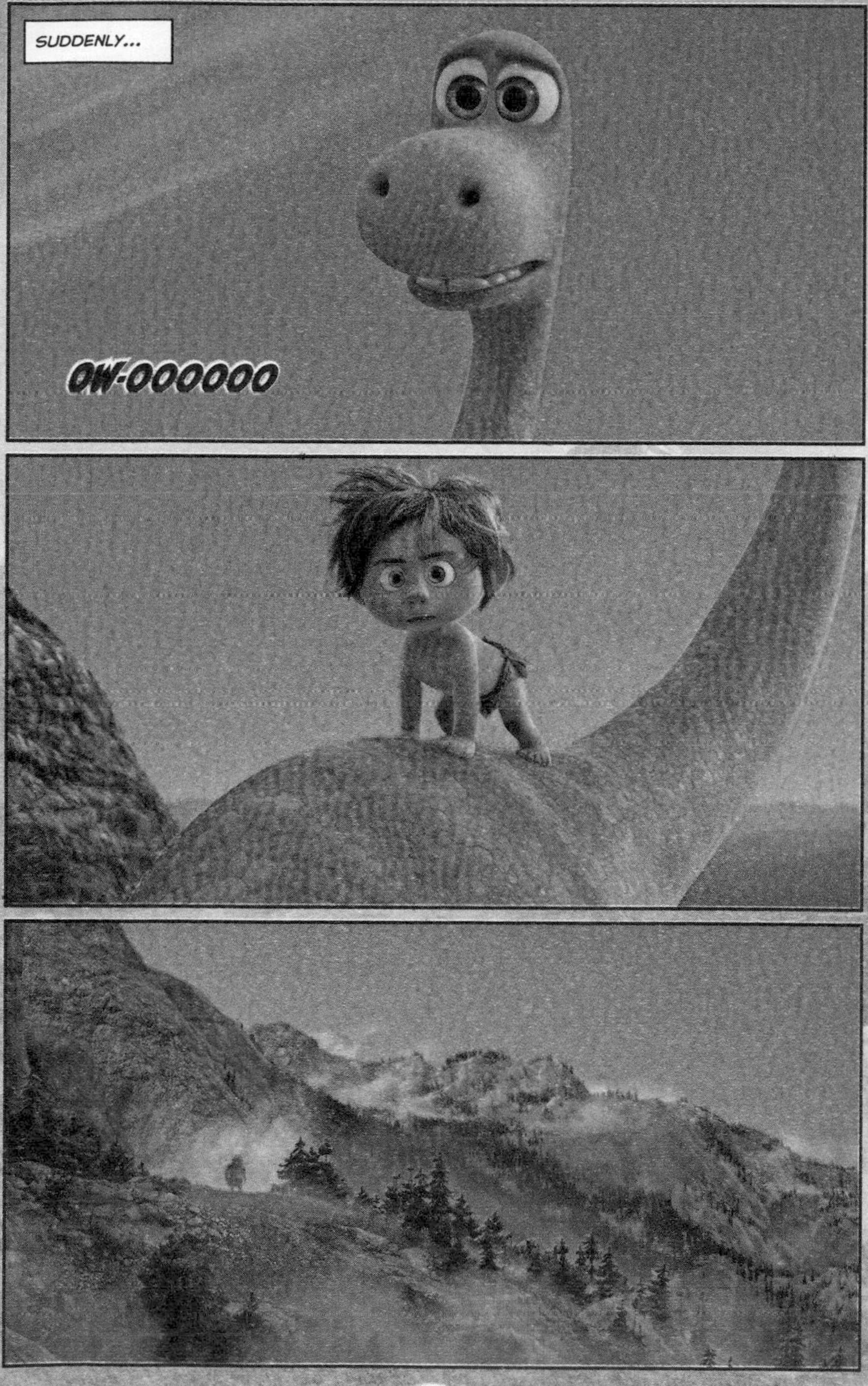
SUDDENLY...
OW-OOOOOO

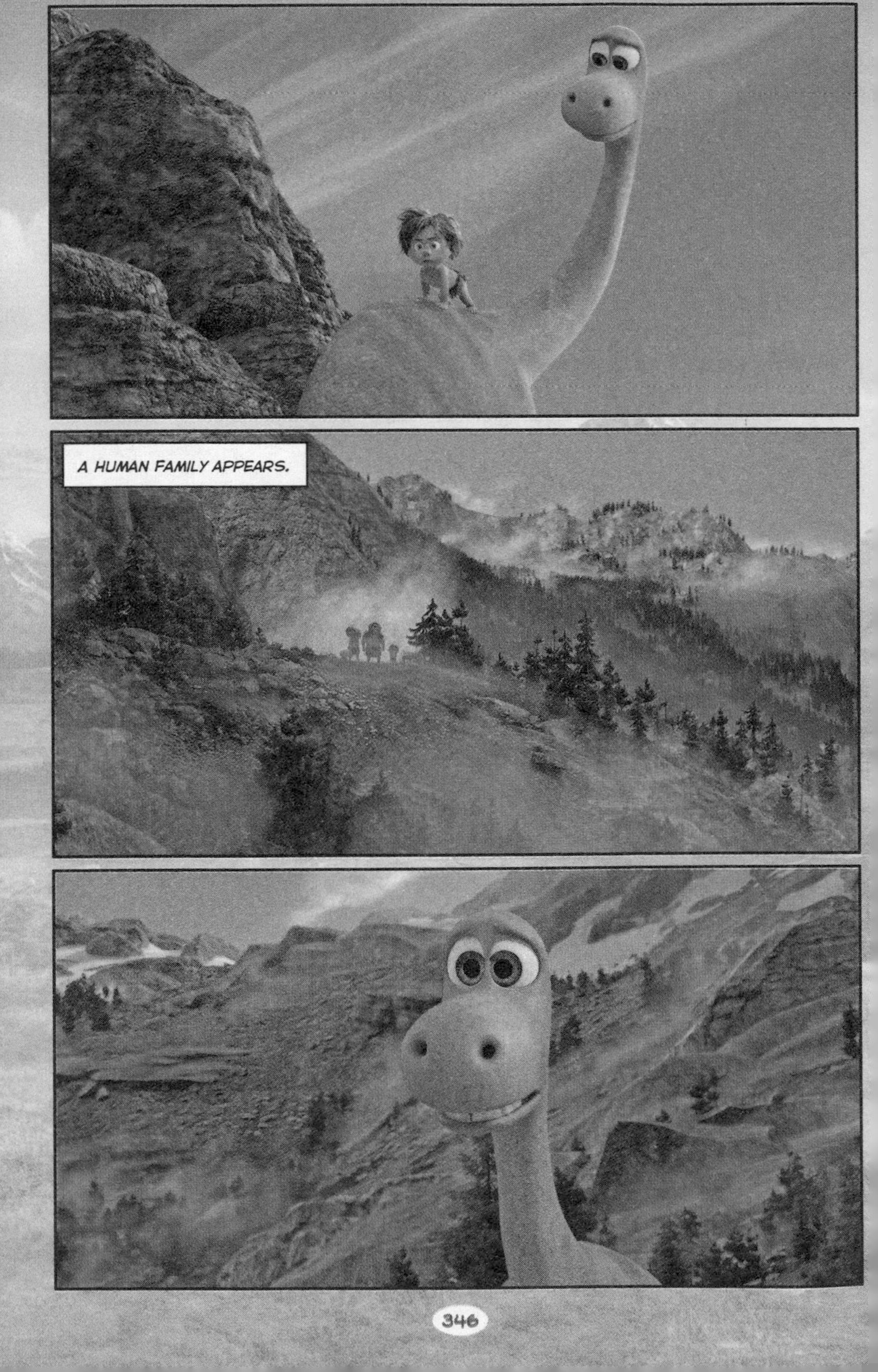
A HUMAN FAMILY APPEARS.

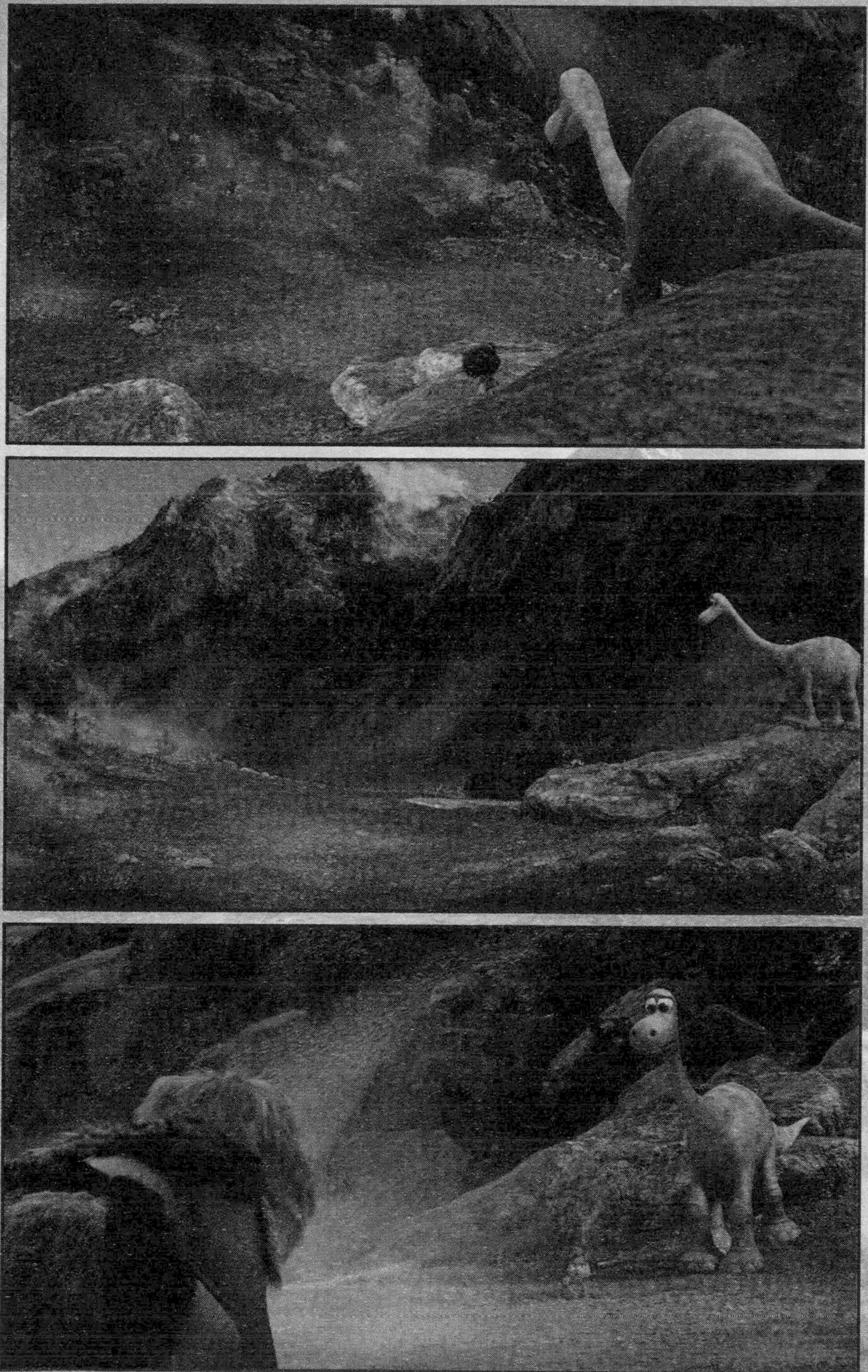

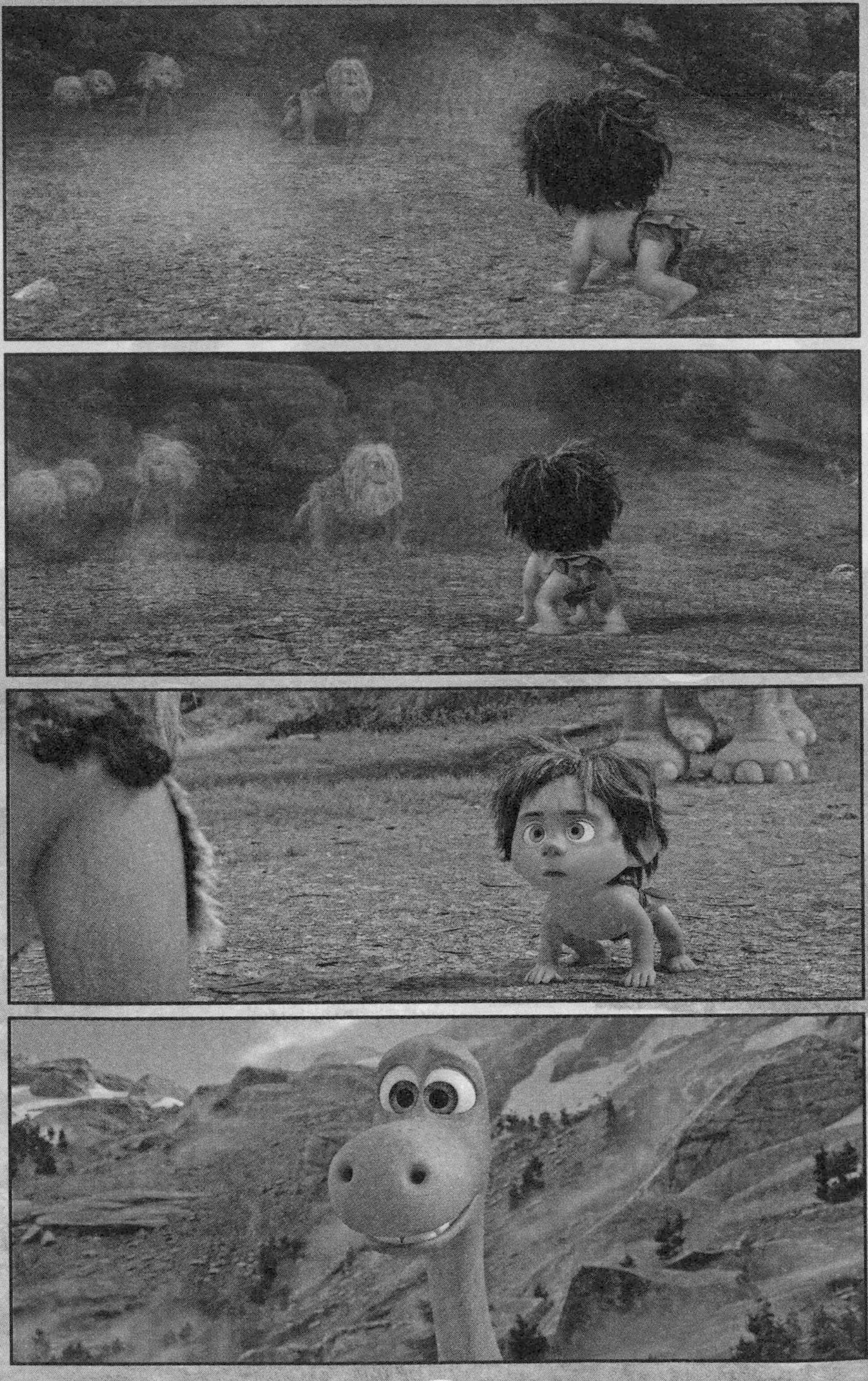

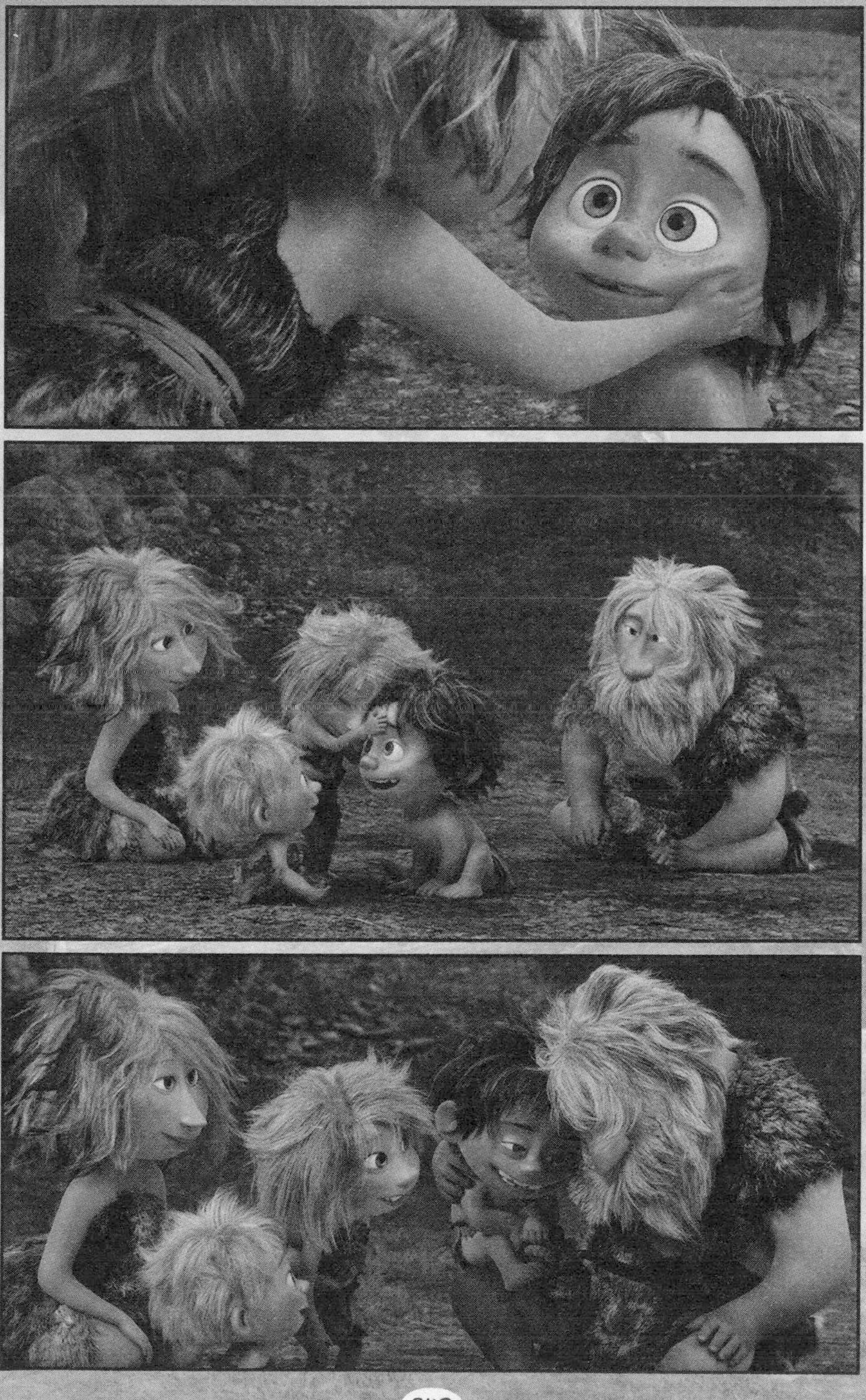

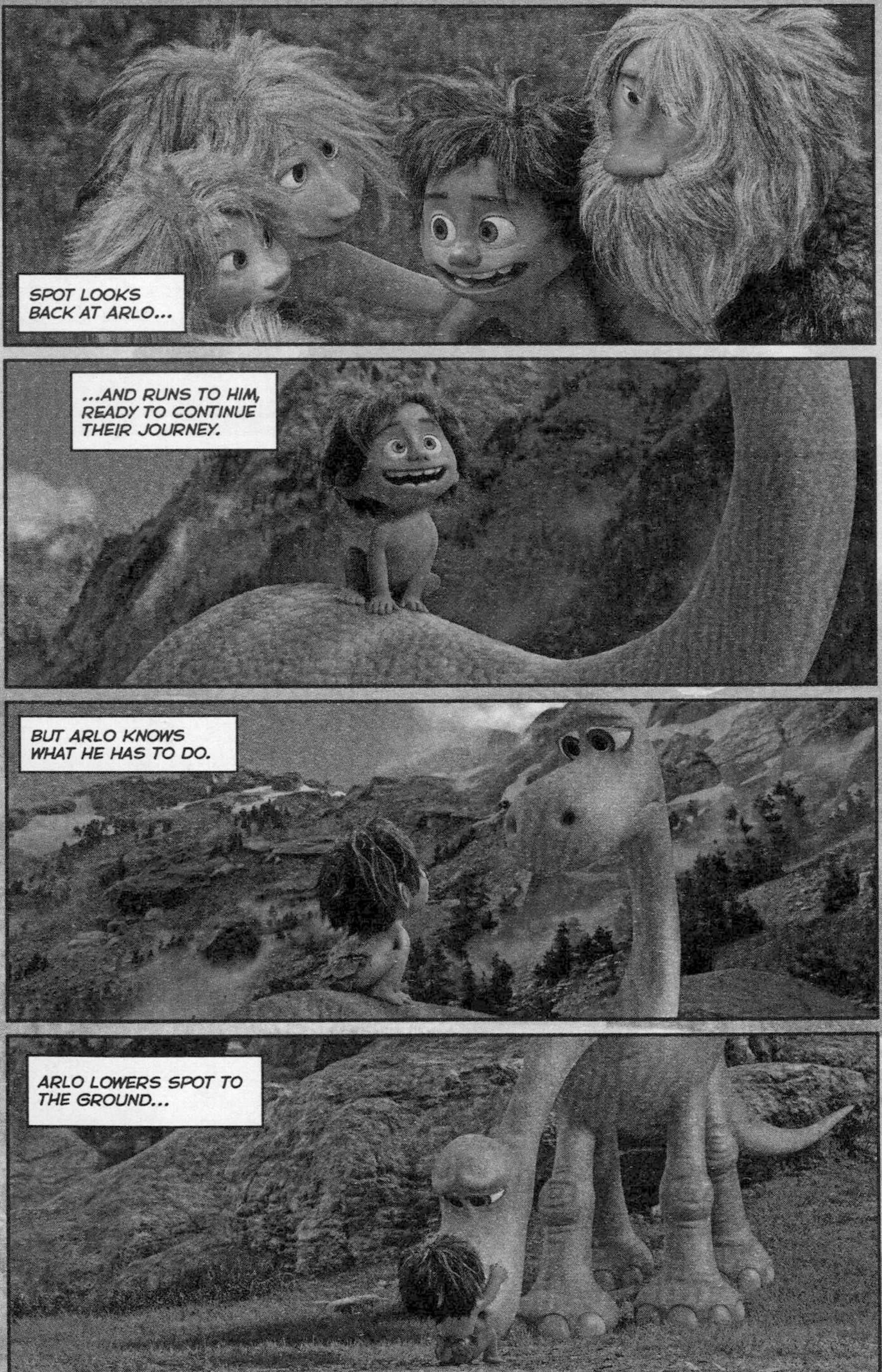
SPOT LOOKS BACK AT ARLO...
...AND RUNS TO HIM, READY TO CONTINUE THEIR JOURNEY.
BUT ARLO KNOWS WHAT HE HAS TO DO.
ARLO LOWERS SPOT TO THE GROUND...

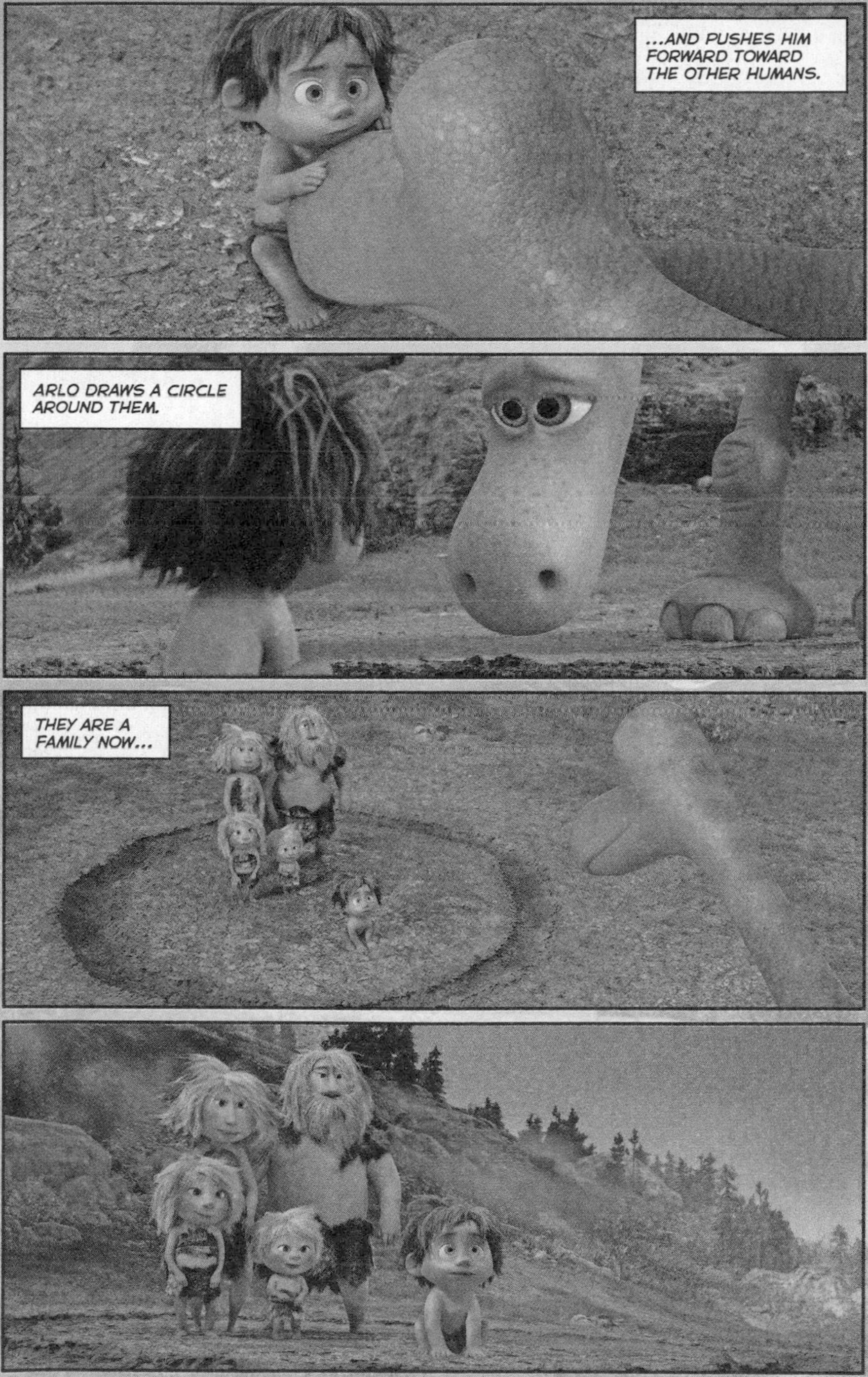
...AND PUSHES HIM FORWARD TOWARD THE OTHER HUMANS.
ARLO DRAWS A CIRCLE AROUND THEM.
THEY ARE A FAMILY NOW...

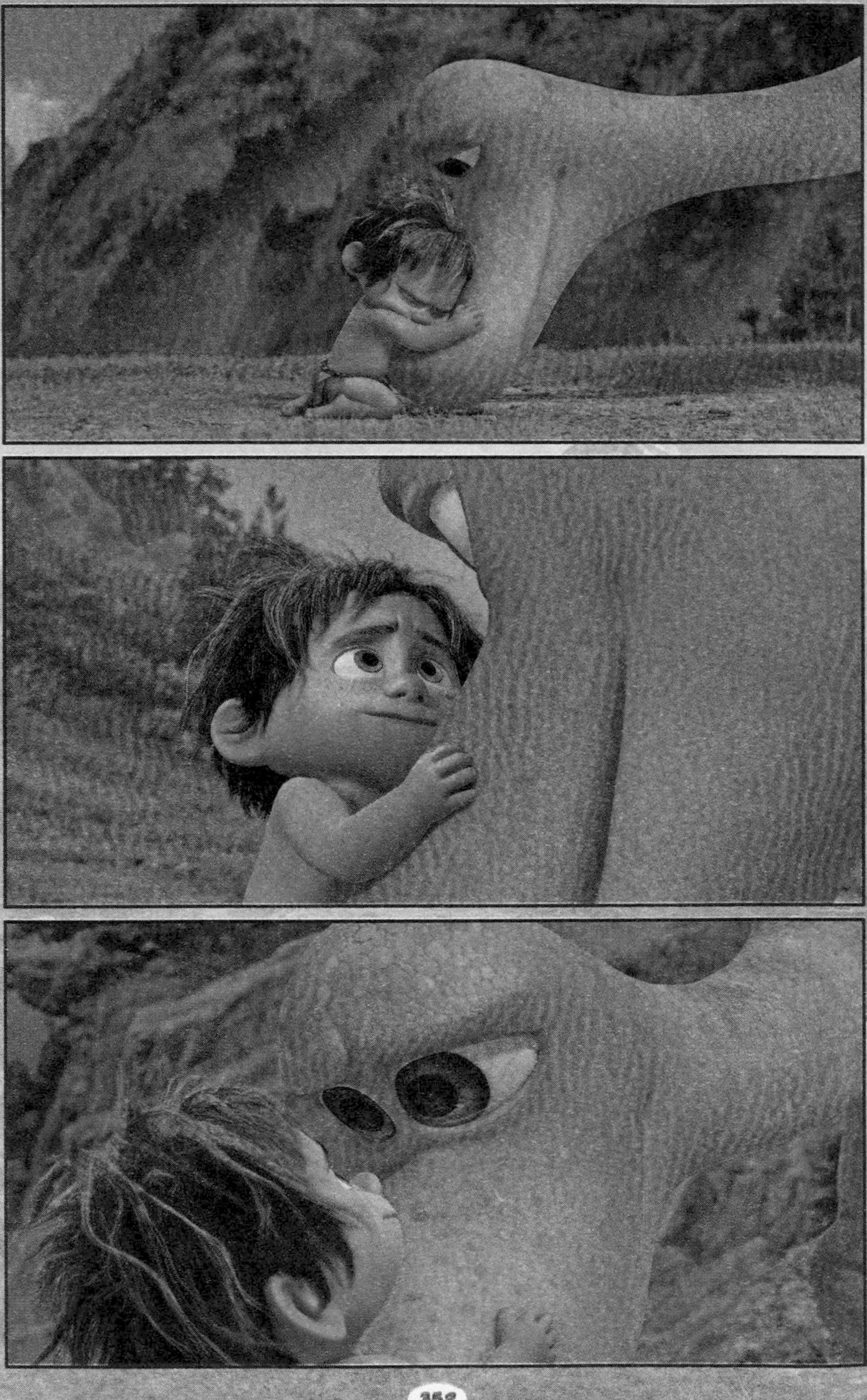

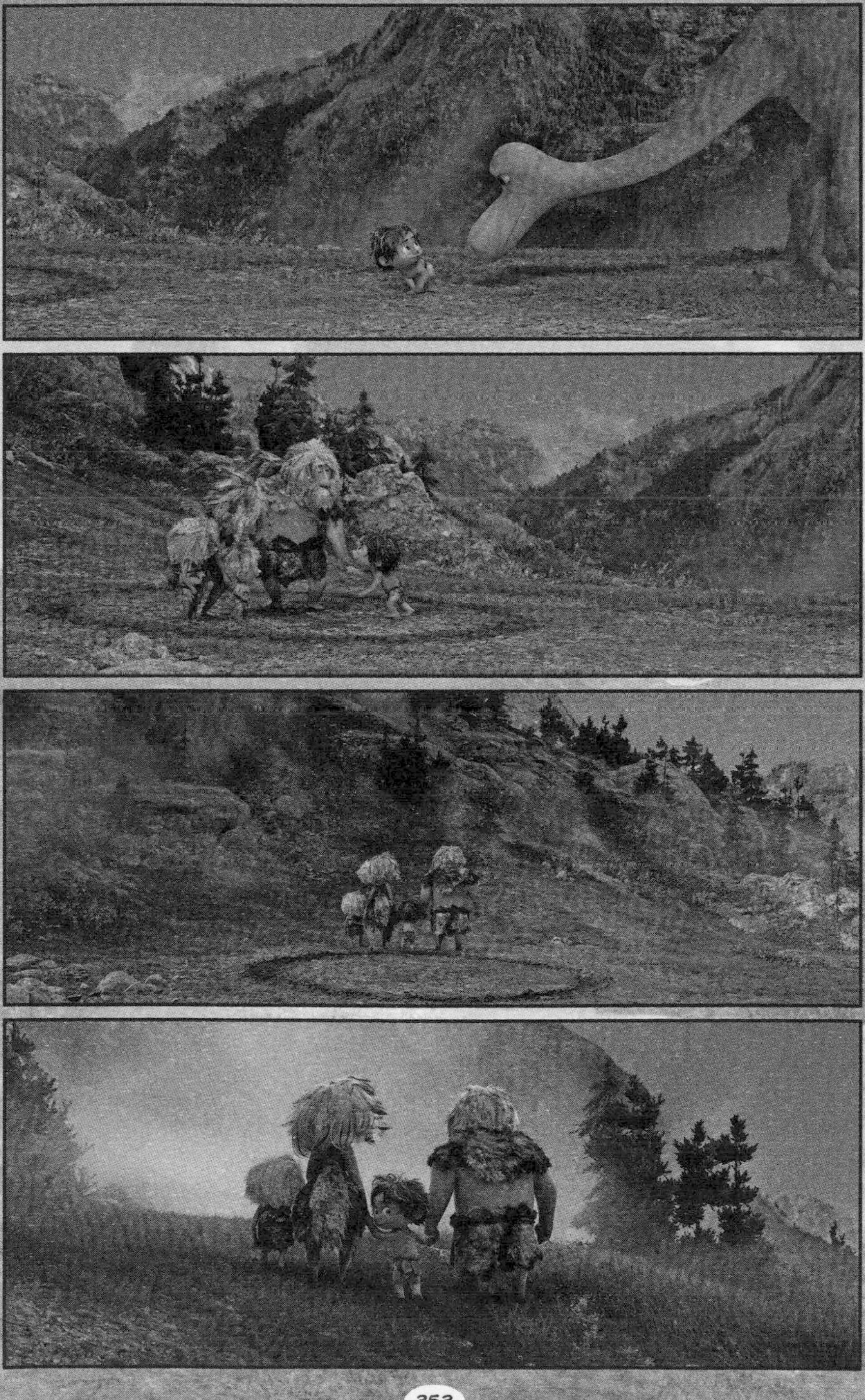

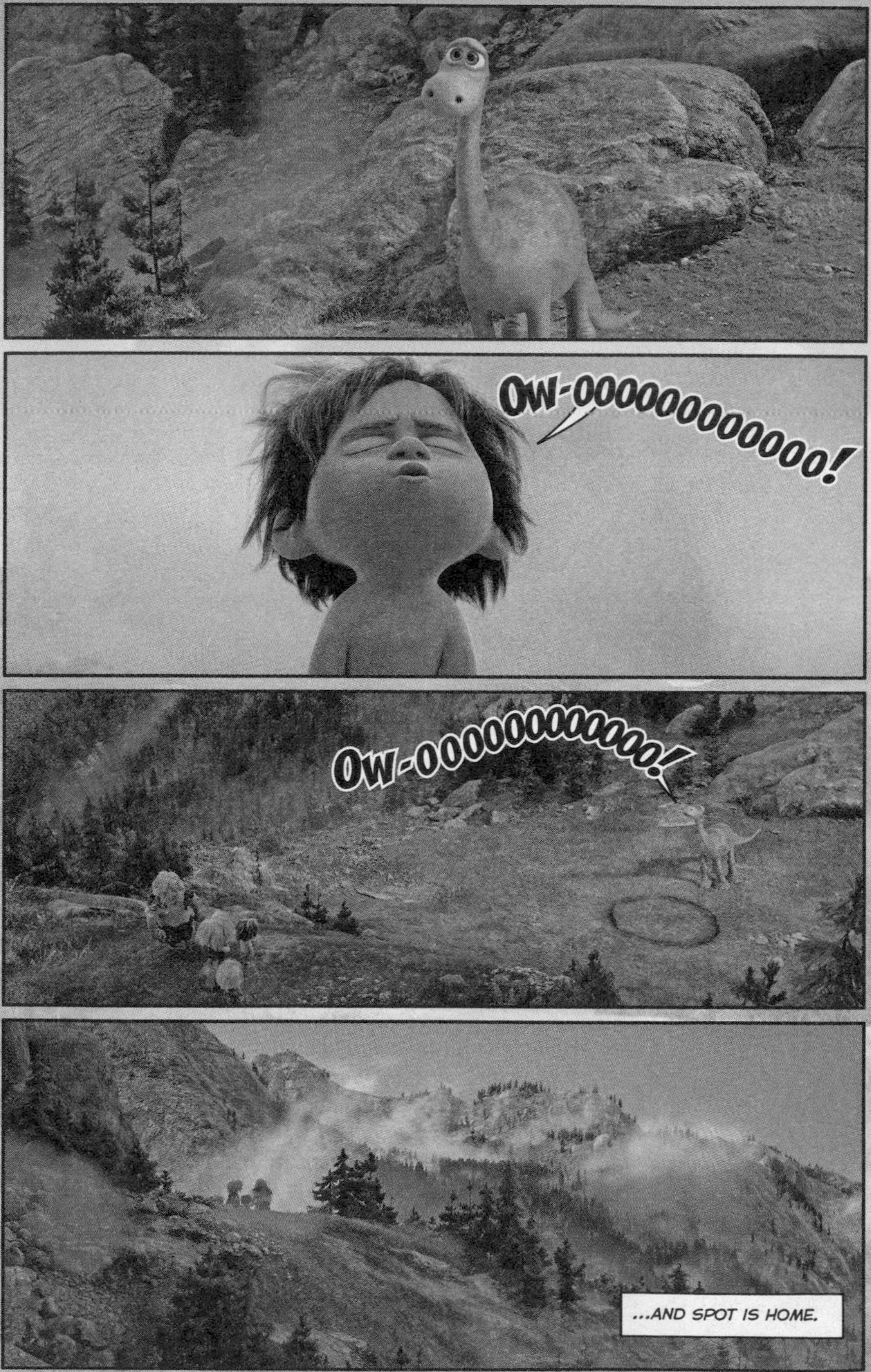
OW-OOOOOOOOOOOO!
OW-OOOOOOOOOOOO!
...AND SPOT IS HOME.

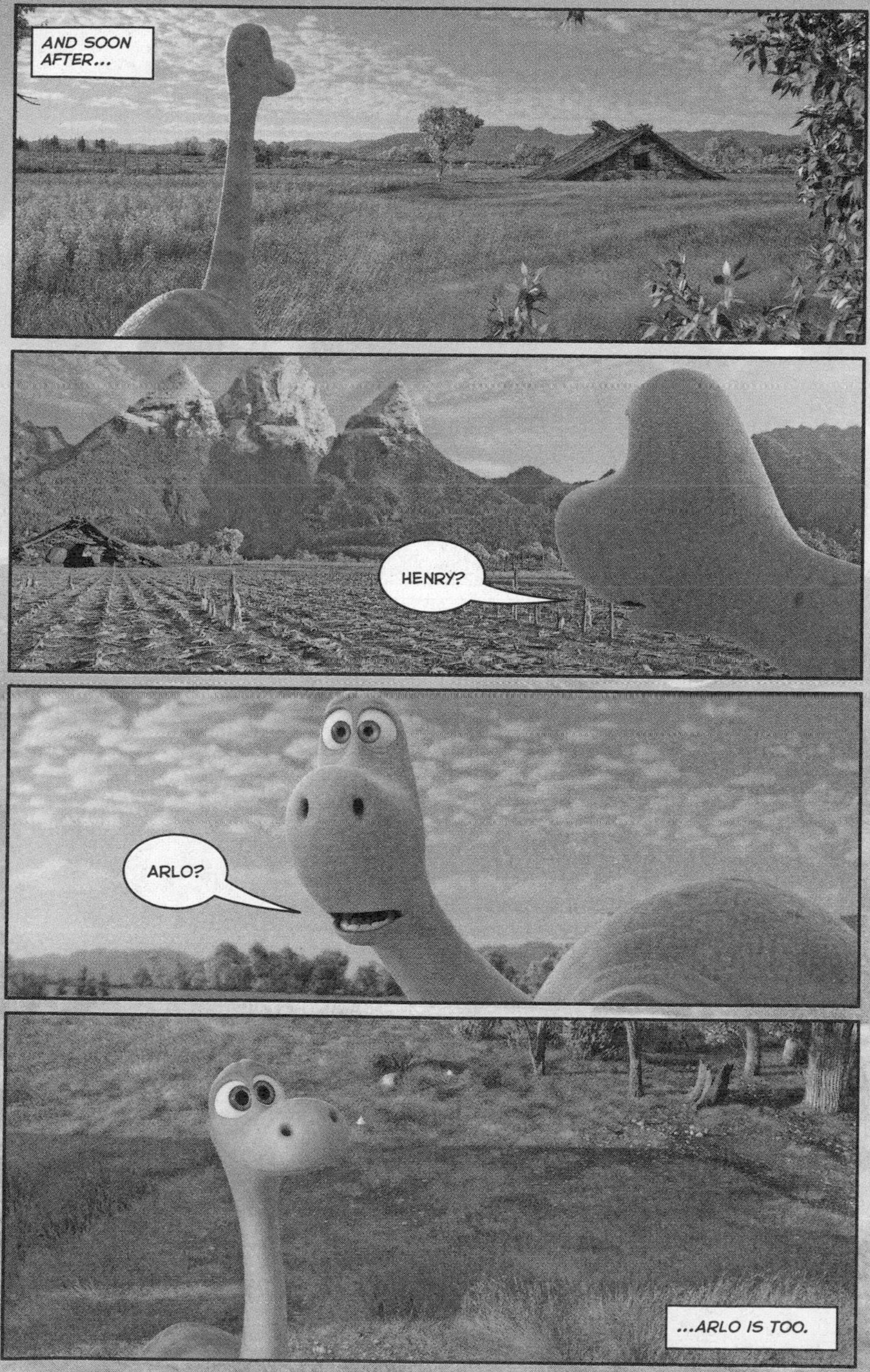
AND SOON AFTER...
HENRY?
ARLO?
...ARLO IS TOO.

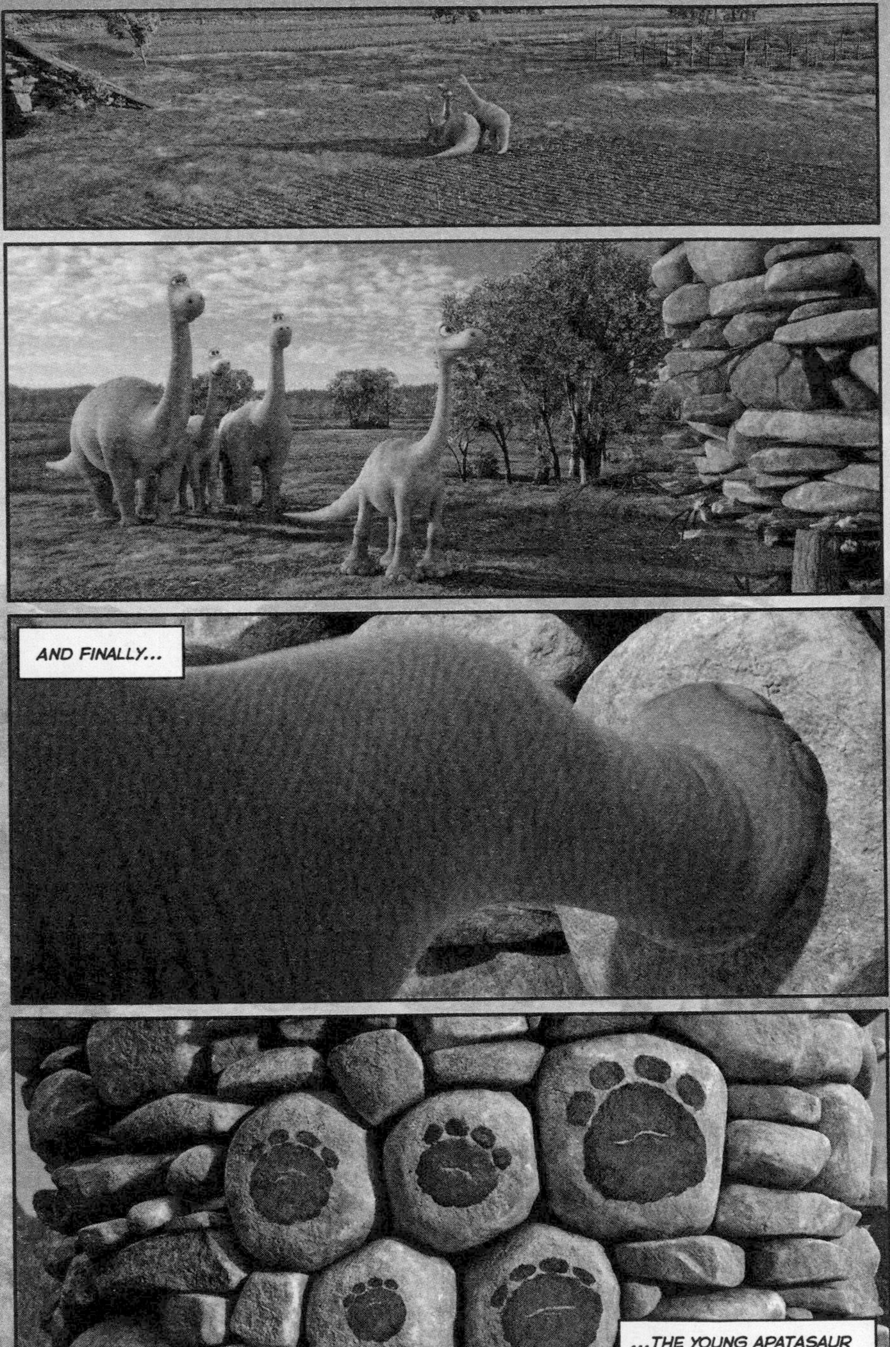
AND FINALLY...
...THE YOUNG APATASAUR MAKES HIS MARK!

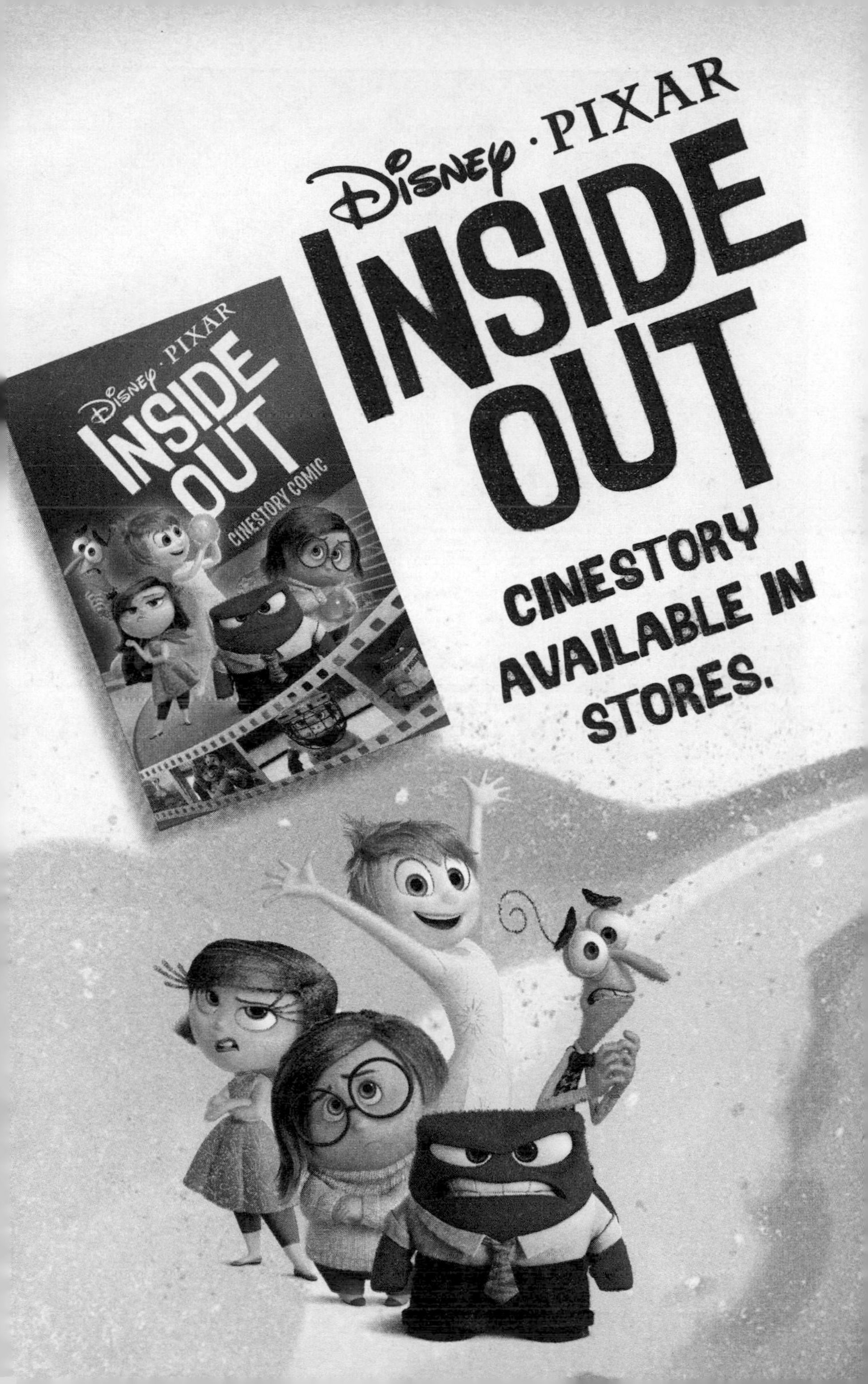
Disney · PIXAR
INSIDE OUT
CINESTORY AVAILABLE IN STORES.
Disney · PIXAR
INSIDE OUT
CINESTORY COMIC

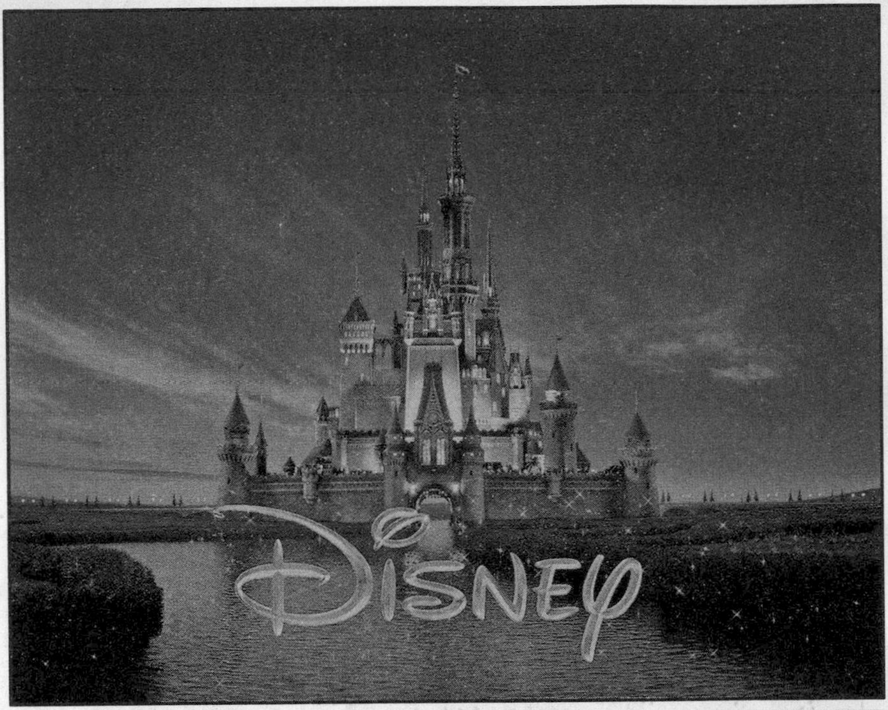
Disney

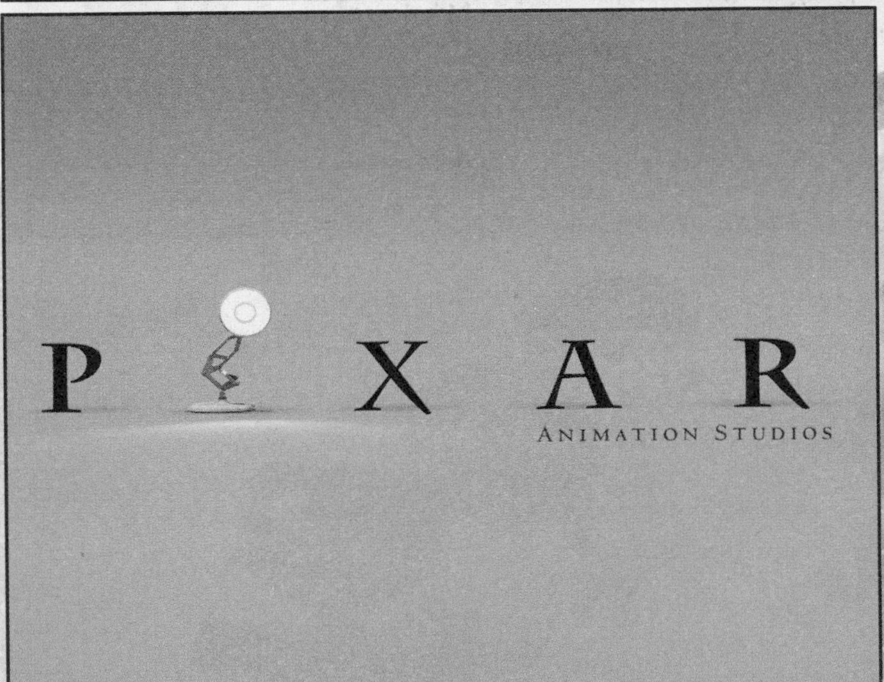
PIXAR
ANIMATION STUDIOS

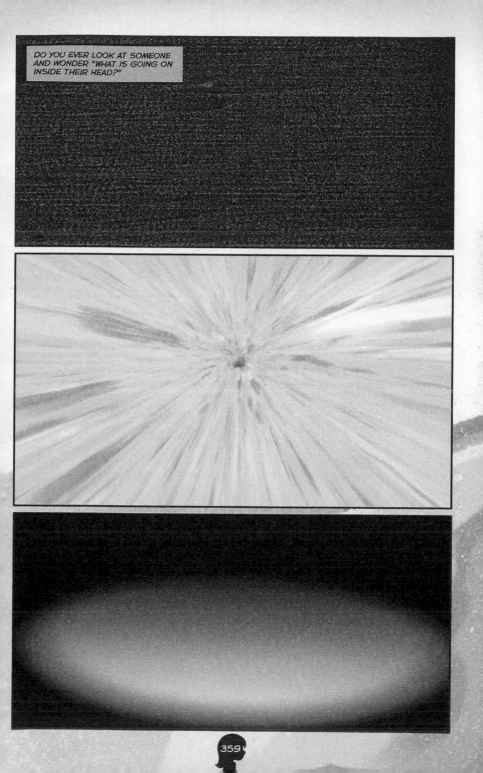

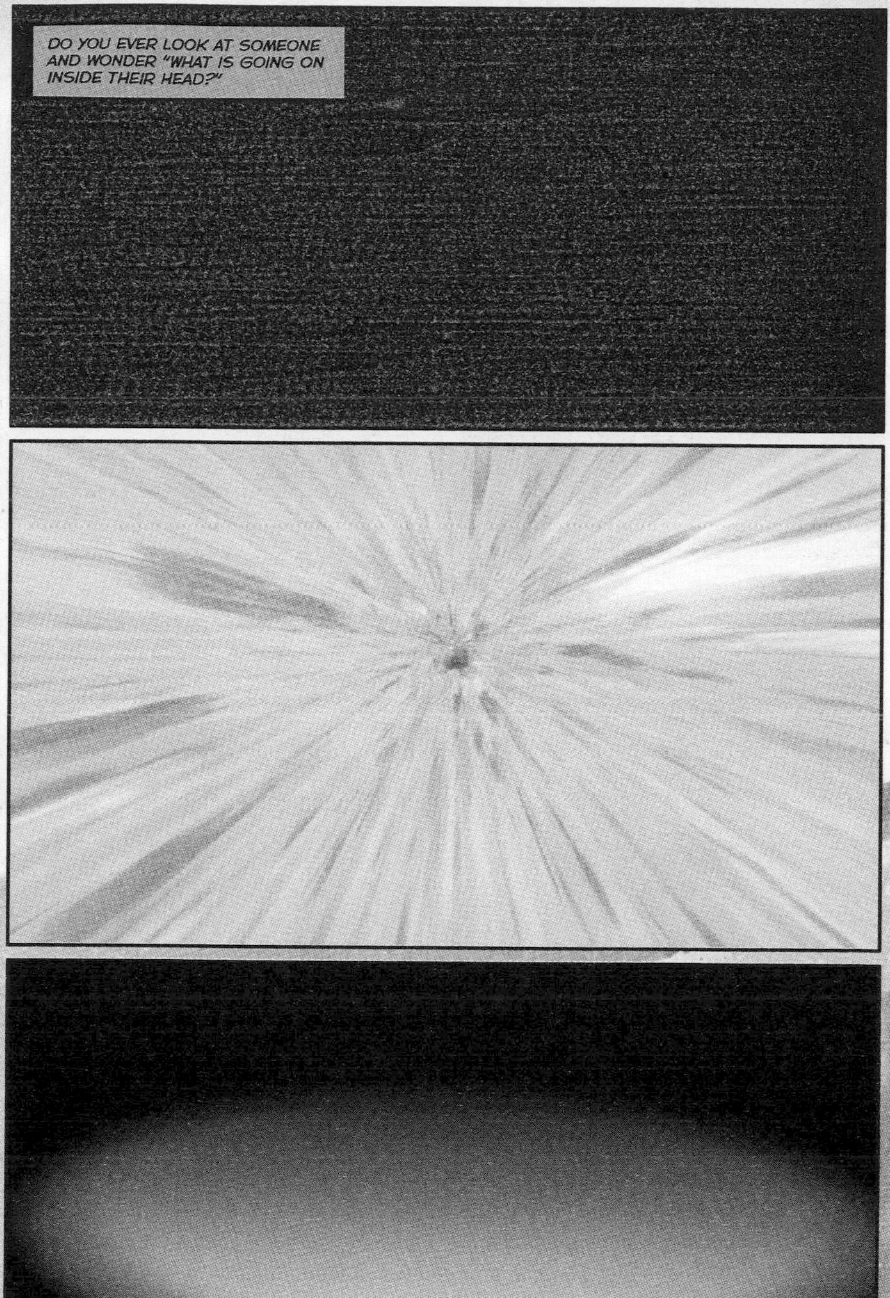
DO YOU EVER LOOK AT SOMEONE AND WONDER "WHAT IS GOING ON INSIDE THEIR HEAD?"

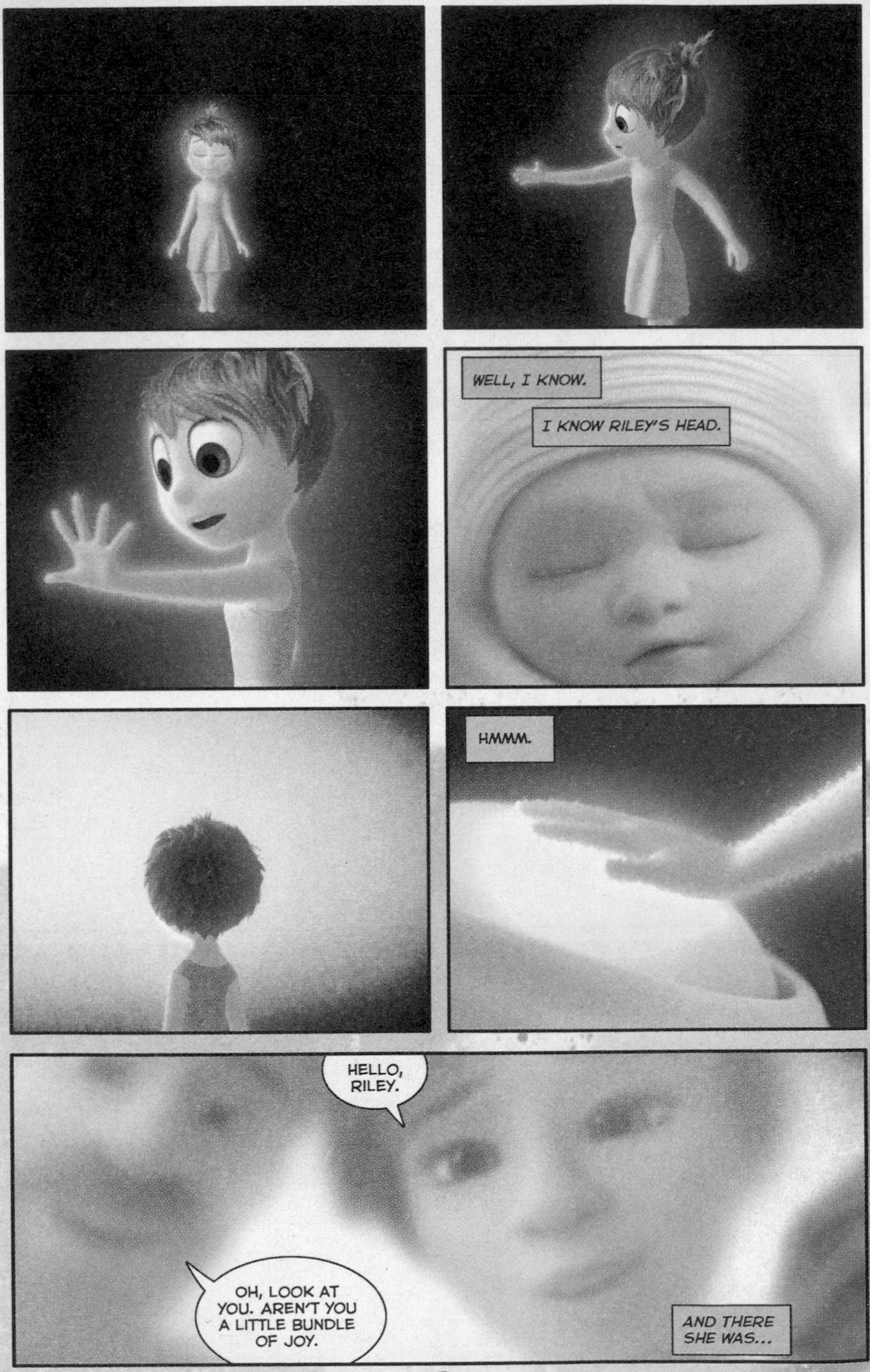
WELL, I KNOW.
I KNOW RILEY'S HEAD.
HMMM.
HELLO, RILEY.
OH, LOOK AT YOU. AREN'T YOU A LITTLE BUNDLE OF JOY.
AND THERE SHE WAS...

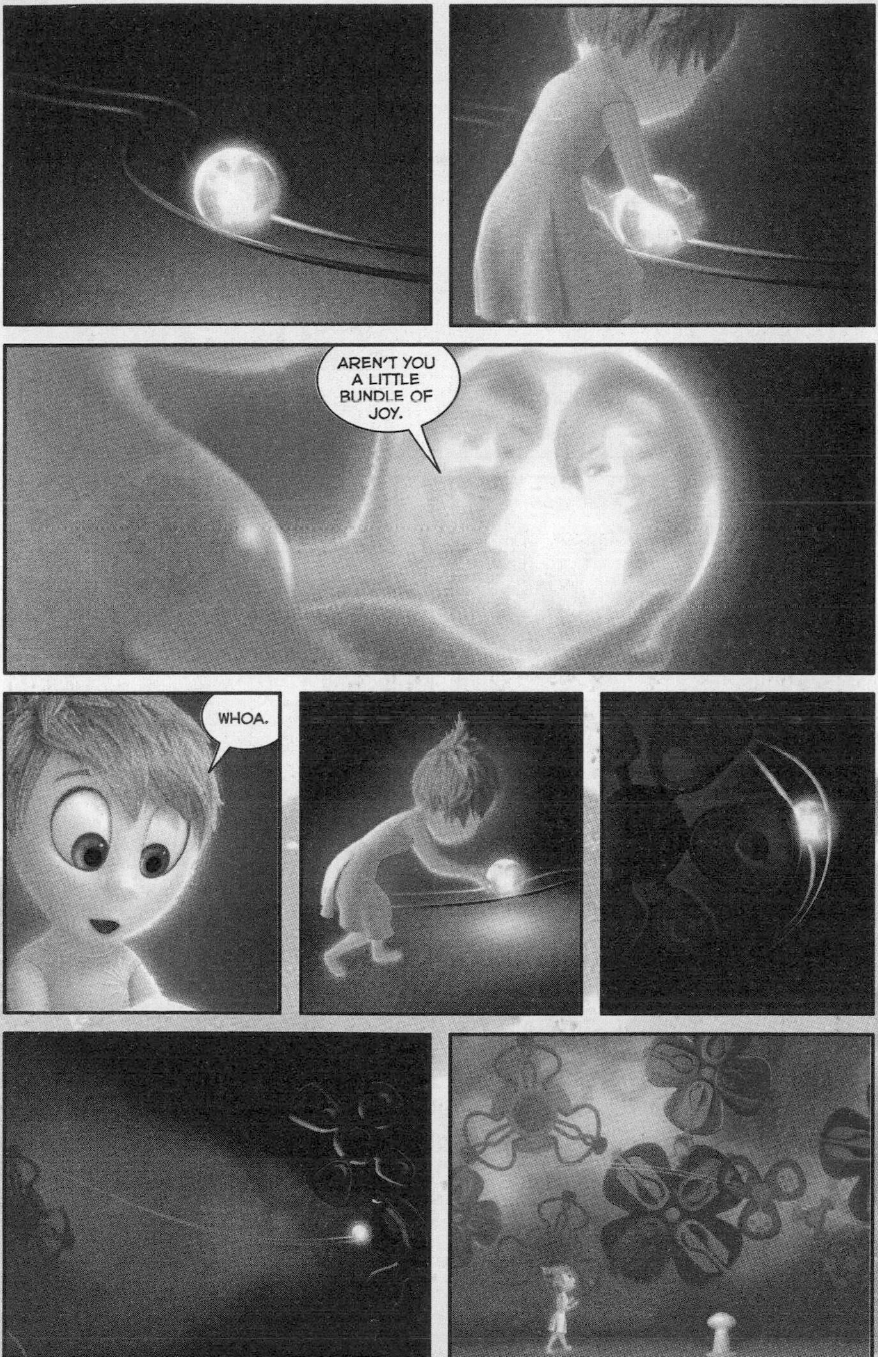
ARE'NT YOU A LITTLE BUNDLE OF JOY.
WHOA.

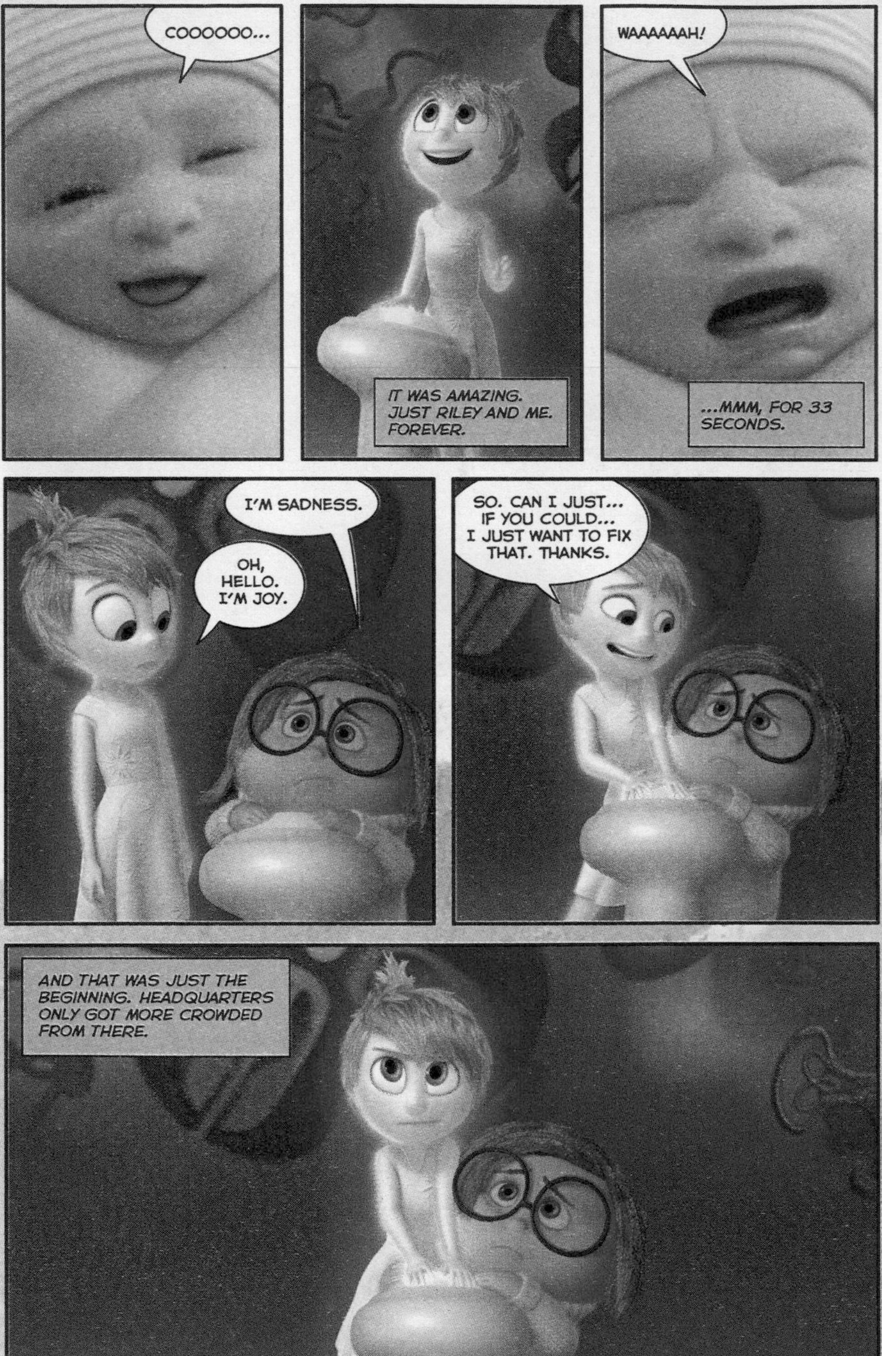
COOOOOO...
IT WAS AMAZING. JUST RILEY AND ME. FOREVER.
WAAAAAAH!
...MMM, FOR 33 SECONDS.
I'M SADNESS.
OH, HELLO. I'M JOY.
SO. CAN I JUST... IF YOU COULD... I JUST WANT TO FIX THAT. THANKS.
AND THAT WAS JUST THE BEGINNING. HEADQUARTERS ONLY GOT MORE CROWDED FROM THERE.

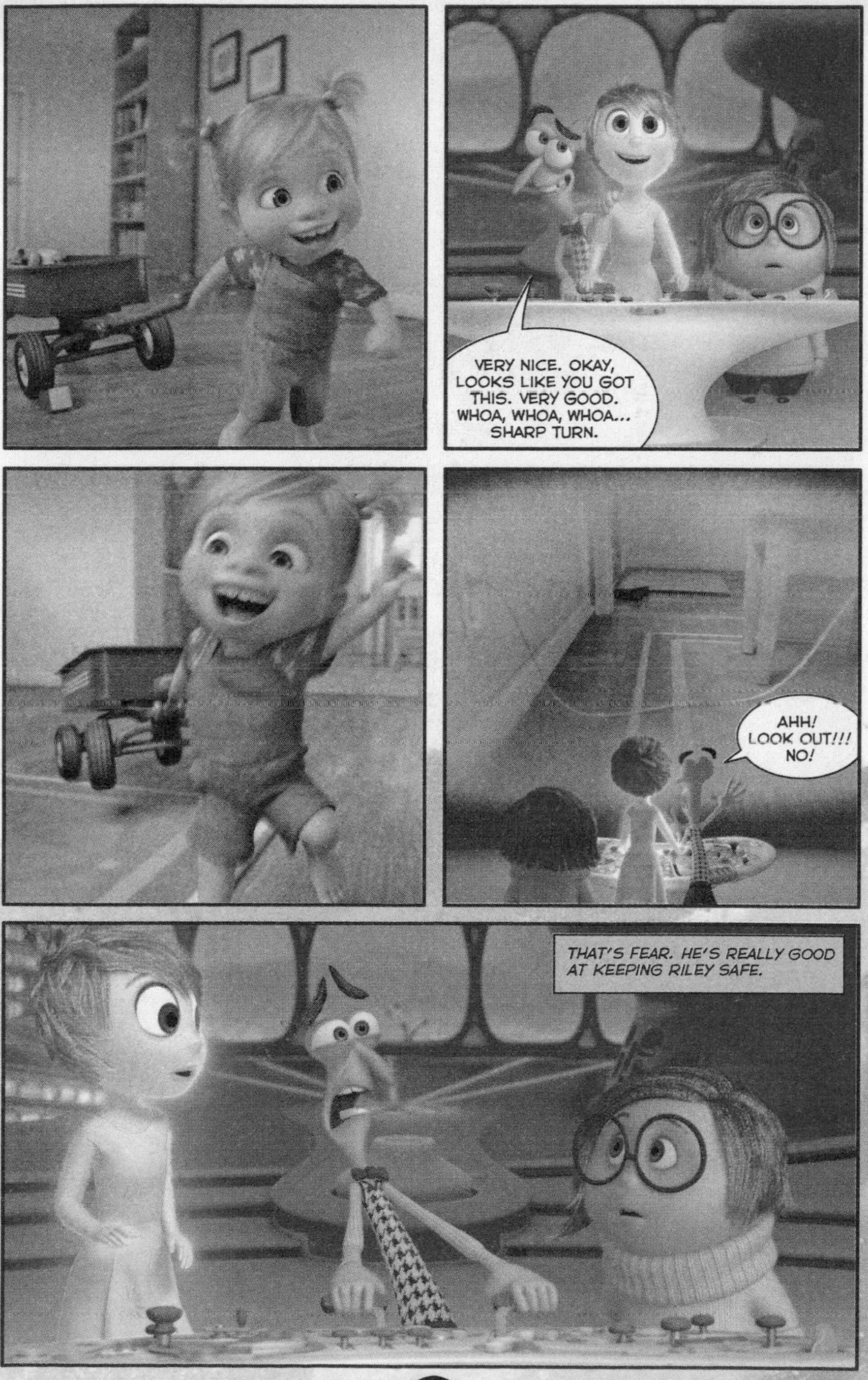
VERY NICE. OKAY, LOOKS LIKE YOU GOT THIS. VERY GOOD. WHOA, WHOA, WHOA... SHARP TURN.
AHH! LOOK OUT!!! NO!
THAT'S FEAR. HE'S REALLY GOOD AT KEEPING RILEY SAFE.

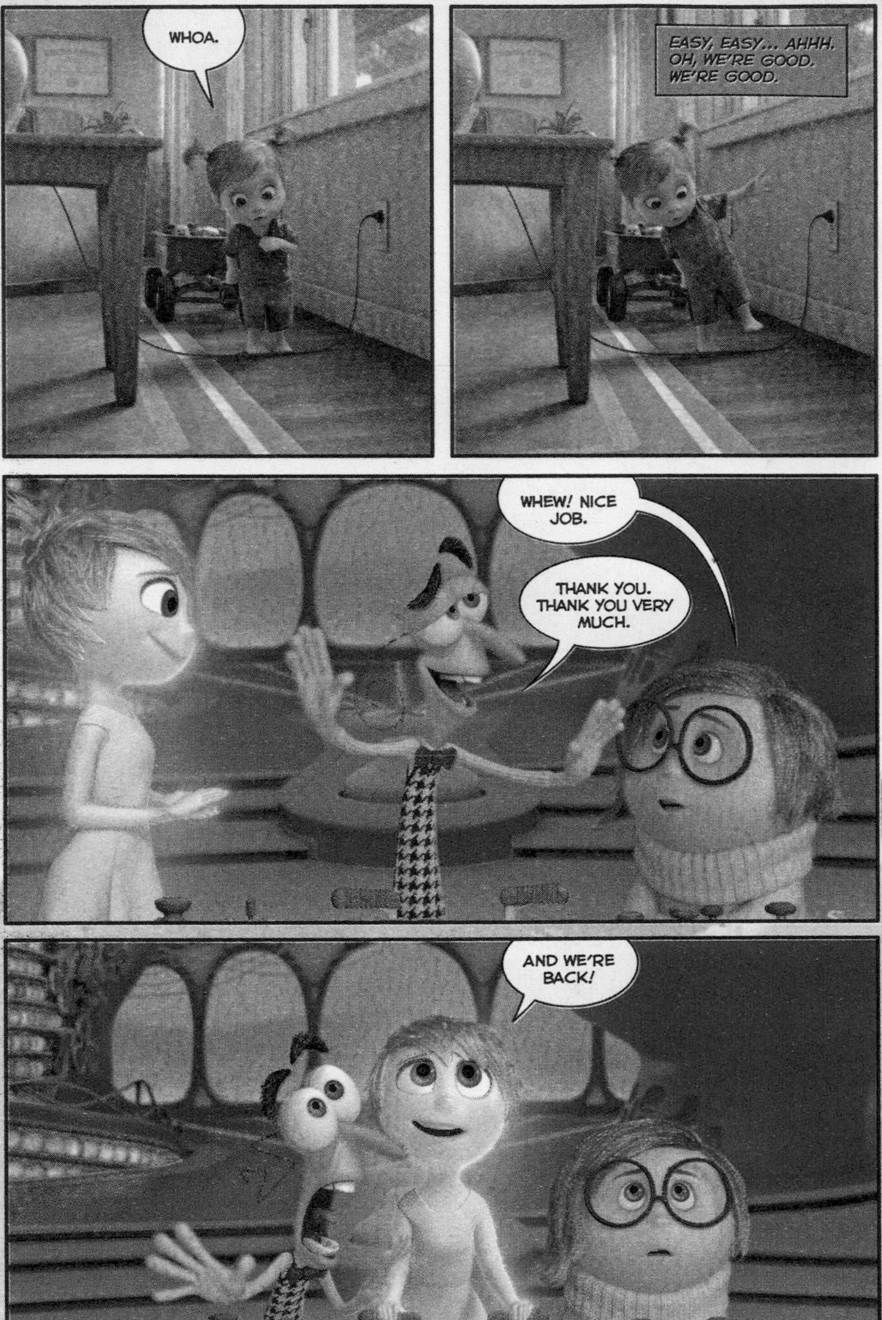
WHOA.
EASY, EASY... AHHH. OH, WE'RE GOOD. WE'RE GOOD.
WHEW! NICE JOB.
THANK YOU. THANK YOU VERY MUCH.
AND WE'RE BACK!

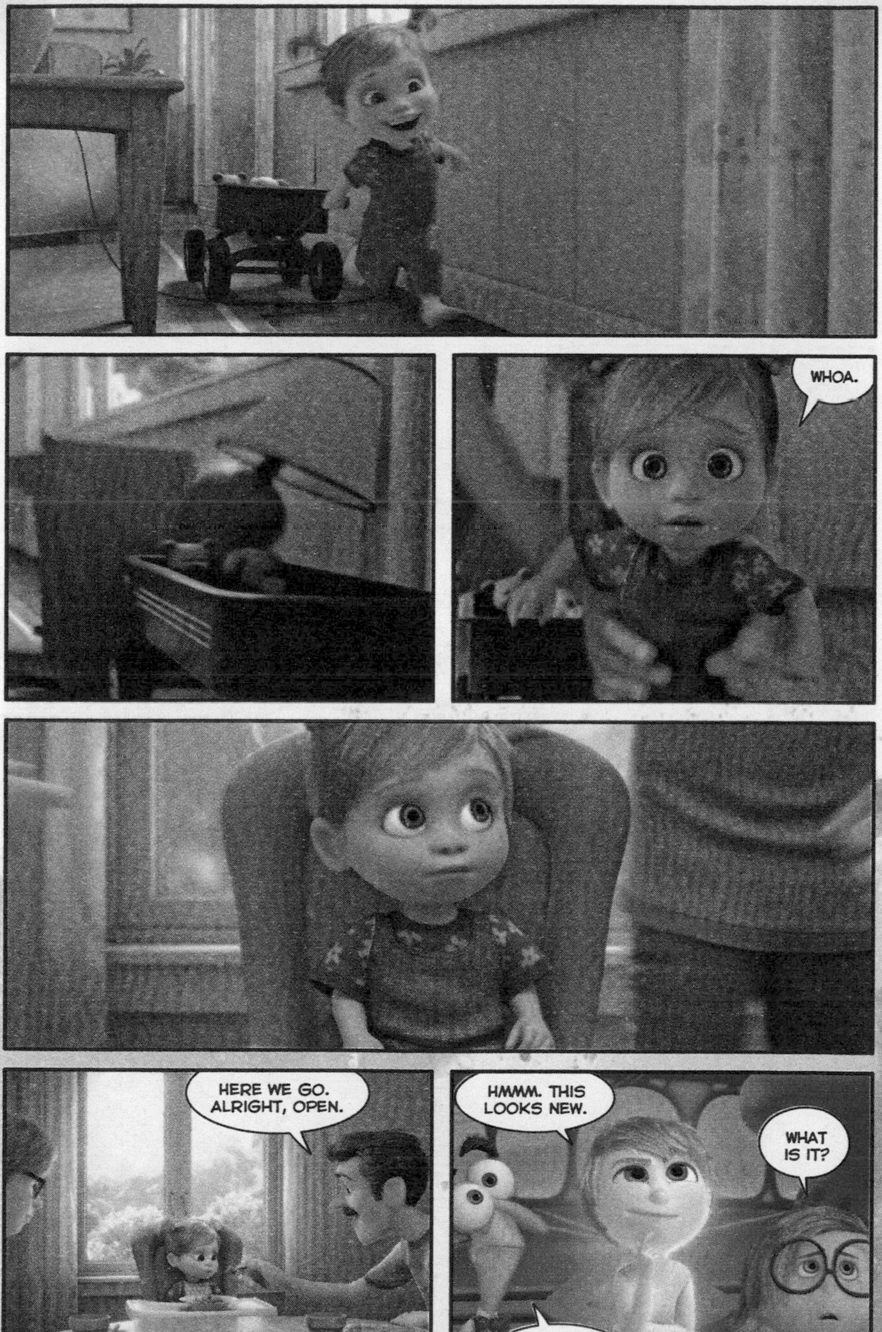
WHOA.
HERE WE GO. ALRIGHT, OPEN.
HMMM. THIS LOOKS NEW.
WHAT IS IT?
DO YOU THINK IT'S SAFE?

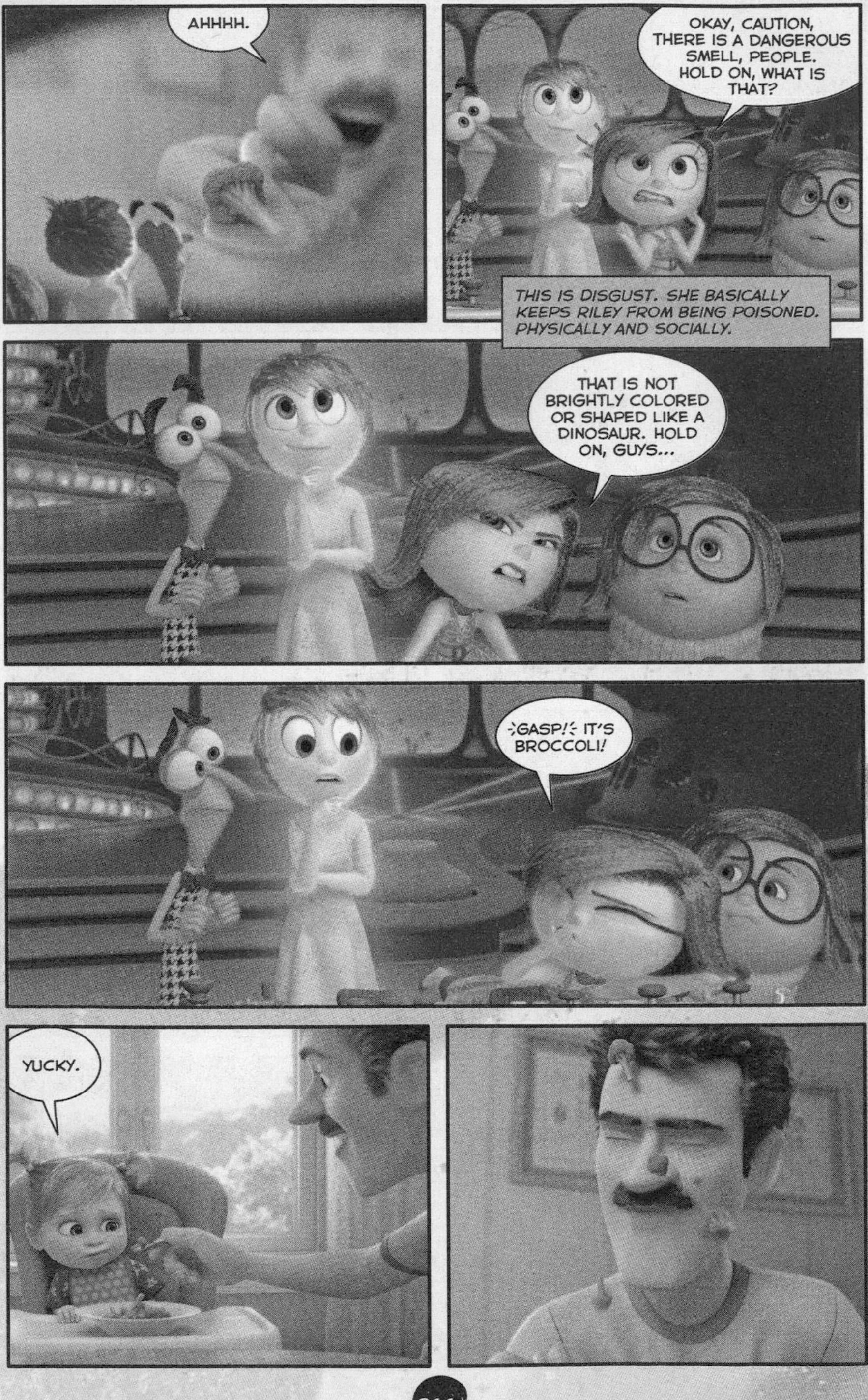
AHHHH.
OKAY, CAUTION, THERE IS A DANGEROUS SMELL, PEOPLE. HOLD ON, WHAT IS THAT?
THIS IS DISGUST. SHE BASICALLY KEEPS RILEY FROM BEING POISONED. PHYSICALLY AND SOCIALLY.
THAT IS NOT BRIGHTLY COLORED OR SHAPED LIKE A DINOSAUR. HOLD ON, GUYS...
-GASP!- IT'S BROCCOLI!
YUCKY.

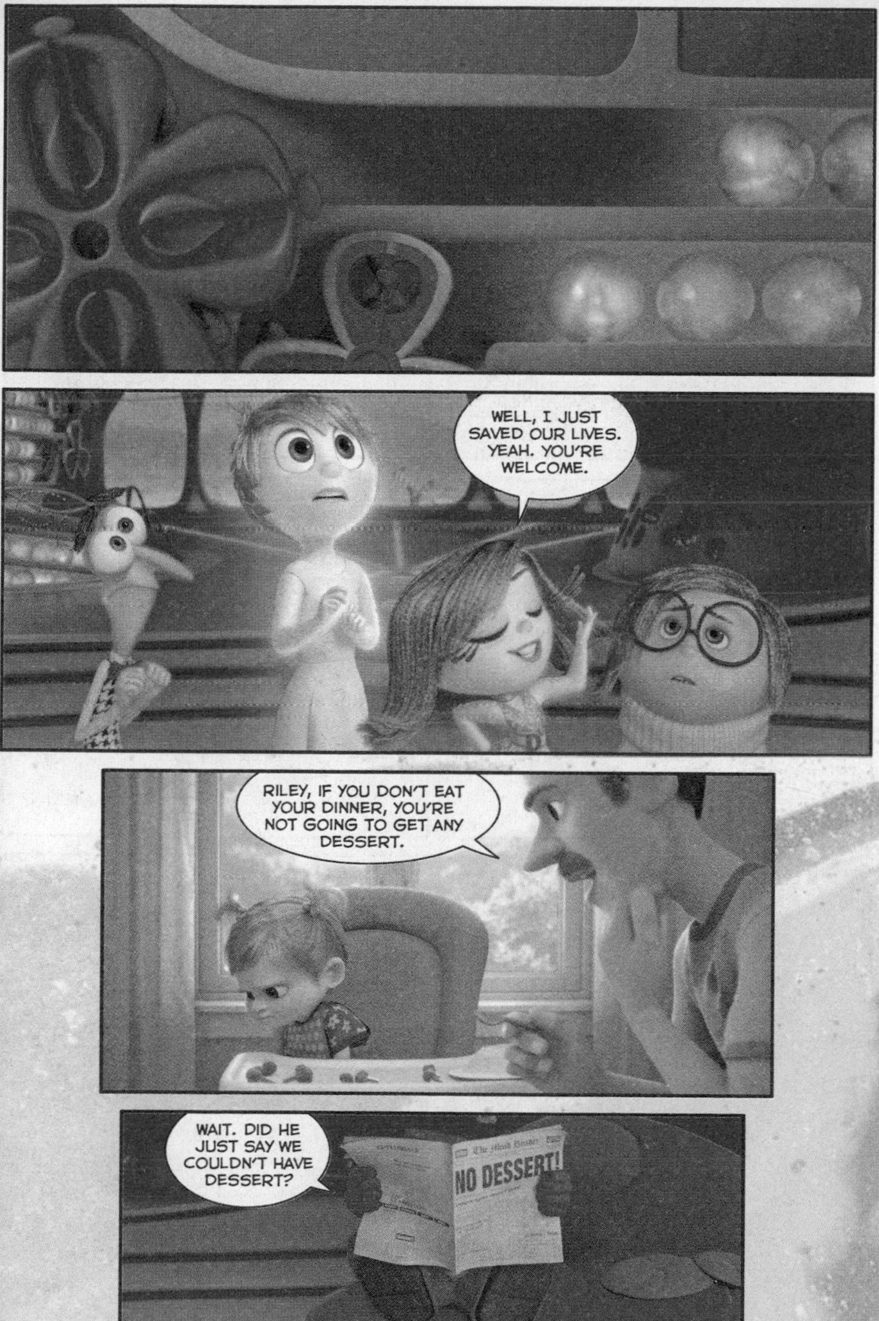
WELL, I JUST SAVED OUR LIVES. YEAH. YOU'RE WELCOME.
RILEY, IF YOU DON'T EAT YOUR DINNER, YOU'RE NOT GOING TO GET ANY DESSERT.
WAIT. DID HE JUST SAY WE COULDN'T HAVE DESSERT?
NO DESSERT!

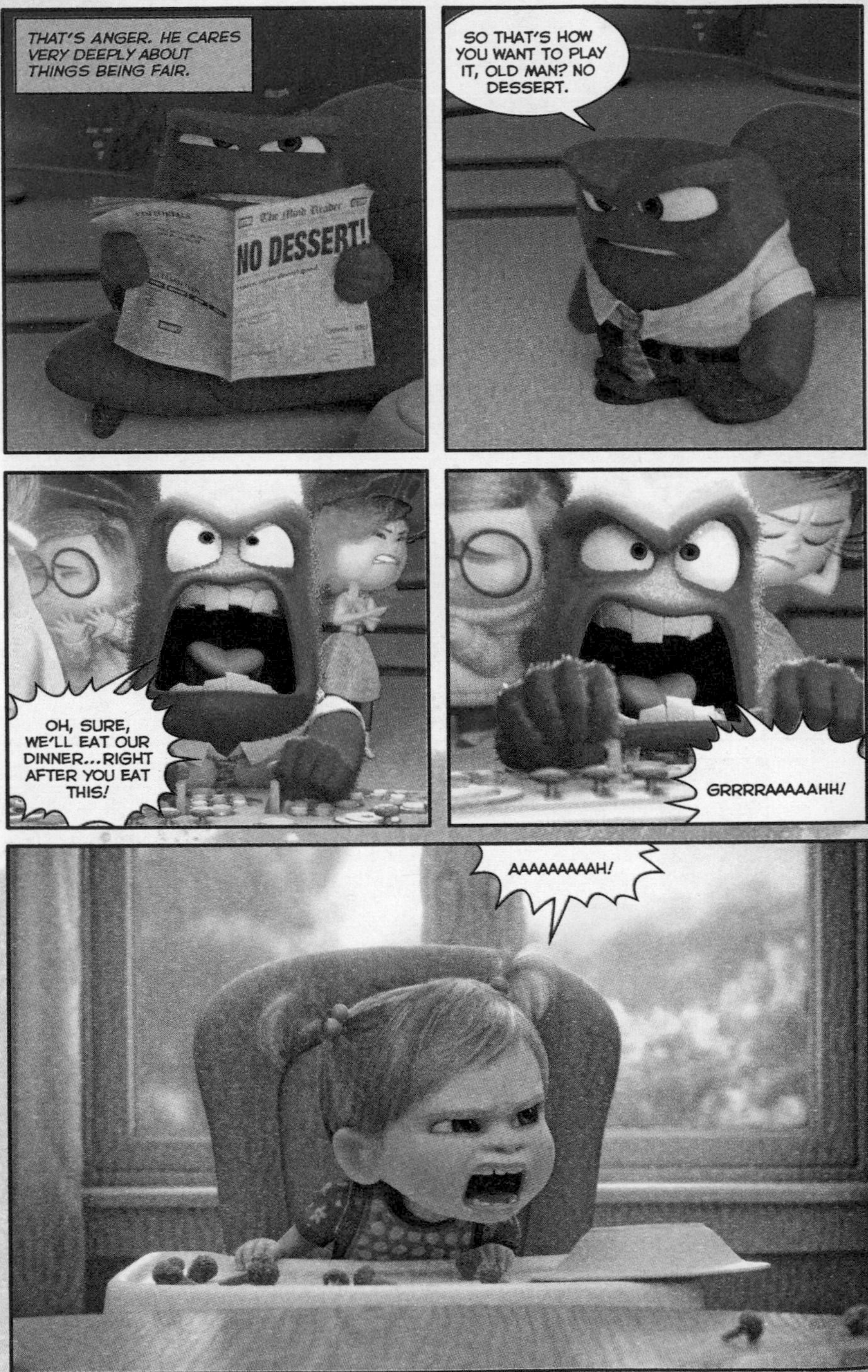
THAT'S ANGER. HE CARES VERY DEEPLY ABOUT THINGS BEING FAIR.
NO DESSERT!
SO THAT'S HOW YOU WANT TO PLAY IT, OLD MAN? NO DESSERT.
OH, SURE, WE'LL EAT OUR DINNER...RIGHT AFTER YOU EAT THIS!
GRRRRAAAAAHH!
AAAAAAAAAH!

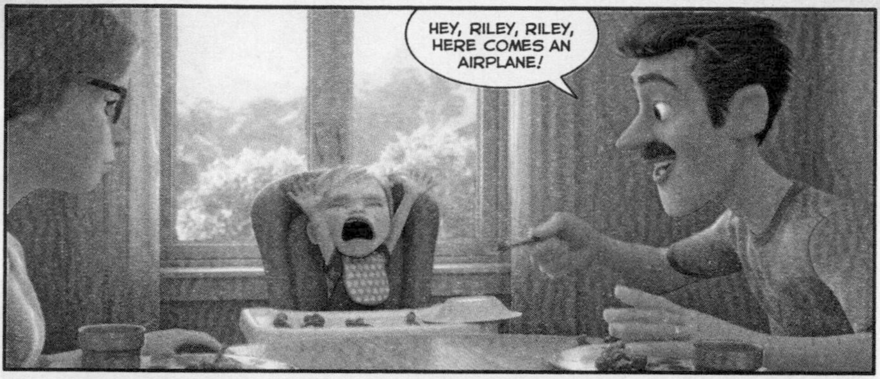
HEY, RILEY, RILEY, HERE COMES AN AIRPLANE!

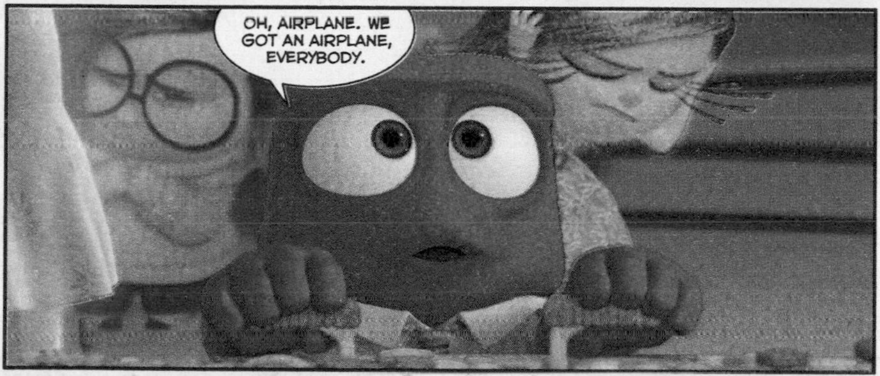
OH, AIRPLANE. WE GOT AN AIRPLANE, EVERYBODY.

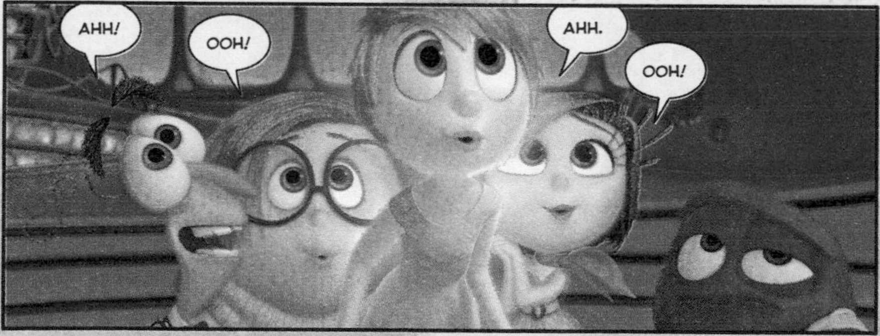
AHH!
OOH!
AHH.
OOH!

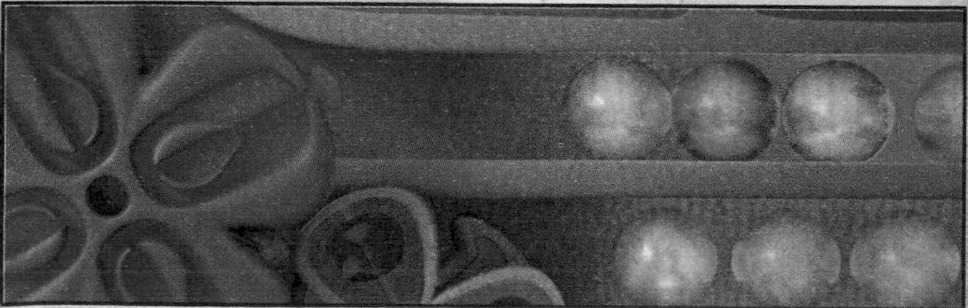

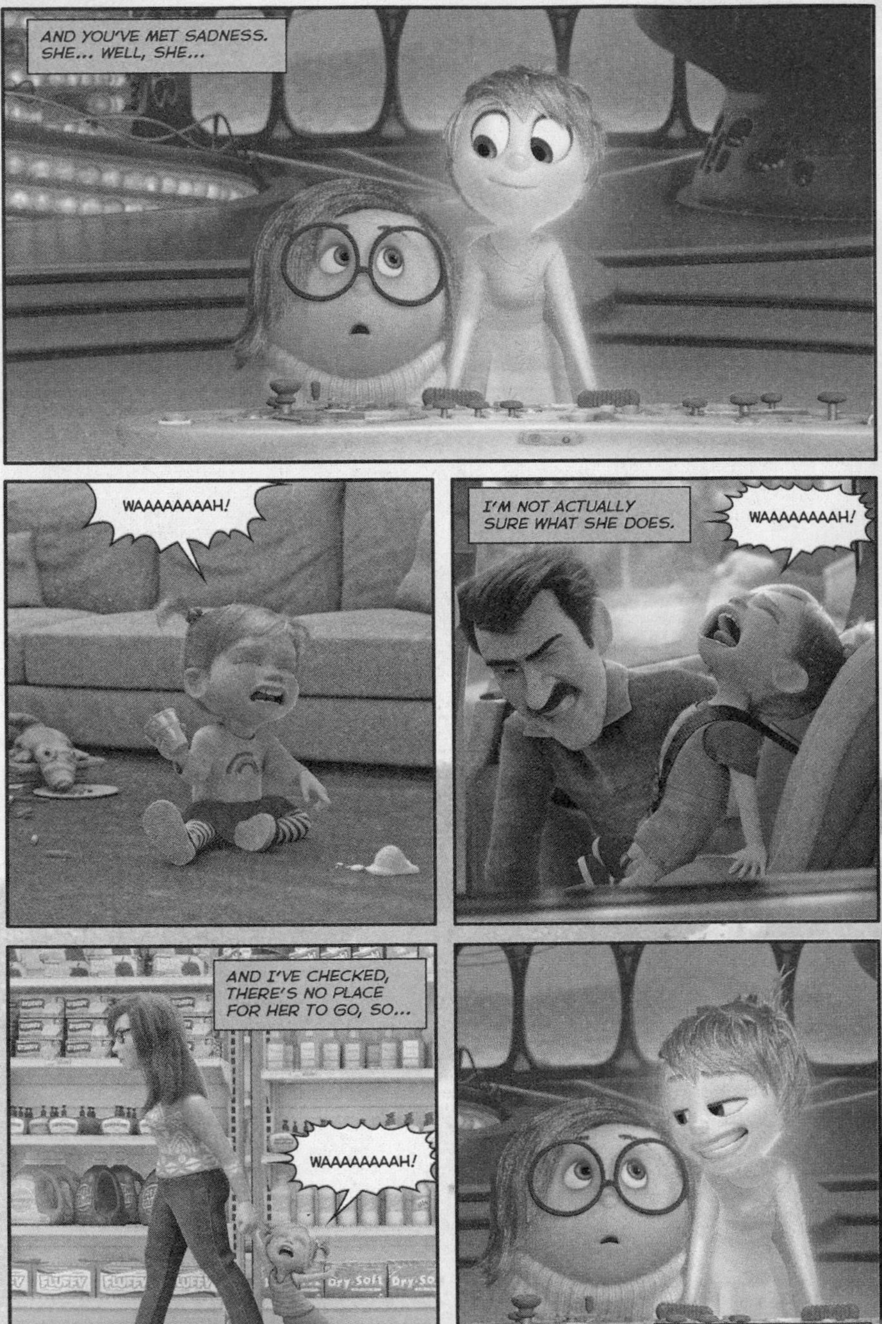
AND YOU'VE MET SADNESS. SHE... WELL, SHE...
WAAAAAAAAAH!
I'M NOT ACTUALLY SURE WHAT SHE DOES.
WAAAAAAAAAH!
AND I'VE CHECKED, THERE'S NO PLACE FOR HER TO GO, SO...
WAAAAAAAAAH!
SHE'S GOOD, WE'RE GOOD. IT'S ALL GREAT!

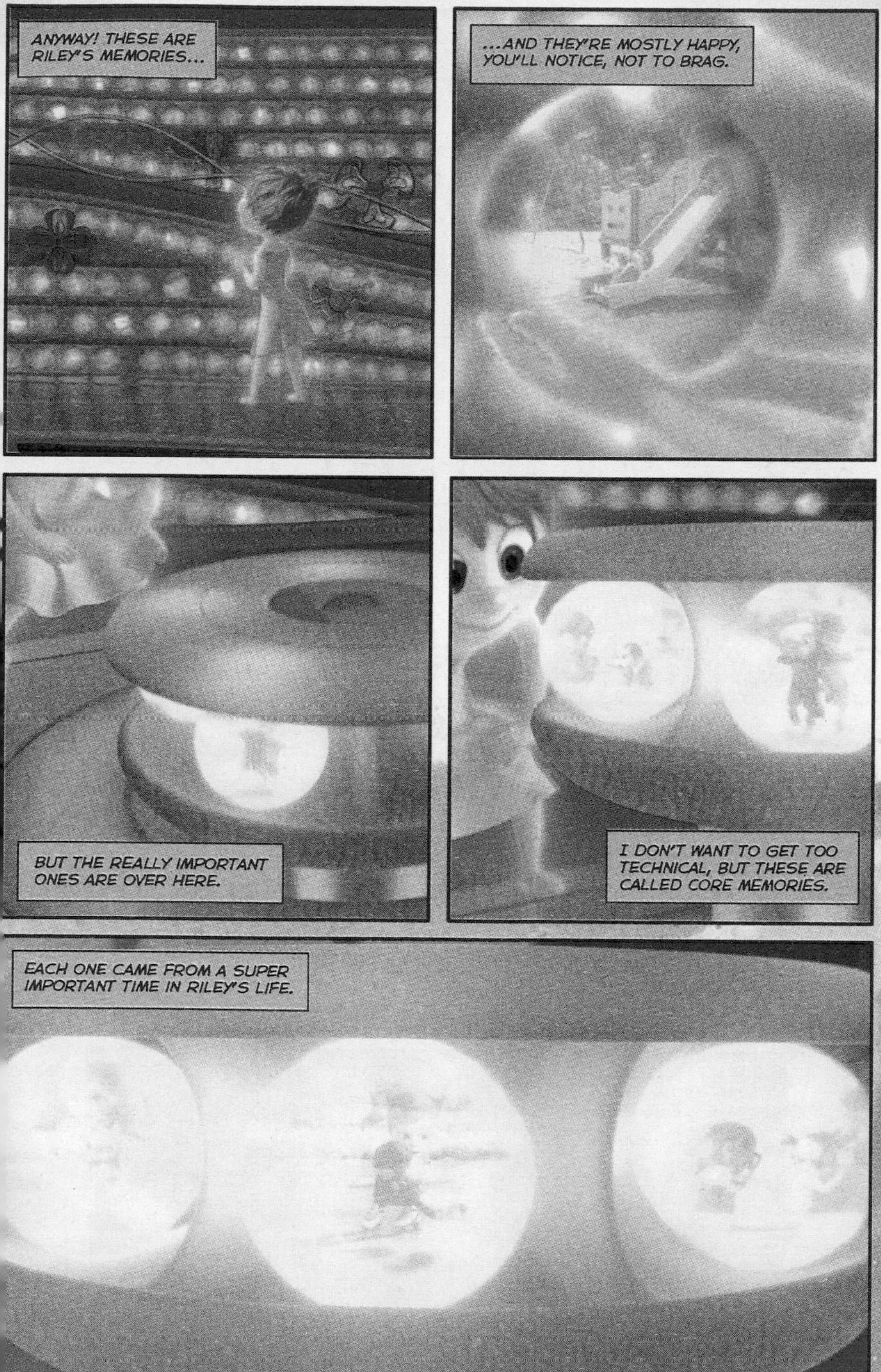
ANYWAY! THESE ARE RILEY'S MEMORIES...
...AND THEY'RE MOSTLY HAPPY, YOU'LL NOTICE, NOT TO BRAG.
BUT THE REALLY IMPORTANT ONES ARE OVER HERE.
I DON'T WANT TO GET TOO TECHNICAL, BUT THESE ARE CALLED CORE MEMORIES.
EACH ONE CAME FROM A SUPER IMPORTANT TIME IN RILEY'S LIFE.

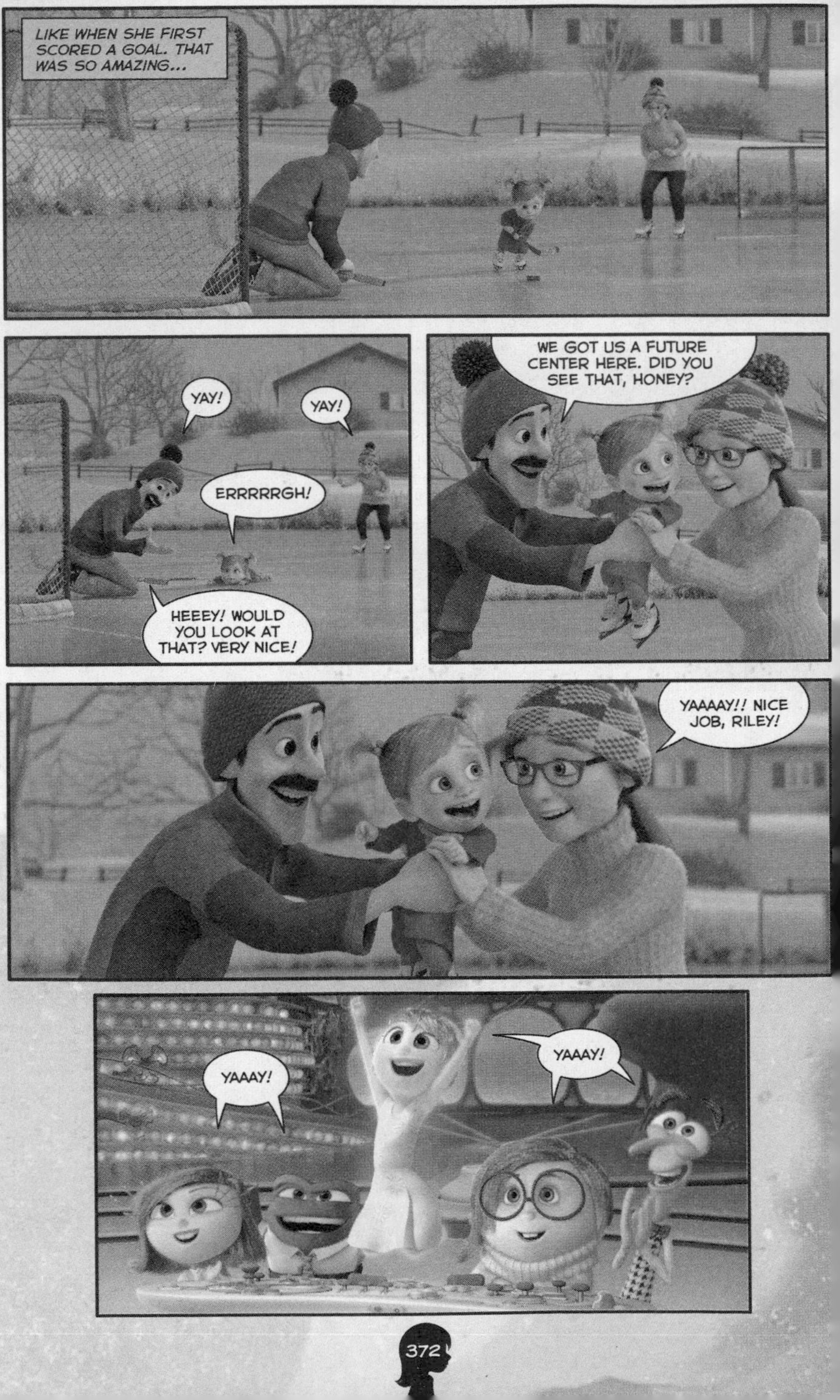
LIKE WHEN SHE FIRST SCORED A GOAL. THAT WAS SO AMAZING...
YAY!
YAY!
ERRRRRGH!
HEEEY! WOULD YOU LOOK AT THAT? VERY NICE!
WE GOT US A FUTURE CENTER HERE. DID YOU SEE THAT, HONEY?
YAAAAY!! NICE JOB, RILEY!
YAAAY!
YAAAY!

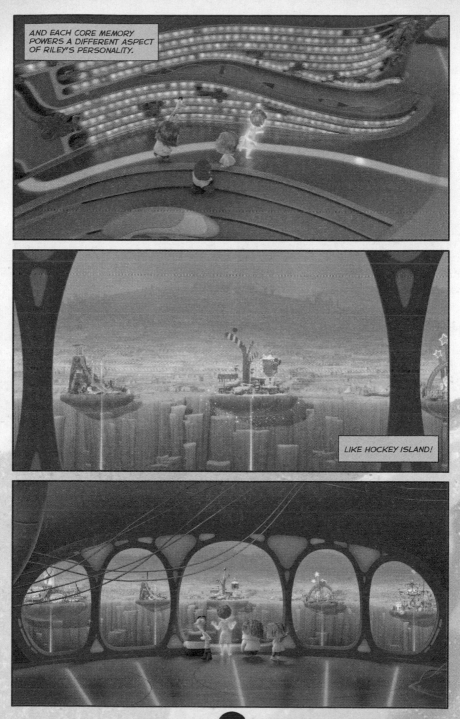

AND EACH CORE MEMORY POWERS A DIFFERENT ASPECT OF RILEY'S PERSONALITY.

LIKE HOCKEY ISLAND!

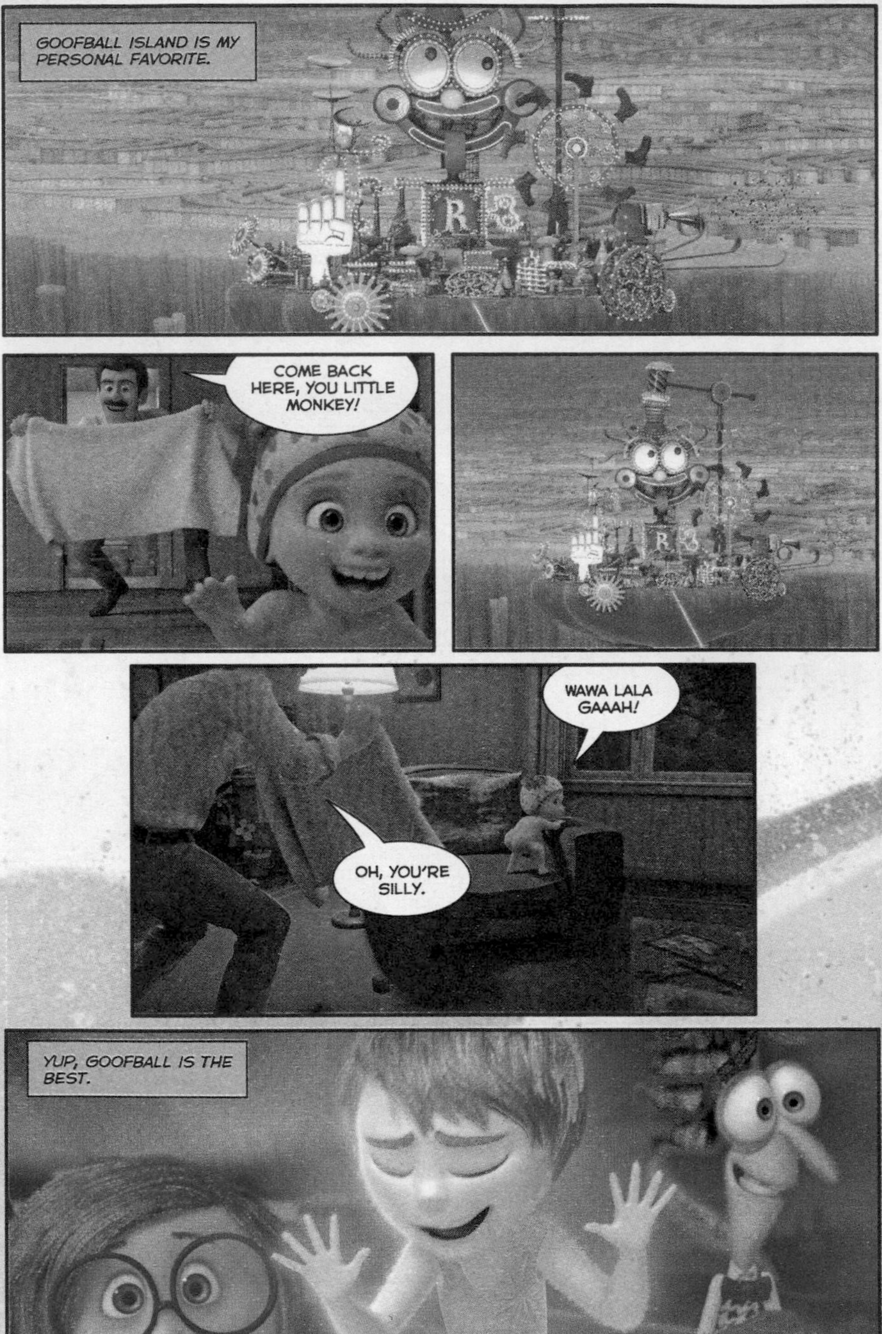
GOOFBALL ISLAND IS MY PERSONAL FAVORITE.
COME BACK HERE, YOU LITTLE MONKEY!
WAWA LALA GAAAH!
OH, YOU'RE SILLY.
YUP, GOOFBALL IS THE BEST.

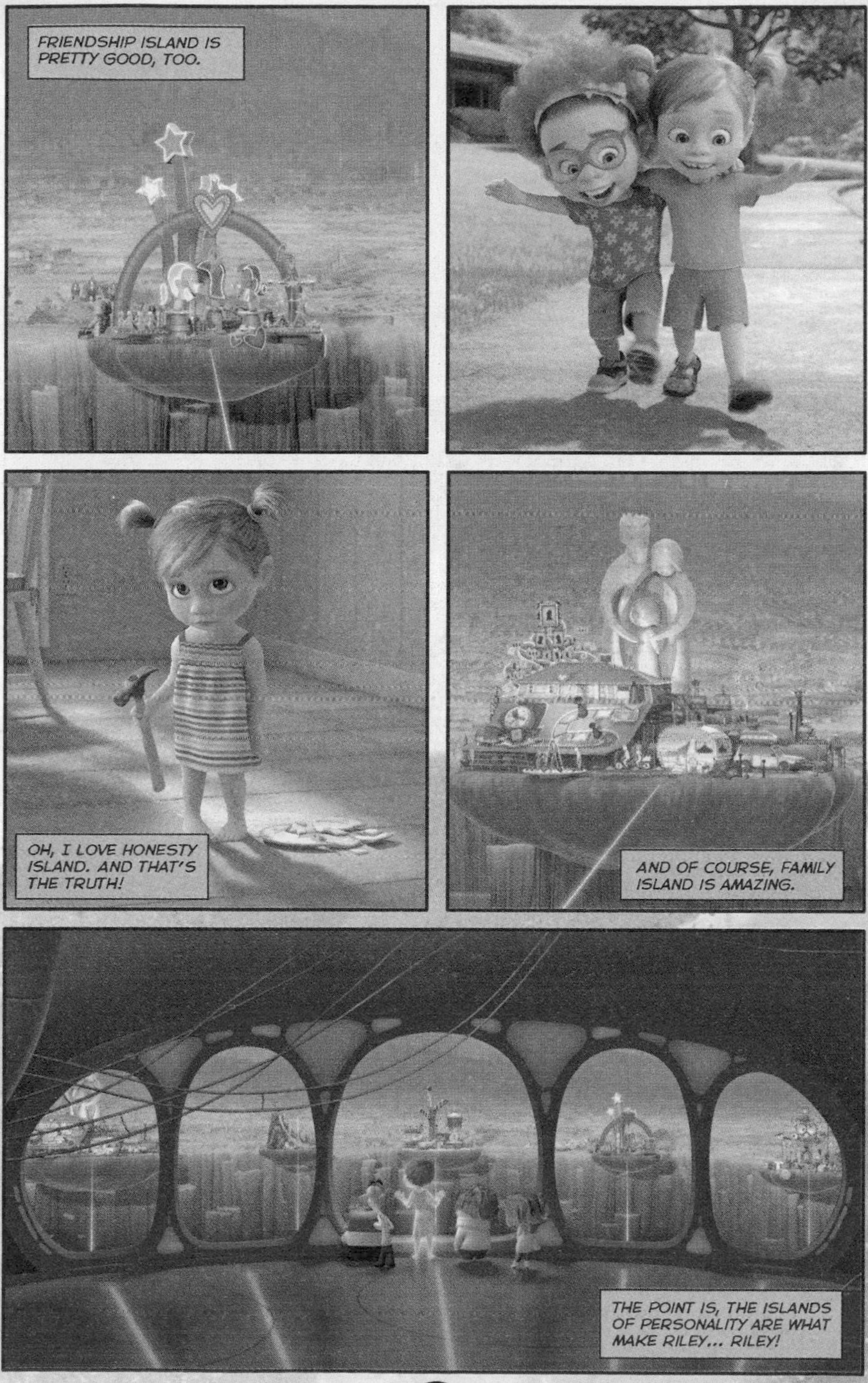
FRIENDSHIP ISLAND IS PRETTY GOOD, TOO.
OH, I LOVE HONESTY ISLAND. AND THAT'S THE TRUTH!
AND OF COURSE, FAMILY ISLAND IS AMAZING.
THE POINT IS, THE ISLANDS OF PERSONALITY ARE WHAT MAKE RILEY... RILEY!

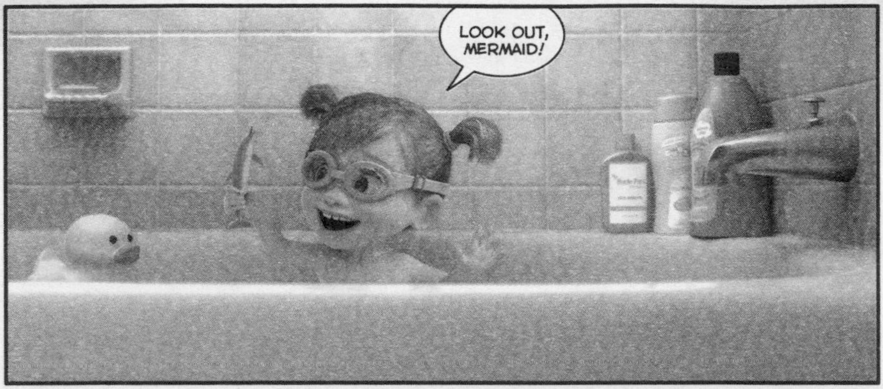
LOOK OUT, MERMAID!

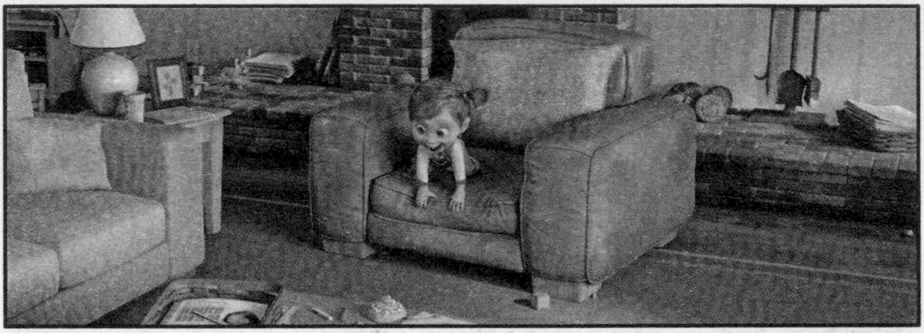

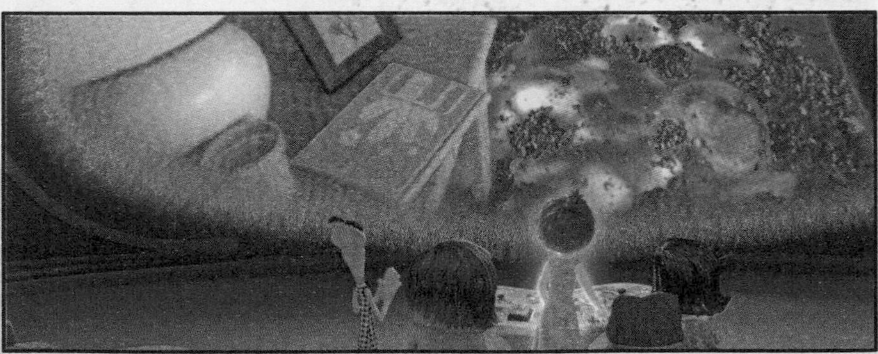

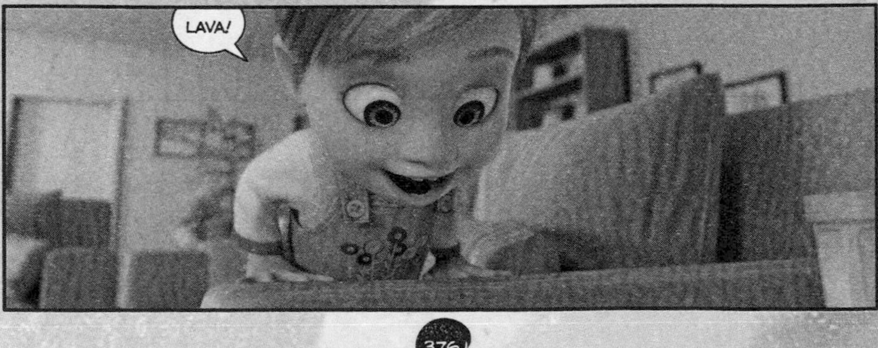
LAVA!

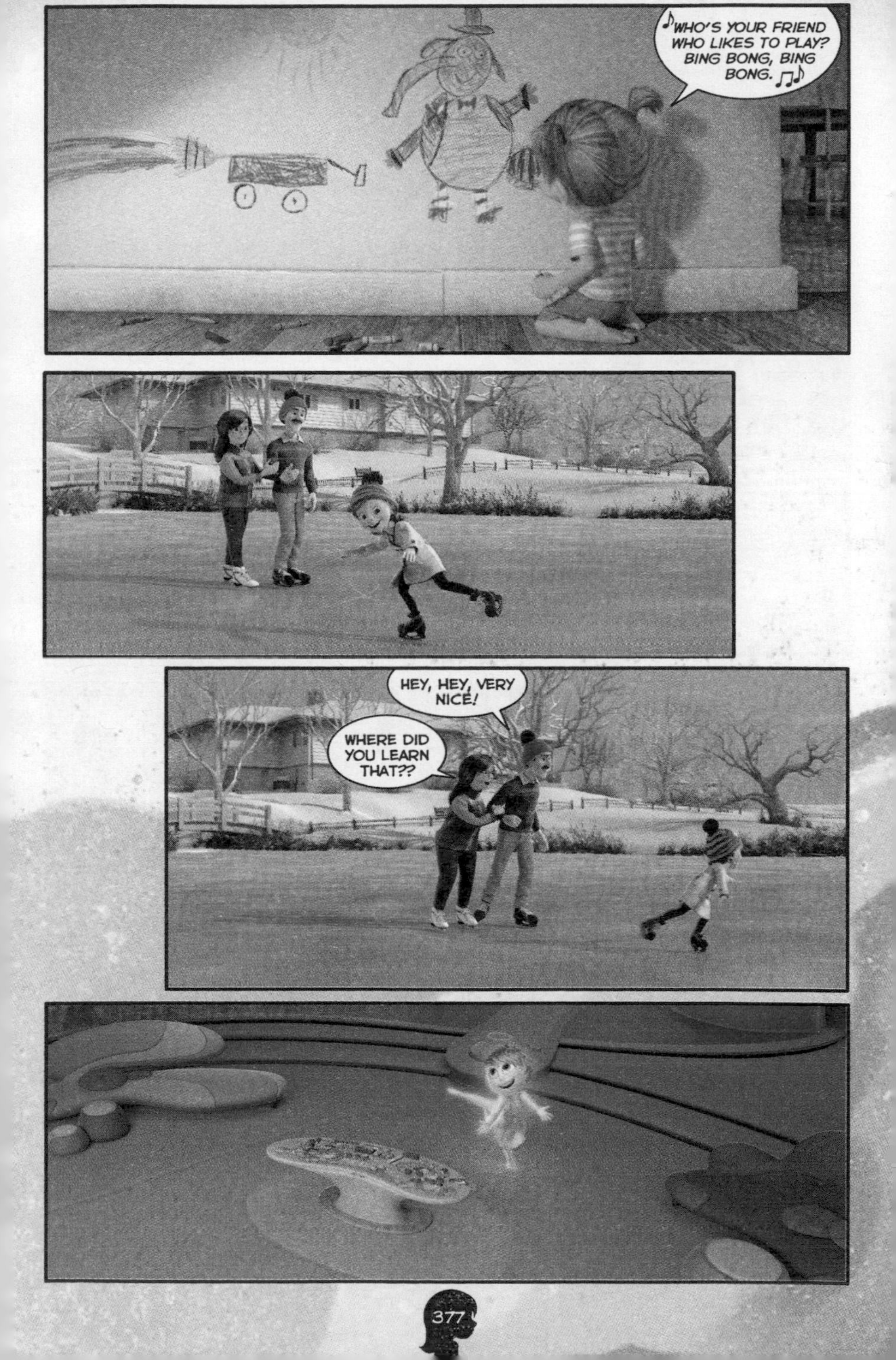
WHO'S YOUR FRIEND WHO LIKES TO PLAY? BING BONG, BING BONG.
HEY, HEY, VERY NICE!
WHERE DID YOU LEARN THAT??

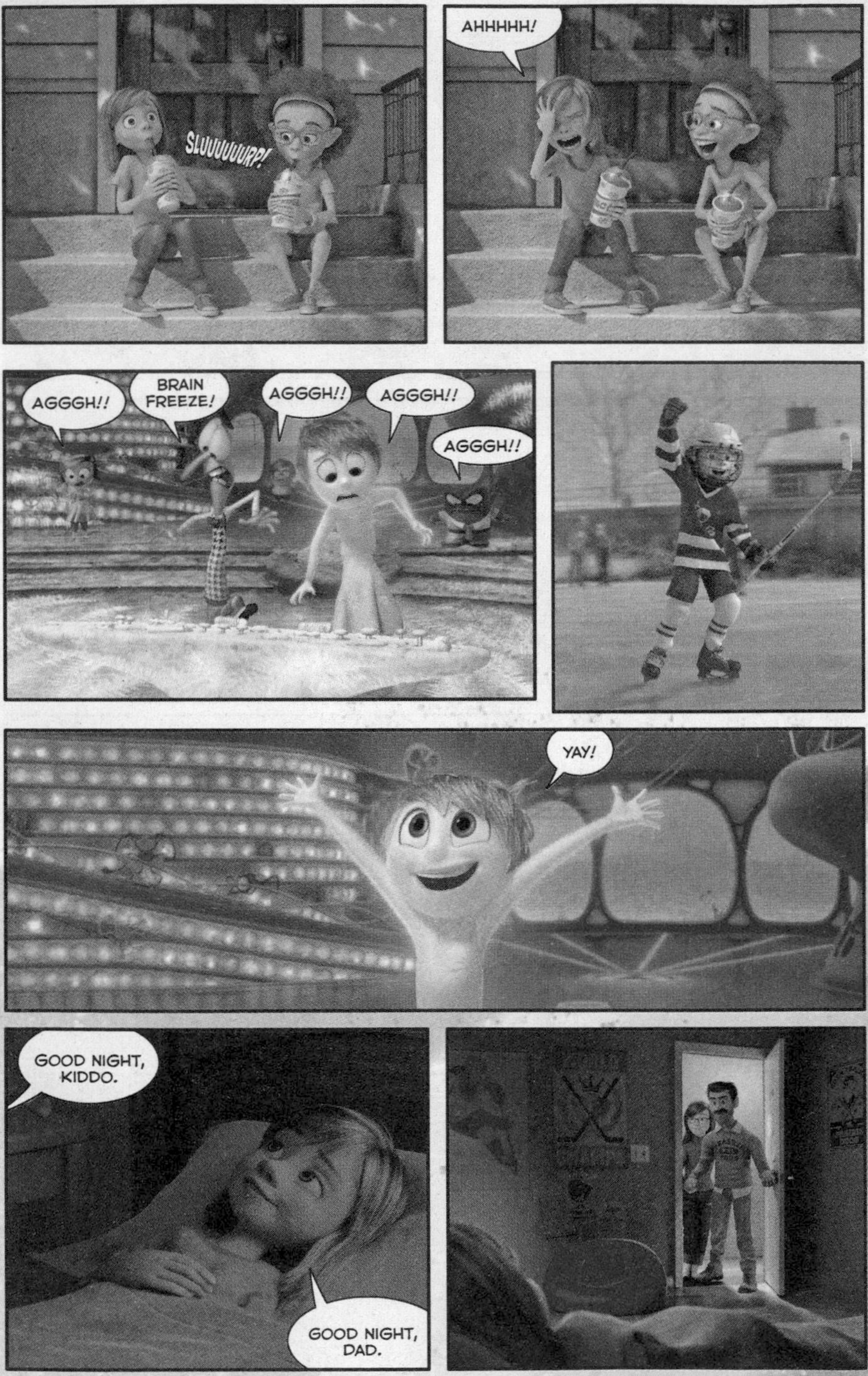
SLUUUUUURP!
AHHHHH!
AGGGH!!
BRAIN FREEZE!
AGGGH!!
AGGGH!!
AGGGH!!
YAY!
GOOD NIGHT, KIDDO.
GOOD NIGHT, DAD.